BIG NATE STAYS CLASSY

Complete Your *Big Nate* Collection

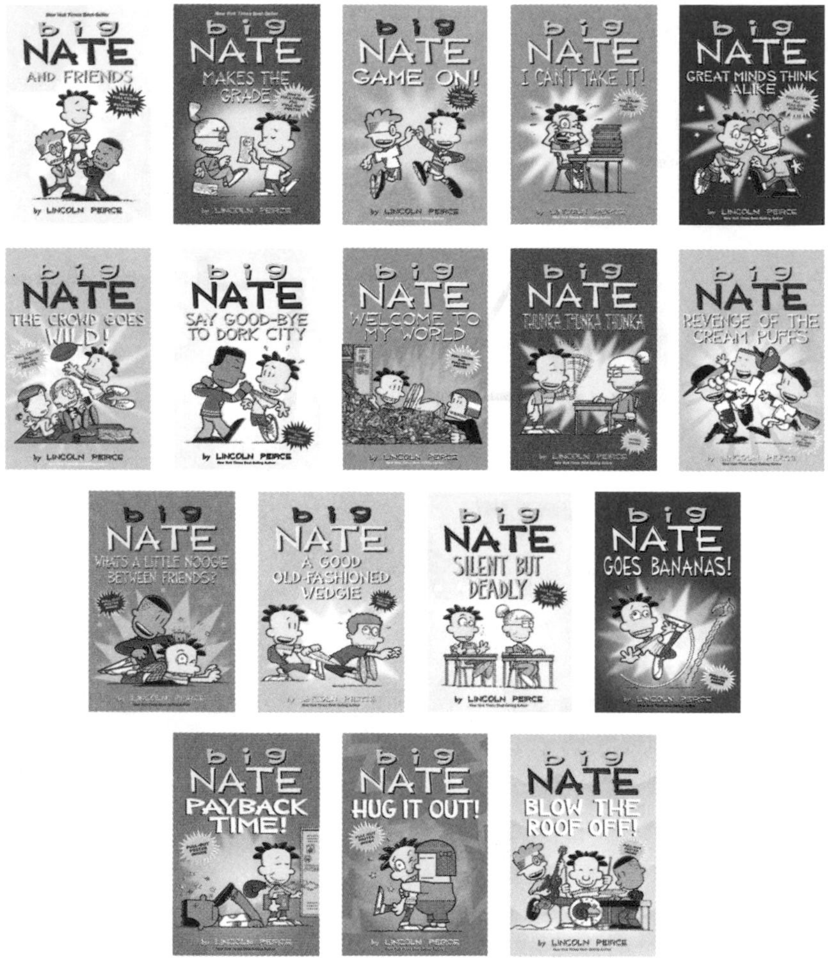
big NATE AND FRIENDS
by LINCOLN PEIRCE
big NATE MAKES THE GRADE
by LINCOLN PEIRCE
big NATE GAME ON!
by LINCOLN PEIRCE
big NATE I CAN'T TAKE IT!
by LINCOLN PEIRCE
big NATE GREAT MINDS THINK ALIKE
by LINCOLN PEIRCE
big NATE THE CROWD GOES WILD!
by LINCOLN PEIRCE
big NATE SAY GOOD-BYE TO DORK CITY
by LINCOLN PEIRCE
big NATE WELCOME TO MY WORLD
by LINCOLN PEIRCE
big NATE THUNKA THUNKA THUNKA
by LINCOLN PEIRCE
big NATE REVENGE OF THE CREAM PUFFS
by LINCOLN PEIRCE
big NATE WHAT'S A LITTLE NOOGIE BETWEEN FRIENDS?
by LINCOLN PEIRCE
big NATE A GOOD OLD-FASHIONED WEDGIE
by LINCOLN PEIRCE
big NATE SILENT BUT DEADLY
by LINCOLN PEIRCE
big NATE GOES BANANAS!
by LINCOLN PEIRCE
big NATE PAYBACK TIME!
by LINCOLN PEIRCE
big NATE HUG IT OUT!
by LINCOLN PEIRCE
big NATE BLOW THE ROOF OFF!
by LINCOLN PEIRCE

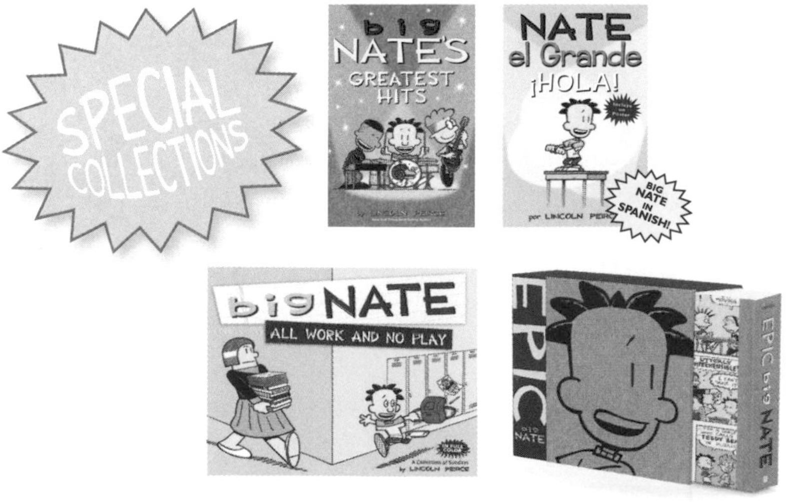
SPECIAL COLLECTIONS
big NATE'S GREATEST HITS
by LINCOLN PEIRCE
NATE el Grande ¡HOLA!
por LINCOLN PEIRCE
BIG NATE IN SPANISH!
big NATE ALL WORK AND NO PLAY
by LINCOLN PEIRCE
EPIC big NATE

big NATE STAYS CLASSY

by LINCOLN PEIRCE

A special collection featuring comics from
Big Nate: From the Top and *Big Nate Out Loud*

Andrews McMeel
PUBLISHING®

Big Nate is distributed internationally by Andrews McMeel Syndication.

Andrews McMeel Publishing
a division of Andrews McMeel Universal
1130 Walnut Street, Kansas City, Missouri 64106

www.andrewsmcmeel.com

20 21 22 23 24 RR2 10 9 8 7 6 5 4 3 2 1

ISBN: 978-1-5248-6176-6

Made by:
LSC Communications US, LLC
Address and location of manufacturer:
1009 Sloan Street
Crawfordsville, IN 47933
1st Printing – 4/3/20

Big Nate can be viewed on the Internet at
www.gocomics.com/big_nate.

big NATE

FROM THE TOP

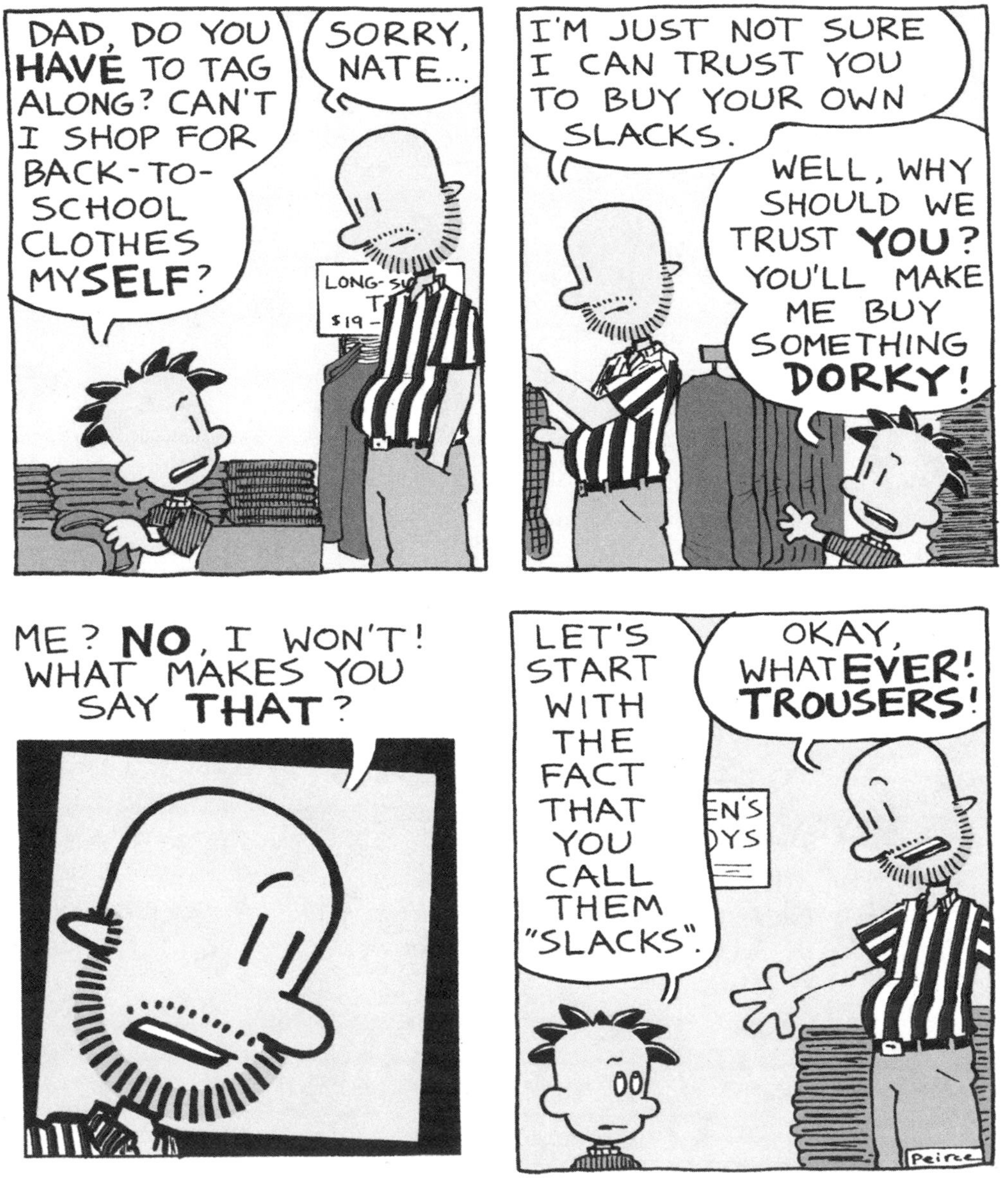
DAD, DO YOU **HAVE** TO TAG ALONG? CAN'T I SHOP FOR BACK-TO-SCHOOL CLOTHES MY**SELF**?
SORRY, NATE...
I'M JUST NOT SURE I CAN TRUST YOU TO BUY YOUR OWN SLACKS.
WELL, WHY SHOULD WE TRUST **YOU**? YOU'LL MAKE ME BUY SOMETHING **DORKY**!
ME? **NO**, I WON'T! WHAT MAKES YOU SAY **THAT**?
LET'S START WITH THE FACT THAT YOU CALL THEM "SLACKS".
OKAY, WHAT**EVER**! **TROUSERS**!
Peirce

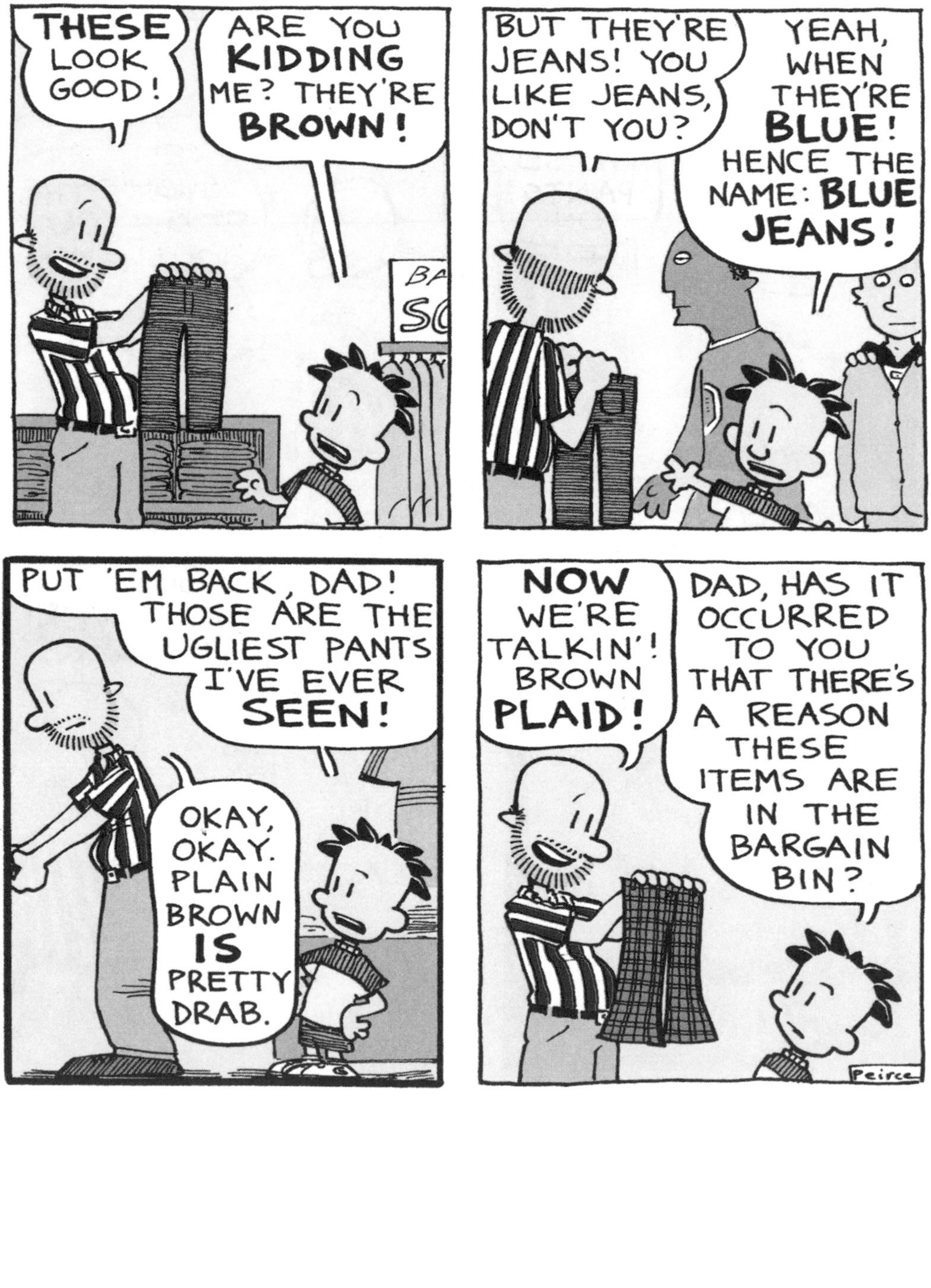
THESE LOOK GOOD!
ARE YOU KIDDING ME? THEY'RE BROWN!
BUT THEY'RE JEANS! YOU LIKE JEANS, DON'T YOU?
YEAH, WHEN THEY'RE BLUE! HENCE THE NAME: BLUE JEANS!
PUT 'EM BACK, DAD! THOSE ARE THE UGLIEST PANTS I'VE EVER SEEN!
OKAY, OKAY. PLAIN BROWN IS PRETTY DRAB.
NOW WE'RE TALKIN'! BROWN PLAID!
DAD, HAS IT OCCURRED TO YOU THAT THERE'S A REASON THESE ITEMS ARE IN THE BARGAIN BIN?
Peirce

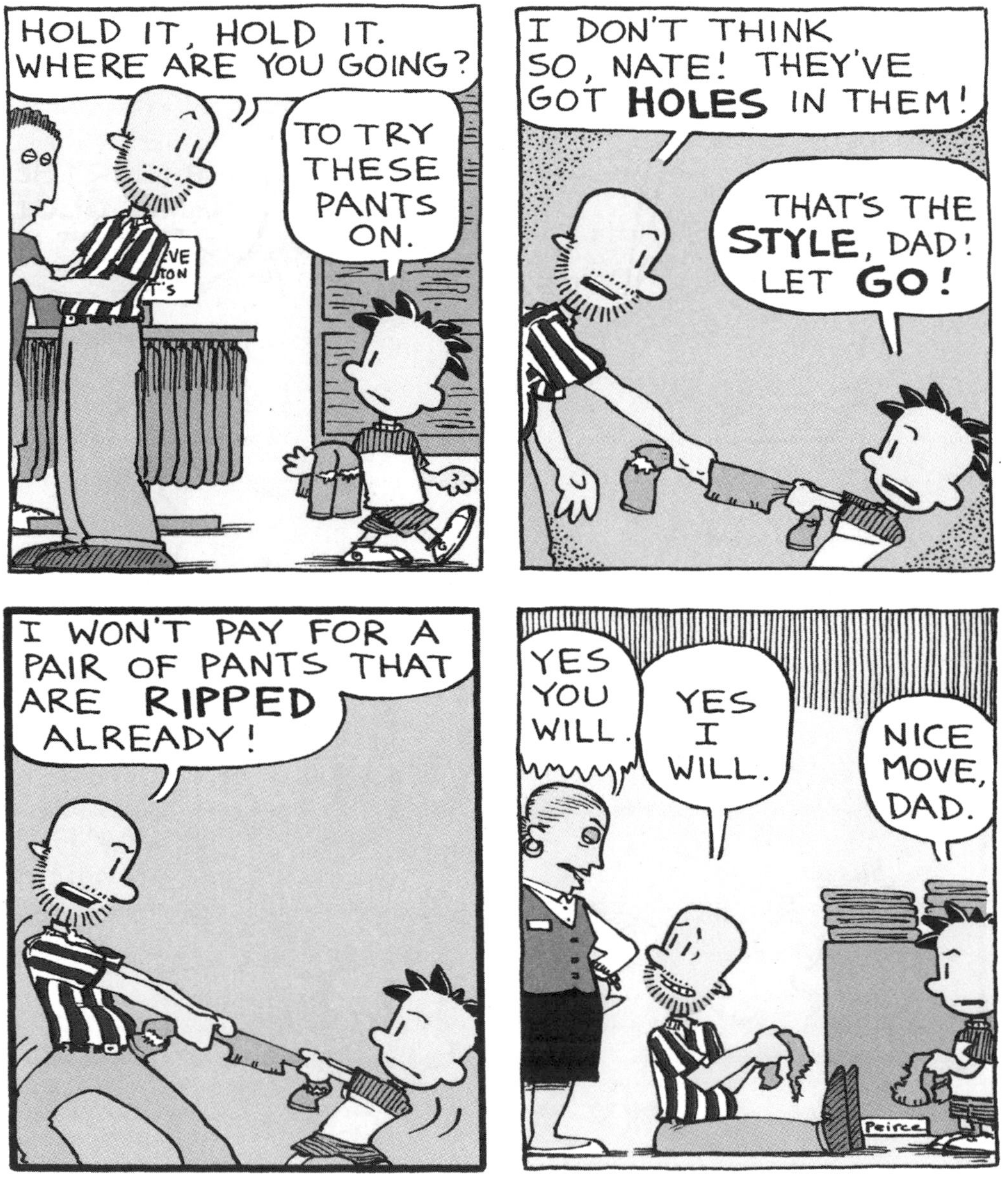
HOLD IT, HOLD IT. WHERE ARE YOU GOING?
TO TRY THESE PANTS ON.
I DON'T THINK SO, NATE! THEY'VE GOT **HOLES** IN THEM!
THAT'S THE **STYLE**, DAD! LET **GO**!
I WON'T PAY FOR A PAIR OF PANTS THAT ARE **RIPPED** ALREADY!
YES YOU WILL.
YES I WILL.
NICE MOVE, DAD.
Peirce

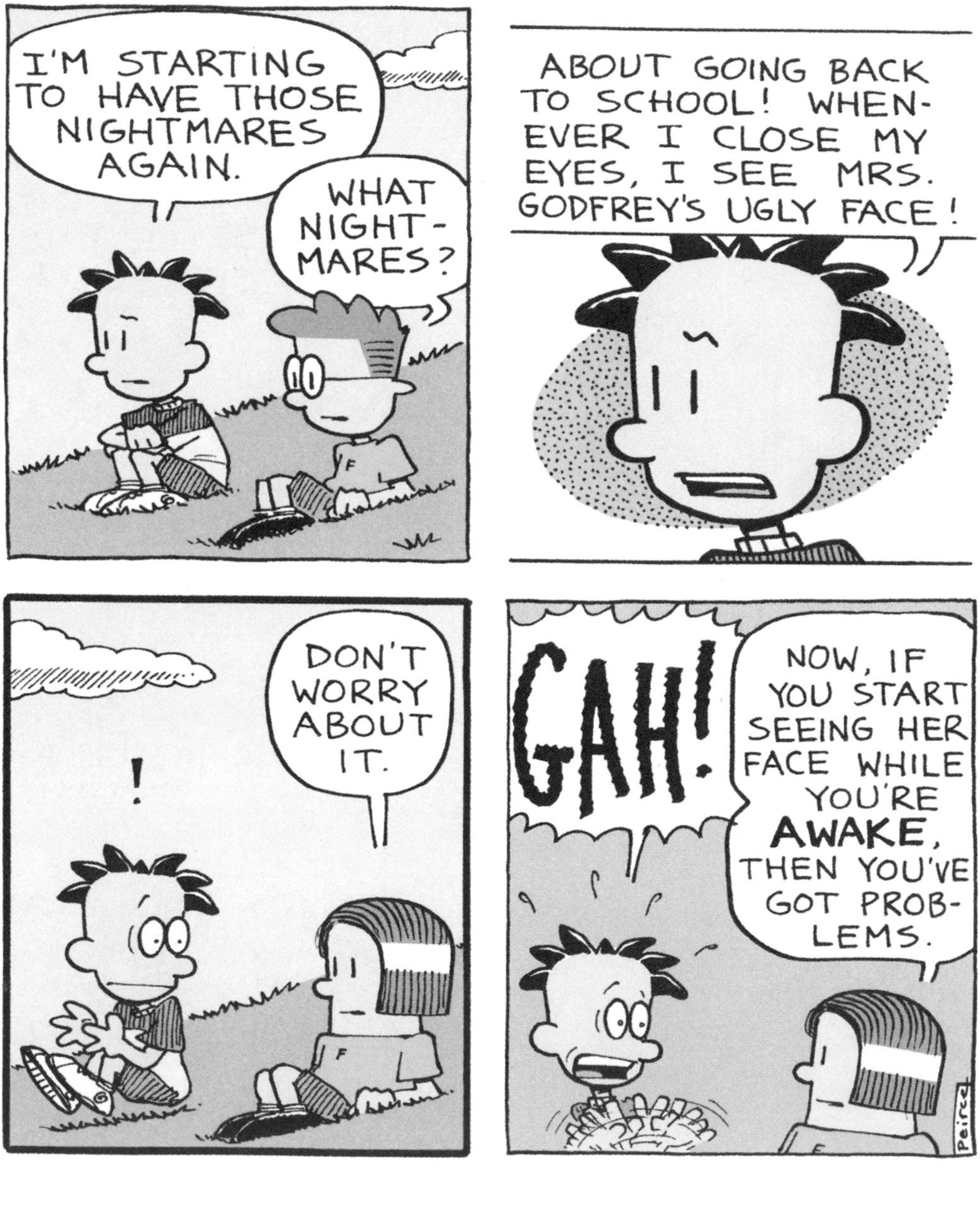
I'M STARTING TO HAVE THOSE NIGHTMARES AGAIN.
WHAT NIGHTMARES?
ABOUT GOING BACK TO SCHOOL! WHENEVER I CLOSE MY EYES, I SEE MRS. GODFREY'S UGLY FACE!
DON'T WORRY ABOUT IT.
!
GAH!
NOW, IF YOU START SEEING HER FACE WHILE YOU'RE **AWAKE**, THEN YOU'VE GOT PROBLEMS.
Peirce

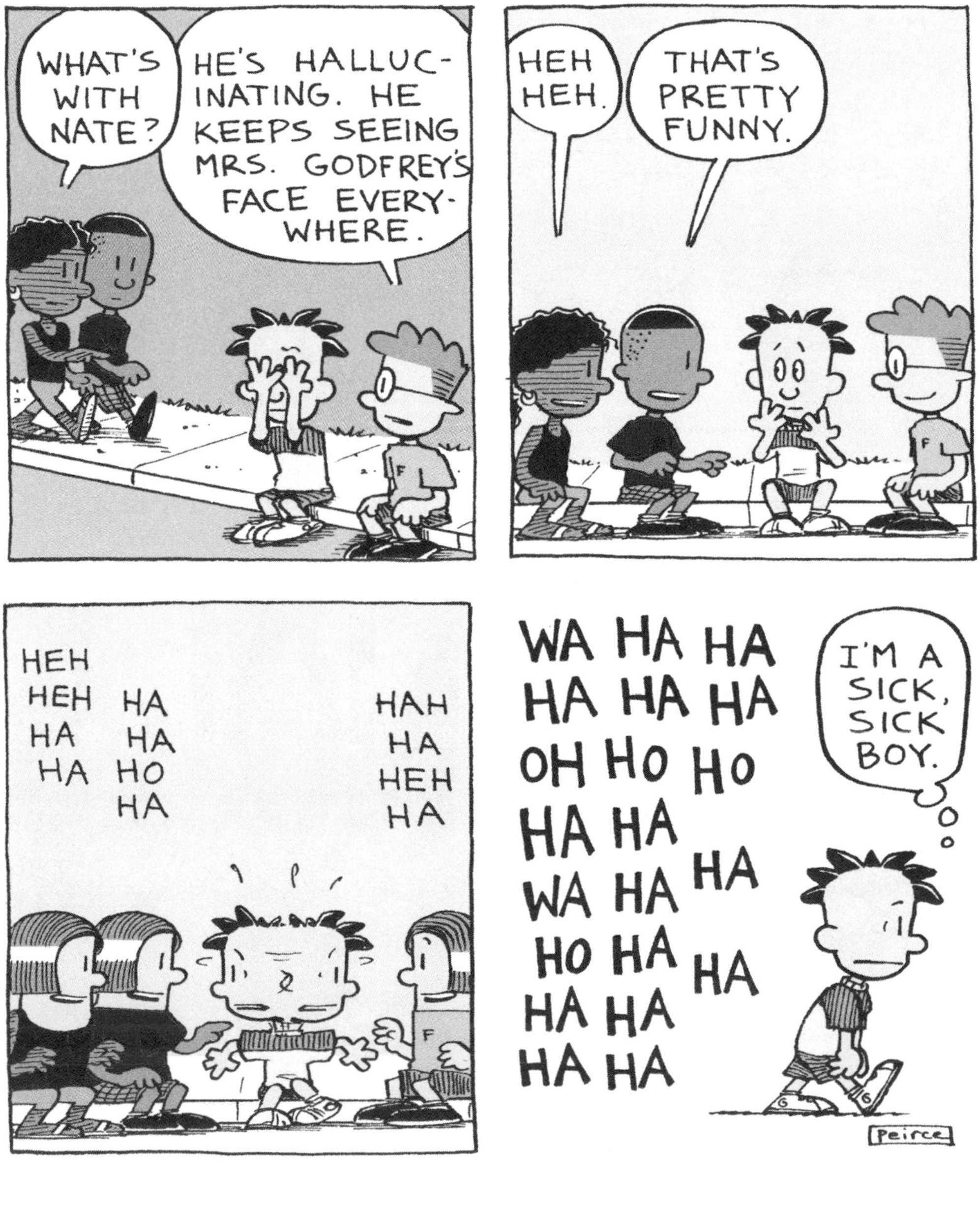
WHAT'S WITH NATE?
HE'S HALLUC-INATING. HE KEEPS SEEING MRS. GODFREY'S FACE EVERY-WHERE.
HEH HEH.
THAT'S PRETTY FUNNY.
HEH HEH HA HA
HA HA HO HA
HAH HA HEH HA
WA HA HA HA HA HA OH HO HO HA HA WA HA HA HO HA HA HA HA HA HA
I'M A SICK, SICK BOY.
peirce

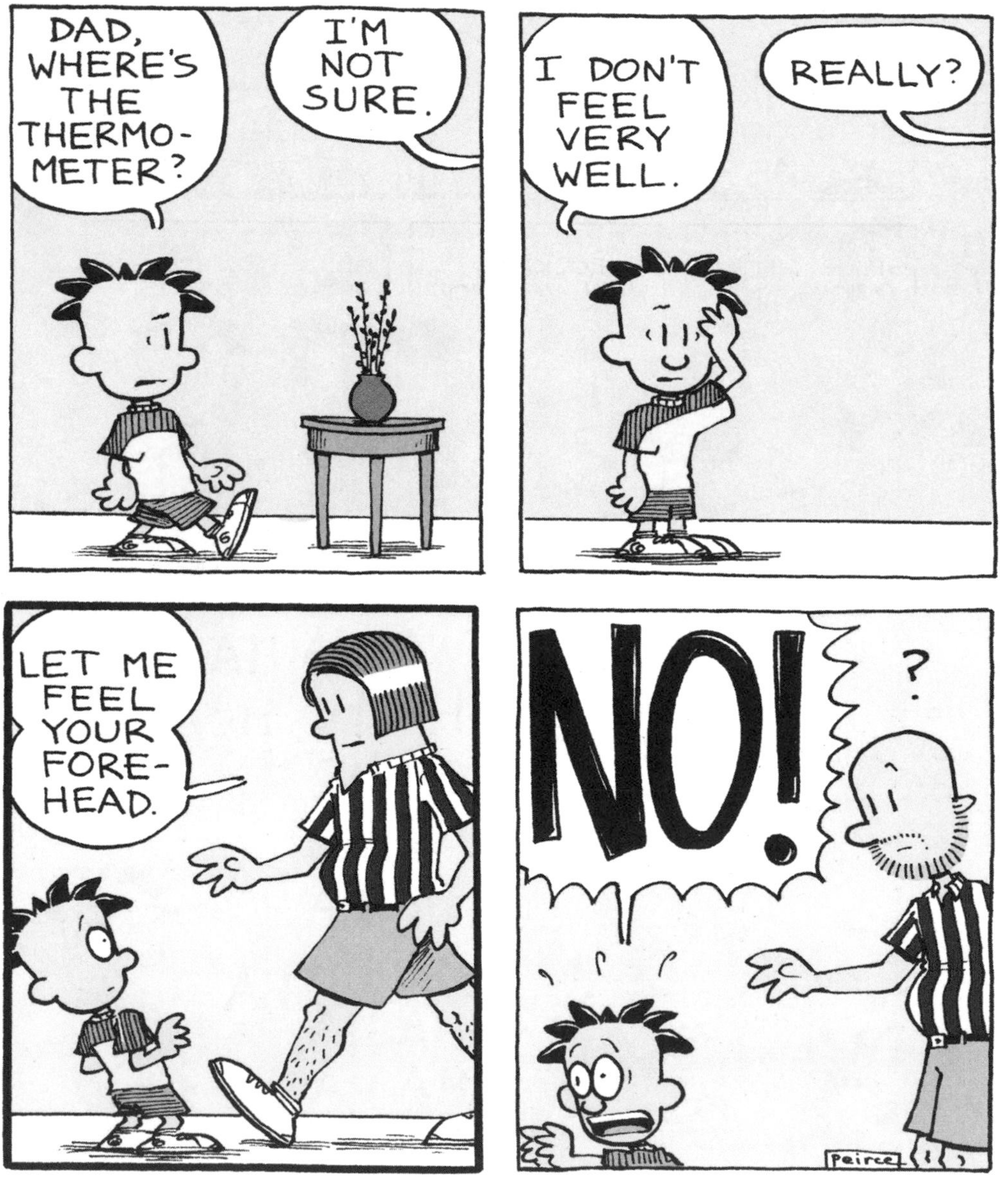
DAD, WHERE'S THE THERMO-METER?
I'M NOT SURE.
I DON'T FEEL VERY WELL.
REALLY?
LET ME FEEL YOUR FORE-HEAD.
NO!
?
peirce

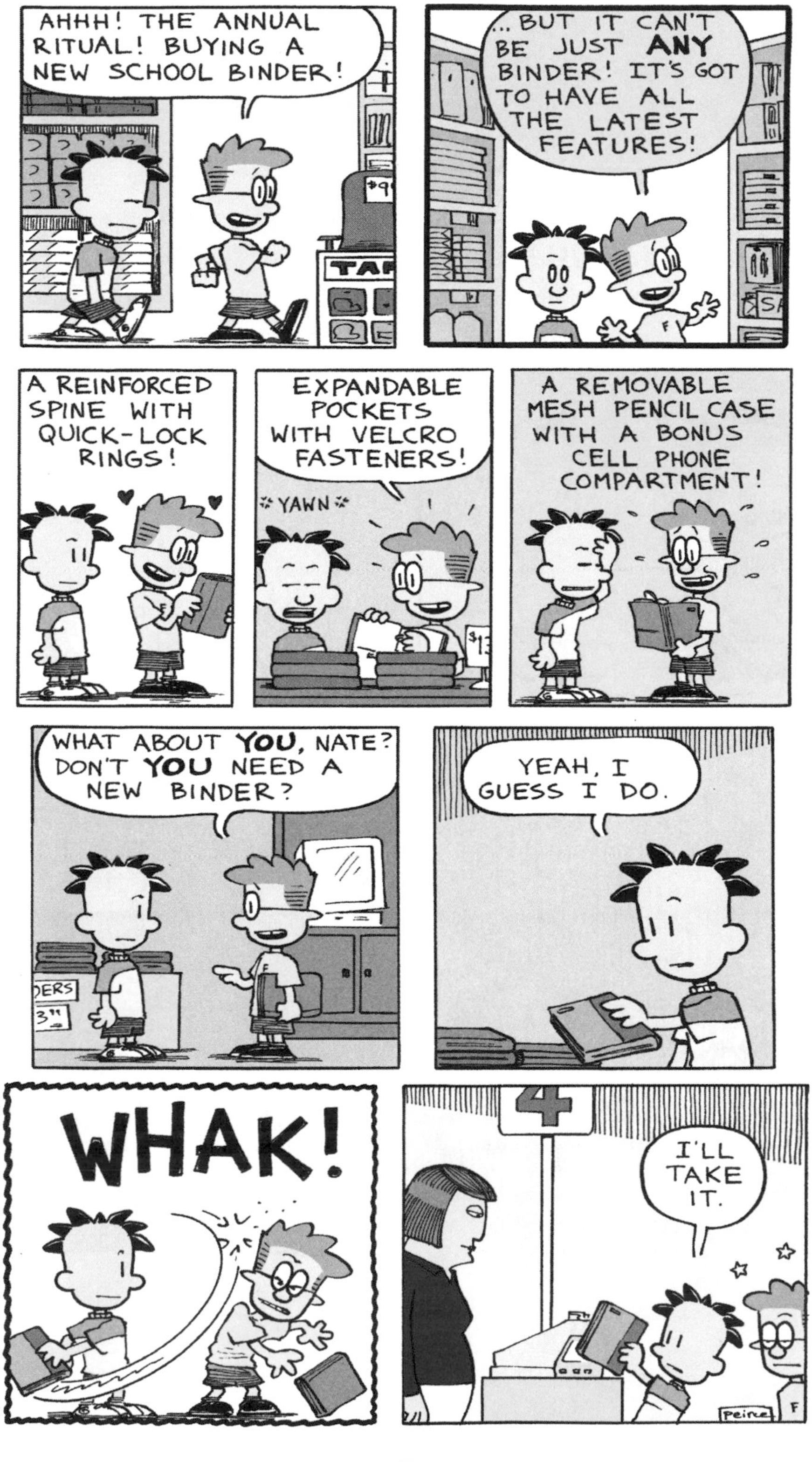

AHHH! THE ANNUAL RITUAL! BUYING A NEW SCHOOL BINDER!
... BUT IT CAN'T BE JUST **ANY** BINDER! IT'S GOT TO HAVE ALL THE LATEST FEATURES!
A REINFORCED SPINE WITH QUICK-LOCK RINGS!
EXPANDABLE POCKETS WITH VELCRO FASTENERS!
YAWN
A REMOVABLE MESH PENCIL CASE WITH A BONUS CELL PHONE COMPARTMENT!
WHAT ABOUT **YOU**, NATE? DON'T **YOU** NEED A NEW BINDER?
YEAH, I GUESS I DO.
WHAK!
4
I'LL TAKE IT.
Peirce

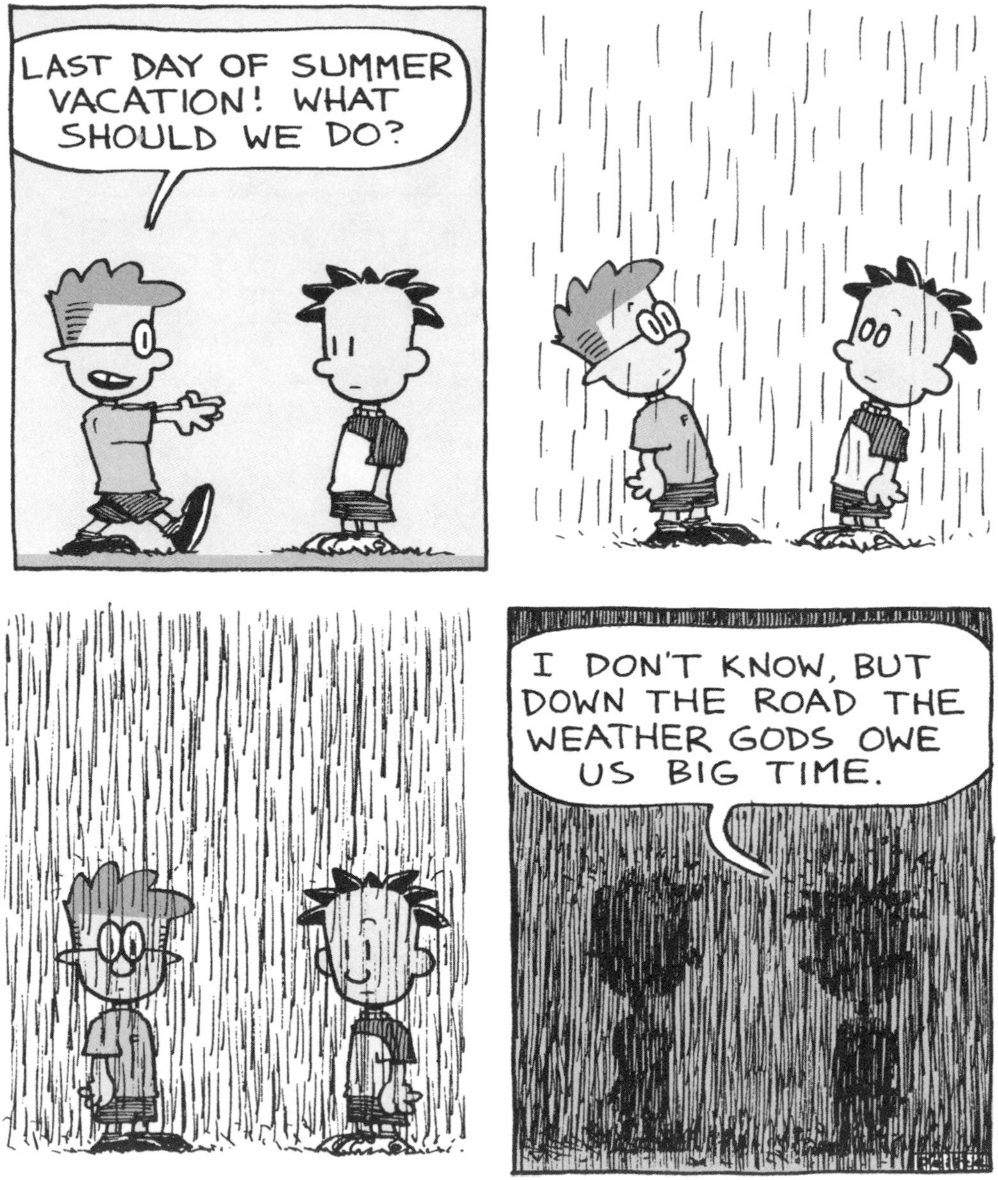
LAST DAY OF SUMMER VACATION! WHAT SHOULD WE DO?
I DON'T KNOW, BUT DOWN THE ROAD THE WEATHER GODS OWE US BIG TIME.

A PRINCIPAL IS NEVER QUITE SO EXCITED AS ON THE FIRST DAY OF SCHOOL!

THERE'S A FEELING OF RENEWAL, A SENSE OF...

IS IT TRUE? **IS IT TRUE?**

OOP. GUESS NOT.

GUYS, HE'S STILL HERE.

⁑ SIGH... ⁑

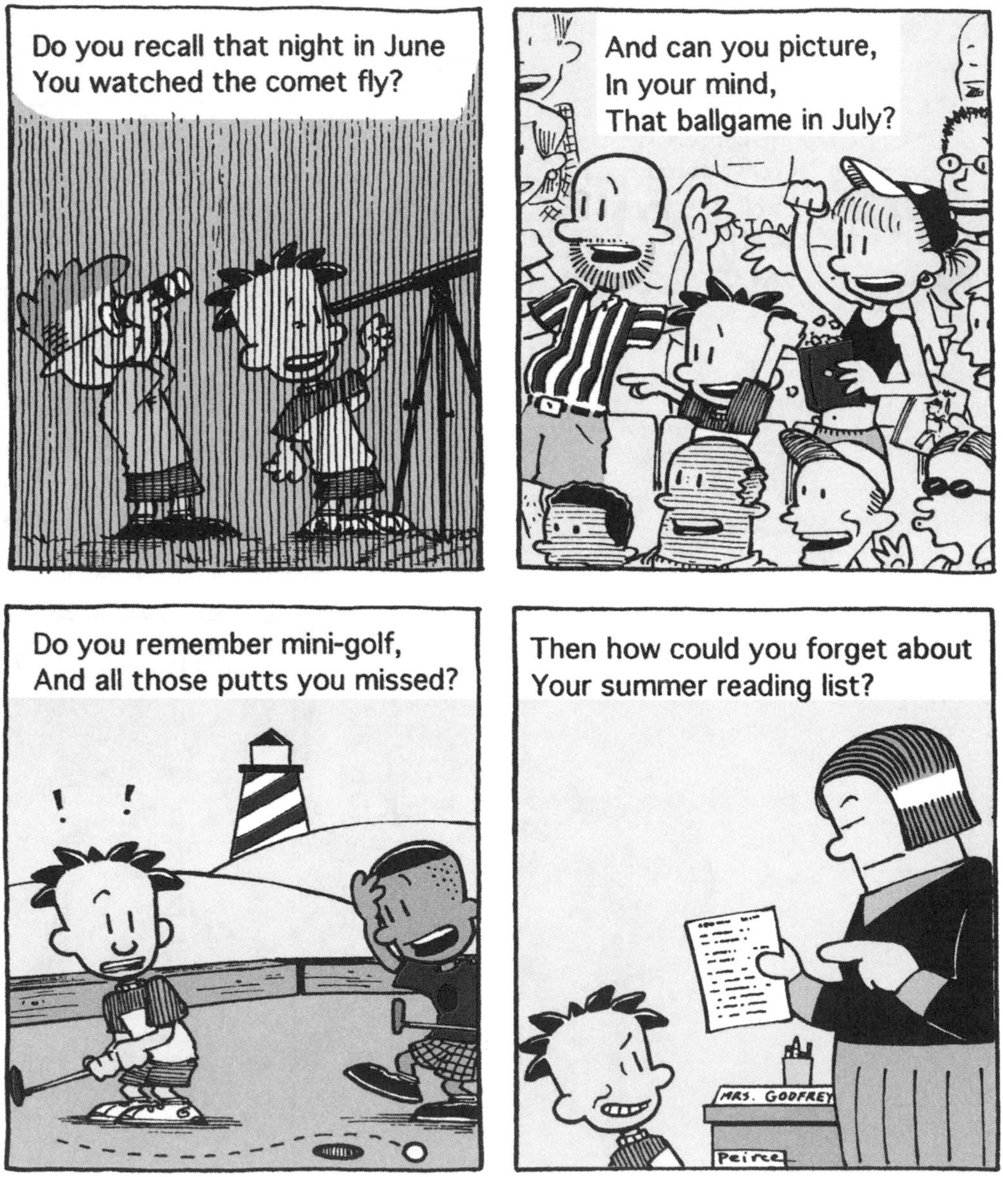
Do you recall that night in June
You watched the comet fly?
And can you picture,
In your mind,
That ballgame in July?
Do you remember mini-golf,
And all those putts you missed?
Then how could you forget about
Your summer reading list?
MRS. GODFREY
Peirce

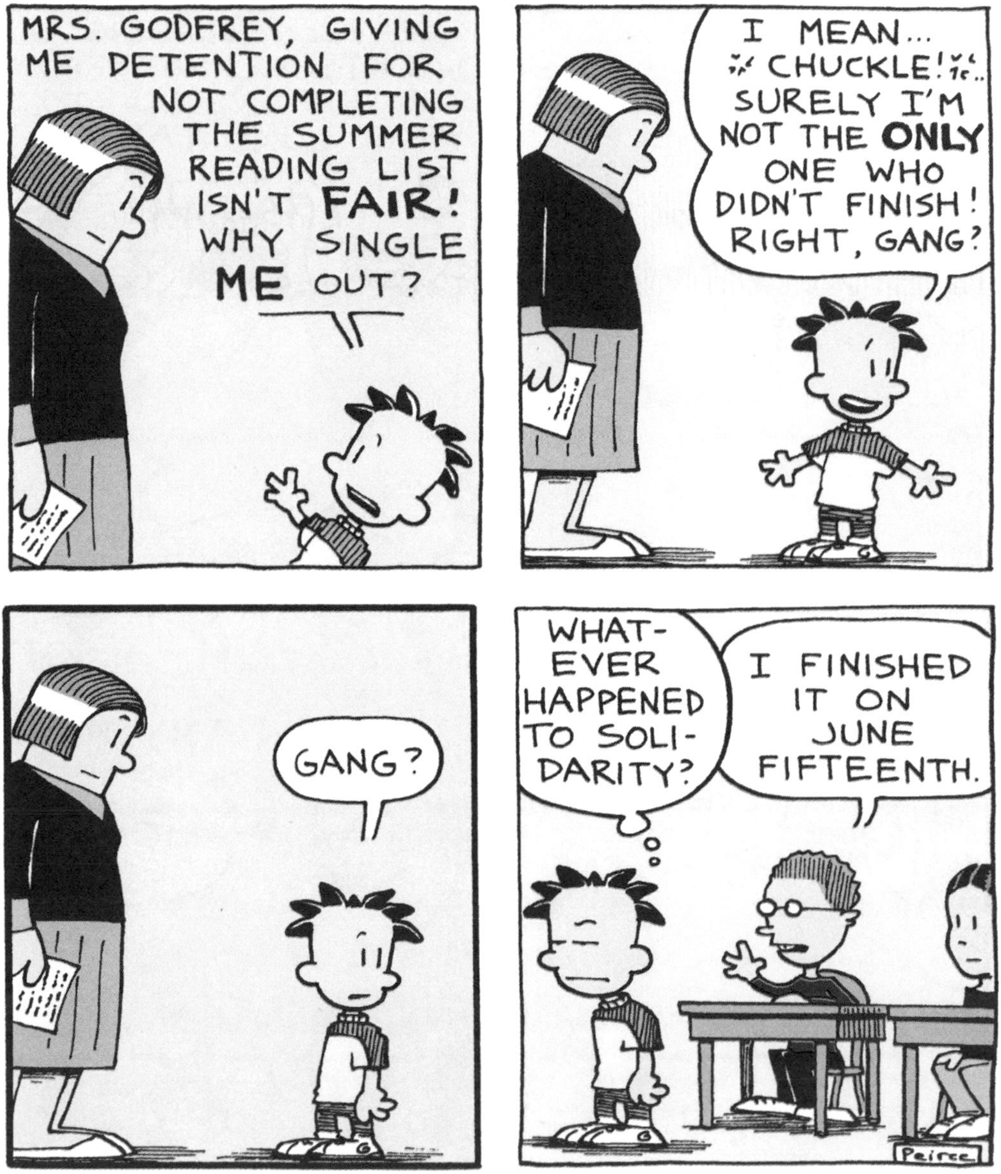
MRS. GODFREY, GIVING ME DETENTION FOR NOT COMPLETING THE SUMMER READING LIST ISN'T FAIR! WHY SINGLE ME OUT?
I MEAN... CHUCKLE! SURELY I'M NOT THE ONLY ONE WHO DIDN'T FINISH! RIGHT, GANG?
GANG?
WHAT-EVER HAPPENED TO SOLI-DARITY?
I FINISHED IT ON JUNE FIFTEENTH.
Peirce

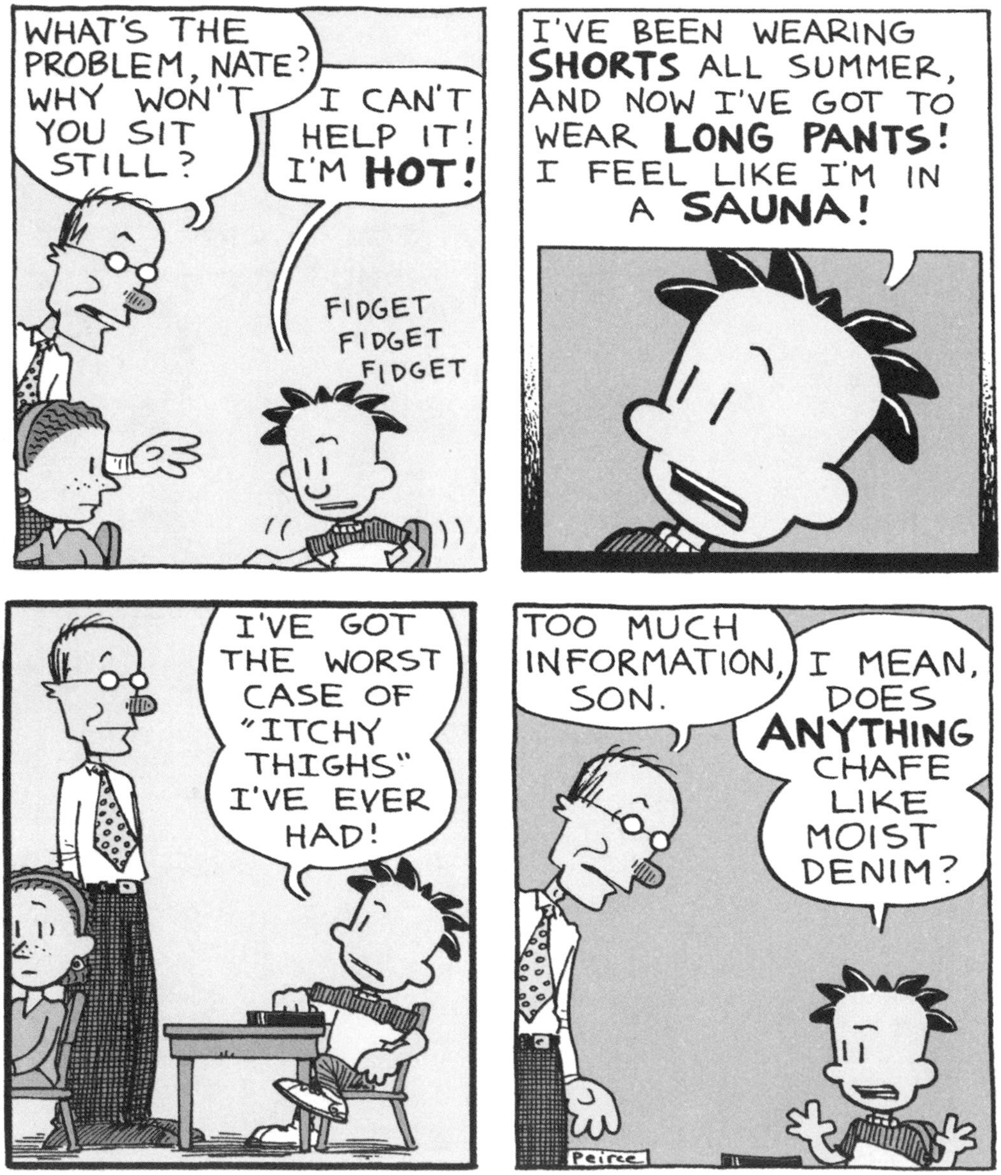
WHAT'S THE PROBLEM, NATE? WHY WON'T YOU SIT STILL?
I CAN'T HELP IT! I'M **HOT**!
FIDGET FIDGET FIDGET
I'VE BEEN WEARING **SHORTS** ALL SUMMER, AND NOW I'VE GOT TO WEAR **LONG PANTS**! I FEEL LIKE I'M IN A **SAUNA**!
I'VE GOT THE WORST CASE OF "ITCHY THIGHS" I'VE EVER HAD!
TOO MUCH INFORMATION, SON.
I MEAN, DOES **ANYTHING** CHAFE LIKE MOIST DENIM?
Peirce

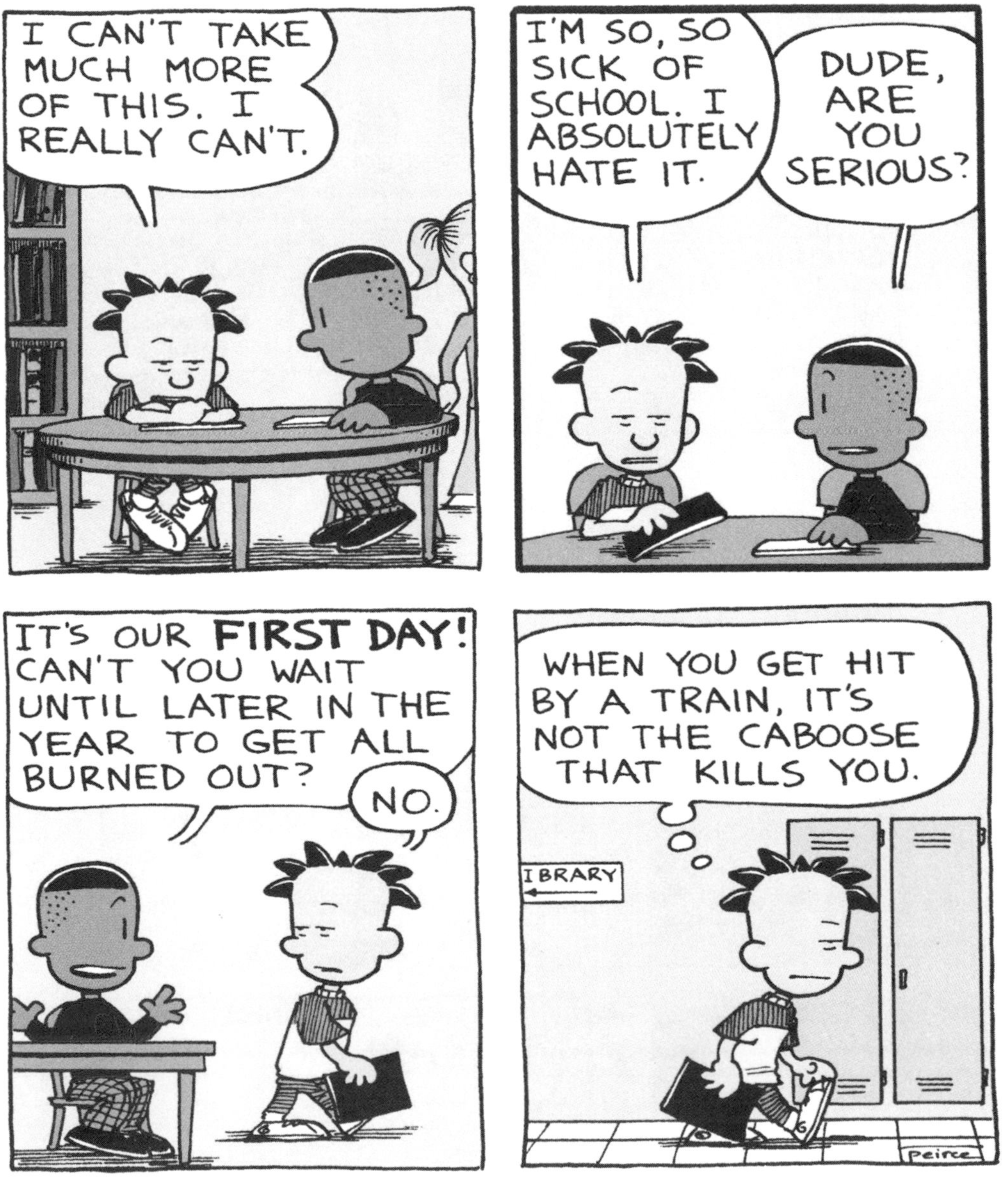
I CAN'T TAKE MUCH MORE OF THIS. I REALLY CAN'T.
I'M SO, SO SICK OF SCHOOL. I ABSOLUTELY HATE IT.
DUDE, ARE YOU SERIOUS?
IT'S OUR **FIRST DAY**! CAN'T YOU WAIT UNTIL LATER IN THE YEAR TO GET ALL BURNED OUT?
NO.
WHEN YOU GET HIT BY A TRAIN, IT'S NOT THE CABOOSE THAT KILLS YOU.
IBRARY
peirce

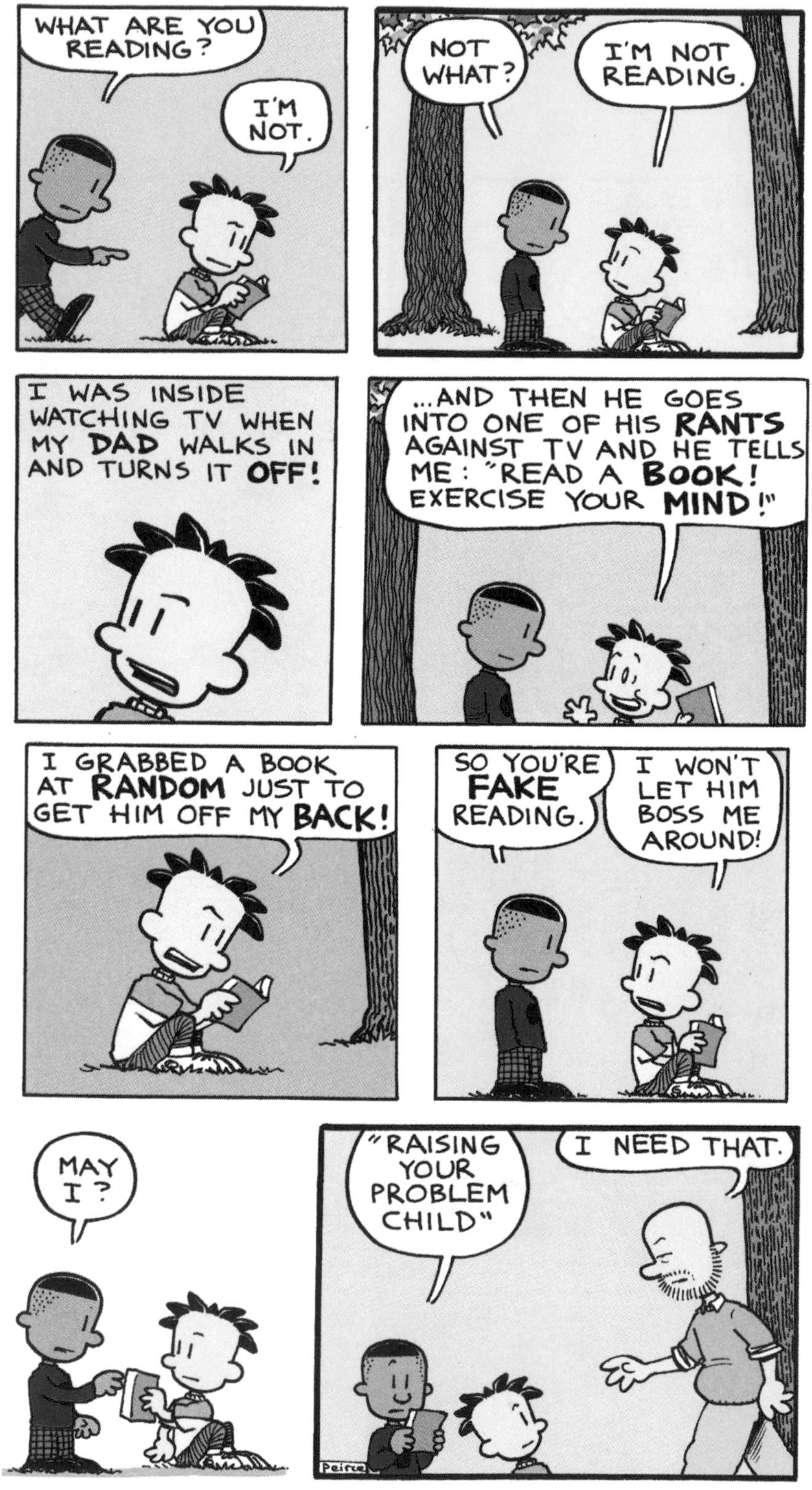
WHAT ARE YOU READING?
I'M NOT.
NOT WHAT?
I'M NOT READING.
I WAS INSIDE WATCHING TV WHEN MY DAD WALKS IN AND TURNS IT OFF!
...AND THEN HE GOES INTO ONE OF HIS RANTS AGAINST TV AND HE TELLS ME: "READ A BOOK! EXERCISE YOUR MIND!"
I GRABBED A BOOK AT RANDOM JUST TO GET HIM OFF MY BACK!
SO YOU'RE FAKE READING.
I WON'T LET HIM BOSS ME AROUND!
MAY I?
"RAISING YOUR PROBLEM CHILD"
I NEED THAT.
Peirce

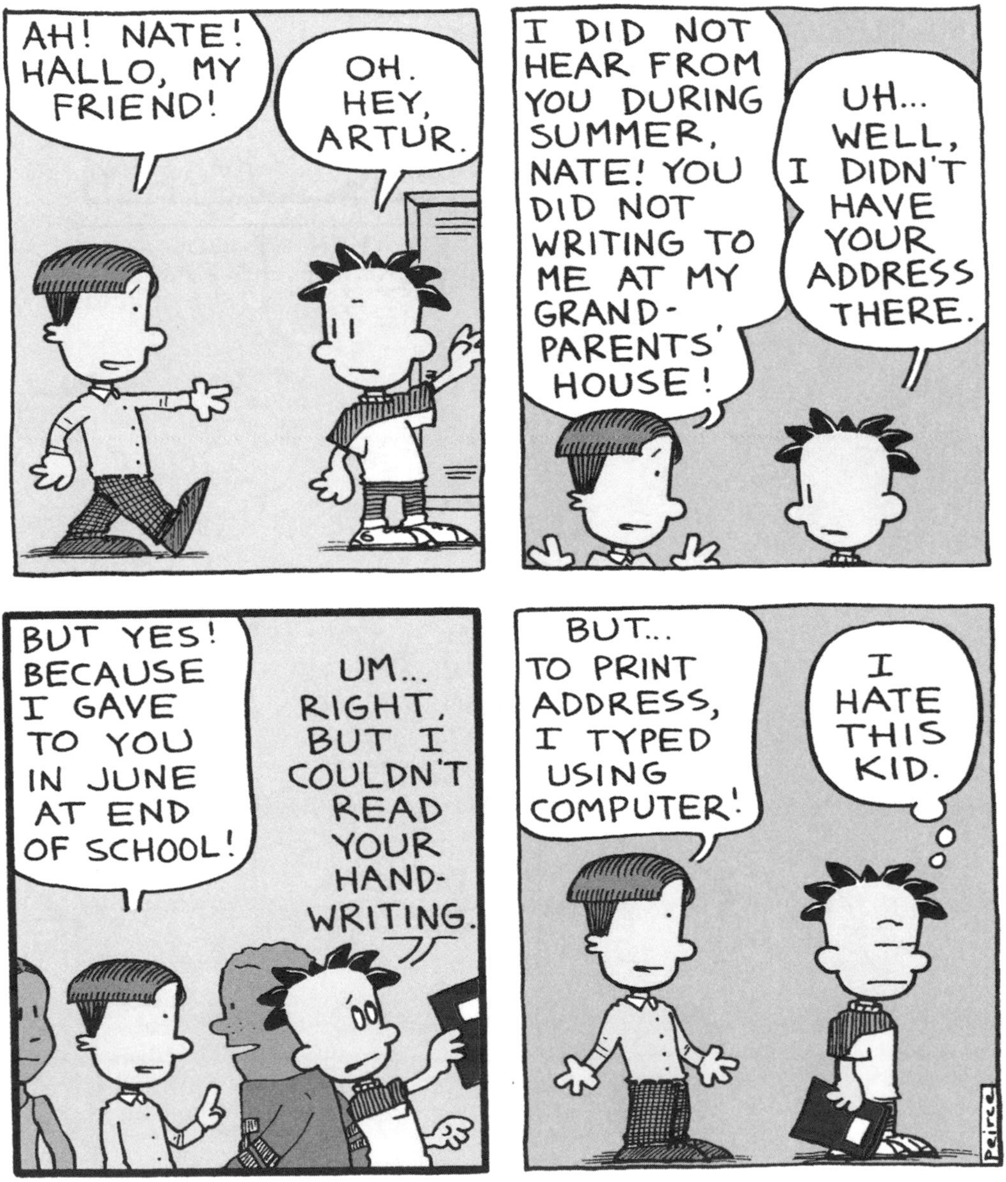
AH! NATE! HALLO, MY FRIEND!
OH. HEY, ARTUR.
I DID NOT HEAR FROM YOU DURING SUMMER, NATE! YOU DID NOT WRITING TO ME AT MY GRAND-PARENTS' HOUSE!
UH... WELL, I DIDN'T HAVE YOUR ADDRESS THERE.
BUT YES! BECAUSE I GAVE TO YOU IN JUNE AT END OF SCHOOL!
UM... RIGHT, BUT I COULDN'T READ YOUR HAND-WRITING.
BUT... TO PRINT ADDRESS, I TYPED USING COMPUTER!
I HATE THIS KID.
Peirce

NATE. HERE. I BROUGHT TO YOU SOUVENIR FROM MY TRIP TO BELARUS.

WOW, A **SNOW GLOBE**! I COL-**LECT** THESE!

YES. AND ON BOTTOM SAYS IT "BELARUS", SO YOU KNOW IS REALLY **FROM** THERE!

WOW... UH... HERE, I GOT A SOUVENIR FOR YOU TOO, ARTUR...

AH.

A **PENCIL**!

SO YOU WERE TO VISITING SOME- WHERE CALLED "TICON- DEROGA"?

RIGHT. NICE TOWN.

24

I DON'T GET IT. WHY IS ARTUR ALWAYS SO NICE TO ME?
BECAUSE HE'S A NICE KID, THAT'S WHY!
BUT WHY WASTE YOUR TIME BEING NICE TO SOMEONE WHO CAN'T STAND YOU? WHAT'S UP WITH THAT?
WELL, SOME PEOPLE...
OOP! HOLD ON!
JENNY, M'LADY!
SOME PEOPLE ARE JUST KIND OF CLUELESS.
Peirce

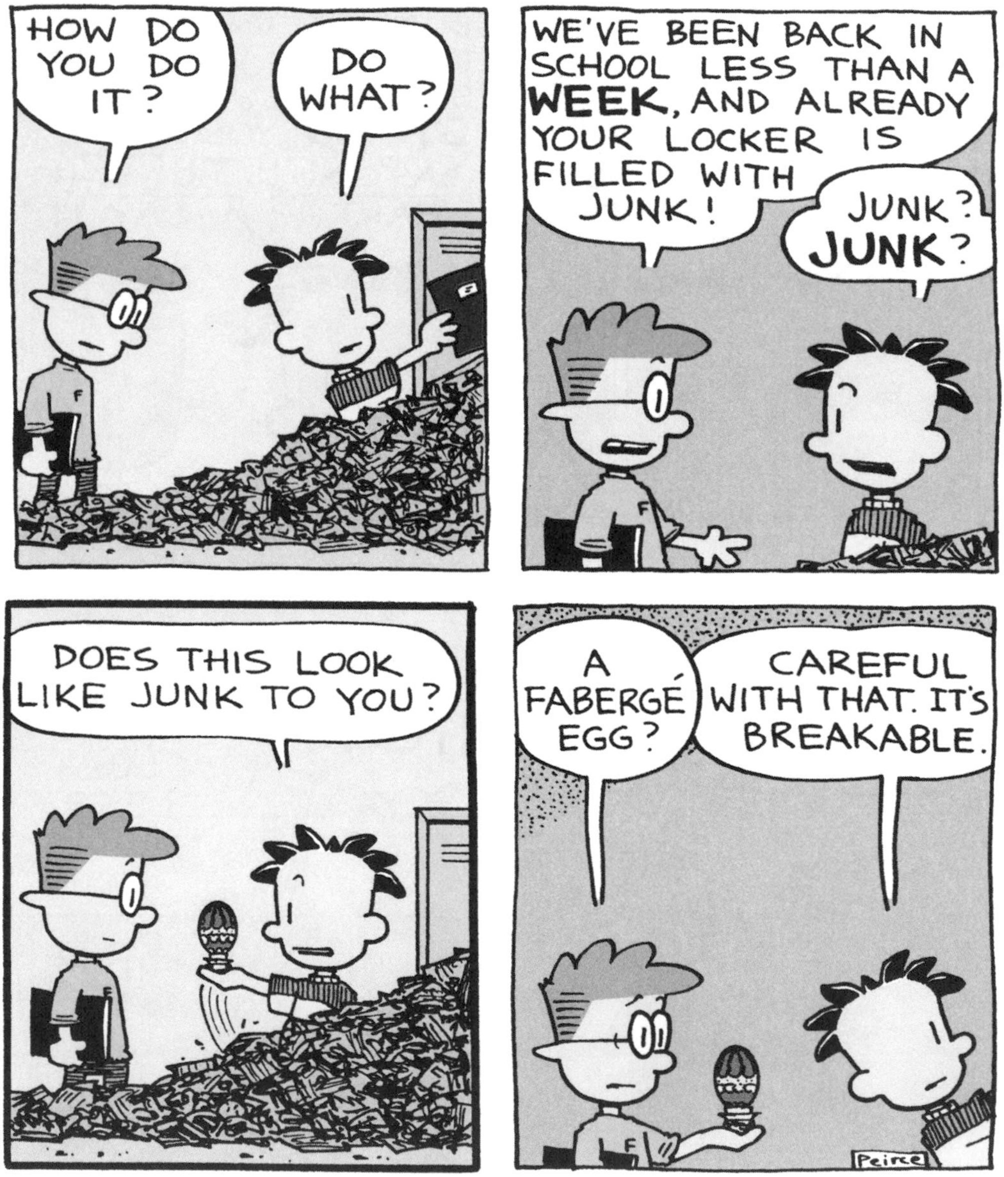
HOW DO YOU DO IT?
DO WHAT?
WE'VE BEEN BACK IN SCHOOL LESS THAN A **WEEK**, AND ALREADY YOUR LOCKER IS FILLED WITH JUNK!
JUNK? **JUNK**?
DOES THIS LOOK LIKE JUNK TO YOU?
A FABERGÉ EGG?
CAREFUL WITH THAT. IT'S BREAKABLE.
Peirce

LET'S SAY YOU JUST FOUND OUT YOU HAVE ONLY 24 HOURS TO LIVE. WHAT WOULD YOU DO?
HOW WOULD YOU SPEND YOUR LAST DAY ON EARTH?
WELL, THAT WOULD DEPEND ON WHAT DAY IT WAS.
WHY WOULD IT MATTER?
IT WOULD MATTER IF IT WAS A SUNDAY. SUNDAY'S MY TV NIGHT.
OF COURSE, IF "FAMILY GUY" WAS A RERUN, THAT WOULD BE A DIFFERENT STORY.
Peirce

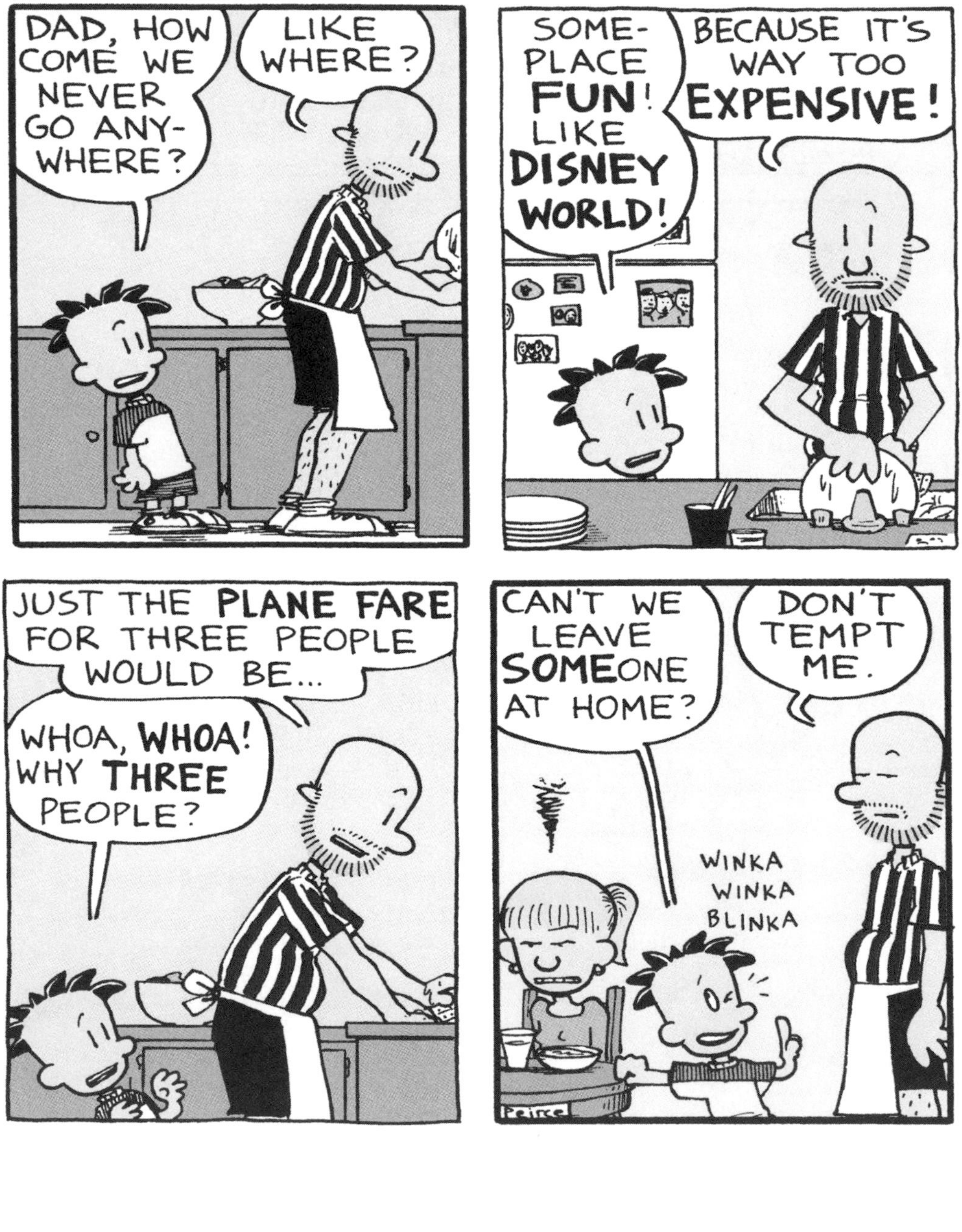
DAD, HOW COME WE NEVER GO ANY-WHERE?
LIKE WHERE?
SOME-PLACE FUN! LIKE DISNEY WORLD!
BECAUSE IT'S WAY TOO EXPENSIVE!
JUST THE PLANE FARE FOR THREE PEOPLE WOULD BE...
WHOA, WHOA! WHY THREE PEOPLE?
CAN'T WE LEAVE SOMEONE AT HOME?
DON'T TEMPT ME.
WINKA WINKA BLINKA
PEIRCE

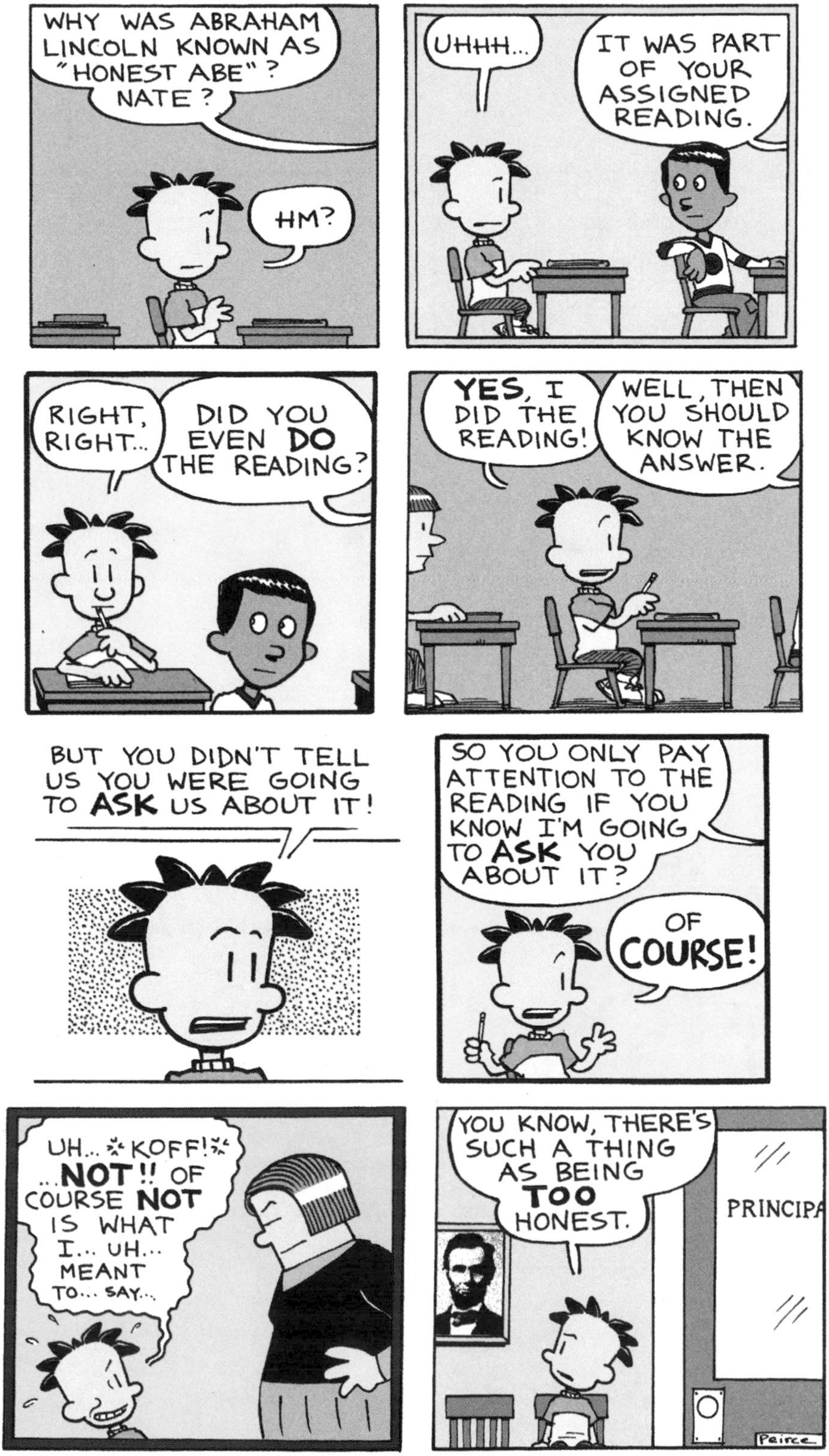
WHY WAS ABRAHAM LINCOLN KNOWN AS "HONEST ABE"? NATE?
HM?
UHHH...
IT WAS PART OF YOUR ASSIGNED READING.
RIGHT, RIGHT...
DID YOU EVEN DO THE READING?
YES, I DID THE READING!
WELL, THEN YOU SHOULD KNOW THE ANSWER.
BUT YOU DIDN'T TELL US YOU WERE GOING TO ASK US ABOUT IT!
SO YOU ONLY PAY ATTENTION TO THE READING IF YOU KNOW I'M GOING TO ASK YOU ABOUT IT?
OF COURSE!
UH... KOFF! ...NOT!! OF COURSE NOT IS WHAT I... UH... MEANT TO... SAY...
YOU KNOW, THERE'S SUCH A THING AS BEING TOO HONEST.
PRINCIPA
Peirce

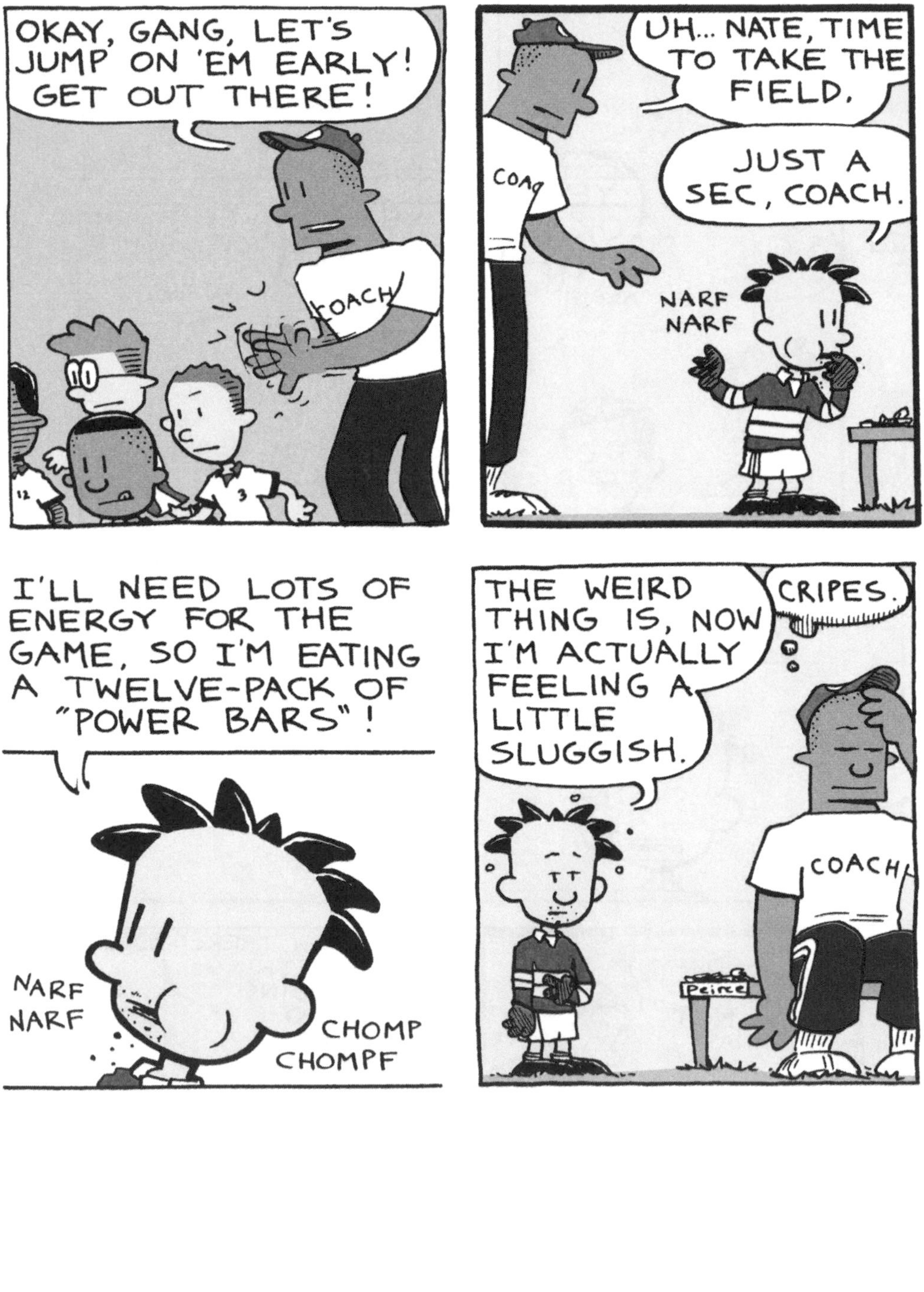
OKAY, GANG, LET'S JUMP ON 'EM EARLY! GET OUT THERE!
COACH
12
3
UH... NATE, TIME TO TAKE THE FIELD.
JUST A SEC, COACH.
COA
NARF NARF
I'LL NEED LOTS OF ENERGY FOR THE GAME, SO I'M EATING A TWELVE-PACK OF "POWER BARS"!
NARF NARF
CHOMP CHOMPF
THE WEIRD THING IS, NOW I'M ACTUALLY FEELING A LITTLE SLUGGISH.
CRIPES.
COACH
Peirce

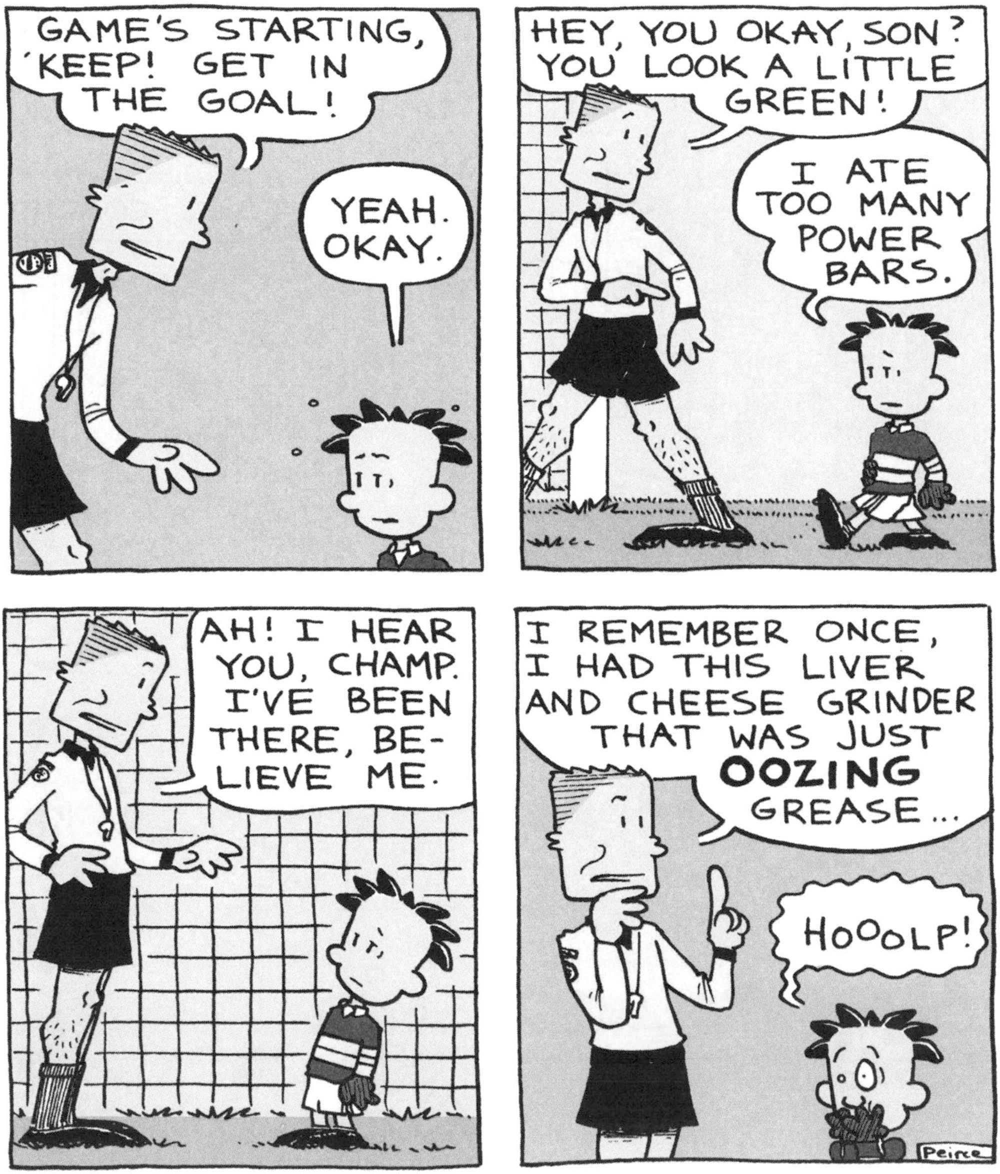
GAME'S STARTING, 'KEEP! GET IN THE GOAL!
YEAH. OKAY.
HEY, YOU OKAY, SON? YOU LOOK A LITTLE GREEN!
I ATE TOO MANY POWER BARS.
AH! I HEAR YOU, CHAMP. I'VE BEEN THERE, BE-LIEVE ME.
I REMEMBER ONCE, I HAD THIS LIVER AND CHEESE GRINDER THAT WAS JUST **OOZING** GREASE...
HOOOLP!
Peirce

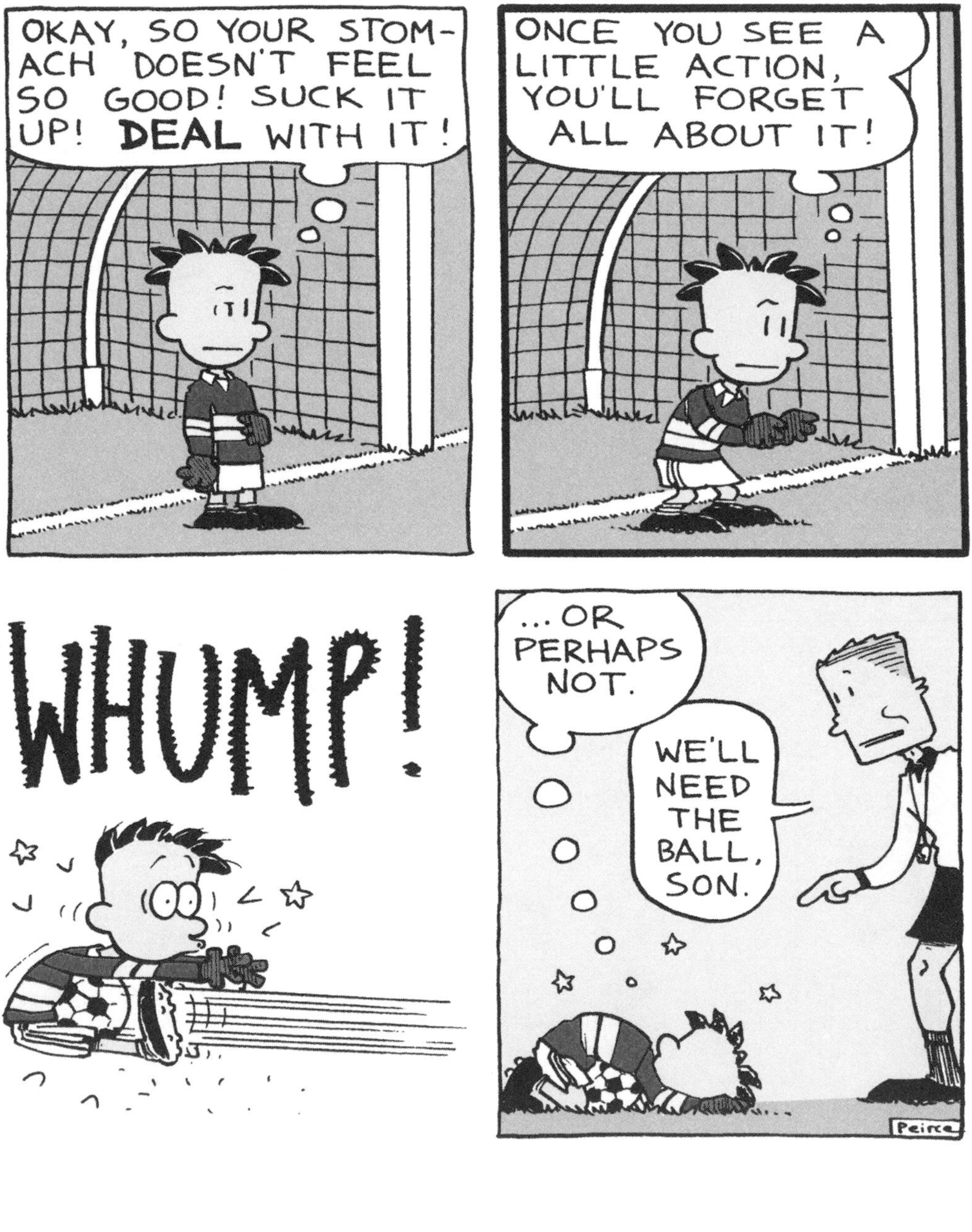
OKAY, SO YOUR STOMACH DOESN'T FEEL SO GOOD! SUCK IT UP! DEAL WITH IT!
ONCE YOU SEE A LITTLE ACTION, YOU'LL FORGET ALL ABOUT IT!
WHUMP!
...OR PERHAPS NOT.
WE'LL NEED THE BALL, SON.
Peirce

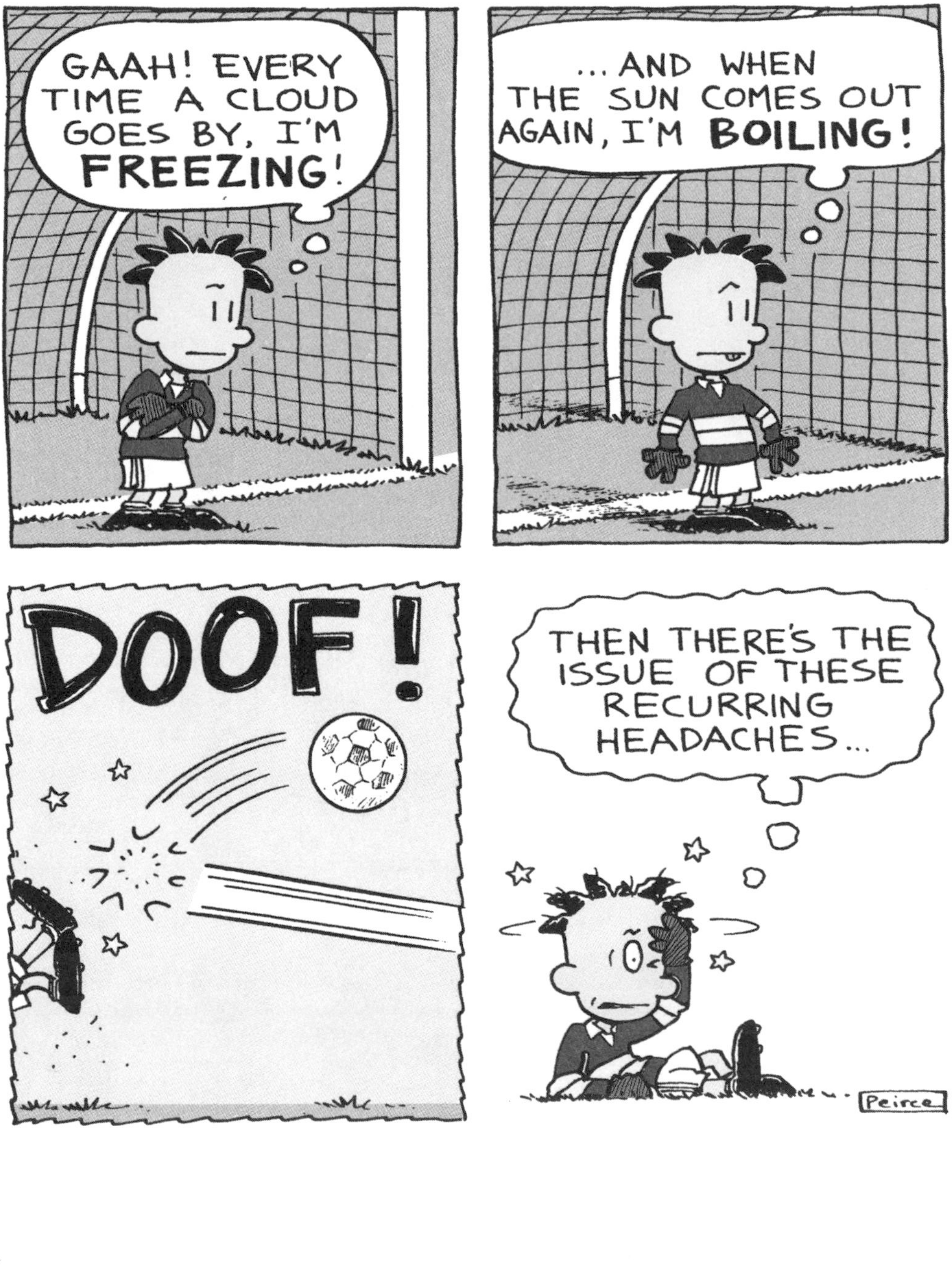
GAAH! EVERY TIME A CLOUD GOES BY, I'M FREEZING!
...AND WHEN THE SUN COMES OUT AGAIN, I'M BOILING!
DOOF!
THEN THERE'S THE ISSUE OF THESE RECURRING HEADACHES...
Peirce

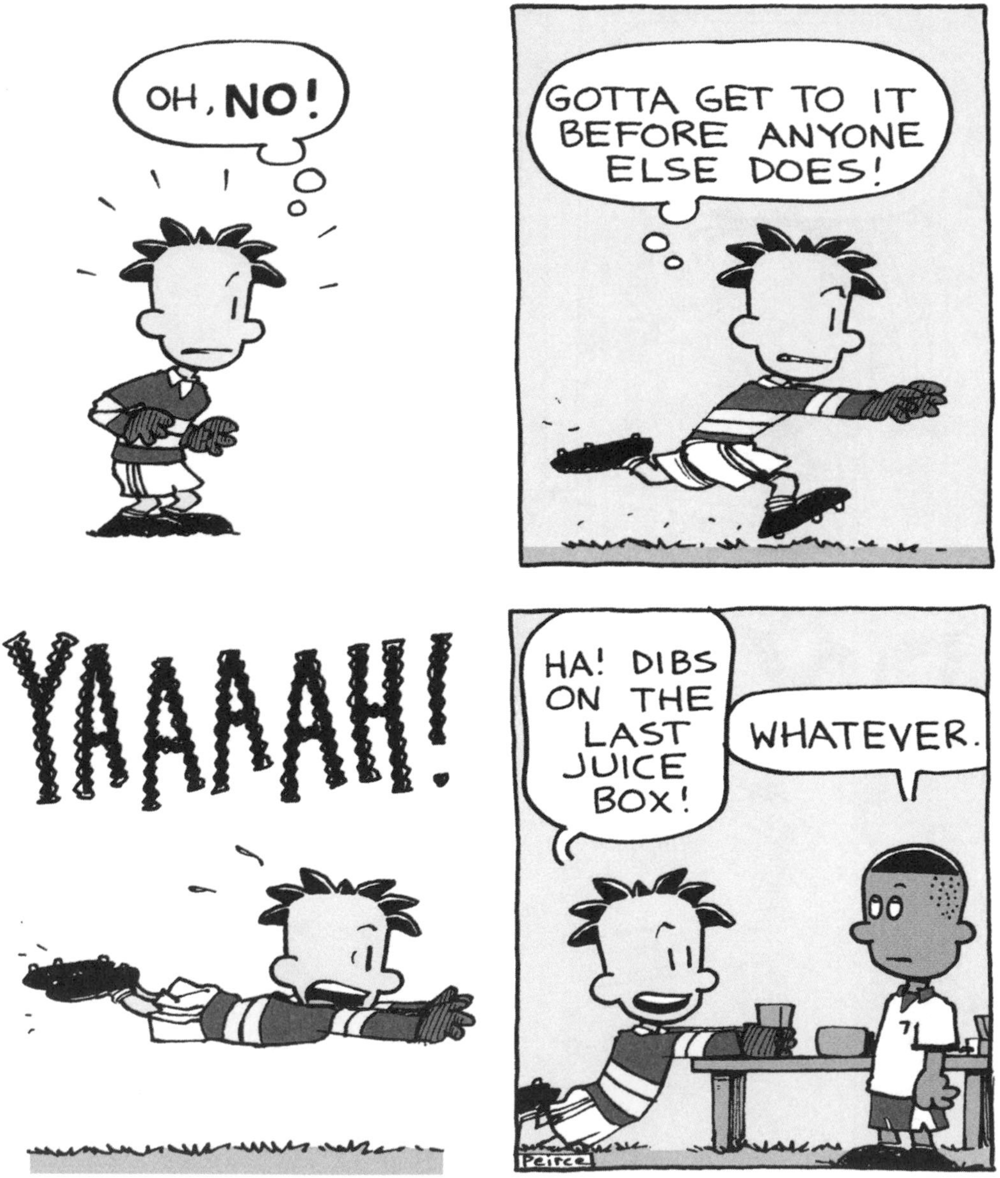

OH, NO!
GOTTA GET TO IT BEFORE ANYONE ELSE DOES!
YAAAAH!
HA! DIBS ON THE LAST JUICE BOX!
WHATEVER.
Peirce

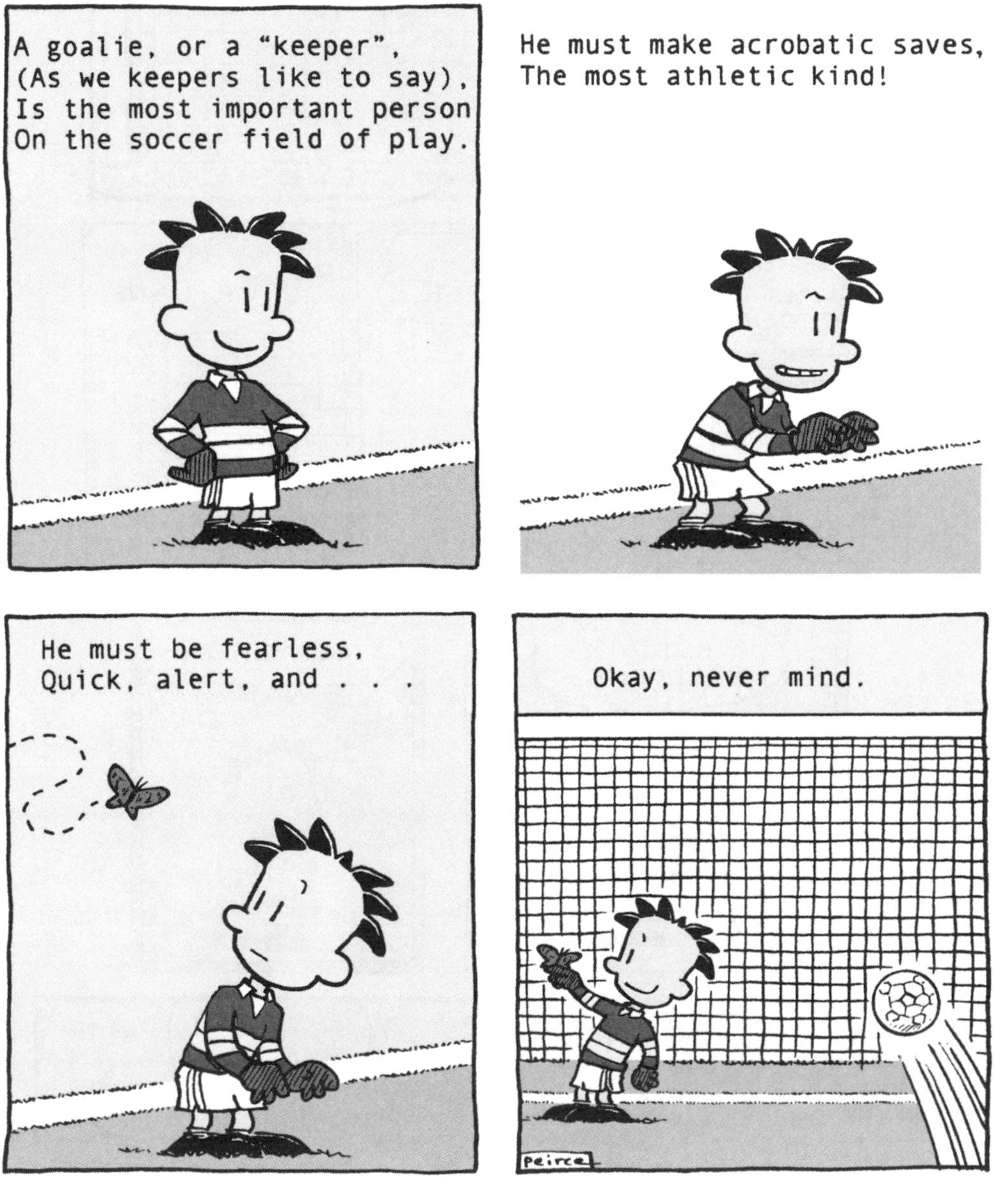
A goalie, or a "keeper",
(As we keepers like to say),
Is the most important person
On the soccer field of play.
He must make acrobatic saves,
The most athletic kind!
He must be fearless,
Quick, alert, and . . .
Okay, never mind.
Peirce

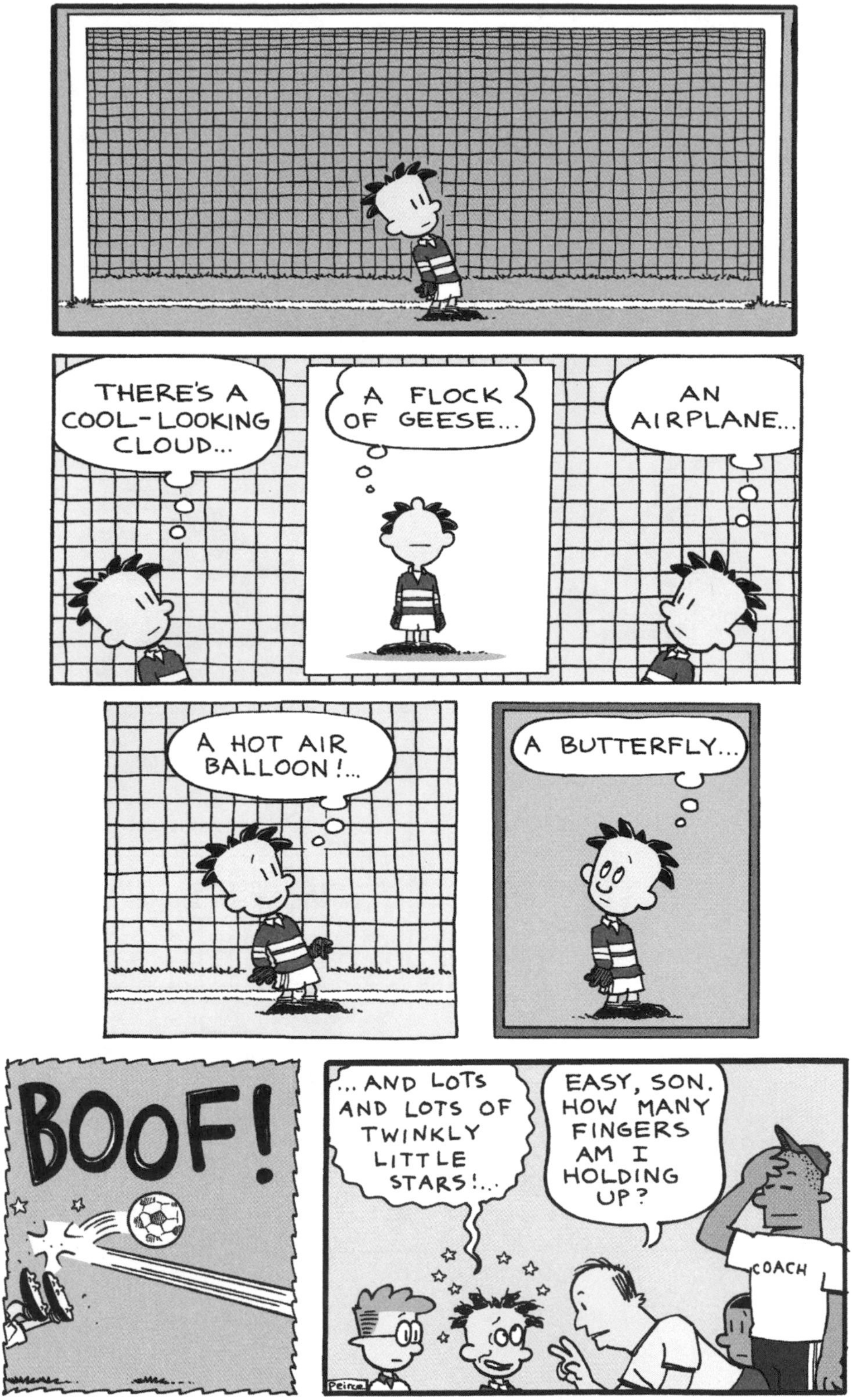
THERE'S A COOL-LOOKING CLOUD...
A FLOCK OF GEESE...
AN AIRPLANE...
A HOT AIR BALLOON!...
A BUTTERFLY...
BOOF!
...AND LOTS AND LOTS OF TWINKLY LITTLE STARS!...
EASY, SON. HOW MANY FINGERS AM I HOLDING UP?
COACH
Peirce

AH! FOR ONCE, I'M READY FOR SCHOOL PICTURE DAY!
I'M NOT GOING TO LET THE SCHOOL PICTURE GUY CATCH ME WITH A STUPID EXPRESSION ON MY FACE! I'VE BEEN **PRACTICING**!
PRACTICING?
HOW DO YOU **PRACTICE** FOR A **PICTURE**?
YOU PRACTICE YOUR **LOOK**! I NOW HAVE MY OWN PERSONAL **LOOK**!
...AND HERE IT IS.
VERY NATURAL.
I THOUGHT THE POINT WAS TO **NOT** LOOK STUPID.
Peirce

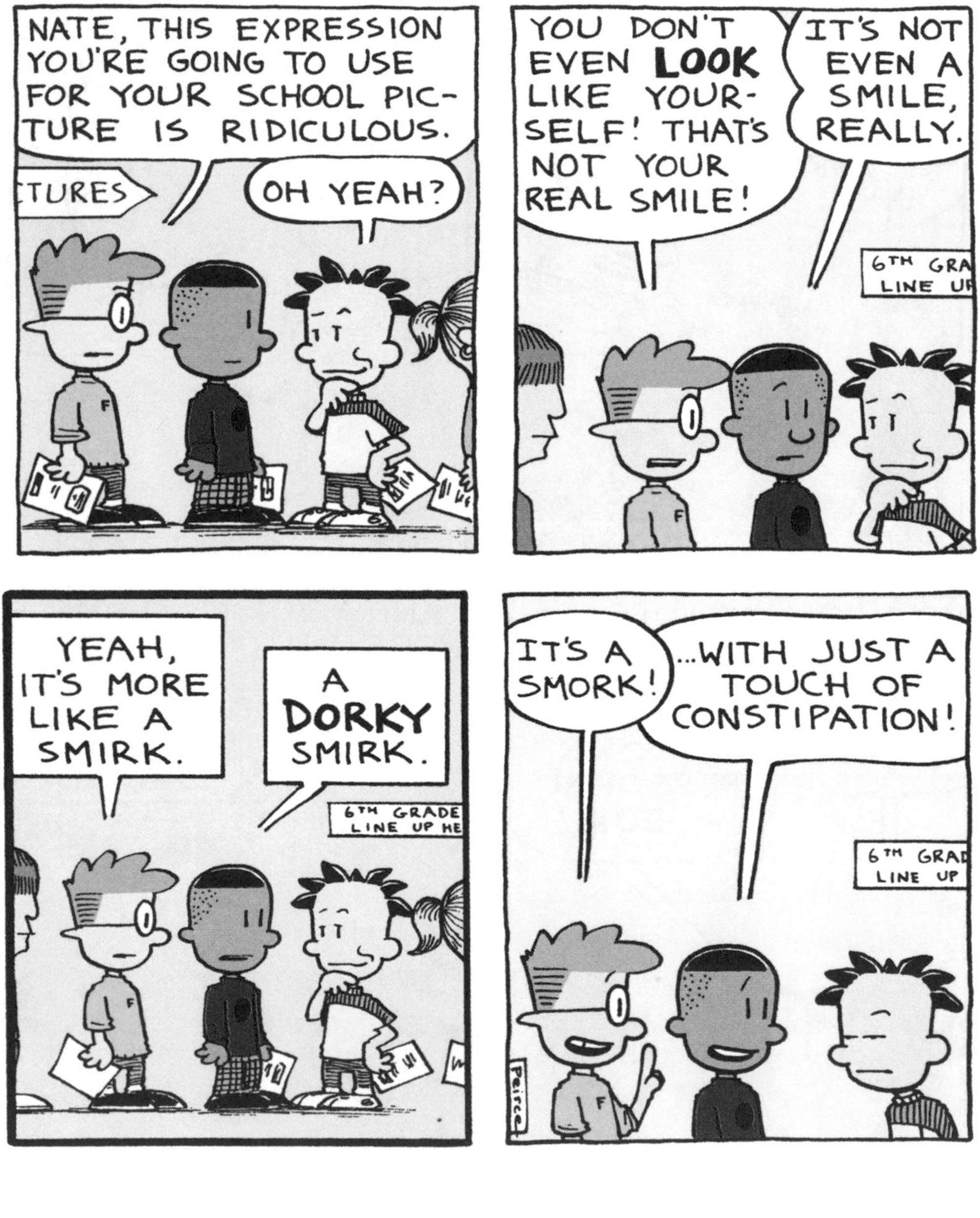
NATE, THIS EXPRESSION YOU'RE GOING TO USE FOR YOUR SCHOOL PICTURE IS RIDICULOUS.
TURES
OH YEAH?
YOU DON'T EVEN LOOK LIKE YOURSELF! THAT'S NOT YOUR REAL SMILE!
IT'S NOT EVEN A SMILE, REALLY.
6TH GRA LINE UP
YEAH, IT'S MORE LIKE A SMIRK.
A DORKY SMIRK.
6TH GRADE LINE UP HE
IT'S A SMORK!
...WITH JUST A TOUCH OF CONSTIPATION!
6TH GRAD LINE UP
Peirce

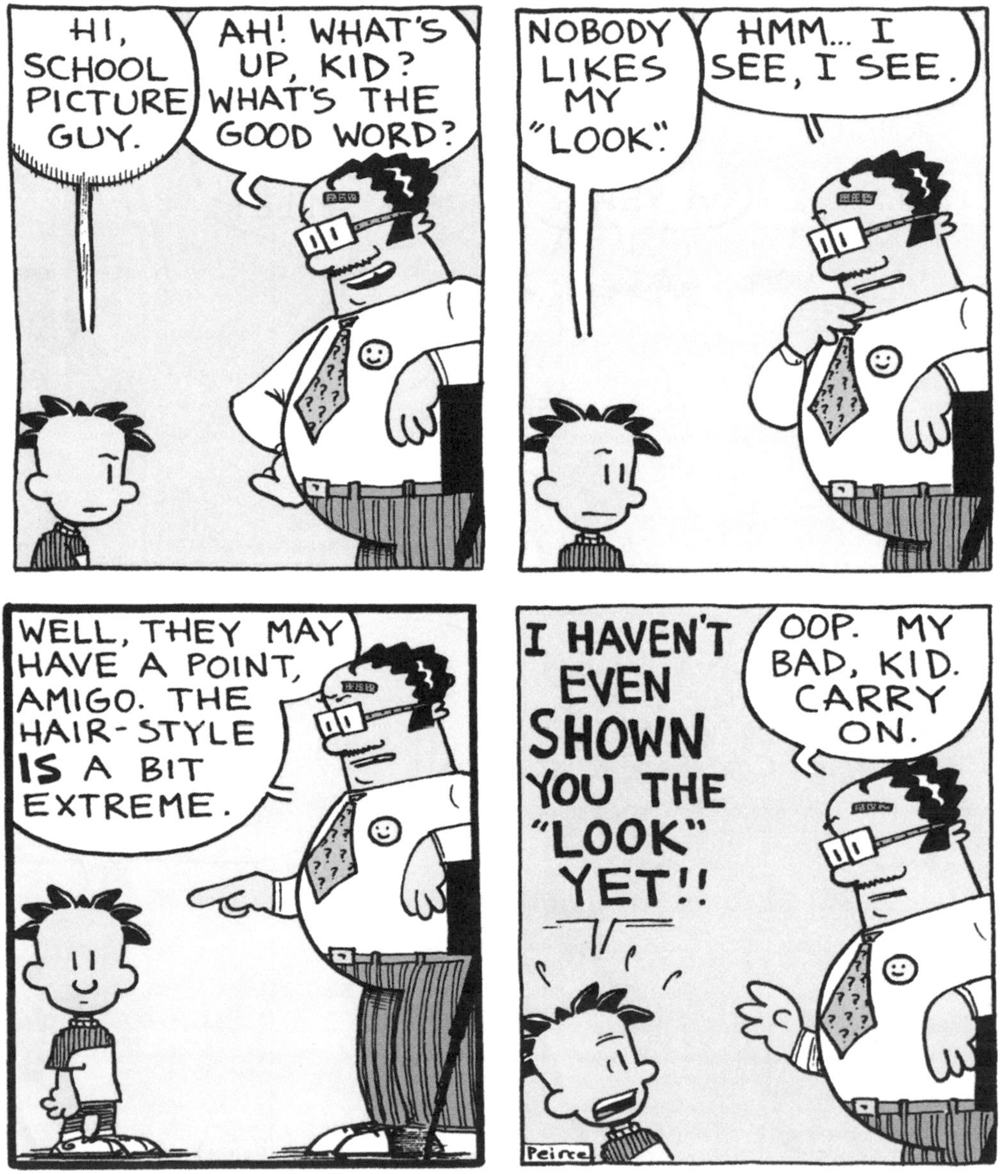
HI, SCHOOL PICTURE GUY.
AH! WHAT'S UP, KID? WHAT'S THE GOOD WORD?
NOBODY LIKES MY "LOOK."
HMM... I SEE, I SEE.
WELL, THEY MAY HAVE A POINT, AMIGO. THE HAIR-STYLE **IS** A BIT EXTREME.
I HAVEN'T EVEN SHOWN YOU THE "LOOK" YET!!
OOP. MY BAD, KID. CARRY ON.
Peirce

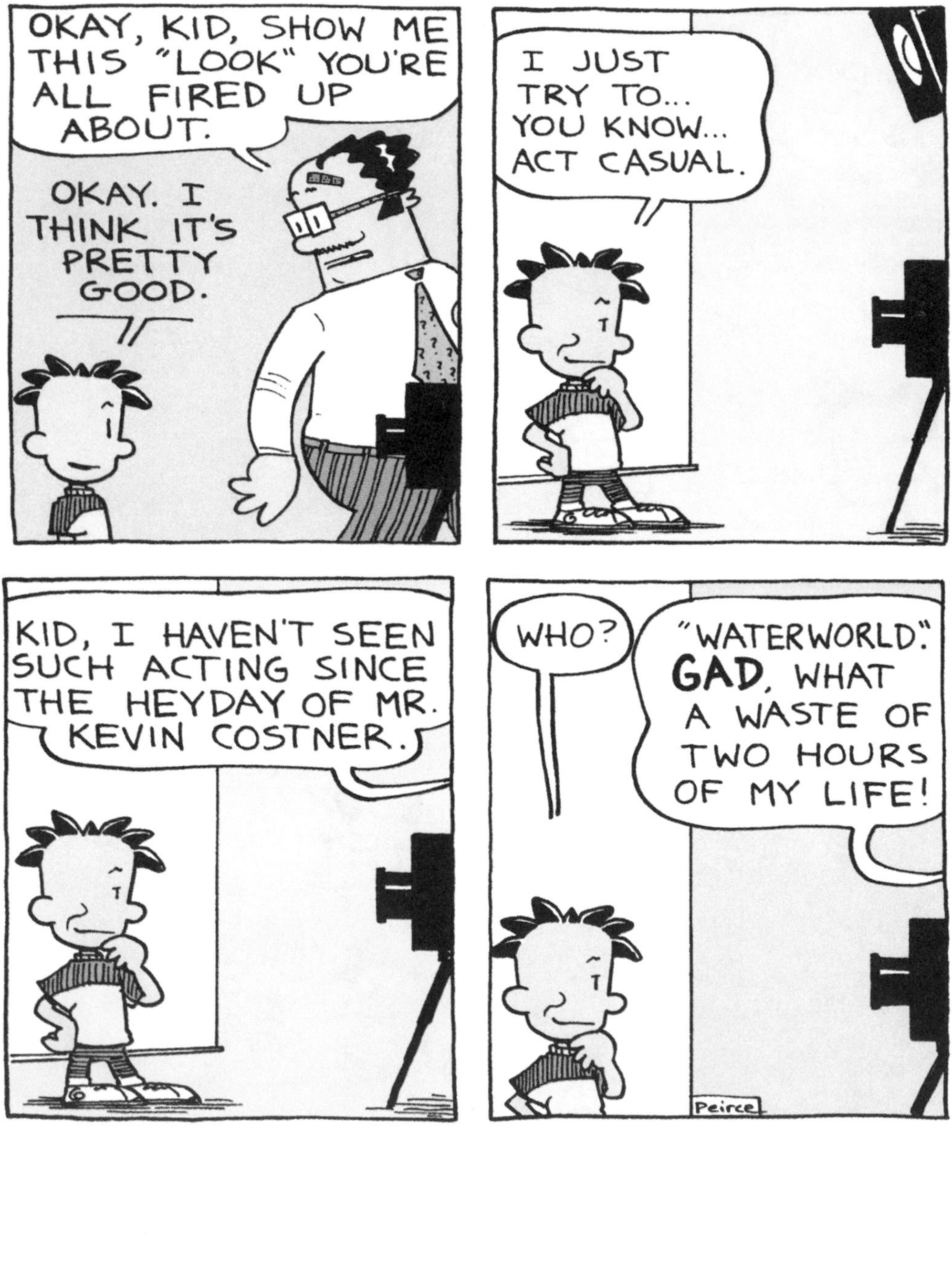
OKAY, KID, SHOW ME THIS "LOOK" YOU'RE ALL FIRED UP ABOUT.
OKAY. I THINK IT'S PRETTY GOOD.
I JUST TRY TO... YOU KNOW... ACT CASUAL.
KID, I HAVEN'T SEEN SUCH ACTING SINCE THE HEYDAY OF MR. KEVIN COSTNER.
"WATERWORLD." GAD, WHAT A WASTE OF TWO HOURS OF MY LIFE!
WHO?
Peirce

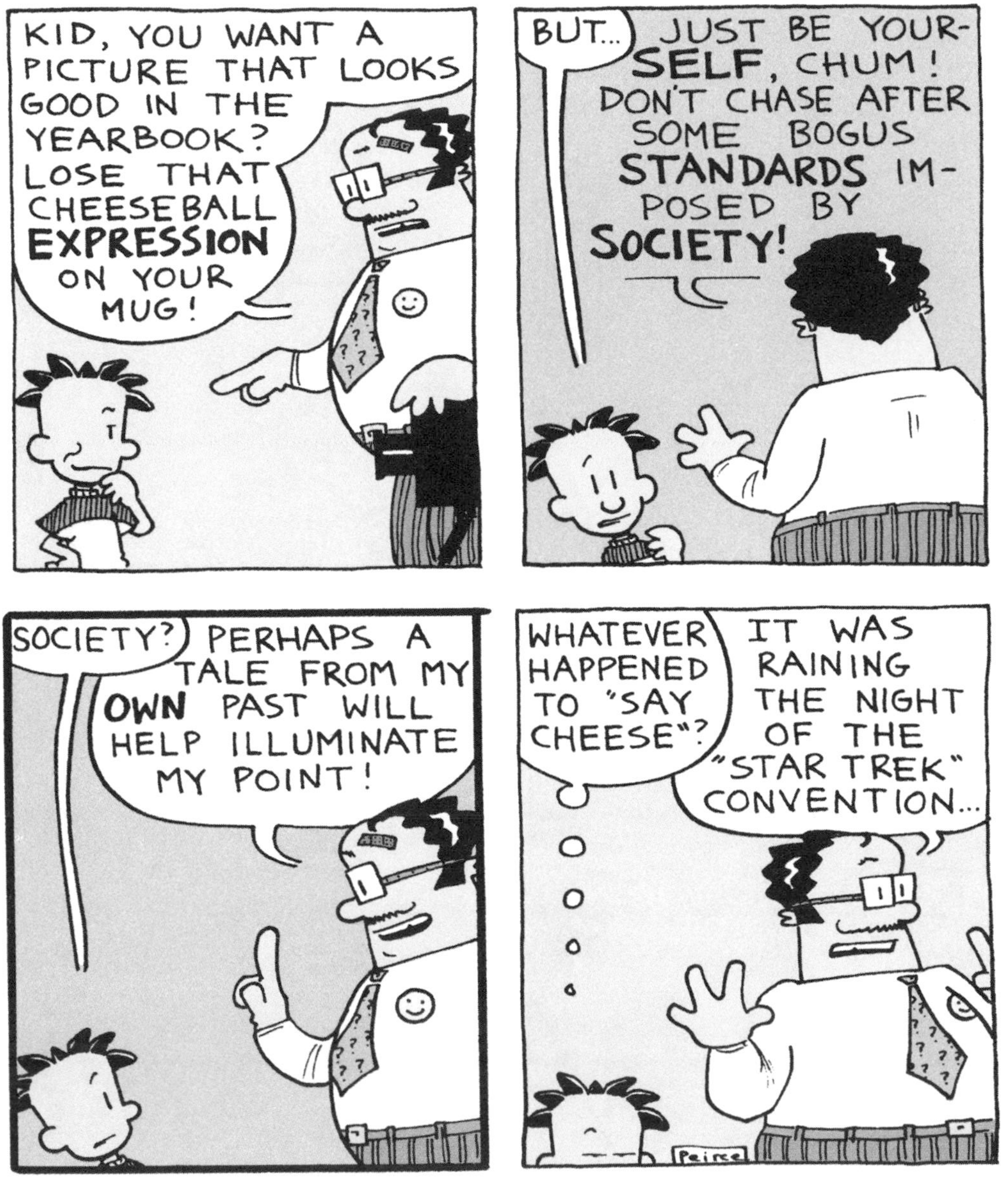
KID, YOU WANT A PICTURE THAT LOOKS GOOD IN THE YEARBOOK? LOSE THAT CHEESEBALL **EXPRESSION** ON YOUR MUG!
BUT...
JUST BE YOUR-**SELF**, CHUM! DON'T CHASE AFTER SOME BOGUS **STANDARDS** IM-POSED BY **SOCIETY**!
SOCIETY?
PERHAPS A TALE FROM MY **OWN** PAST WILL HELP ILLUMINATE MY POINT!
WHATEVER HAPPENED TO "SAY CHEESE"?
IT WAS RAINING THE NIGHT OF THE "STAR TREK" CONVENTION...
Peirce

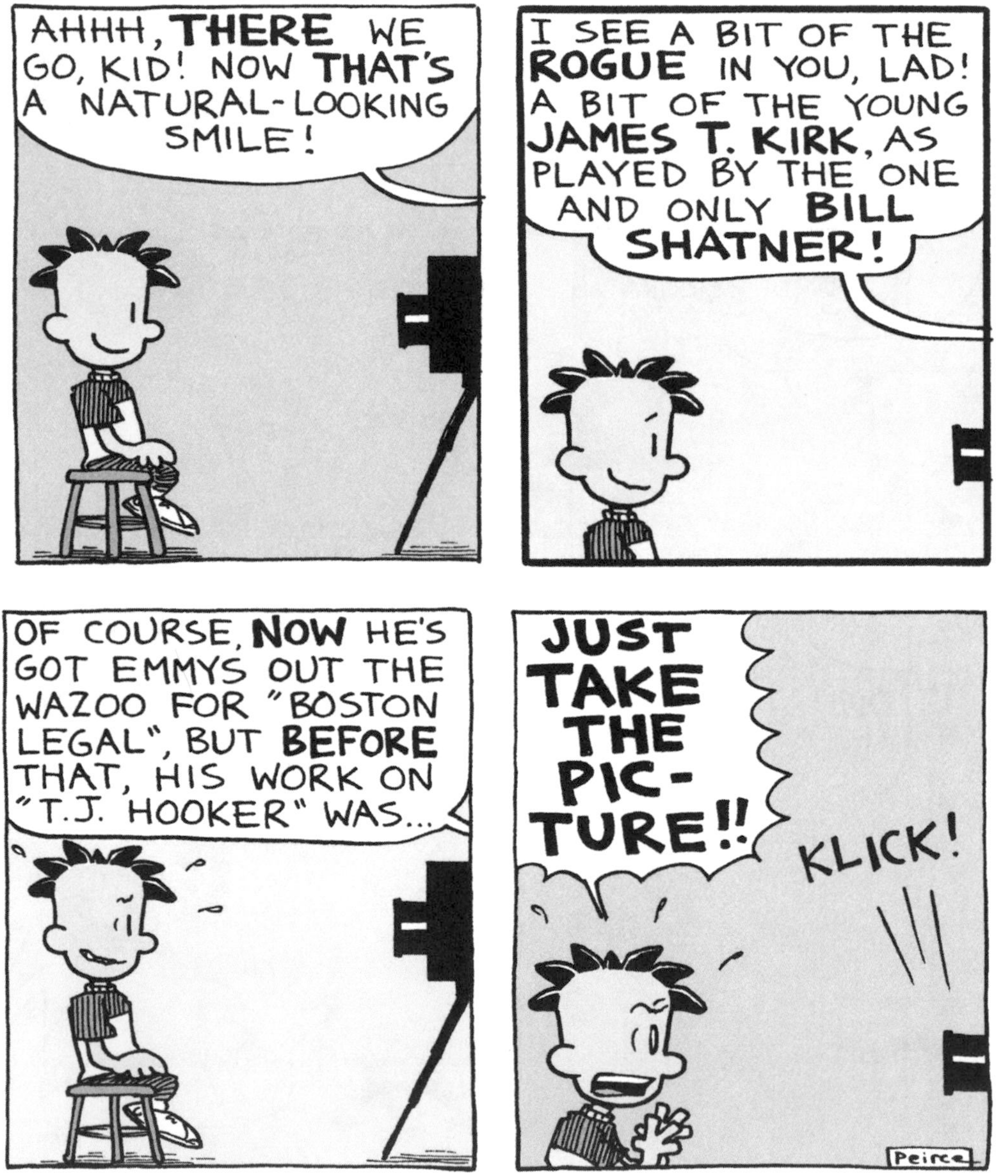
AHHH, THERE WE GO, KID! NOW THAT'S A NATURAL-LOOKING SMILE!
I SEE A BIT OF THE ROGUE IN YOU, LAD! A BIT OF THE YOUNG JAMES T. KIRK, AS PLAYED BY THE ONE AND ONLY BILL SHATNER!
OF COURSE, NOW HE'S GOT EMMYS OUT THE WAZOO FOR "BOSTON LEGAL", BUT BEFORE THAT, HIS WORK ON "T.J. HOOKER" WAS...
JUST TAKE THE PIC-TURE!!
KLICK!
Peirce

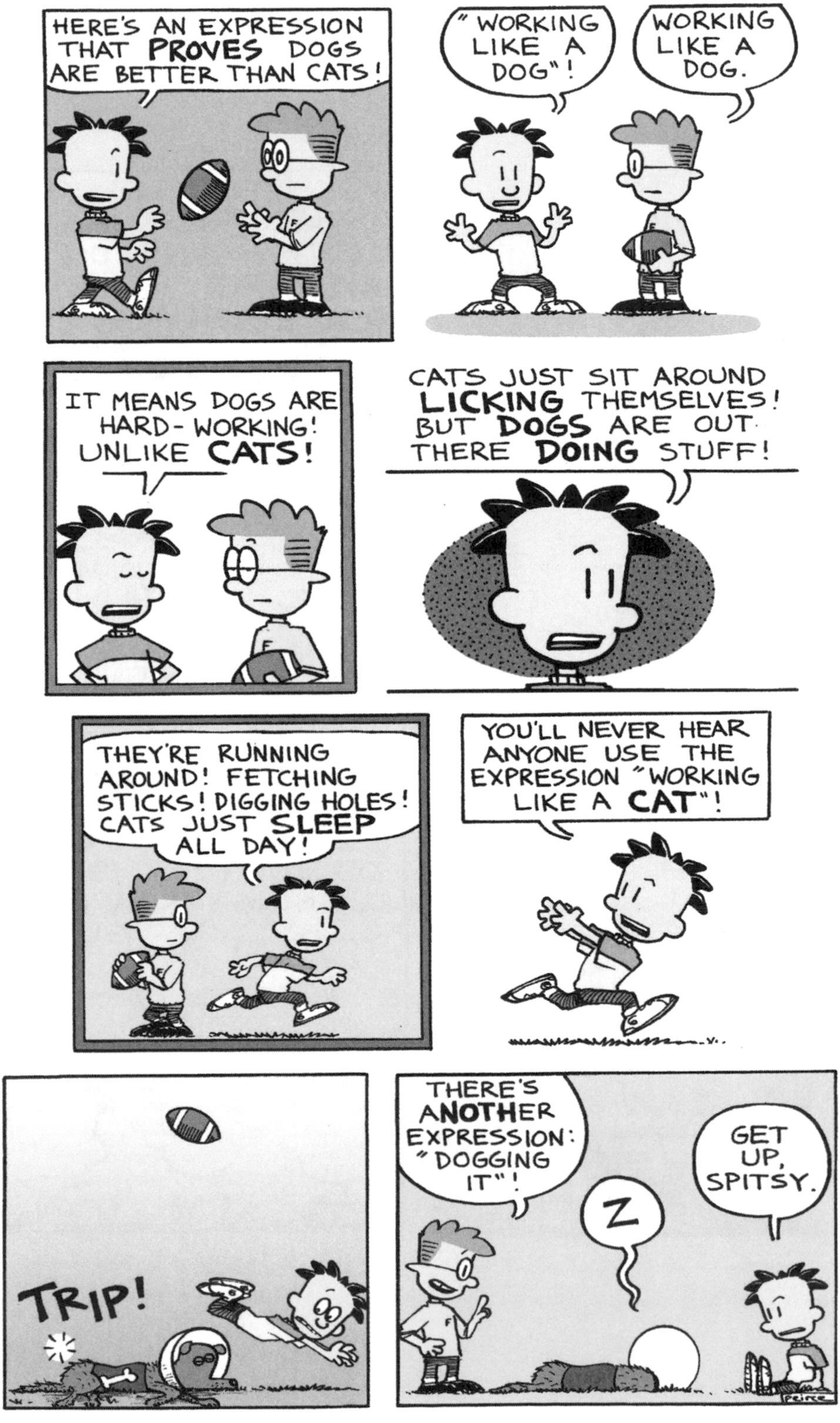
HERE'S AN EXPRESSION THAT PROVES DOGS ARE BETTER THAN CATS!
"WORKING LIKE A DOG"!
WORKING LIKE A DOG.
IT MEANS DOGS ARE HARD-WORKING! UNLIKE CATS!
CATS JUST SIT AROUND LICKING THEMSELVES! BUT DOGS ARE OUT THERE DOING STUFF!
THEY'RE RUNNING AROUND! FETCHING STICKS! DIGGING HOLES! CATS JUST SLEEP ALL DAY!
YOU'LL NEVER HEAR ANYONE USE THE EXPRESSION "WORKING LIKE A CAT"!
TRIP!
THERE'S ANOTHER EXPRESSION: "DOGGING IT"!
Z
GET UP, SPITSY.
peirce

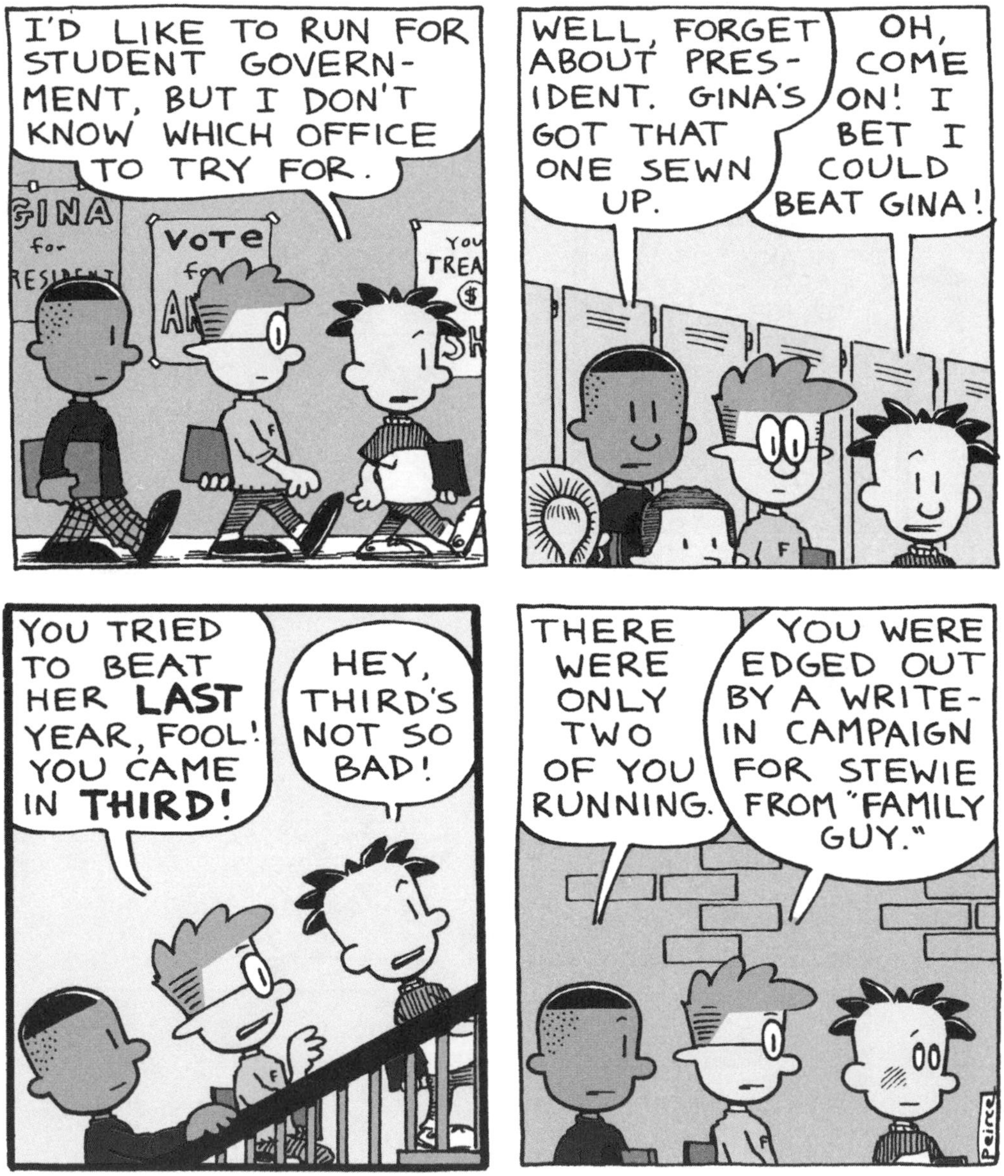
I'D LIKE TO RUN FOR STUDENT GOVERNMENT, BUT I DON'T KNOW WHICH OFFICE TO TRY FOR.
GINA for PRESIDENT
VOTE for
WELL, FORGET ABOUT PRESIDENT. GINA'S GOT THAT ONE SEWN UP.
OH, COME ON! I BET I COULD BEAT GINA!
YOU TRIED TO BEAT HER LAST YEAR, FOOL! YOU CAME IN THIRD!
HEY, THIRD'S NOT SO BAD!
THERE WERE ONLY TWO OF YOU RUNNING.
YOU WERE EDGED OUT BY A WRITE-IN CAMPAIGN FOR STEWIE FROM "FAMILY GUY."
Peirce

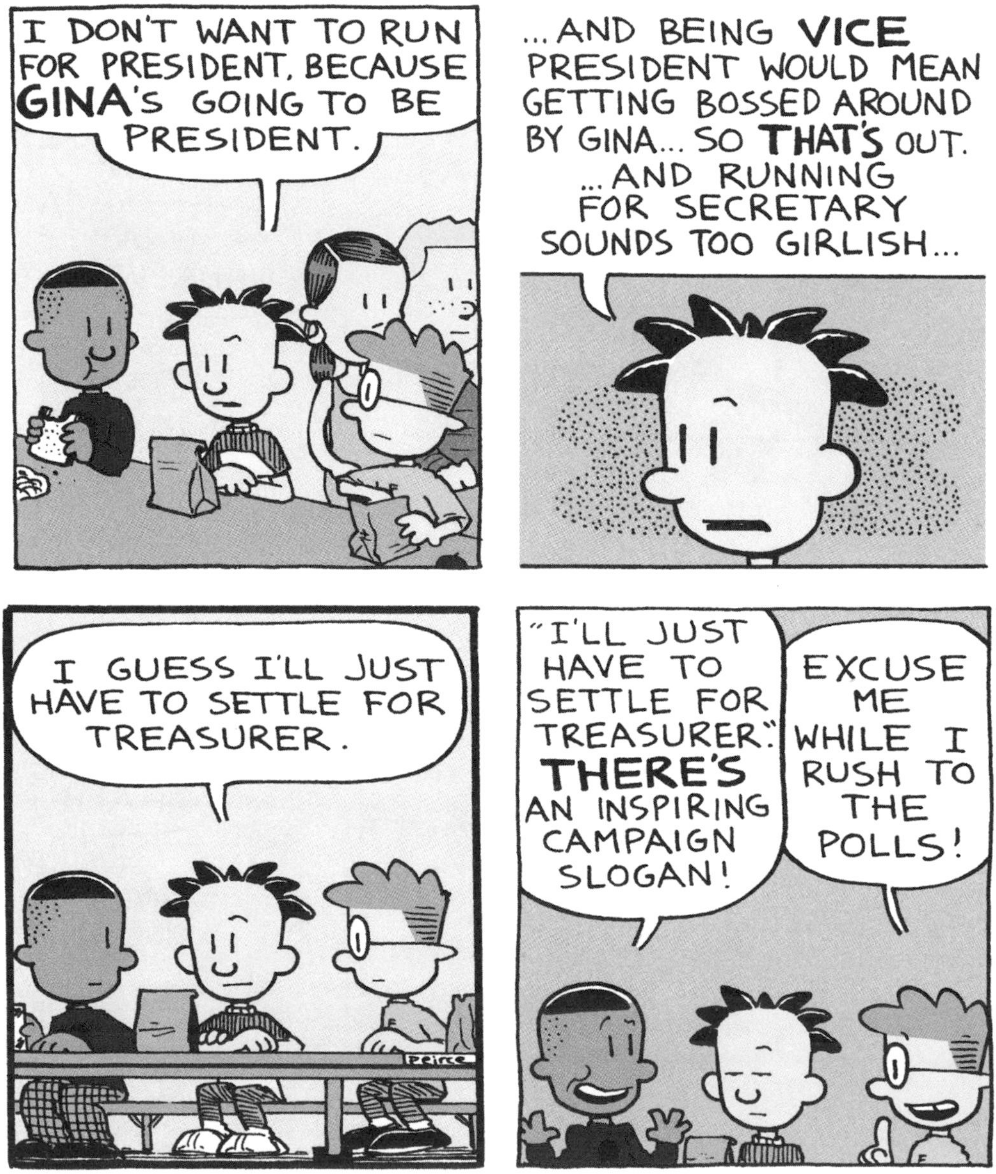
I DON'T WANT TO RUN FOR PRESIDENT, BECAUSE GINA'S GOING TO BE PRESIDENT.
...AND BEING VICE PRESIDENT WOULD MEAN GETTING BOSSED AROUND BY GINA... SO THAT'S OUT.
...AND RUNNING FOR SECRETARY SOUNDS TOO GIRLISH...
I GUESS I'LL JUST HAVE TO SETTLE FOR TREASURER.
PEIRCE
"I'LL JUST HAVE TO SETTLE FOR TREASURER." THERE'S AN INSPIRING CAMPAIGN SLOGAN!
EXCUSE ME WHILE I RUSH TO THE POLLS!

FASTEN YOUR SEAT BELT, SHEILA! I'M RUNNING AGAINST YOU FOR TREASURER!

YOU? REALLY?

YUP, AND I CAN'T WAIT TO GET ELECTED! MY ALLOWANCE JUST DOESN'T GO AS FAR AS IT USED TO!

WHAT? WHOA, **WHOA!**

NATE! YOU CAN'T RAID THE SIXTH GRADE TREASURY FOR YOUR **PERSONAL USE!!**

WELL, **DUH!** I **REALIZE** THAT, SHEILA!

ALL I'M SAYING IS, THE SALARY WILL COME IN HANDY!

UH... MORE BAD NEWS, CHAMP...

I'VE DECIDED NOT TO RUN FOR STUDENT GOVERNMENT.

WHAT CHANGED YOUR MIND?

WELL, YOU DON'T REALLY **DO** ANYTHING IN STUDENT GOVERNMENT! YOU DON'T HAVE ANY **POWER!**

WHAT'S THE POINT IN RUNNING FOR OFFICE IF IT DOESN'T GIVE ME **POWER?** ... OR MONEY?

...OR FAME. FAME IS GOOD.

THERE'S NOTHING LIKE PUBLIC SERVICE.

CERTAINLY NOT IN THIS CASE.

Peirce

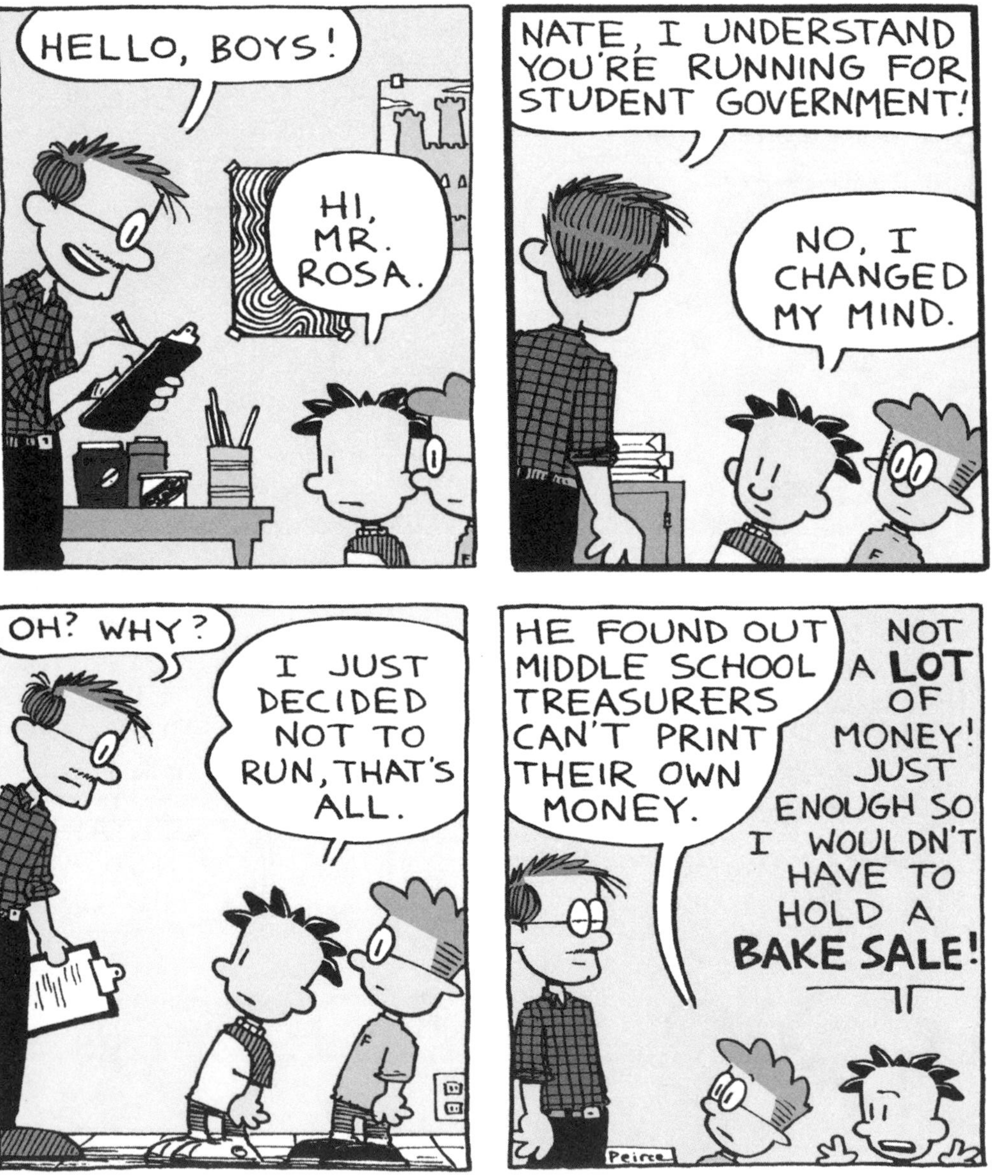
HELLO, BOYS!
HI, MR. ROSA.
NATE, I UNDERSTAND YOU'RE RUNNING FOR STUDENT GOVERNMENT!
NO, I CHANGED MY MIND.
OH? WHY?
I JUST DECIDED NOT TO RUN, THAT'S ALL.
HE FOUND OUT MIDDLE SCHOOL TREASURERS CAN'T PRINT THEIR OWN MONEY.
NOT A LOT OF MONEY! JUST ENOUGH SO I WOULDN'T HAVE TO HOLD A BAKE SALE!
Peirce

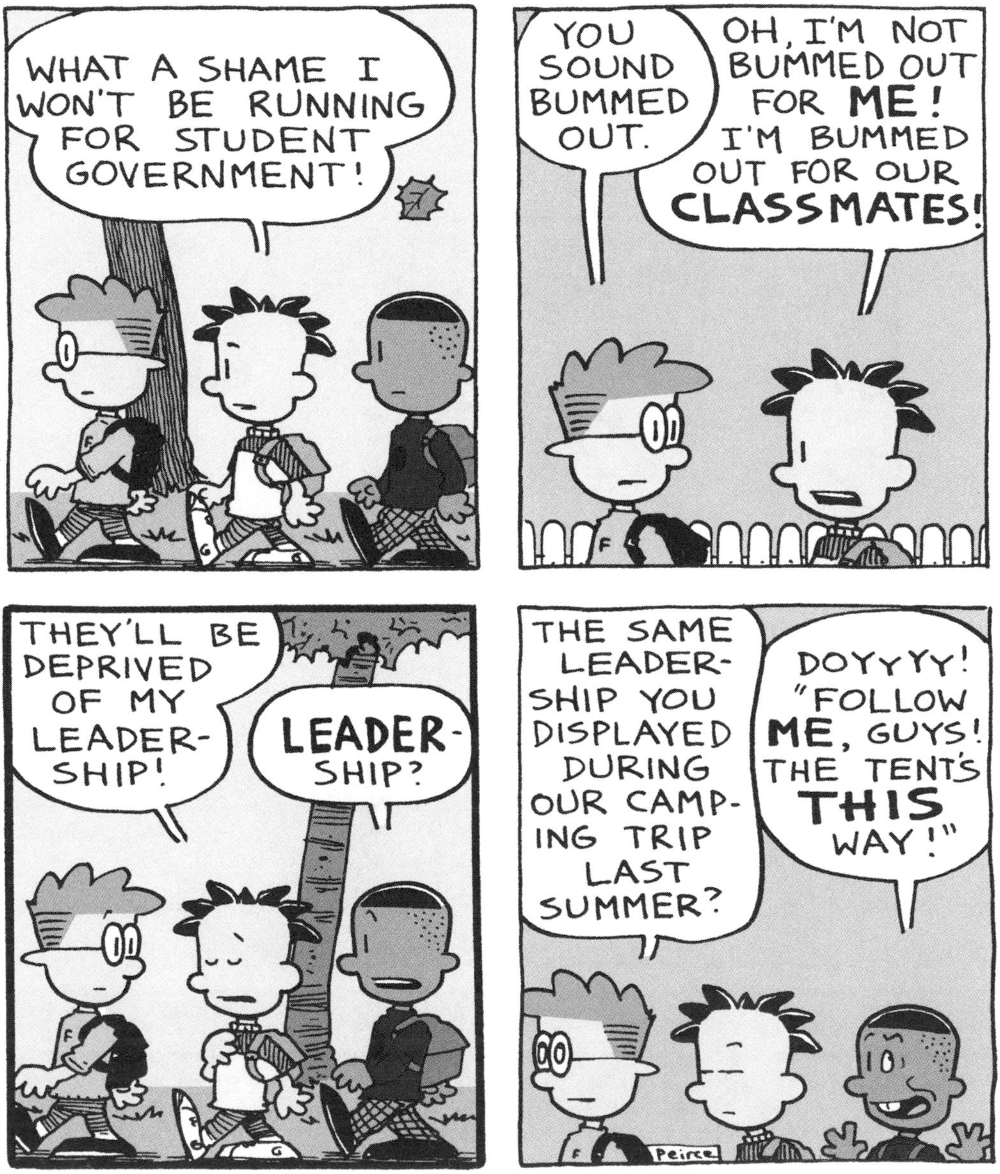
WHAT A SHAME I WON'T BE RUNNING FOR STUDENT GOVERNMENT!
YOU SOUND BUMMED OUT.
OH, I'M NOT BUMMED OUT FOR **ME**! I'M BUMMED OUT FOR OUR **CLASSMATES**!
THEY'LL BE DEPRIVED OF MY LEADER-SHIP!
LEADER-SHIP?
THE SAME LEADER-SHIP YOU DISPLAYED DURING OUR CAMP-ING TRIP LAST SUMMER?
DOYYYY! "FOLLOW **ME**, GUYS! THE TENT'S **THIS** WAY!"
Peirce

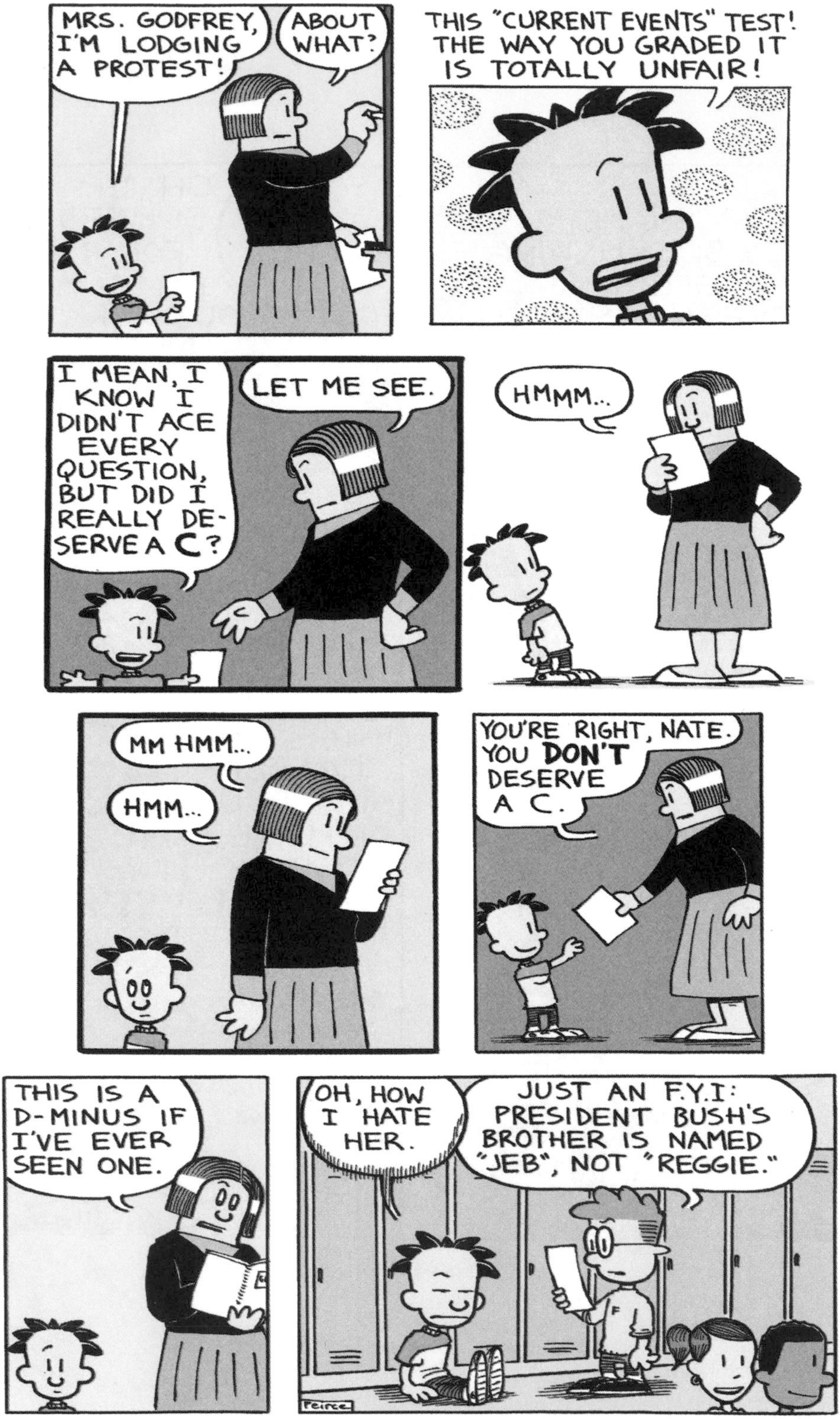
MRS. GODFREY, I'M LODGING A PROTEST!
ABOUT WHAT?
THIS "CURRENT EVENTS" TEST! THE WAY YOU GRADED IT IS TOTALLY UNFAIR!
I MEAN, I KNOW I DIDN'T ACE EVERY QUESTION, BUT DID I REALLY DE-SERVE A C?
LET ME SEE.
HMMM...
MM HMM...
HMM...
YOU'RE RIGHT, NATE. YOU DON'T DESERVE A C.
THIS IS A D-MINUS IF I'VE EVER SEEN ONE.
OH, HOW I HATE HER.
JUST AN F.Y.I: PRESIDENT BUSH'S BROTHER IS NAMED "JEB", NOT "REGGIE."
Peirce

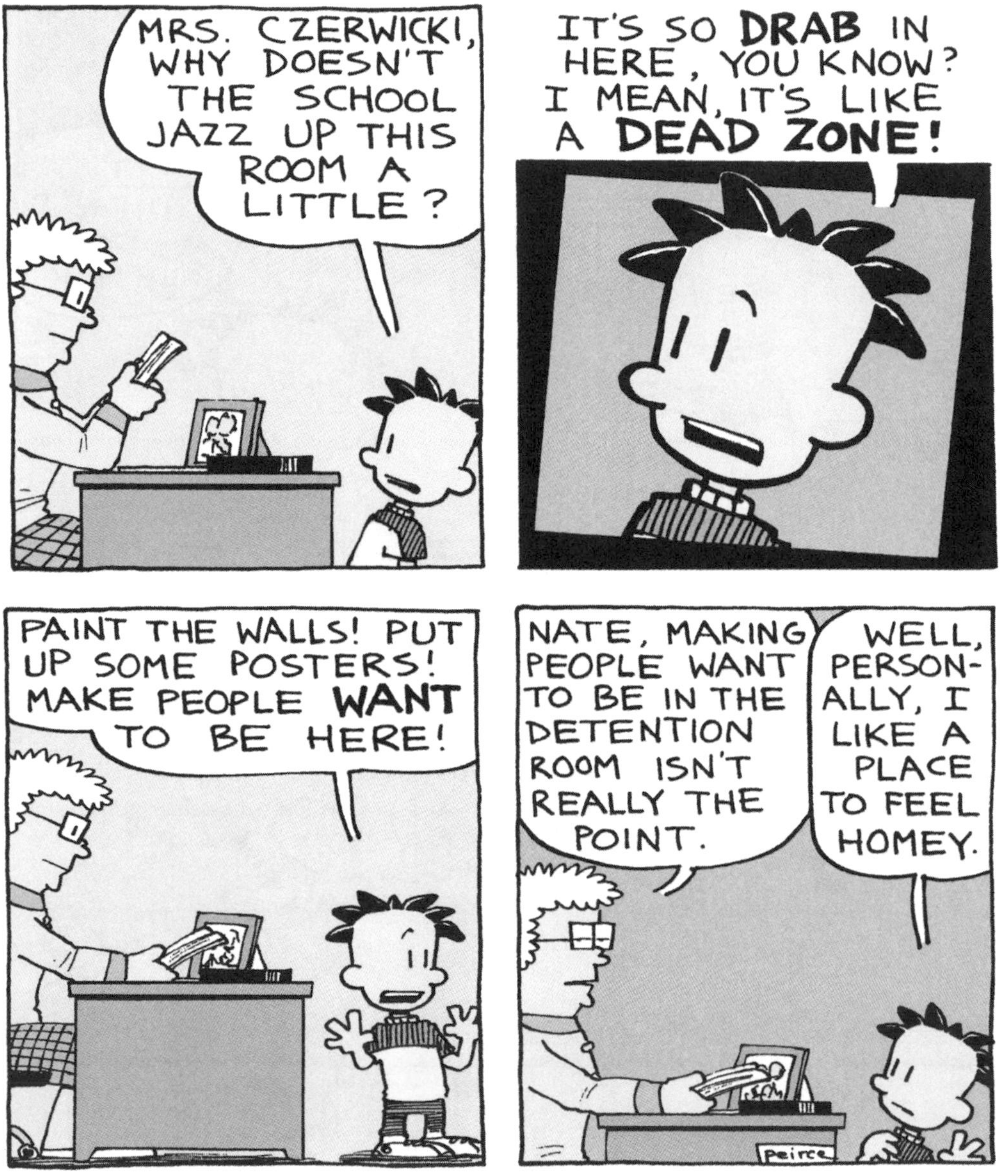
MRS. CZERWICKI, WHY DOESN'T THE SCHOOL JAZZ UP THIS ROOM A LITTLE?
IT'S SO DRAB IN HERE, YOU KNOW? I MEAN, IT'S LIKE A DEAD ZONE!
PAINT THE WALLS! PUT UP SOME POSTERS! MAKE PEOPLE WANT TO BE HERE!
NATE, MAKING PEOPLE WANT TO BE IN THE DETENTION ROOM ISN'T REALLY THE POINT.
WELL, PERSONALLY, I LIKE A PLACE TO FEEL HOMEY.
peirce

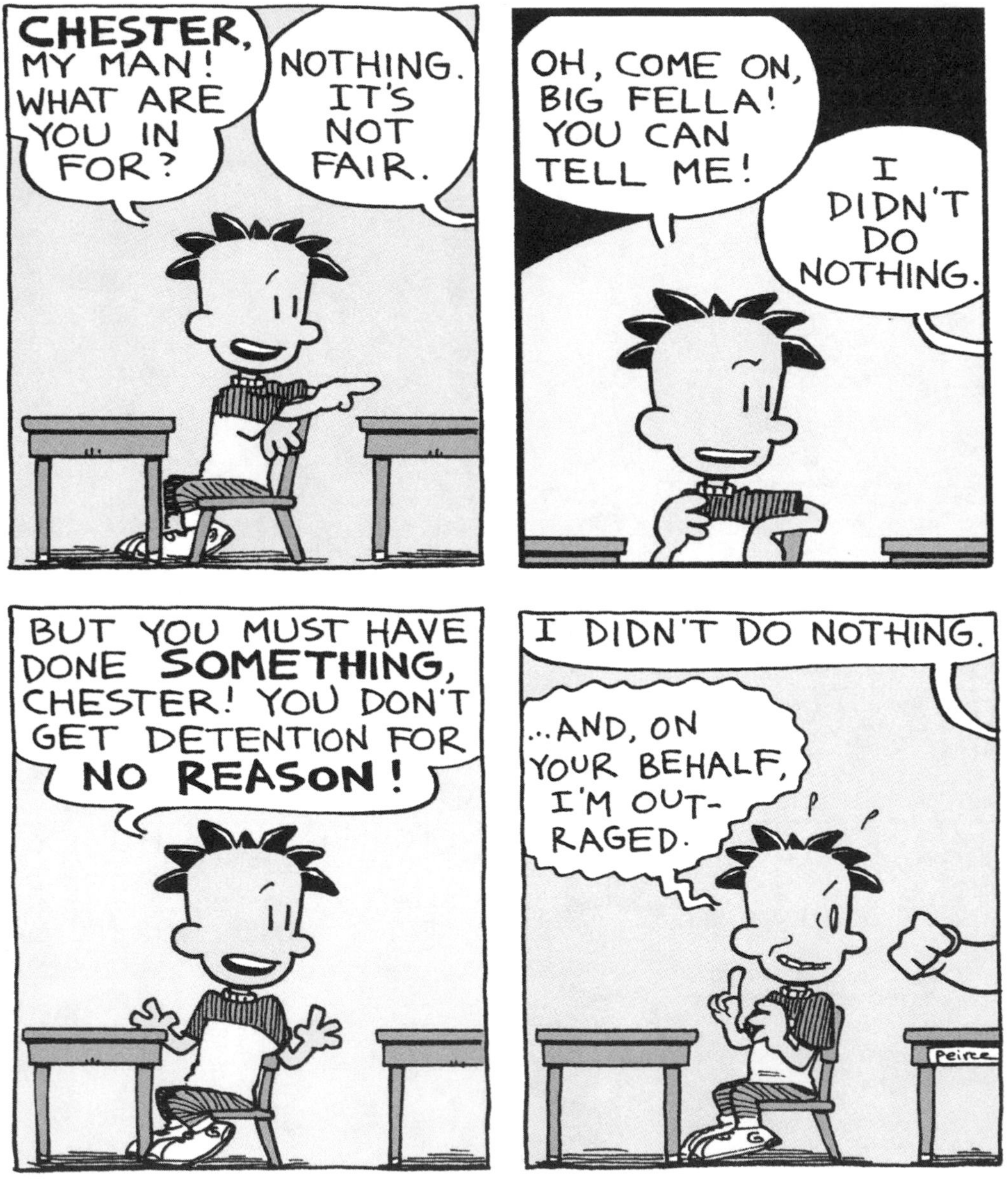
CHESTER, MY MAN! WHAT ARE YOU IN FOR?
NOTHING. IT'S NOT FAIR.
OH, COME ON, BIG FELLA! YOU CAN TELL ME!
I DIDN'T DO NOTHING.
BUT YOU MUST HAVE DONE SOMETHING, CHESTER! YOU DON'T GET DETENTION FOR NO REASON!
I DIDN'T DO NOTHING.
...AND, ON YOUR BEHALF, I'M OUT-RAGED.
Peirce

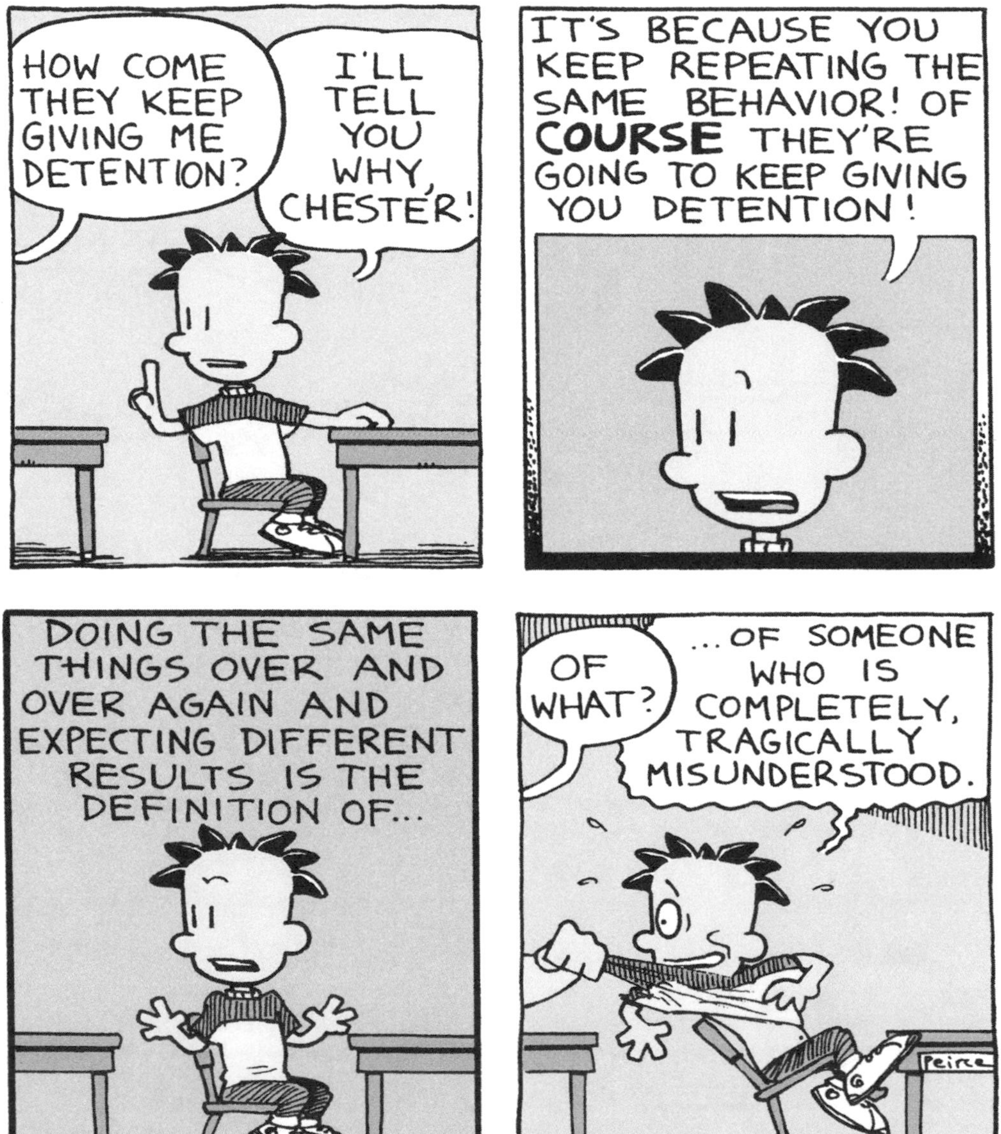
HOW COME THEY KEEP GIVING ME DETENTION?
I'LL TELL YOU WHY, CHESTER!
IT'S BECAUSE YOU KEEP REPEATING THE SAME BEHAVIOR! OF **COURSE** THEY'RE GOING TO KEEP GIVING YOU DETENTION!
DOING THE SAME THINGS OVER AND OVER AGAIN AND EXPECTING DIFFERENT RESULTS IS THE DEFINITION OF...
OF WHAT?
...OF SOMEONE WHO IS COMPLETELY, TRAGICALLY MISUNDERSTOOD.
Peirce

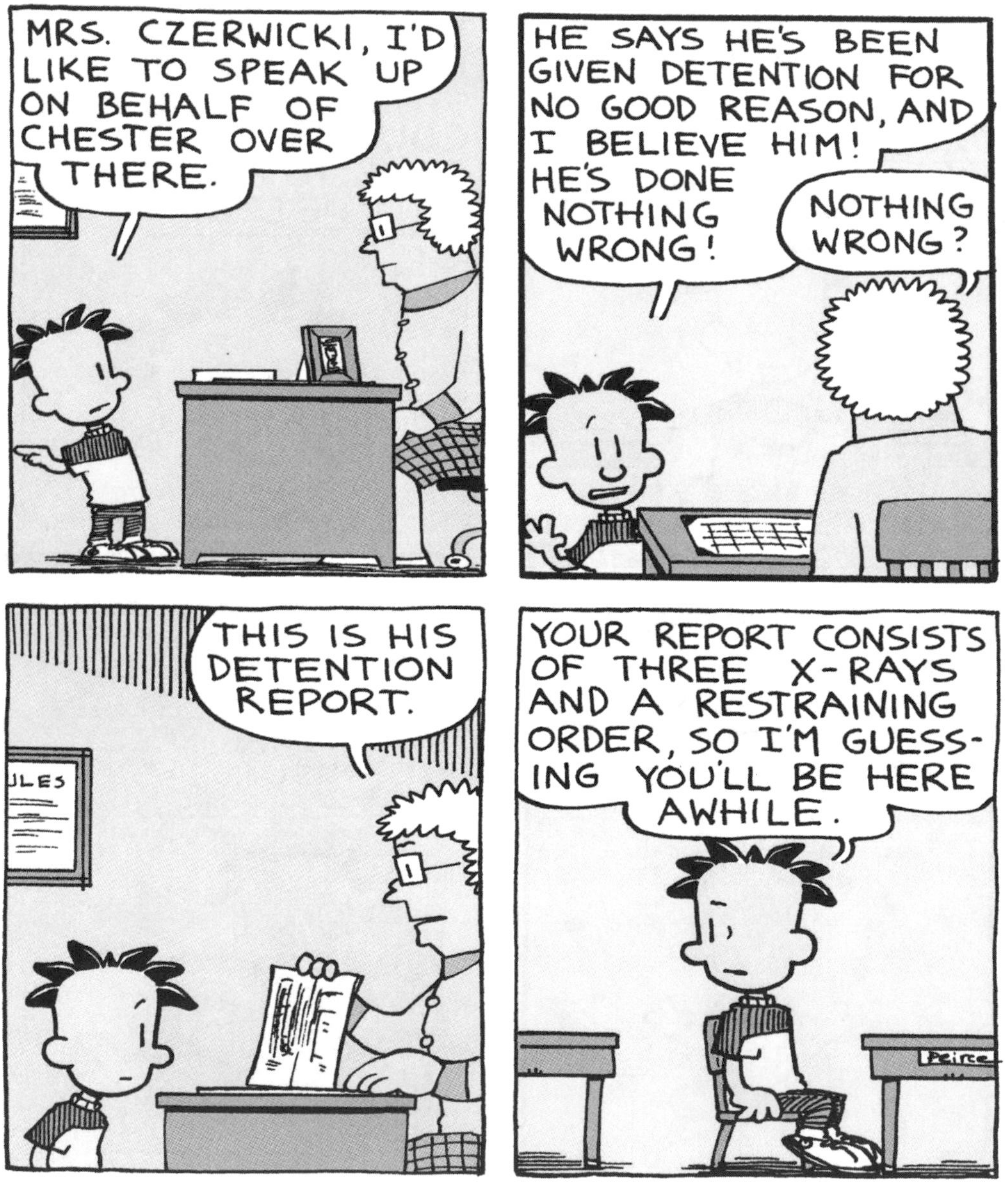
MRS. CZERWICKI, I'D LIKE TO SPEAK UP ON BEHALF OF CHESTER OVER THERE.
HE SAYS HE'S BEEN GIVEN DETENTION FOR NO GOOD REASON, AND I BELIEVE HIM! HE'S DONE NOTHING WRONG!
NOTHING WRONG?
THIS IS HIS DETENTION REPORT.
YOUR REPORT CONSISTS OF THREE X-RAYS AND A RESTRAINING ORDER, SO I'M GUESSING YOU'LL BE HERE AWHILE.

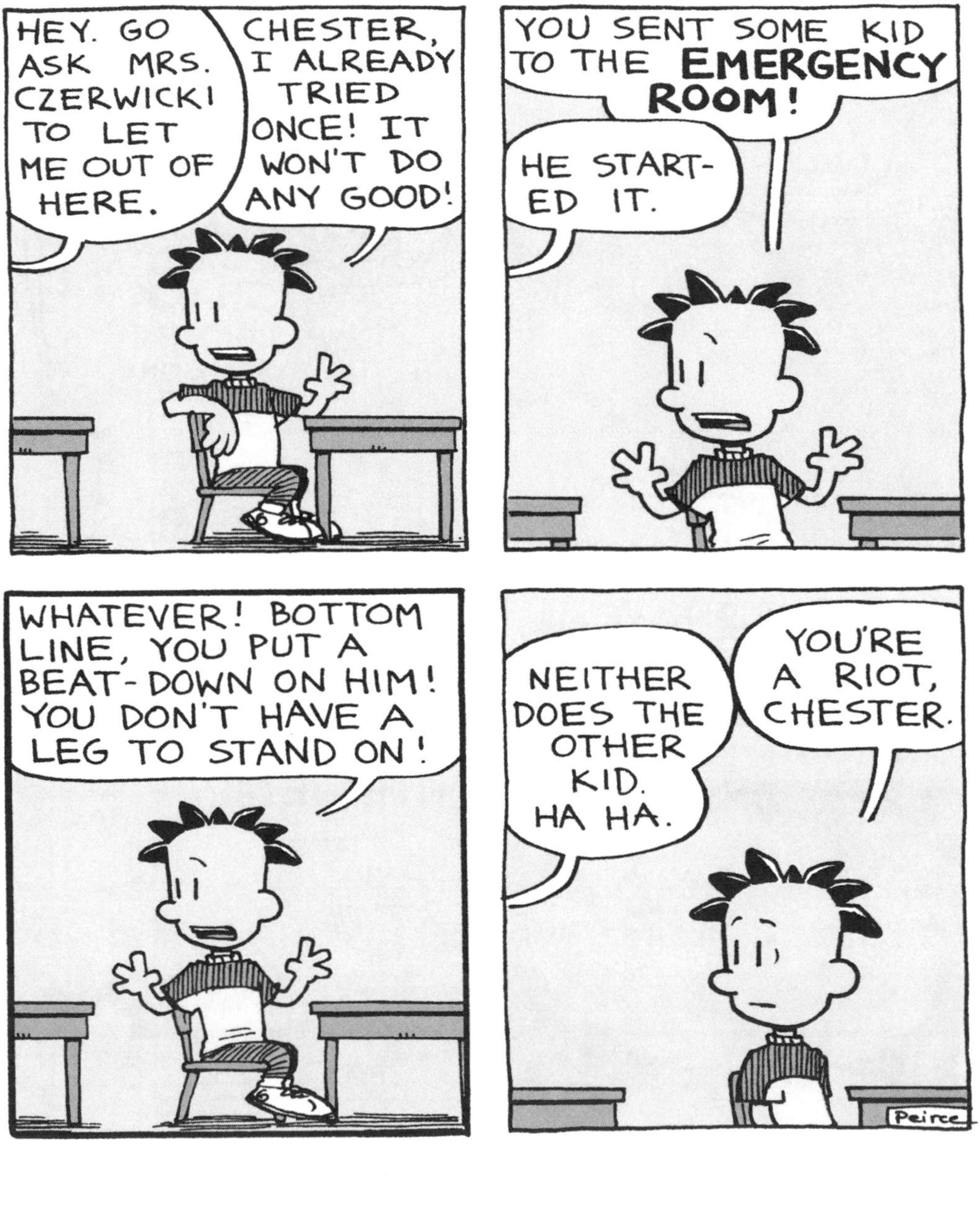
HEY. GO ASK MRS. CZERWICKI TO LET ME OUT OF HERE.
CHESTER, I ALREADY TRIED ONCE! IT WON'T DO ANY GOOD!
YOU SENT SOME KID TO THE EMERGENCY ROOM!
HE STARTED IT.
WHATEVER! BOTTOM LINE, YOU PUT A BEAT-DOWN ON HIM! YOU DON'T HAVE A LEG TO STAND ON!
NEITHER DOES THE OTHER KID. HA HA.
YOU'RE A RIOT, CHESTER.
Peirce

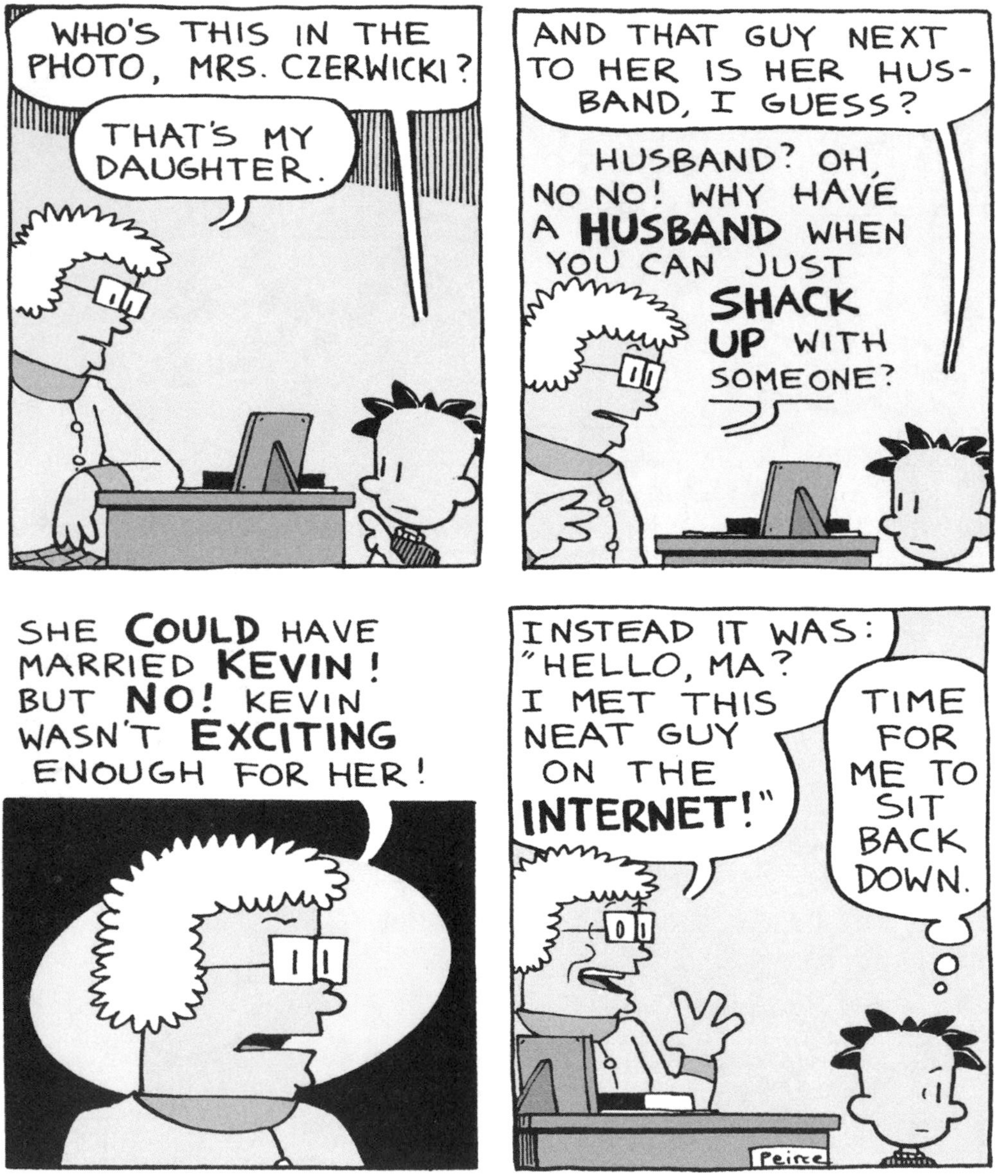
WHO'S THIS IN THE PHOTO, MRS. CZERWICKI?
THAT'S MY DAUGHTER.
AND THAT GUY NEXT TO HER IS HER HUSBAND, I GUESS?
HUSBAND? OH, NO NO! WHY HAVE A HUSBAND WHEN YOU CAN JUST SHACK UP WITH SOMEONE?
SHE COULD HAVE MARRIED KEVIN! BUT NO! KEVIN WASN'T EXCITING ENOUGH FOR HER!
INSTEAD IT WAS: "HELLO, MA? I MET THIS NEAT GUY ON THE INTERNET!"
TIME FOR ME TO SIT BACK DOWN.
Peirce

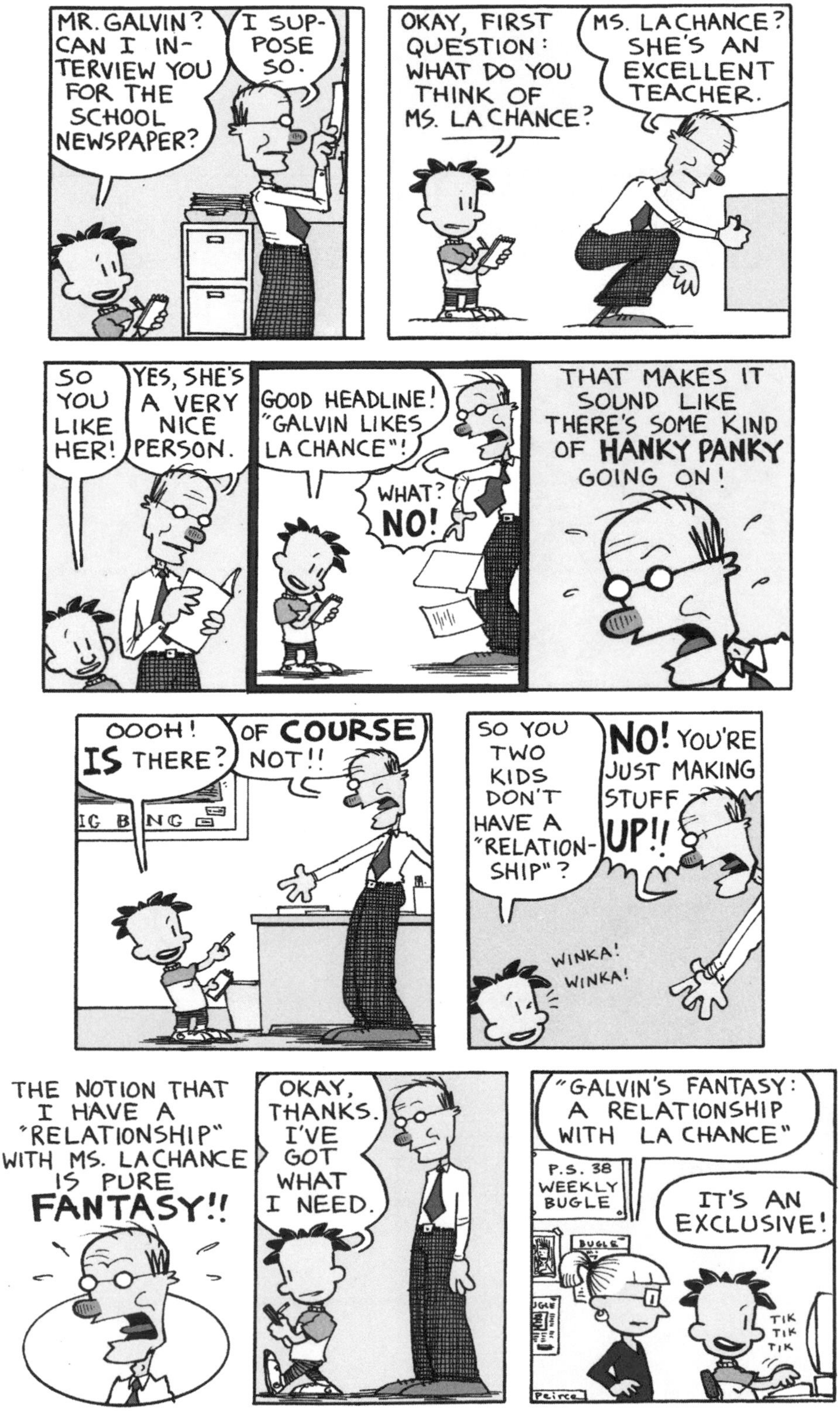
MR. GALVIN? CAN I INTERVIEW YOU FOR THE SCHOOL NEWSPAPER?
I SUPPOSE SO.
OKAY, FIRST QUESTION: WHAT DO YOU THINK OF MS. LA CHANCE?
MS. LA CHANCE? SHE'S AN EXCELLENT TEACHER.
SO YOU LIKE HER!
YES, SHE'S A VERY NICE PERSON.
GOOD HEADLINE! "GALVIN LIKES LA CHANCE"!
WHAT? NO!
THAT MAKES IT SOUND LIKE THERE'S SOME KIND OF HANKY PANKY GOING ON!
OOOH! IS THERE?
OF COURSE NOT!!
SO YOU TWO KIDS DON'T HAVE A "RELATIONSHIP"?
NO! YOU'RE JUST MAKING STUFF UP!!
WINKA! WINKA!
THE NOTION THAT I HAVE A "RELATIONSHIP" WITH MS. LA CHANCE IS PURE FANTASY!!
OKAY, THANKS. I'VE GOT WHAT I NEED.
"GALVIN'S FANTASY: A RELATIONSHIP WITH LA CHANCE"
P.S. 38 WEEKLY BUGLE
BUGLE
IT'S AN EXCLUSIVE!
TIK TIK TIK
Peirce

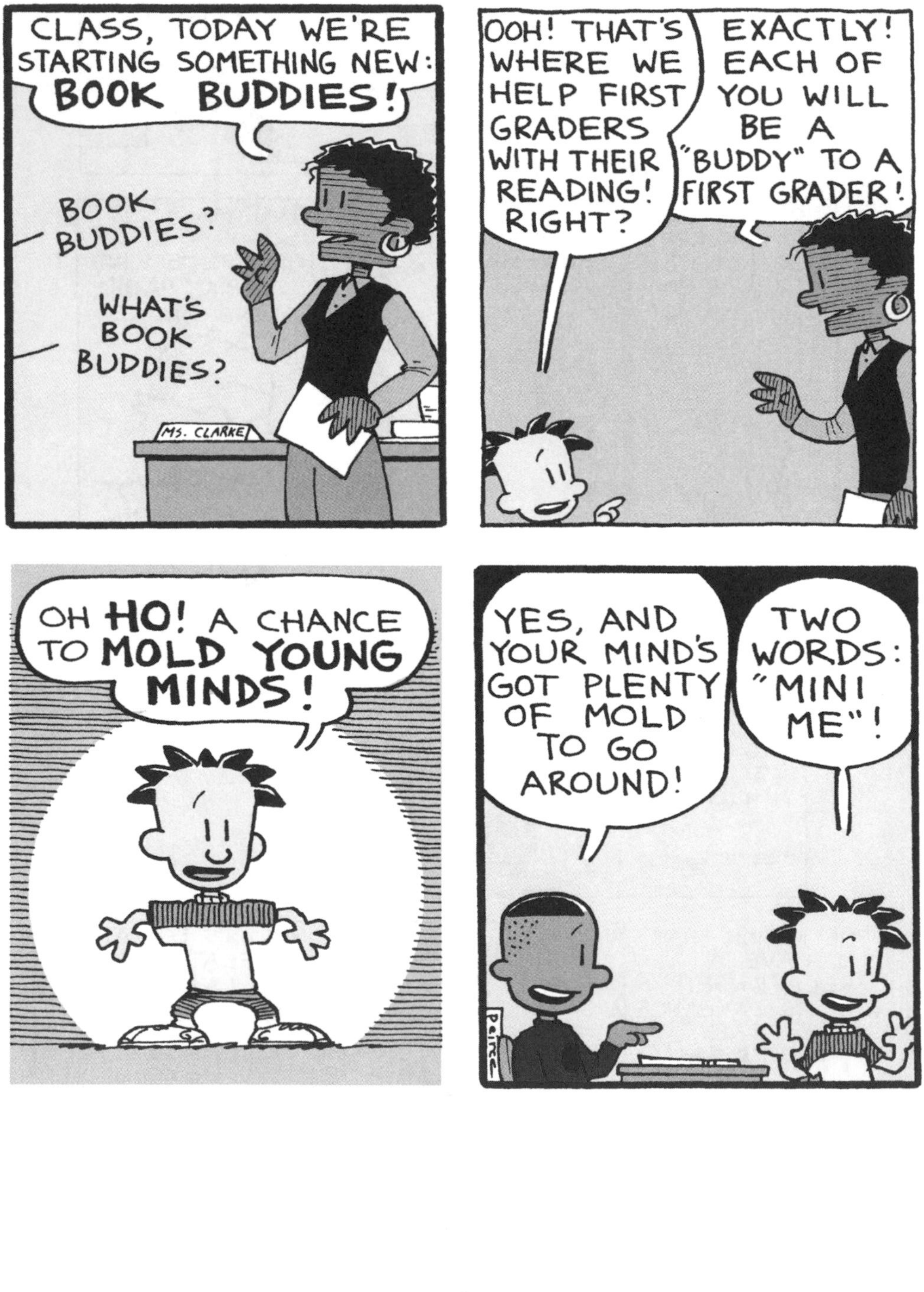
CLASS, TODAY WE'RE STARTING SOMETHING NEW: **BOOK BUDDIES!**
BOOK BUDDIES?
WHAT'S BOOK BUDDIES?
MS. CLARKE
OOH! THAT'S WHERE WE HELP FIRST GRADERS WITH THEIR READING! RIGHT?
EXACTLY! EACH OF YOU WILL BE A "BUDDY" TO A FIRST GRADER!
OH **HO!** A CHANCE TO **MOLD YOUNG MINDS!**
YES, AND YOUR MIND'S GOT PLENTY OF MOLD TO GO AROUND!
TWO WORDS: "MINI ME"!
Peirce

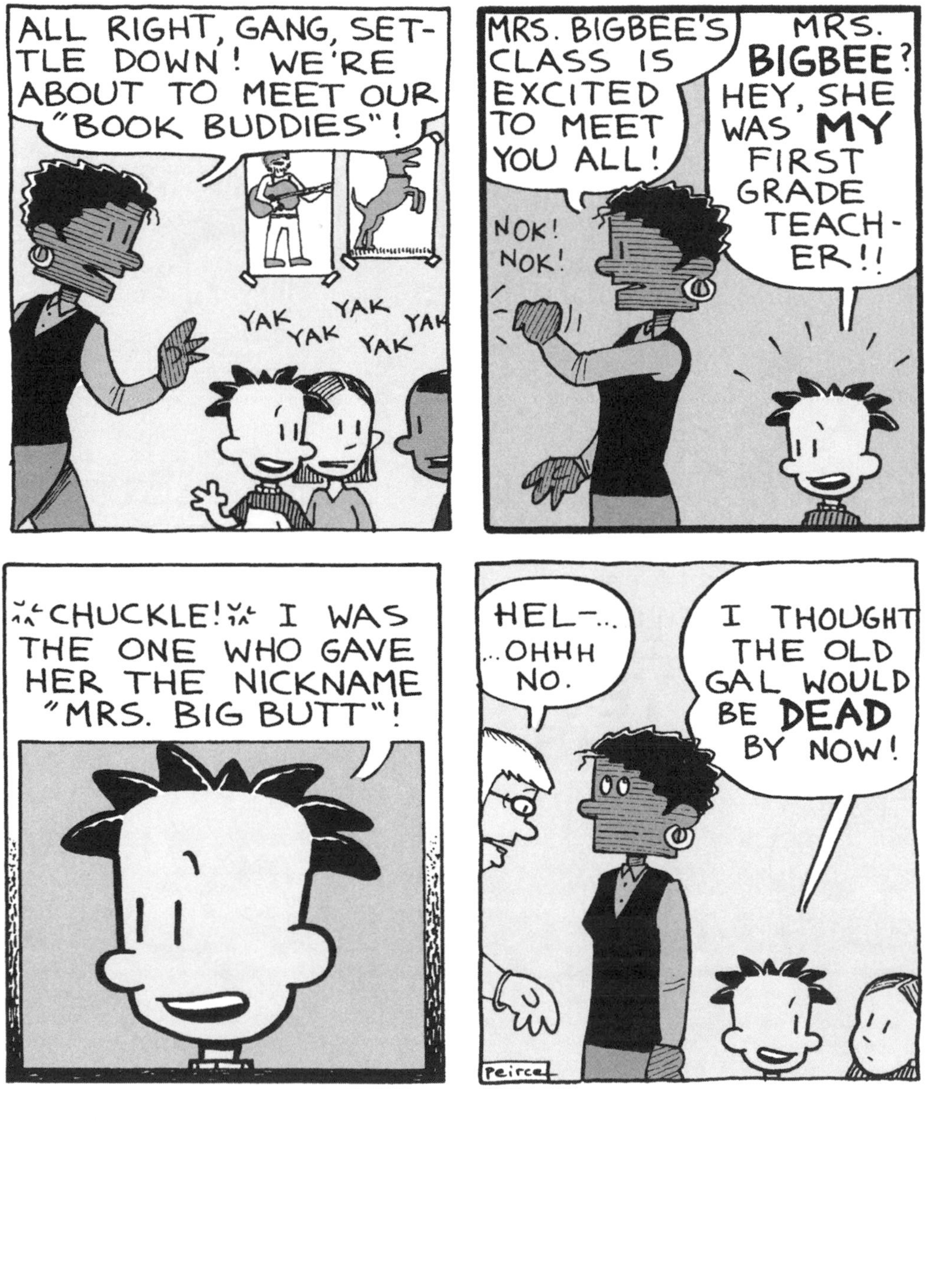
ALL RIGHT, GANG, SETTLE DOWN! WE'RE ABOUT TO MEET OUR "BOOK BUDDIES"!
YAK YAK YAK YAK YAK
MRS. BIGBEE'S CLASS IS EXCITED TO MEET YOU ALL!
NOK! NOK!
MRS. **BIGBEE**? HEY, SHE WAS **MY** FIRST GRADE TEACHER!!
CHUCKLE! I WAS THE ONE WHO GAVE HER THE NICKNAME "MRS. BIG BUTT"!
HEL-...
...OHHH NO.
I THOUGHT THE OLD GAL WOULD BE **DEAD** BY NOW!
Peirce

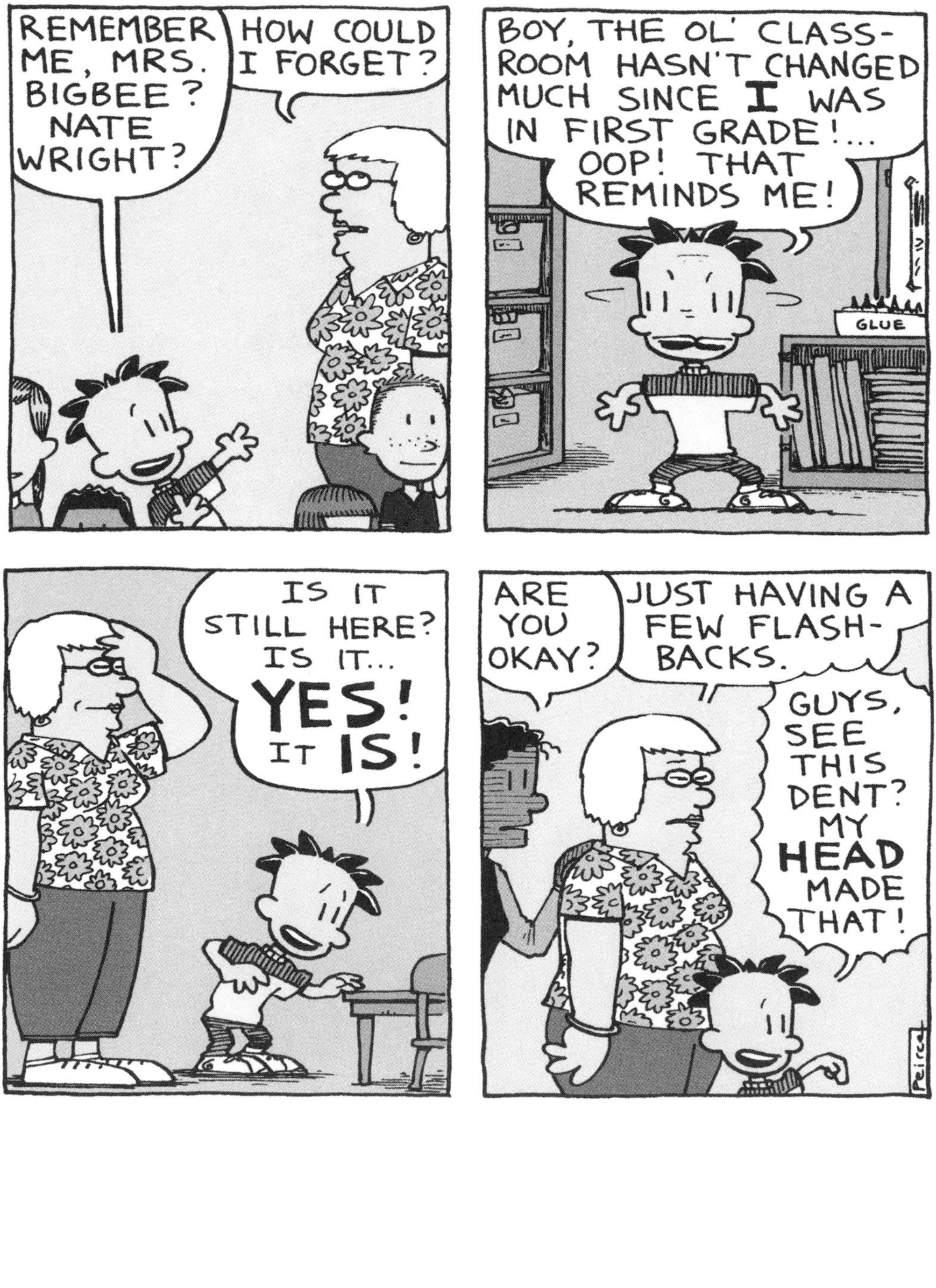
REMEMBER ME, MRS. BIGBEE? NATE WRIGHT?
HOW COULD I FORGET?
BOY, THE OL' CLASSROOM HASN'T CHANGED MUCH SINCE I WAS IN FIRST GRADE!... OOP! THAT REMINDS ME!
GLUE
IS IT STILL HERE? IS IT... YES! IT IS!
ARE YOU OKAY?
JUST HAVING A FEW FLASHBACKS.
GUYS, SEE THIS DENT? MY HEAD MADE THAT!
Peirce

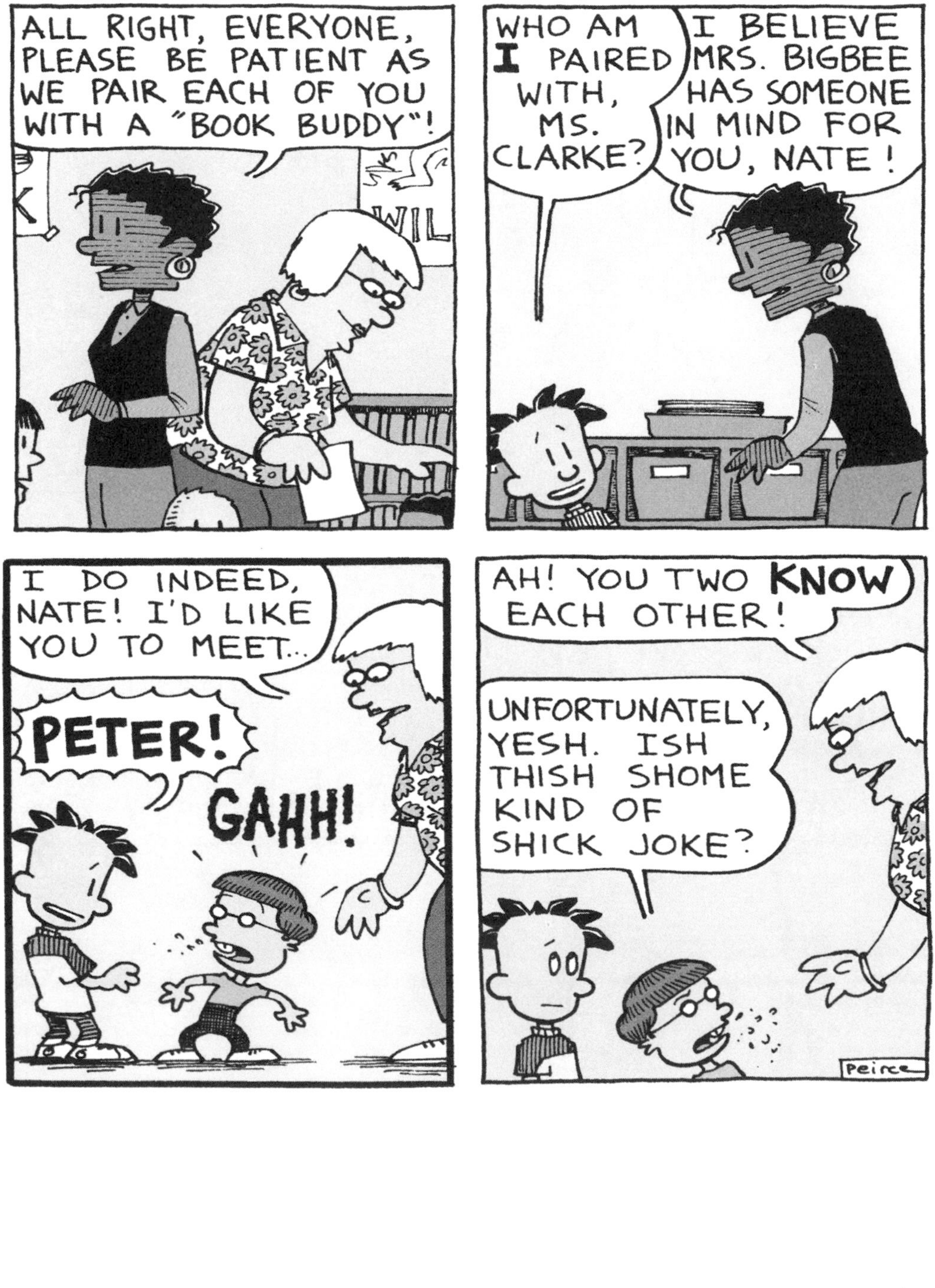

ALL RIGHT, EVERYONE, PLEASE BE PATIENT AS WE PAIR EACH OF YOU WITH A "BOOK BUDDY"!
WHO AM **I** PAIRED WITH, MS. CLARKE?
I BELIEVE MRS. BIGBEE HAS SOMEONE IN MIND FOR YOU, NATE!
I DO INDEED, NATE! I'D LIKE YOU TO MEET...
PETER!
GAHH!
AH! YOU TWO **KNOW** EACH OTHER!
UNFORTUNATELY, YESH. ISH THISH SHOME KIND OF SHICK JOKE?
Peirce

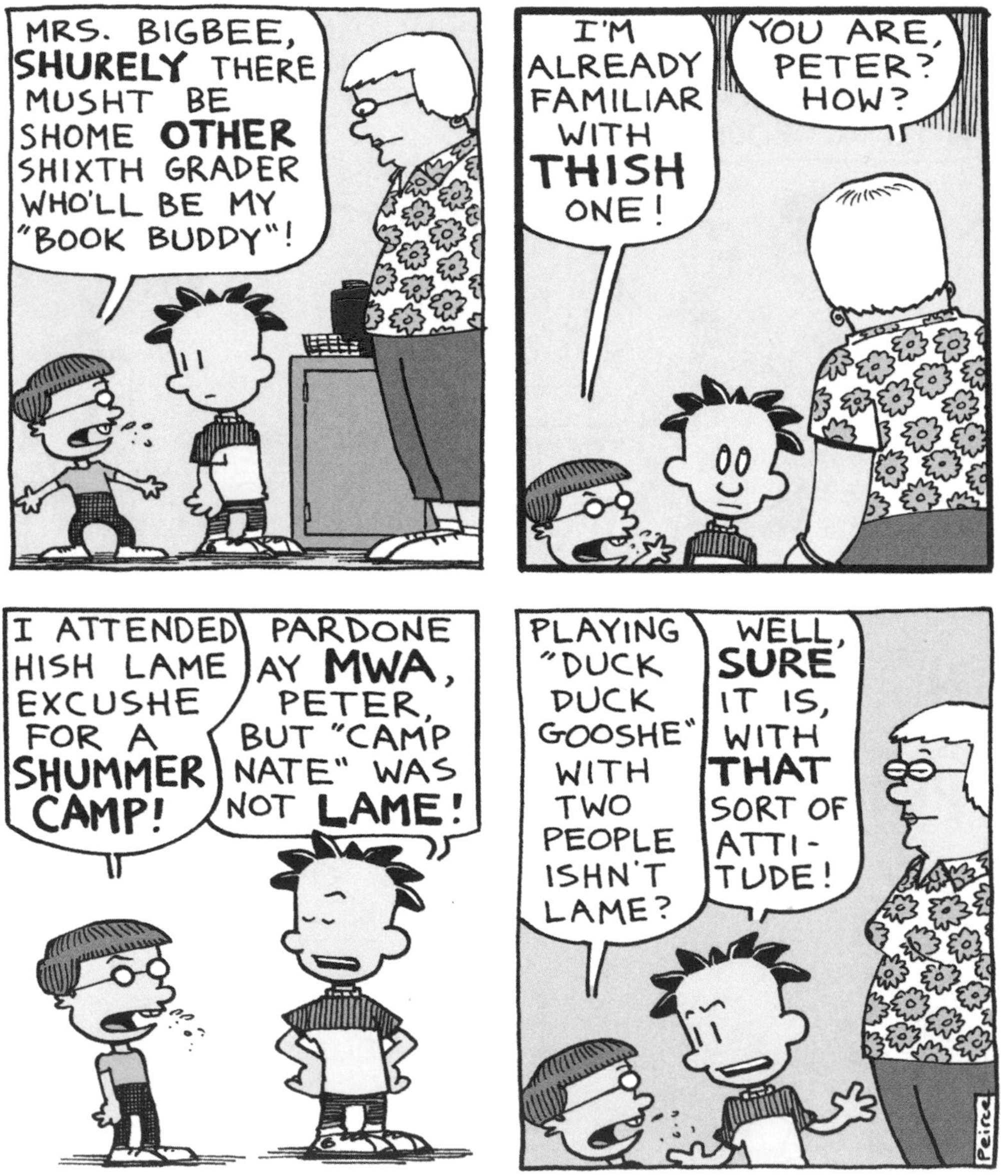
MRS. BIGBEE, **SHURELY** THERE MUSHT BE SHOME **OTHER** SHIXTH GRADER WHO'LL BE MY "BOOK BUDDY"!
I'M ALREADY FAMILIAR WITH **THISH** ONE!
YOU ARE, PETER? HOW?
I ATTENDED HISH LAME EXCUSHE FOR A **SHUMMER CAMP!**
PARDONE AY **MWA**, PETER, BUT "CAMP NATE" WAS NOT **LAME!**
PLAYING "DUCK DUCK GOOSHE" WITH TWO PEOPLE ISHN'T LAME?
WELL, **SURE** IT IS, WITH **THAT** SORT OF ATTITUDE!
Peirce

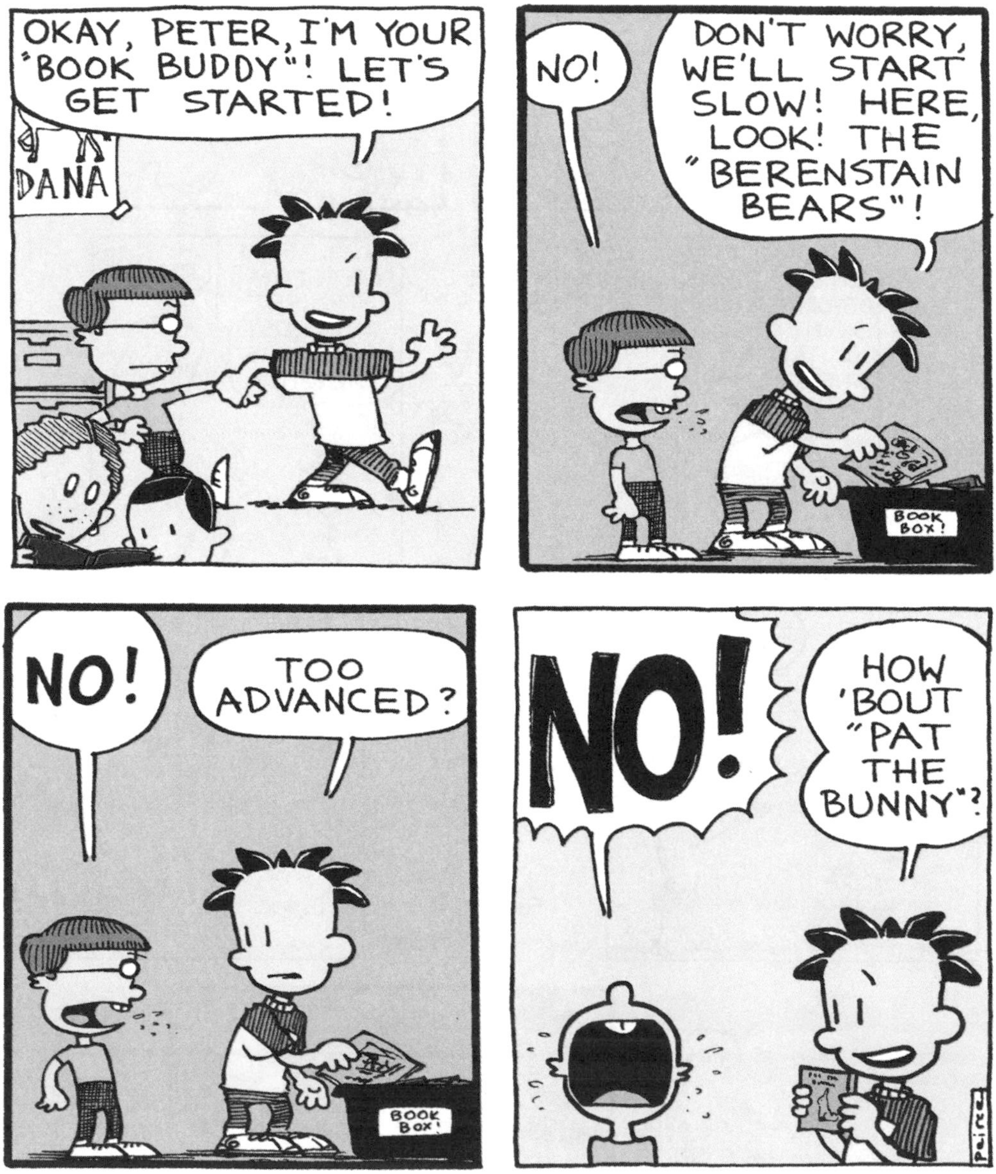
OKAY, PETER, I'M YOUR "BOOK BUDDY"! LET'S GET STARTED!
DANA
NO!
DON'T WORRY, WE'LL START SLOW! HERE, LOOK! THE "BERENSTAIN BEARS"!
BOOK BOX!
NO!
TOO ADVANCED?
BOOK BOX!
NO!
HOW 'BOUT "PAT THE BUNNY"?
Peirce

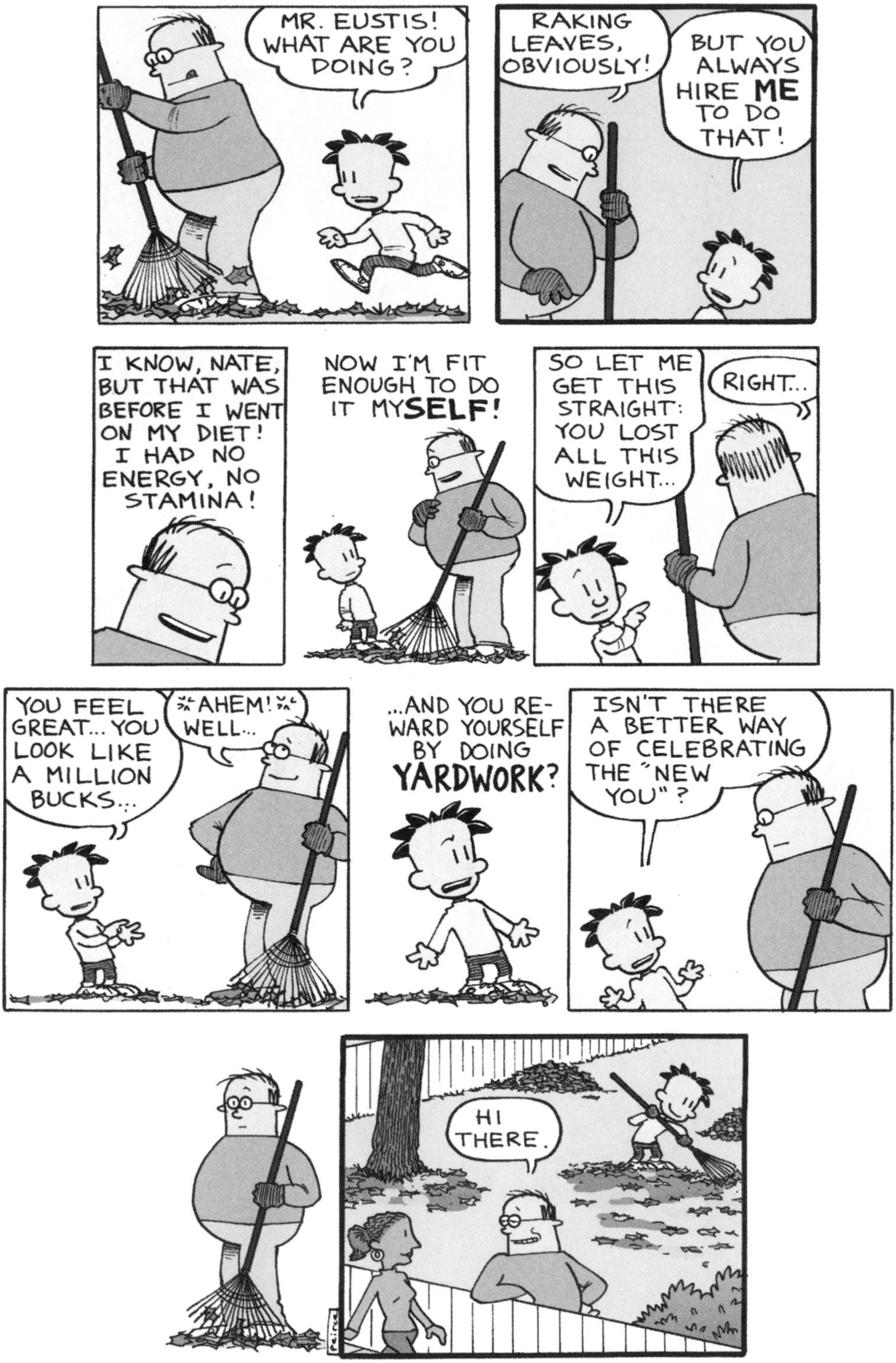
MR. EUSTIS! WHAT ARE YOU DOING?
RAKING LEAVES, OBVIOUSLY!
BUT YOU ALWAYS HIRE **ME** TO DO THAT!
I KNOW, NATE, BUT THAT WAS BEFORE I WENT ON MY DIET! I HAD NO ENERGY, NO STAMINA!
NOW I'M FIT ENOUGH TO DO IT MY**SELF**!
SO LET ME GET THIS STRAIGHT: YOU LOST ALL THIS WEIGHT...
RIGHT...
YOU FEEL GREAT... YOU LOOK LIKE A MILLION BUCKS...
AHEM! WELL...
...AND YOU RE-WARD YOURSELF BY DOING **YARDWORK**?
ISN'T THERE A BETTER WAY OF CELEBRATING THE "NEW YOU"?
HI THERE.
Peirce

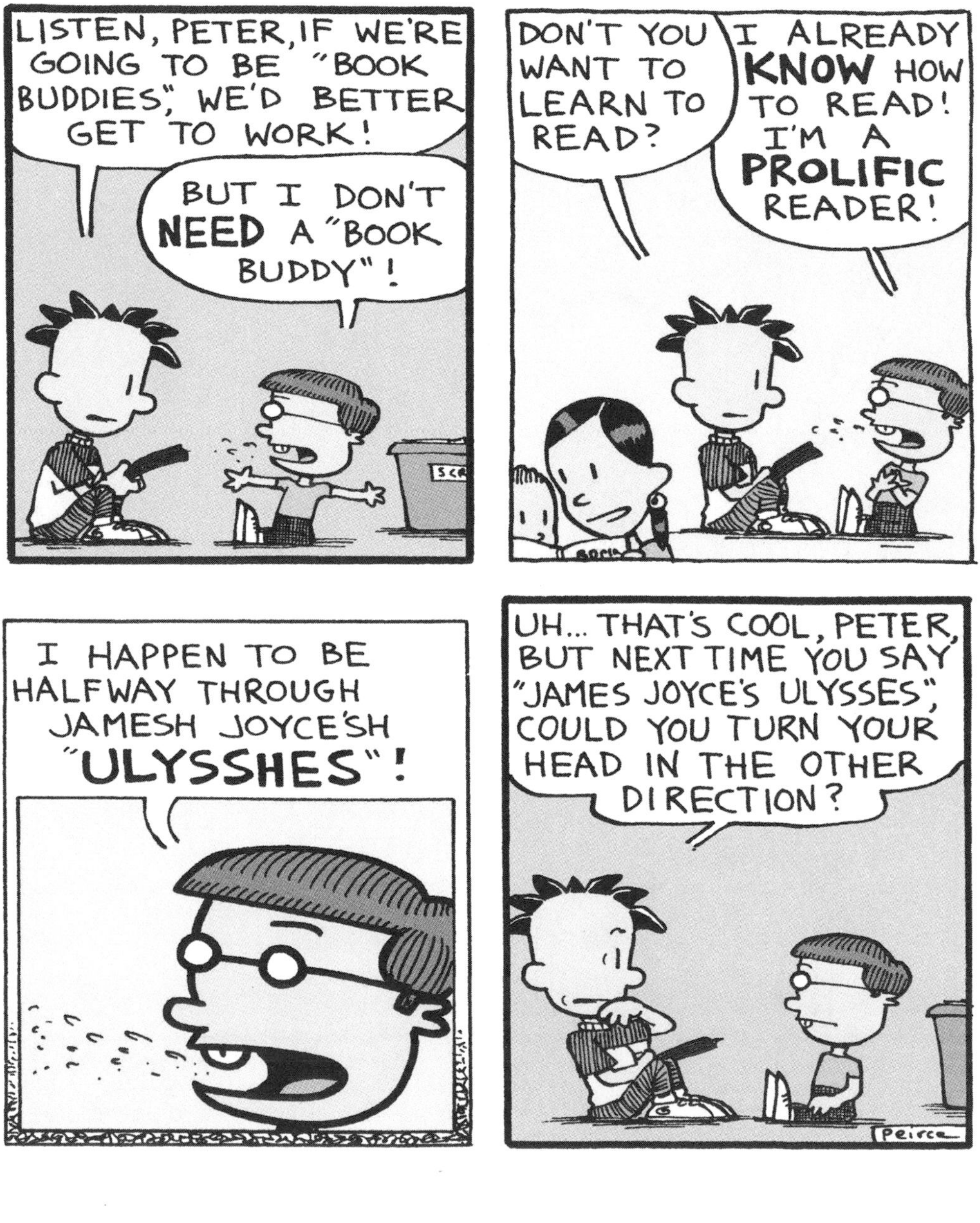
LISTEN, PETER, IF WE'RE GOING TO BE "BOOK BUDDIES", WE'D BETTER GET TO WORK!
BUT I DON'T **NEED** A "BOOK BUDDY"!
DON'T YOU WANT TO LEARN TO READ?
I ALREADY **KNOW** HOW TO READ! I'M A **PROLIFIC** READER!
I HAPPEN TO BE HALFWAY THROUGH JAMESH JOYCE'SH "**ULYSSHES**"!
UH... THAT'S COOL, PETER, BUT NEXT TIME YOU SAY "JAMES JOYCE'S ULYSSES", COULD YOU TURN YOUR HEAD IN THE OTHER DIRECTION?
Peirce

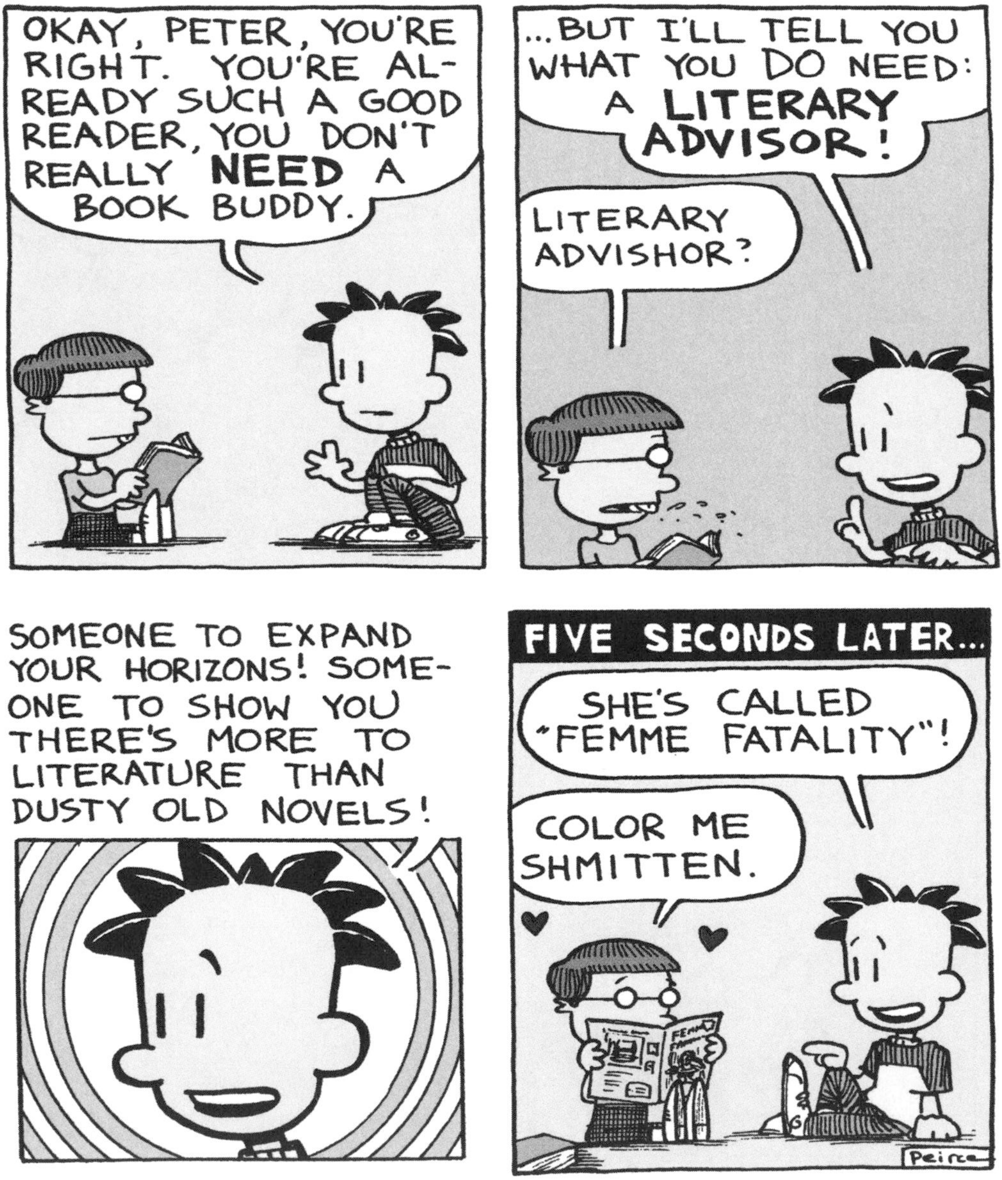
OKAY, PETER, YOU'RE RIGHT. YOU'RE ALREADY SUCH A GOOD READER, YOU DON'T REALLY **NEED** A BOOK BUDDY.
...BUT I'LL TELL YOU WHAT YOU DO NEED: A **LITERARY ADVISOR**!
LITERARY ADVISHOR?
SOMEONE TO EXPAND YOUR HORIZONS! SOMEONE TO SHOW YOU THERE'S MORE TO LITERATURE THAN DUSTY OLD NOVELS!
FIVE SECONDS LATER...
SHE'S CALLED "FEMME FATALITY"!
COLOR ME SHMITTEN.
Peirce

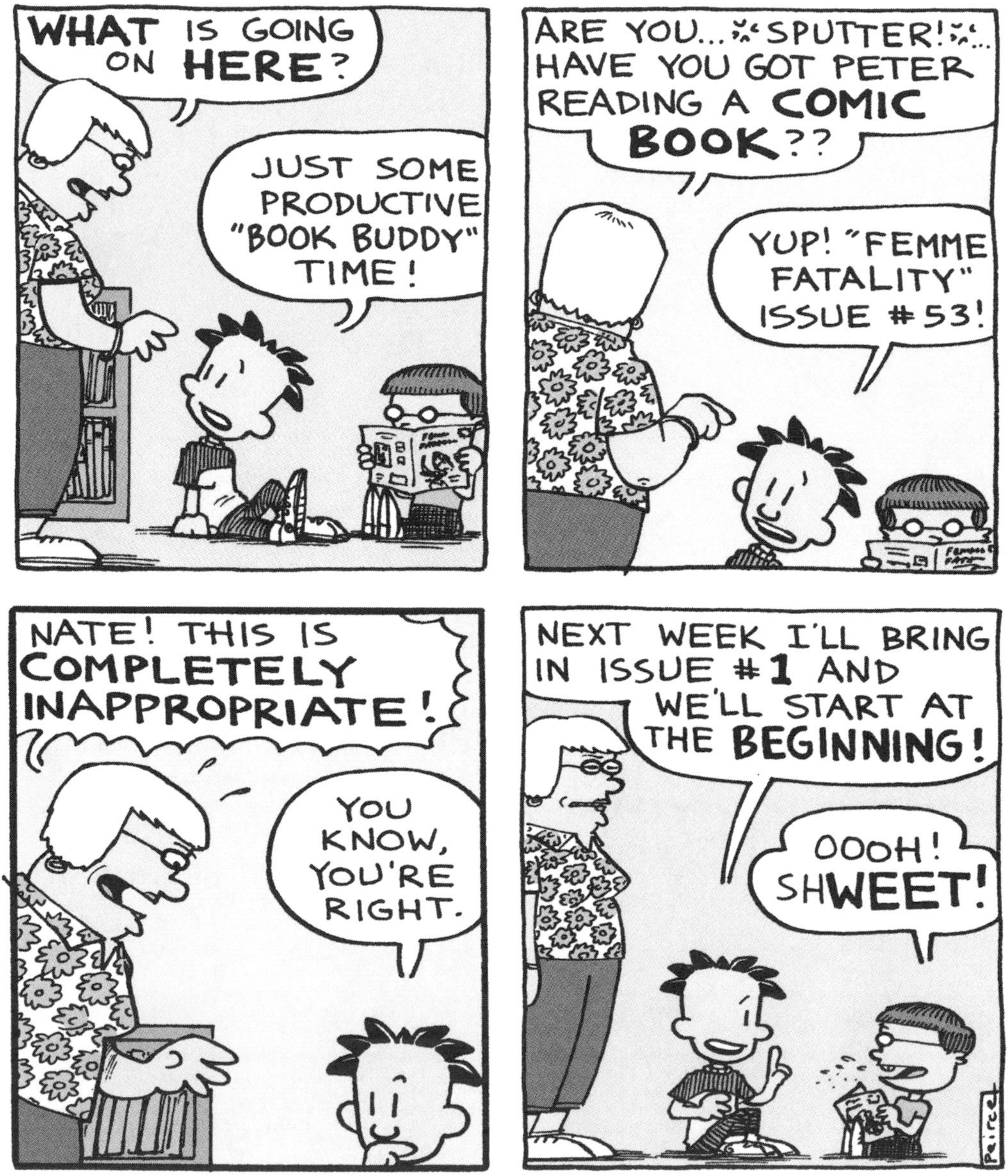
WHAT IS GOING ON HERE?
JUST SOME PRODUCTIVE "BOOK BUDDY" TIME!
ARE YOU... SPUTTER! ... HAVE YOU GOT PETER READING A COMIC BOOK??
YUP! "FEMME FATALITY" ISSUE #53!
NATE! THIS IS COMPLETELY INAPPROPRIATE!
YOU KNOW, YOU'RE RIGHT.
NEXT WEEK I'LL BRING IN ISSUE #1 AND WE'LL START AT THE BEGINNING!
OOOH! SHWEET!
Peirce

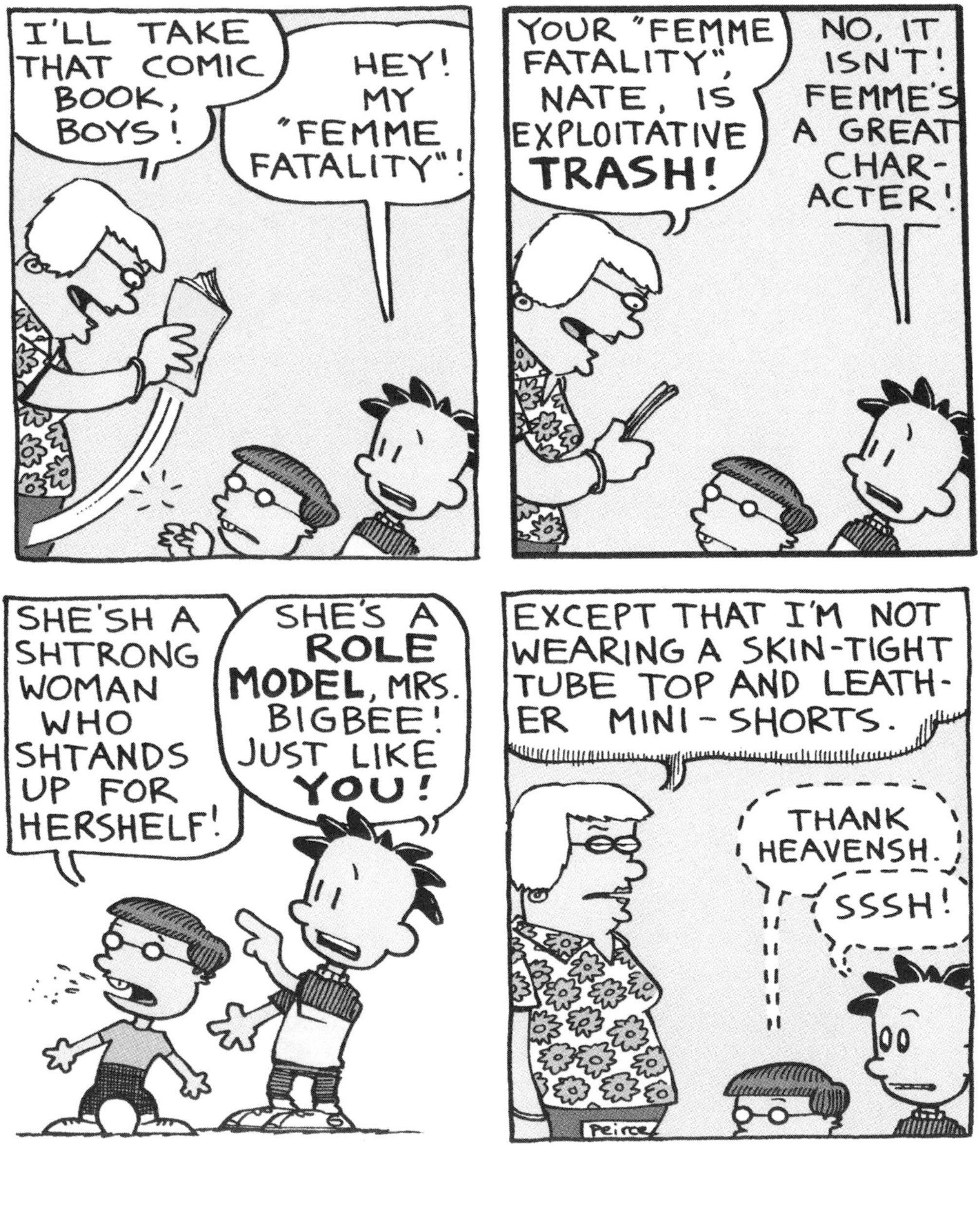
I'LL TAKE THAT COMIC BOOK, BOYS!
HEY! MY "FEMME FATALITY"!
YOUR "FEMME FATALITY", NATE, IS EXPLOITATIVE **TRASH!**
NO, IT ISN'T! FEMME'S A GREAT CHAR-ACTER!
SHE'SH A SHTRONG WOMAN WHO SHTANDS UP FOR HERSHELF!
SHE'S A **ROLE MODEL**, MRS. BIGBEE! JUST LIKE **YOU!**
EXCEPT THAT I'M NOT WEARING A SKIN-TIGHT TUBE TOP AND LEATH-ER MINI-SHORTS.
THANK HEAVENSH.
SSSH!
Peirce

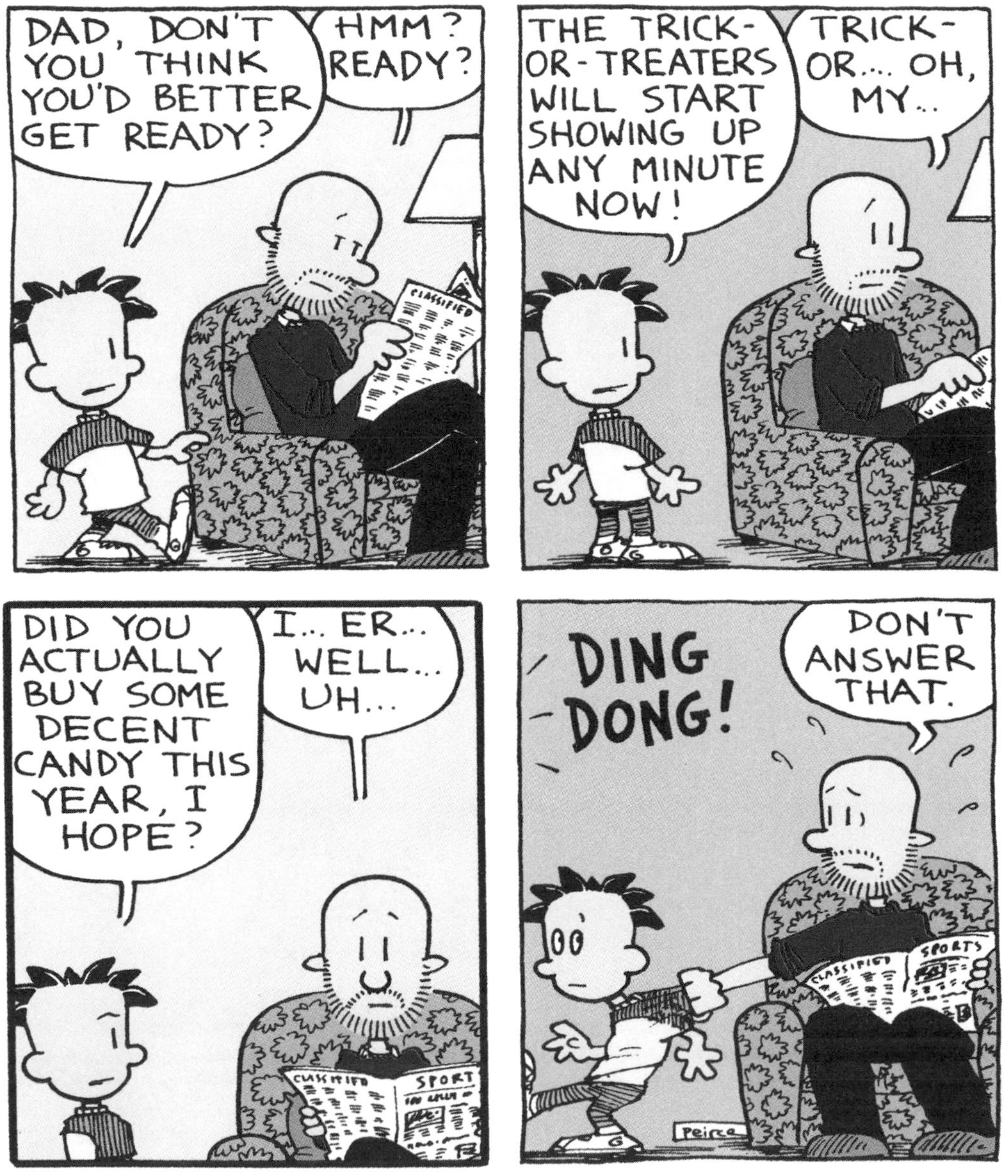
DAD, DON'T YOU THINK YOU'D BETTER GET READY?
HMM? READY?
THE TRICK-OR-TREATERS WILL START SHOWING UP ANY MINUTE NOW!
TRICK-OR.... OH, MY...
DID YOU ACTUALLY BUY SOME DECENT CANDY THIS YEAR, I HOPE?
I... ER... WELL... UH...
DING DONG!
DON'T ANSWER THAT.
Peirce

DING DONG!
DAD! CHOP CHOP! THERE'S TRICK-OR-TREATERS AT THE DOOR!
GULP
WE'VE GOT NOTHING TO GIVE THEM. I FORGOT TO BUY ANY TREATS.
DING DONG!
DING DONG! DING DONG! DING DONG!
DING DONG! DING DONG!
BAM! BAM! BAM
BAM! BAM!
AM!
THIS ISN'T GOING TO BE PRETTY.
BAM!
PEIRCE

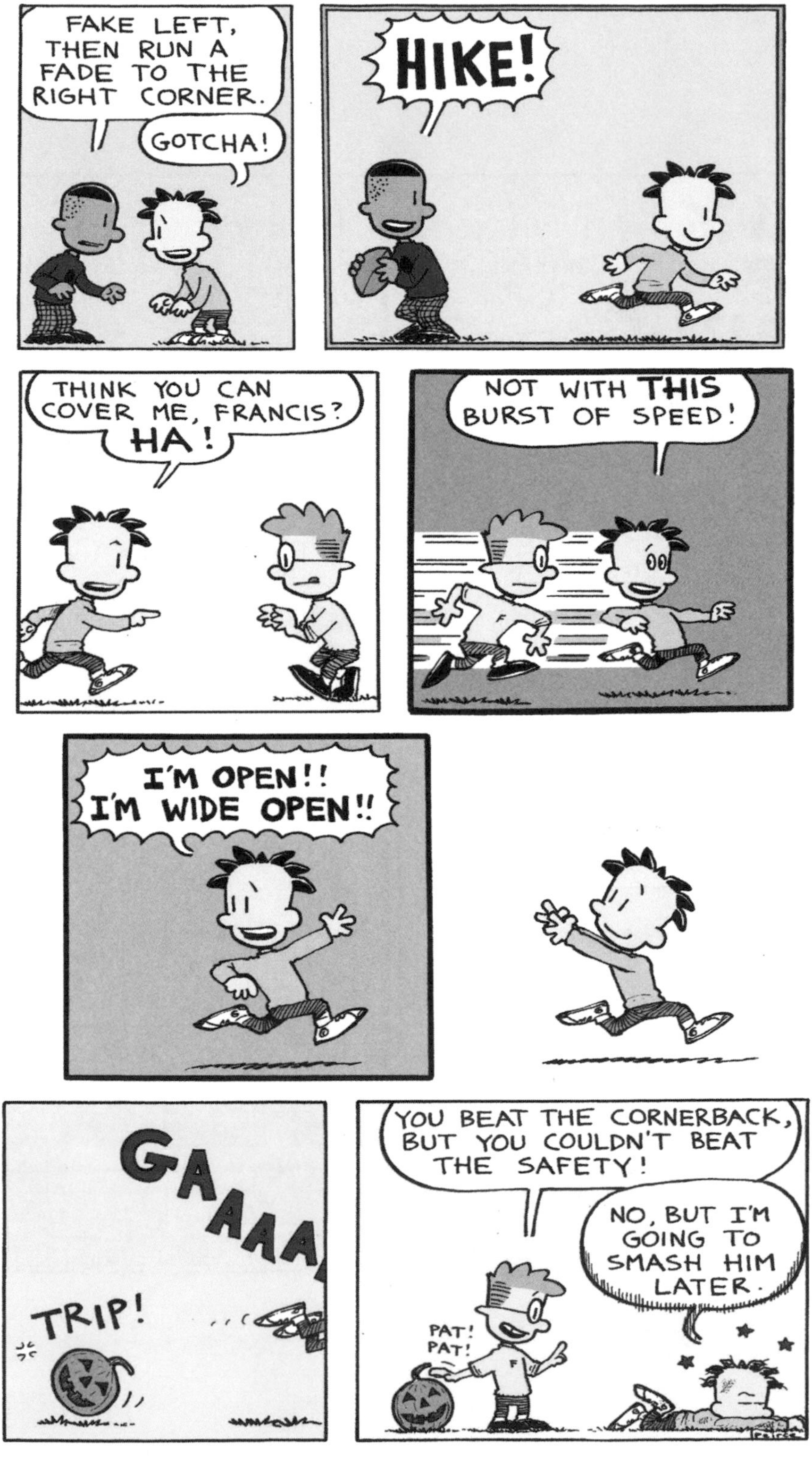
FAKE LEFT, THEN RUN A FADE TO THE RIGHT CORNER.
GOTCHA!
HIKE!
THINK YOU CAN COVER ME, FRANCIS? HA!
NOT WITH THIS BURST OF SPEED!
I'M OPEN!! I'M WIDE OPEN!!
GAAAA
TRIP!
YOU BEAT THE CORNERBACK, BUT YOU COULDN'T BEAT THE SAFETY!
PAT! PAT!
NO, BUT I'M GOING TO SMASH HIM LATER.

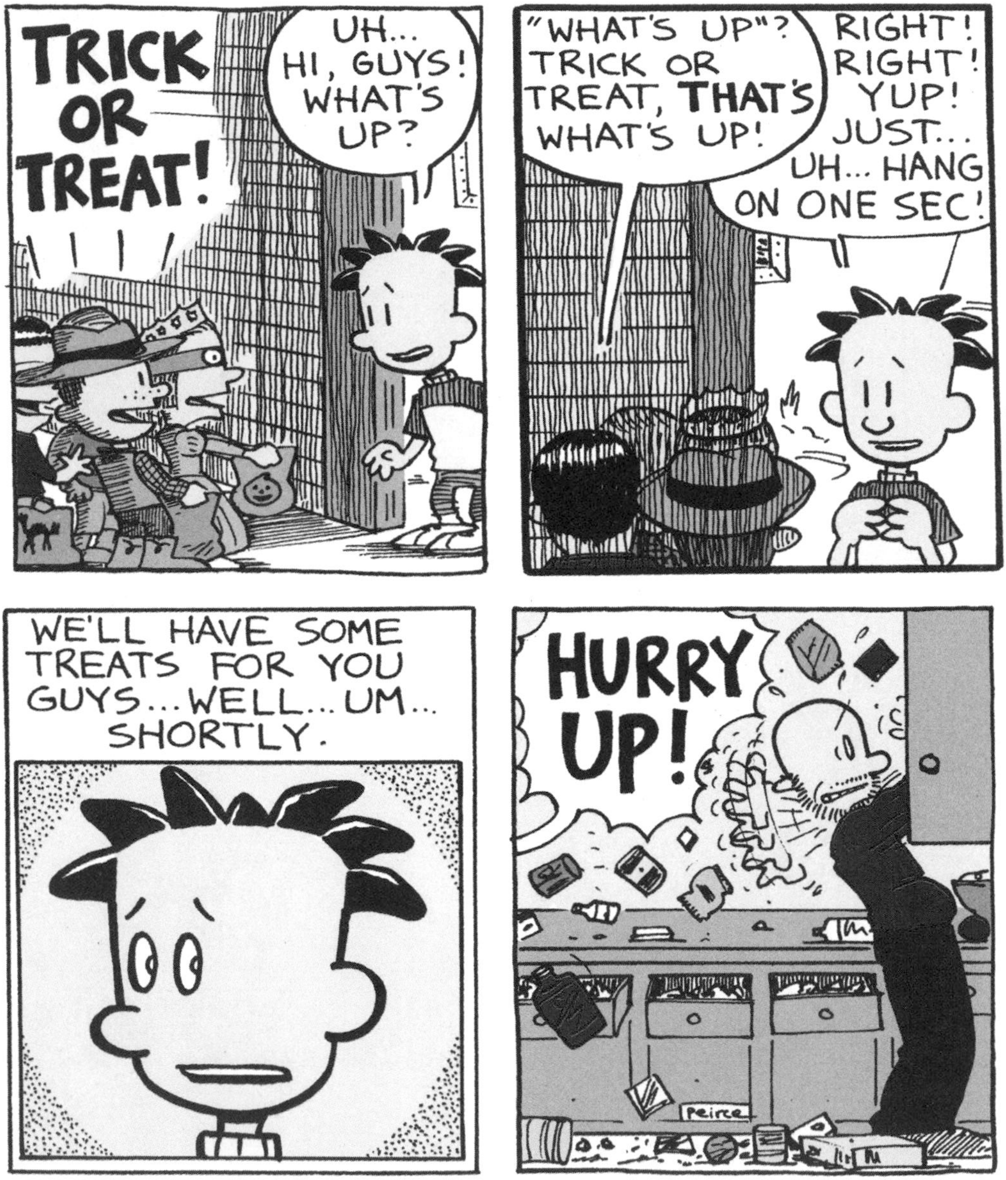
TRICK OR TREAT!
UH... HI, GUYS! WHAT'S UP?
"WHAT'S UP"? TRICK OR TREAT, **THAT'S** WHAT'S UP!
RIGHT! RIGHT! YUP! JUST... UH... HANG ON ONE SEC!
WE'LL HAVE SOME TREATS FOR YOU GUYS... WELL... UM... SHORTLY.
HURRY UP!

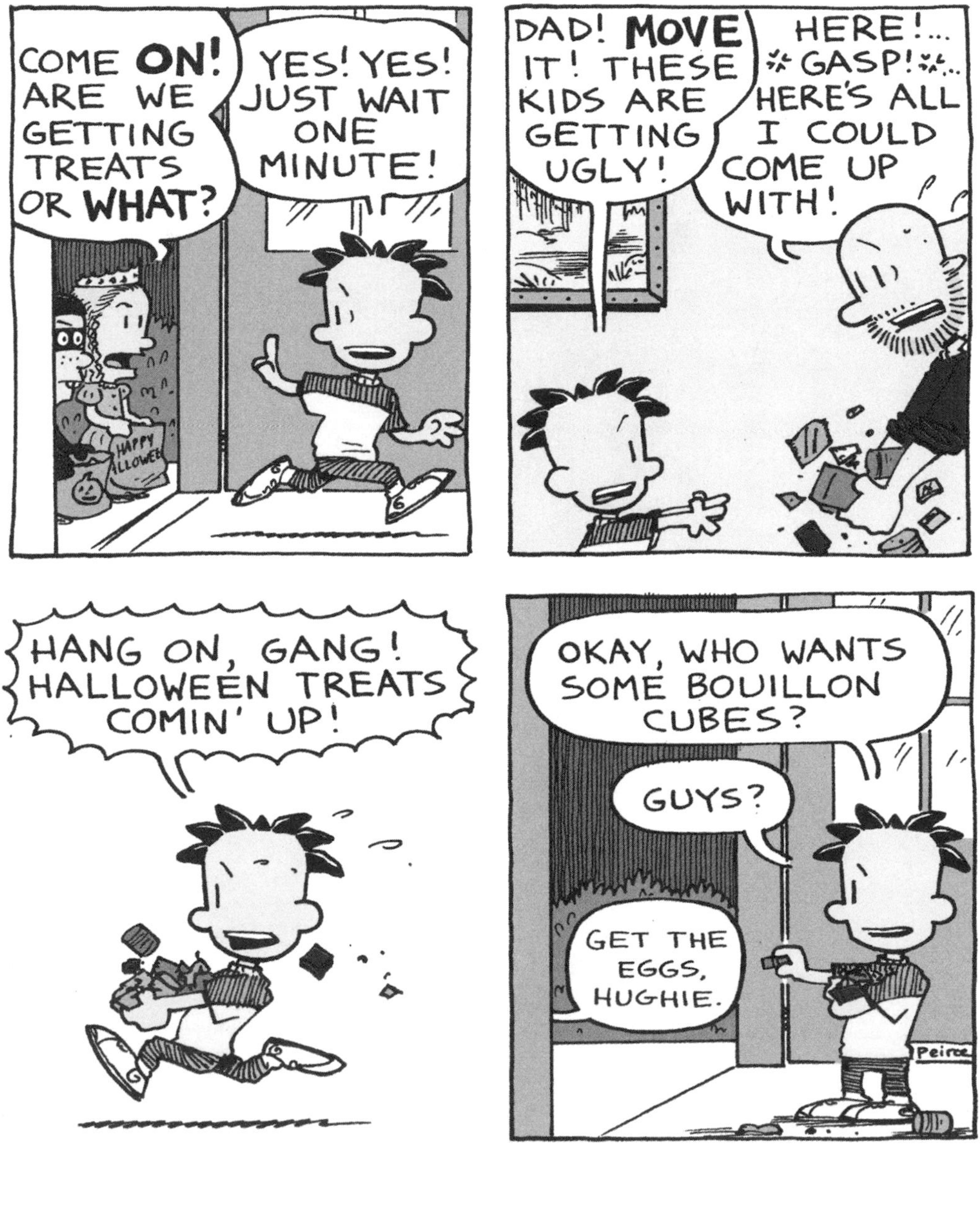
COME ON! ARE WE GETTING TREATS OR WHAT?
YES! YES! JUST WAIT ONE MINUTE!
HAPPY HALLOWEEN
DAD! MOVE IT! THESE KIDS ARE GETTING UGLY!
HERE!... GASP!... HERE'S ALL I COULD COME UP WITH!
HANG ON, GANG! HALLOWEEN TREATS COMIN' UP!
OKAY, WHO WANTS SOME BOUILLON CUBES?
GUYS?
GET THE EGGS, HUGHIE.
Peirce

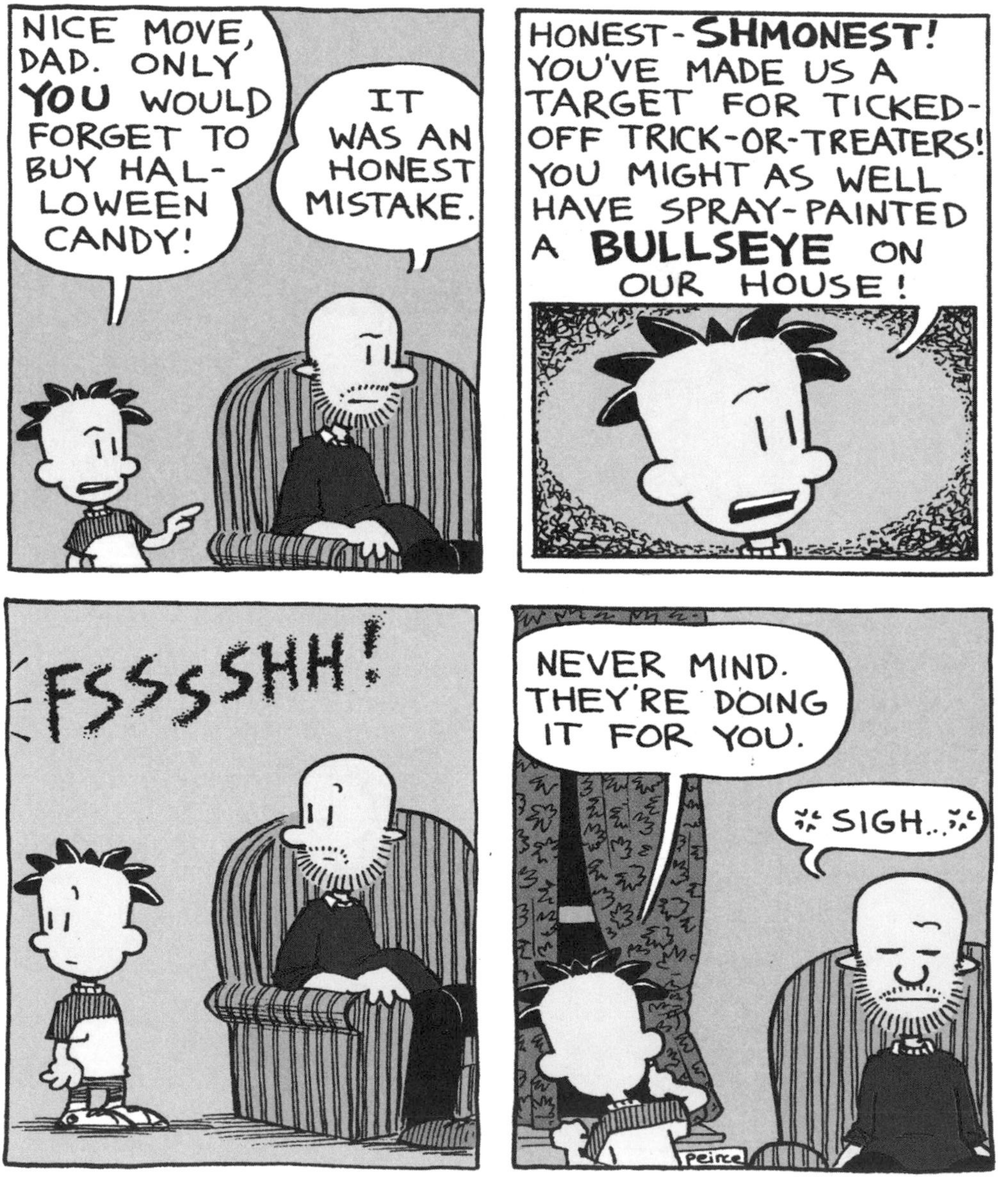
NICE MOVE, DAD. ONLY YOU WOULD FORGET TO BUY HALLOWEEN CANDY!
IT WAS AN HONEST MISTAKE.
HONEST-SHMONEST! YOU'VE MADE US A TARGET FOR TICKED-OFF TRICK-OR-TREATERS! YOU MIGHT AS WELL HAVE SPRAY-PAINTED A BULLSEYE ON OUR HOUSE!
FSSSSHH!
NEVER MIND. THEY'RE DOING IT FOR YOU.
SIGH...
peirce

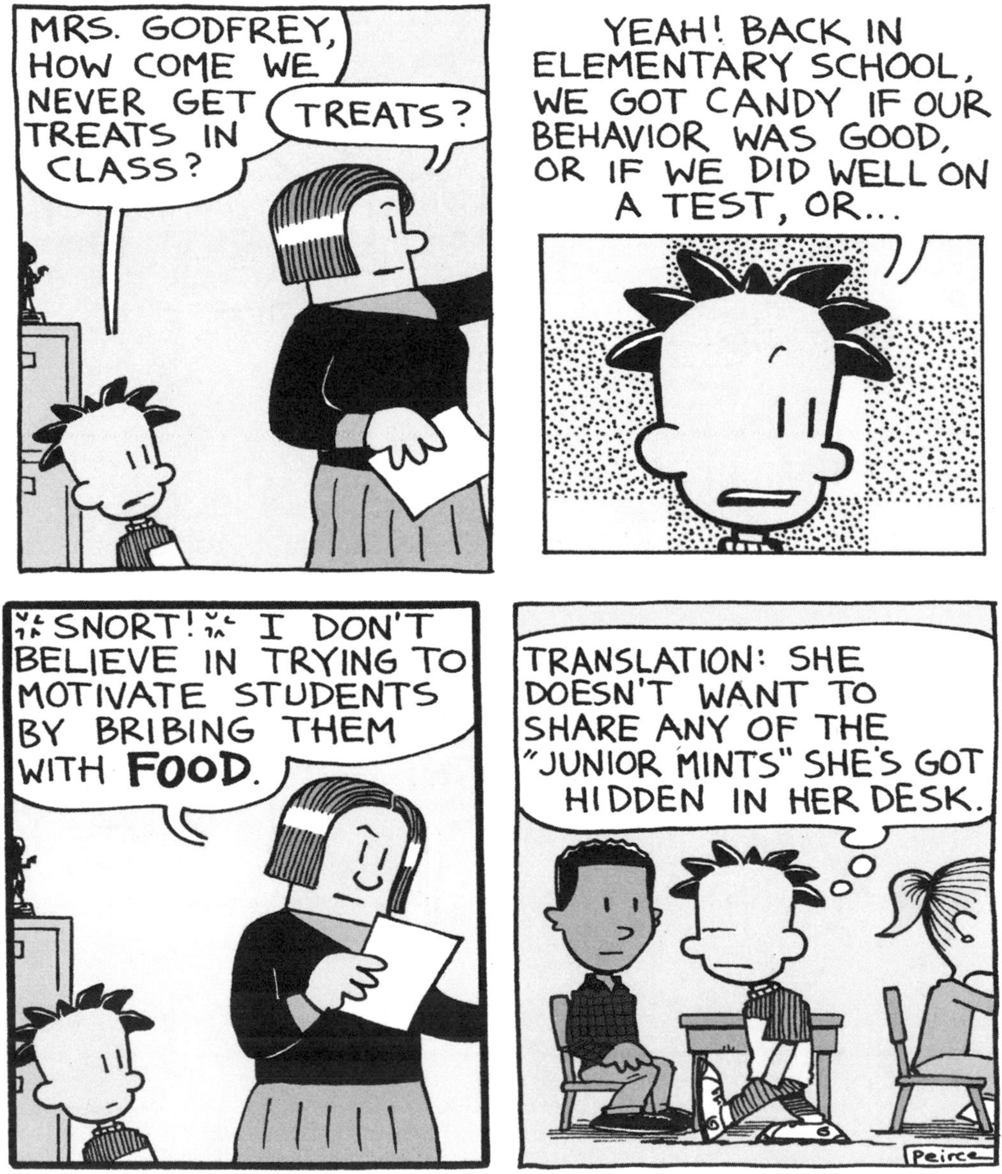
MRS. GODFREY, HOW COME WE NEVER GET TREATS IN CLASS?
TREATS?
YEAH! BACK IN ELEMENTARY SCHOOL, WE GOT CANDY IF OUR BEHAVIOR WAS GOOD, OR IF WE DID WELL ON A TEST, OR...
SNORT! I DON'T BELIEVE IN TRYING TO MOTIVATE STUDENTS BY BRIBING THEM WITH **FOOD**.
TRANSLATION: SHE DOESN'T WANT TO SHARE ANY OF THE "JUNIOR MINTS" SHE'S GOT HIDDEN IN HER DESK.
Peirce

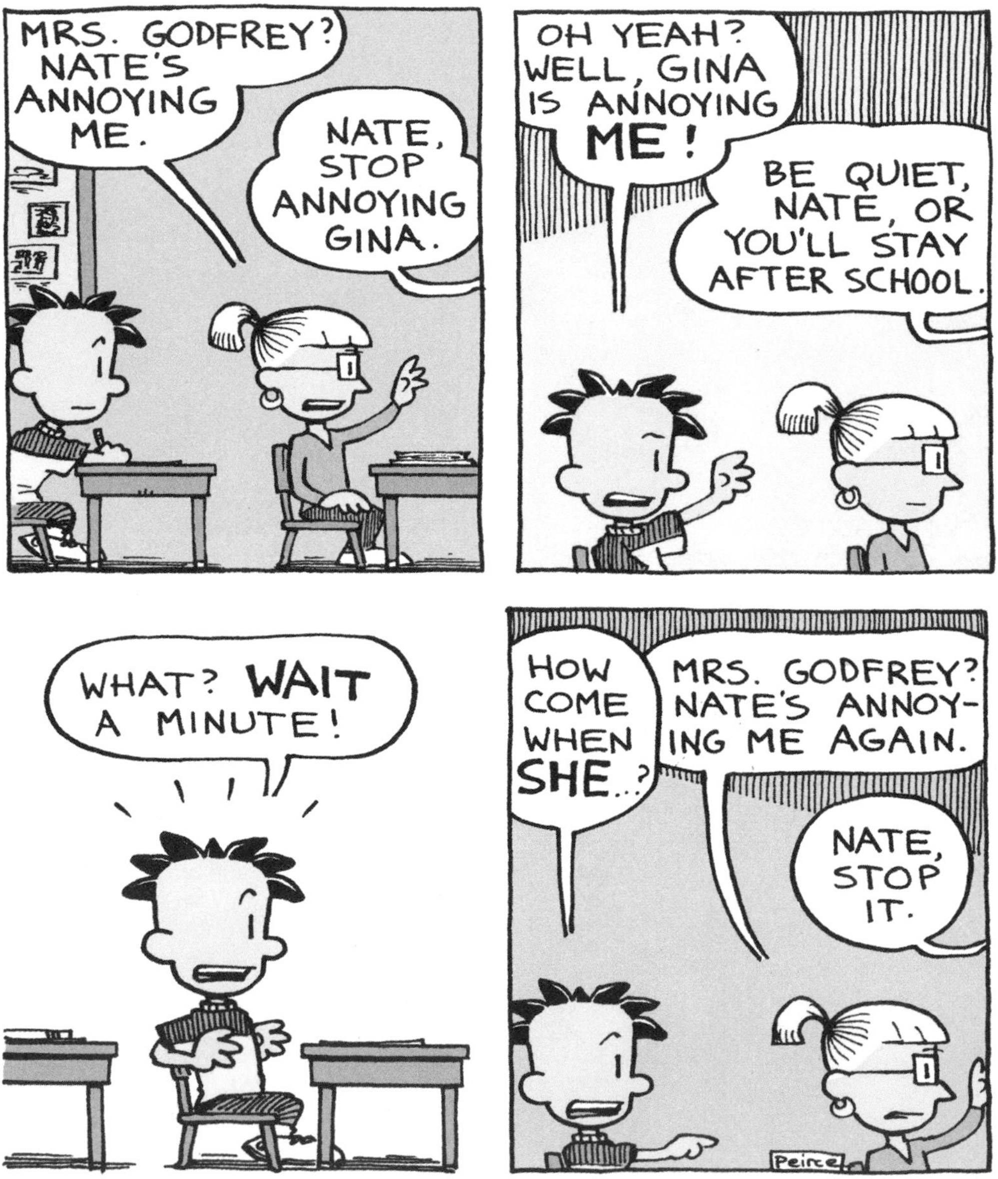
MRS. GODFREY? NATE'S ANNOYING ME.
NATE, STOP ANNOYING GINA.
OH YEAH? WELL, GINA IS ANNOYING **ME**!
BE QUIET, NATE, OR YOU'LL STAY AFTER SCHOOL.
WHAT? **WAIT** A MINUTE!
HOW COME WHEN **SHE**...?
MRS. GODFREY? NATE'S ANNOYING ME AGAIN.
NATE, STOP IT.
Peirce

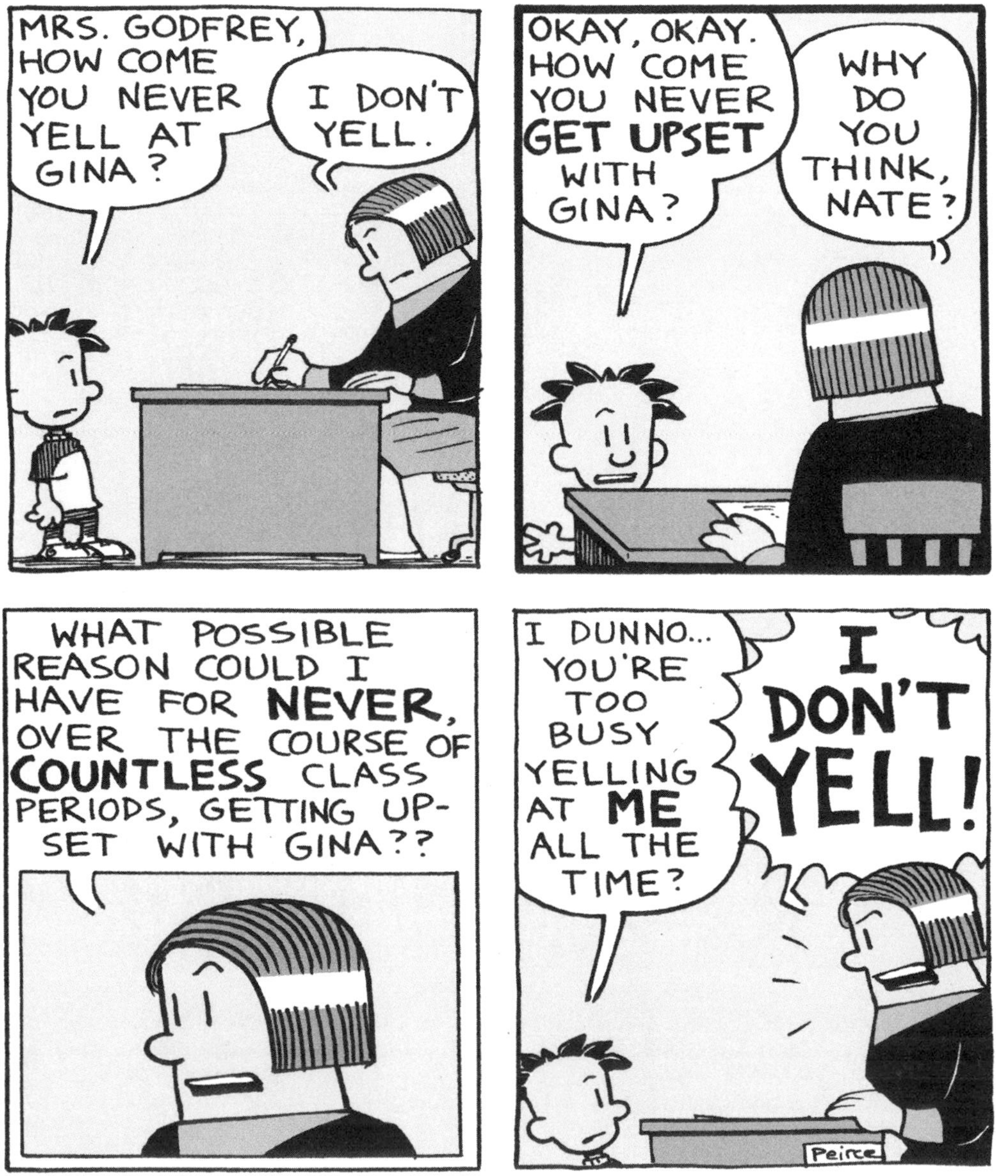
MRS. GODFREY, HOW COME YOU NEVER YELL AT GINA?
I DON'T YELL.
OKAY, OKAY. HOW COME YOU NEVER GET UPSET WITH GINA?
WHY DO YOU THINK, NATE?
WHAT POSSIBLE REASON COULD I HAVE FOR NEVER, OVER THE COURSE OF COUNTLESS CLASS PERIODS, GETTING UPSET WITH GINA??
I DUNNO... YOU'RE TOO BUSY YELLING AT ME ALL THE TIME?
I DON'T YELL!
Peirce

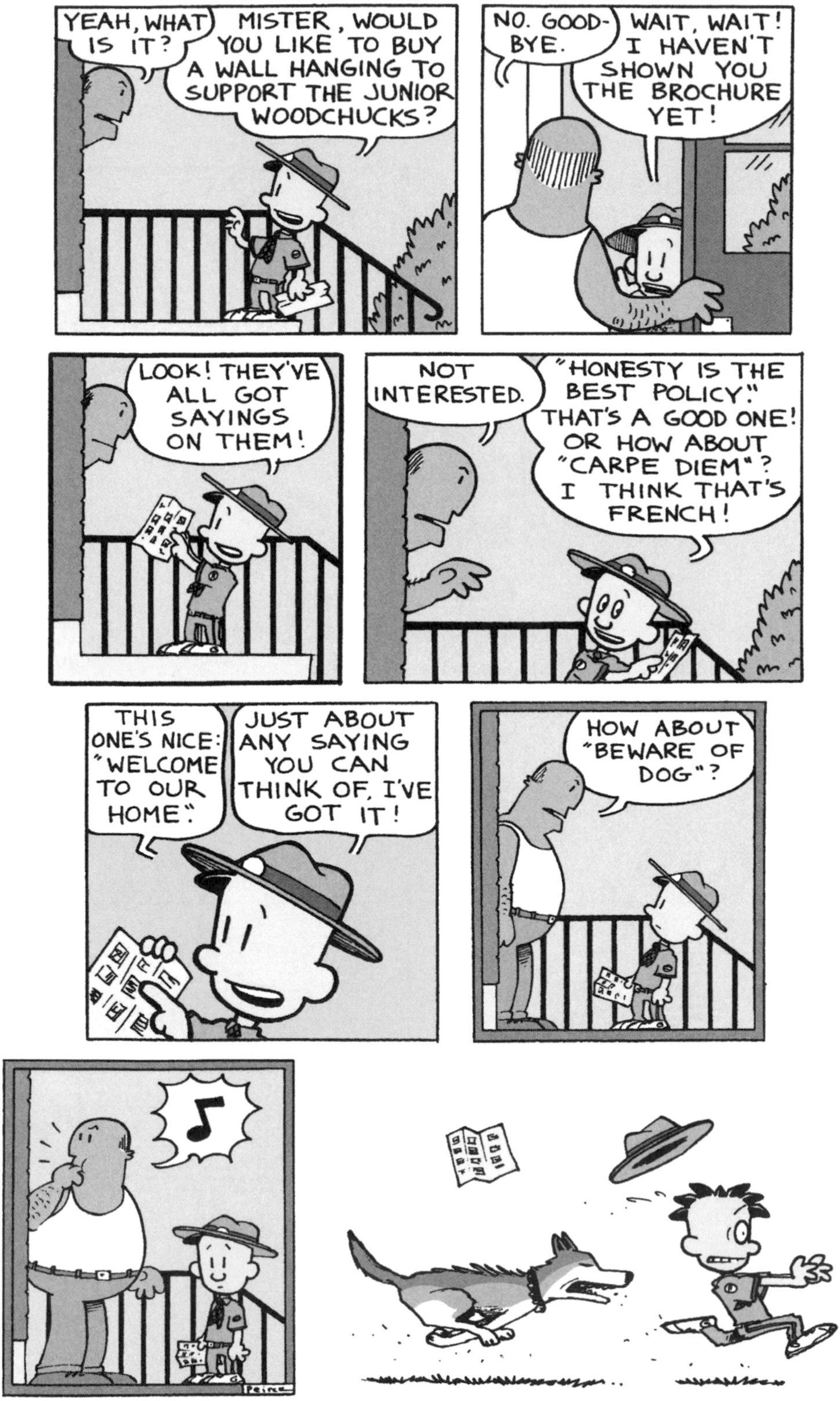
YEAH, WHAT IS IT?
MISTER, WOULD YOU LIKE TO BUY A WALL HANGING TO SUPPORT THE JUNIOR WOODCHUCKS?
NO. GOOD-BYE.
WAIT, WAIT! I HAVEN'T SHOWN YOU THE BROCHURE YET!
LOOK! THEY'VE ALL GOT SAYINGS ON THEM!
NOT INTERESTED.
"HONESTY IS THE BEST POLICY." THAT'S A GOOD ONE! OR HOW ABOUT "CARPE DIEM"? I THINK THAT'S FRENCH!
THIS ONE'S NICE: "WELCOME TO OUR HOME."
JUST ABOUT ANY SAYING YOU CAN THINK OF, I'VE GOT IT!
HOW ABOUT "BEWARE OF DOG"?
PEIRCE

ACCORDING TO THIS ARTICLE, WOMEN ARE ATTRACTED TO "BAD BOYS"!

THERE'S SOMETHING ABOUT A REBEL THAT THE LADIES FIND IRRESISTIBLE! HMMM!...

GENTS, I DO BELIEVE I'M GETTING ANOTHER BRILLIANT IDEA!

"ANOTHER"?

YUP! THE HITS JUST KEEP ON COMIN'!

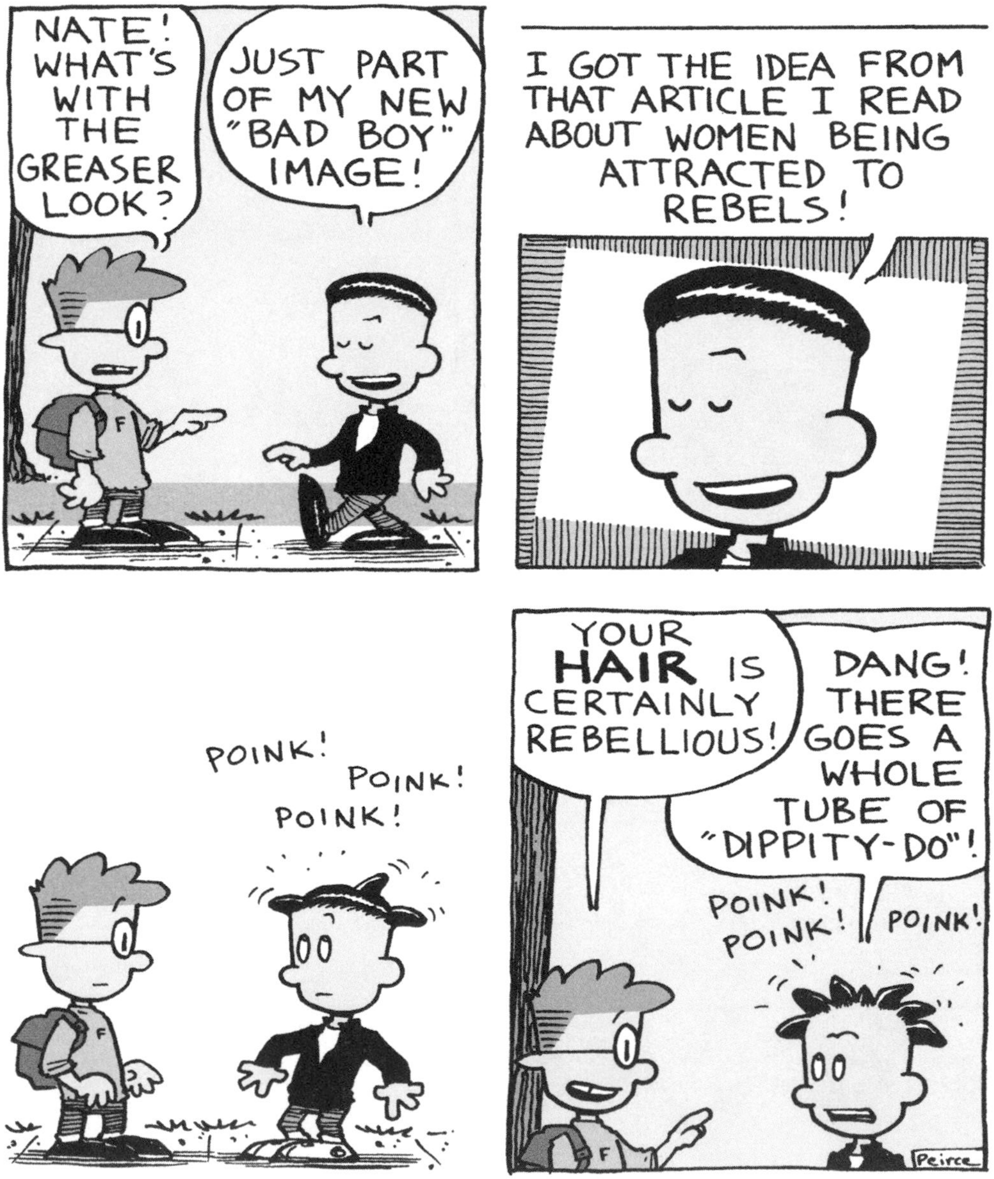
NATE! WHAT'S WITH THE GREASER LOOK?
JUST PART OF MY NEW "BAD BOY" IMAGE!
I GOT THE IDEA FROM THAT ARTICLE I READ ABOUT WOMEN BEING ATTRACTED TO REBELS!
POINK! POINK! POINK!
YOUR **HAIR** IS CERTAINLY REBELLIOUS!
DANG! THERE GOES A WHOLE TUBE OF "DIPPITY-DO"!
POINK! POINK! POINK!
Peirce

A LEATHER JACKET?
HE'S A "BAD BOY".
YOU'RE ACTUALLY FOLLOWING THROUGH ON THAT DUMB IDEA?
DUMB IDEA? IT'S RIGHT HERE IN BLACK AND WHITE!
"FOR A MULTITUDE OF REASONS, WOMEN ARE OFTEN ATTRACTED TO "BAD BOYS"– MEN WHO SIMPLY AREN'T GOOD FOR THEM."
COSMO
THAT'S YOU, ALL RIGHT!
YEAH, YOU'RE GOOD FOR **NOTHING!**
HI, LADIES.
Peirce

JENNY! CHECK IT OUT! I'M A "BAD BOY"!
A WHAT?
A BAD BOY! I'M DANGEROUS, BABY! I'M BAD TO THE BONE!
YOU?
HA HA HA HA HA
HA HA HA HA HA
HA HA HA
I'M HAVING TROUBLE GETTING MY BADNESS ACROSS.
WELL, THERE'S A DIF-FERENCE BETWEEN "BAD" AND "LAME."

WHAT'S UP, LADIES?
UH... NOTHING.
HEY! WE DIDN'T INVITE YOU TO SIT WITH US!
IN**VITE** ME? LISTEN, I'M A "BAD BOY"!
I SIT WHEREVER I **WANT** TO SIT!
...AND RIGHT ABOUT NOW, THE COT IN THE NURSE'S OFFICE SOUNDS PRETTY GOOD.
Peirce

UH... NATE?
YUP?
WHY ARE YOU WEARING A LEATHER JACKET OVER YOUR SMOCK?
BECAUSE I'M A BAD BOY!
YOU'RE A BAD BOY?
CORRECT!
SON, I HAVEN'T SEEN A LESS CONVINCING "BAD" SINCE MICHAEL JACKSON.
WHO?
Peirce

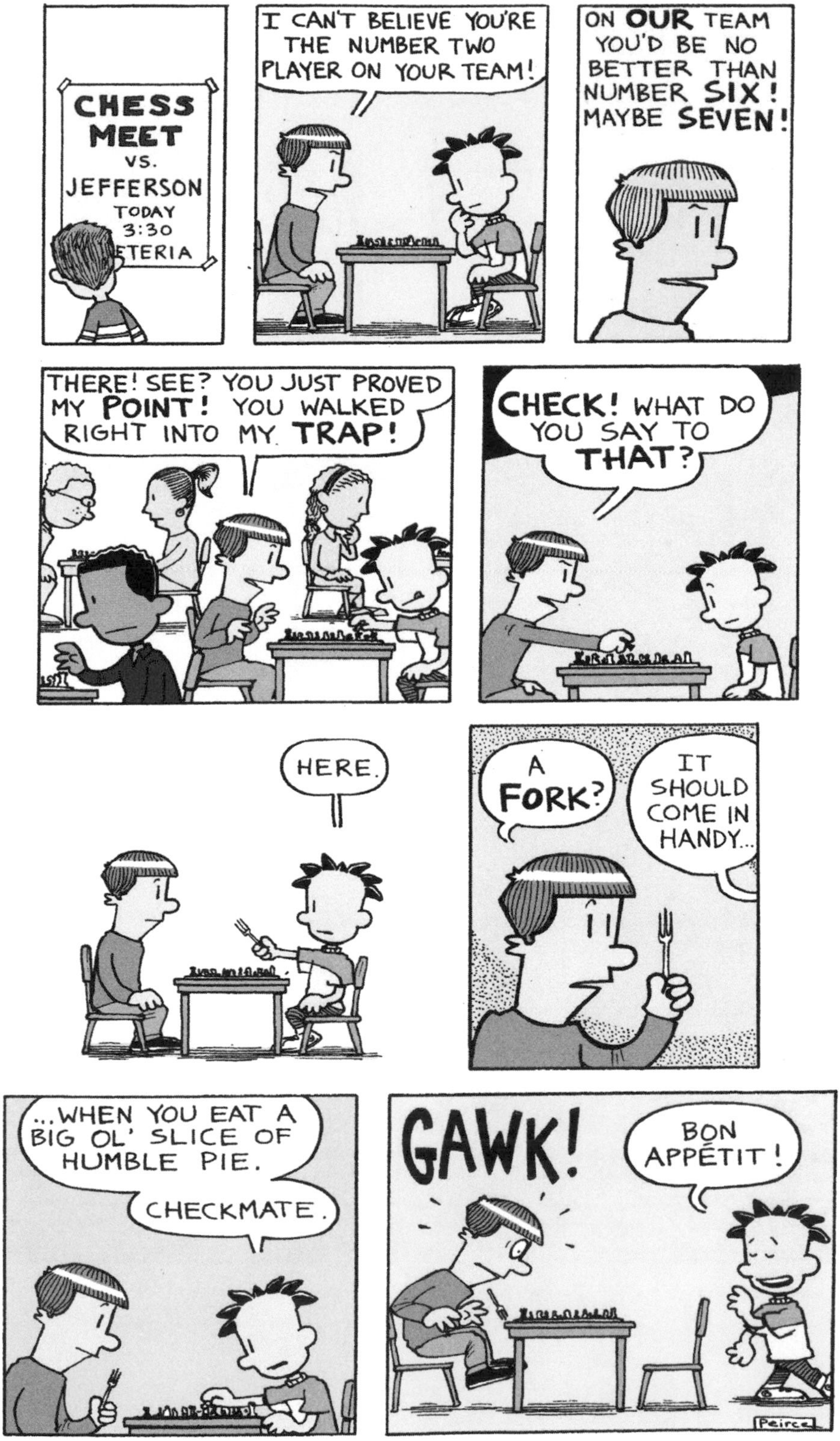
CHESS MEET
VS.
JEFFERSON
TODAY
3:30
ETERIA
I CAN'T BELIEVE YOU'RE THE NUMBER TWO PLAYER ON YOUR TEAM!
ON OUR TEAM YOU'D BE NO BETTER THAN NUMBER SIX! MAYBE SEVEN!
THERE! SEE? YOU JUST PROVED MY POINT! YOU WALKED RIGHT INTO MY TRAP!
CHECK! WHAT DO YOU SAY TO THAT?
HERE.
A FORK?
IT SHOULD COME IN HANDY...
...WHEN YOU EAT A BIG OL' SLICE OF HUMBLE PIE.
CHECKMATE.
GAWK!
BON APPÉTIT!
Peirce

REMEMBER THAT SUB WE HAD LAST SPRING?

MRS. ESTERHAUS!

OH, YEAH! WAS **SHE** IN OVER HER HEAD!

FOR THREE DAYS WE DID NOTHING IN CLASS BUT PLAY "HANGMAN"! IT WAS **GREAT!**

THINK WE COULD GET HER BACK?

WELL, MAYBE. IF ONE OF THE **REAL** TEACHERS GOT SICK OR SOMETHING.

HMMM... RIGHT...

...AND BY THE WAY, THAT WAS JUST A STATEMENT OF FACT, NOT A...

FIRST, WE'LL NEED A DART GUN.

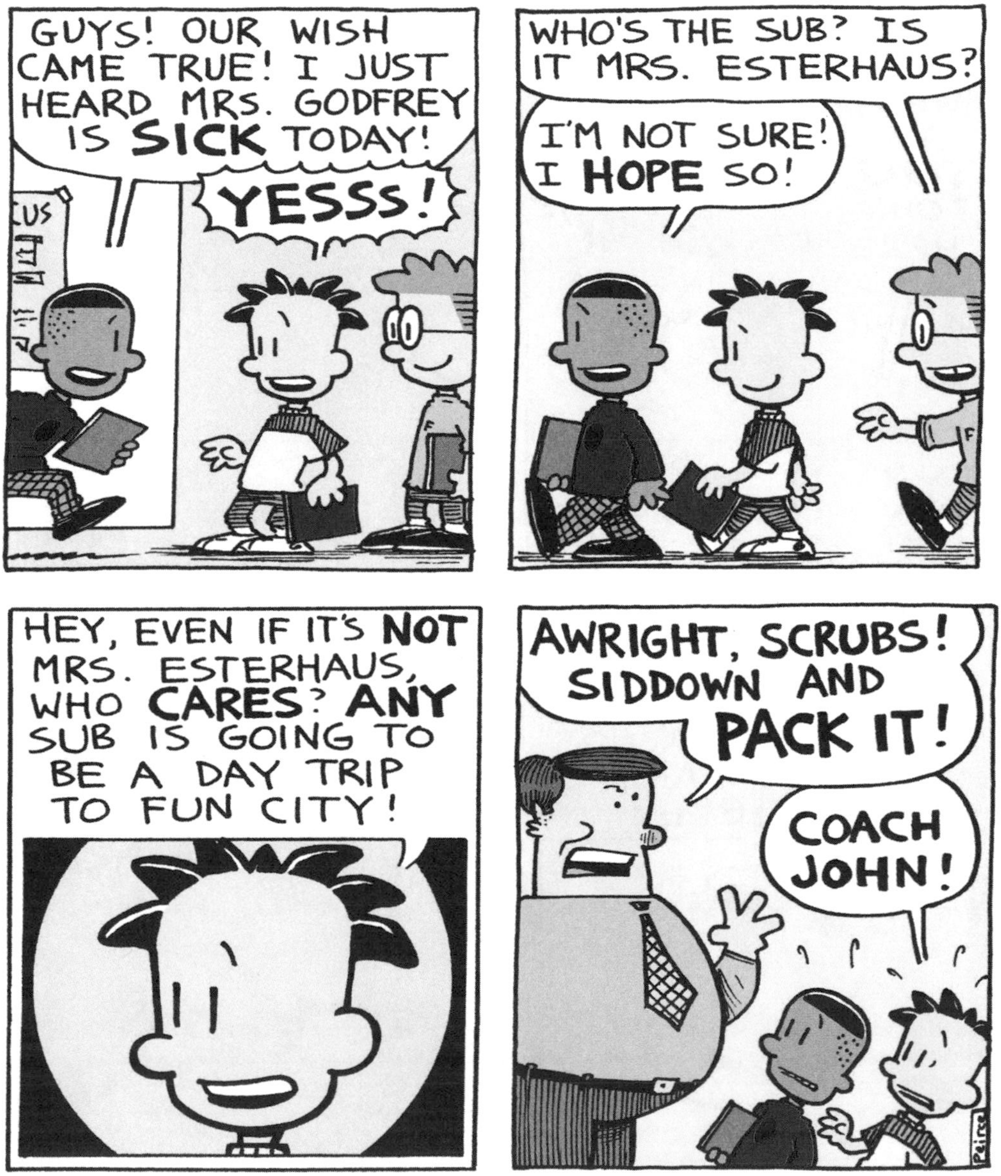
GUYS! OUR WISH CAME TRUE! I JUST HEARD MRS. GODFREY IS SICK TODAY!
YESSS!
WHO'S THE SUB? IS IT MRS. ESTERHAUS?
I'M NOT SURE! I HOPE SO!
HEY, EVEN IF IT'S NOT MRS. ESTERHAUS, WHO CARES? ANY SUB IS GOING TO BE A DAY TRIP TO FUN CITY!
AWRIGHT, SCRUBS! SIDDOWN AND PACK IT!
COACH JOHN!
Peirce

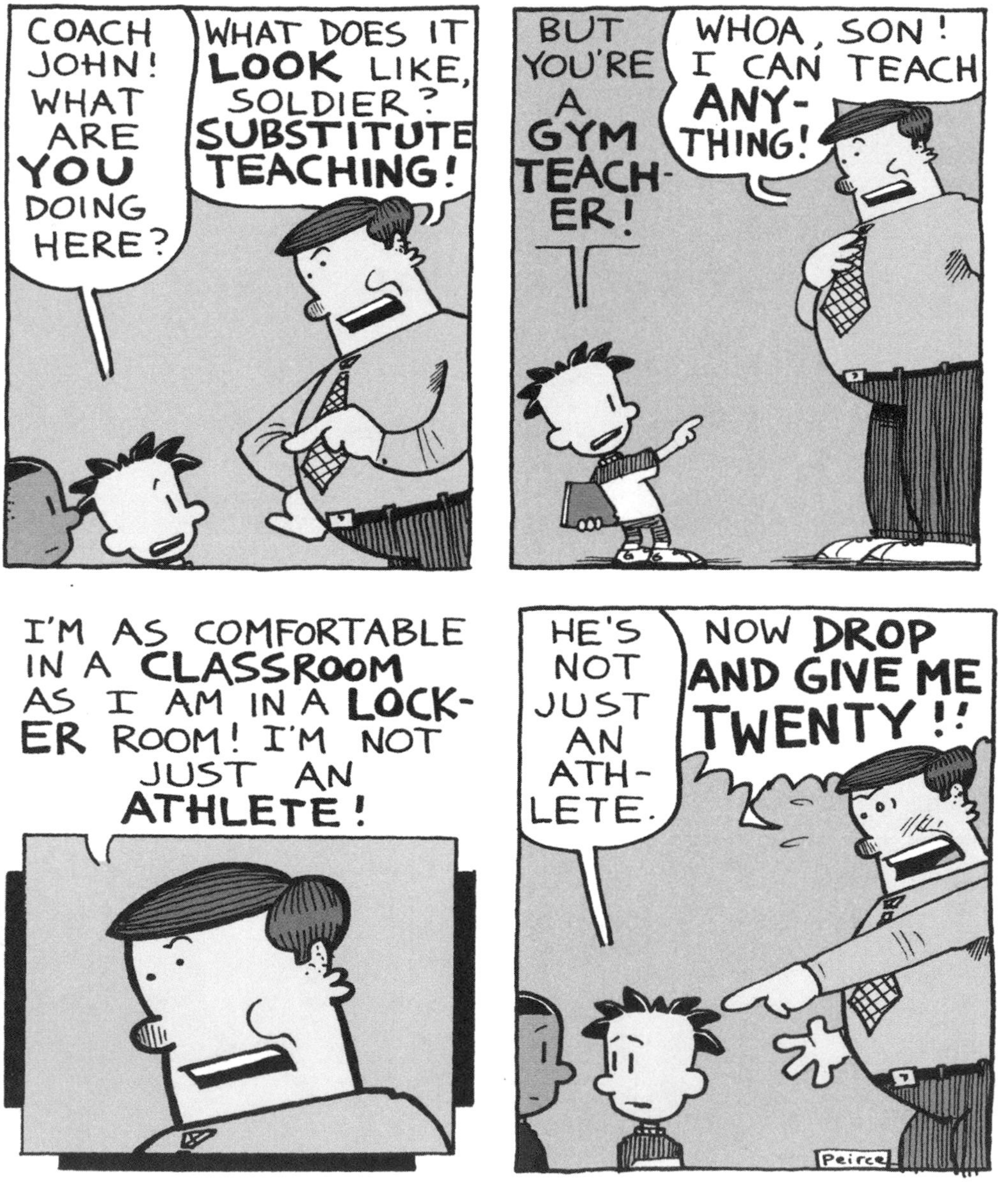
COACH JOHN! WHAT ARE YOU DOING HERE?
WHAT DOES IT LOOK LIKE, SOLDIER? SUBSTITUTE TEACHING!
BUT YOU'RE A GYM TEACHER!
WHOA, SON! I CAN TEACH ANYTHING!
I'M AS COMFORTABLE IN A CLASSROOM AS I AM IN A LOCKER ROOM! I'M NOT JUST AN ATHLETE!
HE'S NOT JUST AN ATHLETE.
NOW DROP AND GIVE ME TWENTY!!
Peirce

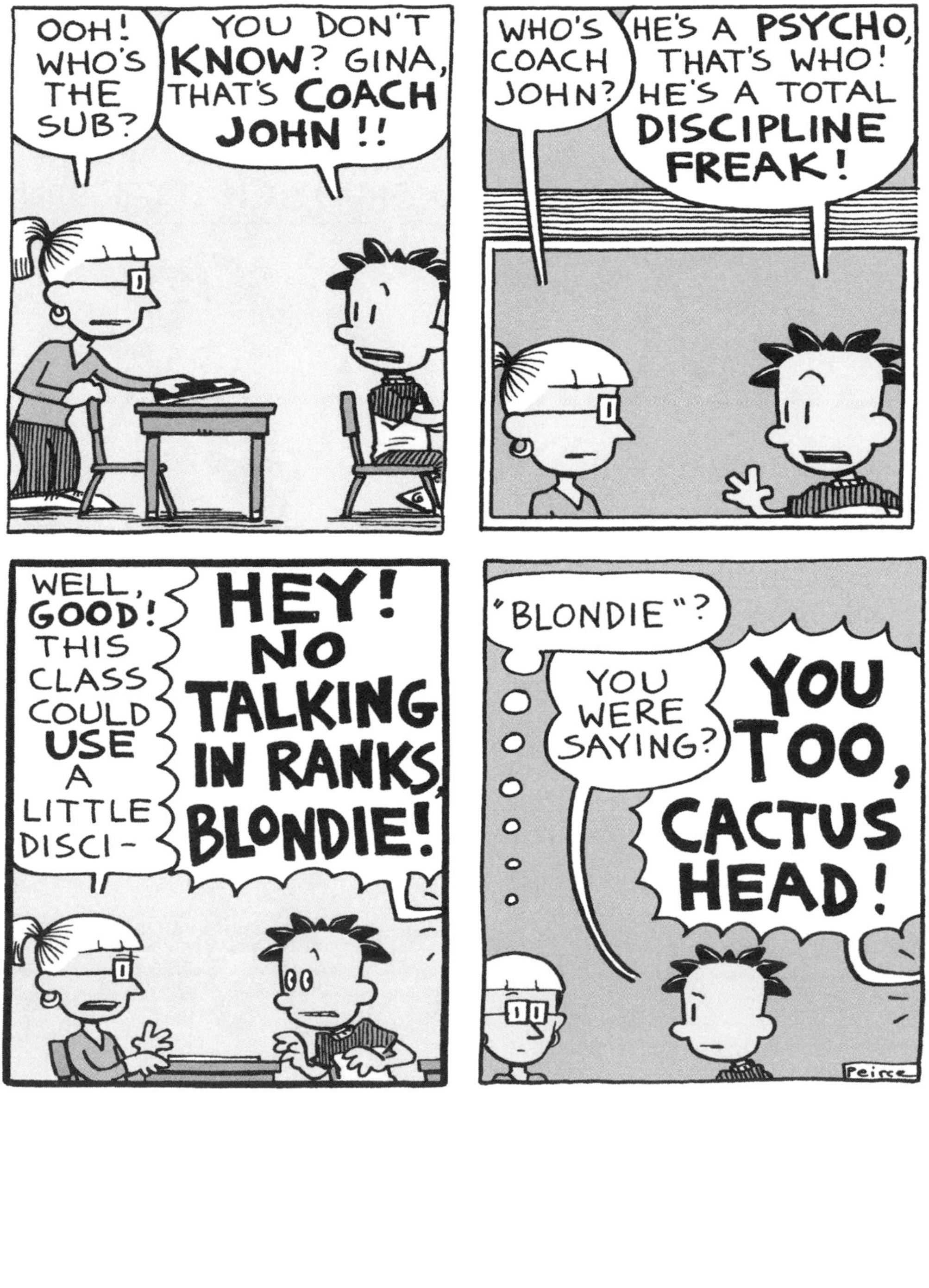
OOH! WHO'S THE SUB?
YOU DON'T KNOW? GINA, THAT'S COACH JOHN!!
WHO'S COACH JOHN?
HE'S A PSYCHO, THAT'S WHO! HE'S A TOTAL DISCIPLINE FREAK!
WELL, GOOD! THIS CLASS COULD USE A LITTLE DISCI-
HEY! NO TALKING IN RANKS, BLONDIE!
"BLONDIE"?
YOU WERE SAYING?
YOU TOO, CACTUS HEAD!
Peirce

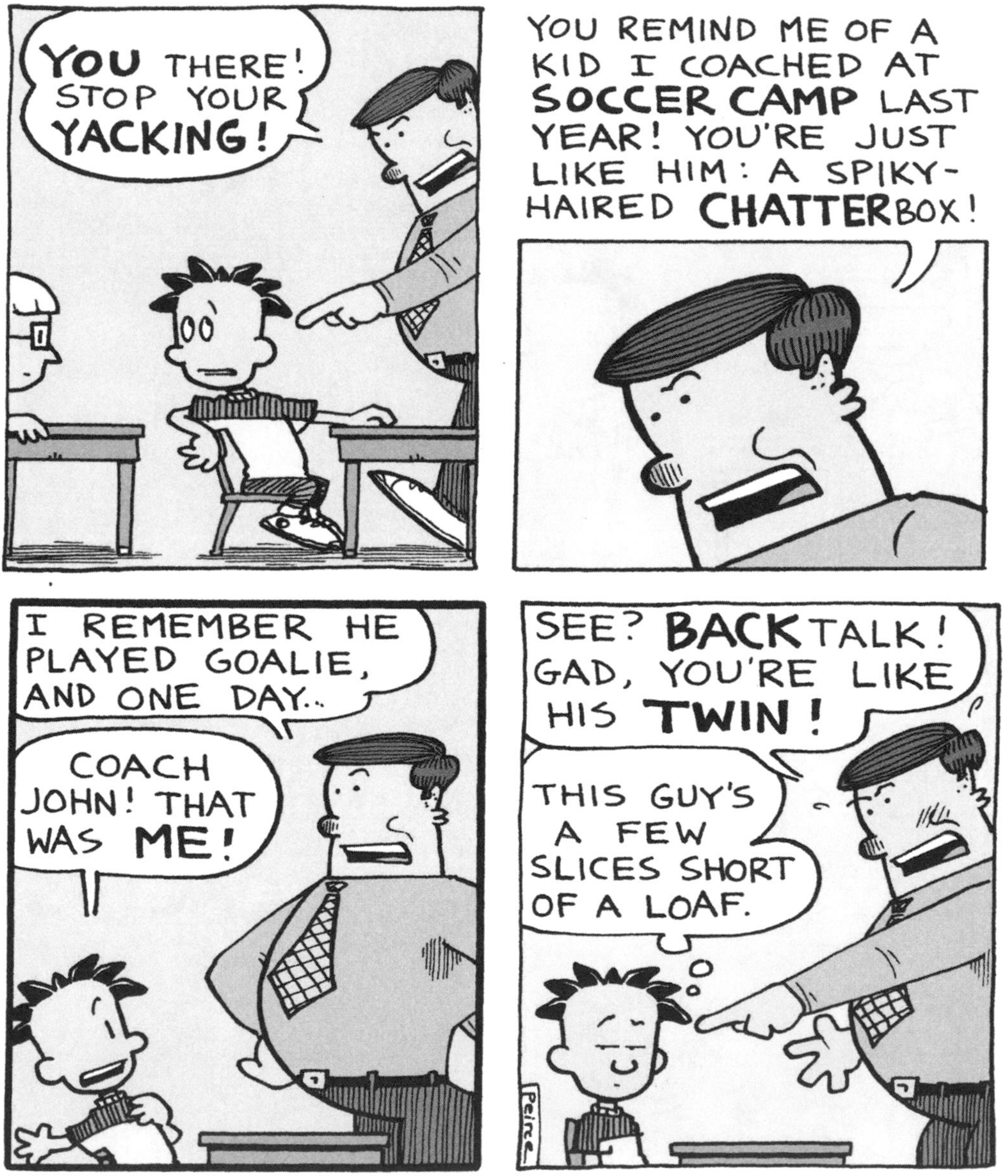
YOU THERE! STOP YOUR YACKING!
YOU REMIND ME OF A KID I COACHED AT SOCCER CAMP LAST YEAR! YOU'RE JUST LIKE HIM: A SPIKY-HAIRED CHATTERBOX!
I REMEMBER HE PLAYED GOALIE, AND ONE DAY...
COACH JOHN! THAT WAS ME!
SEE? BACKTALK! GAD, YOU'RE LIKE HIS TWIN!
THIS GUY'S A FEW SLICES SHORT OF A LOAF.
Peirce

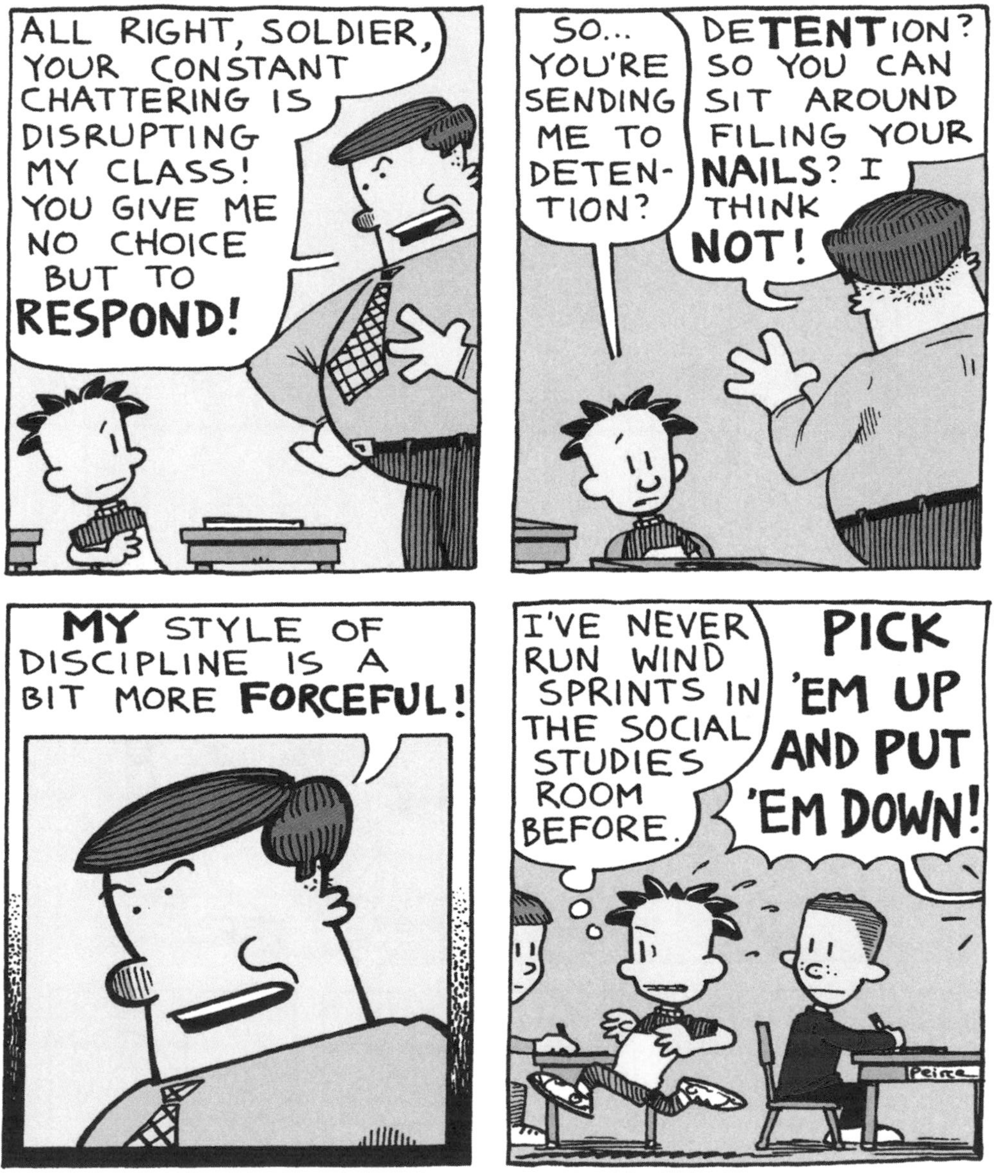
ALL RIGHT, SOLDIER, YOUR CONSTANT CHATTERING IS DISRUPTING MY CLASS! YOU GIVE ME NO CHOICE BUT TO RESPOND!
SO... YOU'RE SENDING ME TO DETEN-TION?
DETENTION? SO YOU CAN SIT AROUND FILING YOUR NAILS? I THINK NOT!
MY STYLE OF DISCIPLINE IS A BIT MORE FORCEFUL!
I'VE NEVER RUN WIND SPRINTS IN THE SOCIAL STUDIES ROOM BEFORE.
PICK 'EM UP AND PUT 'EM DOWN!
Peirce

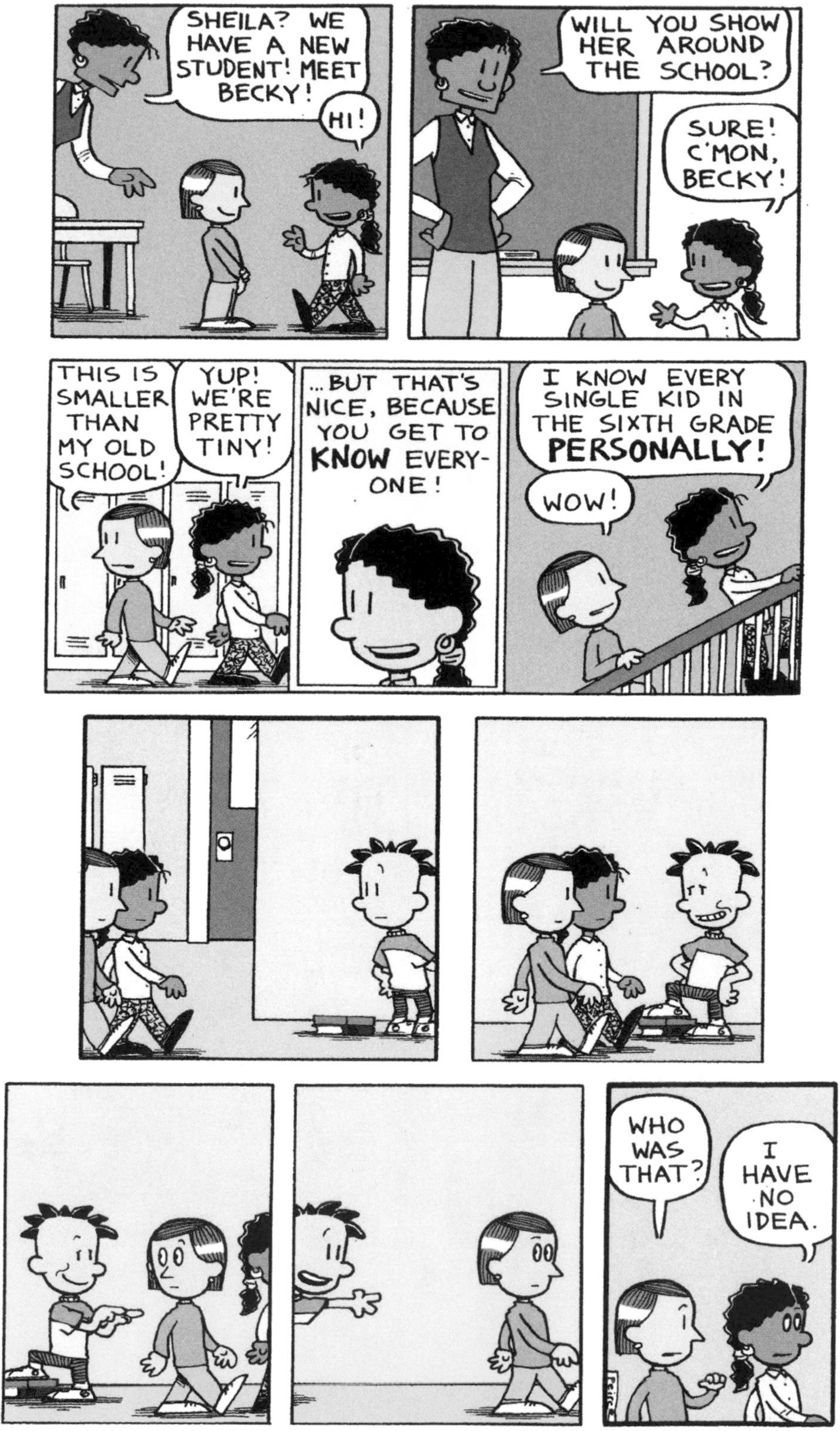
SHEILA? WE HAVE A NEW STUDENT! MEET BECKY!
HI!
WILL YOU SHOW HER AROUND THE SCHOOL?
SURE! C'MON, BECKY!
THIS IS SMALLER THAN MY OLD SCHOOL!
YUP! WE'RE PRETTY TINY!
...BUT THAT'S NICE, BECAUSE YOU GET TO KNOW EVERYONE!
I KNOW EVERY SINGLE KID IN THE SIXTH GRADE PERSONALLY!
WOW!
WHO WAS THAT?
I HAVE NO IDEA.

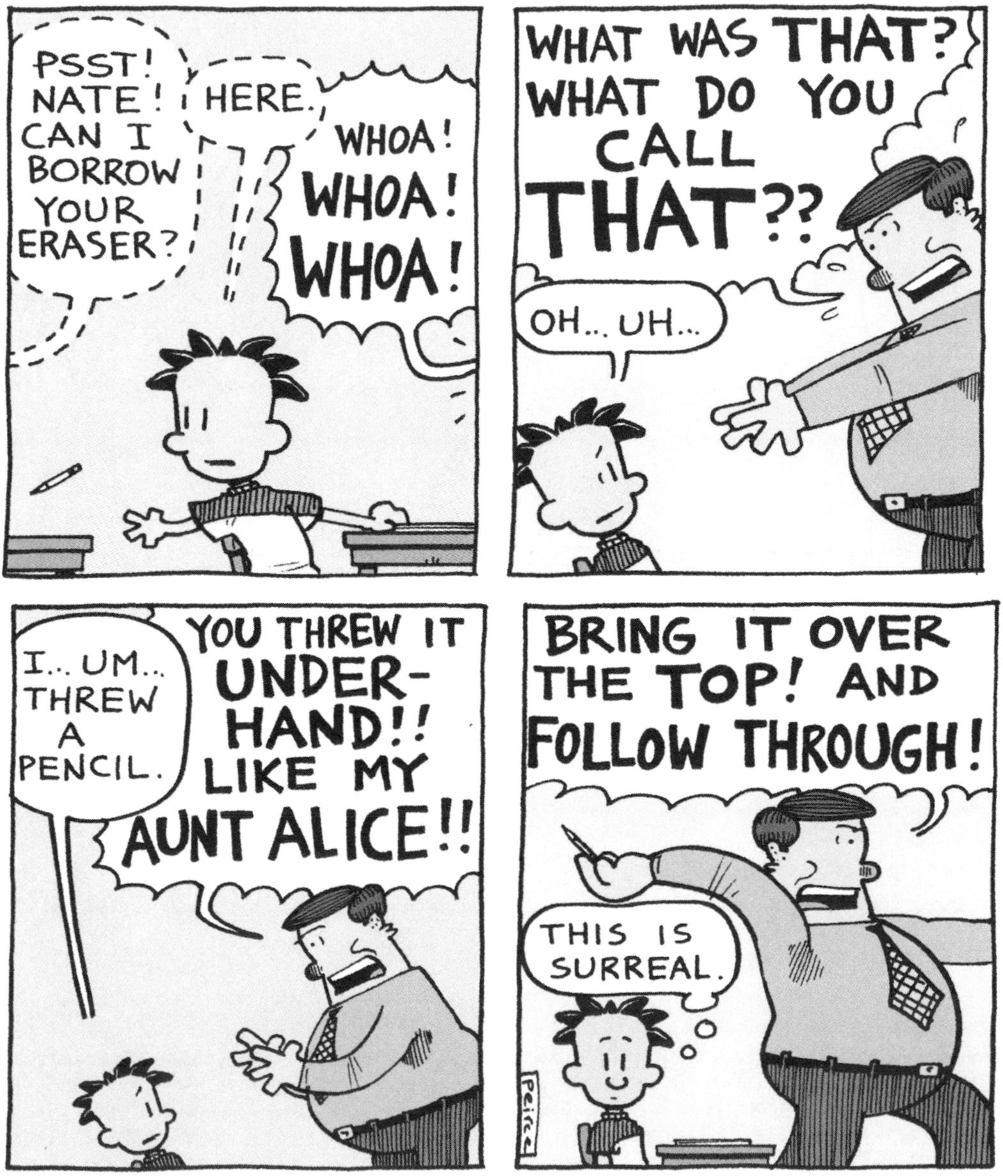
PSST! NATE! CAN I BORROW YOUR ERASER?
HERE.
WHOA! WHOA! WHOA!
WHAT WAS THAT? WHAT DO YOU CALL THAT??
OH... UH...
I... UM... THREW A PENCIL.
YOU THREW IT UNDER-HAND!! LIKE MY AUNT ALICE!!
BRING IT OVER THE TOP! AND FOLLOW THROUGH!
THIS IS SURREAL.
PEIRCE

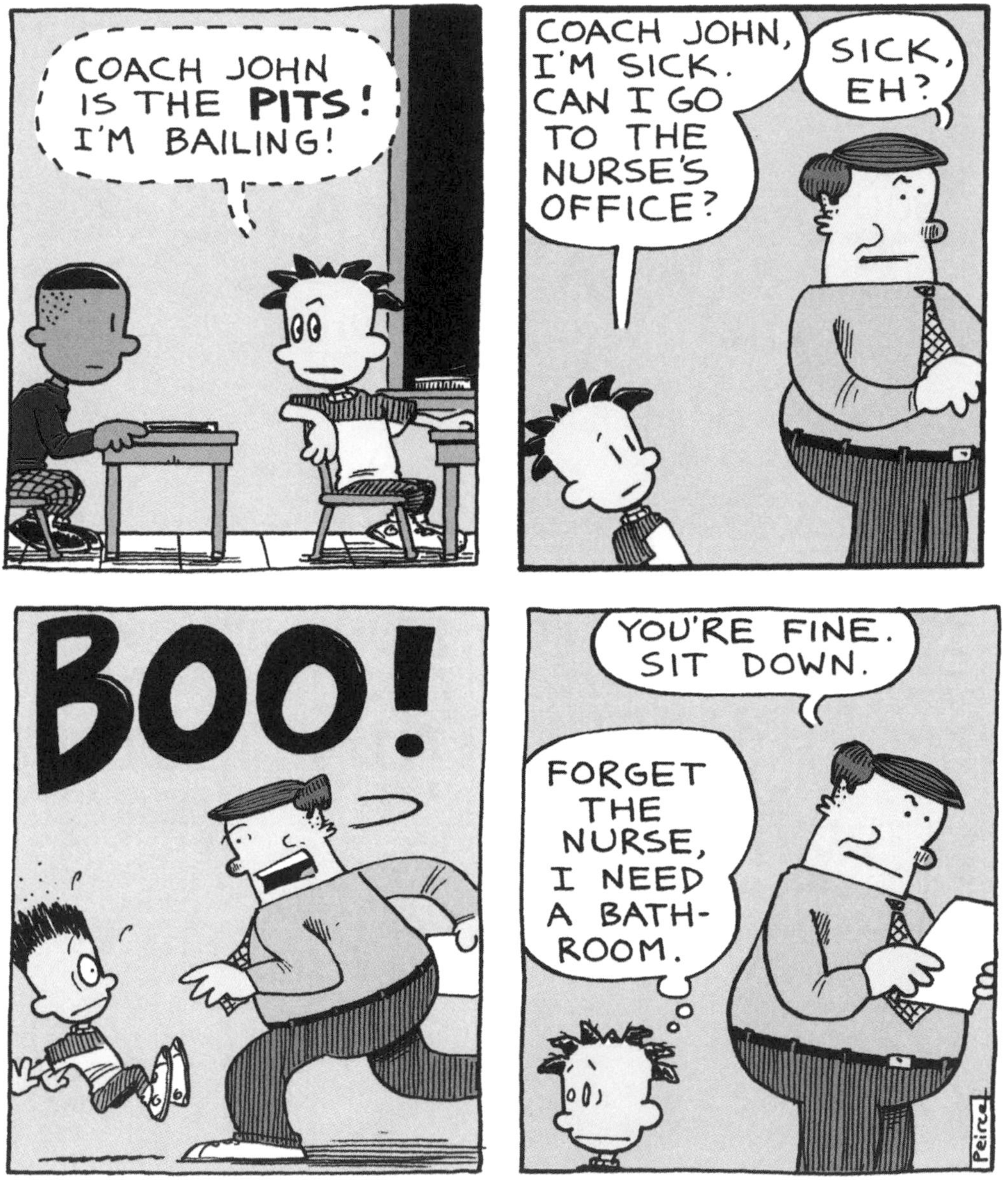
COACH JOHN IS THE **PITS**! I'M BAILING!
COACH JOHN, I'M SICK. CAN I GO TO THE NURSE'S OFFICE?
SICK, EH?
BOO!
YOU'RE FINE. SIT DOWN.
FORGET THE NURSE, I NEED A BATH-ROOM.
Peirce

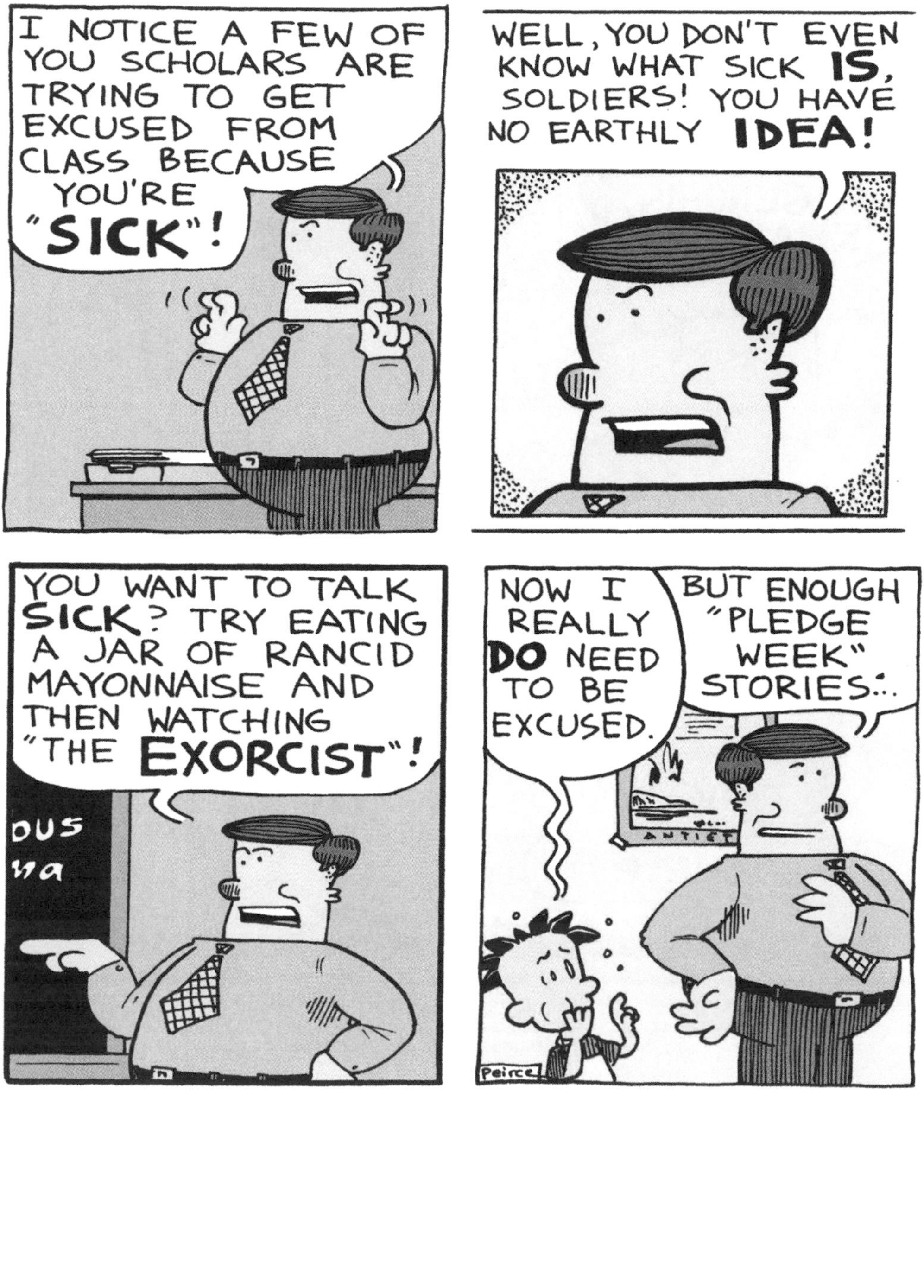
I NOTICE A FEW OF YOU SCHOLARS ARE TRYING TO GET EXCUSED FROM CLASS BECAUSE YOU'RE "SICK"!
WELL, YOU DON'T EVEN KNOW WHAT SICK IS, SOLDIERS! YOU HAVE NO EARTHLY IDEA!
YOU WANT TO TALK SICK? TRY EATING A JAR OF RANCID MAYONNAISE AND THEN WATCHING "THE EXORCIST"!
BUT ENOUGH "PLEDGE WEEK" STORIES...
NOW I REALLY DO NEED TO BE EXCUSED.
Peirce

COACH JOHN IS THE WORST SUBSTITUTE TEACHER EVER! IT'S LIKE HAVING SOCIAL STUDIES WITH GENGHIS KHAN!
I THINK I MIGHT ACTUALLY PREFER MRS. GODFR–...
WAIT! DON'T SAY IT!
BUT IT'S TRUE!
NO! BITE YOUR TONGUE!
I CAN'T HELP IT!
GET A-HOLD OF YOURSELF!
NO!
WHAT THE...?
SLAP
SLAP
SLAP
SLAP
SLAP
Peirce

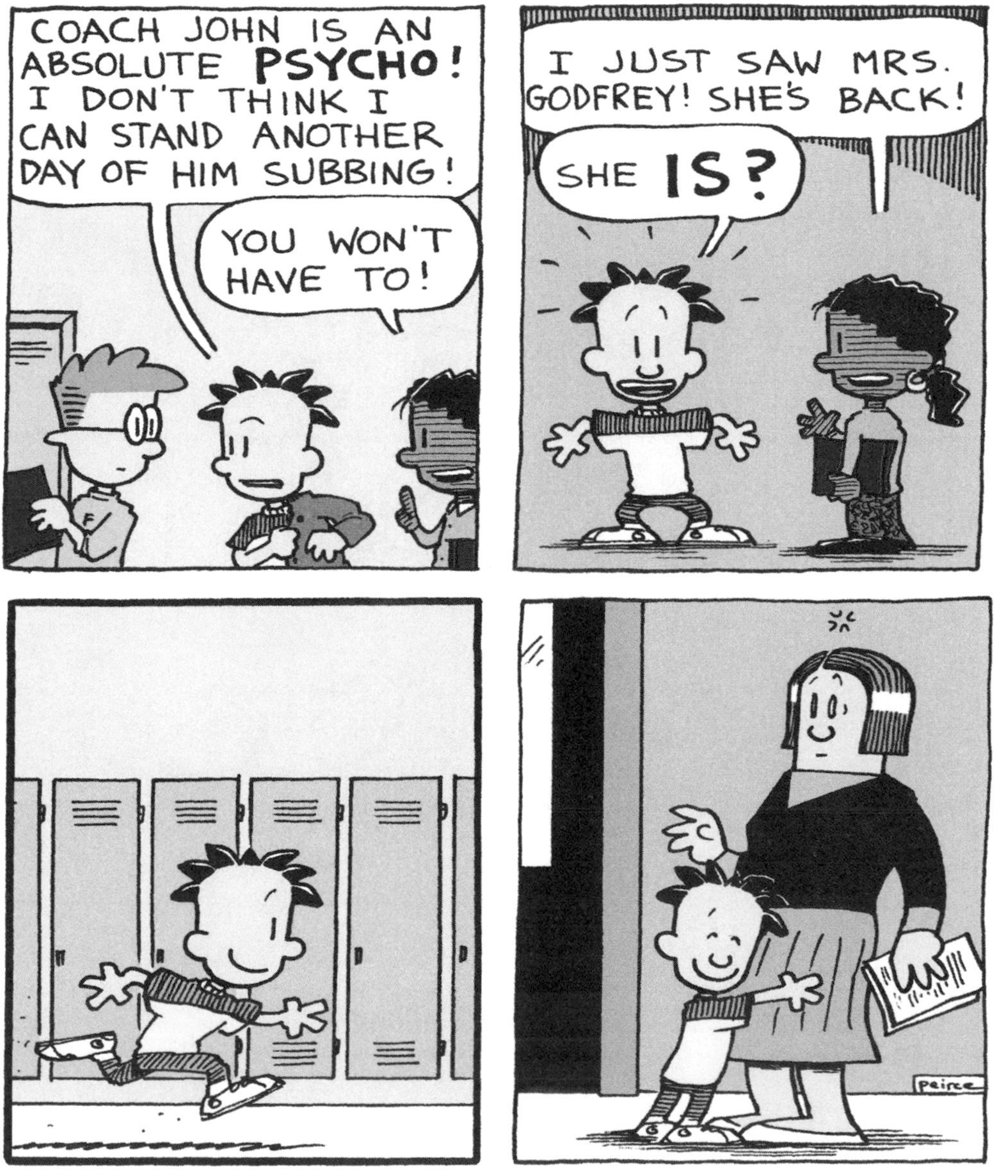
COACH JOHN IS AN ABSOLUTE PSYCHO! I DON'T THINK I CAN STAND ANOTHER DAY OF HIM SUBBING!
YOU WON'T HAVE TO!
I JUST SAW MRS. GODFREY! SHE'S BACK!
SHE IS?
peirce

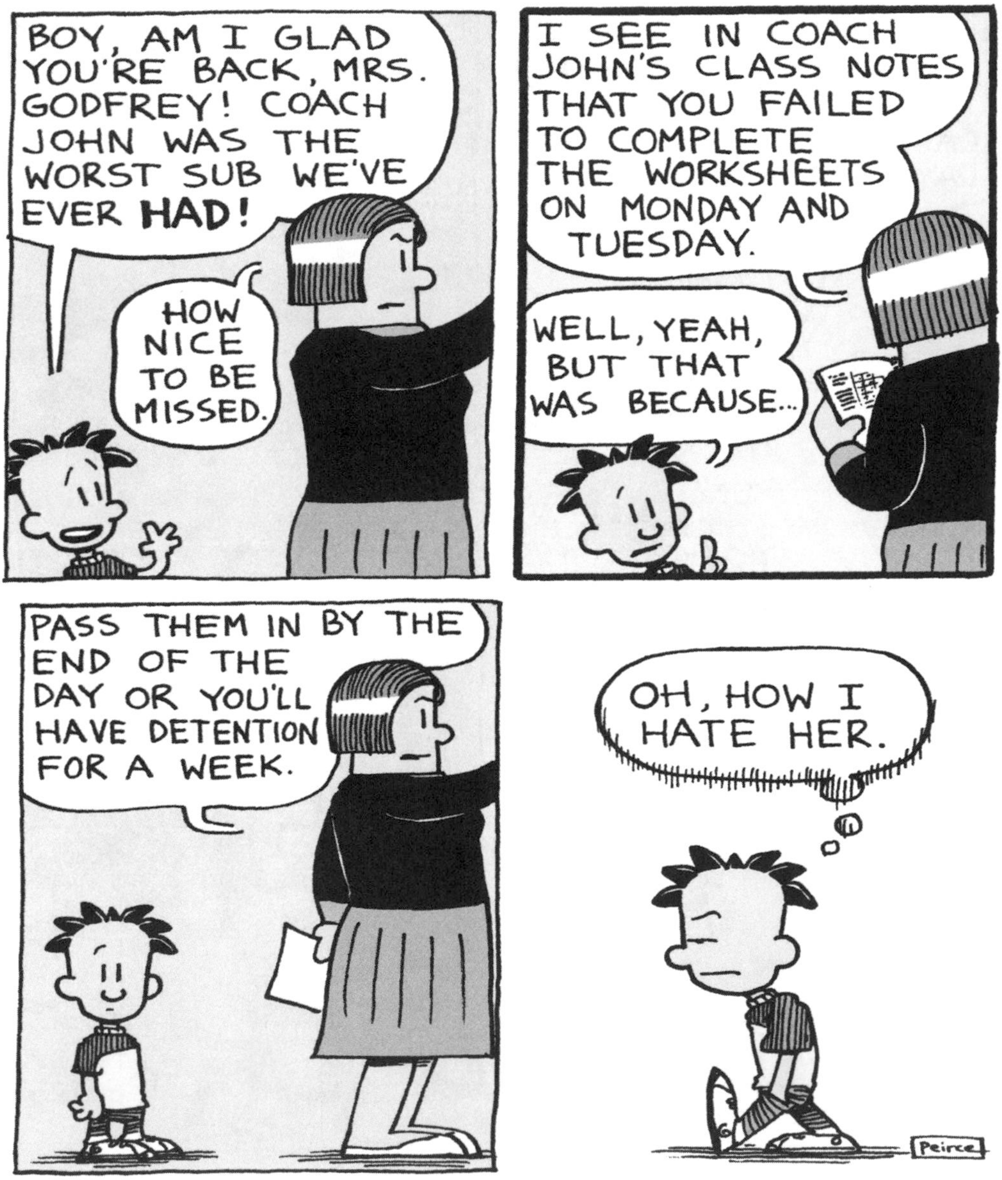
BOY, AM I GLAD YOU'RE BACK, MRS. GODFREY! COACH JOHN WAS THE WORST SUB WE'VE EVER **HAD!**
HOW NICE TO BE MISSED.
I SEE IN COACH JOHN'S CLASS NOTES THAT YOU FAILED TO COMPLETE THE WORKSHEETS ON MONDAY AND TUESDAY.
WELL, YEAH, BUT THAT WAS BECAUSE...
PASS THEM IN BY THE END OF THE DAY OR YOU'LL HAVE DETENTION FOR A WEEK.
OH, HOW I HATE HER.
Peirce

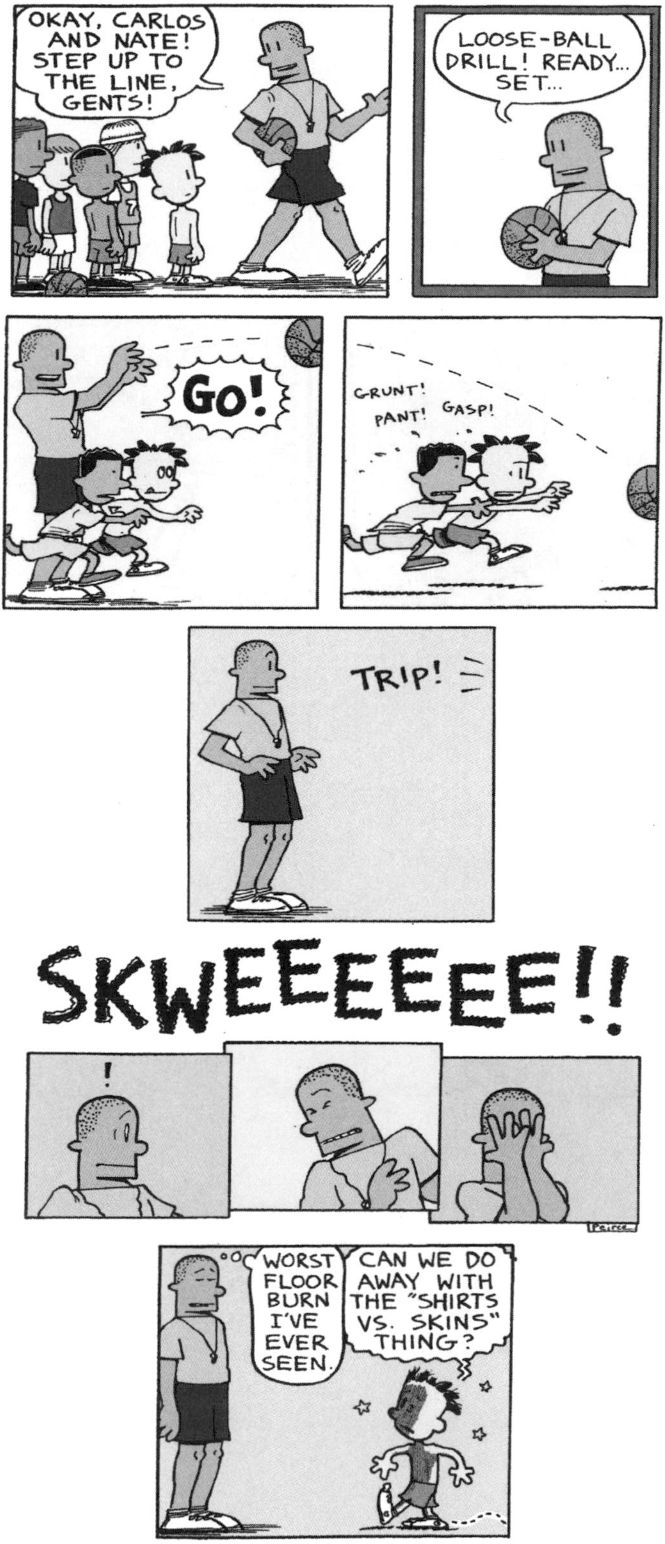
OKAY, CARLOS AND NATE! STEP UP TO THE LINE, GENTS!
LOOSE-BALL DRILL! READY... SET...
GO!
GRUNT!
PANT!
GASP!
TRIP!
SKWEEEEEEE!!
!
WORST FLOOR BURN I'VE EVER SEEN.
CAN WE DO AWAY WITH THE "SHIRTS VS. SKINS" THING?

DAD, CAN I HAVE A FEW BUCKS TO BUY HOT LUNCH?
NOT TODAY, NATE.
WE'VE GOT TO WORK OUR WAY THROUGH THESE THANKSGIVING LEFTOVERS!
EAT HEARTY.
Peirce
HEARTY HAR HAR.
PLEASE TELL ME THAT'S CRAN-BERRY SAUCE.
SCHOO
BUS

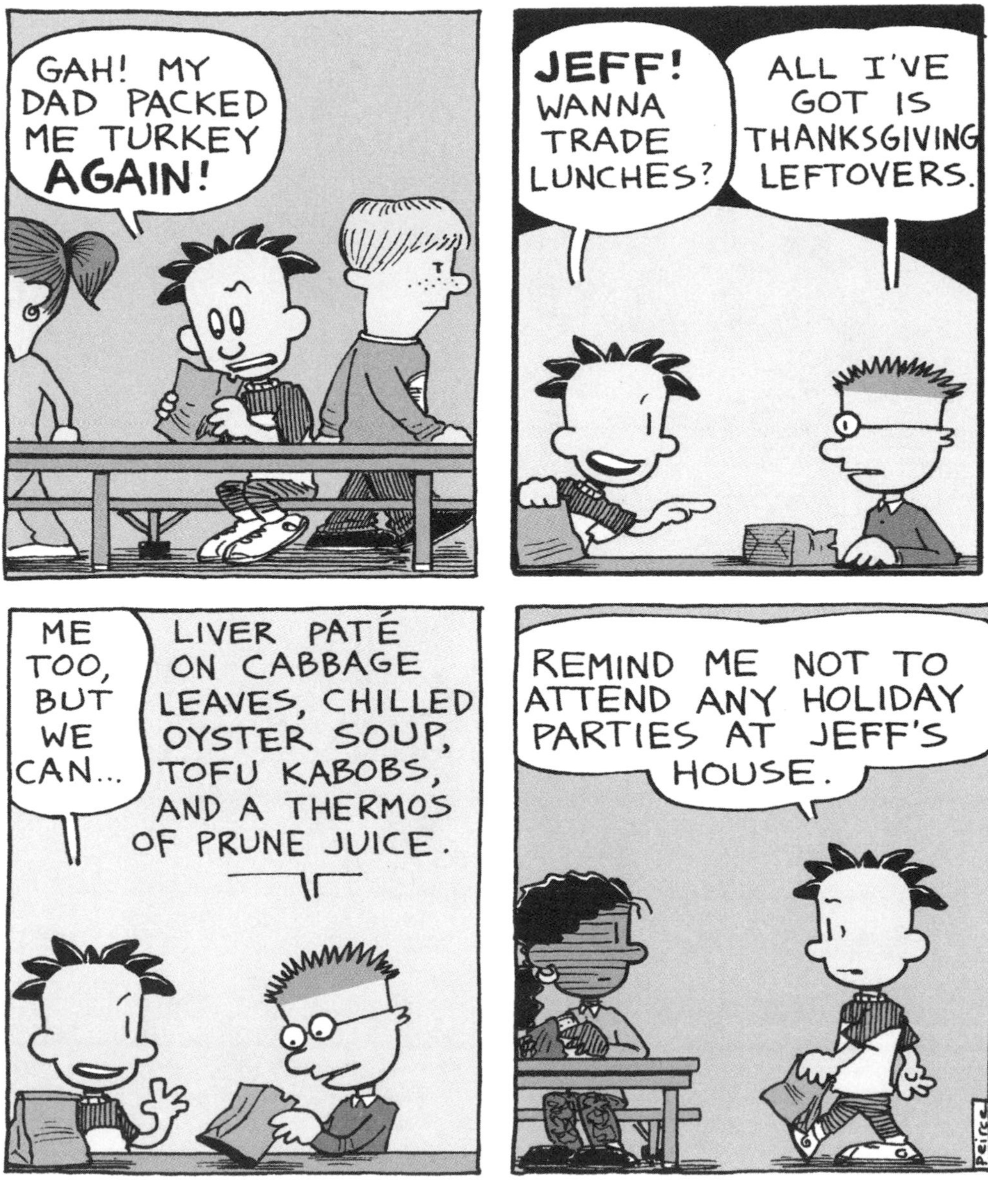
GAH! MY DAD PACKED ME TURKEY **AGAIN!**
JEFF! WANNA TRADE LUNCHES?
ALL I'VE GOT IS THANKSGIVING LEFTOVERS.
ME TOO, BUT WE CAN...
LIVER PATÉ ON CABBAGE LEAVES, CHILLED OYSTER SOUP, TOFU KABOBS, AND A THERMOS OF PRUNE JUICE.
REMIND ME NOT TO ATTEND ANY HOLIDAY PARTIES AT JEFF'S HOUSE.
Peirce

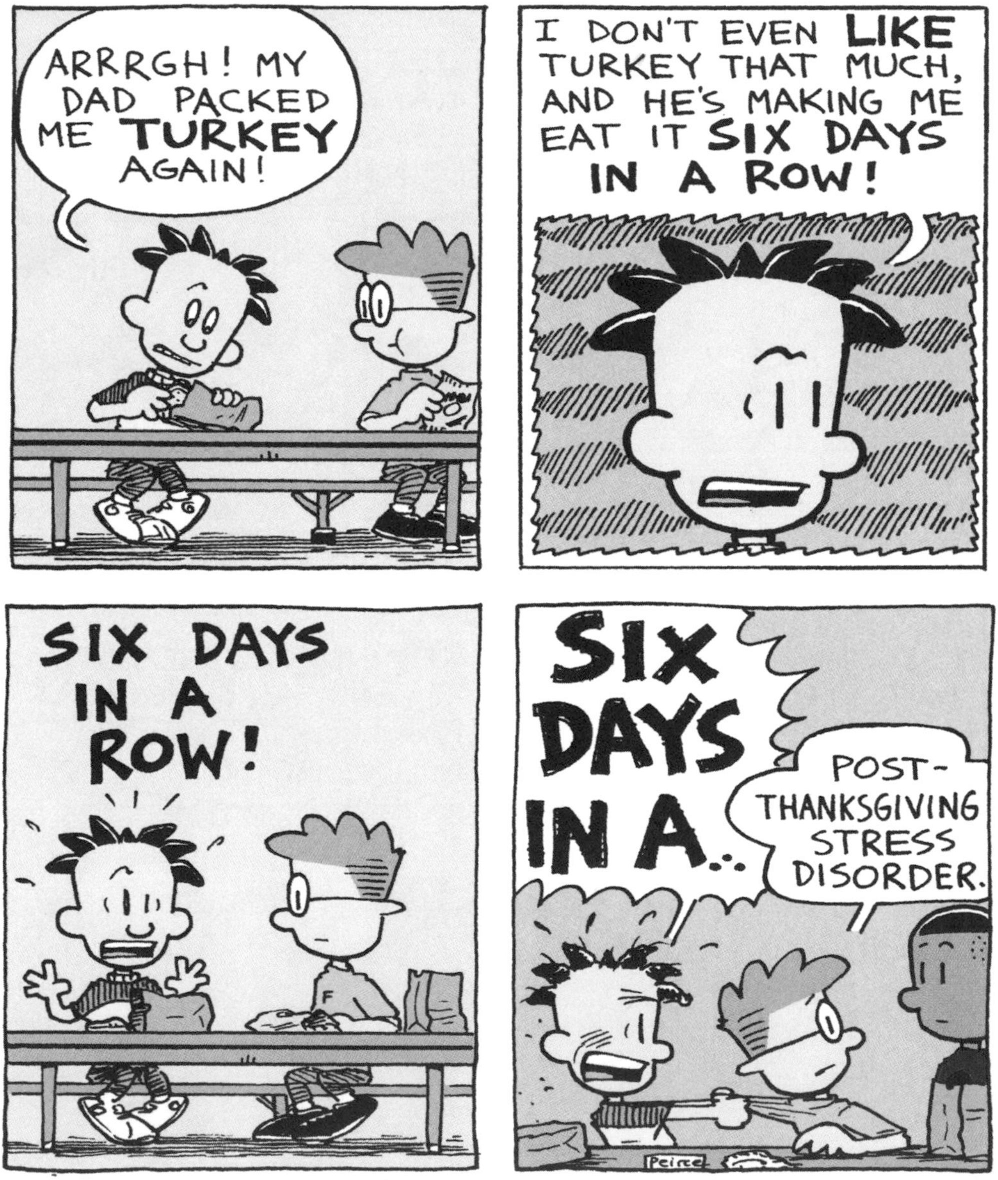

ARRRGH! MY DAD PACKED ME TURKEY AGAIN!
I DON'T EVEN LIKE TURKEY THAT MUCH, AND HE'S MAKING ME EAT IT SIX DAYS IN A ROW!
SIX DAYS IN A ROW!
SIX DAYS IN A...
POST-THANKSGIVING STRESS DISORDER.
Peirce

TEDDY! WANNA SWAP LUNCHES?
SURE!
YES! GOOD! HERE YOU GO! DONE DEAL! NO "TAKE BACKS"!
ZIP!
ZWIP!
HA! FINALLY I GET TO EAT SOMETHING OTHER THAN...
...TURKEY?
TURKEY **SALAD**. WELCOME TO MY NIGHT-MARE.
peirce

DAD, NO TURKEY FOR LUNCH TODAY! I'M **DONE** WITH TURKEY!
NO TURKEY?
NO TURKEY DRUM-STICKS?
NO!
NO TURKEY SANDWICHES?
NO!
NO TURKEY SALAD?
NO!
NO MOUTH-WATERING CHOCOLATE CHIP TURKOOKIES?
NO!
Peirce

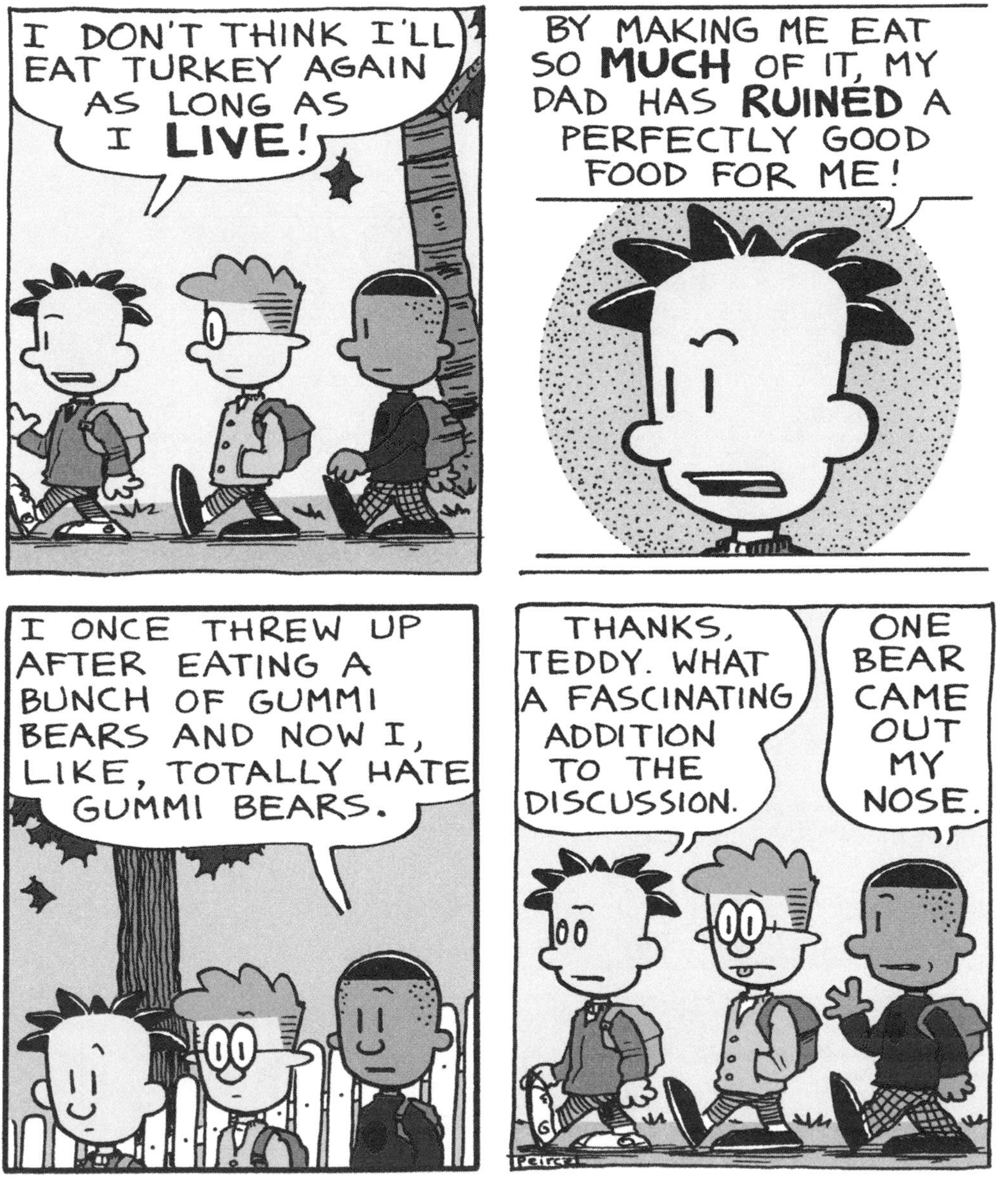
I DON'T THINK I'LL EAT TURKEY AGAIN AS LONG AS I **LIVE**!
BY MAKING ME EAT SO **MUCH** OF IT, MY DAD HAS **RUINED** A PERFECTLY GOOD FOOD FOR ME!
I ONCE THREW UP AFTER EATING A BUNCH OF GUMMI BEARS AND NOW I, LIKE, TOTALLY HATE GUMMI BEARS.
THANKS, TEDDY. WHAT A FASCINATING ADDITION TO THE DISCUSSION.
ONE BEAR CAME OUT MY NOSE.
Peirce

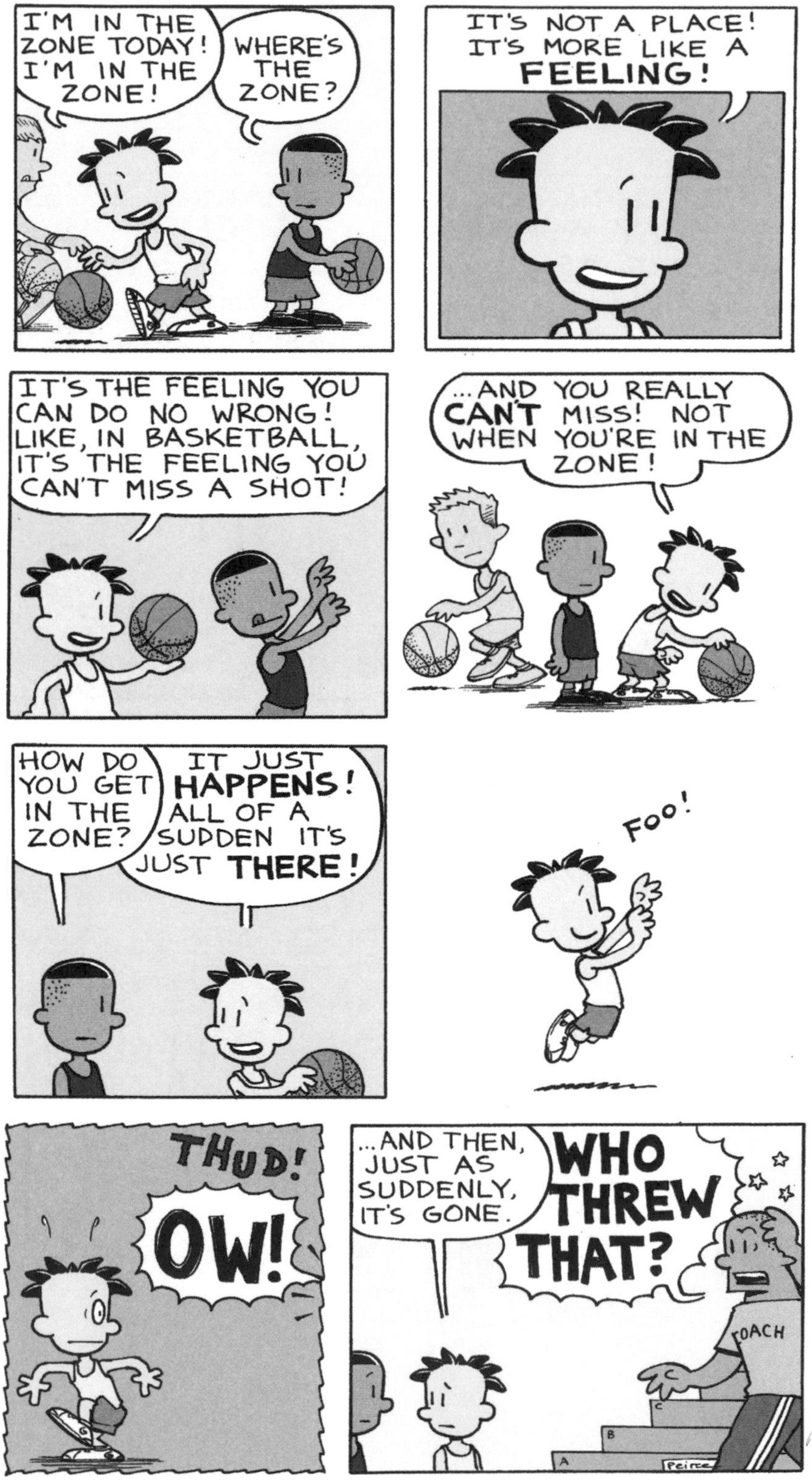
I'M IN THE ZONE TODAY! I'M IN THE ZONE!
WHERE'S THE ZONE?
IT'S NOT A PLACE! IT'S MORE LIKE A **FEELING**!
IT'S THE FEELING YOU CAN DO NO WRONG! LIKE, IN BASKETBALL, IT'S THE FEELING YOU CAN'T MISS A SHOT!
...AND YOU REALLY **CAN'T** MISS! NOT WHEN YOU'RE IN THE ZONE!
HOW DO YOU GET IN THE ZONE?
IT JUST **HAPPENS**! ALL OF A SUDDEN IT'S JUST **THERE**!
FOO!
THUD!
OW!
...AND THEN, JUST AS SUDDENLY, IT'S GONE.
WHO THREW THAT?
OACH
C
B
A
Peirce

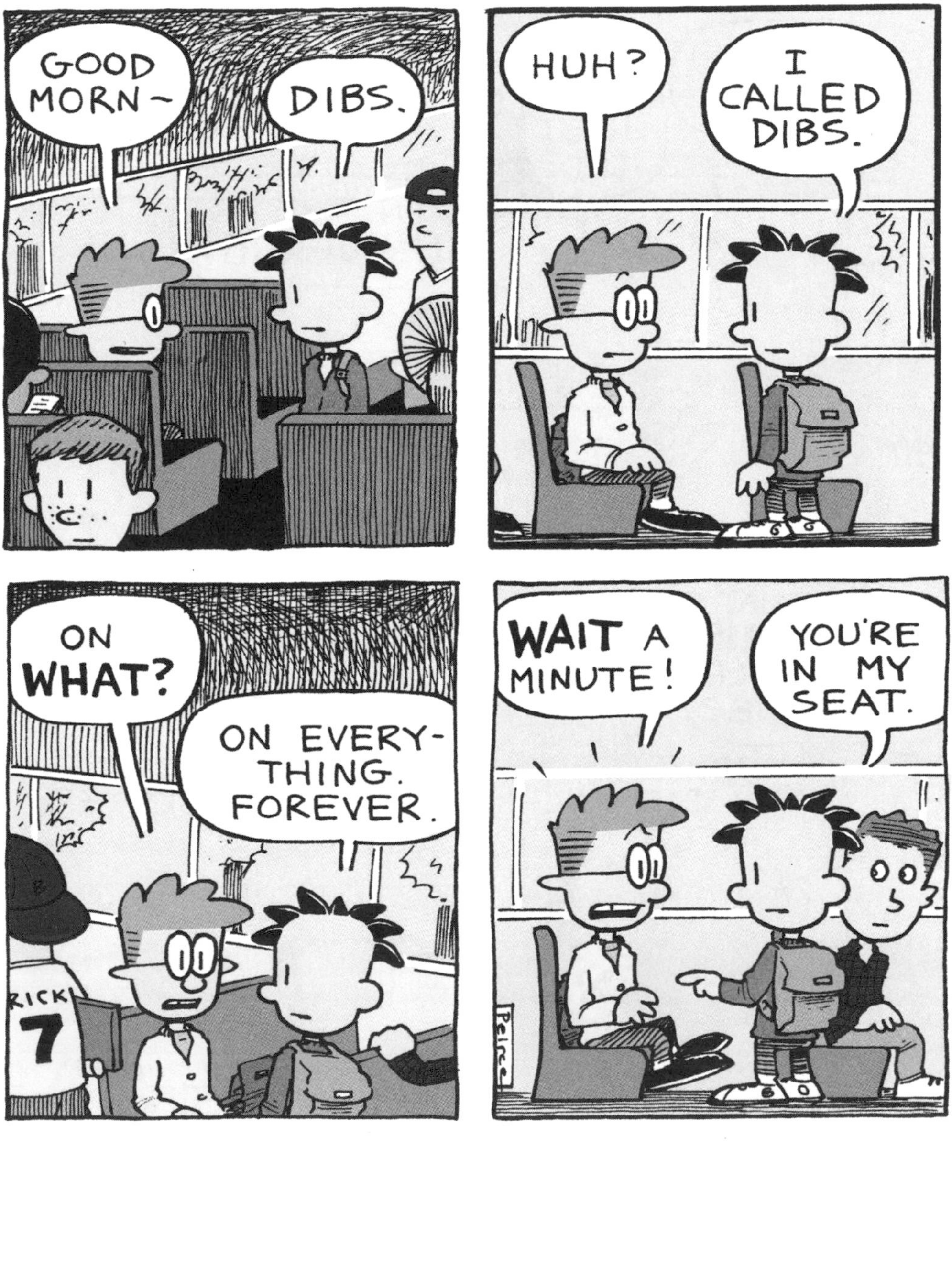
GOOD MORN~
DIBS.
HUH?
I CALLED DIBS.
ON WHAT?
ON EVERY-THING. FOREVER.
RICK
7
WAIT A MINUTE!
YOU'RE IN MY SEAT.
Peirce

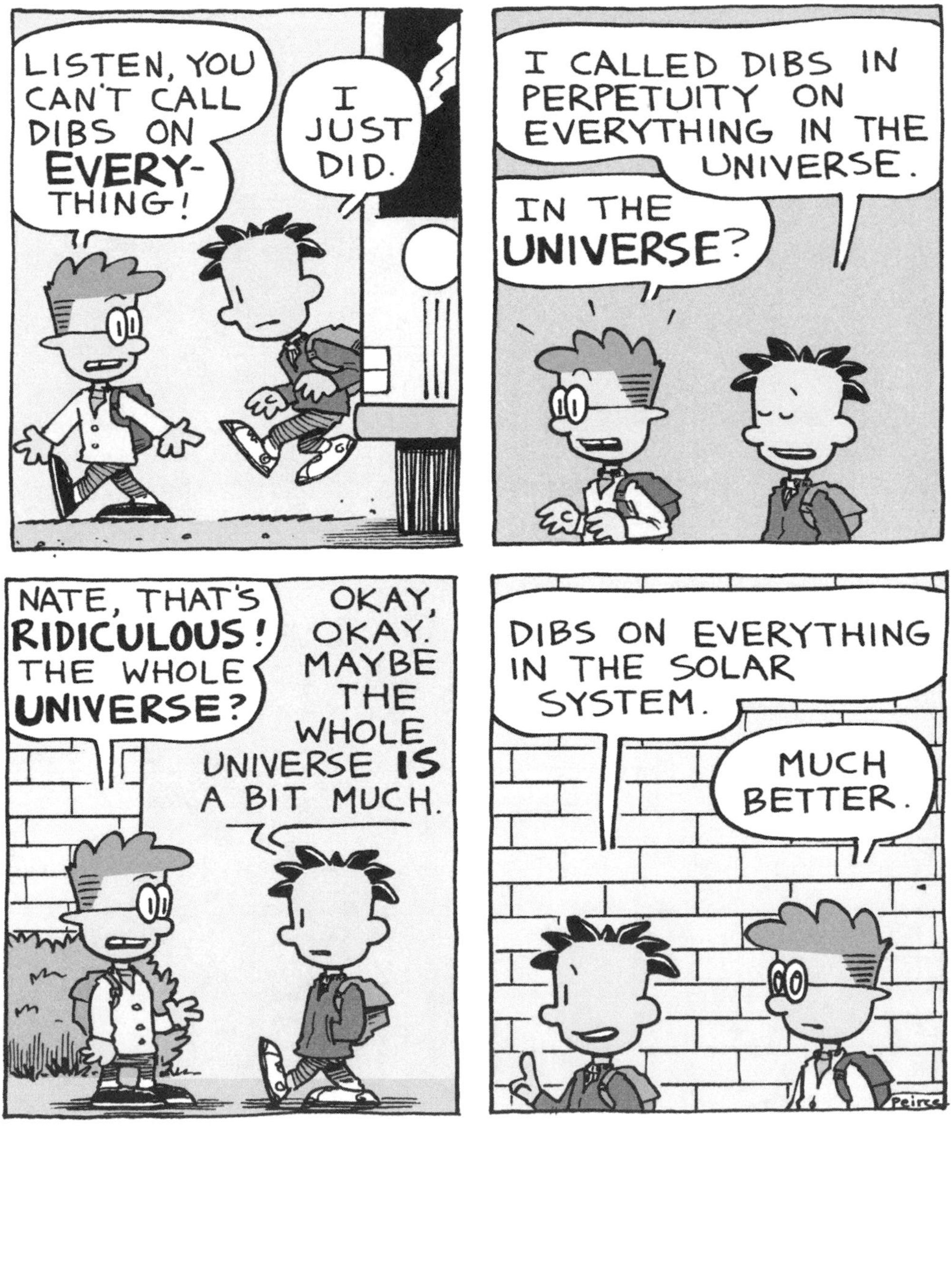

LISTEN, YOU CAN'T CALL DIBS ON EVERY-THING!
I JUST DID.
I CALLED DIBS IN PERPETUITY ON EVERYTHING IN THE UNIVERSE.
IN THE UNIVERSE?
NATE, THAT'S RIDICULOUS! THE WHOLE UNIVERSE?
OKAY, OKAY. MAYBE THE WHOLE UNIVERSE IS A BIT MUCH.
DIBS ON EVERYTHING IN THE SOLAR SYSTEM.
MUCH BETTER.
Peirce

NO, YOU CAN'T!
'S JUST SO STUPID!
I ALREADY DID!
HEY, SHUT UP, SCRUB!
GENTS, GENTS! WHAT'S THE PROB?
NATE CALLED DIBS ON EVERY-THING! YOU JUST CAN'T DO THAT!
YOU'RE JUST MAD 'CAUSE I BEAT YOU TO IT!
HE'S RIGHT, NATE, YOU CAN'T DO THAT.
... BECAUSE I CALLED DIBS ON EVERYTHING YESTERDAY!
YOU'VE BEEN OUT-DIBBED!
WHAT? HOLD IT! WITNESSES! I WANT WITNESSES!
Peirce

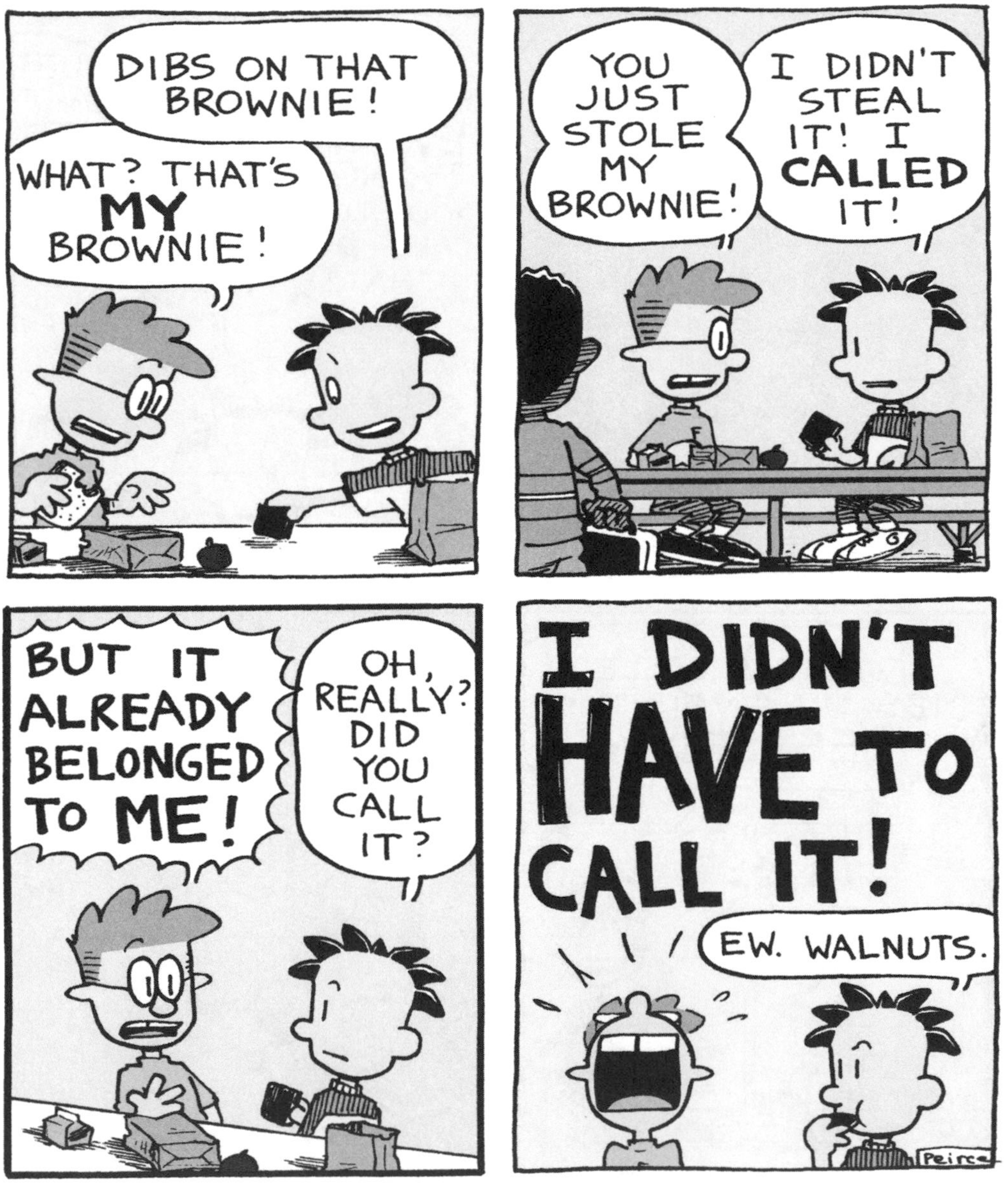
DIBS ON THAT BROWNIE!
WHAT? THAT'S **MY** BROWNIE!
YOU JUST STOLE MY BROWNIE!
I DIDN'T STEAL IT! I **CALLED** IT!
BUT IT ALREADY BELONGED TO **ME**!
OH, REALLY? DID YOU CALL IT?
I DIDN'T **HAVE** TO CALL IT!
EW. WALNUTS.
Peirce

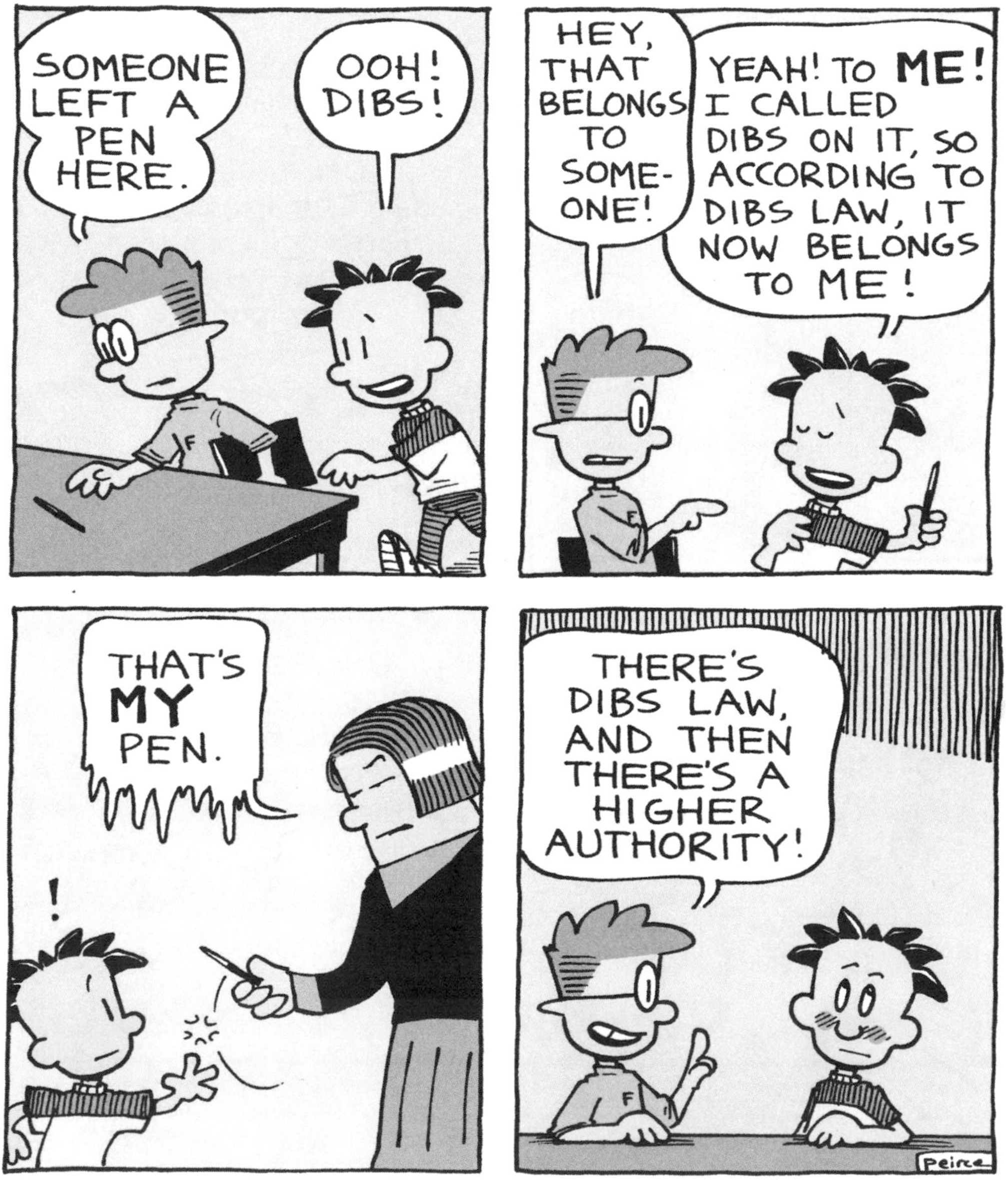
SOMEONE LEFT A PEN HERE.
OOH! DIBS!
HEY, THAT BELONGS TO SOME-ONE!
YEAH! TO ME! I CALLED DIBS ON IT, SO ACCORDING TO DIBS LAW, IT NOW BELONGS TO ME!
THAT'S MY PEN.
!
THERE'S DIBS LAW, AND THEN THERE'S A HIGHER AUTHORITY!
Peirce

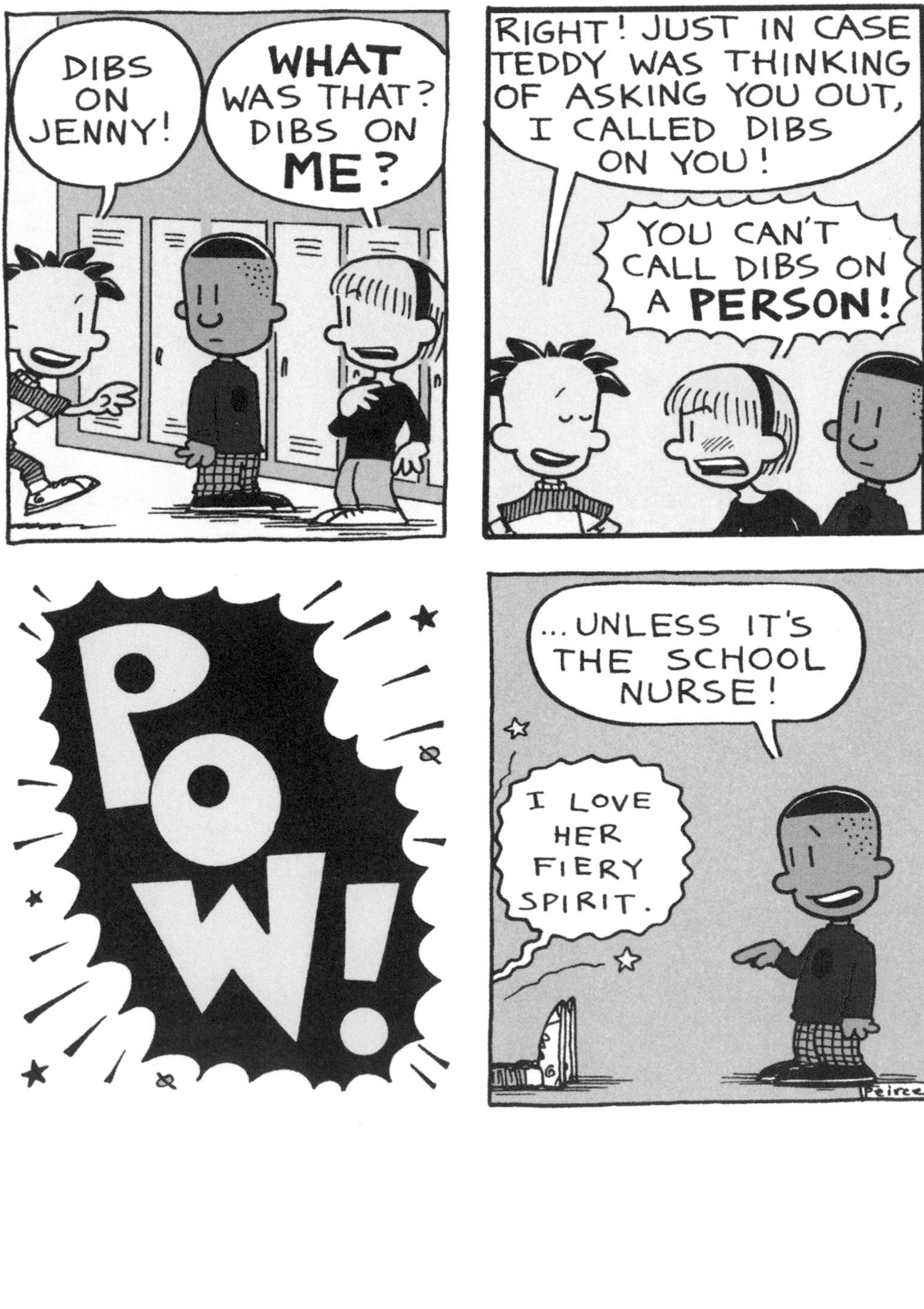
DIBS ON JENNY!
WHAT WAS THAT? DIBS ON ME?
RIGHT! JUST IN CASE TEDDY WAS THINKING OF ASKING YOU OUT, I CALLED DIBS ON YOU!
YOU CAN'T CALL DIBS ON A PERSON!
POW!
...UNLESS IT'S THE SCHOOL NURSE!
I LOVE HER FIERY SPIRIT.
Peirce

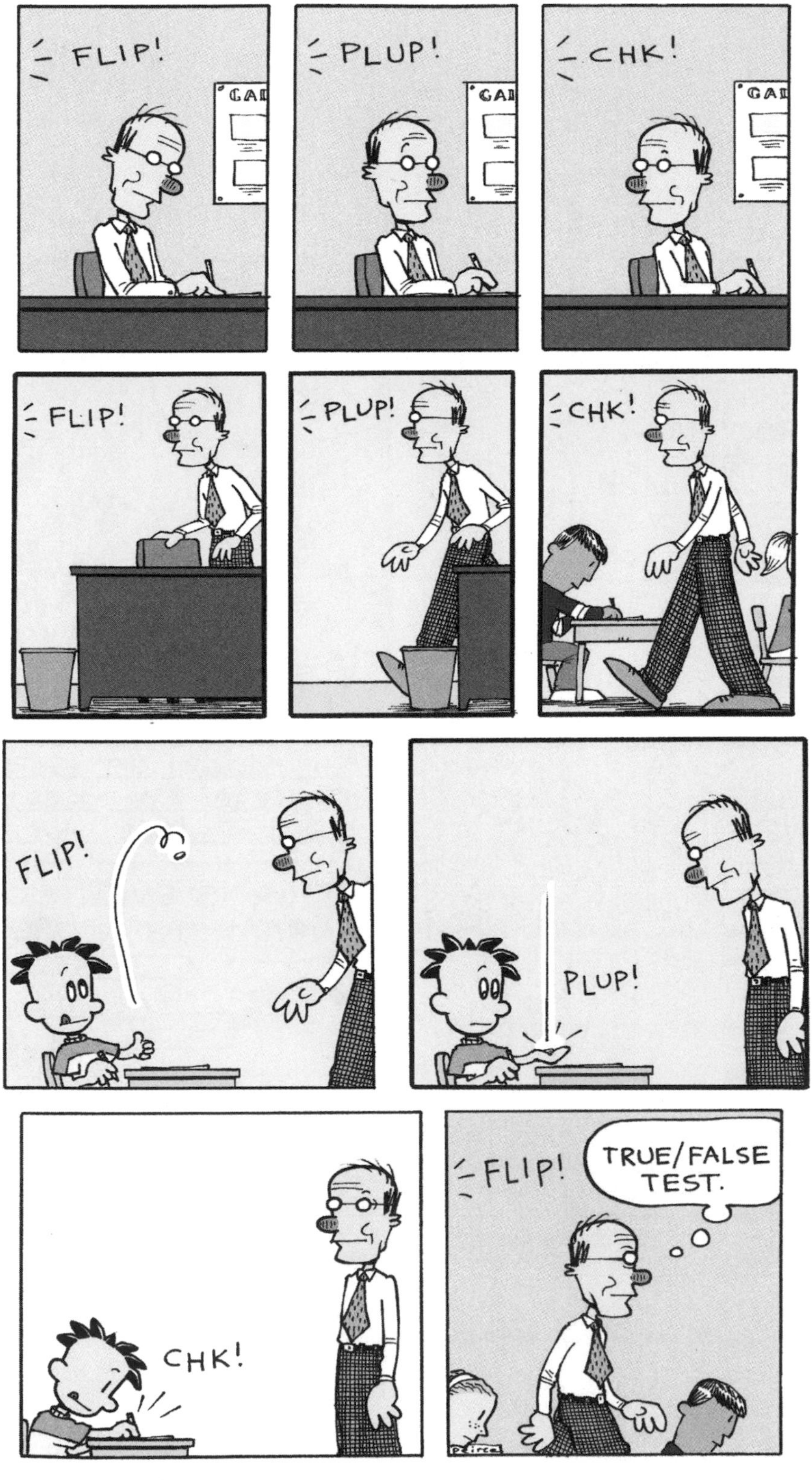
FLIP!
PLUP!
CHK!
FLIP!
PLUP!
CHK!
FLIP!
PLUP!
CHK!
FLIP!
TRUE/FALSE TEST.

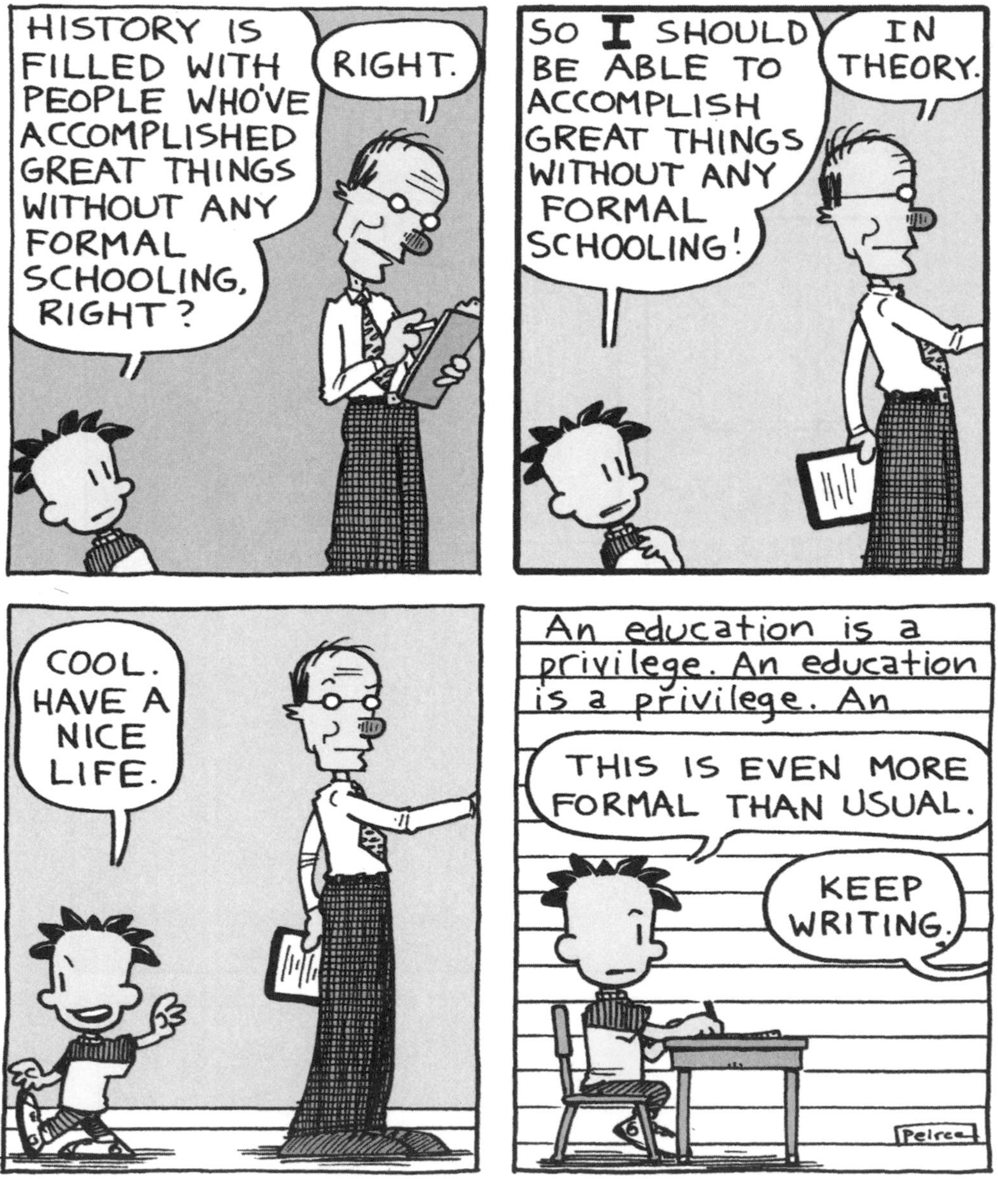
HISTORY IS FILLED WITH PEOPLE WHO'VE ACCOMPLISHED GREAT THINGS WITHOUT ANY FORMAL SCHOOLING, RIGHT?
RIGHT.
SO I SHOULD BE ABLE TO ACCOMPLISH GREAT THINGS WITHOUT ANY FORMAL SCHOOLING!
IN THEORY.
COOL. HAVE A NICE LIFE.
An education is a privilege. An education is a privilege. An
THIS IS EVEN MORE FORMAL THAN USUAL.
KEEP WRITING.
Peirce

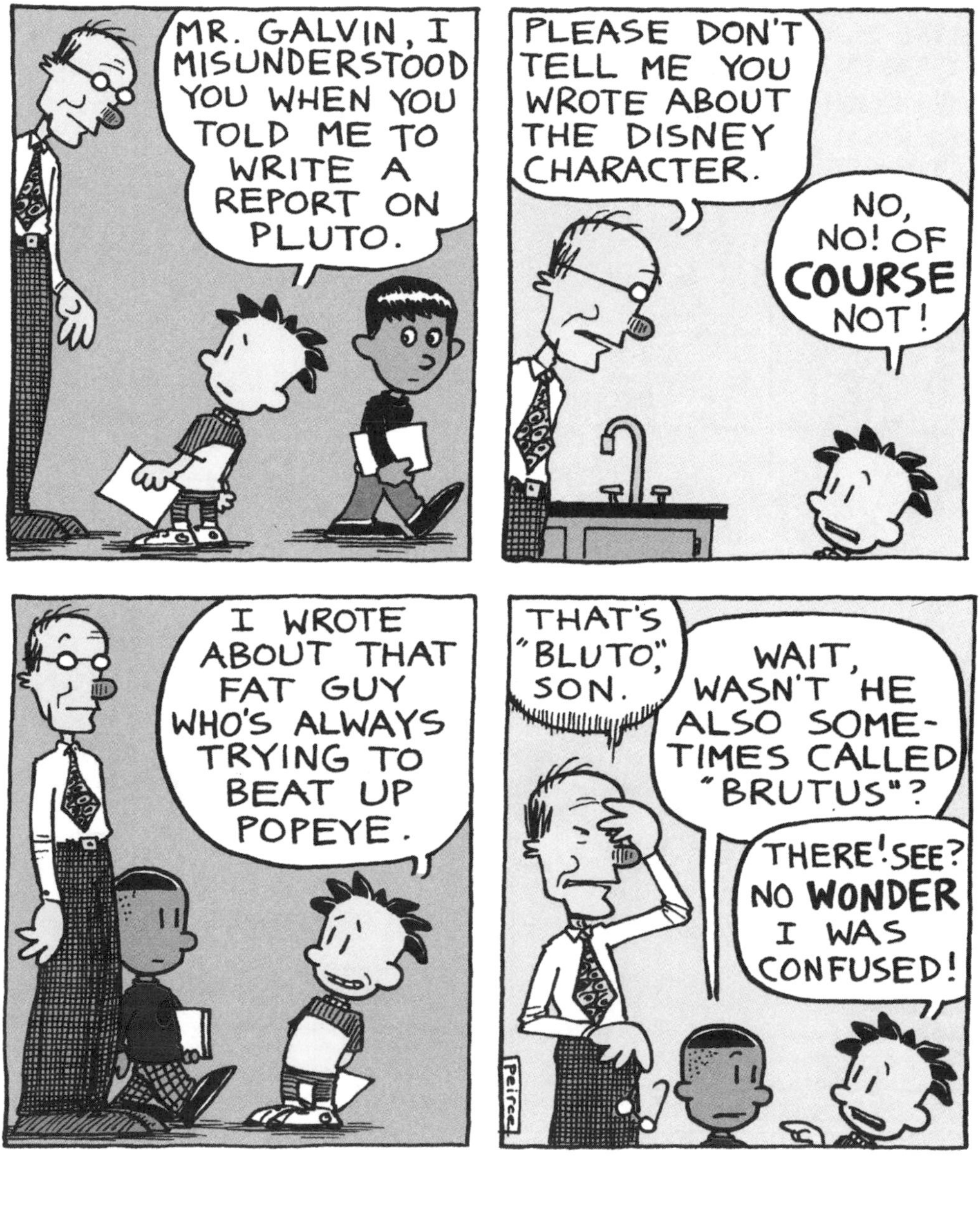
MR. GALVIN, I MISUNDERSTOOD YOU WHEN YOU TOLD ME TO WRITE A REPORT ON PLUTO.
PLEASE DON'T TELL ME YOU WROTE ABOUT THE DISNEY CHARACTER.
NO, NO! OF **COURSE** NOT!
I WROTE ABOUT THAT FAT GUY WHO'S ALWAYS TRYING TO BEAT UP POPEYE.
THAT'S "BLUTO," SON.
WAIT, WASN'T HE ALSO SOMETIMES CALLED "BRUTUS"?
THERE! SEE? NO **WONDER** I WAS CONFUSED!
Peirce

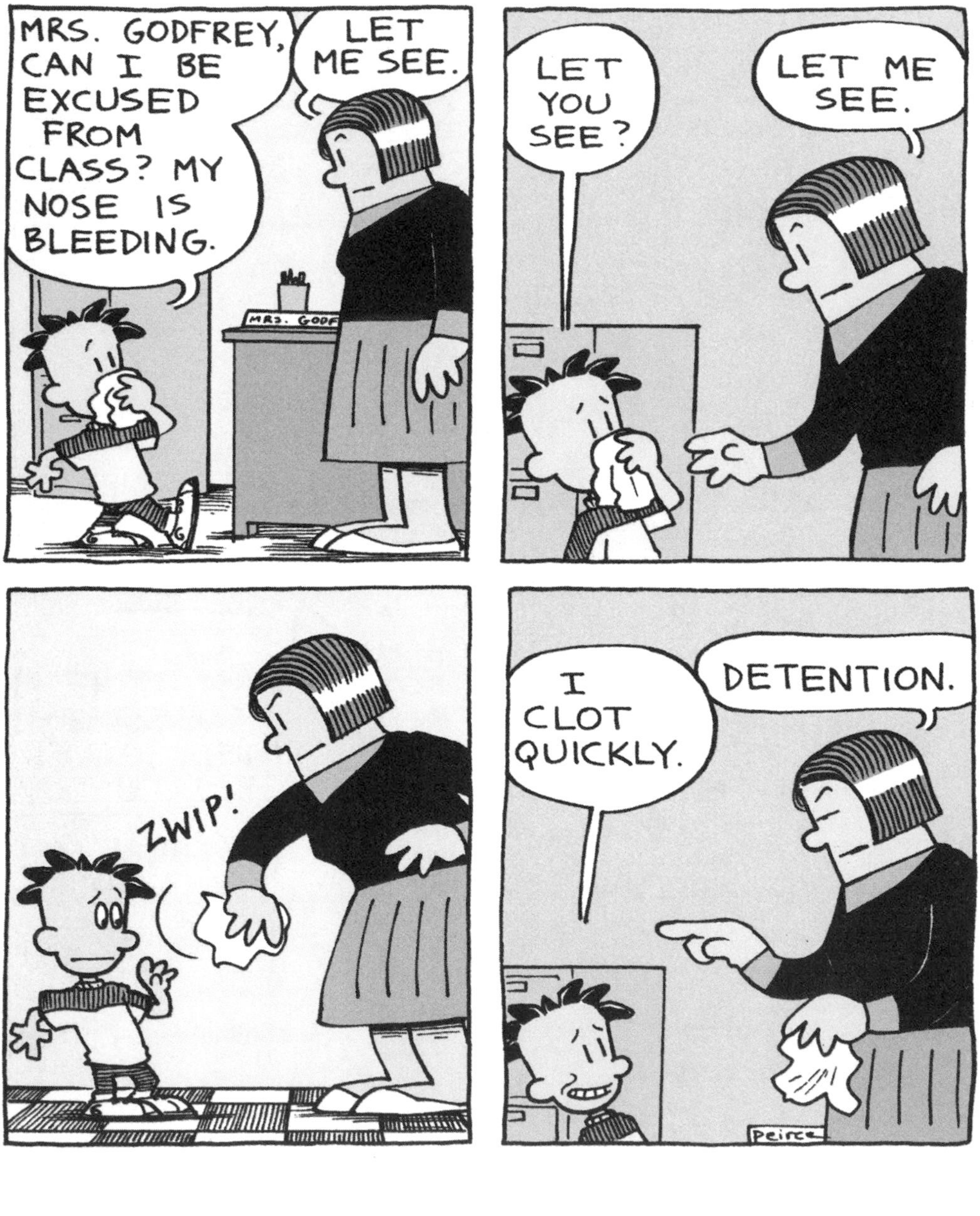
MRS. GODFREY, CAN I BE EXCUSED FROM CLASS? MY NOSE IS BLEEDING.
LET ME SEE.
MRS. GODF
LET YOU SEE?
LET ME SEE.
ZWIP!
I CLOT QUICKLY.
DETENTION.
Peirce

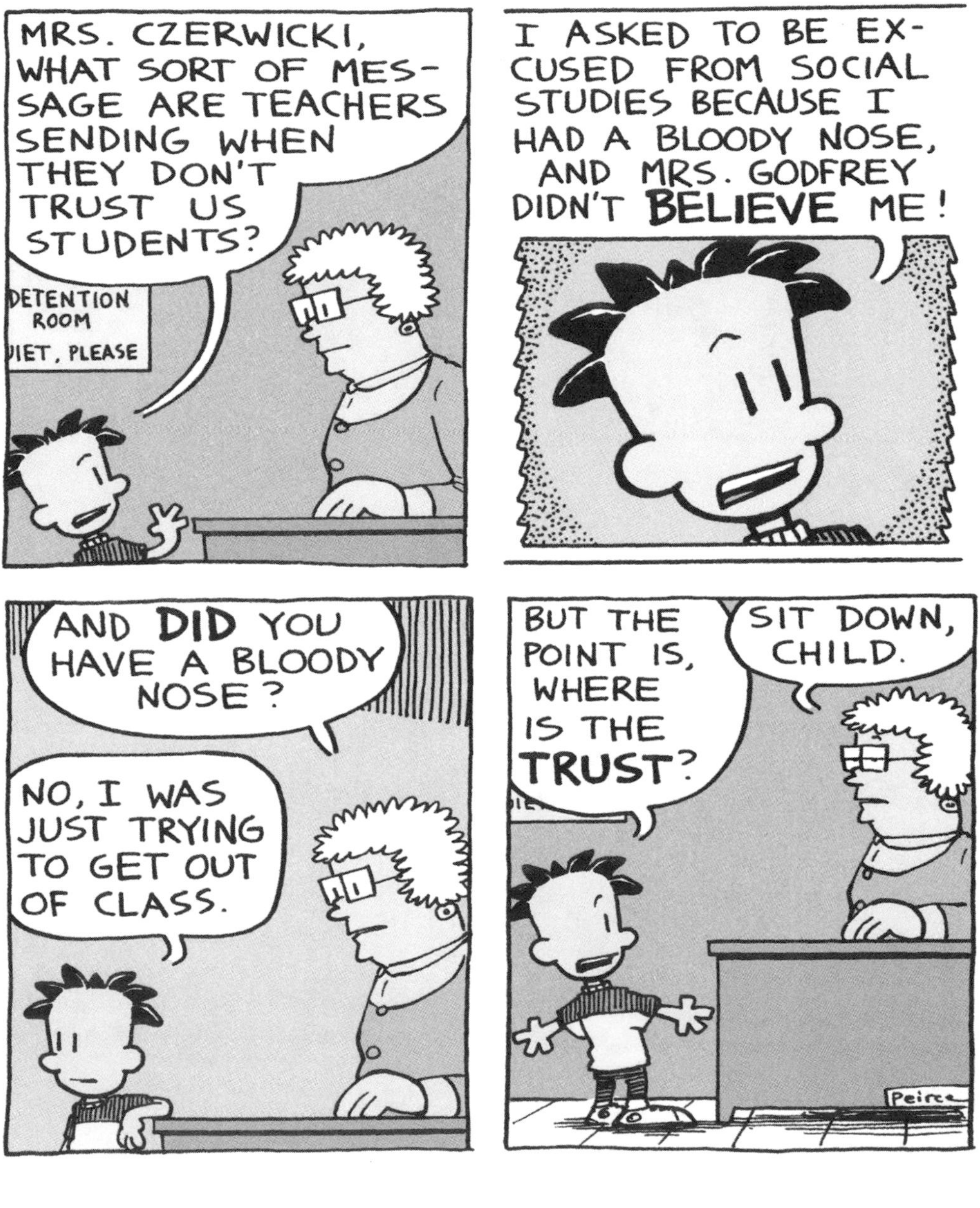
MRS. CZERWICKI, WHAT SORT OF MESSAGE ARE TEACHERS SENDING WHEN THEY DON'T TRUST US STUDENTS?
DETENTION ROOM
IET, PLEASE
I ASKED TO BE EXCUSED FROM SOCIAL STUDIES BECAUSE I HAD A BLOODY NOSE, AND MRS. GODFREY DIDN'T BELIEVE ME!
AND DID YOU HAVE A BLOODY NOSE?
NO, I WAS JUST TRYING TO GET OUT OF CLASS.
BUT THE POINT IS, WHERE IS THE TRUST?
SIT DOWN, CHILD.
Peirce

WOW! COOL DRAWING!
I'VE BEEN WORKING ON IT ALL PERIOD!
THIS MAY VERY WELL BE THE BEST PIECE OF ART I'VE EVER MADE!
UNFORTUNATELY, YOU MADE IT DURING SOCIAL STUDIES.
...KOFF!... ...WHICH IS WHY IT'S A PICTURE OF THE GETTYSBURG ADDRESS!
WITH NINJAS?
Peirce

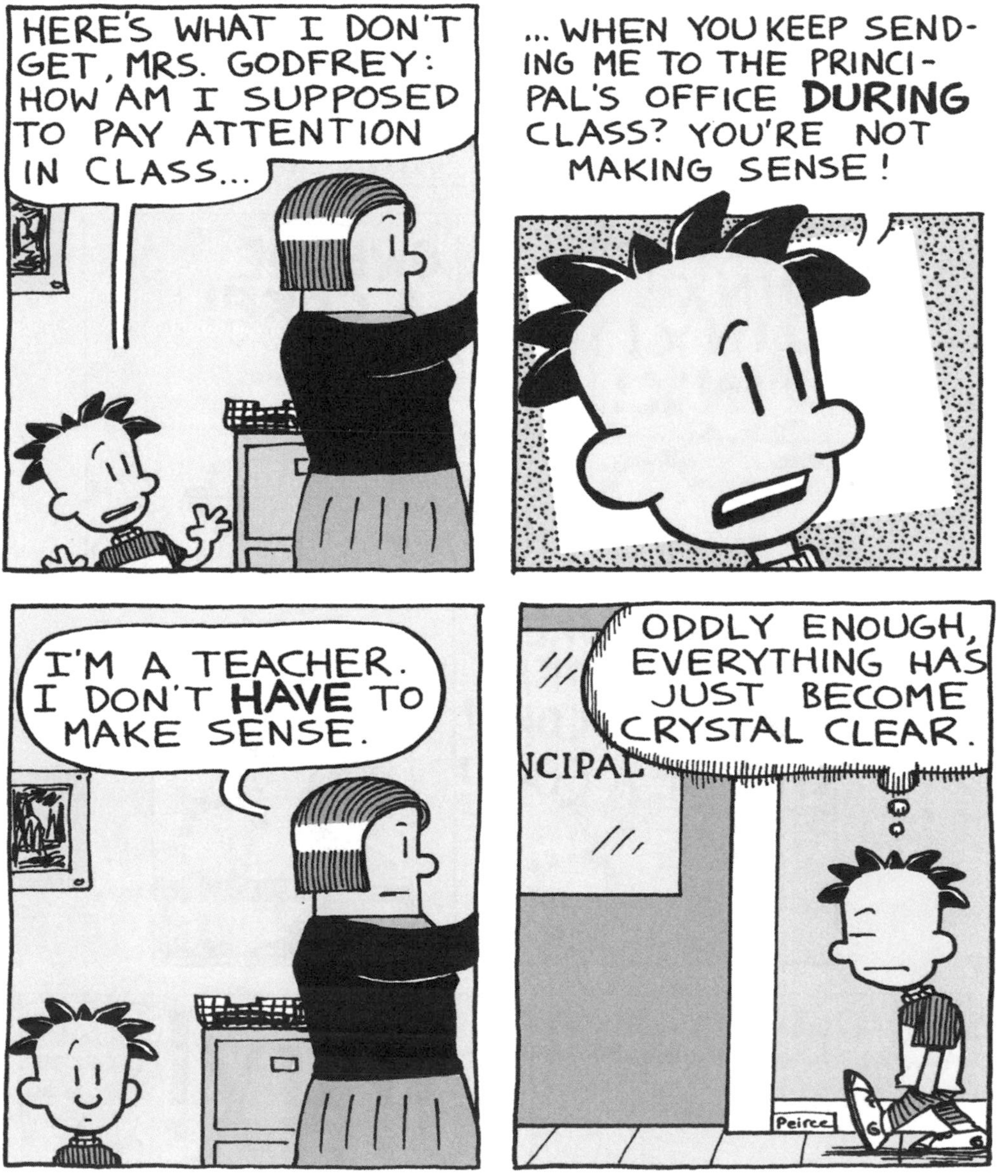
HERE'S WHAT I DON'T GET, MRS. GODFREY: HOW AM I SUPPOSED TO PAY ATTENTION IN CLASS...
... WHEN YOU KEEP SENDING ME TO THE PRINCIPAL'S OFFICE **DURING** CLASS? YOU'RE NOT MAKING SENSE!
I'M A TEACHER. I DON'T **HAVE** TO MAKE SENSE.
NCIPAL
ODDLY ENOUGH, EVERYTHING HAS JUST BECOME CRYSTAL CLEAR.
Peirce

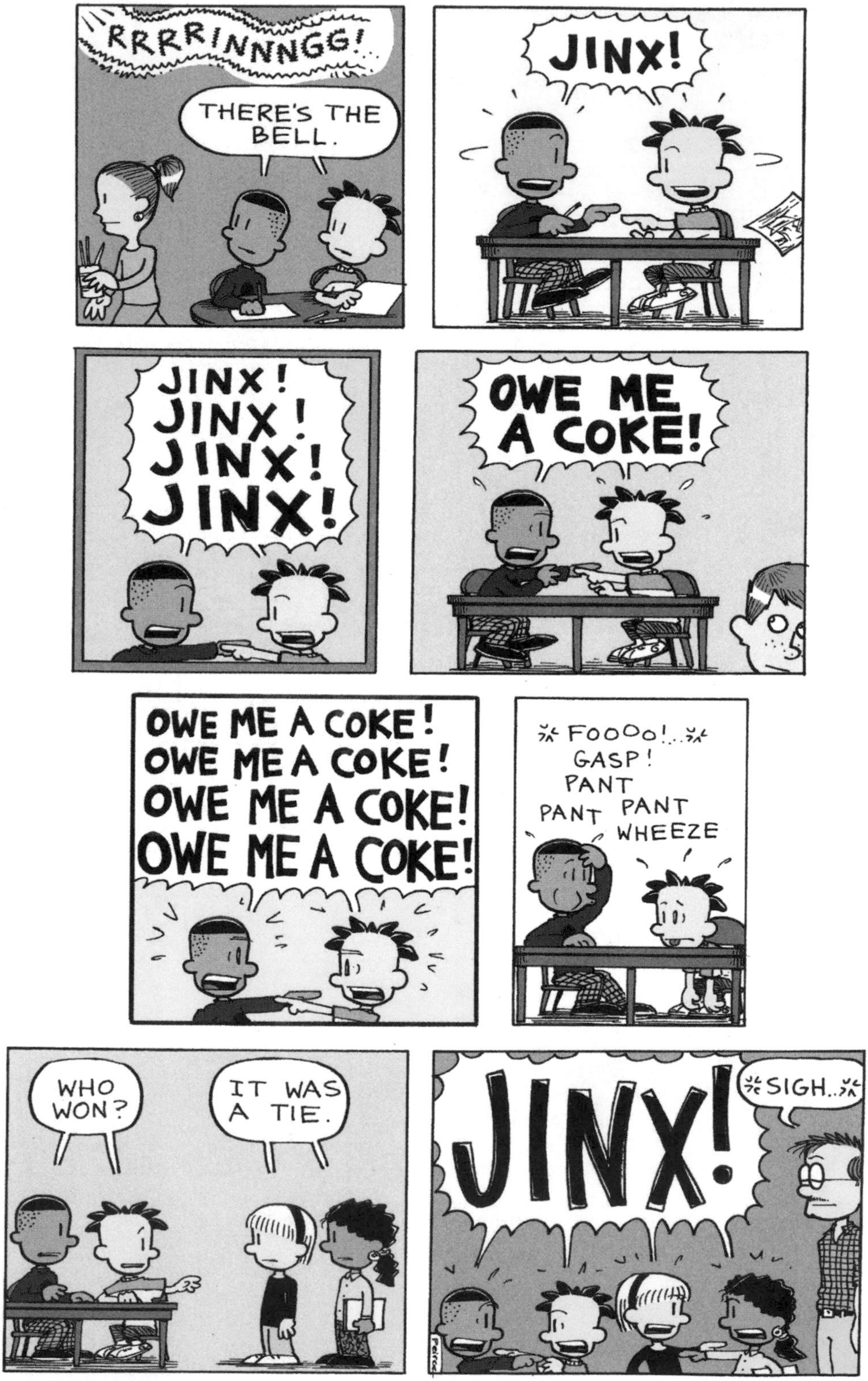
RRRRINNNGG!
THERE'S THE BELL.
JINX!
JINX! JINX! JINX! JINX!
OWE ME A COKE!
OWE ME A COKE! OWE ME A COKE! OWE ME A COKE! OWE ME A COKE!
FOOOO!.. GASP! PANT PANT PANT WHEEZE
WHO WON?
IT WAS A TIE.
JINX!
SIGH..

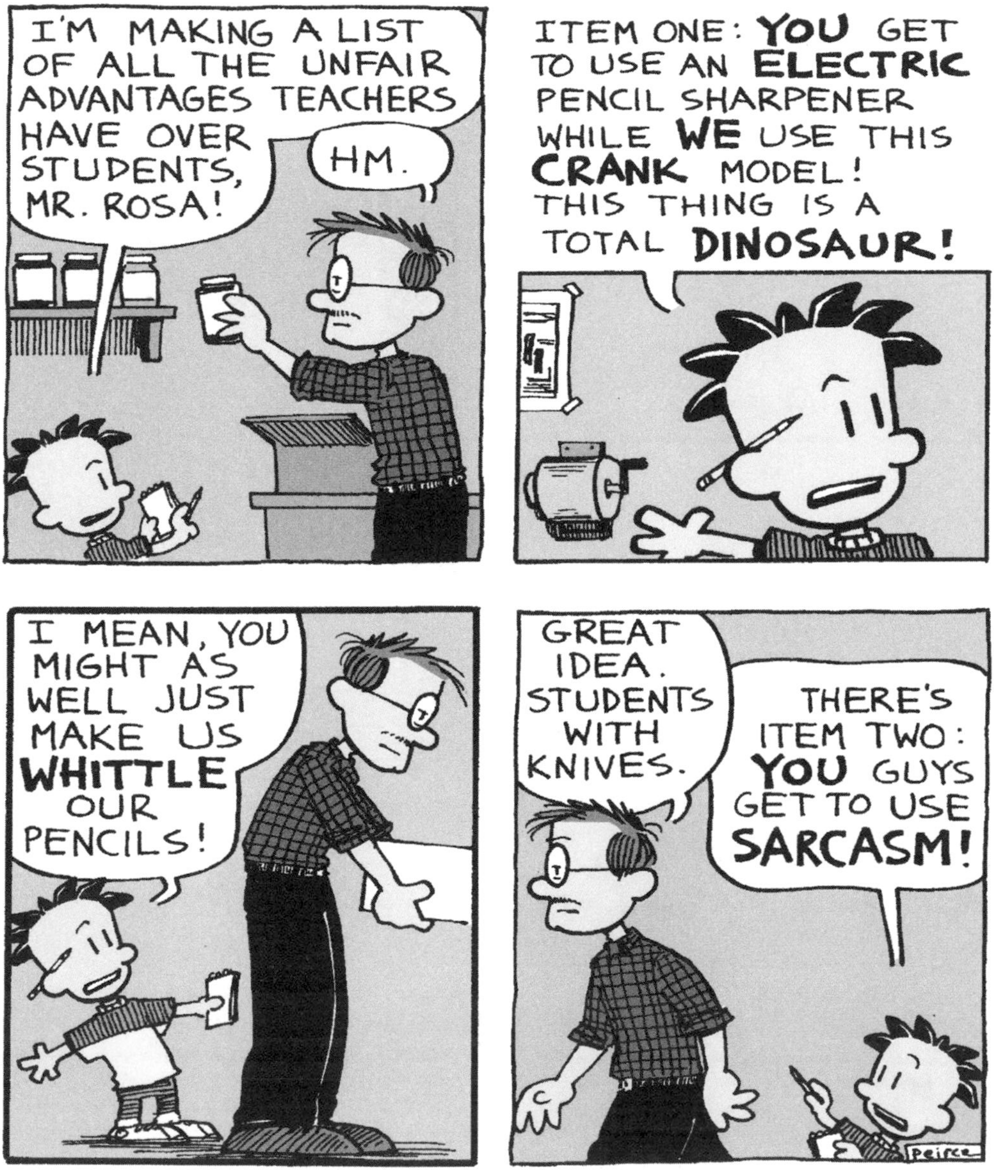
I'M MAKING A LIST OF ALL THE UNFAIR ADVANTAGES TEACHERS HAVE OVER STUDENTS, MR. ROSA!
HM.
ITEM ONE: YOU GET TO USE AN ELECTRIC PENCIL SHARPENER WHILE WE USE THIS CRANK MODEL! THIS THING IS A TOTAL DINOSAUR!
I MEAN, YOU MIGHT AS WELL JUST MAKE US WHITTLE OUR PENCILS!
GREAT IDEA. STUDENTS WITH KNIVES.
THERE'S ITEM TWO: YOU GUYS GET TO USE SARCASM!
Peirce

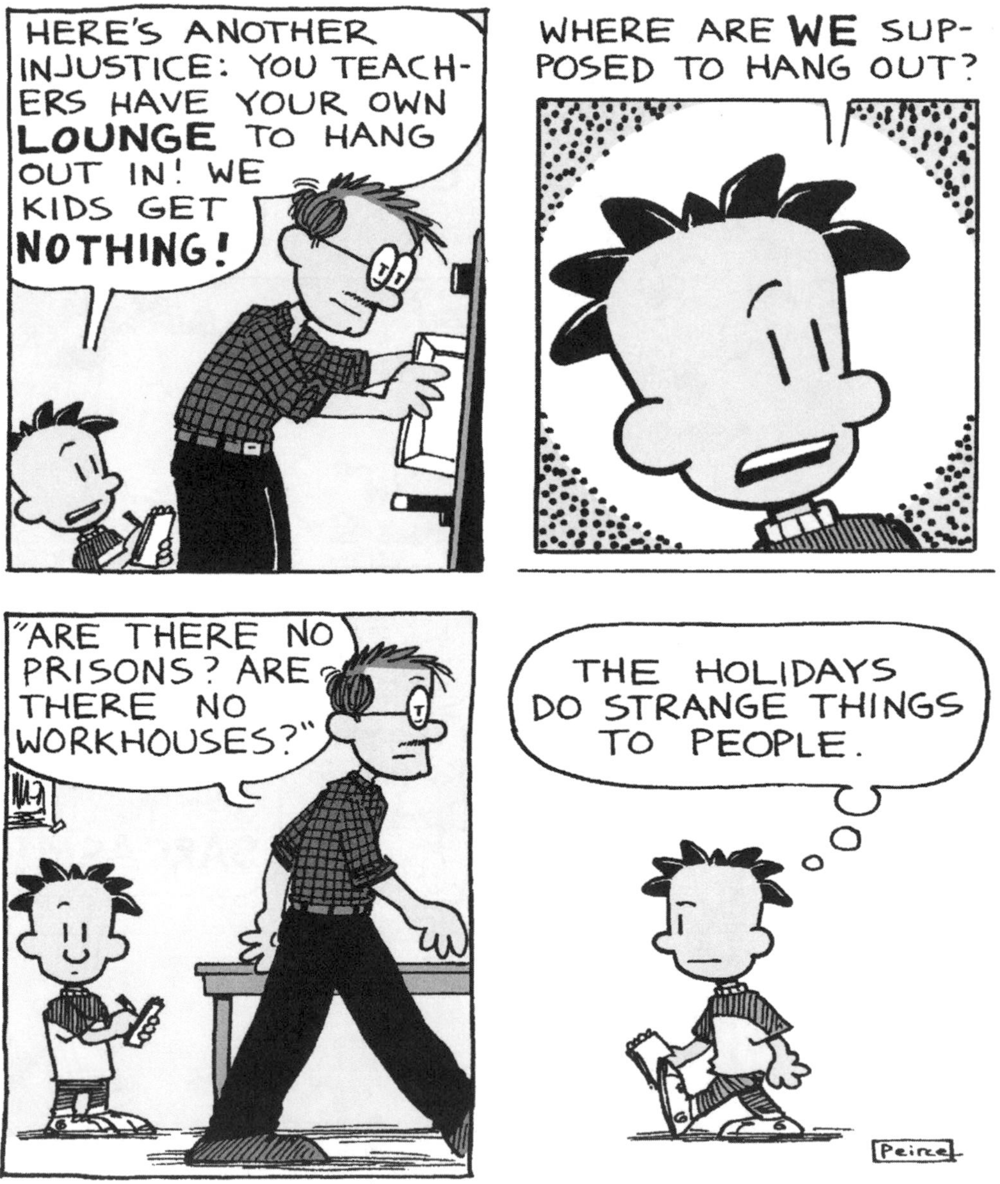
HERE'S ANOTHER INJUSTICE: YOU TEACHERS HAVE YOUR OWN LOUNGE TO HANG OUT IN! WE KIDS GET NOTHING!
WHERE ARE WE SUPPOSED TO HANG OUT?
"ARE THERE NO PRISONS? ARE THERE NO WORKHOUSES?"
THE HOLIDAYS DO STRANGE THINGS TO PEOPLE.
Peirce

HERE'S ANOTHER THING THAT'S NOT FAIR: WE STUDENTS GET NOTHING FOR BEING HERE! YOU TEACHERS GET PAID!
"PAID."
HEH HEH... WE GET "PAID." HEH HA HA..
HA HA HA HA HA HA
WE'RE ROLLING IN IT!
HA HA HA
HA HA HA
HA HA
HA HA HA HA HA
I'M RICH!
HA HA HA
HA
THEY ALL ACT THIS WAY WHEN ANYONE MENTIONS MONEY.
Peirce

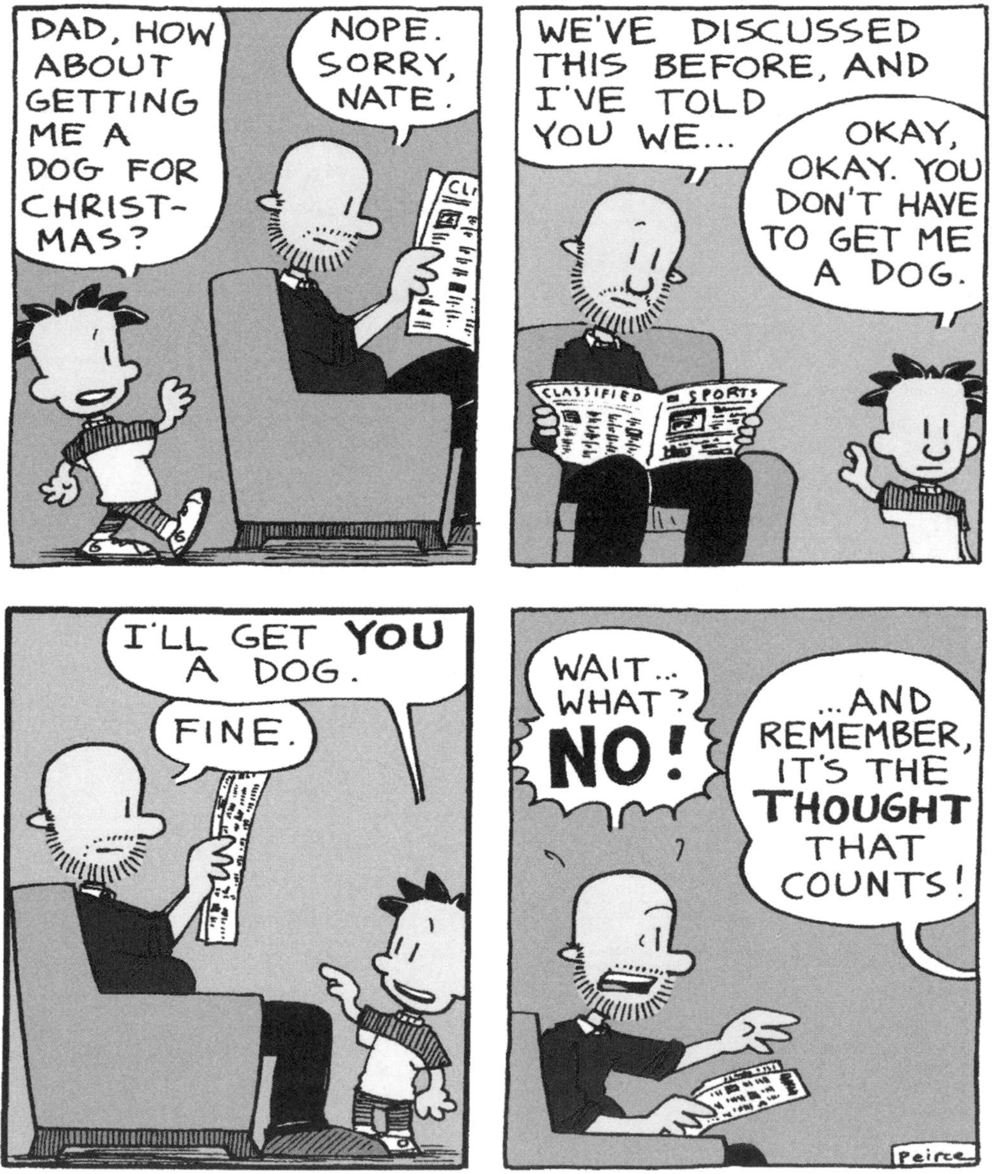
DAD, HOW ABOUT GETTING ME A DOG FOR CHRIST-MAS?
NOPE. SORRY, NATE.
WE'VE DISCUSSED THIS BEFORE, AND I'VE TOLD YOU WE...
OKAY, OKAY. YOU DON'T HAVE TO GET ME A DOG.
I'LL GET **YOU** A DOG.
FINE.
WAIT... WHAT? **NO!**
...AND REMEMBER, IT'S THE **THOUGHT** THAT COUNTS!
Peirce

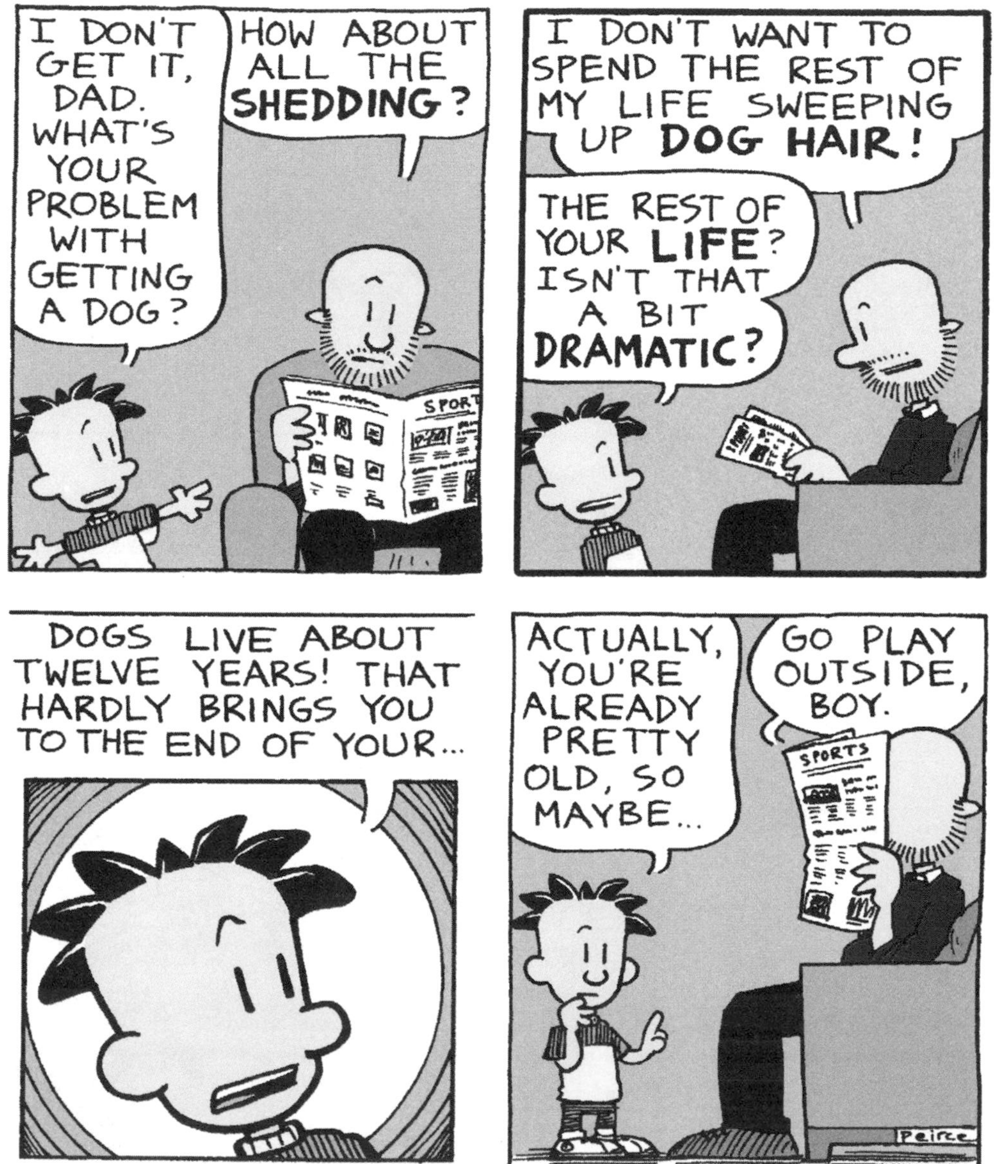
I DON'T GET IT, DAD. WHAT'S YOUR PROBLEM WITH GETTING A DOG?
HOW ABOUT ALL THE SHEDDING?
SPORT
I DON'T WANT TO SPEND THE REST OF MY LIFE SWEEPING UP DOG HAIR!
THE REST OF YOUR LIFE? ISN'T THAT A BIT DRAMATIC?
DOGS LIVE ABOUT TWELVE YEARS! THAT HARDLY BRINGS YOU TO THE END OF YOUR...
ACTUALLY, YOU'RE ALREADY PRETTY OLD, SO MAYBE...
GO PLAY OUTSIDE, BOY.
SPORTS
Peirce

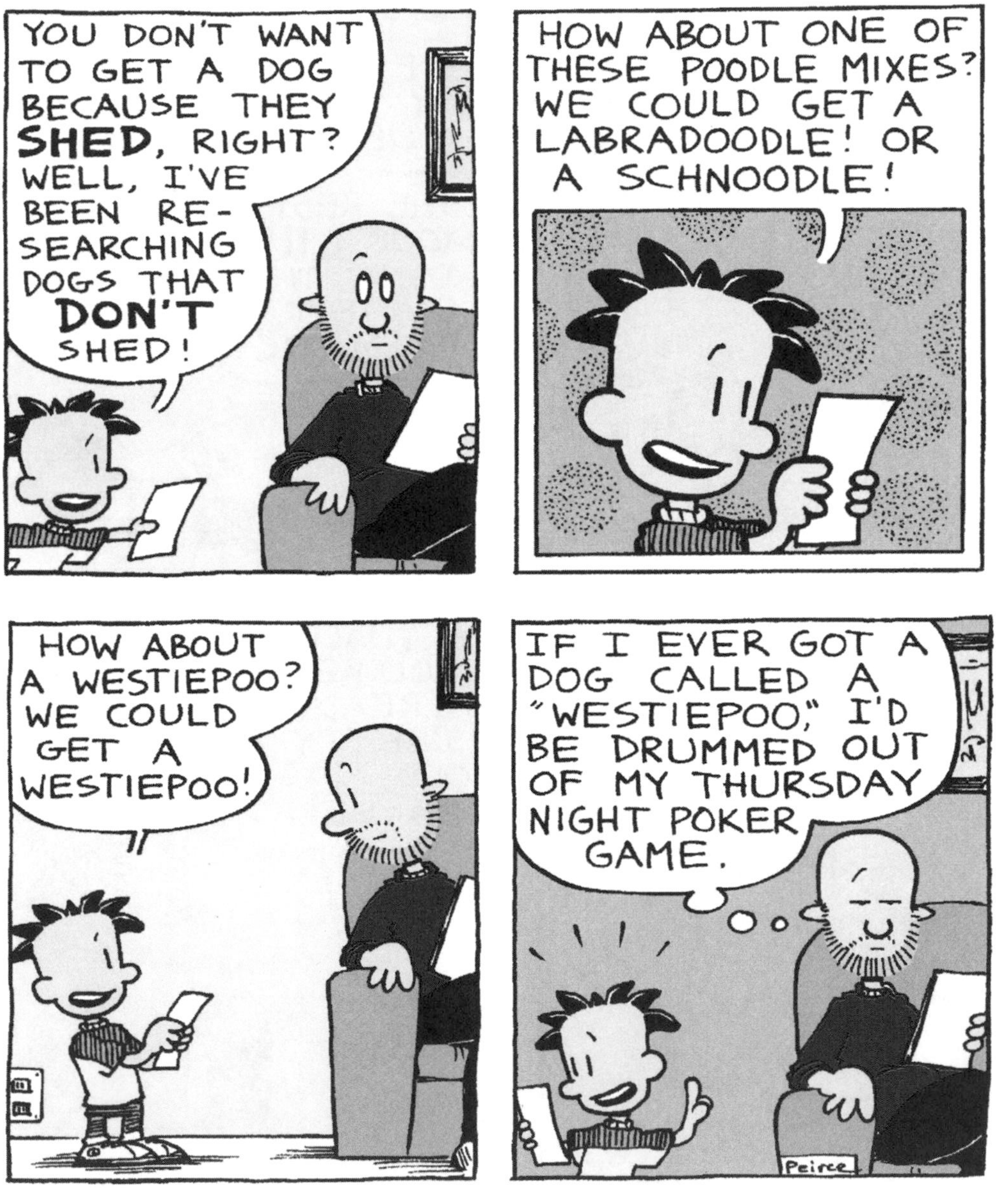
YOU DON'T WANT TO GET A DOG BECAUSE THEY SHED, RIGHT? WELL, I'VE BEEN RE-SEARCHING DOGS THAT DON'T SHED!
HOW ABOUT ONE OF THESE POODLE MIXES? WE COULD GET A LABRADOODLE! OR A SCHNOODLE!
HOW ABOUT A WESTIEPOO? WE COULD GET A WESTIEPOO!
IF I EVER GOT A DOG CALLED A "WESTIEPOO," I'D BE DRUMMED OUT OF MY THURSDAY NIGHT POKER GAME.
Peirce

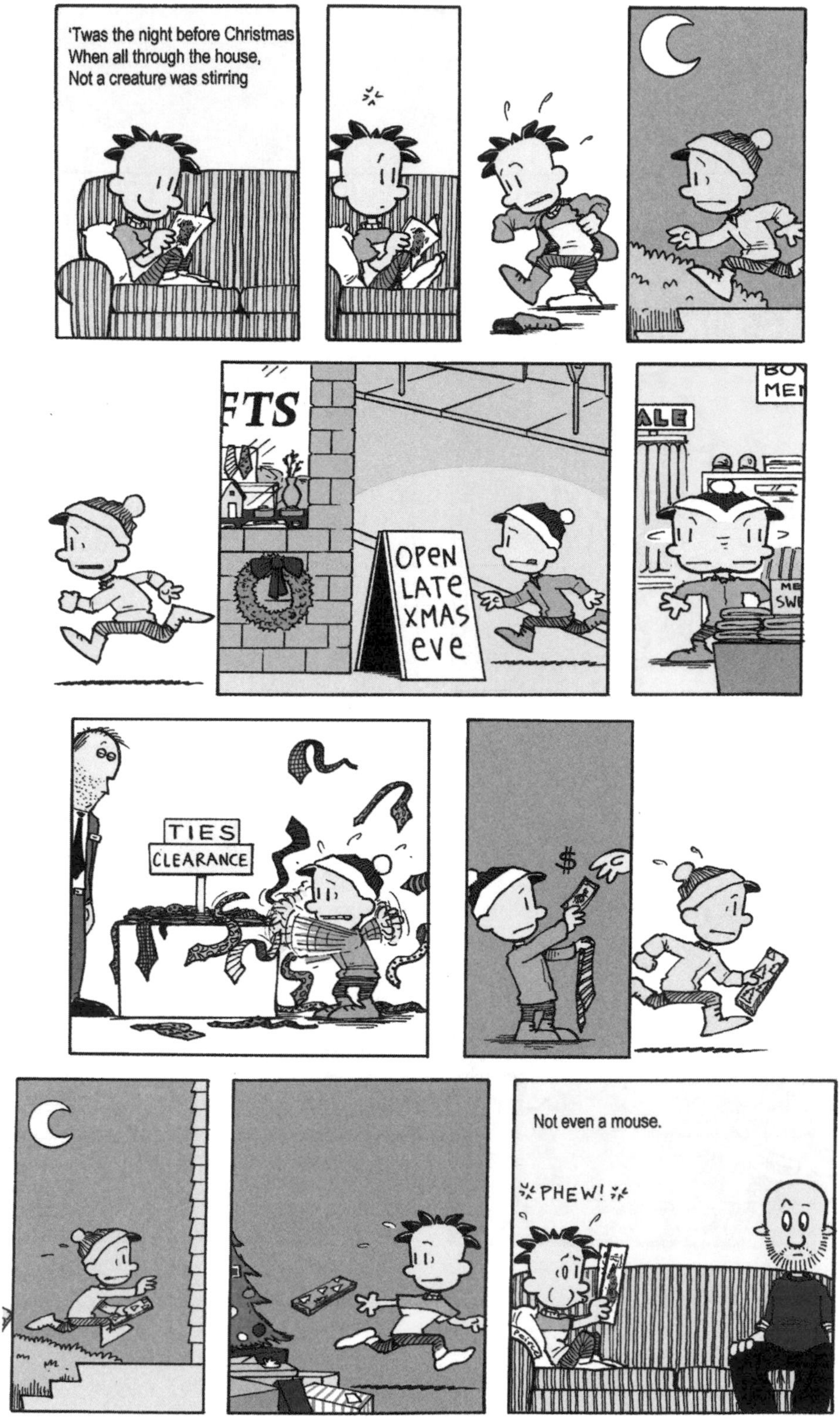
'Twas the night before Christmas
When all through the house,
Not a creature was stirring
FTS
OPEN LATE XMAS eve
ALE
TIES
CLEARANCE
$
Not even a mouse.
PHEW!

"TO NATE, FROM DAD"! HMM, WHAT COULD THIS BE?
WHA...? IT'S... IS THIS A COLLAR? IT'S A COLLAR!
IT'S A BELT.
YOU GOT ME A COLLAR! WHICH MEANS YOU ALSO GOT ME A DOG!
IT'S A BELT.
HERE, BOY!!
IT'S A BELT.
Peirce

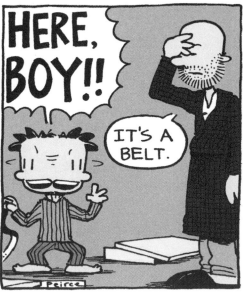

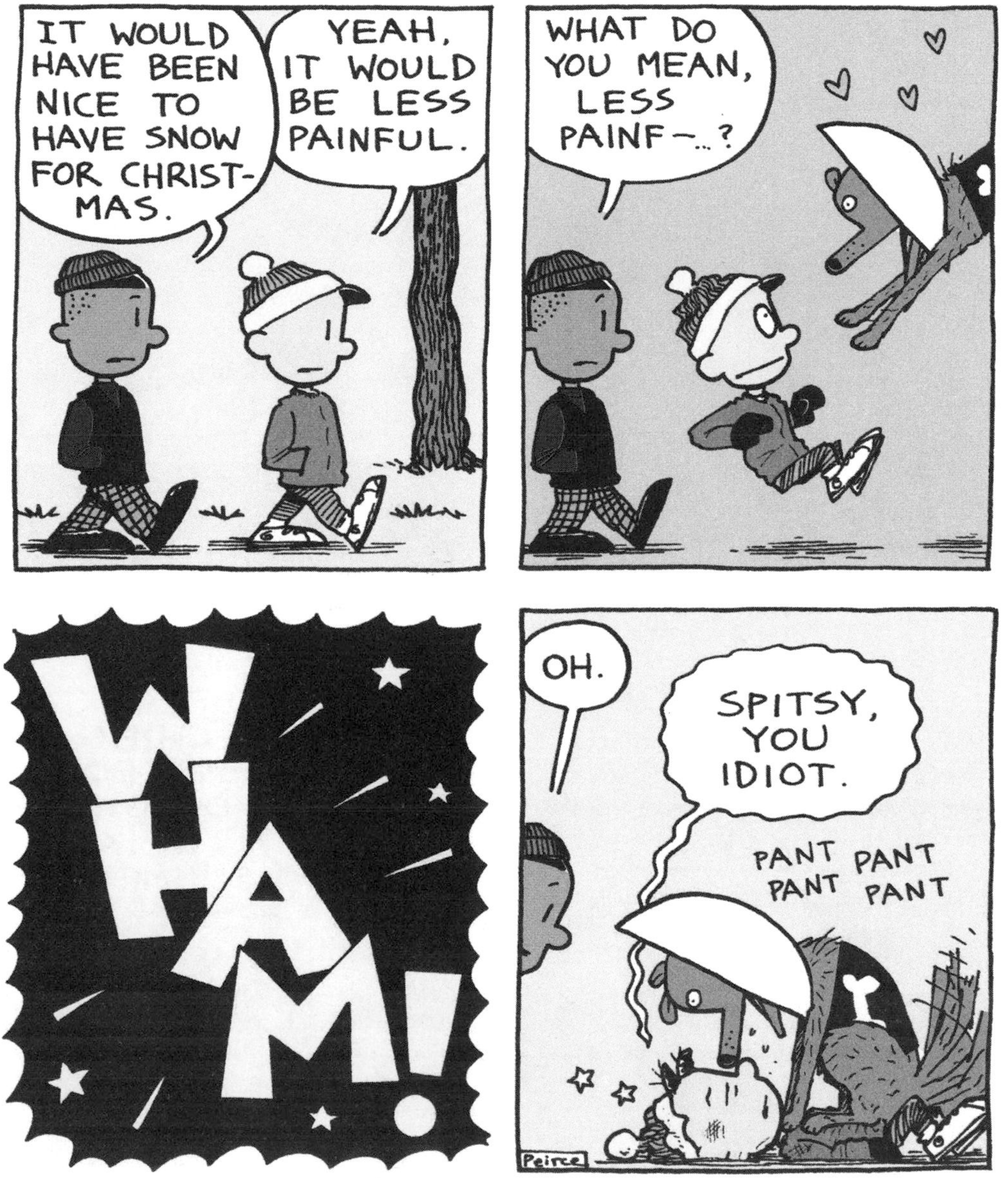
IT WOULD HAVE BEEN NICE TO HAVE SNOW FOR CHRISTMAS.
YEAH, IT WOULD BE LESS PAINFUL.
WHAT DO YOU MEAN, LESS PAINF—...?
WHAM!
OH.
SPITSY, YOU IDIOT.
PANT PANT PANT PANT
Peirce

HEY! A SNOW-FLAKE!
WHAT? NO!
DON'T YOU WANT IT TO SNOW?
NOT NOW! NOT DURING VACATION!
IT'S SUPPOSED TO SNOW DURING SCHOOL! THEN IT'S A SNOW DAY AND WE GET TO STAY HOME! THIS IS A TOTAL WASTE OF A SNOWSTORM!
WHO DOES ONE COM-PLAIN TO ABOUT MISTIMED WEATHER EVENTS?
HELLO, CAN I SPEAK TO CHIEF METEOR-OLOGIST WINK SUMMERS?

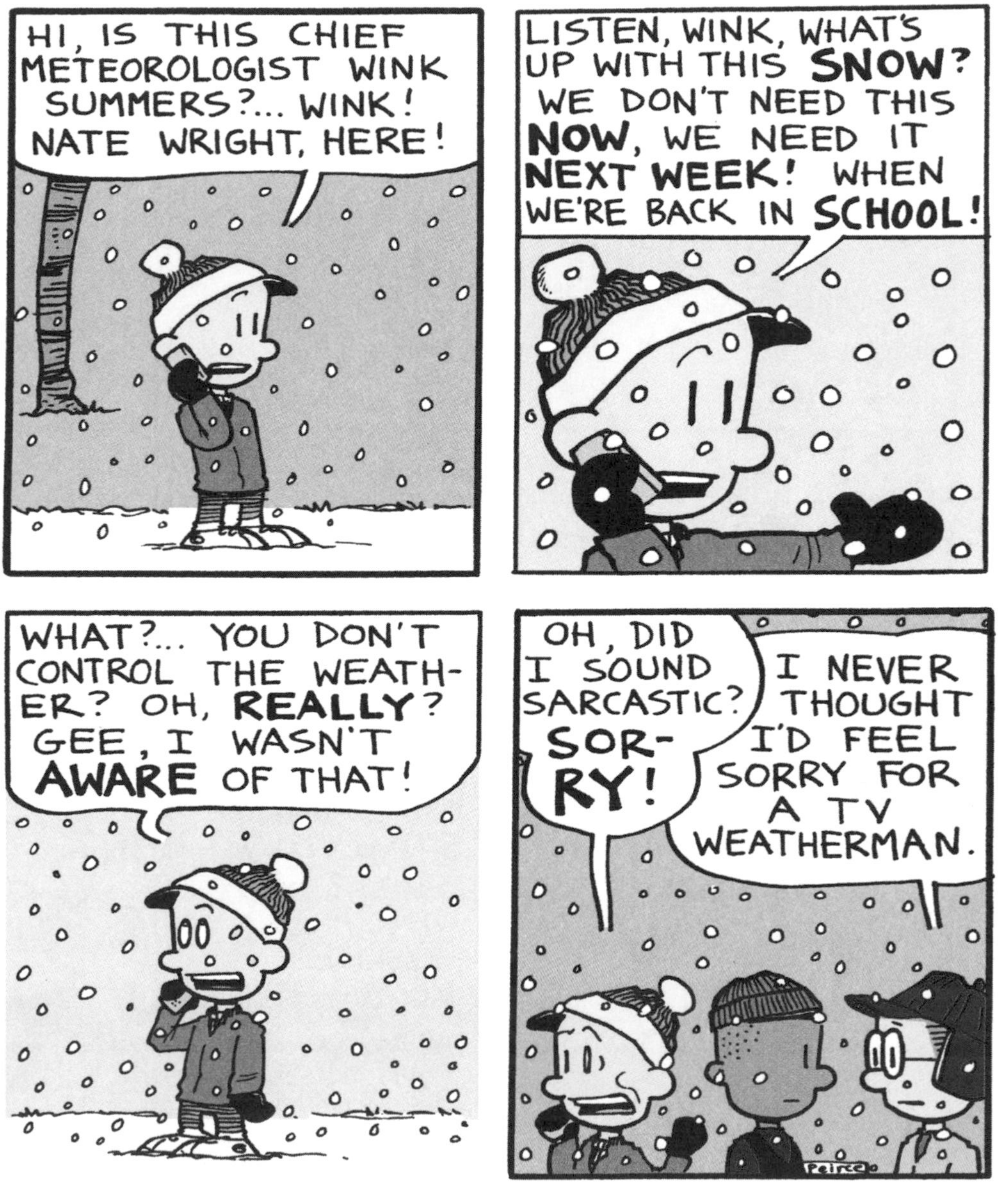
HI, IS THIS CHIEF METEOROLOGIST WINK SUMMERS?... WINK! NATE WRIGHT, HERE!
LISTEN, WINK, WHAT'S UP WITH THIS SNOW? WE DON'T NEED THIS NOW, WE NEED IT NEXT WEEK! WHEN WE'RE BACK IN SCHOOL!
WHAT?... YOU DON'T CONTROL THE WEATHER? OH, REALLY? GEE, I WASN'T AWARE OF THAT!
OH, DID I SOUND SARCASTIC? SOR-RY!
I NEVER THOUGHT I'D FEEL SORRY FOR A TV WEATHERMAN.
Peirce

LISTEN, WINK, SINCE I'VE GOT YOU ON THE PHONE, LET ME GIVE YOU SOME FEEDBACK ON LAST NIGHT'S FORECAST.

THAT BLUE BLAZER WASN'T REALLY DOING YOU ANY FAVORS, DUDE. IT MADE YOU LOOK A LITTLE PUDGY.

THEN AGAIN, YOU **ARE** A LITTLE PUDGY, WINK. I MEAN, YOU REALLY PACKED ON THE POUNDS AFTER THAT BABE WHO DOES THE MOVIE RE- VIEWS DUMPED YOU.

YOU'RE BET- TER OFF WITHOUT HER, MAN. SHE ONLY GAVE **ONE STAR** TO "SNAKES ON A PLANE"!

HANG UP, WINK!

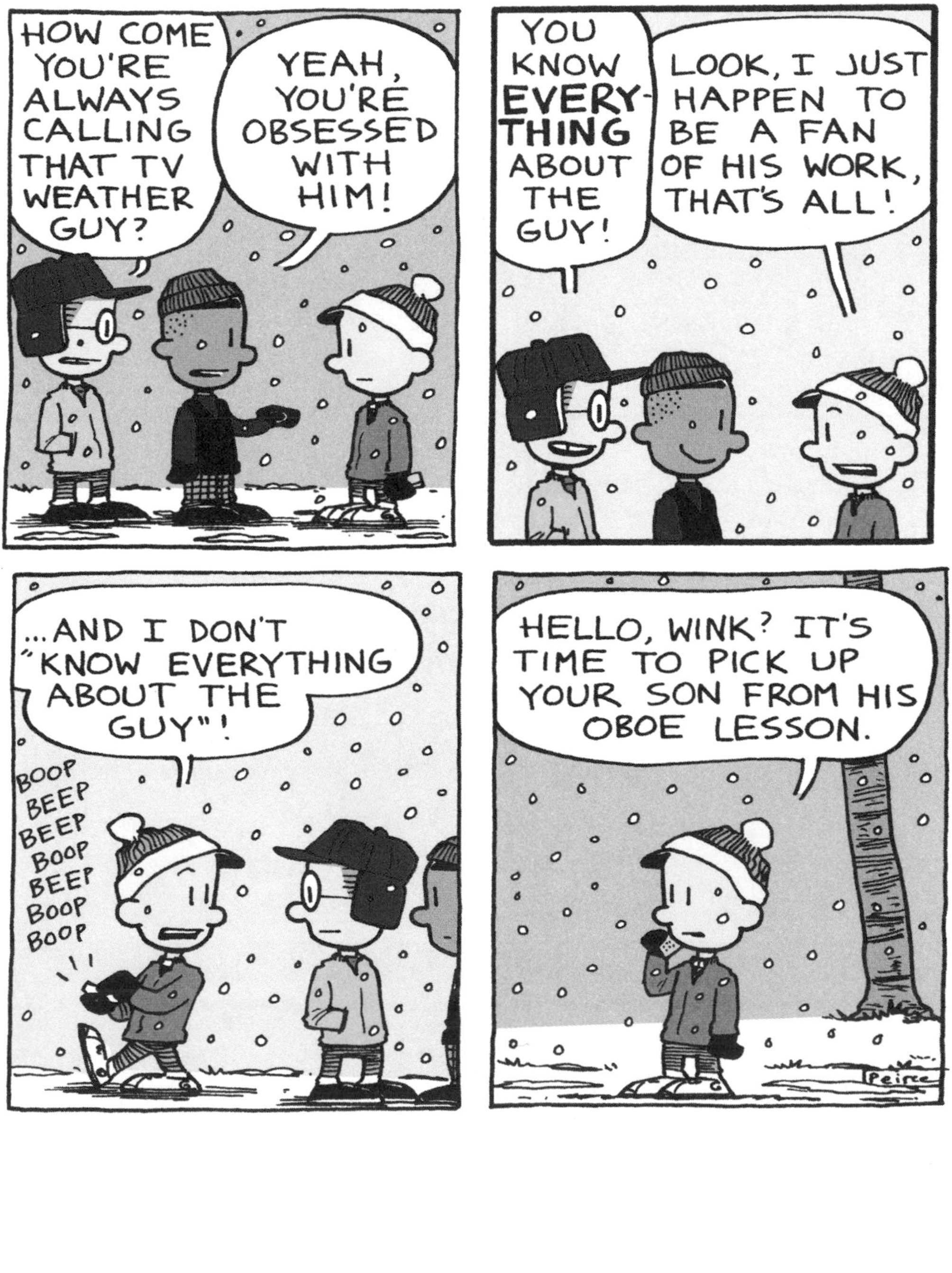
HOW COME YOU'RE ALWAYS CALLING THAT TV WEATHER GUY?
YEAH, YOU'RE OBSESSED WITH HIM!
YOU KNOW EVERY-THING ABOUT THE GUY!
LOOK, I JUST HAPPEN TO BE A FAN OF HIS WORK, THAT'S ALL!
...AND I DON'T "KNOW EVERYTHING ABOUT THE GUY"!
BOOP BEEP BEEP BOOP BEEP BOOP BOOP
HELLO, WINK? IT'S TIME TO PICK UP YOUR SON FROM HIS OBOE LESSON.
Peirce

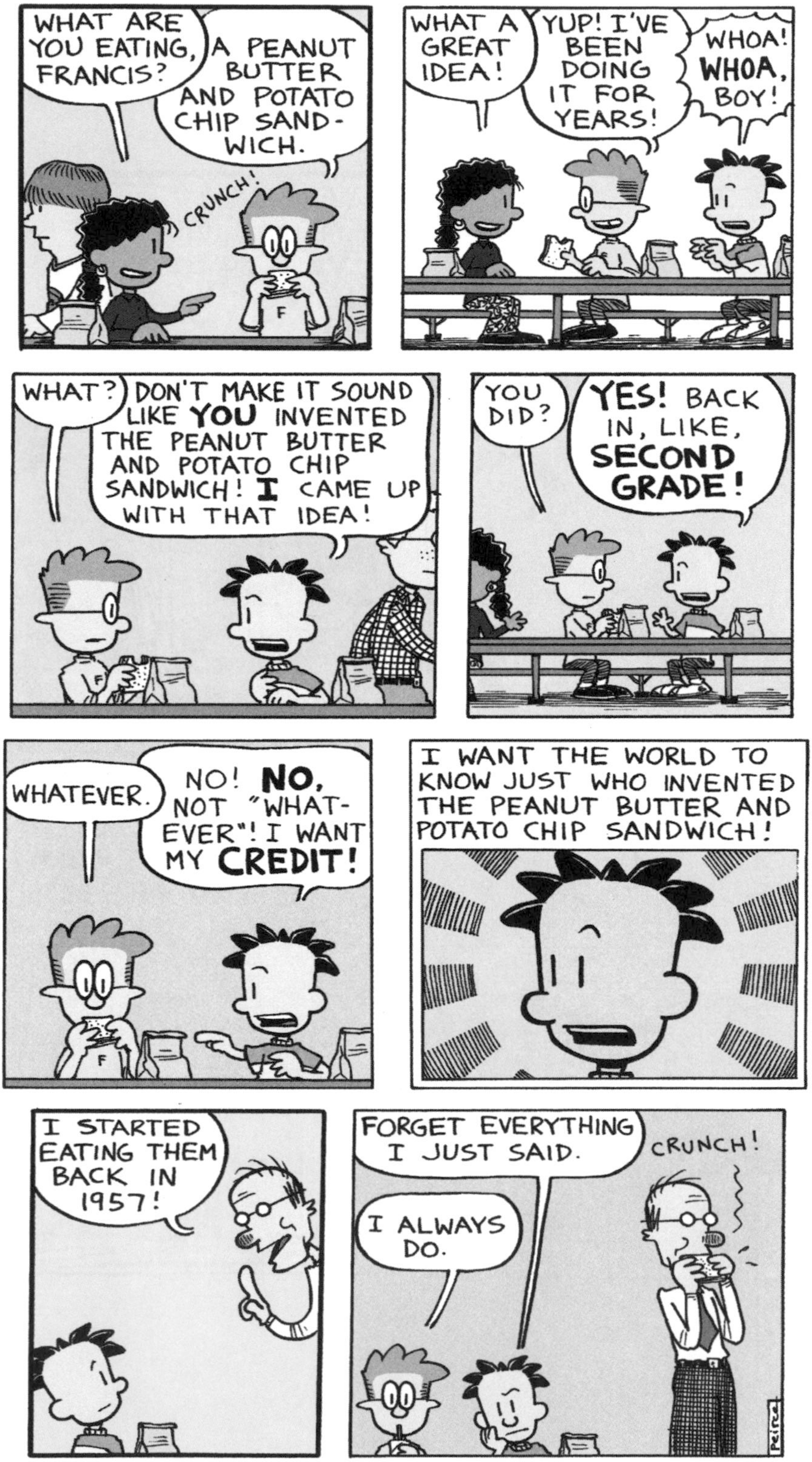
WHAT ARE YOU EATING, FRANCIS?
A PEANUT BUTTER AND POTATO CHIP SAND-WICH.
CRUNCH!
WHAT A GREAT IDEA!
YUP! I'VE BEEN DOING IT FOR YEARS!
WHOA! WHOA, BOY!
WHAT?
DON'T MAKE IT SOUND LIKE YOU INVENTED THE PEANUT BUTTER AND POTATO CHIP SANDWICH! I CAME UP WITH THAT IDEA!
YOU DID?
YES! BACK IN, LIKE, SECOND GRADE!
WHATEVER.
NO! NO, NOT "WHAT-EVER"! I WANT MY CREDIT!
I WANT THE WORLD TO KNOW JUST WHO INVENTED THE PEANUT BUTTER AND POTATO CHIP SANDWICH!
I STARTED EATING THEM BACK IN 1957!
FORGET EVERYTHING I JUST SAID.
I ALWAYS DO.
CRUNCH!

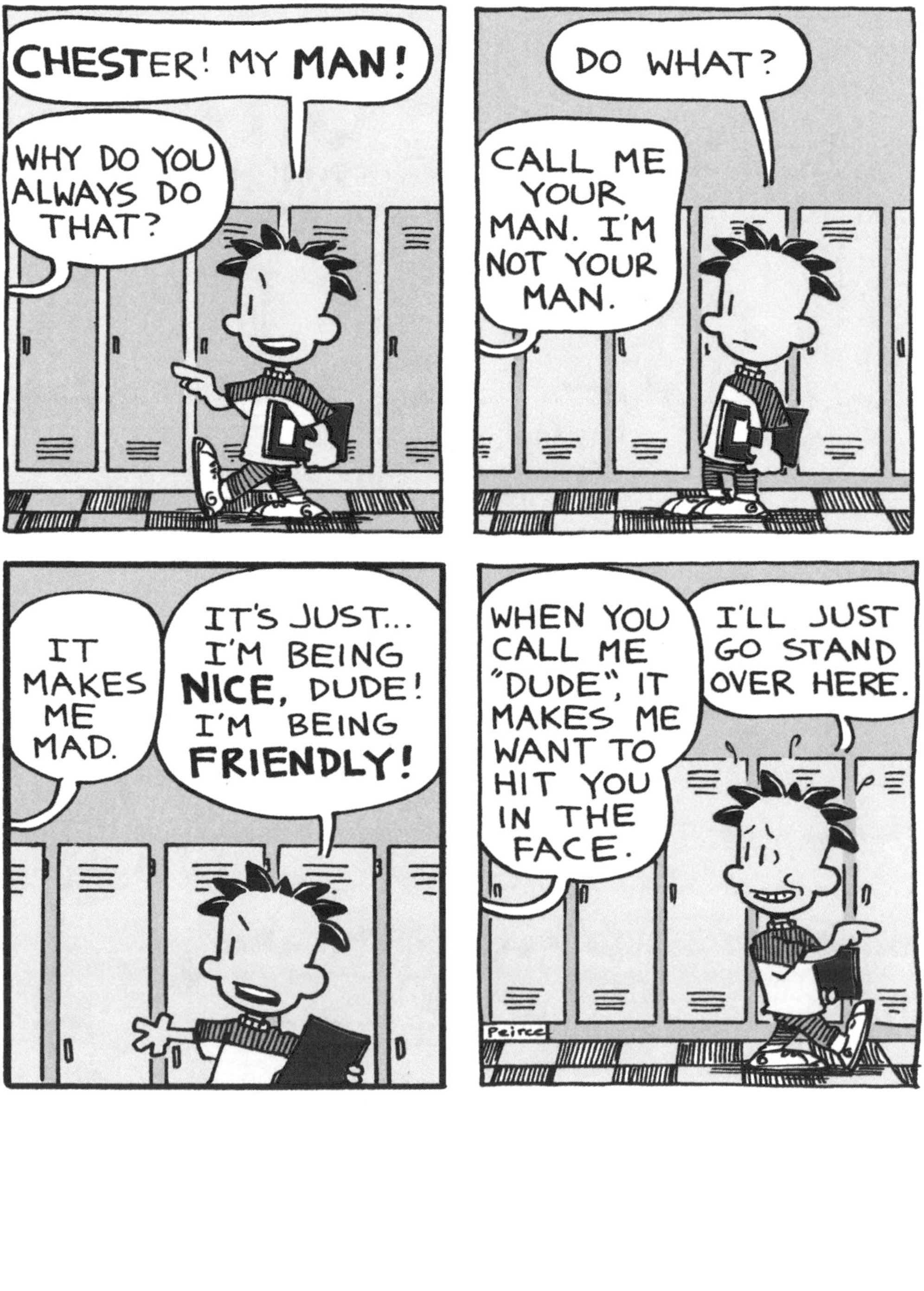
CHESTER! MY MAN!
WHY DO YOU ALWAYS DO THAT?
DO WHAT?
CALL ME YOUR MAN. I'M NOT YOUR MAN.
IT'S JUST... I'M BEING NICE, DUDE! I'M BEING FRIENDLY!
IT MAKES ME MAD.
WHEN YOU CALL ME "DUDE", IT MAKES ME WANT TO HIT YOU IN THE FACE.
I'LL JUST GO STAND OVER HERE.
Peirce

HOW MUCH DO YOU THINK CHESTER WEIGHS?
HMM... I'D SAY ABOUT...
CHOMP!
CRUNCH! CHOMPF! NARF! NARGH!
BURRP!
ABOUT FIVE POUNDS MORE THAN HE DID A SECOND AGO.
DID HE JUST EAT AN ENTIRE CHICK-EN?
BONES AND ALL.
Peirce

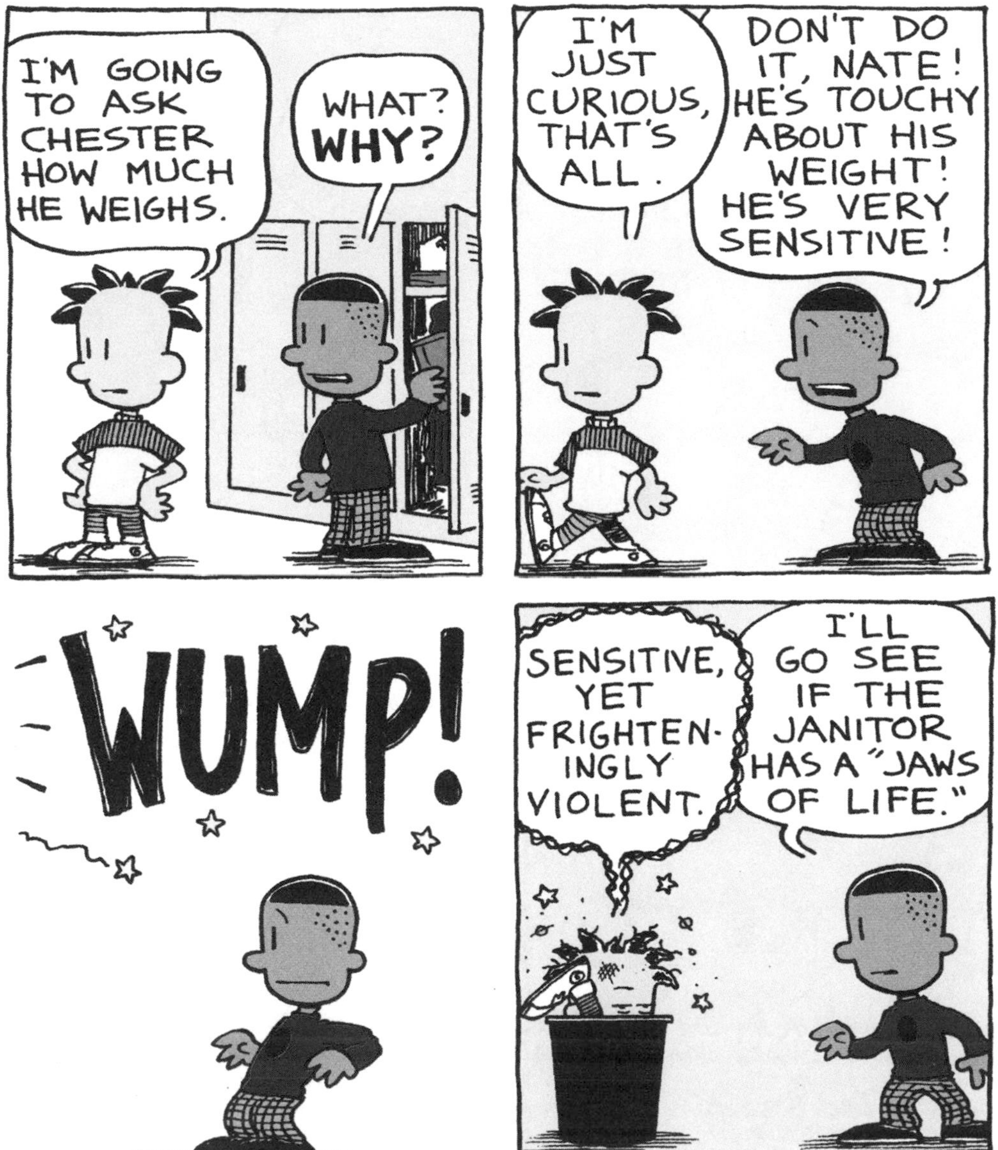
I'M GOING TO ASK CHESTER HOW MUCH HE WEIGHS.
WHAT? WHY?
I'M JUST CURIOUS, THAT'S ALL.
DON'T DO IT, NATE! HE'S TOUCHY ABOUT HIS WEIGHT! HE'S VERY SENSITIVE!
WUMP!
SENSITIVE, YET FRIGHTEN-INGLY VIOLENT.
I'LL GO SEE IF THE JANITOR HAS A "JAWS OF LIFE."
Peirce

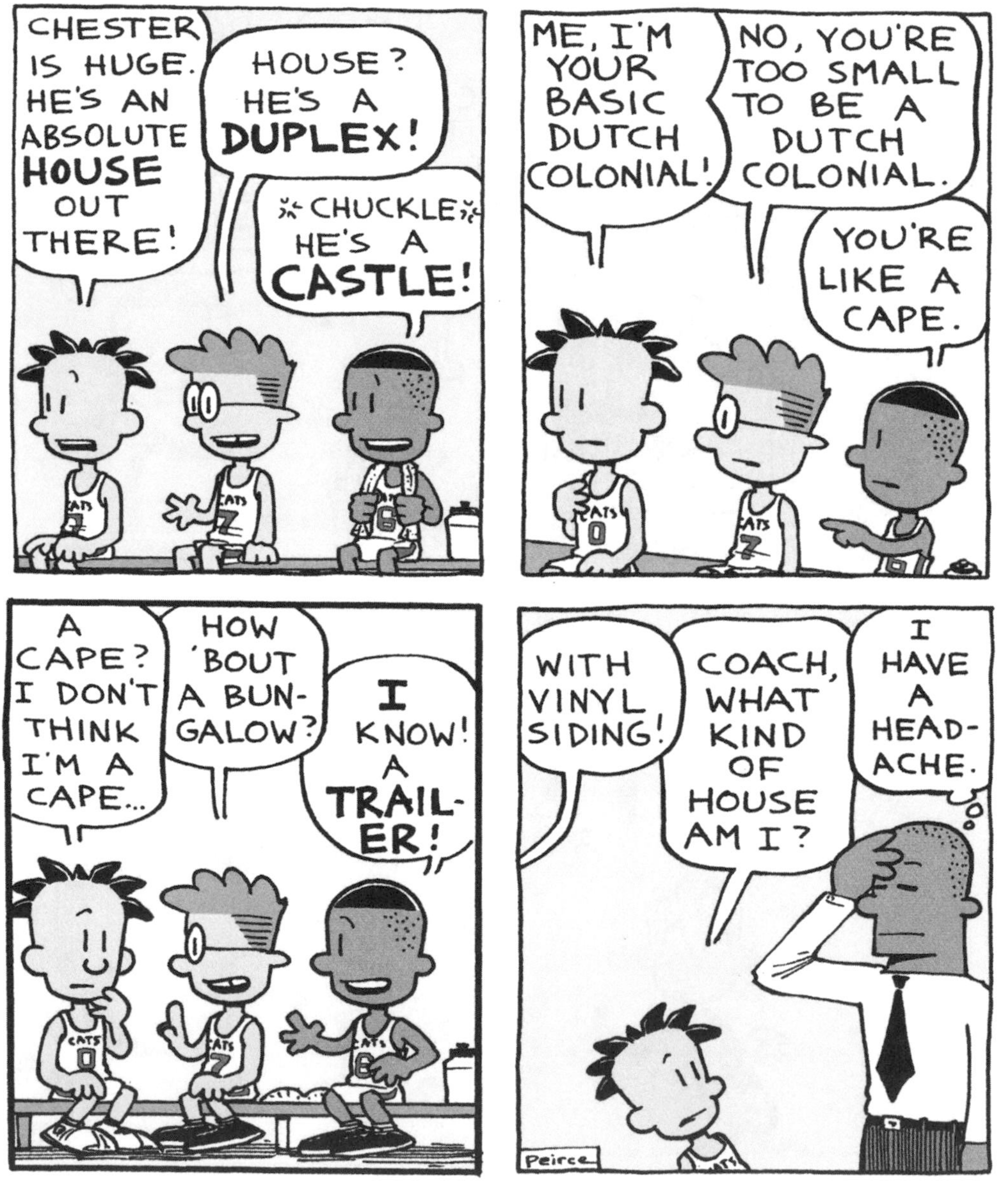
CHESTER IS HUGE. HE'S AN ABSOLUTE **HOUSE** OUT THERE!
HOUSE? HE'S A **DUPLEX**!
CHUCKLE HE'S A **CASTLE**!
ME, I'M YOUR BASIC DUTCH COLONIAL!
NO, YOU'RE TOO SMALL TO BE A DUTCH COLONIAL.
YOU'RE LIKE A CAPE.
A CAPE? I DON'T THINK I'M A CAPE...
HOW 'BOUT A BUNGALOW?
I KNOW! A **TRAILER**!
WITH VINYL SIDING!
COACH, WHAT KIND OF HOUSE AM I?
I HAVE A HEADACHE.
Peirce

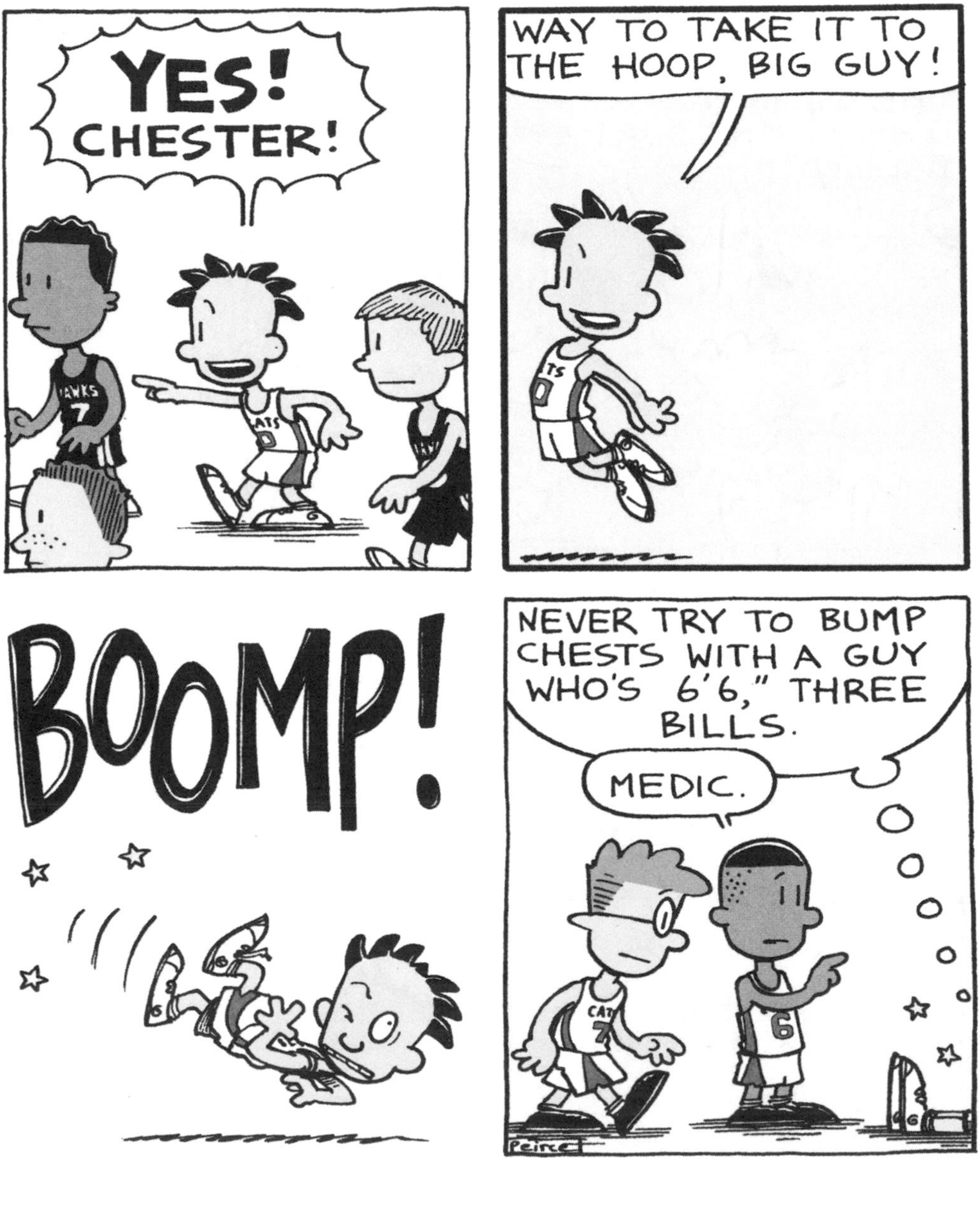
YES! CHESTER!
WAY TO TAKE IT TO THE HOOP, BIG GUY!
BOOMP!
NEVER TRY TO BUMP CHESTS WITH A GUY WHO'S 6'6," THREE BILLS.
MEDIC.
Peirce

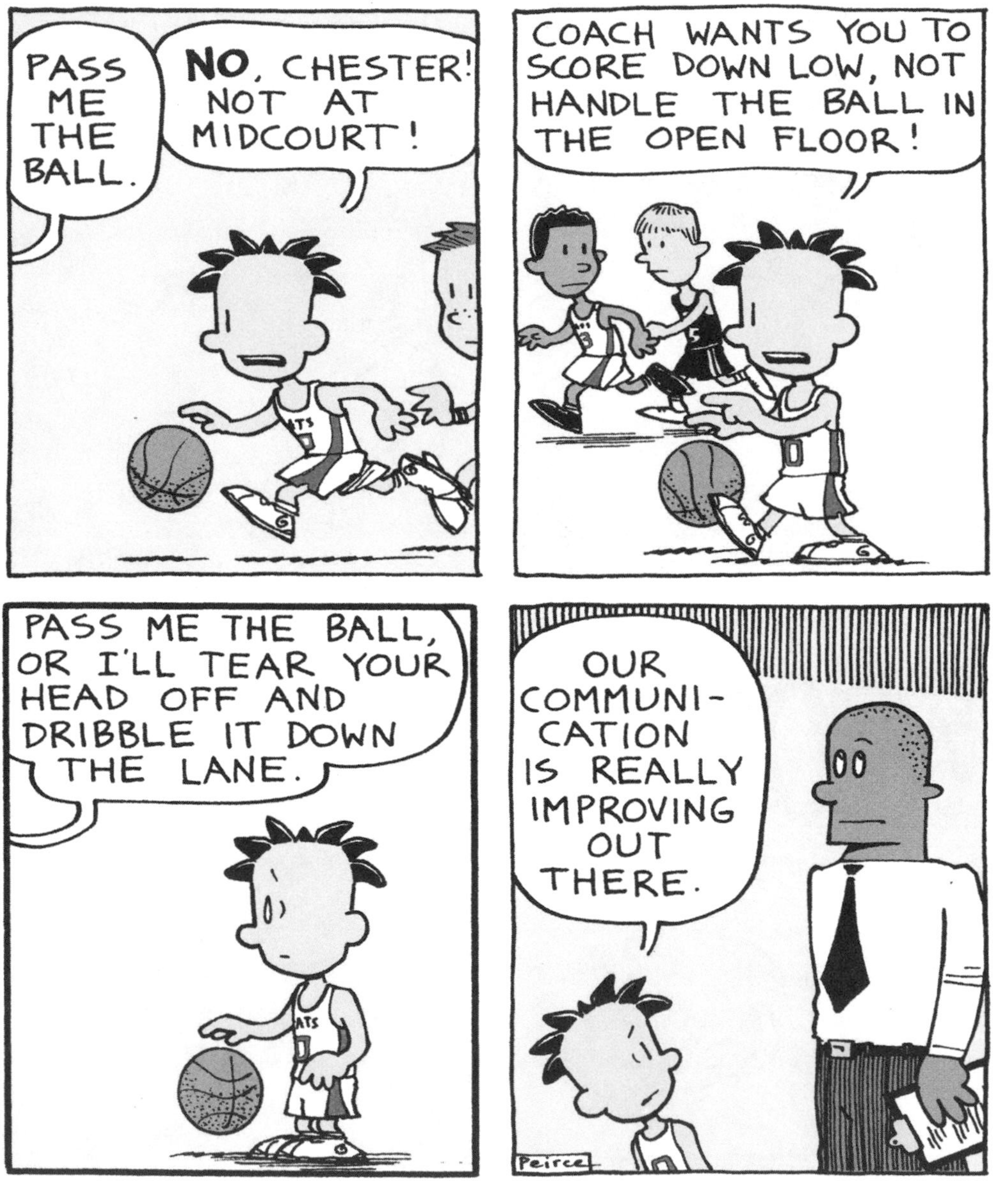
PASS ME THE BALL.
NO, CHESTER! NOT AT MIDCOURT!
COACH WANTS YOU TO SCORE DOWN LOW, NOT HANDLE THE BALL IN THE OPEN FLOOR!
PASS ME THE BALL, OR I'LL TEAR YOUR HEAD OFF AND DRIBBLE IT DOWN THE LANE.
OUR COMMUNI-CATION IS REALLY IMPROVING OUT THERE.
Peirce

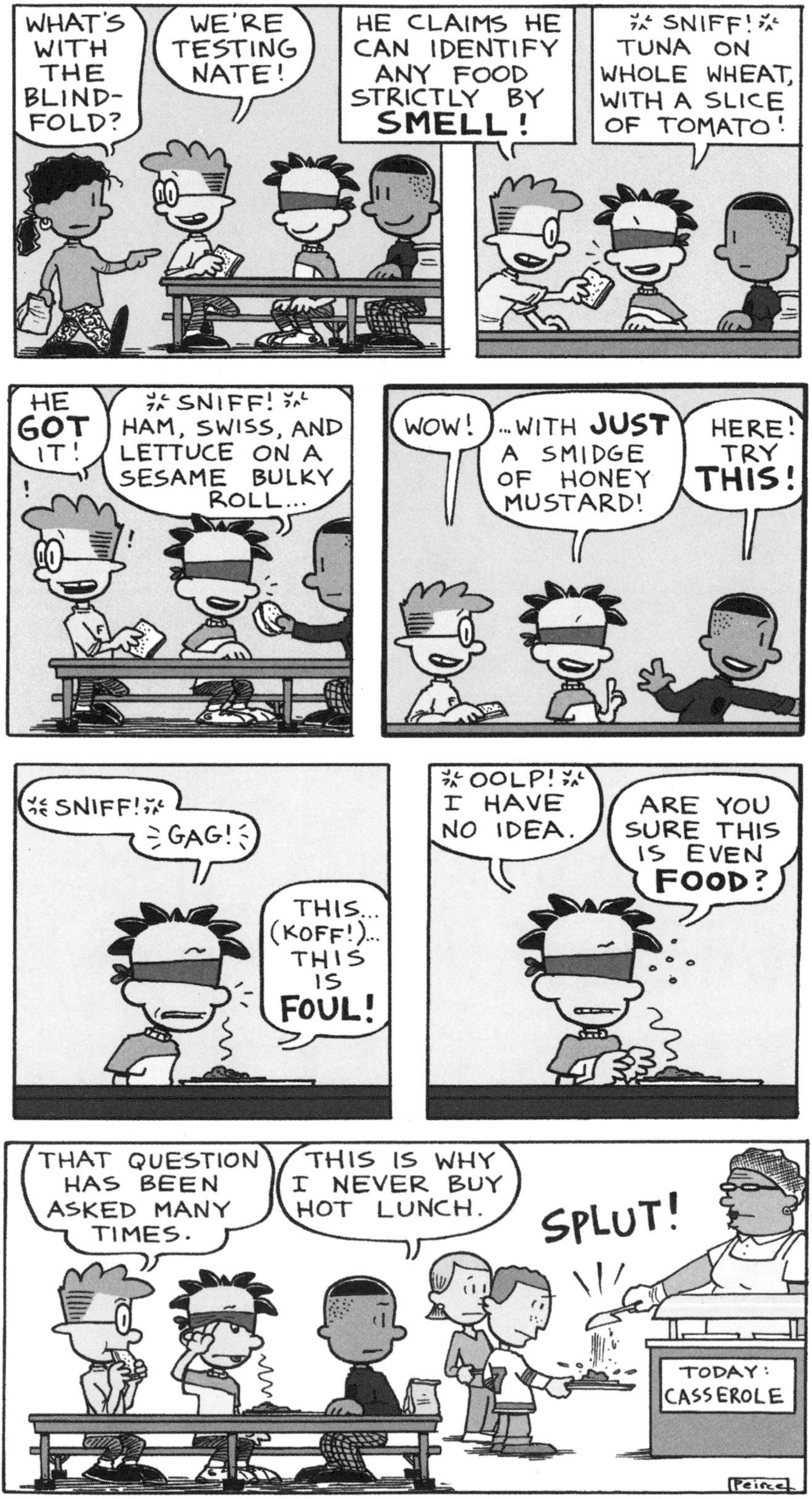
WHAT'S WITH THE BLIND-FOLD?
WE'RE TESTING NATE!
HE CLAIMS HE CAN IDENTIFY ANY FOOD STRICTLY BY SMELL!
SNIFF! TUNA ON WHOLE WHEAT, WITH A SLICE OF TOMATO!
HE GOT IT!
SNIFF! HAM, SWISS, AND LETTUCE ON A SESAME BULKY ROLL...
WOW!
...WITH JUST A SMIDGE OF HONEY MUSTARD!
HERE! TRY THIS!
SNIFF!
GAG!
THIS... (KOFF!)... THIS IS FOUL!
OOLP! I HAVE NO IDEA.
ARE YOU SURE THIS IS EVEN FOOD?
THAT QUESTION HAS BEEN ASKED MANY TIMES.
THIS IS WHY I NEVER BUY HOT LUNCH.
SPLUT!
TODAY: CASSEROLE
Peirce

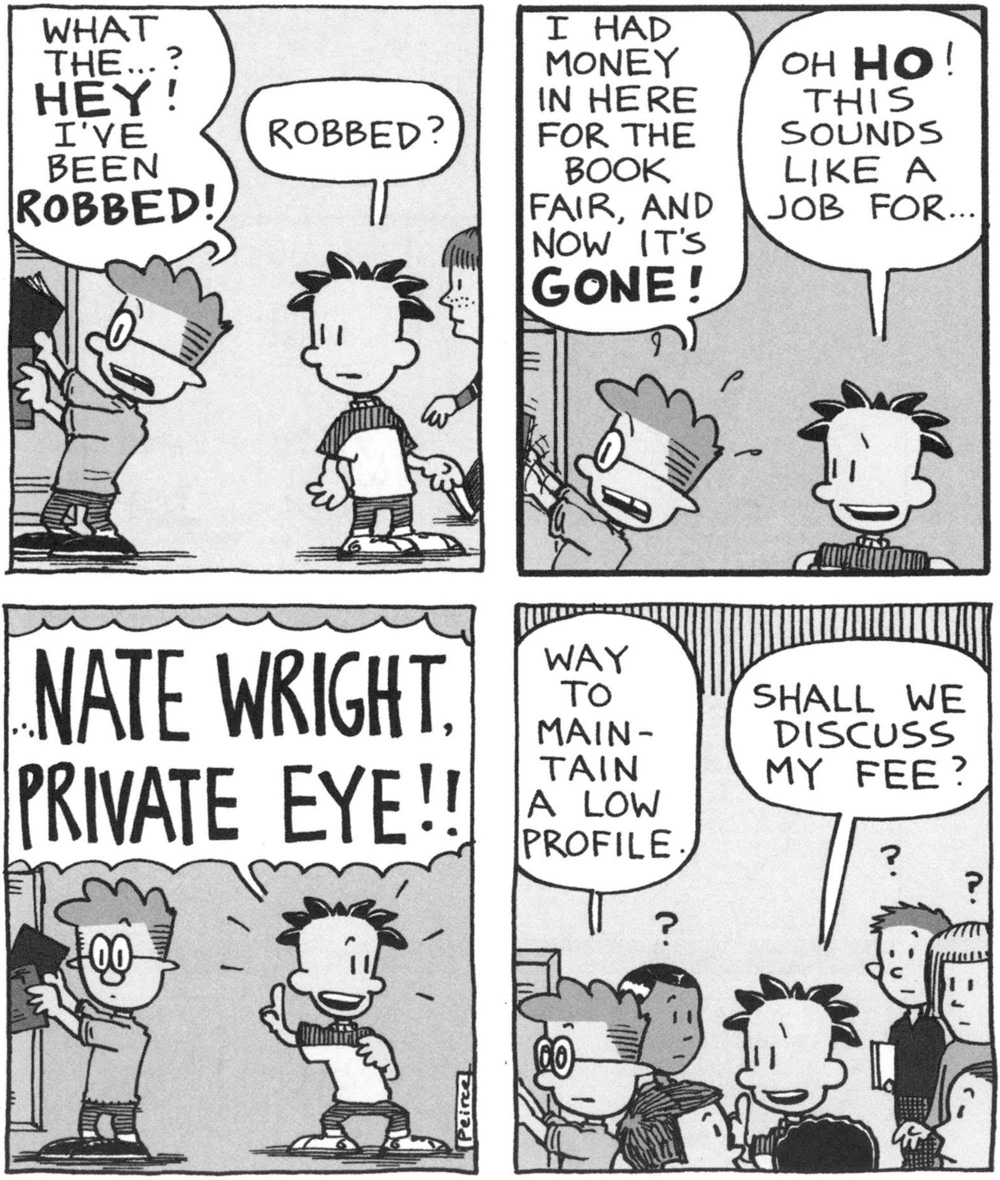
WHAT THE...? HEY! I'VE BEEN ROBBED!
ROBBED?
I HAD MONEY IN HERE FOR THE BOOK FAIR, AND NOW IT'S GONE!
OH HO! THIS SOUNDS LIKE A JOB FOR...
...NATE WRIGHT, PRIVATE EYE!!
Peirce
WAY TO MAIN-TAIN A LOW PROFILE.
SHALL WE DISCUSS MY FEE?
?
?
?

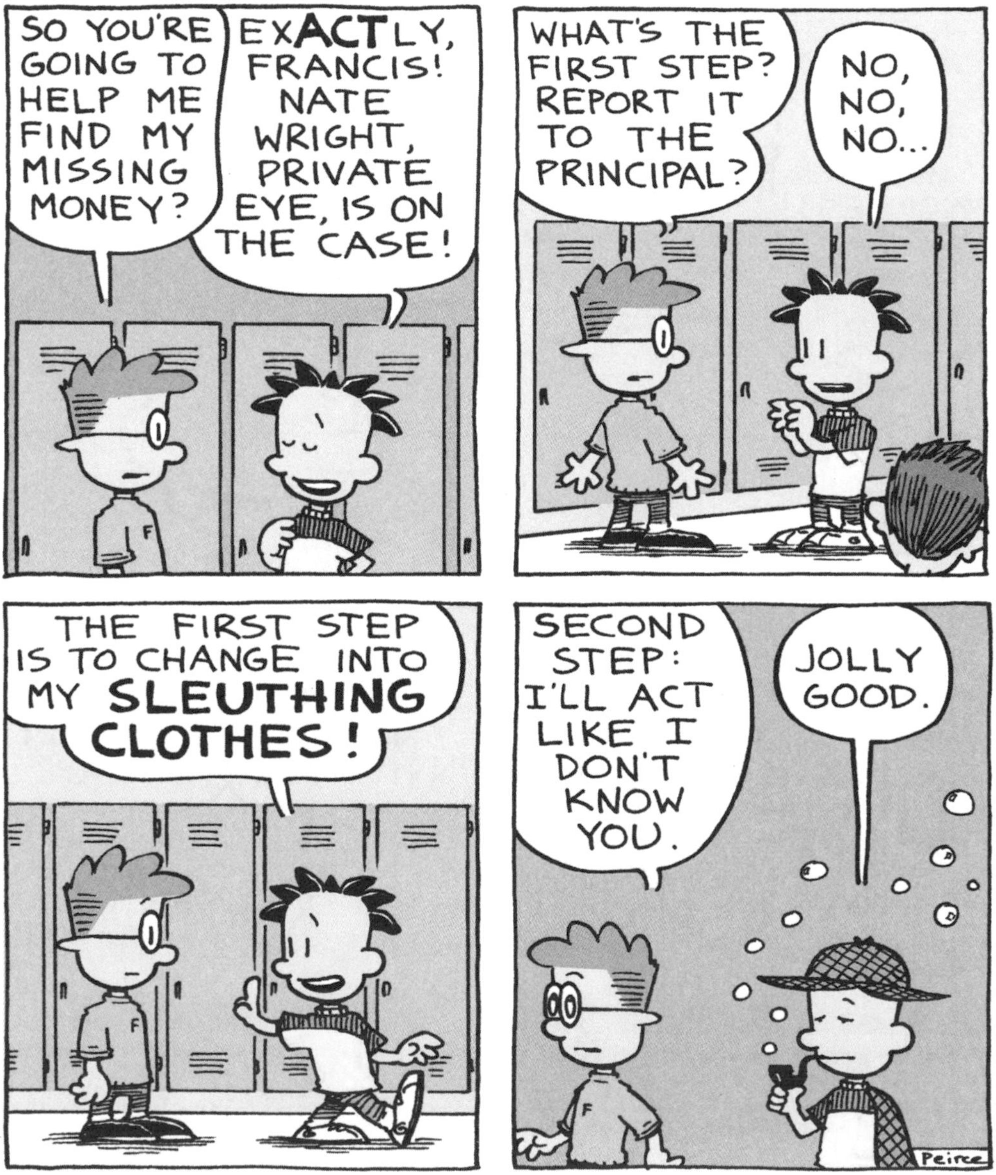
SO YOU'RE GOING TO HELP ME FIND MY MISSING MONEY?
EXACTLY, FRANCIS! NATE WRIGHT, PRIVATE EYE, IS ON THE CASE!
WHAT'S THE FIRST STEP? REPORT IT TO THE PRINCIPAL?
NO, NO, NO...
THE FIRST STEP IS TO CHANGE INTO MY SLEUTHING CLOTHES!
SECOND STEP: I'LL ACT LIKE I DON'T KNOW YOU.
JOLLY GOOD.
Peirce

WHO ARE YOU SUPPOSED TO BE, SHERLOCK HOLMES?
I CAN BE ANYONE, DEAR BOY.
SPANIS CLUB
Fies
THURS. FEB.
LIKE ALL GREAT DETECTIVES, I AM A CHAMELEON! I CAN CHANGE MY IDENTITY AT WILL!
I'VE MASTERED THE ART OF ADAPTING TO MY SURROUNDINGS, SO THAT I'M SCARCELY NOTICED!
I CAN BECOME ALMOST INVISIBLE.
HEY, WHO'S THE LOSER IN THE CAPE?
HA HA HA HA HA HA HA HA HA HA
Peirce

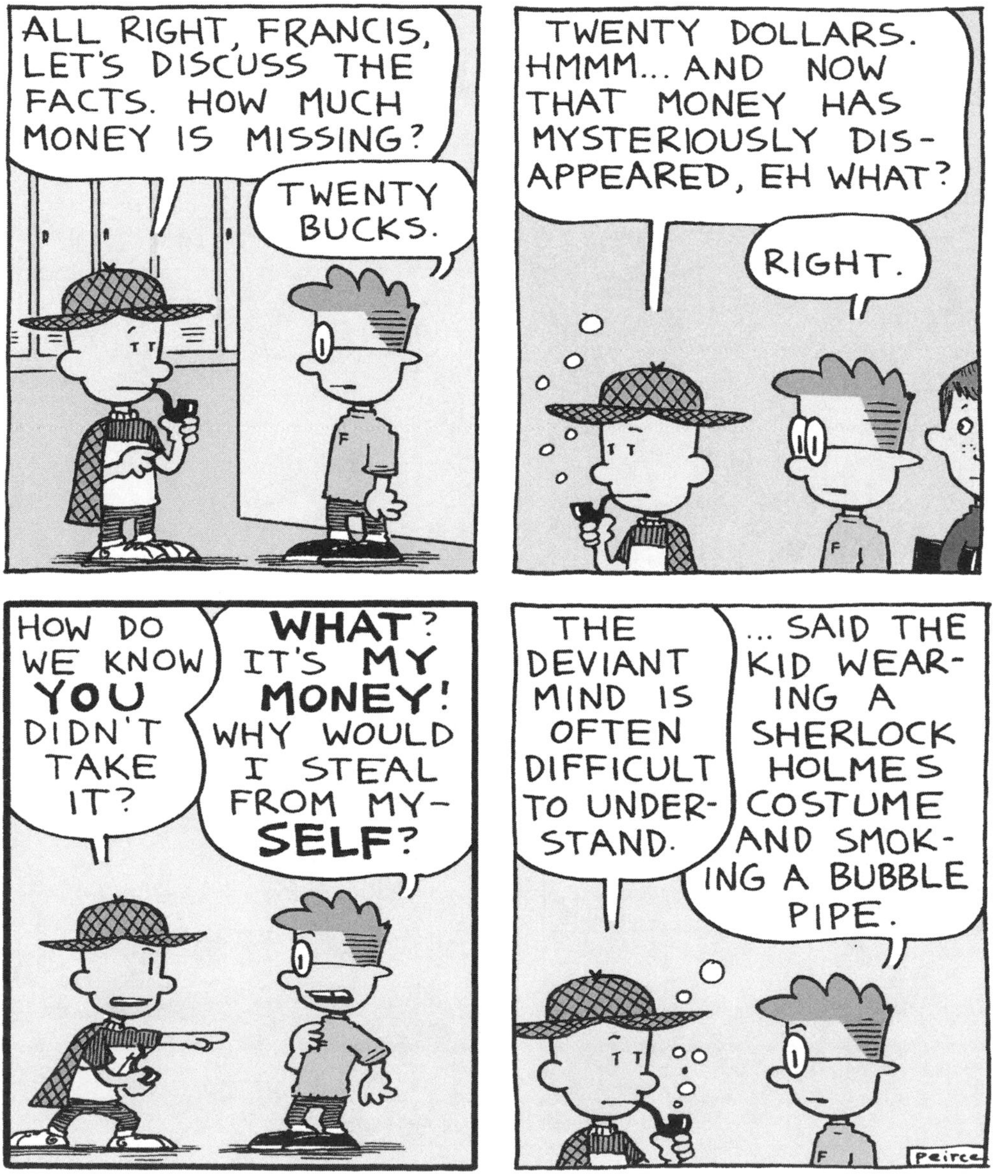
ALL RIGHT, FRANCIS, LET'S DISCUSS THE FACTS. HOW MUCH MONEY IS MISSING?
TWENTY BUCKS.
TWENTY DOLLARS. HMMM... AND NOW THAT MONEY HAS MYSTERIOUSLY DIS-APPEARED, EH WHAT?
RIGHT.
HOW DO WE KNOW **YOU** DIDN'T TAKE IT?
WHAT? IT'S **MY MONEY**! WHY WOULD I STEAL FROM MY-**SELF**?
THE DEVIANT MIND IS OFTEN DIFFICULT TO UNDER-STAND.
... SAID THE KID WEAR-ING A SHERLOCK HOLMES COSTUME AND SMOK-ING A BUBBLE PIPE.
Peirce

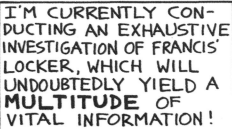

FRANCIS! I HEARD YOU HAD SOME MONEY STOLEN!

NEVER FEAR, SHEILA! THE CULPRIT **WILL** BE CAUGHT!

I'M CURRENTLY CON-DUCTING AN EXHAUSTIVE INVESTIGATION OF FRANCIS' LOCKER, WHICH WILL UNDOUBTEDLY YIELD A **MULTITUDE** OF VITAL INFORMATION!

UH.... THAT'S **MY** LOCKER.

FOR A DETECTIVE, HE'S SURPRISINGLY CLUELESS.

OH, I'M NOT SURPRISED.

HI.

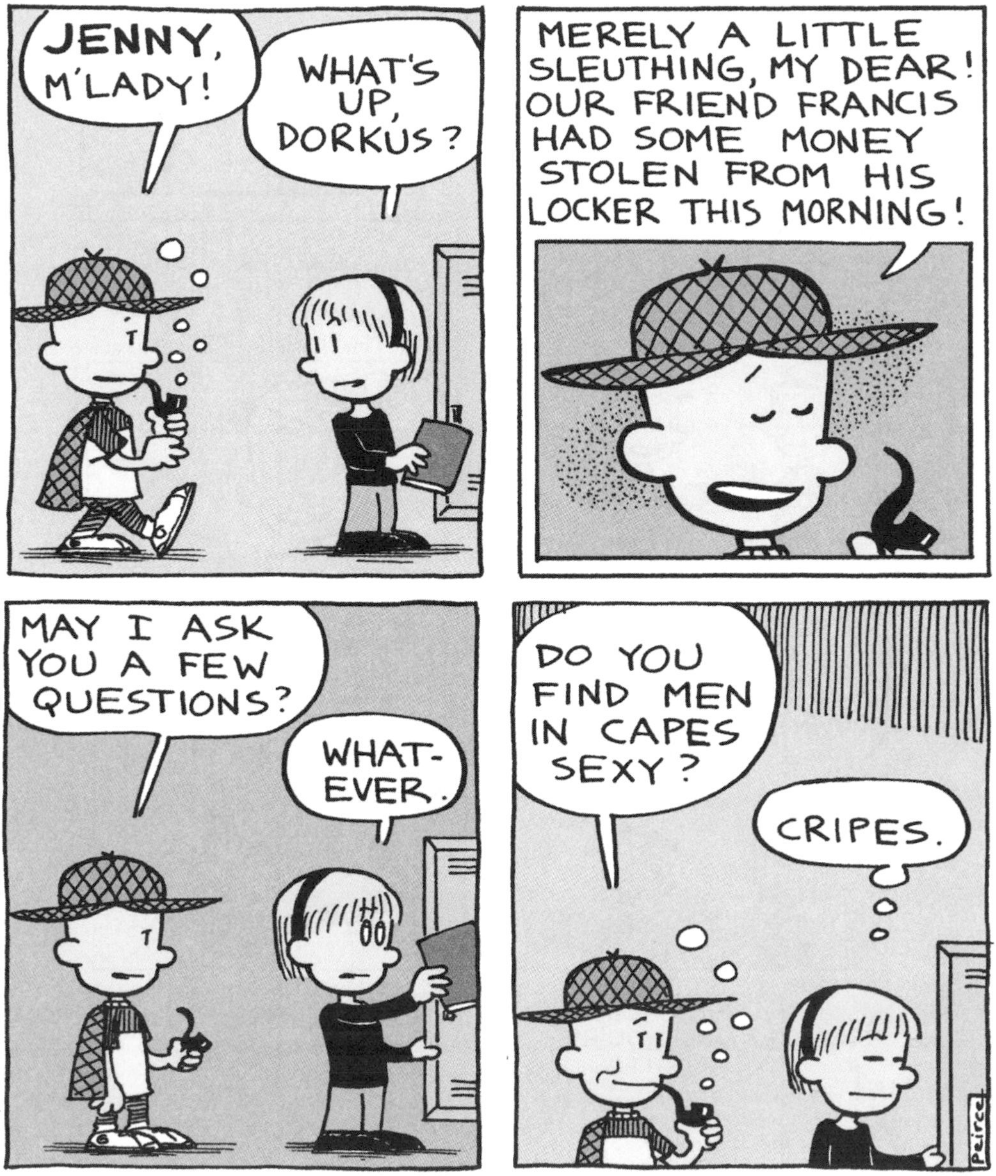
JENNY, M'LADY!
WHAT'S UP, DORKUS?
MERELY A LITTLE SLEUTHING, MY DEAR! OUR FRIEND FRANCIS HAD SOME MONEY STOLEN FROM HIS LOCKER THIS MORNING!
MAY I ASK YOU A FEW QUESTIONS?
WHAT-EVER.
DO YOU FIND MEN IN CAPES SEXY?
CRIPES.
Peirce

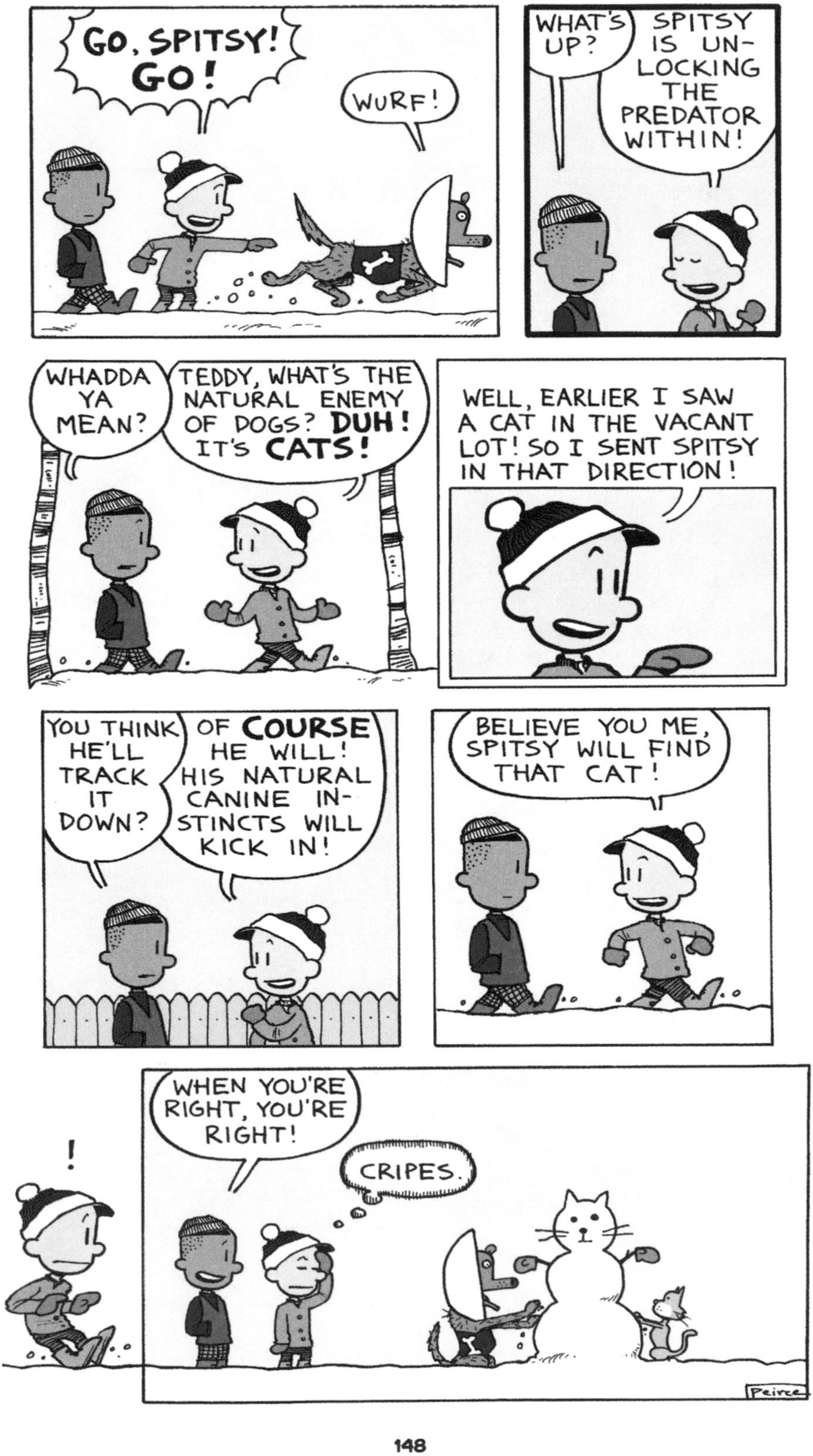
GO, SPITSY! GO!
WURF!
WHAT'S UP?
SPITSY IS UN-LOCKING THE PREDATOR WITHIN!
WHADDA YA MEAN?
TEDDY, WHAT'S THE NATURAL ENEMY OF DOGS? DUH! IT'S CATS!
WELL, EARLIER I SAW A CAT IN THE VACANT LOT! SO I SENT SPITSY IN THAT DIRECTION!
YOU THINK HE'LL TRACK IT DOWN?
OF COURSE HE WILL! HIS NATURAL CANINE IN-STINCTS WILL KICK IN!
BELIEVE YOU ME, SPITSY WILL FIND THAT CAT!
!
WHEN YOU'RE RIGHT, YOU'RE RIGHT!
CRIPES.
Peirce

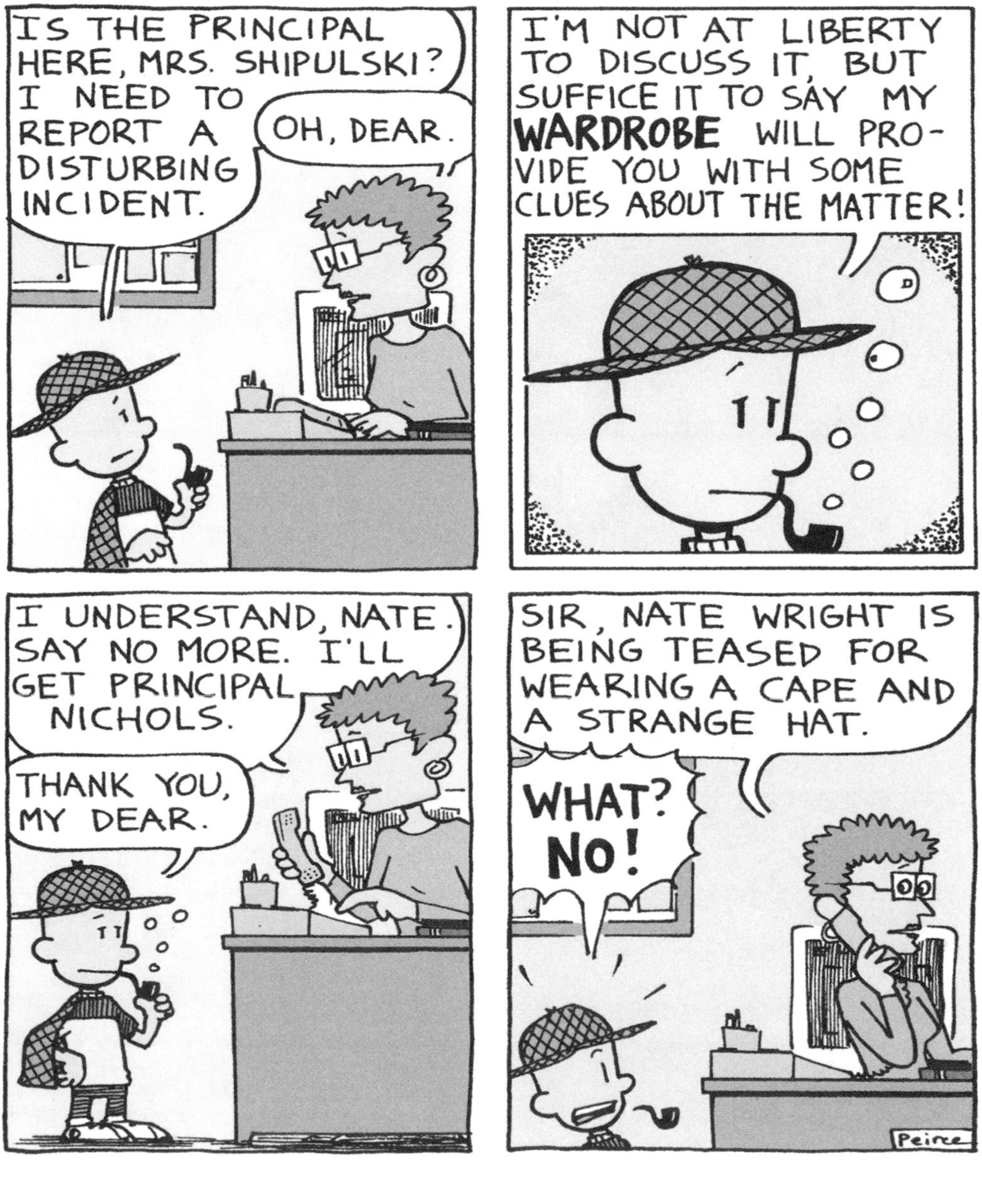
IS THE PRINCIPAL HERE, MRS. SHIPULSKI? I NEED TO REPORT A DISTURBING INCIDENT.
OH, DEAR.
I'M NOT AT LIBERTY TO DISCUSS IT, BUT SUFFICE IT TO SAY MY WARDROBE WILL PROVIDE YOU WITH SOME CLUES ABOUT THE MATTER!
I UNDERSTAND, NATE. SAY NO MORE. I'LL GET PRINCIPAL NICHOLS.
THANK YOU, MY DEAR.
SIR, NATE WRIGHT IS BEING TEASED FOR WEARING A CAPE AND A STRANGE HAT.
WHAT? NO!
Peirce

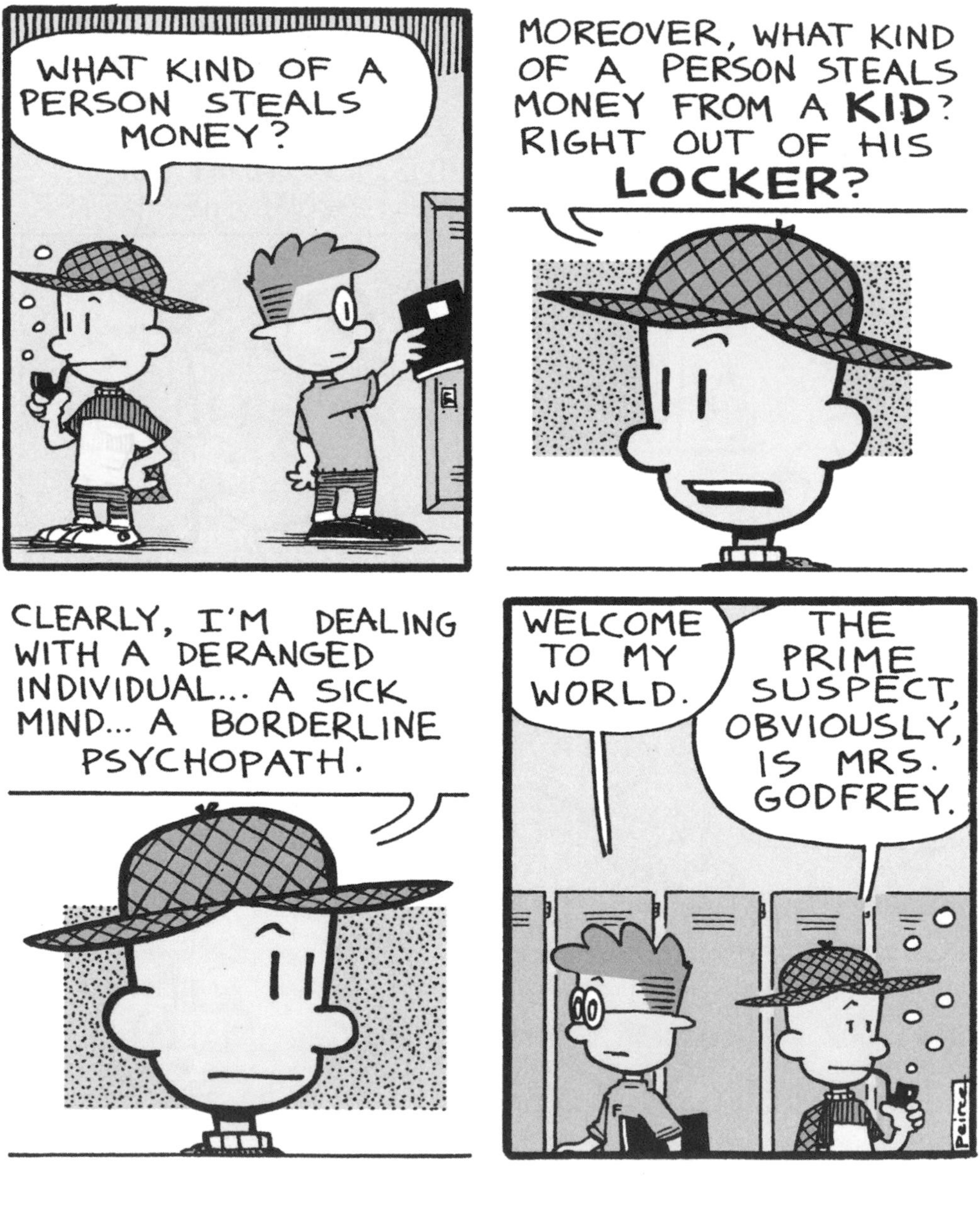
WHAT KIND OF A PERSON STEALS MONEY?
MOREOVER, WHAT KIND OF A PERSON STEALS MONEY FROM A **KID**? RIGHT OUT OF HIS **LOCKER**?
CLEARLY, I'M DEALING WITH A DERANGED INDIVIDUAL... A SICK MIND... A BORDERLINE PSYCHOPATH.
WELCOME TO MY WORLD.
THE PRIME SUSPECT, OBVIOUSLY, IS MRS. GODFREY.
Peirce

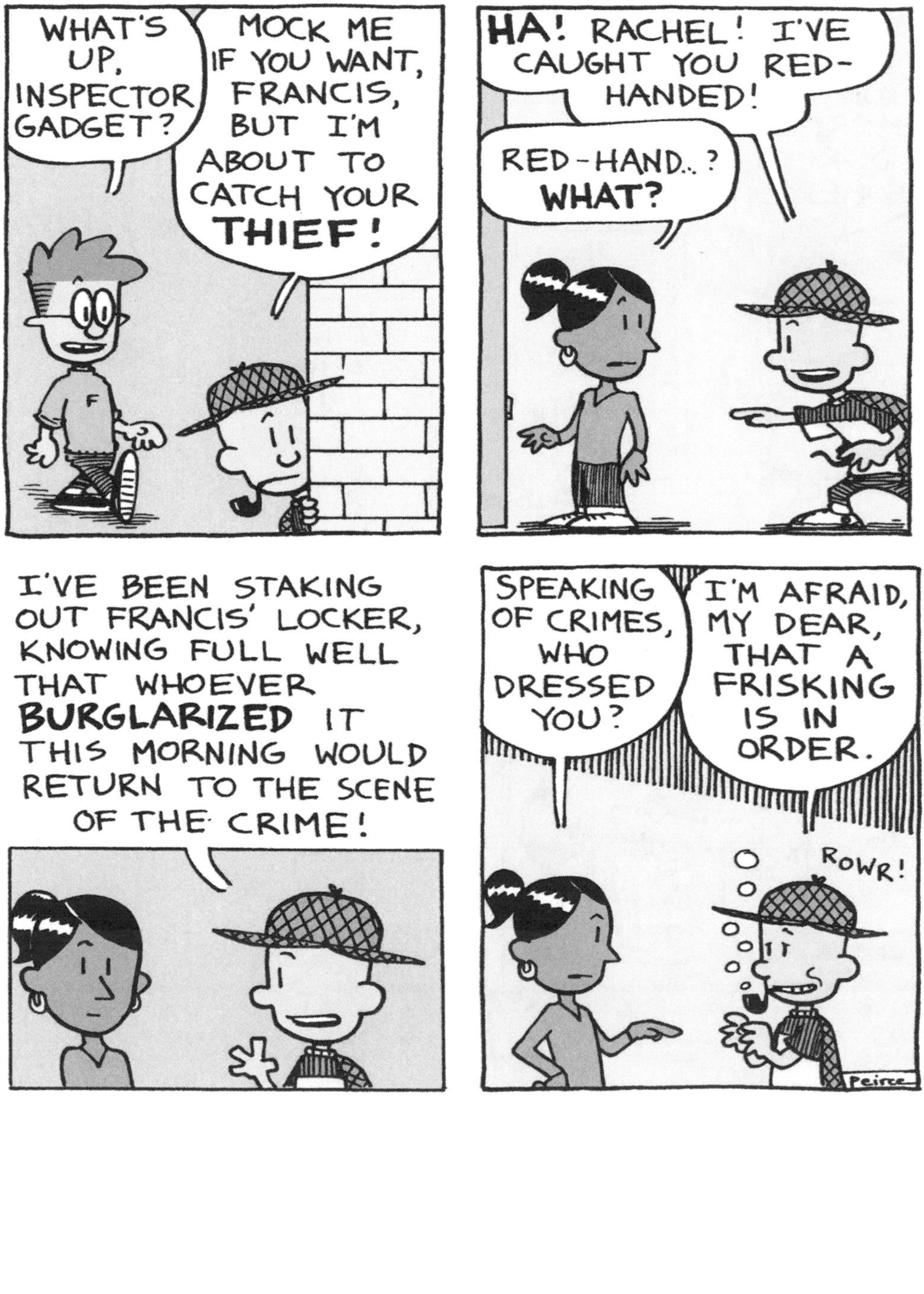
WHAT'S UP, INSPECTOR GADGET?
MOCK ME IF YOU WANT, FRANCIS, BUT I'M ABOUT TO CATCH YOUR THIEF!
HA! RACHEL! I'VE CAUGHT YOU RED-HANDED!
RED-HAND...? WHAT?
I'VE BEEN STAKING OUT FRANCIS' LOCKER, KNOWING FULL WELL THAT WHOEVER BURGLARIZED IT THIS MORNING WOULD RETURN TO THE SCENE OF THE CRIME!
SPEAKING OF CRIMES, WHO DRESSED YOU?
I'M AFRAID, MY DEAR, THAT A FRISKING IS IN ORDER.
ROWR!
Peirce

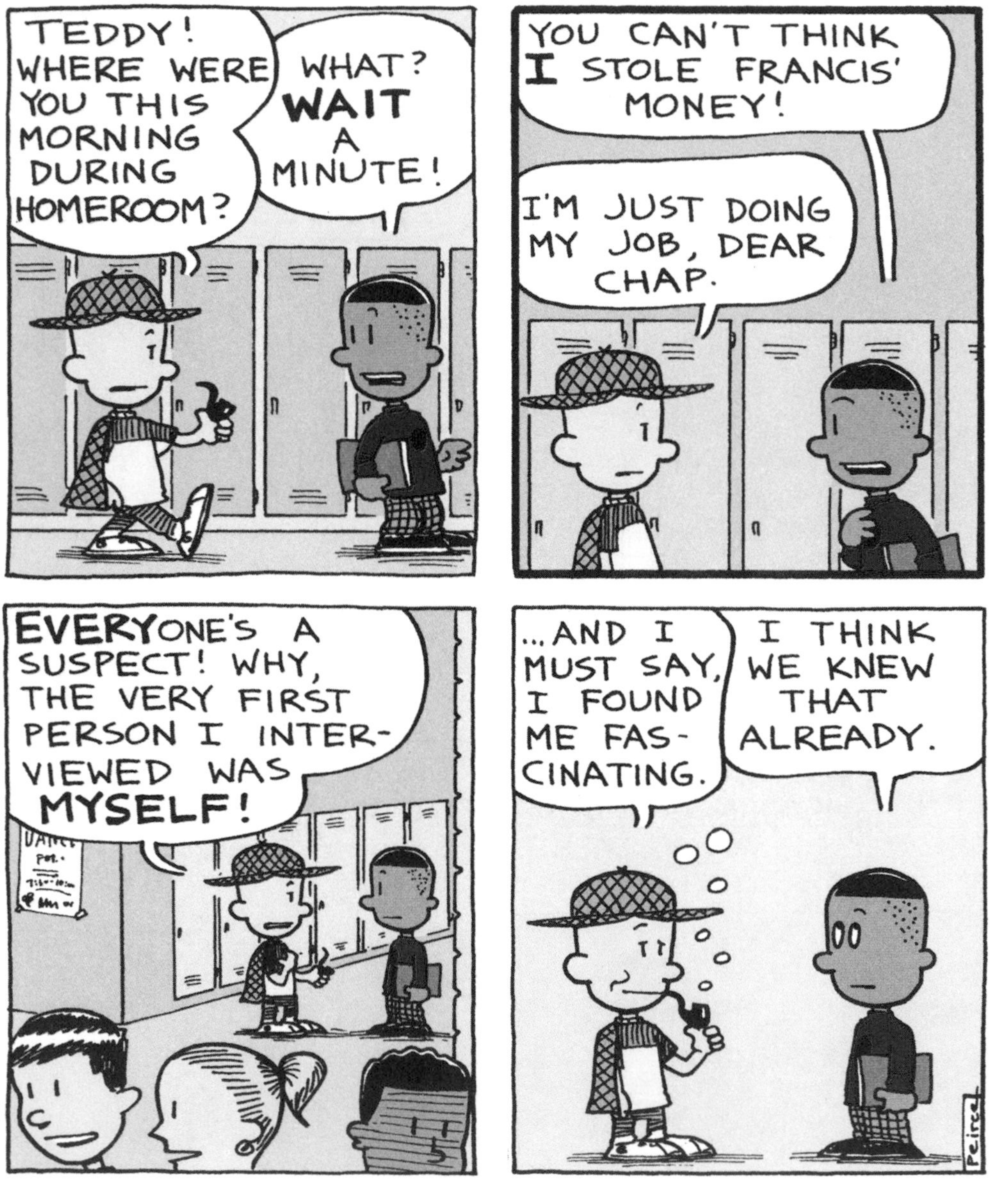
TEDDY! WHERE WERE YOU THIS MORNING DURING HOMEROOM?
WHAT? WAIT A MINUTE!
YOU CAN'T THINK I STOLE FRANCIS' MONEY!
I'M JUST DOING MY JOB, DEAR CHAP.
EVERYONE'S A SUSPECT! WHY, THE VERY FIRST PERSON I INTER-VIEWED WAS MYSELF!
...AND I MUST SAY, I FOUND ME FAS-CINATING.
I THINK WE KNEW THAT ALREADY.
Peirce

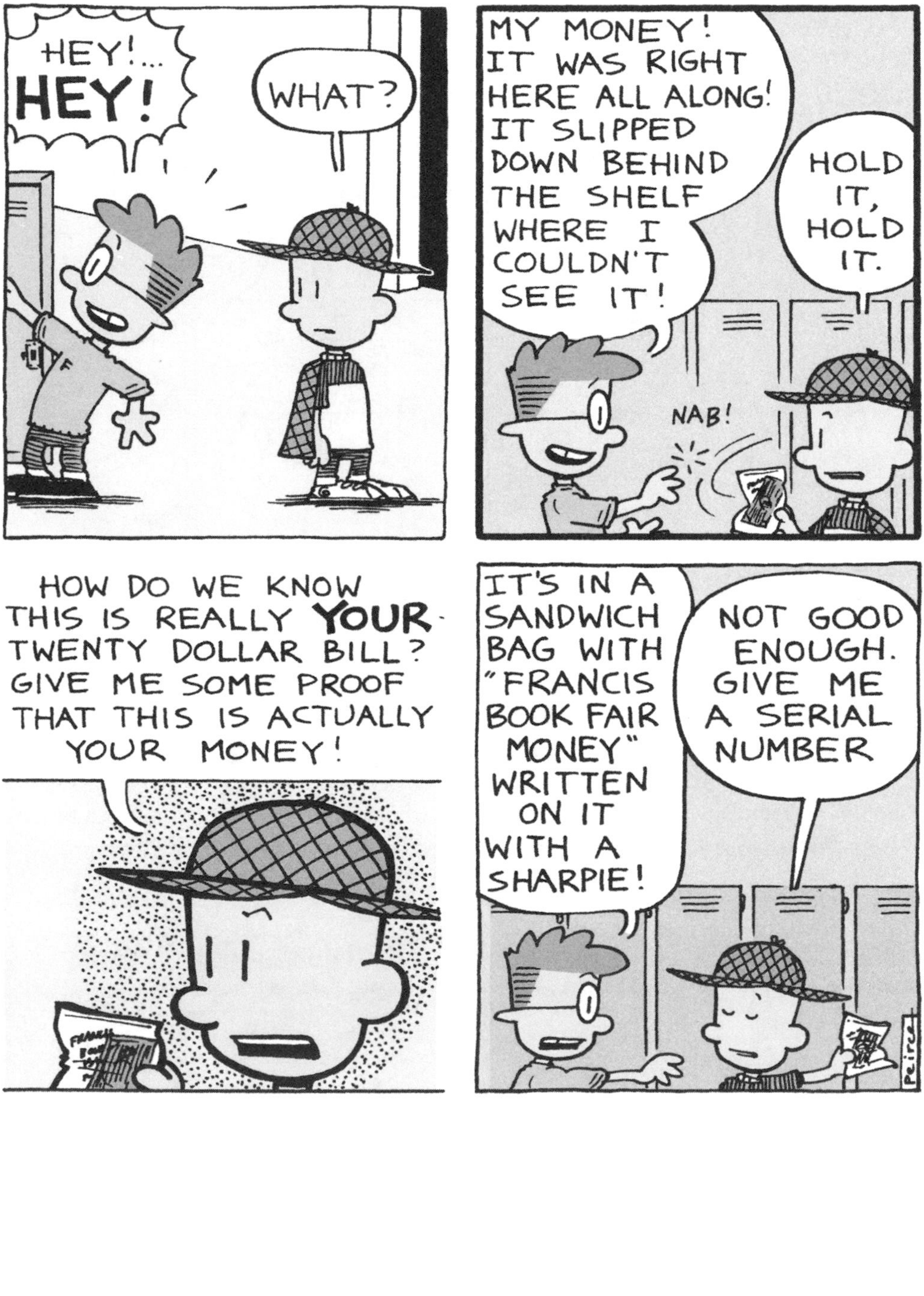
HEY!... HEY!
WHAT?
MY MONEY! IT WAS RIGHT HERE ALL ALONG! IT SLIPPED DOWN BEHIND THE SHELF WHERE I COULDN'T SEE IT!
HOLD IT, HOLD IT.
NAB!
HOW DO WE KNOW THIS IS REALLY YOUR TWENTY DOLLAR BILL? GIVE ME SOME PROOF THAT THIS IS ACTUALLY YOUR MONEY!
IT'S IN A SANDWICH BAG WITH "FRANCIS BOOK FAIR MONEY" WRITTEN ON IT WITH A SHARPIE!
NOT GOOD ENOUGH. GIVE ME A SERIAL NUMBER
Peirce

ALL'S WELL THAT ENDS WELL, EH WHAT? ANOTHER CASE SOLVED!
CASE? THERE WAS NO CASE!
THE MONEY WAS RIGHT HERE IN MY LOCKER THE WHOLE TIME!
...WHICH YOU WOULDN'T HAVE REALIZED WITHOUT MY STELLAR DETECTIVE WORK!
BUT YOU DIDN'T DO ANYTHING! ALL YOU DID WAS WALK AROUND WITH THAT STUPID PIPE!
NO NEED TO THANK ME.
THANK YOU??
YOU'RE QUITE WELCOME, OLD BEAN.
Peirce

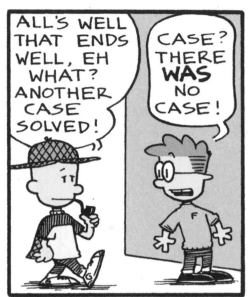

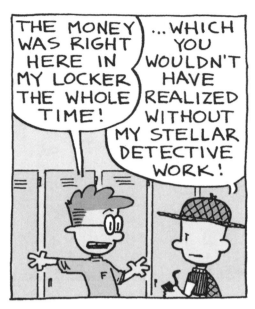

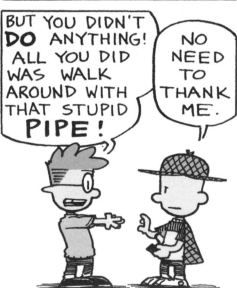

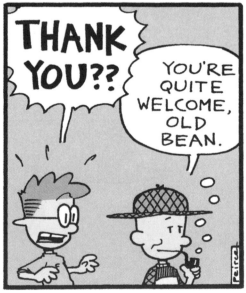

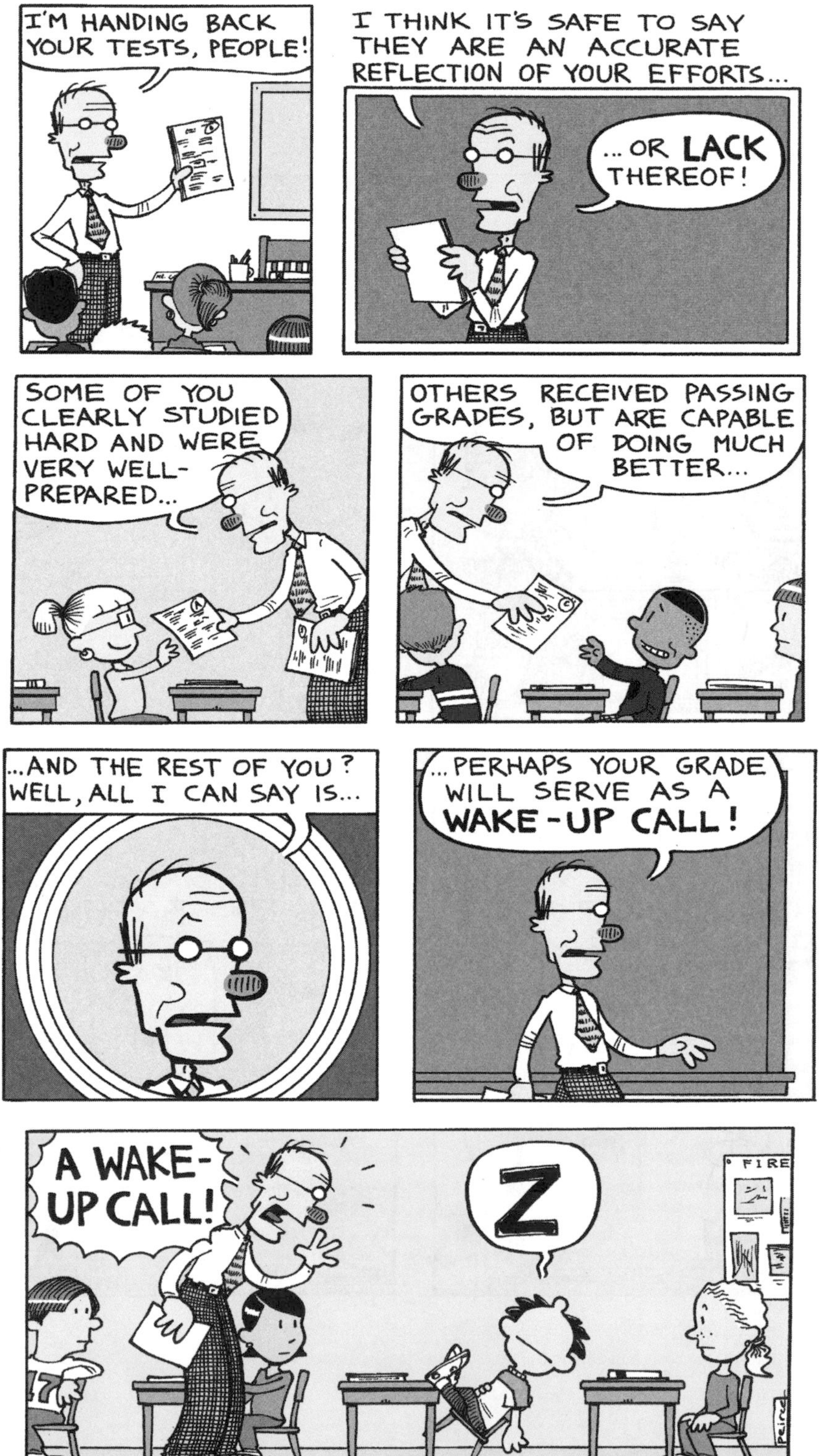

I'M HANDING BACK YOUR TESTS, PEOPLE!
I THINK IT'S SAFE TO SAY THEY ARE AN ACCURATE REFLECTION OF YOUR EFFORTS...
... OR LACK THEREOF!
SOME OF YOU CLEARLY STUDIED HARD AND WERE VERY WELL-PREPARED...
OTHERS RECEIVED PASSING GRADES, BUT ARE CAPABLE OF DOING MUCH BETTER...
...AND THE REST OF YOU? WELL, ALL I CAN SAY IS...
... PERHAPS YOUR GRADE WILL SERVE AS A WAKE-UP CALL!
A WAKE-UP CALL!
Z
FIRE

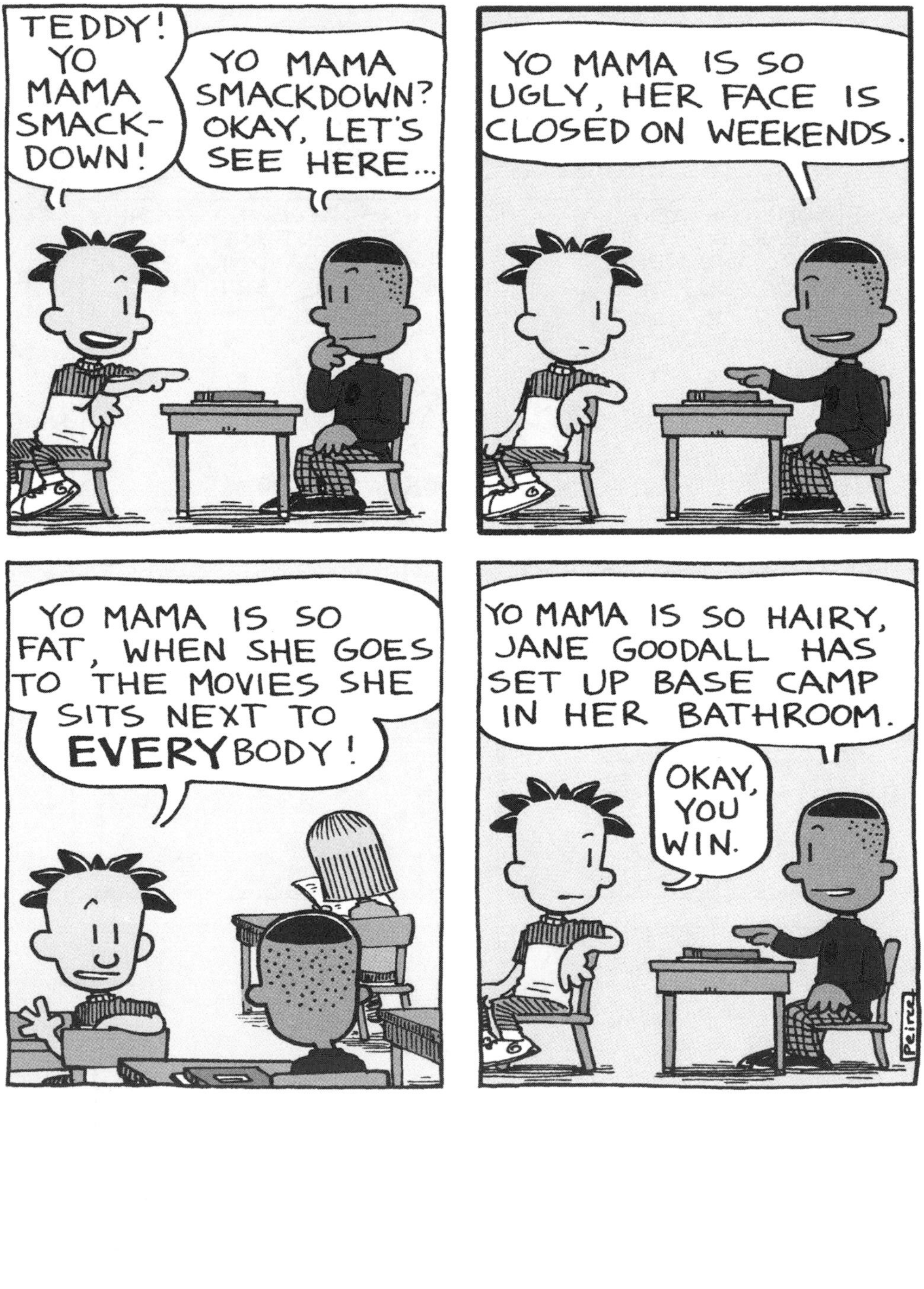
TEDDY! YO MAMA SMACK-DOWN!
YO MAMA SMACKDOWN? OKAY, LET'S SEE HERE...
YO MAMA IS SO UGLY, HER FACE IS CLOSED ON WEEKENDS.
YO MAMA IS SO FAT, WHEN SHE GOES TO THE MOVIES SHE SITS NEXT TO EVERYBODY!
YO MAMA IS SO HAIRY, JANE GOODALL HAS SET UP BASE CAMP IN HER BATHROOM.
OKAY, YOU WIN.
Peirce

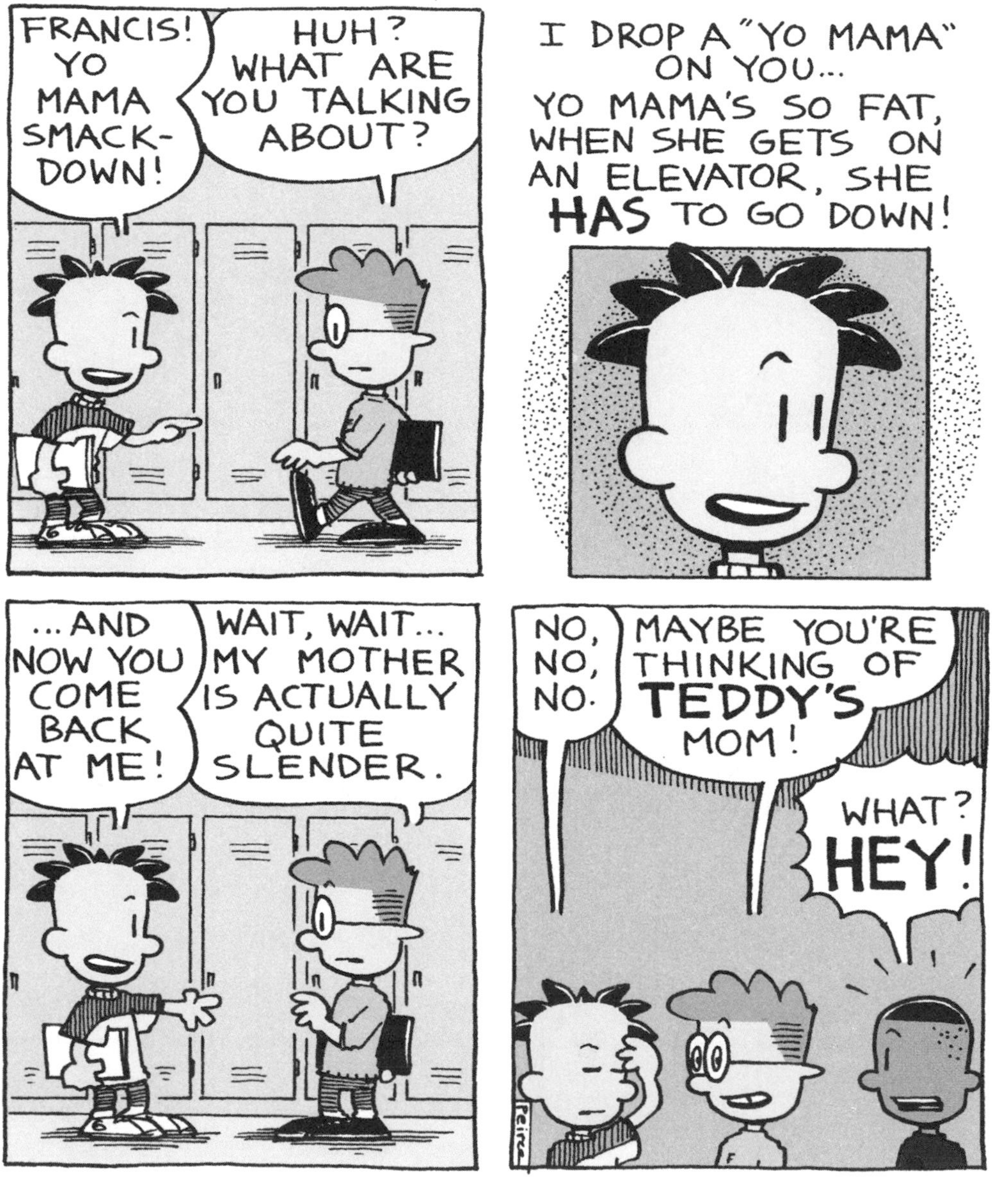
FRANCIS! YO MAMA SMACK-DOWN!
HUH? WHAT ARE YOU TALKING ABOUT?
I DROP A "YO MAMA" ON YOU... YO MAMA'S SO FAT, WHEN SHE GETS ON AN ELEVATOR, SHE **HAS** TO GO DOWN!
...AND NOW YOU COME BACK AT ME!
WAIT, WAIT... MY MOTHER IS ACTUALLY QUITE SLENDER.
NO, NO, NO.
MAYBE YOU'RE THINKING OF **TEDDY'S** MOM!
WHAT? **HEY!**
Peirce

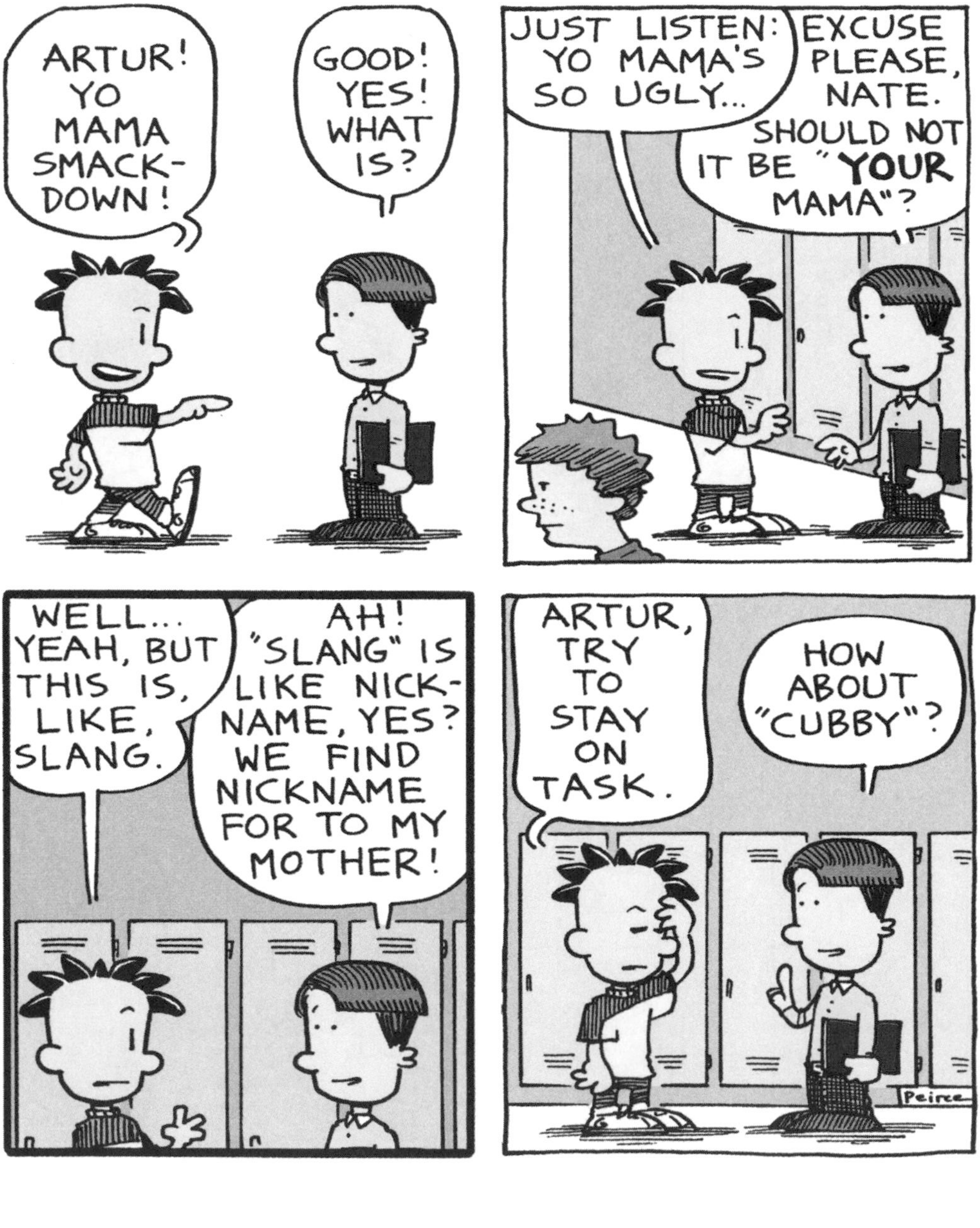
ARTUR! YO MAMA SMACK-DOWN!
GOOD! YES! WHAT IS?
JUST LISTEN: YO MAMA'S SO UGLY...
EXCUSE PLEASE, NATE.
SHOULD NOT IT BE "YOUR MAMA"?
WELL... YEAH, BUT THIS IS, LIKE, SLANG.
AH! "SLANG" IS LIKE NICK-NAME, YES? WE FIND NICKNAME FOR TO MY MOTHER!
ARTUR, TRY TO STAY ON TASK.
HOW ABOUT "CUBBY"?
Peirce

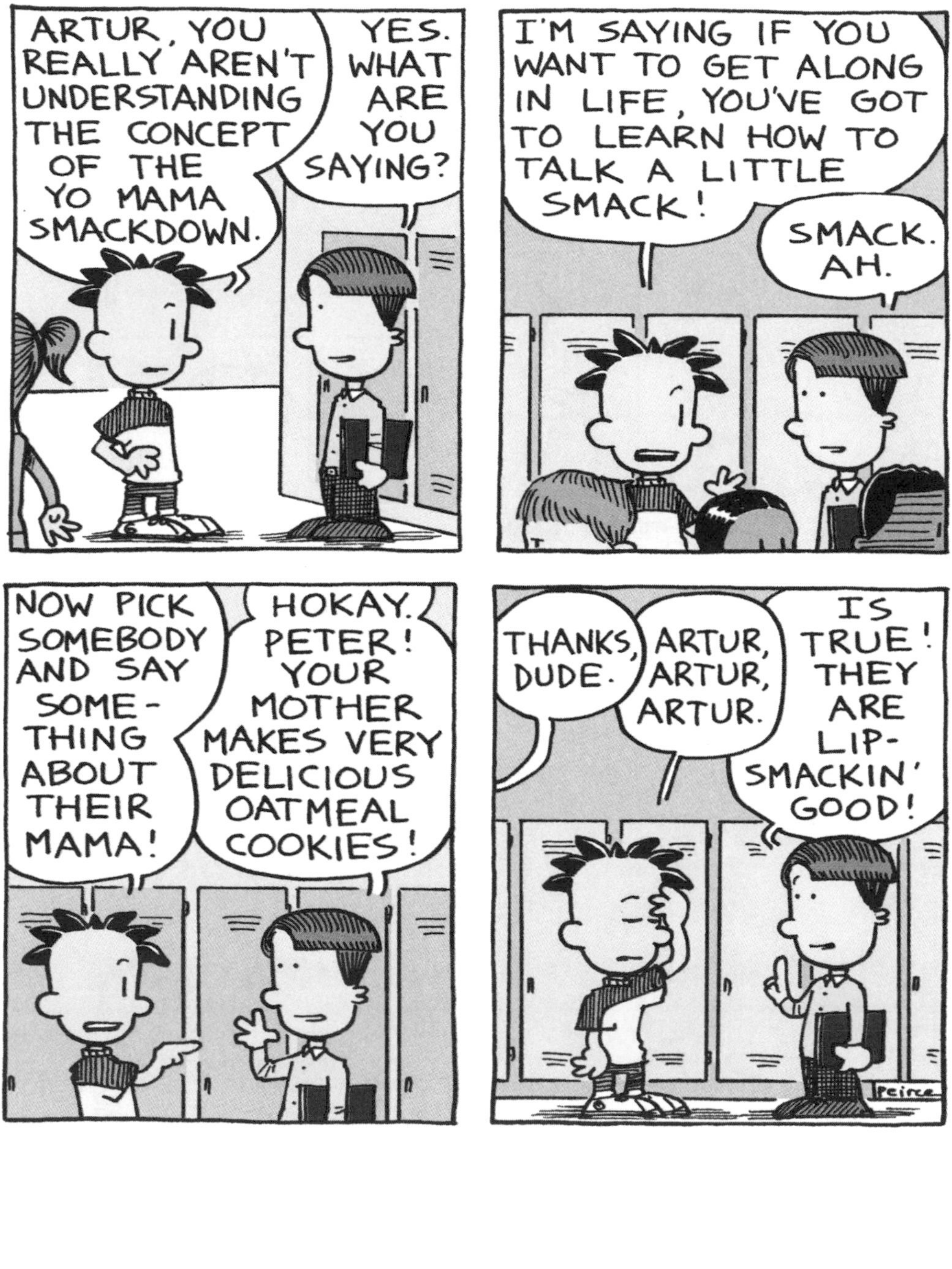
ARTUR, YOU REALLY AREN'T UNDERSTANDING THE CONCEPT OF THE YO MAMA SMACKDOWN.
YES. WHAT ARE YOU SAYING?
I'M SAYING IF YOU WANT TO GET ALONG IN LIFE, YOU'VE GOT TO LEARN HOW TO TALK A LITTLE SMACK!
SMACK. AH.
NOW PICK SOMEBODY AND SAY SOME-THING ABOUT THEIR MAMA!
HOKAY. PETER! YOUR MOTHER MAKES VERY DELICIOUS OATMEAL COOKIES!
THANKS, DUDE.
ARTUR, ARTUR, ARTUR.
IS TRUE! THEY ARE LIP-SMACKIN' GOOD!
peirce

WHAT'S UP, GENTS?

I'M TRYING TO TEACH ARTUR THE FINER POINTS OF THE YO MAMA SMACKDOWN.

AM NOT DOING GOOD SO FAR.

JUST WATCH ME, ARTUR! JUST DO WHAT I DO!

I'LL THROW DOWN SOME **KILLER** YO MAMAS AT THE NEXT PERSON TO COME AROUND THE CORNER!

Peirce

THIS OUGHTA BE GOOD!

CH-CHESTER!

WHUT?

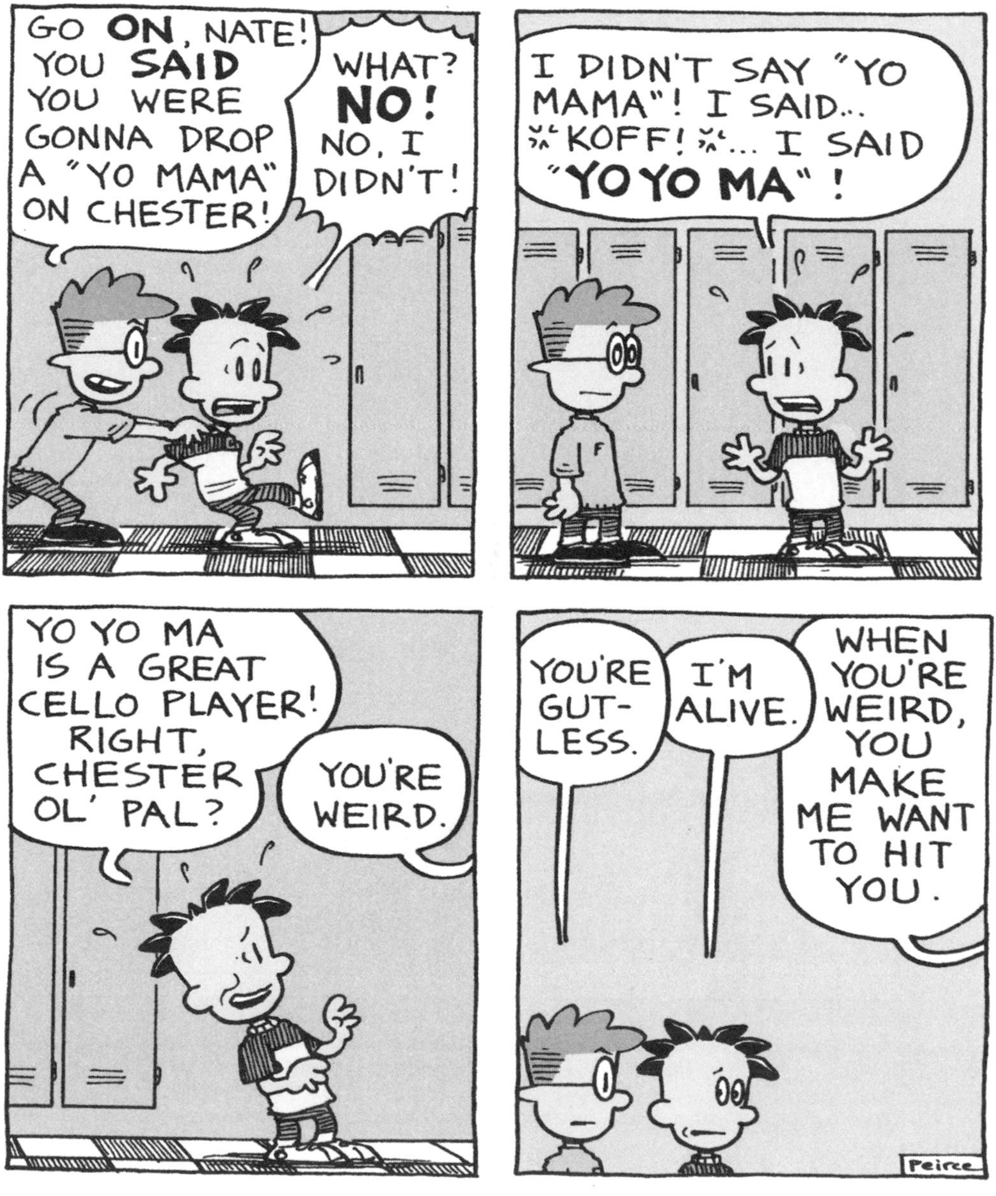
GO ON, NATE! YOU SAID YOU WERE GONNA DROP A "YO MAMA" ON CHESTER!
WHAT? NO! NO, I DIDN'T!
I DIDN'T SAY "YO MAMA"! I SAID... KOFF! ... I SAID "YO YO MA"!
YO YO MA IS A GREAT CELLO PLAYER! RIGHT, CHESTER OL' PAL?
YOU'RE WEIRD.
YOU'RE GUT-LESS.
I'M ALIVE.
WHEN YOU'RE WEIRD, YOU MAKE ME WANT TO HIT YOU.
Peirce

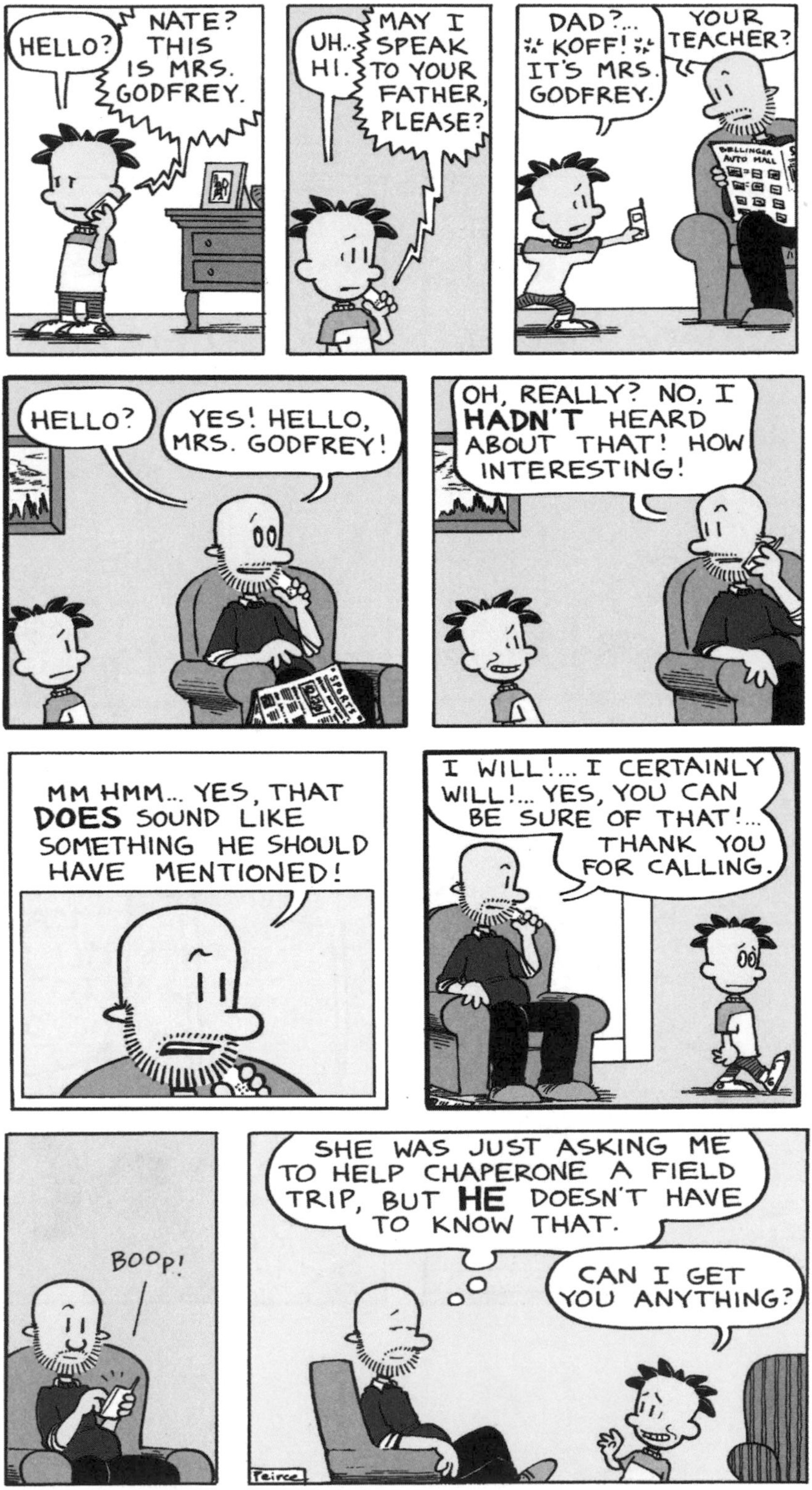
HELLO?
NATE? THIS IS MRS. GODFREY.
UH... HI.
MAY I SPEAK TO YOUR FATHER, PLEASE?
DAD?... KOFF! IT'S MRS. GODFREY.
YOUR TEACHER?
BELLINGER AUTO MALL
HELLO?
YES! HELLO, MRS. GODFREY!
SPORTS
OH, REALLY? NO, I HADN'T HEARD ABOUT THAT! HOW INTERESTING!
MM HMM... YES, THAT DOES SOUND LIKE SOMETHING HE SHOULD HAVE MENTIONED!
I WILL!... I CERTAINLY WILL!... YES, YOU CAN BE SURE OF THAT!... THANK YOU FOR CALLING.
BOOP!
SHE WAS JUST ASKING ME TO HELP CHAPERONE A FIELD TRIP, BUT HE DOESN'T HAVE TO KNOW THAT.
CAN I GET YOU ANYTHING?
Peirce

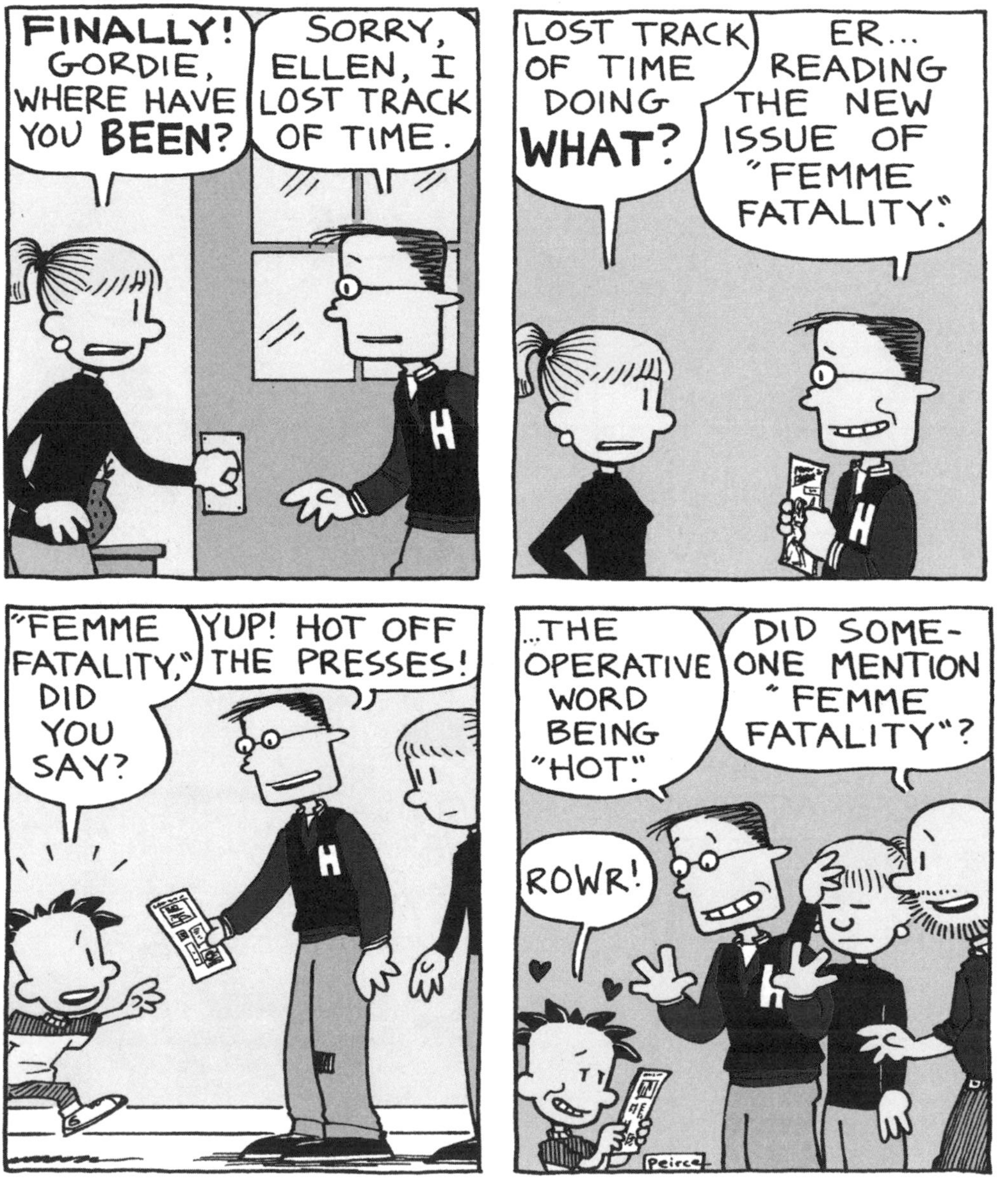
FINALLY! GORDIE, WHERE HAVE YOU BEEN?
SORRY, ELLEN, I LOST TRACK OF TIME.
LOST TRACK OF TIME DOING WHAT?
ER... READING THE NEW ISSUE OF "FEMME FATALITY."
"FEMME FATALITY," DID YOU SAY?
YUP! HOT OFF THE PRESSES!
...THE OPERATIVE WORD BEING "HOT."
DID SOME-ONE MENTION "FEMME FATALITY"?
ROWR!
Peirce

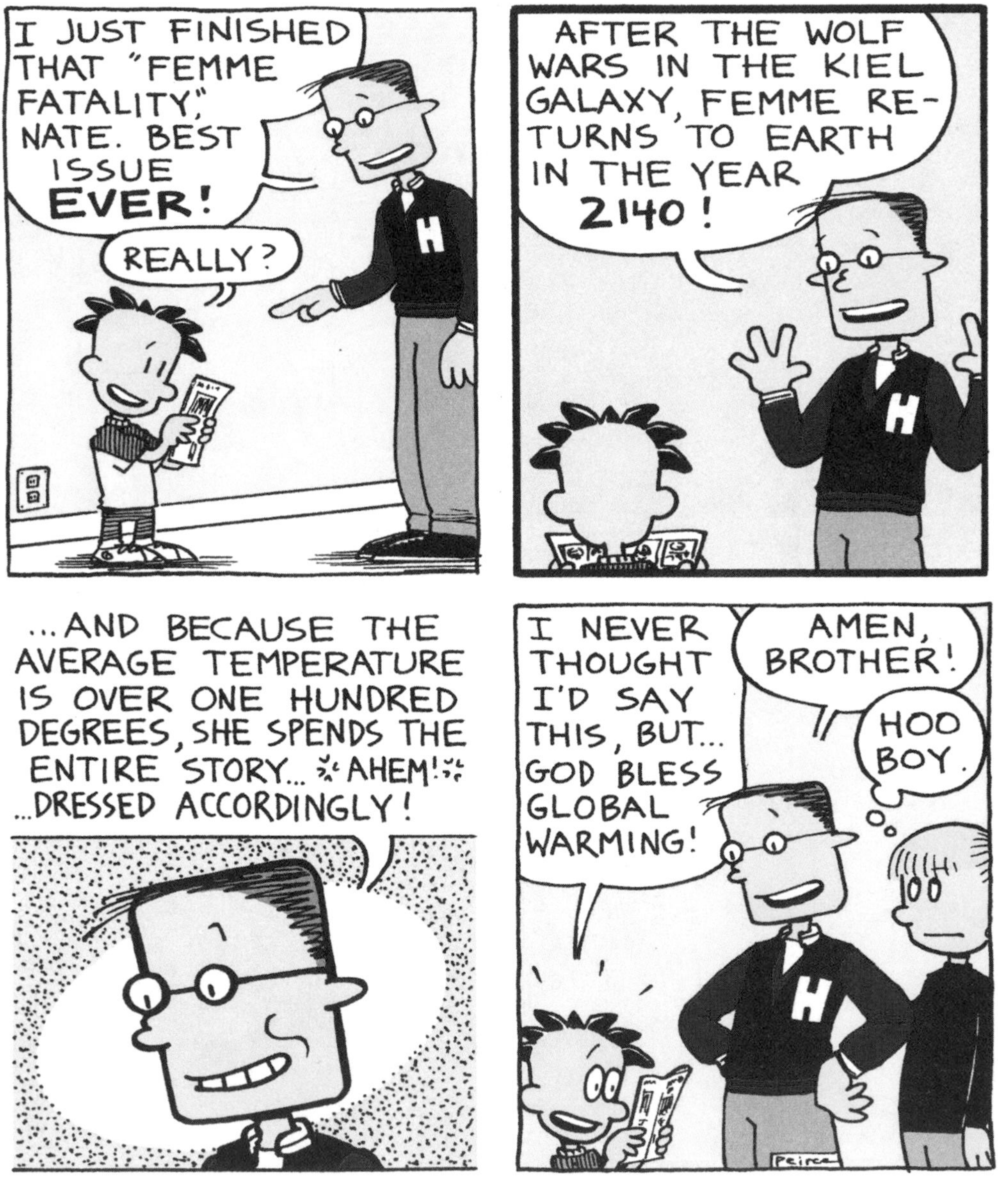
I JUST FINISHED THAT "FEMME FATALITY," NATE. BEST ISSUE EVER!
REALLY?
AFTER THE WOLF WARS IN THE KIEL GALAXY, FEMME RE-TURNS TO EARTH IN THE YEAR 2140!
...AND BECAUSE THE AVERAGE TEMPERATURE IS OVER ONE HUNDRED DEGREES, SHE SPENDS THE ENTIRE STORY... AHEM! ...DRESSED ACCORDINGLY!
I NEVER THOUGHT I'D SAY THIS, BUT... GOD BLESS GLOBAL WARMING!
AMEN, BROTHER!
HOO BOY.
Peirce

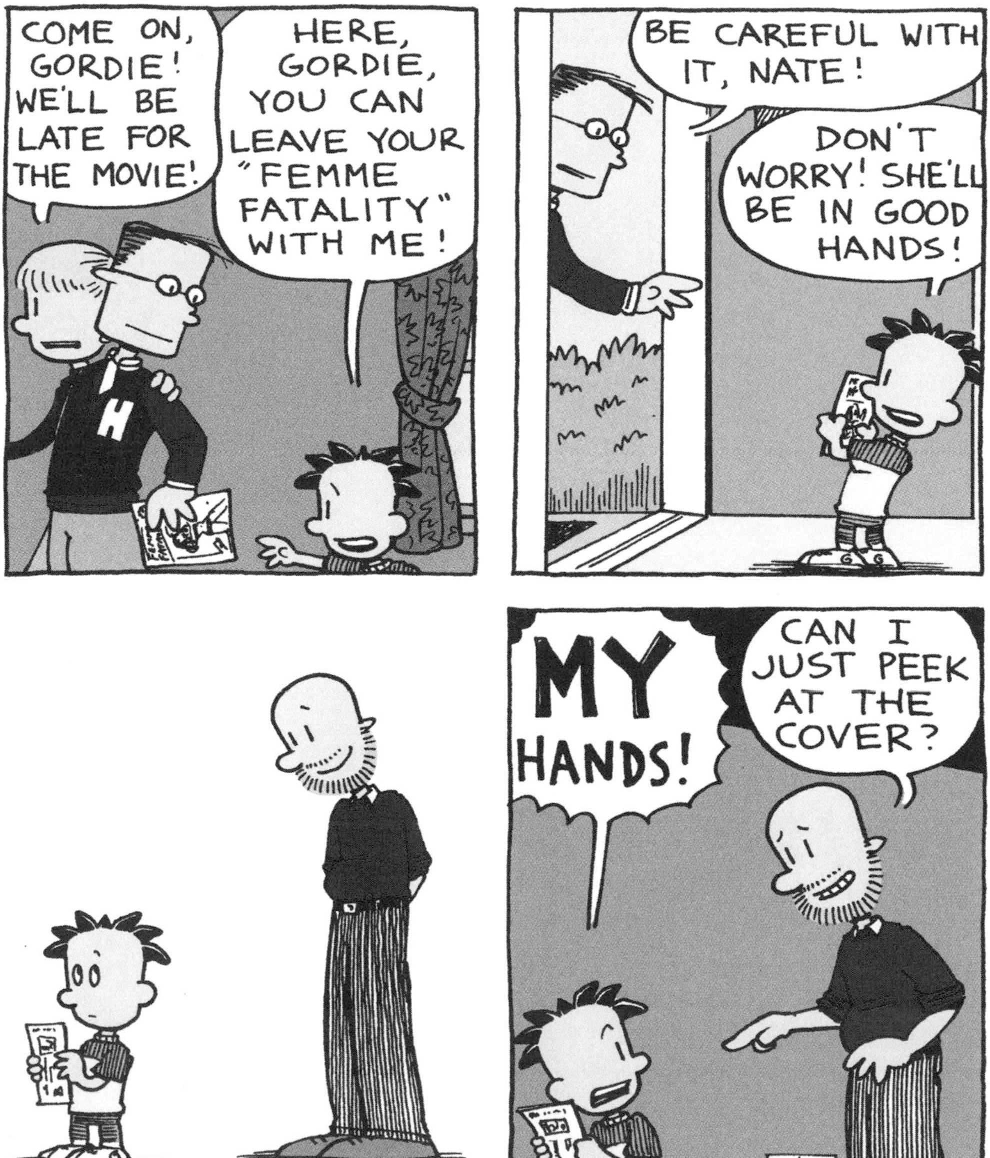
COME ON, GORDIE! WE'LL BE LATE FOR THE MOVIE!
HERE, GORDIE, YOU CAN LEAVE YOUR "FEMME FATALITY" WITH ME!
BE CAREFUL WITH IT, NATE!
DON'T WORRY! SHE'LL BE IN GOOD HANDS!
MY HANDS!
CAN I JUST PEEK AT THE COVER?
Peirce

GORDIE WAS RIGHT! THAT WAS THE BEST ISSUE OF "FEMME FATALITY" **EVER**!

YOU'RE DONE WITH IT? **YES!**

MY TURN! LEMME SEE, LEMME SEE!

WHOA, **WHOA**! I'M ONLY DONE **READ**-ING IT!

GAZING LONGINGLY AT THE MAGNIFICENT ART-WORK UNTIL EVERY IMAGE IS SEARED INTO MY BRAIN WILL TAKE MORE **TIME**!

HOW MUCH MORE TIME?

DAYS. PERHAPS WEEKS.

ROWR!

Peirce

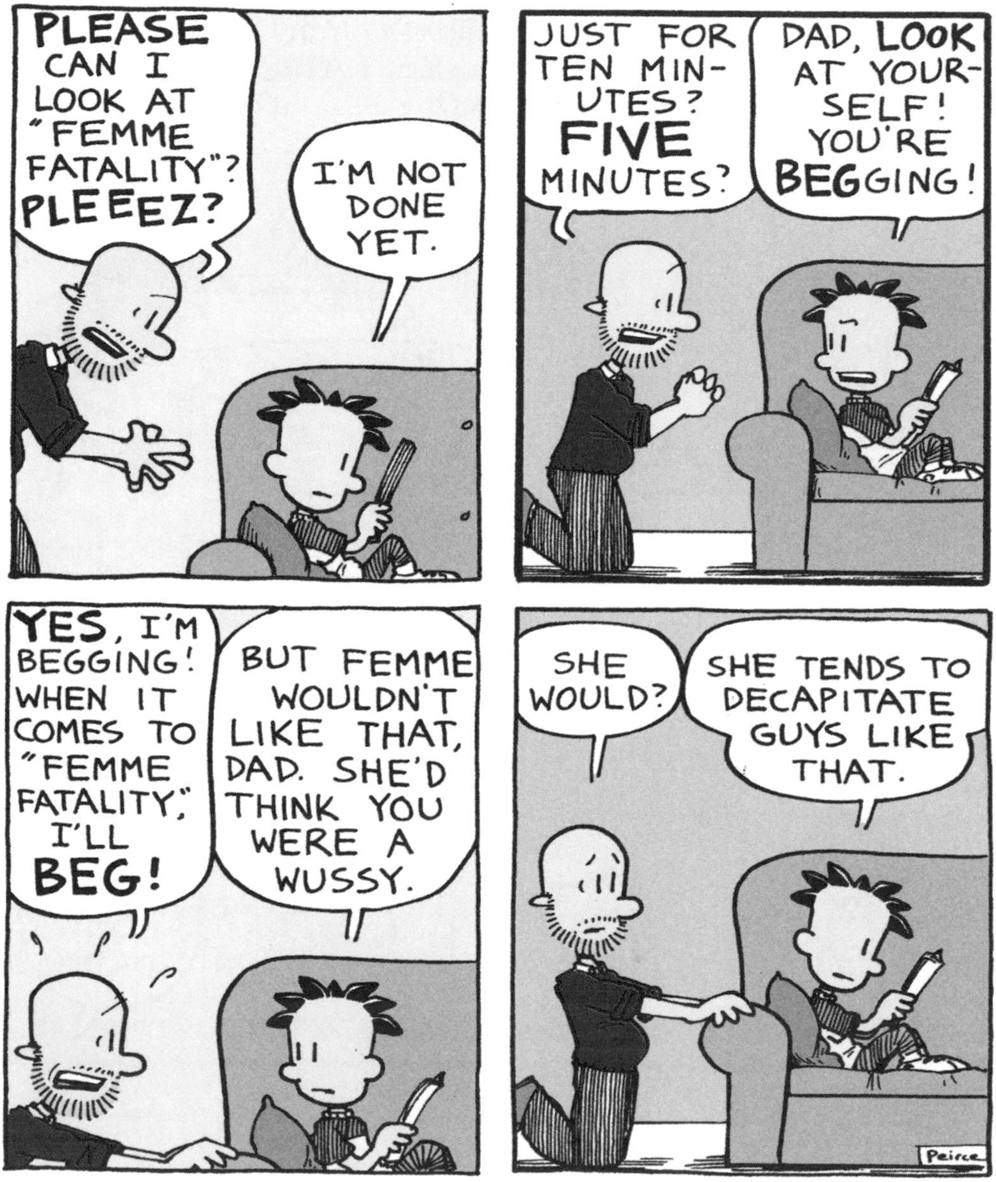
PLEASE CAN I LOOK AT "FEMME FATALITY"? PLEEEZ?
I'M NOT DONE YET.
JUST FOR TEN MIN-UTES? FIVE MINUTES?
DAD, LOOK AT YOUR-SELF! YOU'RE BEGGING!
YES, I'M BEGGING! WHEN IT COMES TO "FEMME FATALITY," I'LL BEG!
BUT FEMME WOULDN'T LIKE THAT, DAD. SHE'D THINK YOU WERE A WUSSY.
SHE WOULD?
SHE TENDS TO DECAPITATE GUYS LIKE THAT.
Peirce

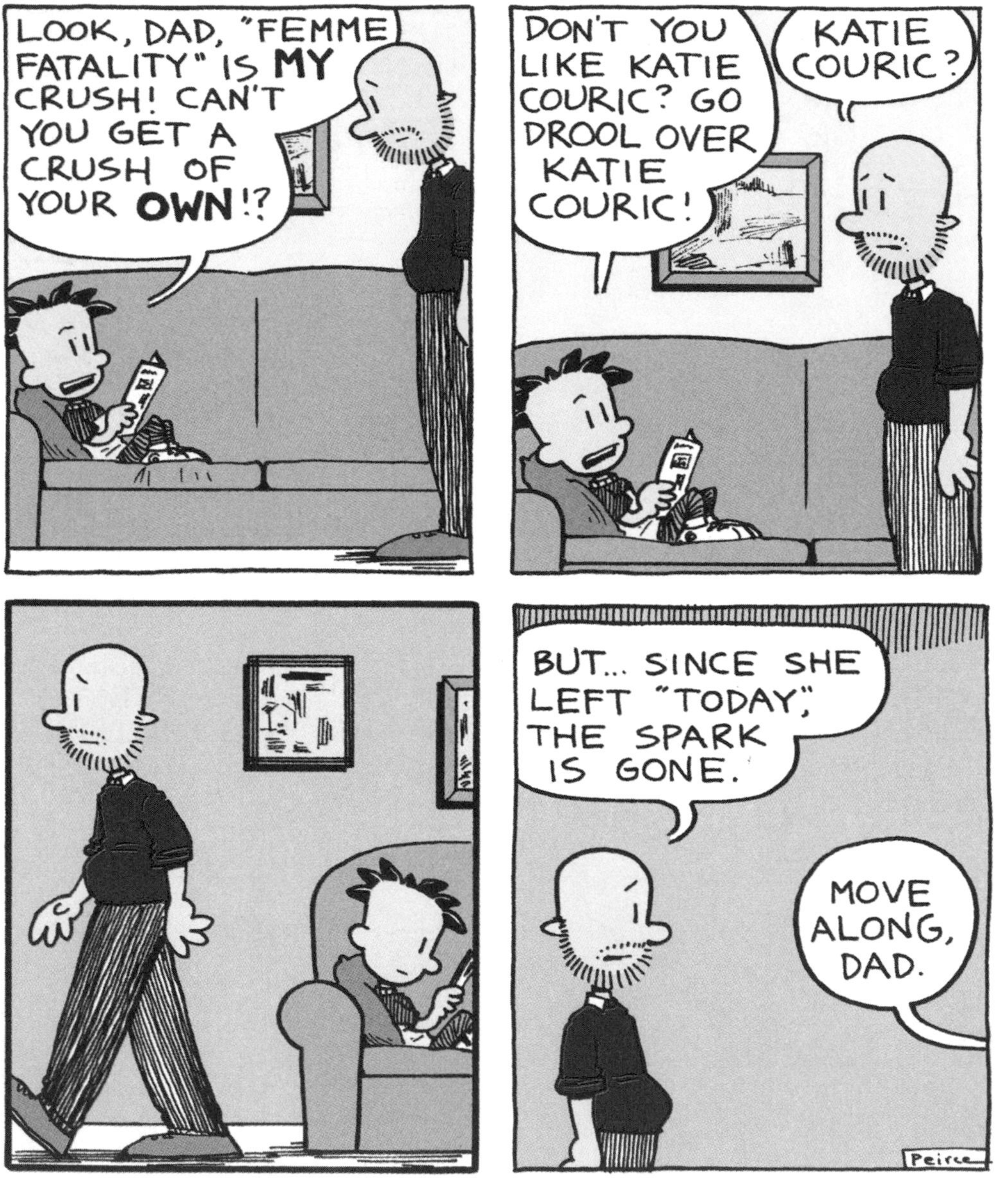
LOOK, DAD, "FEMME FATALITY" IS **MY** CRUSH! CAN'T YOU GET A CRUSH OF YOUR **OWN**!?
DON'T YOU LIKE KATIE COURIC? GO DROOL OVER KATIE COURIC!
KATIE COURIC?
BUT... SINCE SHE LEFT "TODAY," THE SPARK IS GONE.
MOVE ALONG, DAD.
Peirce

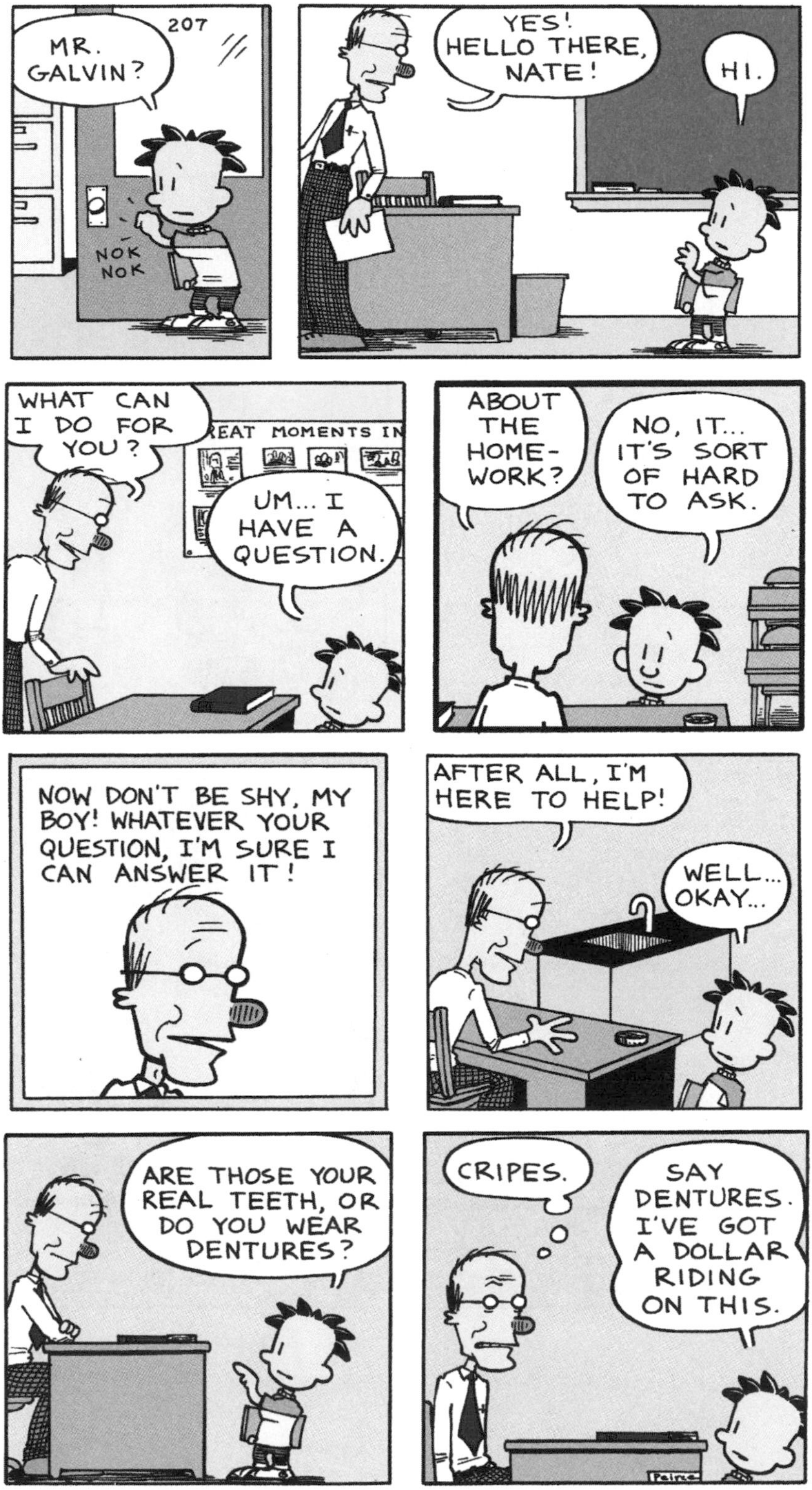
207
MR. GALVIN?
NOK NOK
YES! HELLO THERE, NATE!
HI.
WHAT CAN I DO FOR YOU?
REAT MOMENTS IN
UM... I HAVE A QUESTION.
ABOUT THE HOME-WORK?
NO, IT... IT'S SORT OF HARD TO ASK.
NOW DON'T BE SHY, MY BOY! WHATEVER YOUR QUESTION, I'M SURE I CAN ANSWER IT!
AFTER ALL, I'M HERE TO HELP!
WELL... OKAY...
ARE THOSE YOUR REAL TEETH, OR DO YOU WEAR DENTURES?
CRIPES.
SAY DENTURES. I'VE GOT A DOLLAR RIDING ON THIS.

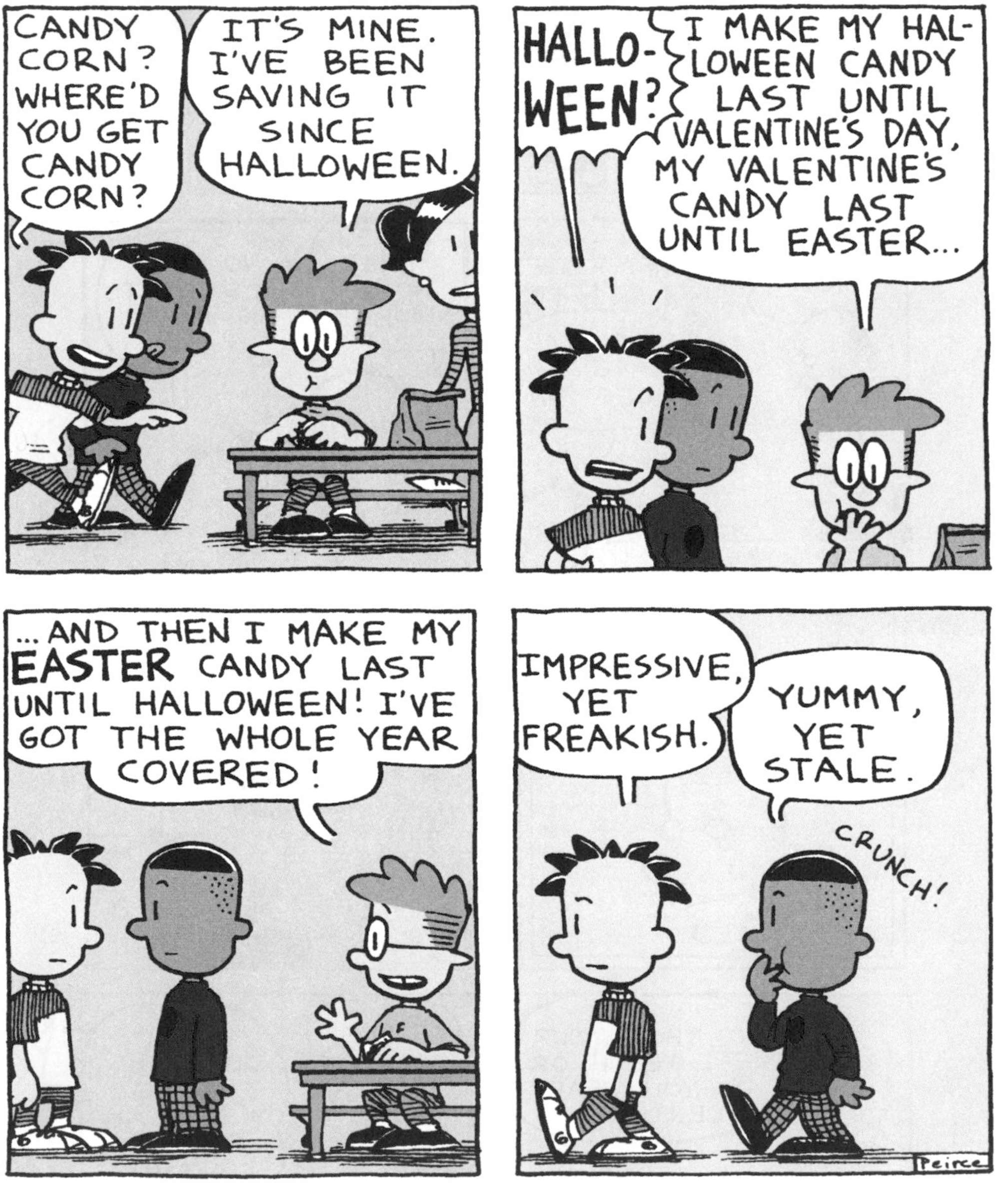
CANDY CORN? WHERE'D YOU GET CANDY CORN?
IT'S MINE. I'VE BEEN SAVING IT SINCE HALLOWEEN.
HALLO-WEEN?
I MAKE MY HALLOWEEN CANDY LAST UNTIL VALENTINE'S DAY, MY VALENTINE'S CANDY LAST UNTIL EASTER...
...AND THEN I MAKE MY EASTER CANDY LAST UNTIL HALLOWEEN! I'VE GOT THE WHOLE YEAR COVERED!
IMPRESSIVE, YET FREAKISH.
YUMMY, YET STALE.
CRUNCH!
Peirce

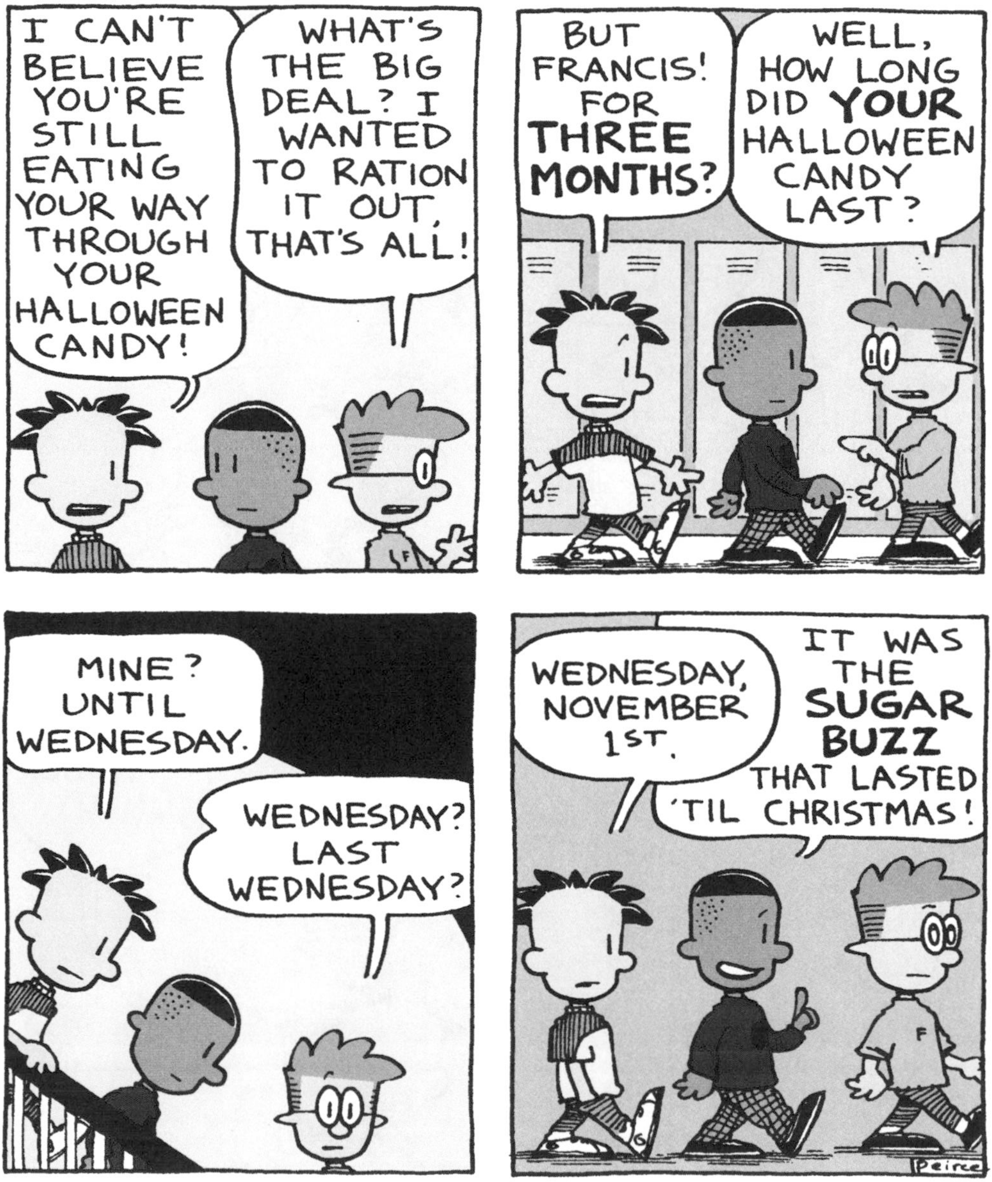
I CAN'T BELIEVE YOU'RE STILL EATING YOUR WAY THROUGH YOUR HALLOWEEN CANDY!
WHAT'S THE BIG DEAL? I WANTED TO RATION IT OUT, THAT'S ALL!
BUT FRANCIS! FOR THREE MONTHS?
WELL, HOW LONG DID YOUR HALLOWEEN CANDY LAST?
MINE? UNTIL WEDNESDAY.
WEDNESDAY? LAST WEDNESDAY?
WEDNESDAY, NOVEMBER 1ST.
IT WAS THE SUGAR BUZZ THAT LASTED 'TIL CHRISTMAS!
Peirce

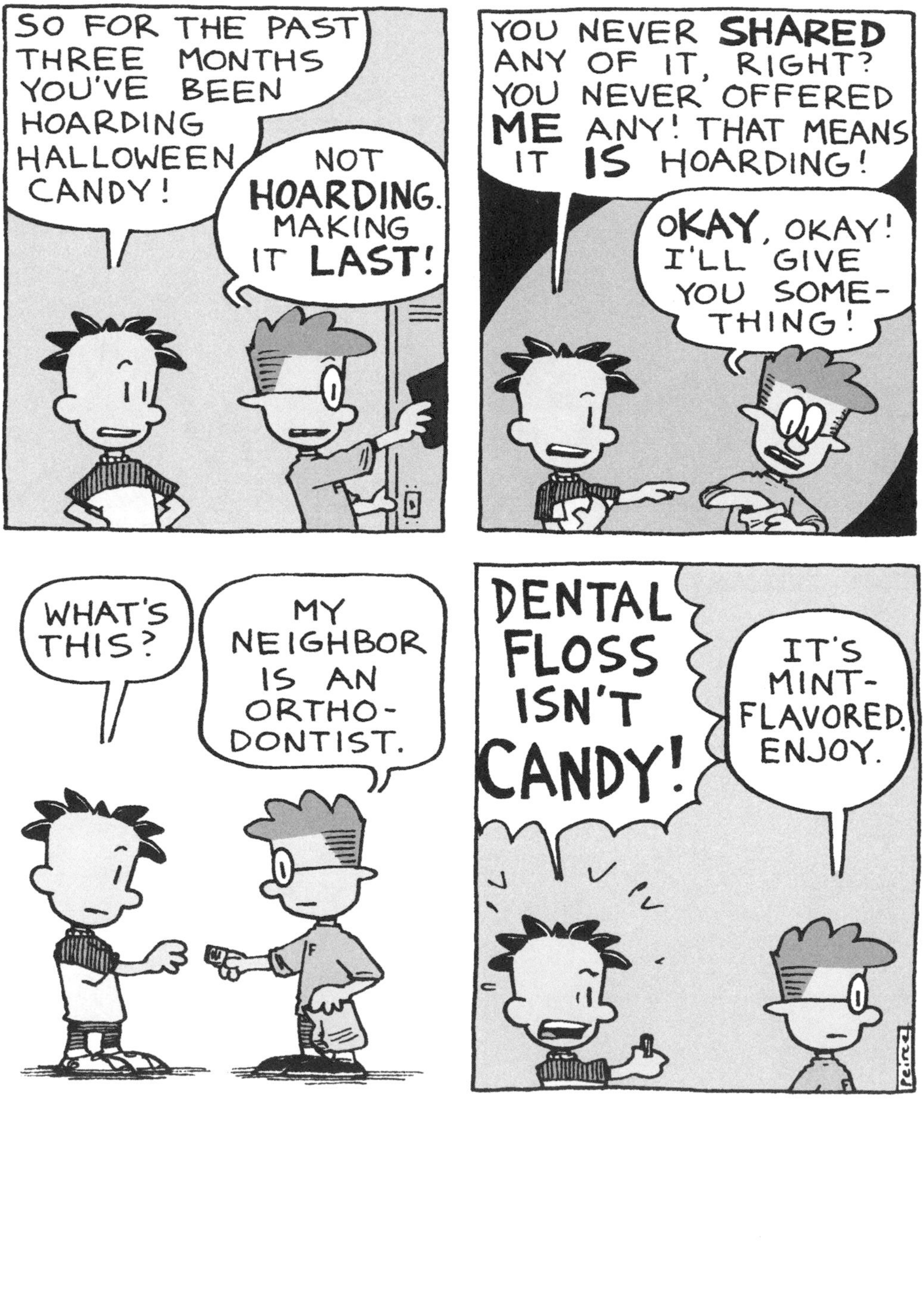
SO FOR THE PAST THREE MONTHS YOU'VE BEEN HOARDING HALLOWEEN CANDY!
NOT HOARDING. MAKING IT LAST!
YOU NEVER SHARED ANY OF IT, RIGHT? YOU NEVER OFFERED ME ANY! THAT MEANS IT IS HOARDING!
OKAY, OKAY! I'LL GIVE YOU SOME-THING!
WHAT'S THIS?
MY NEIGHBOR IS AN ORTHO-DONTIST.
DENTAL FLOSS ISN'T CANDY!
IT'S MINT-FLAVORED. ENJOY.
peirce

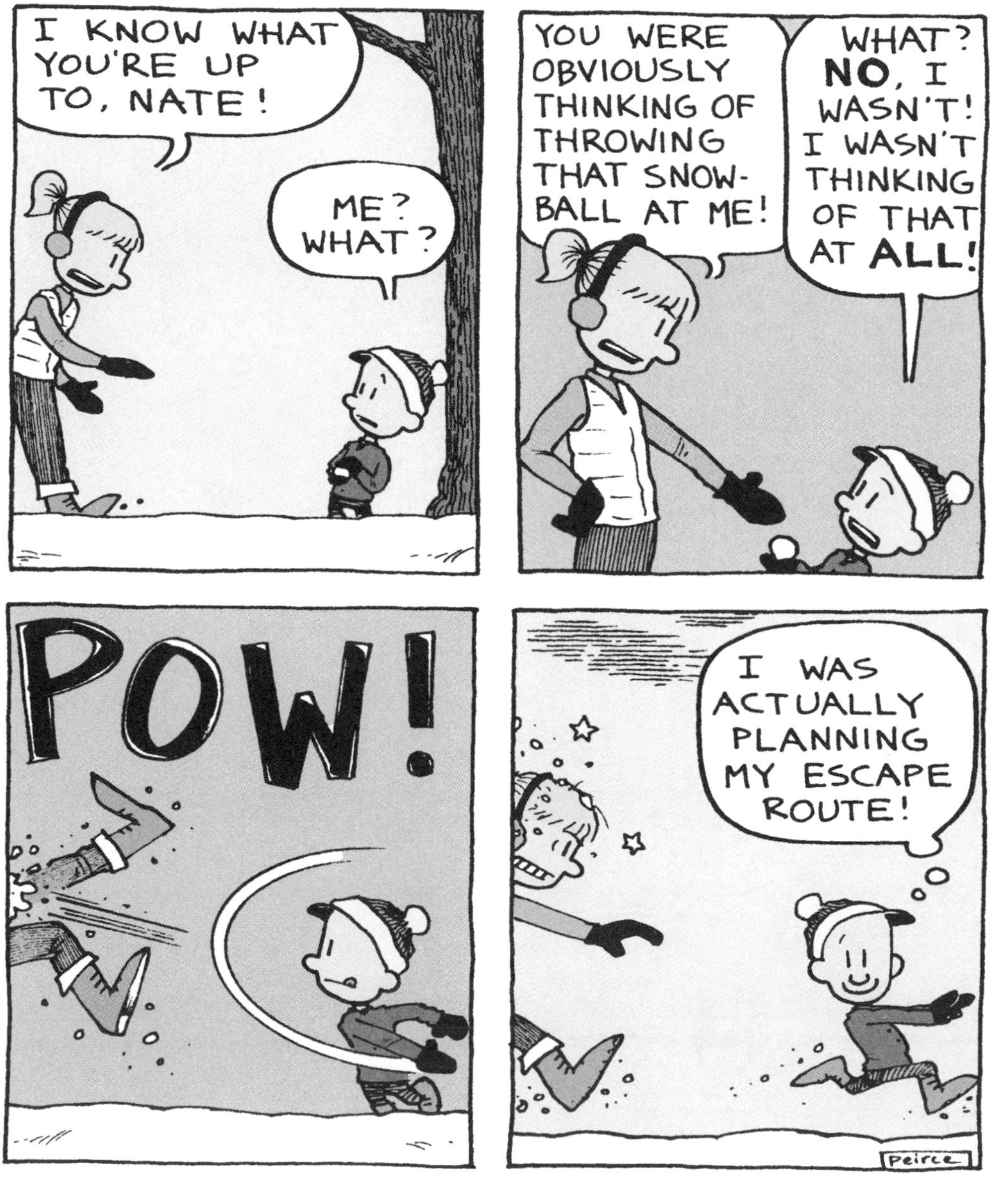
I KNOW WHAT YOU'RE UP TO, NATE!
ME? WHAT?
YOU WERE OBVIOUSLY THINKING OF THROWING THAT SNOW-BALL AT ME!
WHAT? **NO**, I WASN'T! I WASN'T THINKING OF THAT AT **ALL**!
POW!
I WAS ACTUALLY PLANNING MY ESCAPE ROUTE!
Peirce

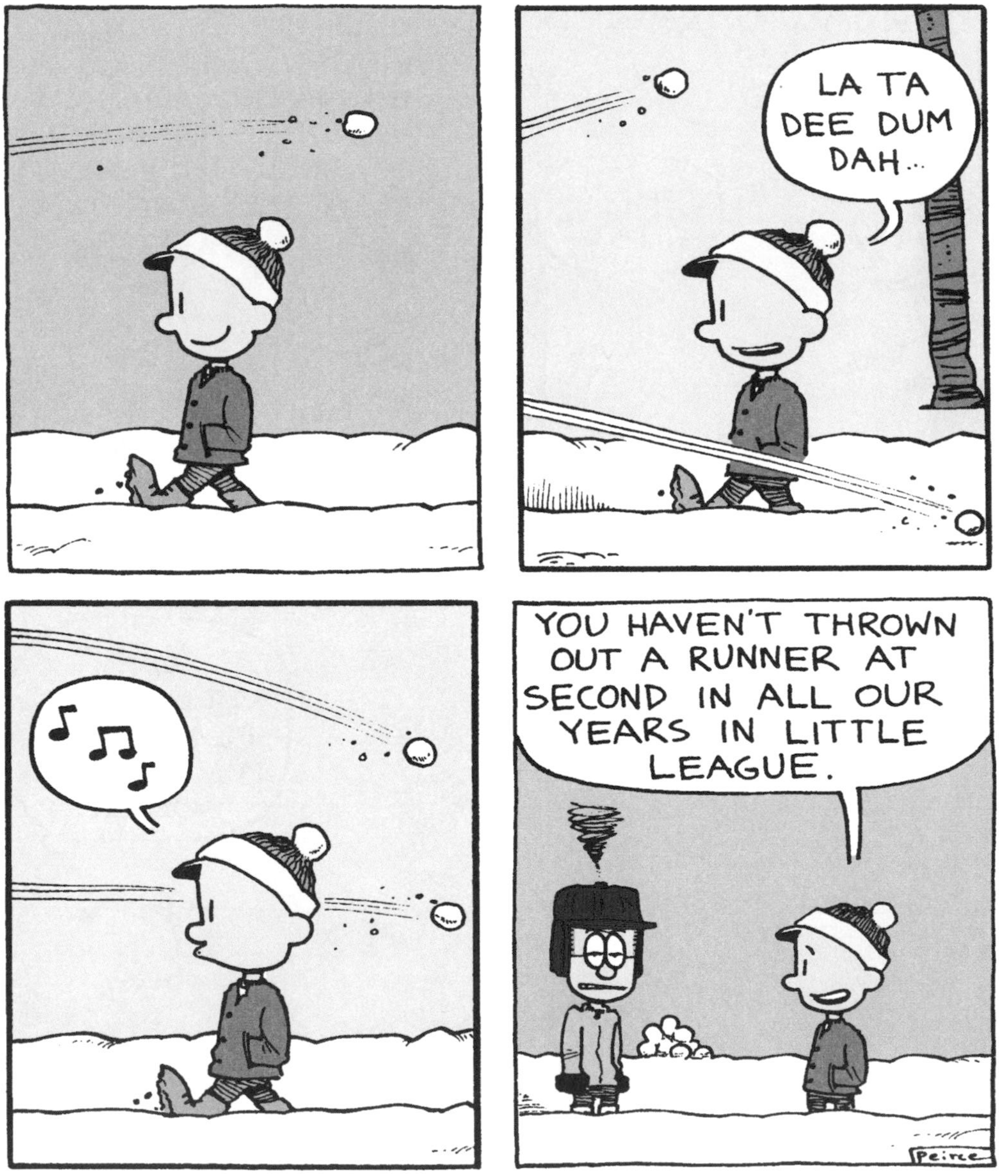
LA TA DEE DUM DAH...
YOU HAVEN'T THROWN OUT A RUNNER AT SECOND IN ALL OUR YEARS IN LITTLE LEAGUE.
Peirce

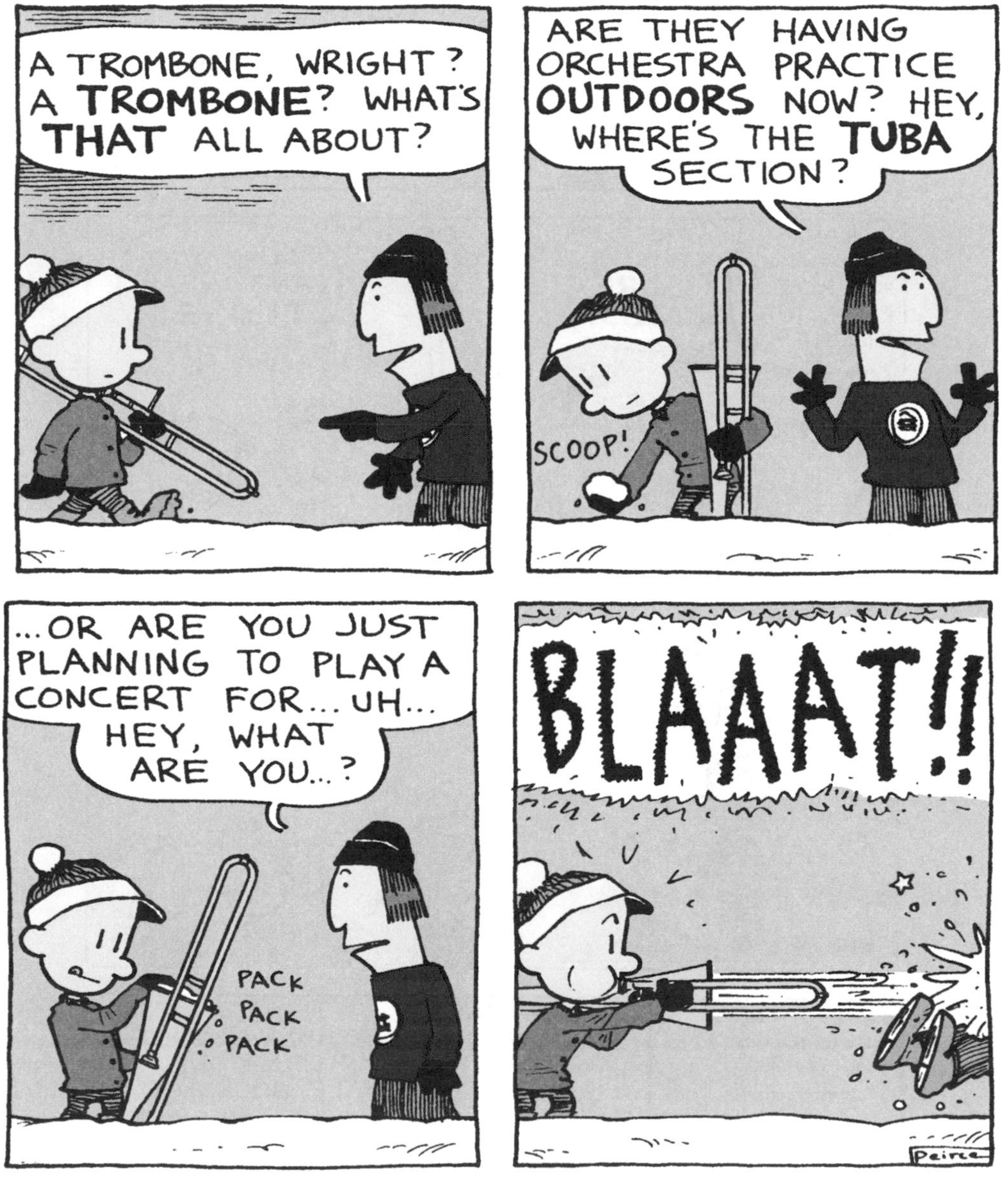

A TROMBONE, WRIGHT? A TROMBONE? WHAT'S THAT ALL ABOUT?
ARE THEY HAVING ORCHESTRA PRACTICE OUTDOORS NOW? HEY, WHERE'S THE TUBA SECTION?
SCOOP!
...OR ARE YOU JUST PLANNING TO PLAY A CONCERT FOR... UH... HEY, WHAT ARE YOU...?
PACK
PACK
PACK
BLAAAT!!
Peirce

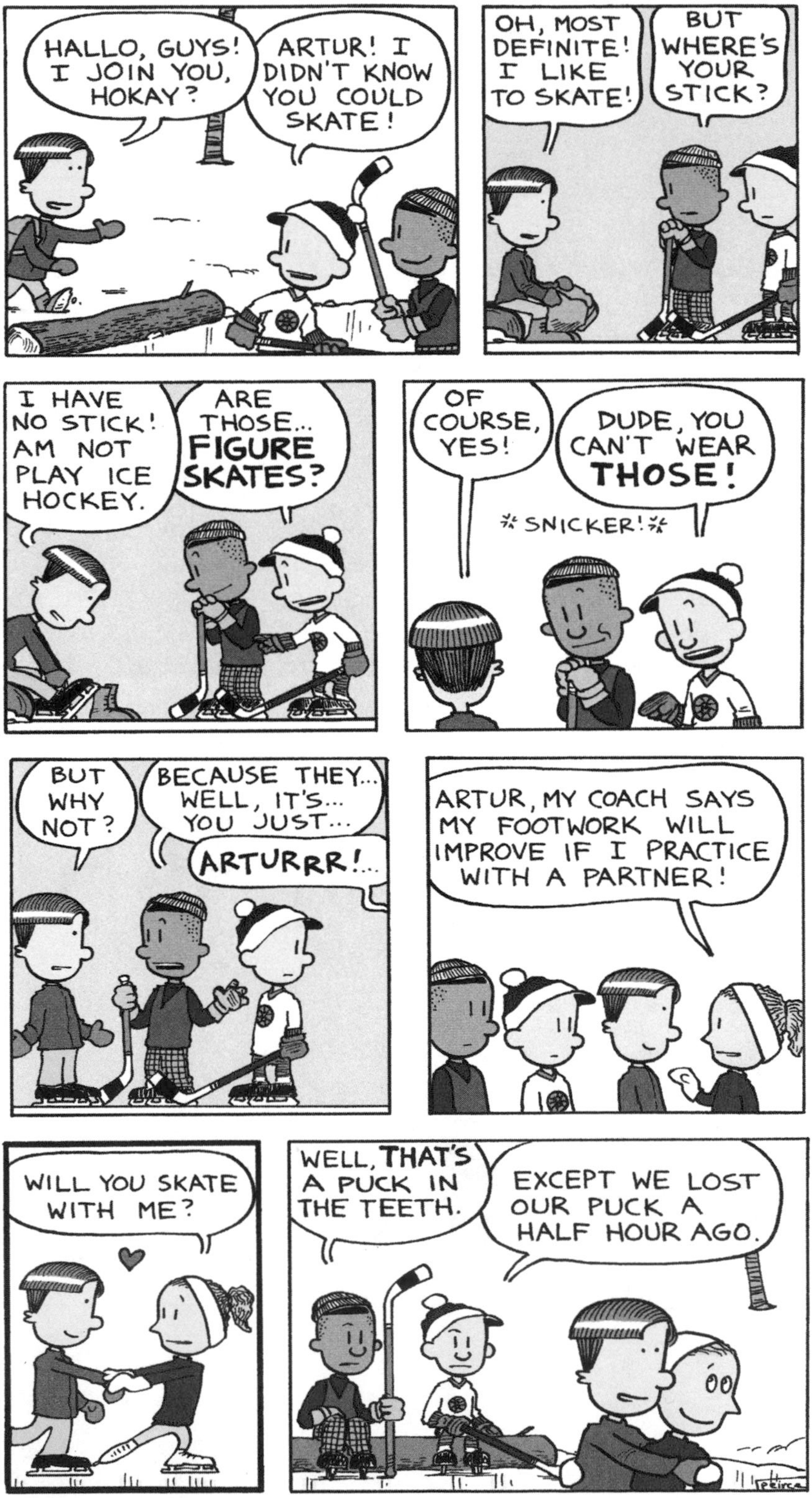

HALLO, GUYS! I JOIN YOU, HOKAY?
ARTUR! I DIDN'T KNOW YOU COULD SKATE!
OH, MOST DEFINITE! I LIKE TO SKATE!
BUT WHERE'S YOUR STICK?
I HAVE NO STICK! AM NOT PLAY ICE HOCKEY.
ARE THOSE... FIGURE SKATES?
OF COURSE, YES!
DUDE, YOU CAN'T WEAR THOSE!
SNICKER!
BUT WHY NOT?
BECAUSE THEY... WELL, IT'S... YOU JUST...
ARTURRR!...
ARTUR, MY COACH SAYS MY FOOTWORK WILL IMPROVE IF I PRACTICE WITH A PARTNER!
WILL YOU SKATE WITH ME?
WELL, THAT'S A PUCK IN THE TEETH.
EXCEPT WE LOST OUR PUCK A HALF HOUR AGO.
peirce

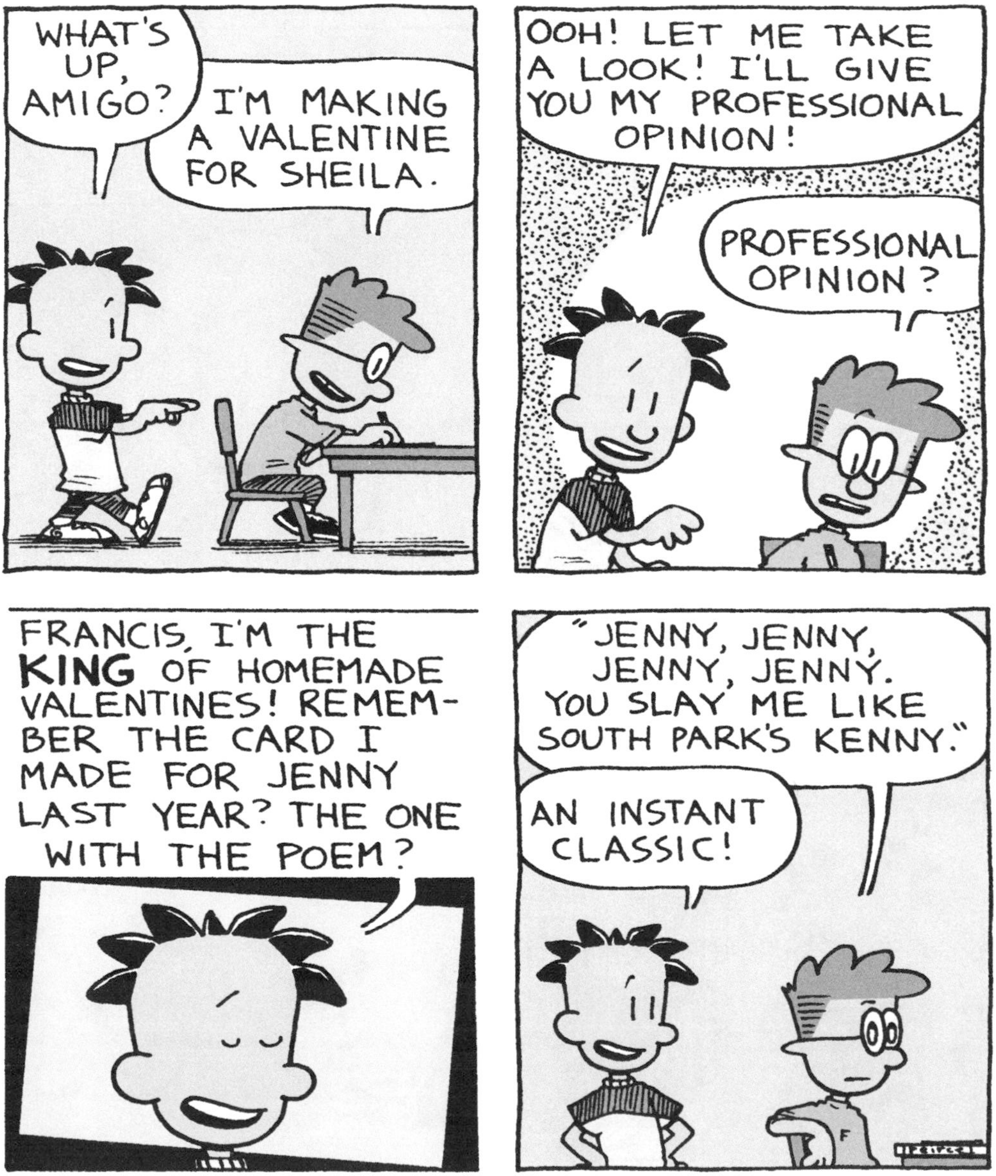

WHAT'S UP, AMIGO?
I'M MAKING A VALENTINE FOR SHEILA.
OOH! LET ME TAKE A LOOK! I'LL GIVE YOU MY PROFESSIONAL OPINION!
PROFESSIONAL OPINION?
FRANCIS, I'M THE **KING** OF HOMEMADE VALENTINES! REMEMBER THE CARD I MADE FOR JENNY LAST YEAR? THE ONE WITH THE POEM?
"JENNY, JENNY, JENNY, JENNY. YOU SLAY ME LIKE SOUTH PARK'S KENNY."
AN INSTANT CLASSIC!

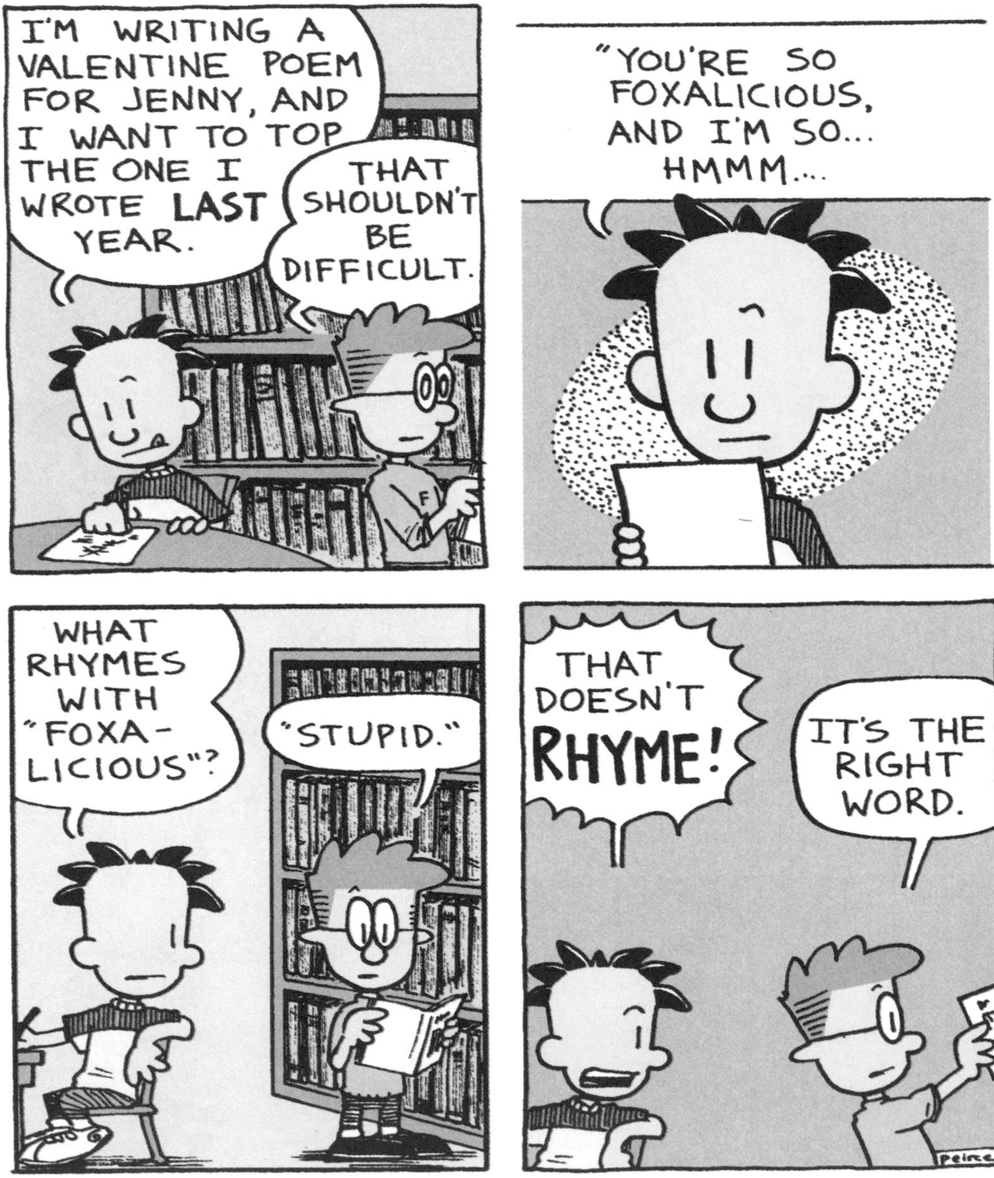
I'M WRITING A VALENTINE POEM FOR JENNY, AND I WANT TO TOP THE ONE I WROTE LAST YEAR.
THAT SHOULDN'T BE DIFFICULT.
"YOU'RE SO FOXALICIOUS, AND I'M SO... HMMM....
WHAT RHYMES WITH "FOXA-LICIOUS"?
"STUPID."
THAT DOESN'T RHYME!
IT'S THE RIGHT WORD.
peirce

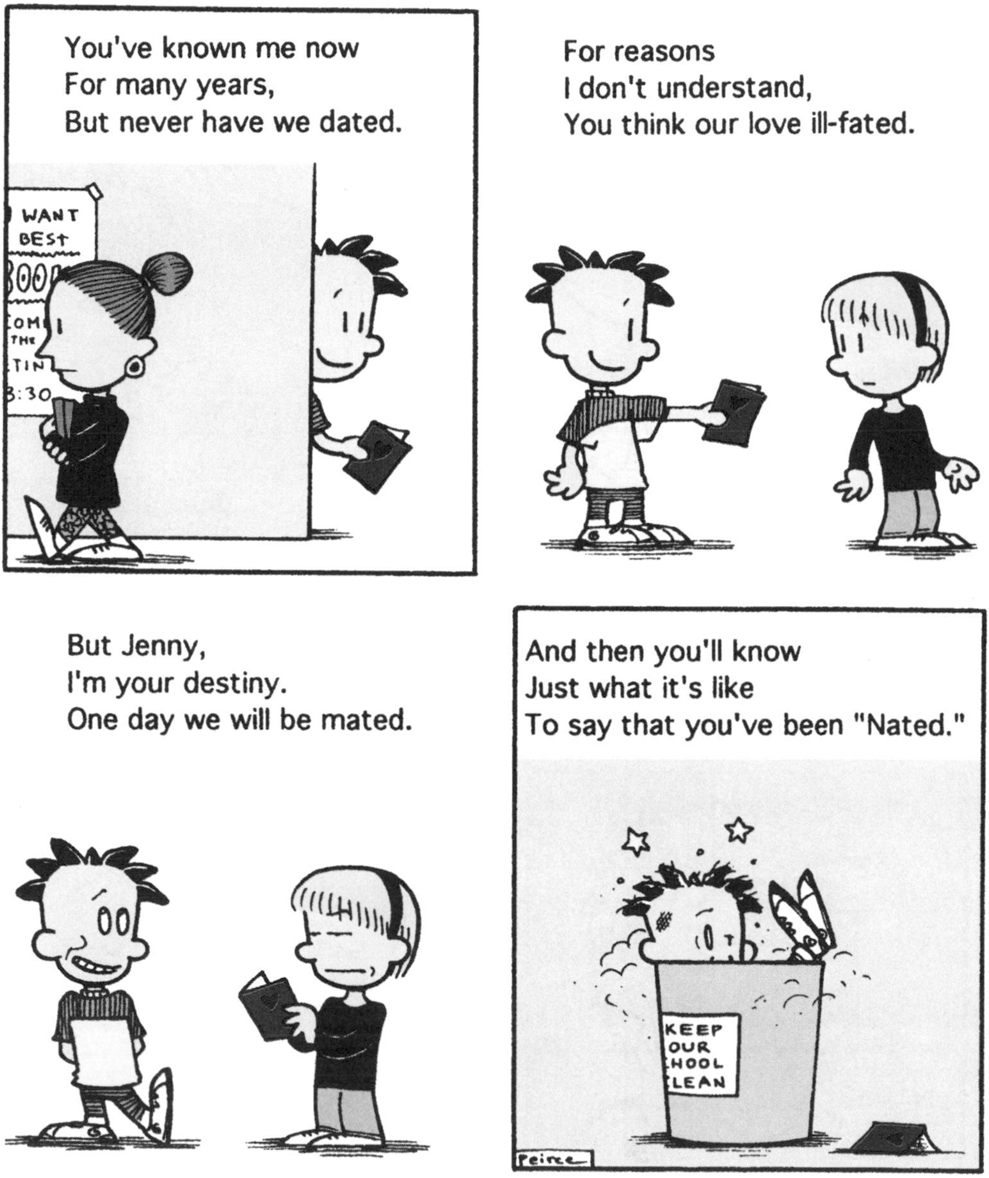
You've known me now
For many years,
But never have we dated.
WANT
BEST
For reasons
I don't understand,
You think our love ill-fated.
But Jenny,
I'm your destiny.
One day we will be mated.
And then you'll know
Just what it's like
To say that you've been "Nated."
KEEP
OUR
Peirce

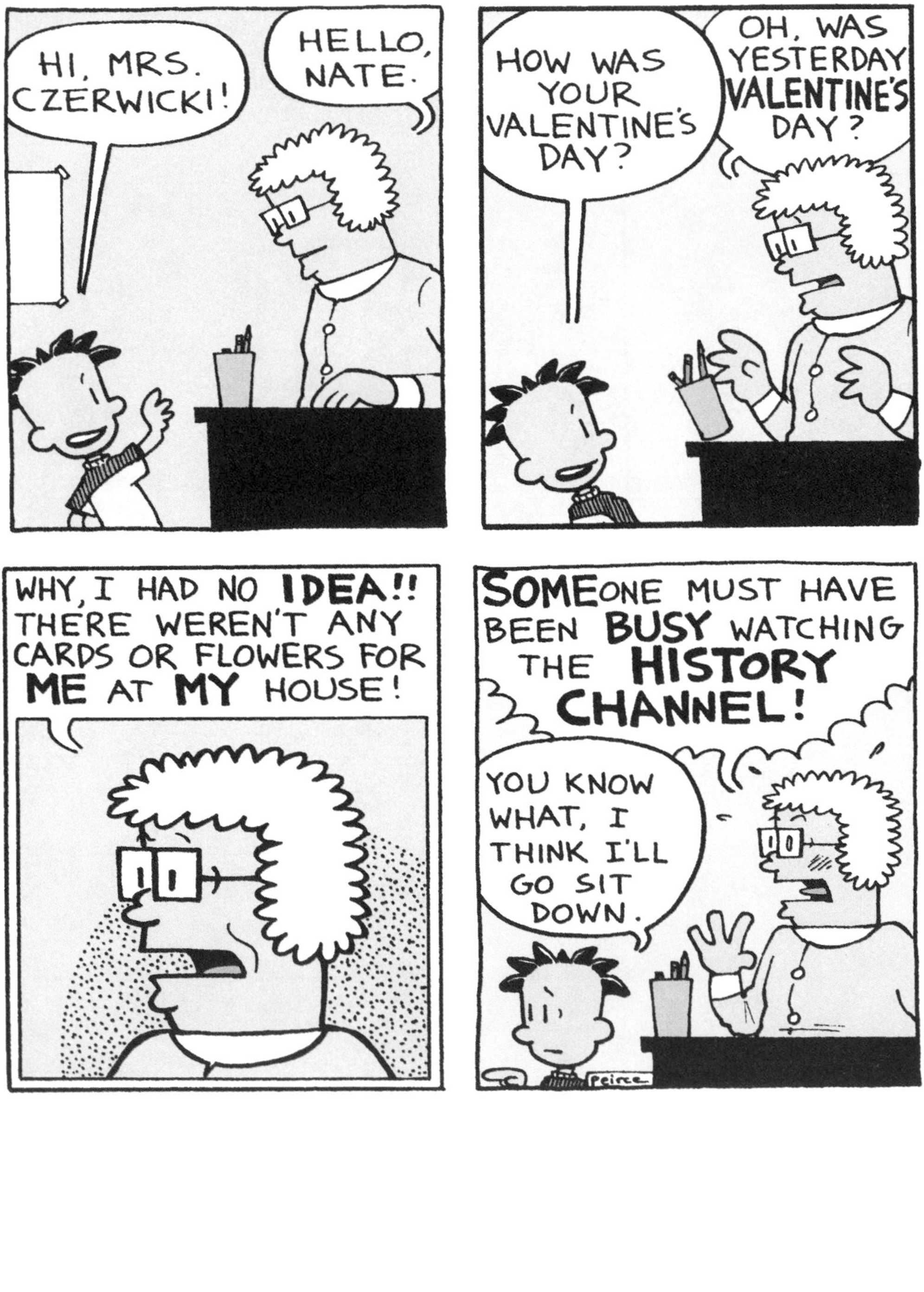
HI, MRS. CZERWICKI!
HELLO, NATE.
HOW WAS YOUR VALENTINE'S DAY?
OH, WAS YESTERDAY VALENTINE'S DAY?
WHY, I HAD NO IDEA!! THERE WEREN'T ANY CARDS OR FLOWERS FOR ME AT MY HOUSE!
SOMEONE MUST HAVE BEEN BUSY WATCHING THE HISTORY CHANNEL!
YOU KNOW WHAT, I THINK I'LL GO SIT DOWN.
Peirce

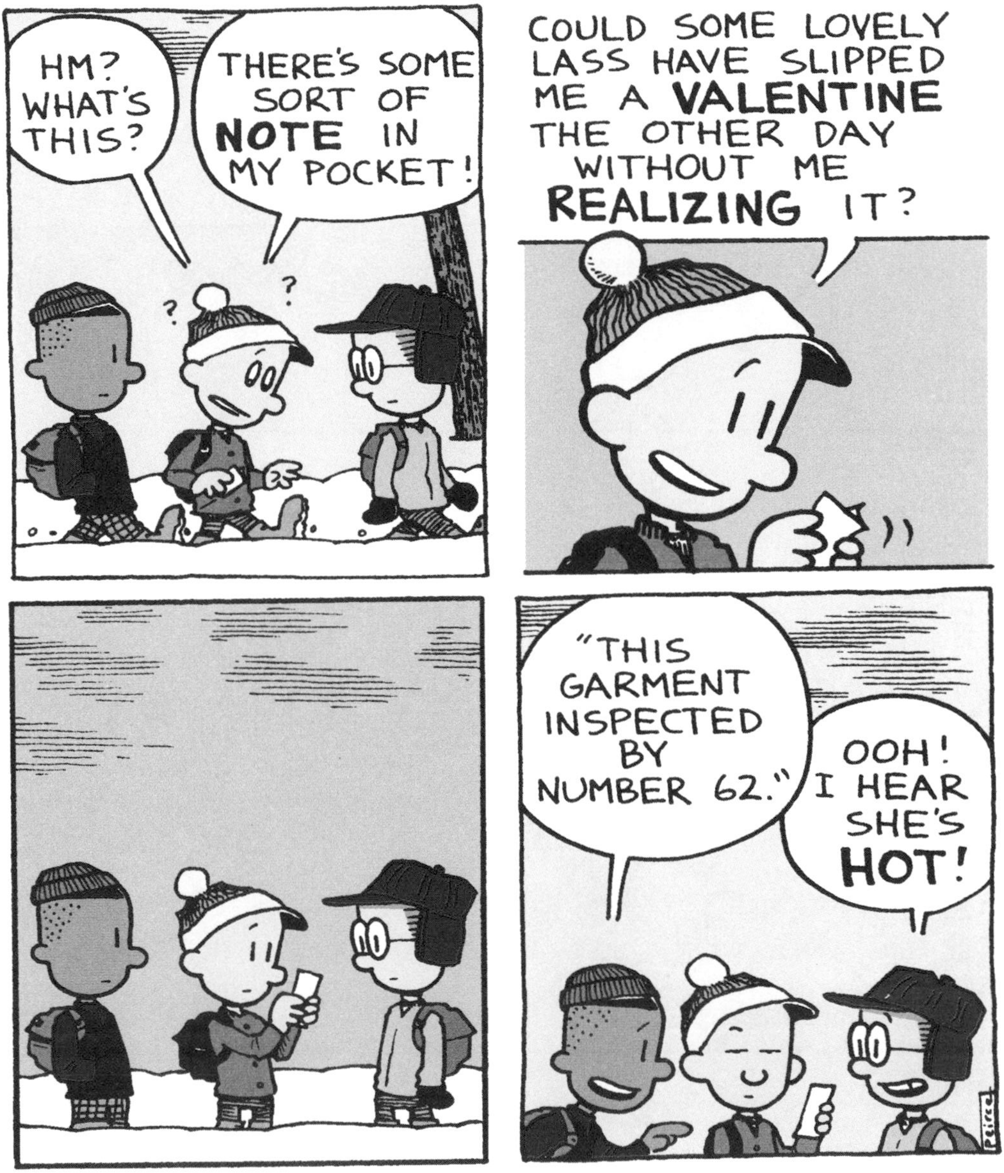
HM? WHAT'S THIS?
THERE'S SOME SORT OF **NOTE** IN MY POCKET!
COULD SOME LOVELY LASS HAVE SLIPPED ME A **VALENTINE** THE OTHER DAY WITHOUT ME **REALIZING** IT?
"THIS GARMENT INSPECTED BY NUMBER 62."
OOH! I HEAR SHE'S **HOT**!
Peirce

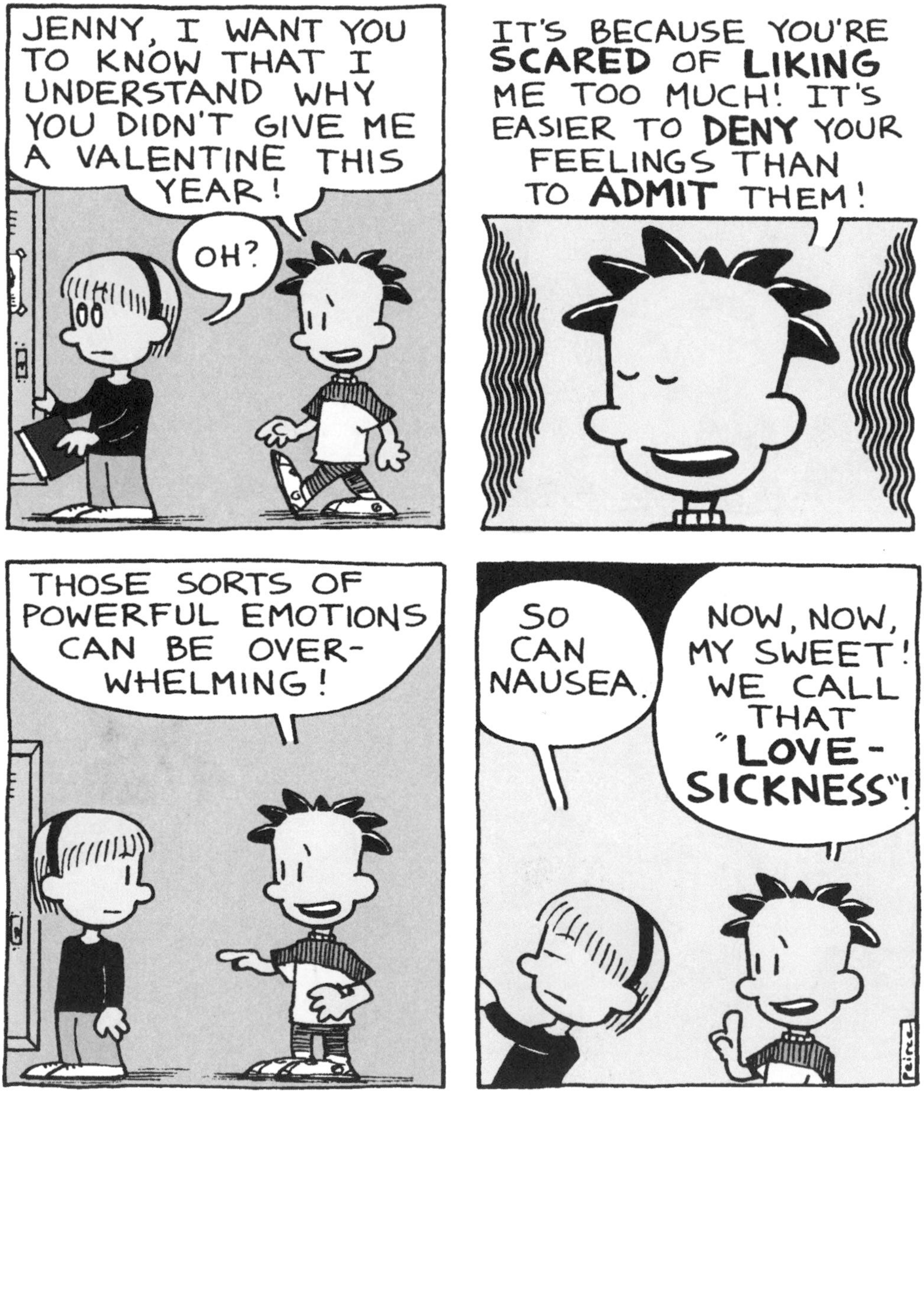
JENNY, I WANT YOU TO KNOW THAT I UNDERSTAND WHY YOU DIDN'T GIVE ME A VALENTINE THIS YEAR!
OH?
IT'S BECAUSE YOU'RE **SCARED** OF **LIKING** ME TOO MUCH! IT'S EASIER TO **DENY** YOUR FEELINGS THAN TO **ADMIT** THEM!
THOSE SORTS OF POWERFUL EMOTIONS CAN BE OVER-WHELMING!
SO CAN NAUSEA.
NOW, NOW, MY SWEET! WE CALL THAT "**LOVE-SICKNESS**"!
Peirce

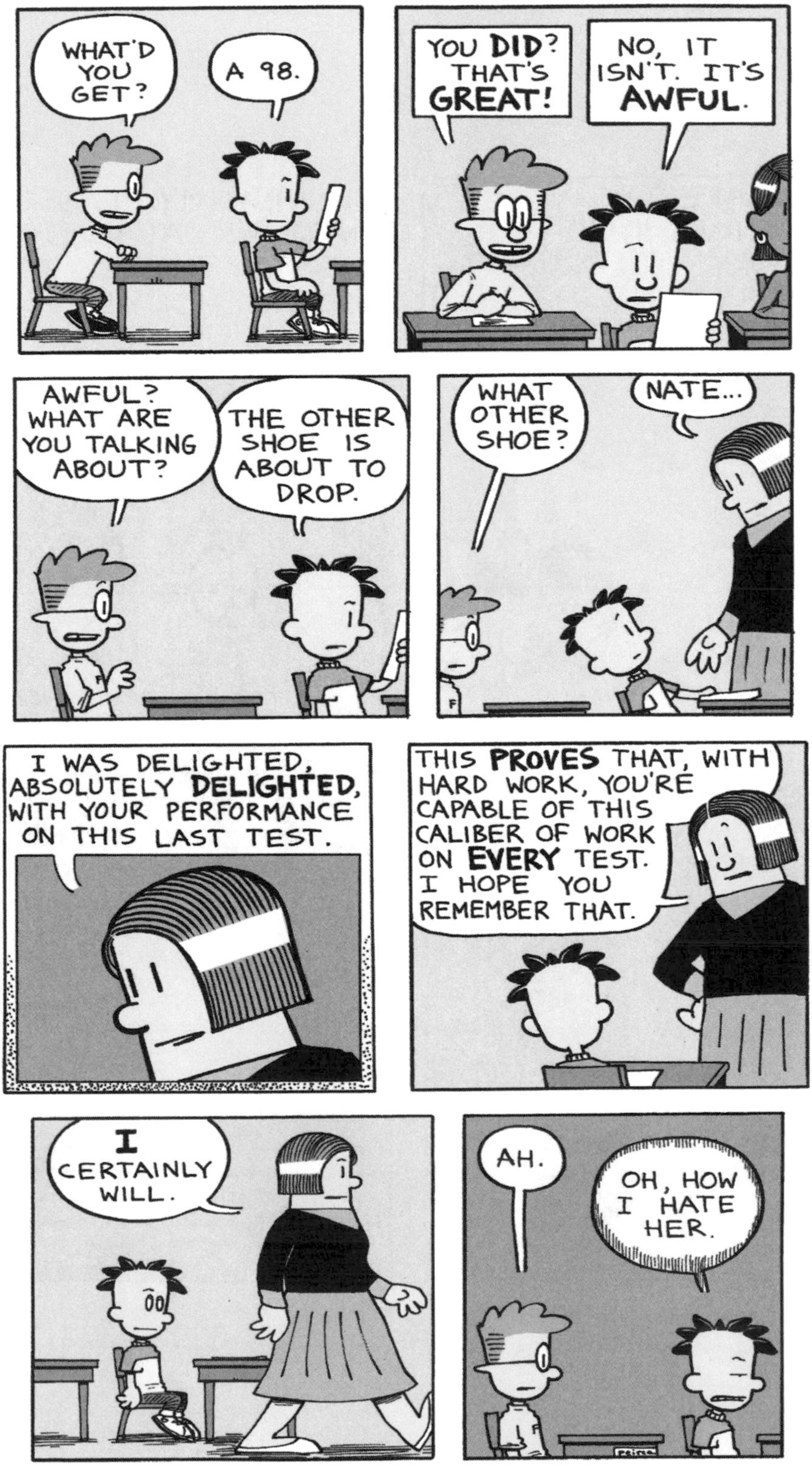
WHAT'D YOU GET?
A 98.
YOU DID? THAT'S GREAT!
NO, IT ISN'T. IT'S AWFUL.
AWFUL? WHAT ARE YOU TALKING ABOUT?
THE OTHER SHOE IS ABOUT TO DROP.
WHAT OTHER SHOE?
NATE...
I WAS DELIGHTED, ABSOLUTELY DELIGHTED, WITH YOUR PERFORMANCE ON THIS LAST TEST.
THIS PROVES THAT, WITH HARD WORK, YOU'RE CAPABLE OF THIS CALIBER OF WORK ON EVERY TEST. I HOPE YOU REMEMBER THAT.
I CERTAINLY WILL.
AH.
OH, HOW I HATE HER.

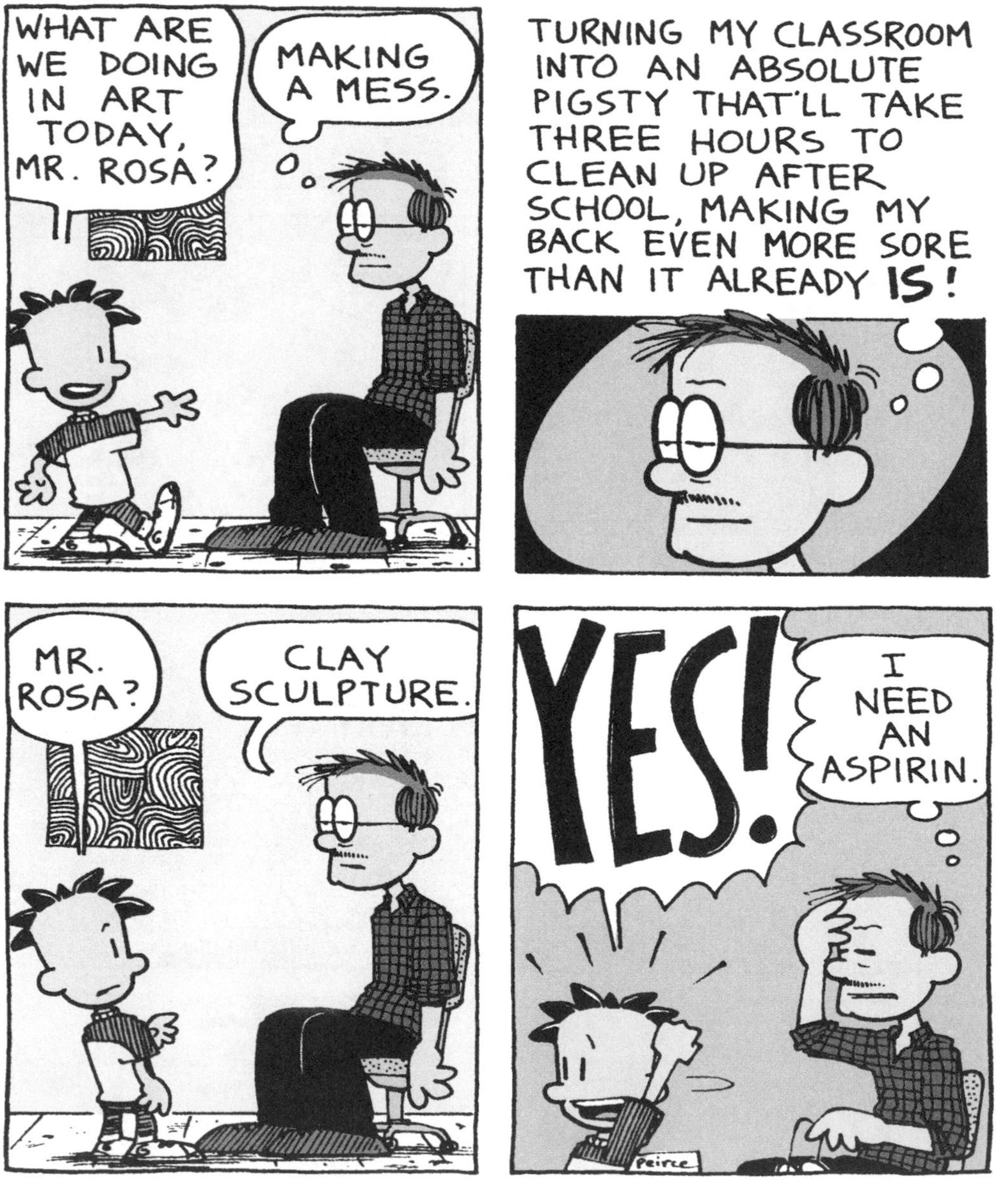
WHAT ARE WE DOING IN ART TODAY, MR. ROSA?
MAKING A MESS.
TURNING MY CLASSROOM INTO AN ABSOLUTE PIGSTY THAT'LL TAKE THREE HOURS TO CLEAN UP AFTER SCHOOL, MAKING MY BACK EVEN MORE SORE THAN IT ALREADY IS!
MR. ROSA?
CLAY SCULPTURE.
YES!
I NEED AN ASPIRIN.
Peirce

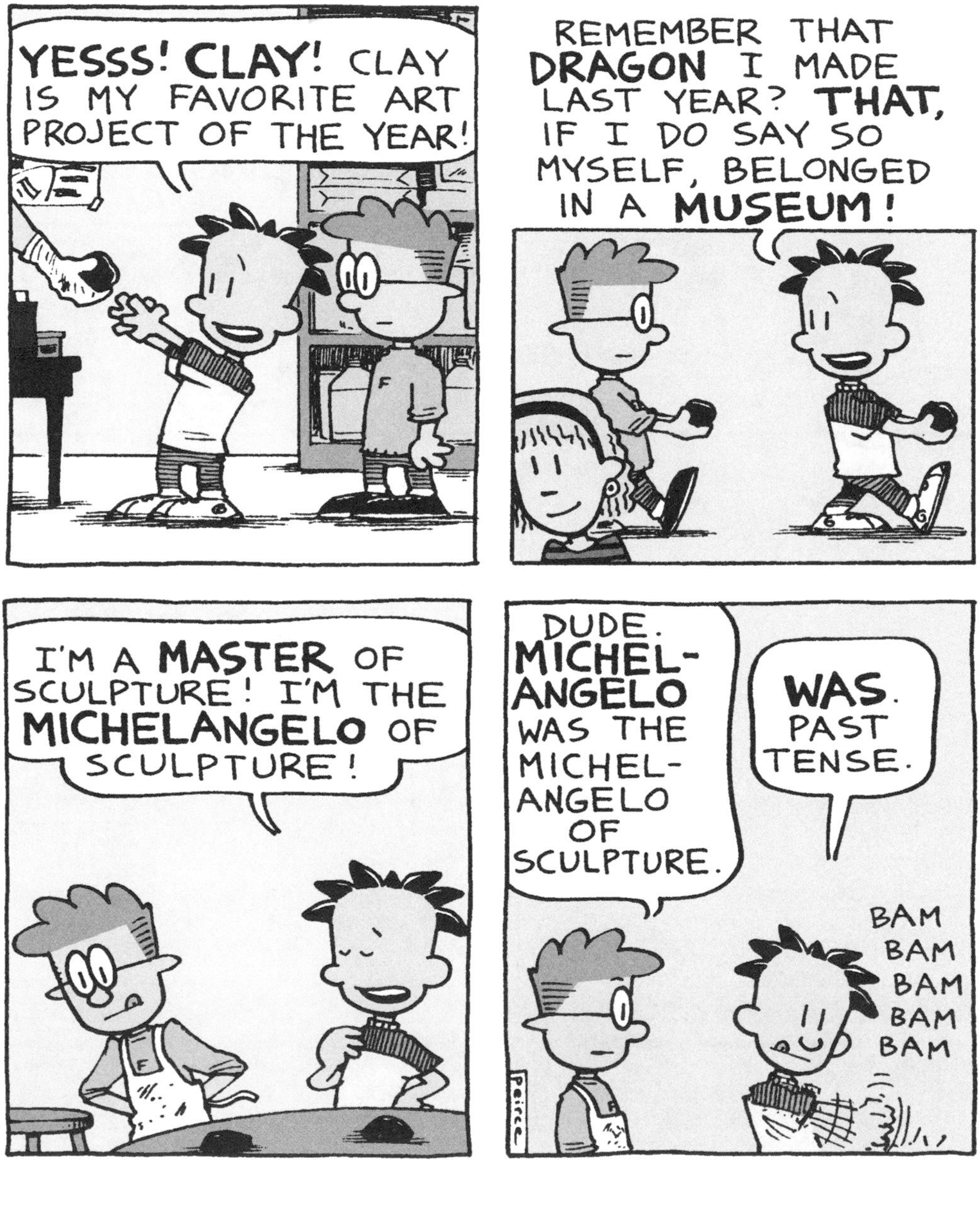
YESSS! CLAY! CLAY IS MY FAVORITE ART PROJECT OF THE YEAR!
REMEMBER THAT DRAGON I MADE LAST YEAR? THAT, IF I DO SAY SO MYSELF, BELONGED IN A MUSEUM!
I'M A MASTER OF SCULPTURE! I'M THE MICHELANGELO OF SCULPTURE!
DUDE. MICHEL-ANGELO WAS THE MICHEL-ANGELO OF SCULPTURE.
WAS. PAST TENSE.
BAM BAM BAM BAM BAM BAM
Peirce

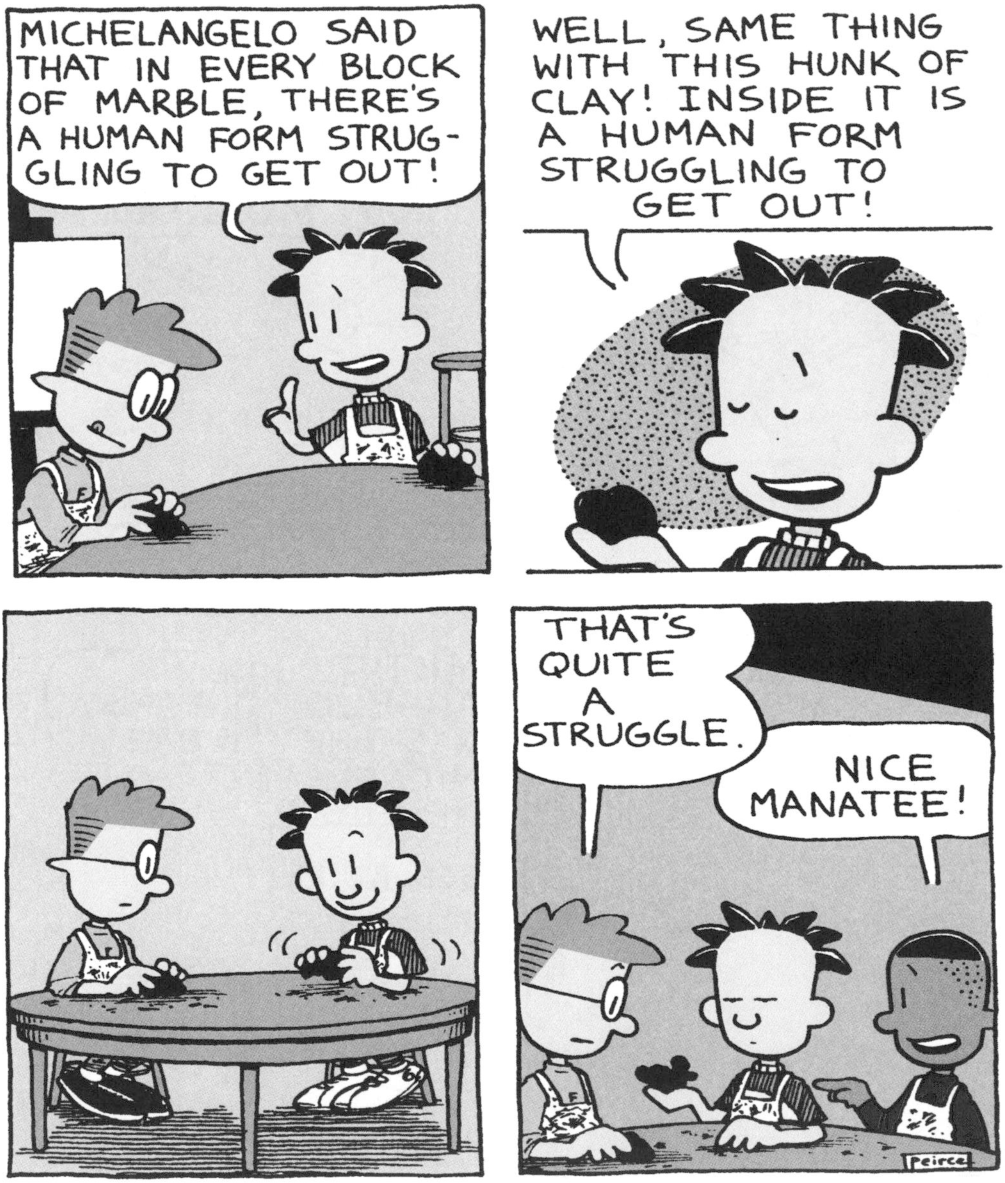
MICHELANGELO SAID THAT IN EVERY BLOCK OF MARBLE, THERE'S A HUMAN FORM STRUG-GLING TO GET OUT!
WELL, SAME THING WITH THIS HUNK OF CLAY! INSIDE IT IS A HUMAN FORM STRUGGLING TO GET OUT!
THAT'S QUITE A STRUGGLE.
NICE MANATEE!
Peirce

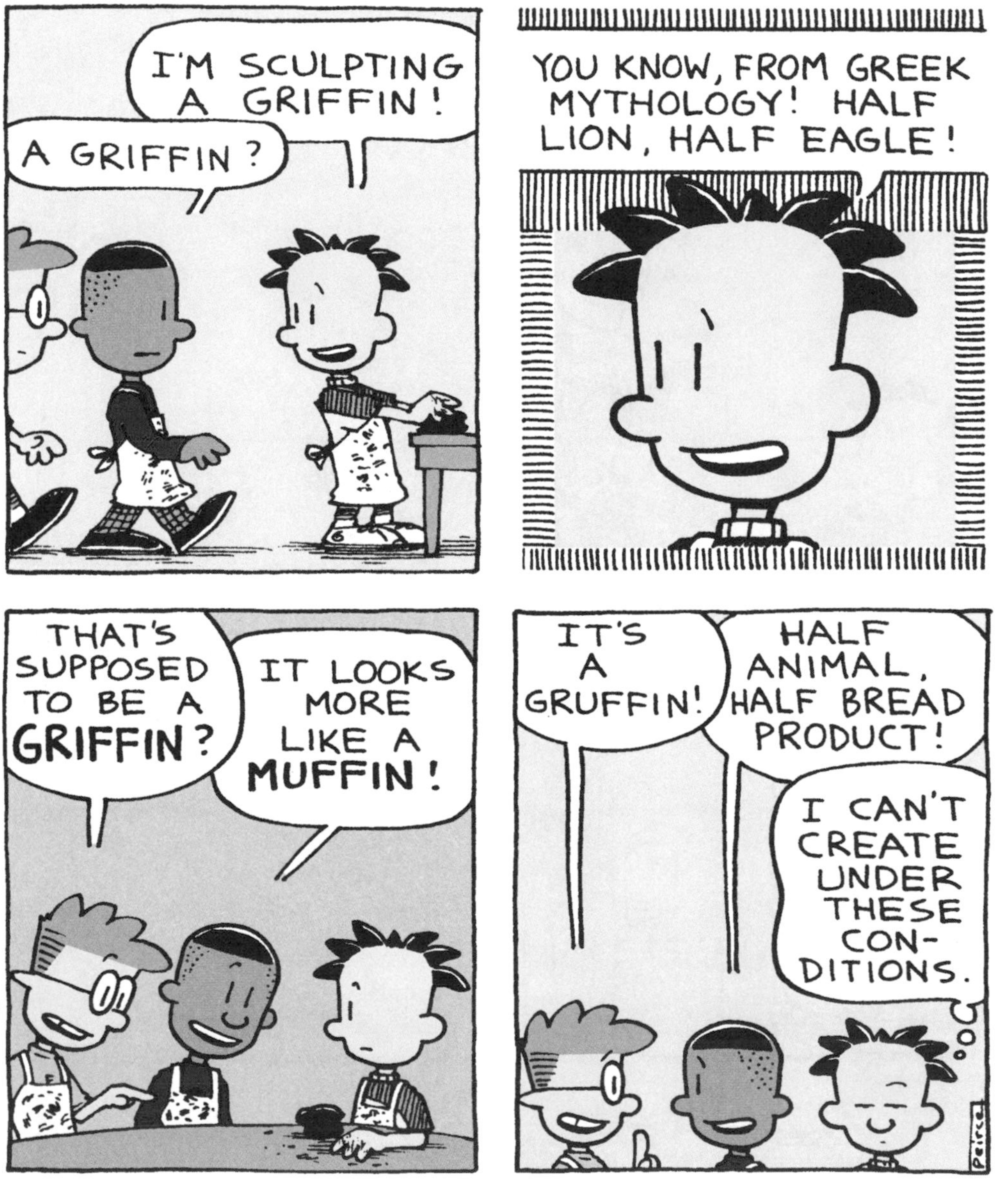
A GRIFFIN?
I'M SCULPTING A GRIFFIN!
YOU KNOW, FROM GREEK MYTHOLOGY! HALF LION, HALF EAGLE!
THAT'S SUPPOSED TO BE A GRIFFIN?
IT LOOKS MORE LIKE A MUFFIN!
IT'S A GRUFFIN!
HALF ANIMAL, HALF BREAD PRODUCT!
I CAN'T CREATE UNDER THESE CON-DITIONS.
Peirce

MR. ROSA, MY CLAY'S GETTING ALL CRUMBLY!
IT'S DRYING OUT. YOU NEED TO KEEP IT MOIST.
HOCCH...
PTOO!
NATE, THERE'S A MARVELOUS INVENTION OVER THERE CALLED A "FAUCET."
I'M NOT THIRSTY.
SMOOSH
SMASH
MASH
Peirce

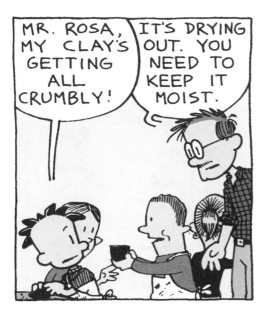

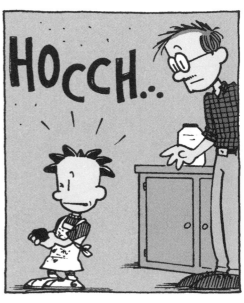

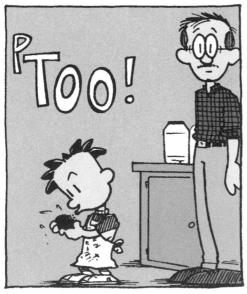

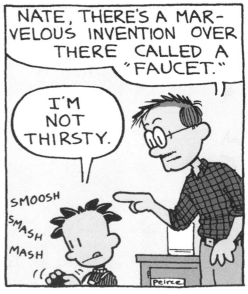

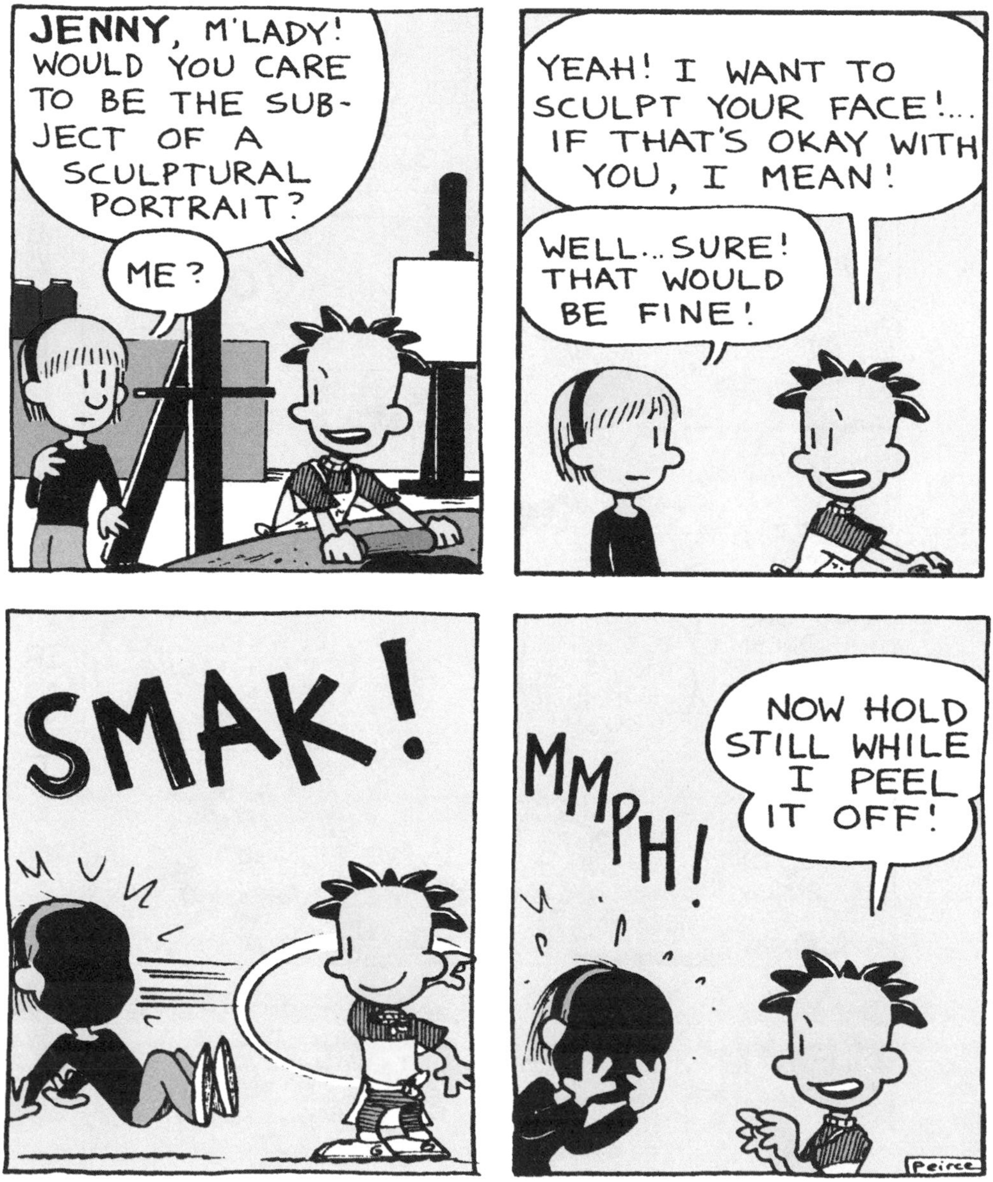
JENNY, M'LADY! WOULD YOU CARE TO BE THE SUBJECT OF A SCULPTURAL PORTRAIT?
ME?
YEAH! I WANT TO SCULPT YOUR FACE!... IF THAT'S OKAY WITH YOU, I MEAN!
WELL...SURE! THAT WOULD BE FINE!
SMAK!
MMPH!
NOW HOLD STILL WHILE I PEEL IT OFF!
Peirce

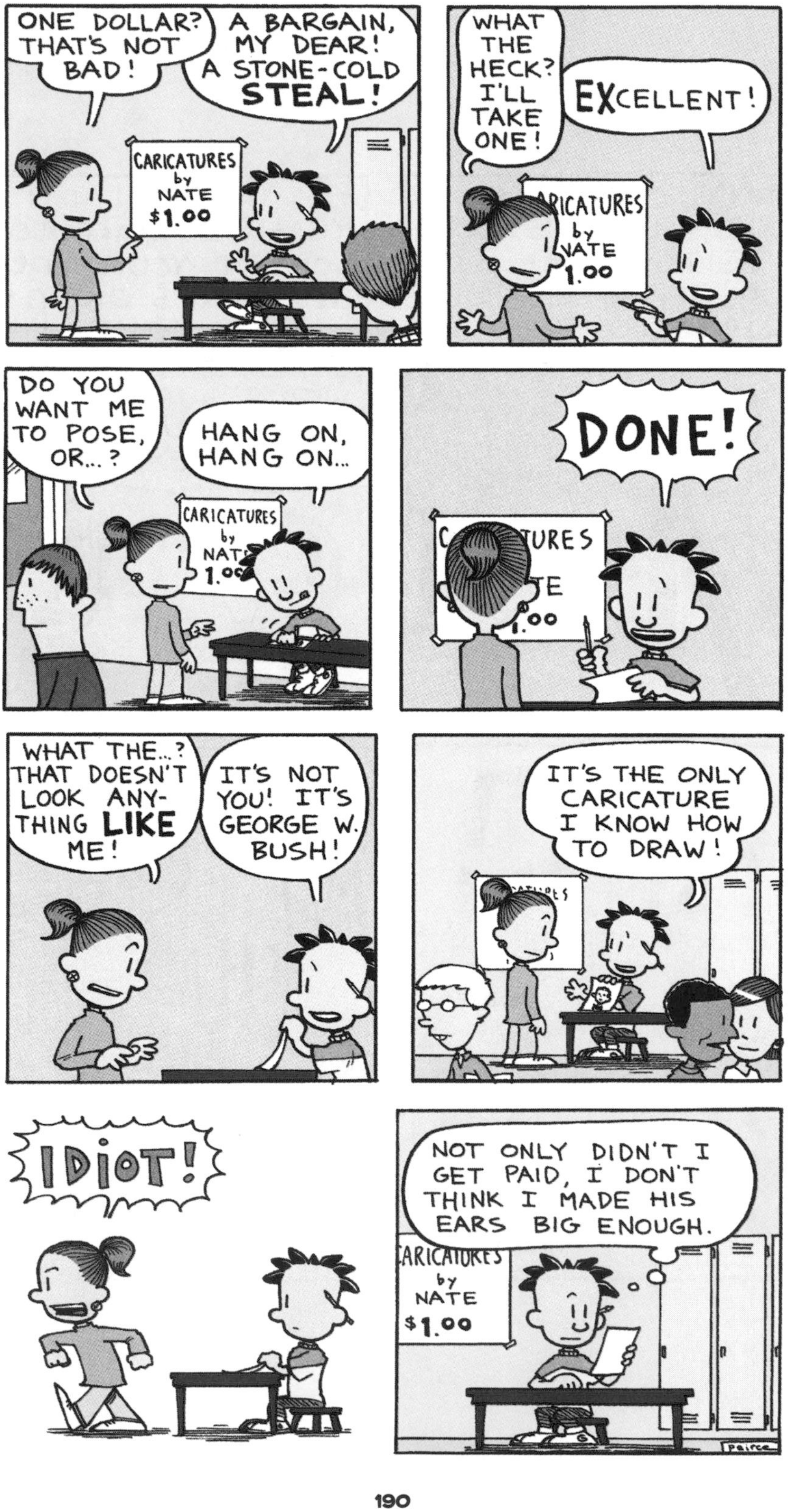
ONE DOLLAR? THAT'S NOT BAD!
A BARGAIN, MY DEAR! A STONE-COLD STEAL!
CARICATURES by NATE $1.00
WHAT THE HECK? I'LL TAKE ONE!
EXCELLENT!
DO YOU WANT ME TO POSE, OR...?
HANG ON, HANG ON...
CARICATURES by NATE $1.00
DONE!
WHAT THE...? THAT DOESN'T LOOK ANYTHING LIKE ME!
IT'S NOT YOU! IT'S GEORGE W. BUSH!
IT'S THE ONLY CARICATURE I KNOW HOW TO DRAW!
IDIOT!
NOT ONLY DIDN'T I GET PAID, I DON'T THINK I MADE HIS EARS BIG ENOUGH.
CARICATURES by NATE $1.00
PEIRCE

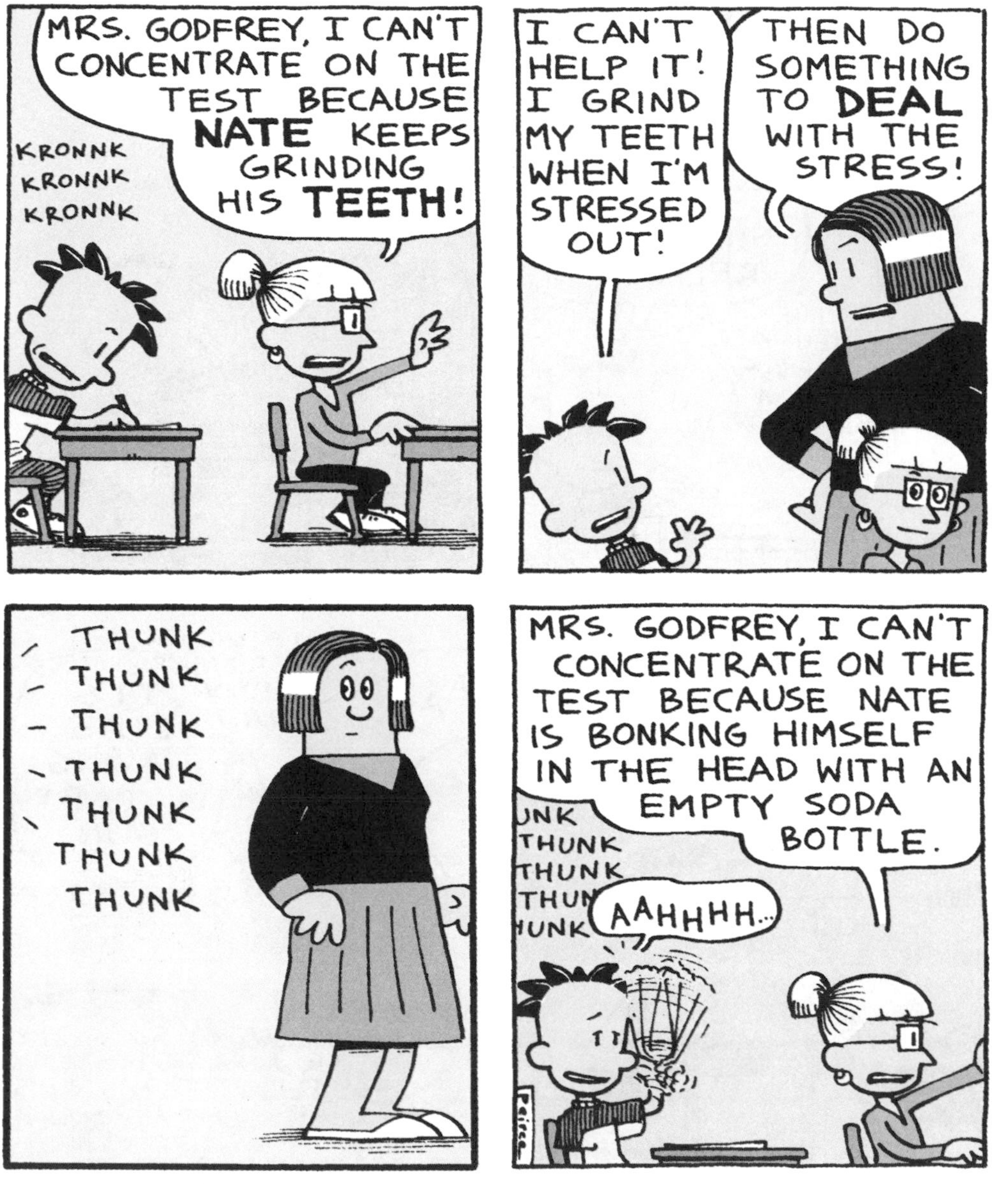
KRONNK KRONNK KRONNK
MRS. GODFREY, I CAN'T CONCENTRATE ON THE TEST BECAUSE NATE KEEPS GRINDING HIS TEETH!
I CAN'T HELP IT! I GRIND MY TEETH WHEN I'M STRESSED OUT!
THEN DO SOMETHING TO DEAL WITH THE STRESS!
THUNK THUNK THUNK THUNK THUNK THUNK THUNK
MRS. GODFREY, I CAN'T CONCENTRATE ON THE TEST BECAUSE NATE IS BONKING HIMSELF IN THE HEAD WITH AN EMPTY SODA BOTTLE.
AAHHHH...

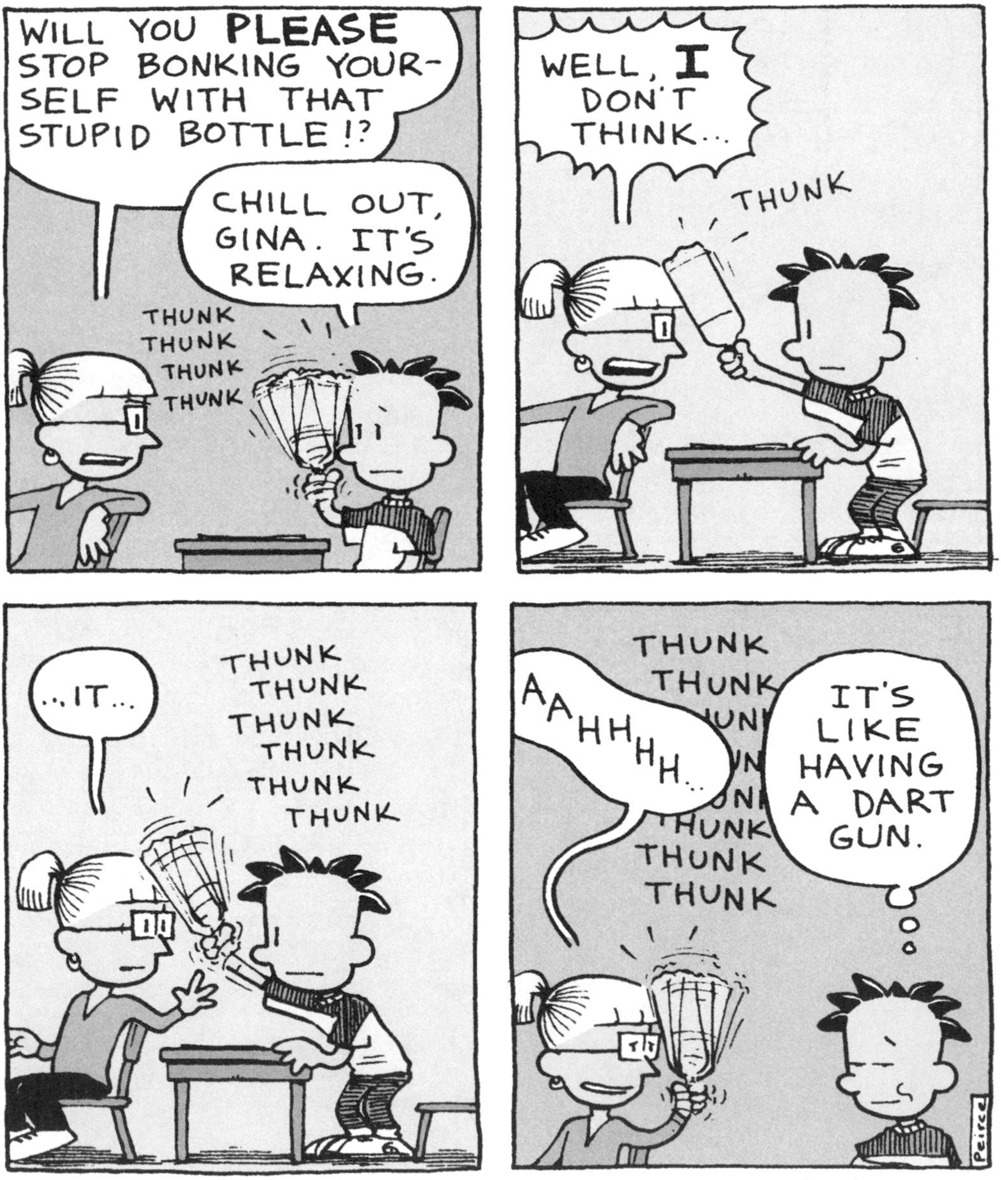
WILL YOU PLEASE STOP BONKING YOURSELF WITH THAT STUPID BOTTLE!?
CHILL OUT, GINA. IT'S RELAXING.
THUNK THUNK THUNK THUNK
WELL, I DON'T THINK...
THUNK
...IT...
THUNK THUNK THUNK THUNK THUNK THUNK
THUNK THUNK
AAHHHHH...
IT'S LIKE HAVING A DART GUN.
THUNK THUNK
Peirce

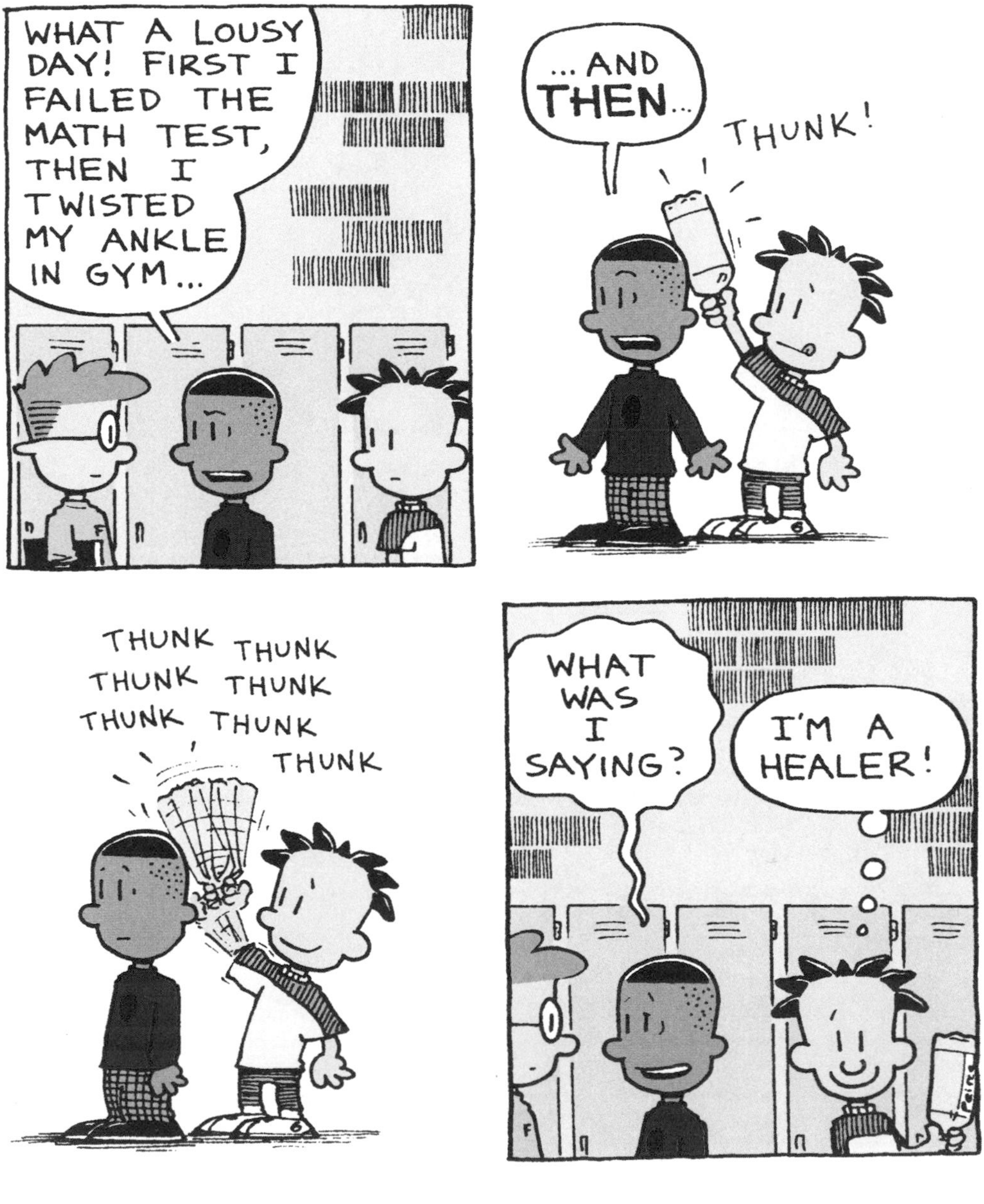
WHAT A LOUSY DAY! FIRST I FAILED THE MATH TEST, THEN I TWISTED MY ANKLE IN GYM...
...AND THEN...
THUNK!
THUNK THUNK
THUNK THUNK
THUNK THUNK
THUNK
WHAT WAS I SAYING?
I'M A HEALER!

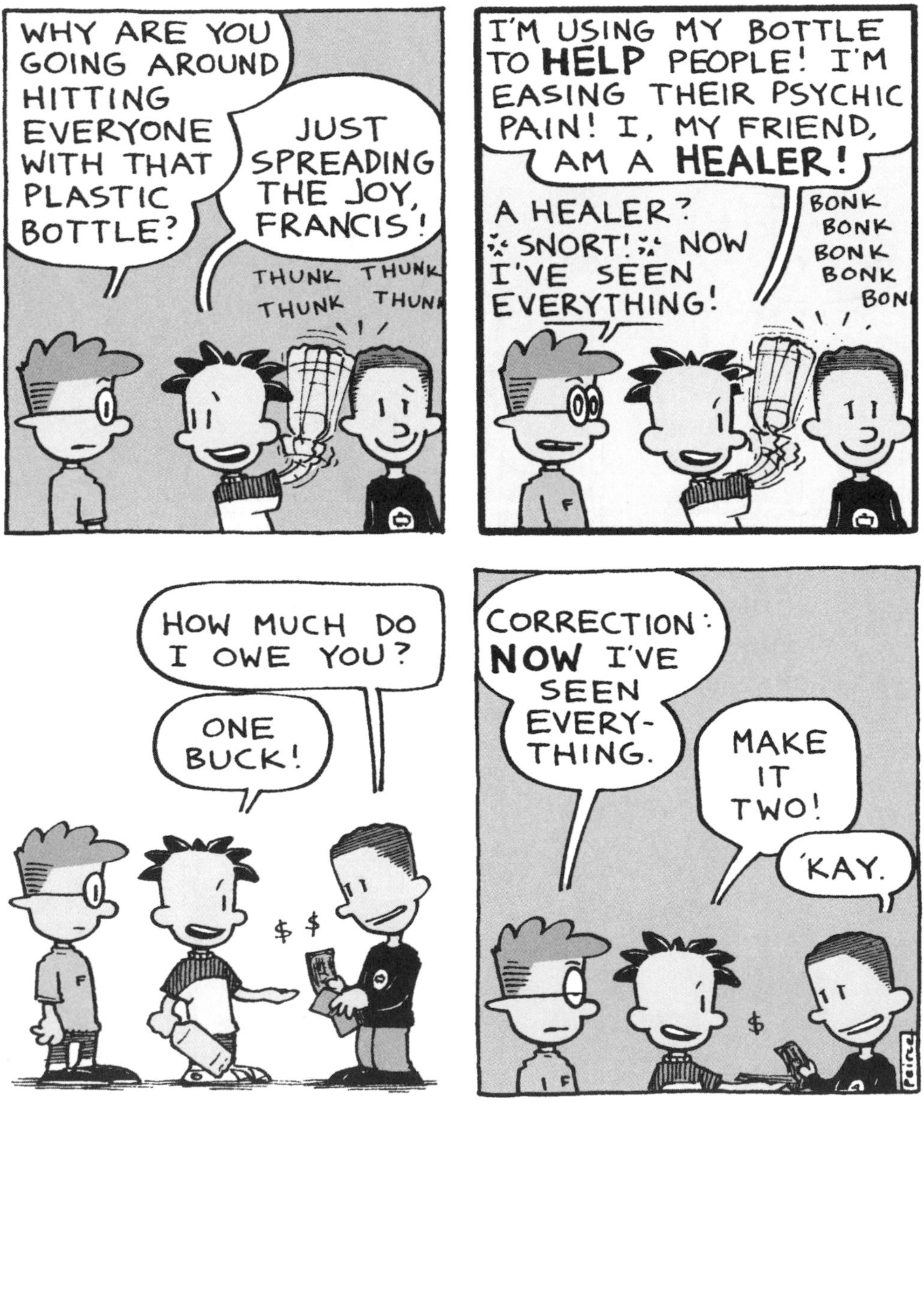
WHY ARE YOU GOING AROUND HITTING EVERYONE WITH THAT PLASTIC BOTTLE?
JUST SPREADING THE JOY, FRANCIS!
THUNK THUNK THUNK THUNK
I'M USING MY BOTTLE TO **HELP** PEOPLE! I'M EASING THEIR PSYCHIC PAIN! I, MY FRIEND, AM A **HEALER**!
A HEALER? SNORT! NOW I'VE SEEN EVERYTHING!
BONK BONK BONK BONK
HOW MUCH DO I OWE YOU?
ONE BUCK!
$ $
CORRECTION: **NOW** I'VE SEEN EVERY-THING.
MAKE IT TWO!
'KAY.
$
Peirce

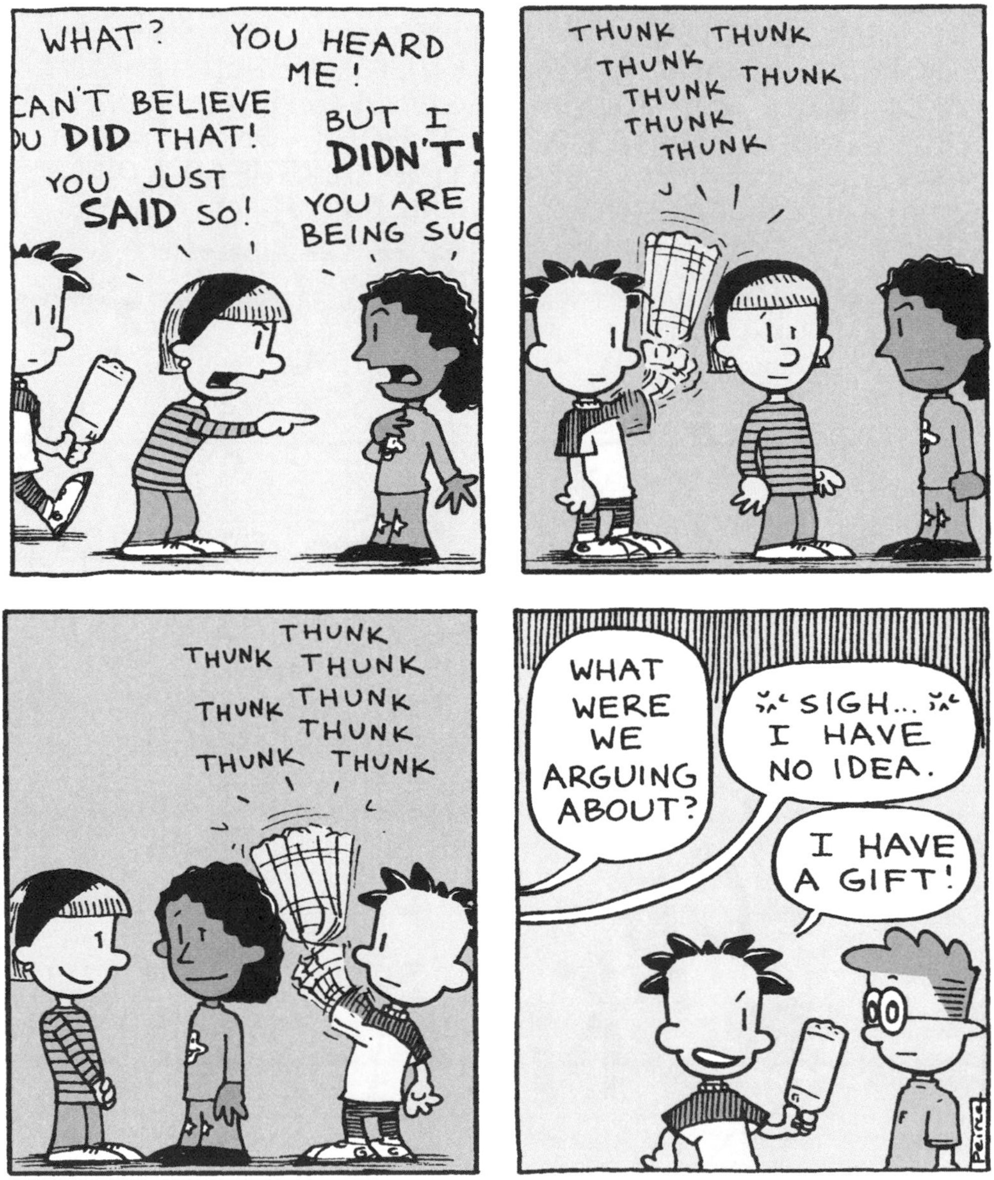
WHAT?
YOU HEARD ME!
CAN'T BELIEVE
U DID THAT!
BUT I DIDN'T!
YOU JUST SAID SO!
YOU ARE BEING SU
THUNK THUNK THUNK THUNK THUNK THUNK THUNK
THUNK THUNK THUNK THUNK THUNK THUNK THUNK THUNK
WHAT WERE WE ARGUING ABOUT?
SIGH... I HAVE NO IDEA.
I HAVE A GIFT!

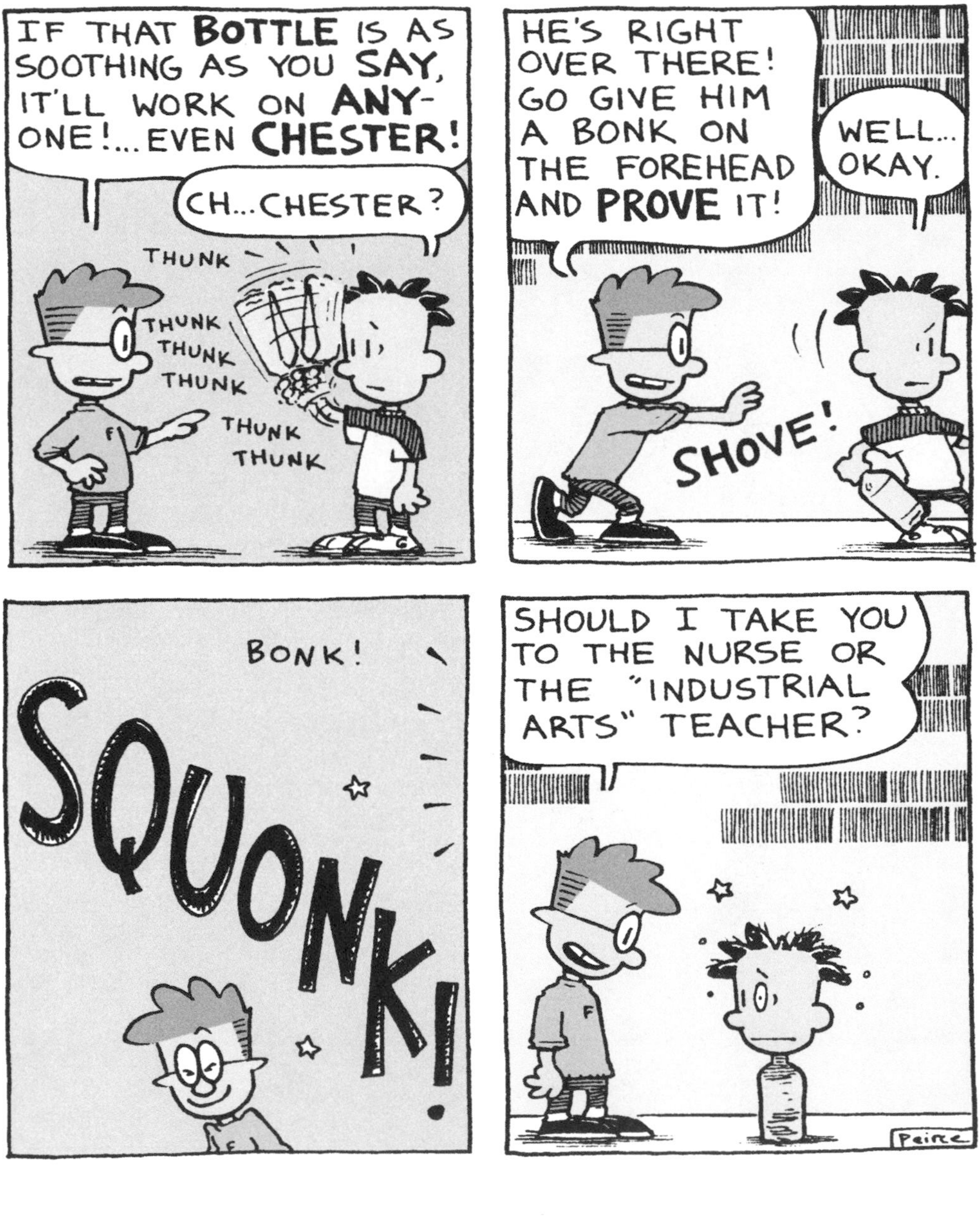
IF THAT BOTTLE IS AS SOOTHING AS YOU SAY, IT'LL WORK ON ANY-ONE!... EVEN CHESTER!
CH... CHESTER?
THUNK
THUNK
THUNK
THUNK
THUNK
THUNK
HE'S RIGHT OVER THERE! GO GIVE HIM A BONK ON THE FOREHEAD AND PROVE IT!
WELL... OKAY.
SHOVE!
BONK!
SQUONK!
SHOULD I TAKE YOU TO THE NURSE OR THE "INDUSTRIAL ARTS" TEACHER?
Peirce

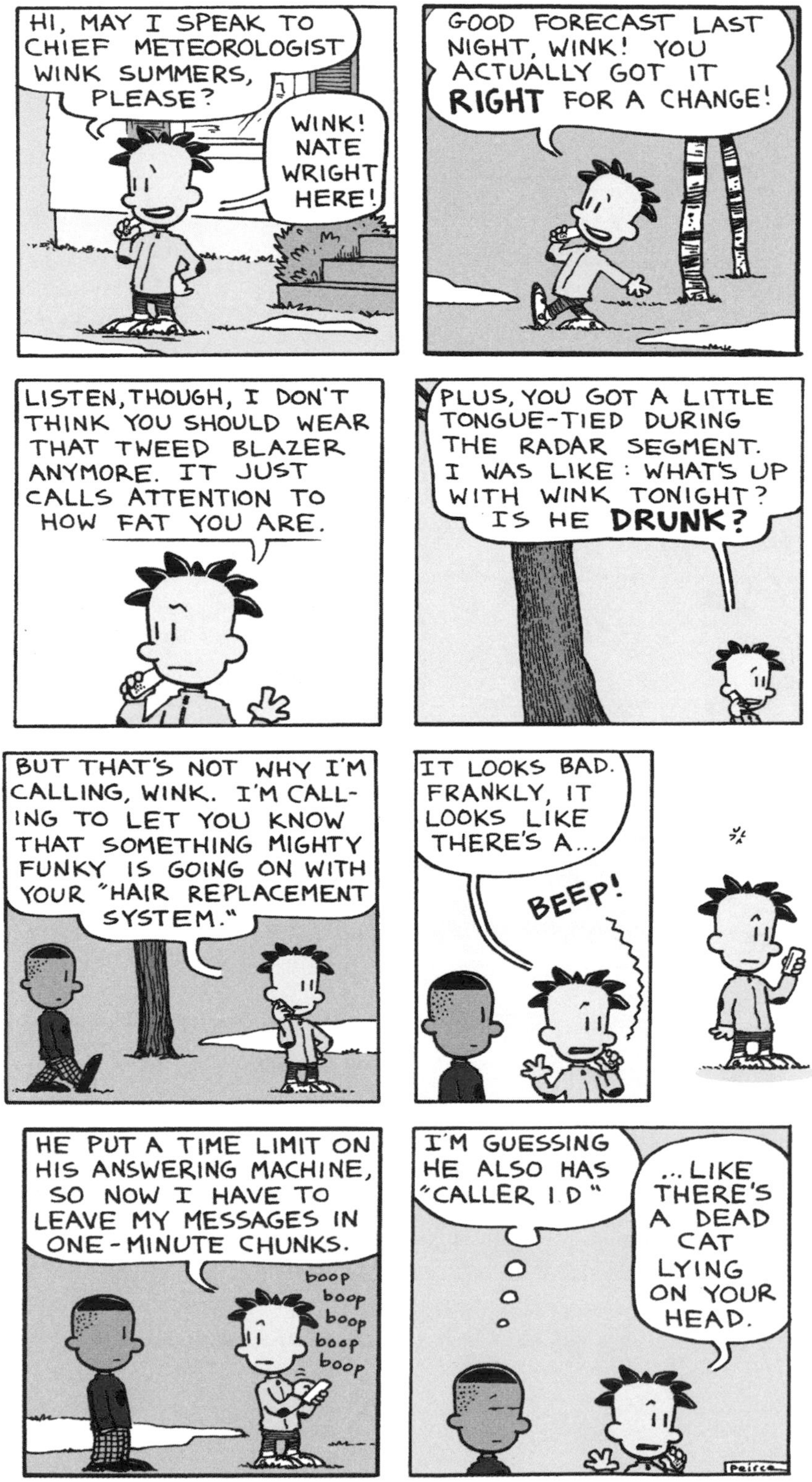
HI, MAY I SPEAK TO CHIEF METEOROLOGIST WINK SUMMERS, PLEASE?
WINK! NATE WRIGHT HERE!
GOOD FORECAST LAST NIGHT, WINK! YOU ACTUALLY GOT IT RIGHT FOR A CHANGE!
LISTEN, THOUGH, I DON'T THINK YOU SHOULD WEAR THAT TWEED BLAZER ANYMORE. IT JUST CALLS ATTENTION TO HOW FAT YOU ARE.
PLUS, YOU GOT A LITTLE TONGUE-TIED DURING THE RADAR SEGMENT. I WAS LIKE: WHAT'S UP WITH WINK TONIGHT? IS HE DRUNK?
BUT THAT'S NOT WHY I'M CALLING, WINK. I'M CALLING TO LET YOU KNOW THAT SOMETHING MIGHTY FUNKY IS GOING ON WITH YOUR "HAIR REPLACEMENT SYSTEM."
IT LOOKS BAD. FRANKLY, IT LOOKS LIKE THERE'S A...
BEEP!
HE PUT A TIME LIMIT ON HIS ANSWERING MACHINE, SO NOW I HAVE TO LEAVE MY MESSAGES IN ONE-MINUTE CHUNKS.
boop boop boop boop boop
I'M GUESSING HE ALSO HAS "CALLER I.D."
...LIKE THERE'S A DEAD CAT LYING ON YOUR HEAD.
Peirce

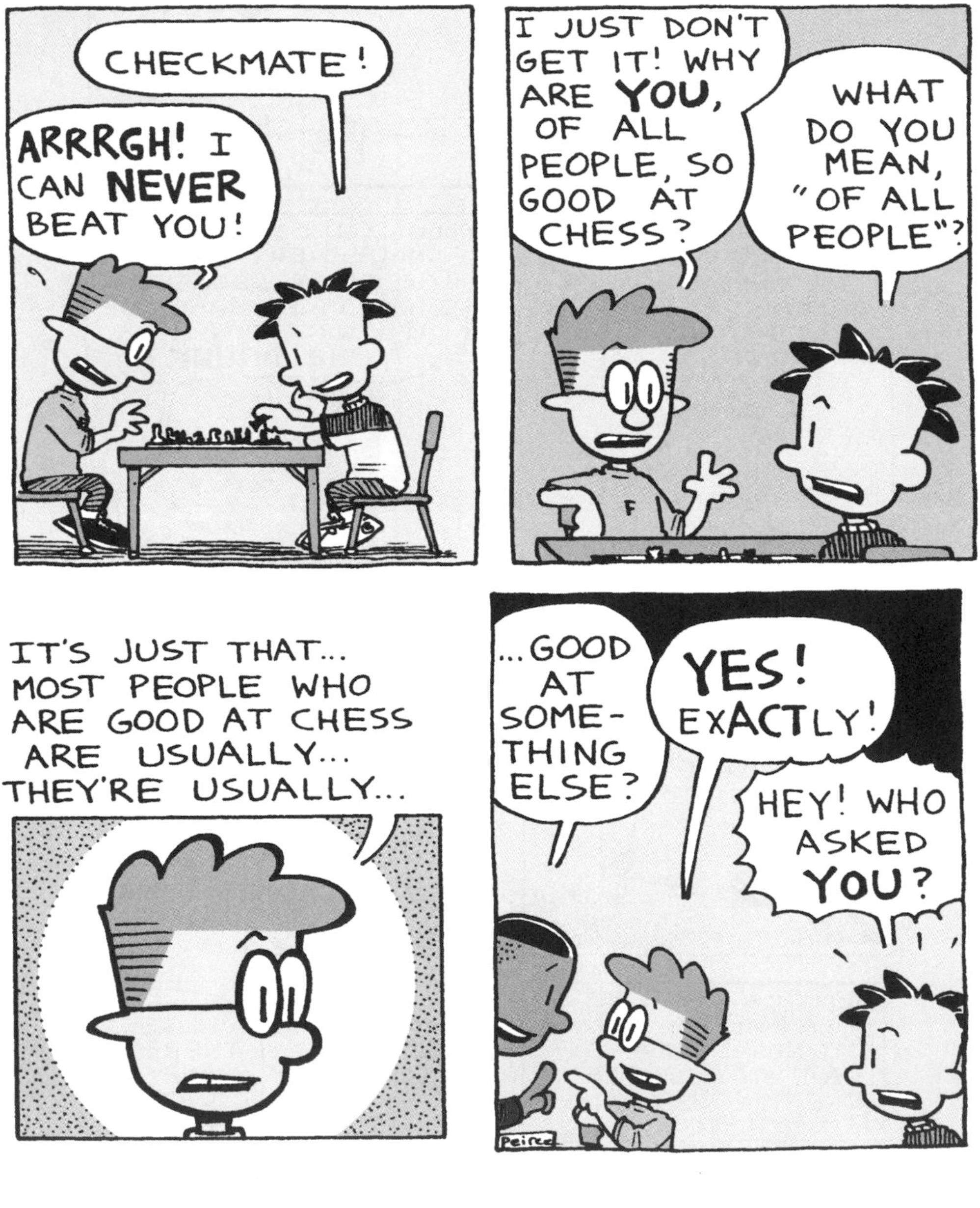
CHECKMATE!
ARRRGH! I CAN NEVER BEAT YOU!
I JUST DON'T GET IT! WHY ARE YOU, OF ALL PEOPLE, SO GOOD AT CHESS?
WHAT DO YOU MEAN, "OF ALL PEOPLE"?
IT'S JUST THAT... MOST PEOPLE WHO ARE GOOD AT CHESS ARE USUALLY... THEY'RE USUALLY...
...GOOD AT SOME-THING ELSE?
YES! EXACTLY!
HEY! WHO ASKED YOU?
F
Peirce

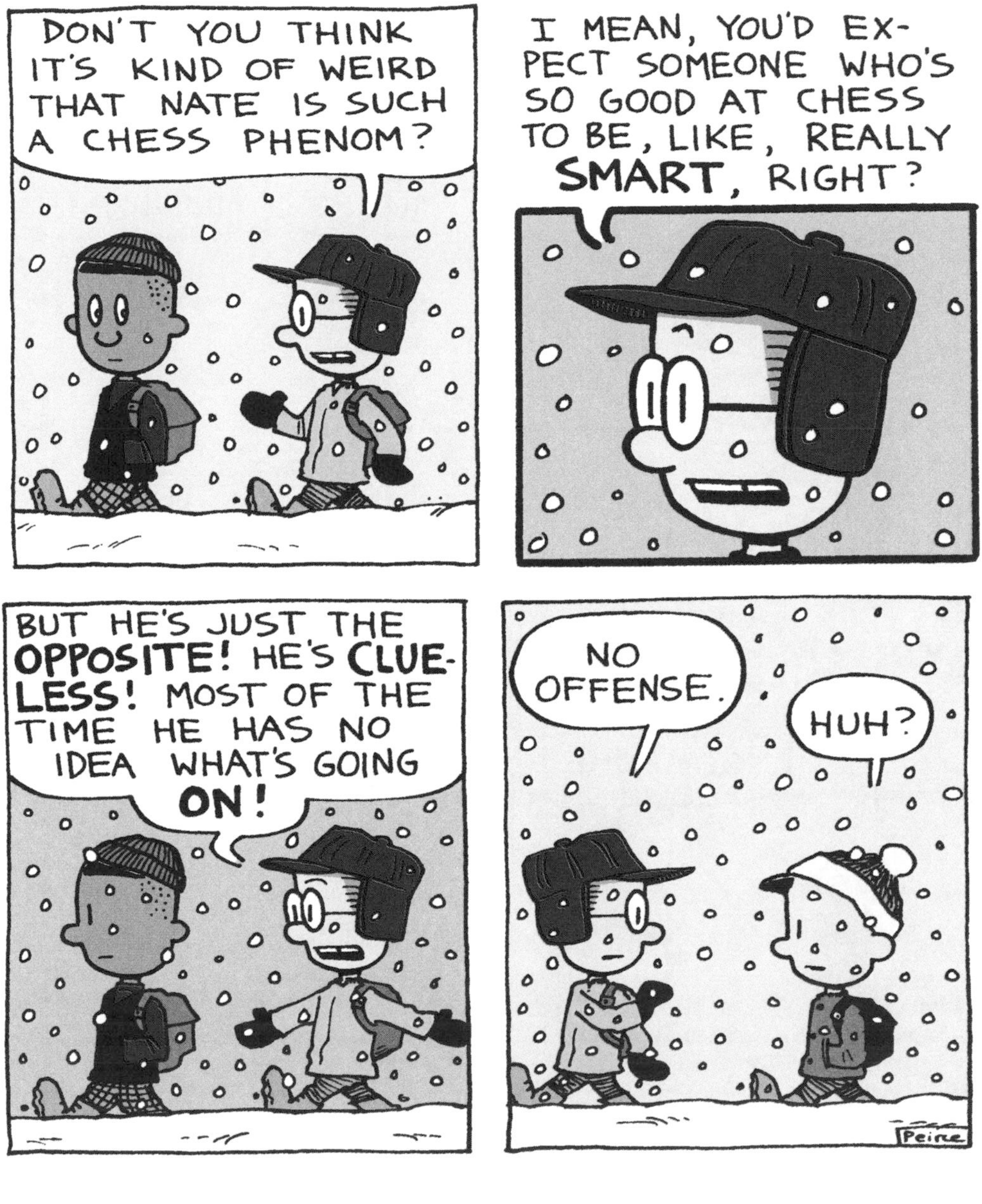
DON'T YOU THINK IT'S KIND OF WEIRD THAT NATE IS SUCH A CHESS PHENOM?
I MEAN, YOU'D EXPECT SOMEONE WHO'S SO GOOD AT CHESS TO BE, LIKE, REALLY SMART, RIGHT?
BUT HE'S JUST THE OPPOSITE! HE'S CLUELESS! MOST OF THE TIME HE HAS NO IDEA WHAT'S GOING ON!
NO OFFENSE.
HUH?
Peirce

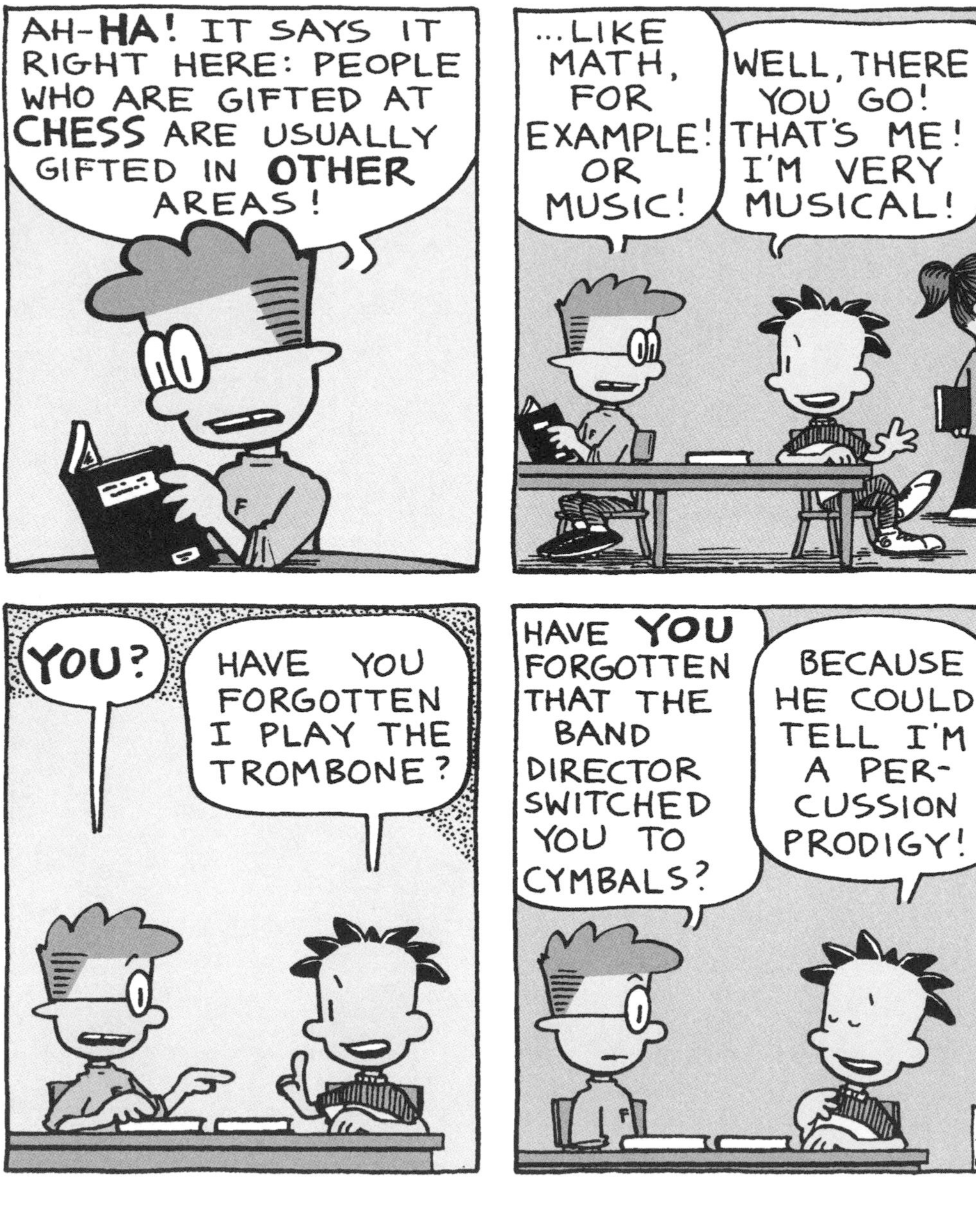
AH-**HA**! IT SAYS IT RIGHT HERE: PEOPLE WHO ARE GIFTED AT **CHESS** ARE USUALLY GIFTED IN **OTHER** AREAS!
...LIKE MATH, FOR EXAMPLE! OR MUSIC!
WELL, THERE YOU GO! THAT'S ME! I'M VERY MUSICAL!
YOU?
HAVE YOU FORGOTTEN I PLAY THE TROMBONE?
HAVE **YOU** FORGOTTEN THAT THE BAND DIRECTOR SWITCHED YOU TO CYMBALS?
BECAUSE HE COULD TELL I'M A PER-CUSSION PRODIGY!
Peirce

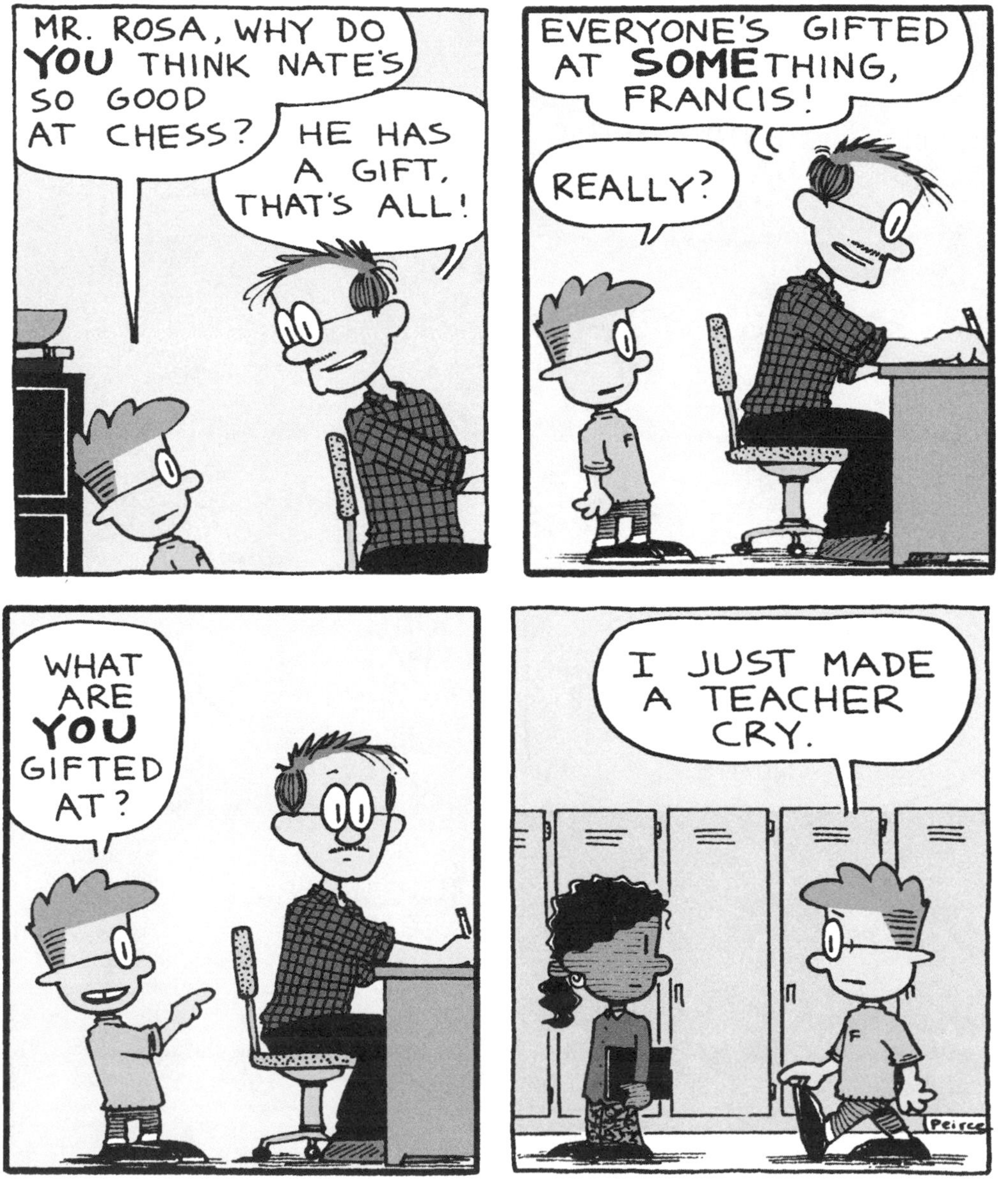
MR. ROSA, WHY DO **YOU** THINK NATE'S SO GOOD AT CHESS?
HE HAS A GIFT, THAT'S ALL!
EVERYONE'S GIFTED AT **SOME**THING, FRANCIS!
REALLY?
WHAT ARE **YOU** GIFTED AT?
I JUST MADE A TEACHER CRY.
Peirce

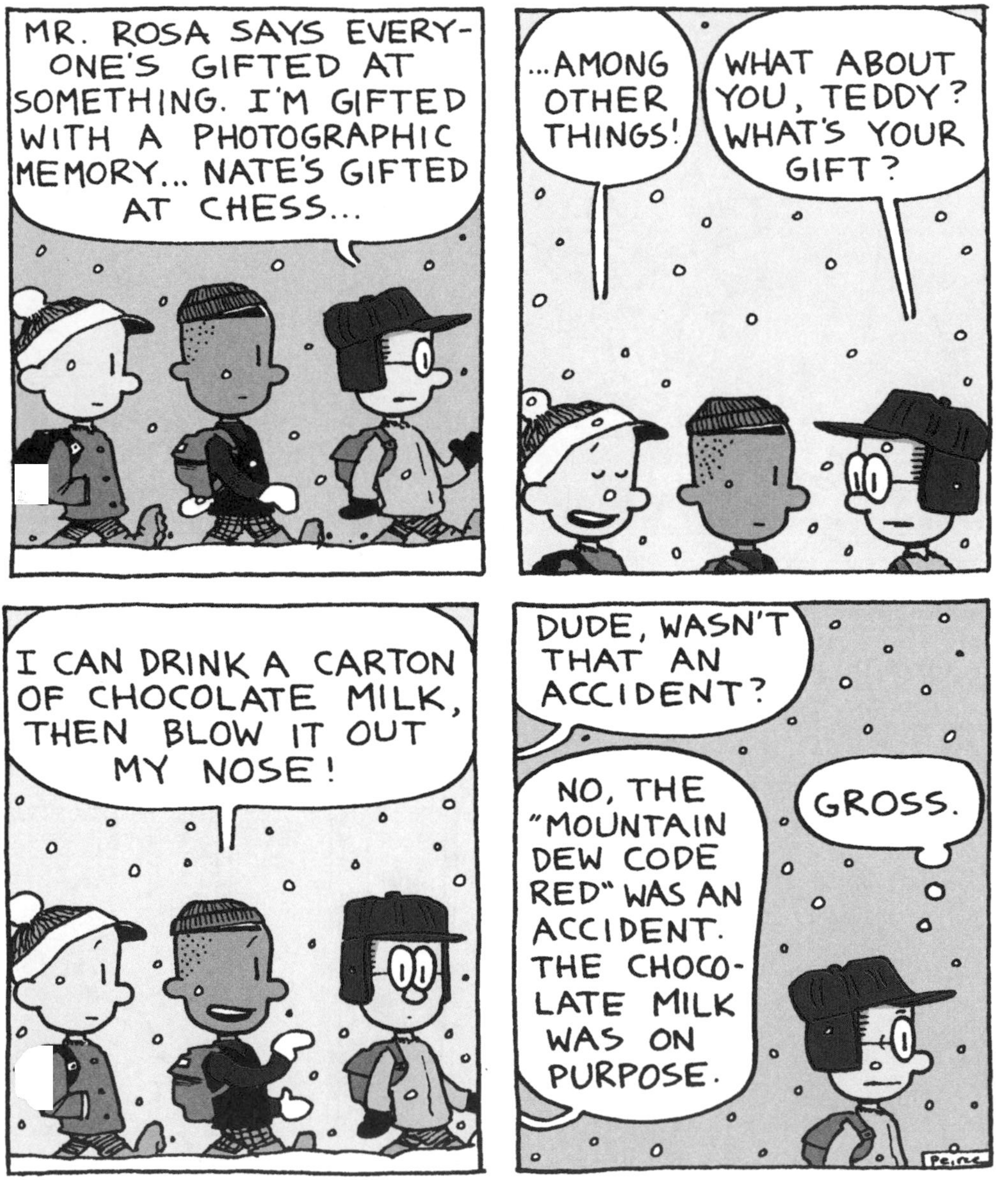
MR. ROSA SAYS EVERY-ONE'S GIFTED AT SOMETHING. I'M GIFTED WITH A PHOTOGRAPHIC MEMORY... NATE'S GIFTED AT CHESS...
...AMONG OTHER THINGS!
WHAT ABOUT YOU, TEDDY? WHAT'S YOUR GIFT?
I CAN DRINK A CARTON OF CHOCOLATE MILK, THEN BLOW IT OUT MY NOSE!
DUDE, WASN'T THAT AN ACCIDENT?
NO, THE "MOUNTAIN DEW CODE RED" WAS AN ACCIDENT. THE CHOCO-LATE MILK WAS ON PURPOSE.
GROSS.
PEIRCE

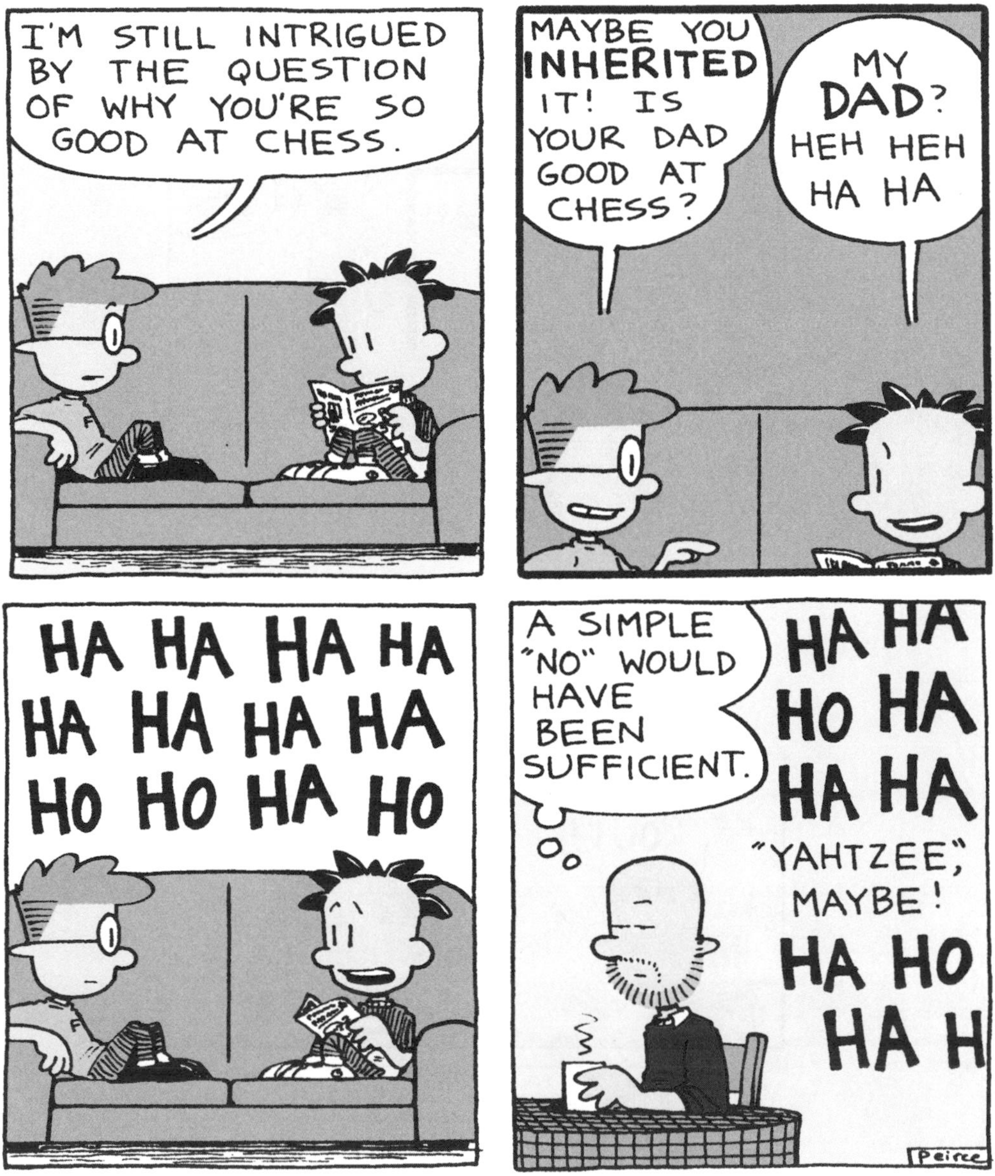
I'M STILL INTRIGUED BY THE QUESTION OF WHY YOU'RE SO GOOD AT CHESS.
MAYBE YOU INHERITED IT! IS YOUR DAD GOOD AT CHESS?
MY DAD? HEH HEH HA HA
HA HA HA HA HA HA HA HA HO HO HA HO
A SIMPLE "NO" WOULD HAVE BEEN SUFFICIENT.
HA HA HO HA HA HA
"YAHTZEE," MAYBE!
HA HO HA H
Peirce

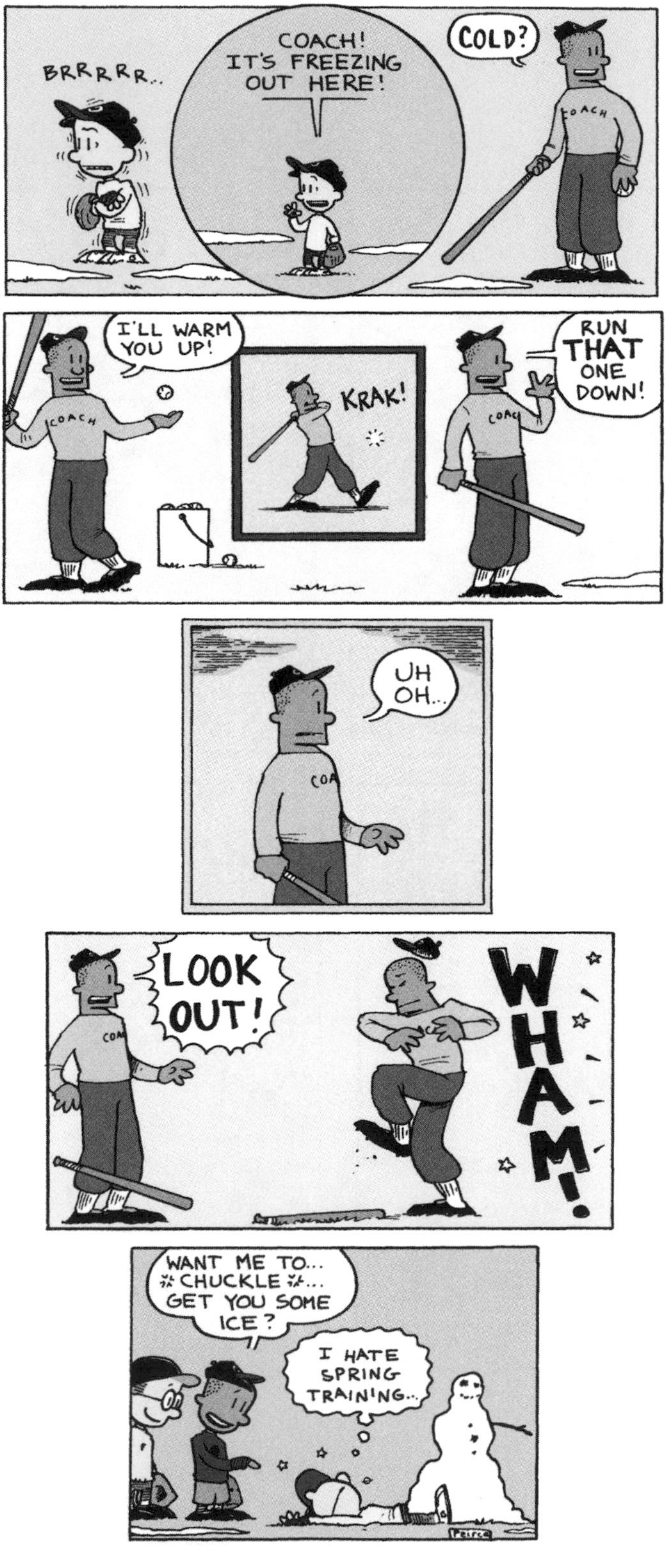
BRRRRR..
COACH! IT'S FREEZING OUT HERE!
COLD?
COACH
I'LL WARM YOU UP!
COACH
KRAK!
RUN THAT ONE DOWN!
UH OH...
LOOK OUT!
WHAM!
WANT ME TO... CHUCKLE... GET YOU SOME ICE?
I HATE SPRING TRAINING...
Peirce

WHAT'S WITH THE CAMERA?

I'VE JOINED THE YEARBOOK STAFF! I'M IN CHARGE OF CANDIDS!

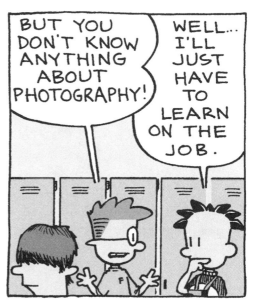

BUT YOU DON'T KNOW ANYTHING ABOUT PHOTOGRAPHY!

WELL... I'LL JUST HAVE TO LEARN ON THE JOB.

YOU NEED A MENTOR.

YES!... A MENTOR! AND I KNOW JUST THE PERSON!

RRINNG!

MOTHER! PHONE!

FIRE TORPEDOES, MISTER SULU.

AYE, CAPTAIN.

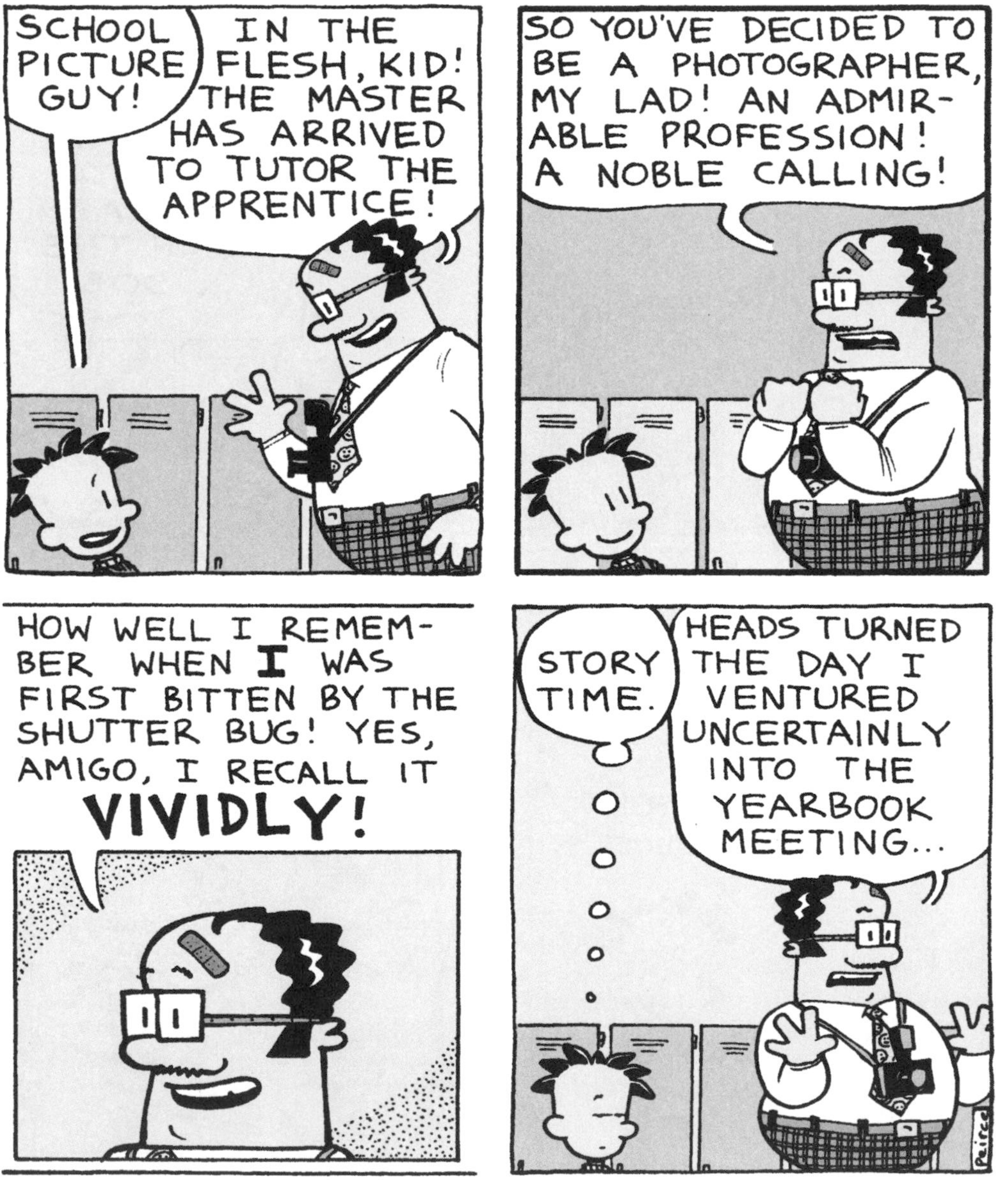
SCHOOL PICTURE GUY!
IN THE FLESH, KID! THE MASTER HAS ARRIVED TO TUTOR THE APPRENTICE!
SO YOU'VE DECIDED TO BE A PHOTOGRAPHER, MY LAD! AN ADMIRABLE PROFESSION! A NOBLE CALLING!
HOW WELL I REMEMBER WHEN I WAS FIRST BITTEN BY THE SHUTTER BUG! YES, AMIGO, I RECALL IT VIVIDLY!
STORY TIME.
HEADS TURNED THE DAY I VENTURED UNCERTAINLY INTO THE YEARBOOK MEETING...
PEIRCE

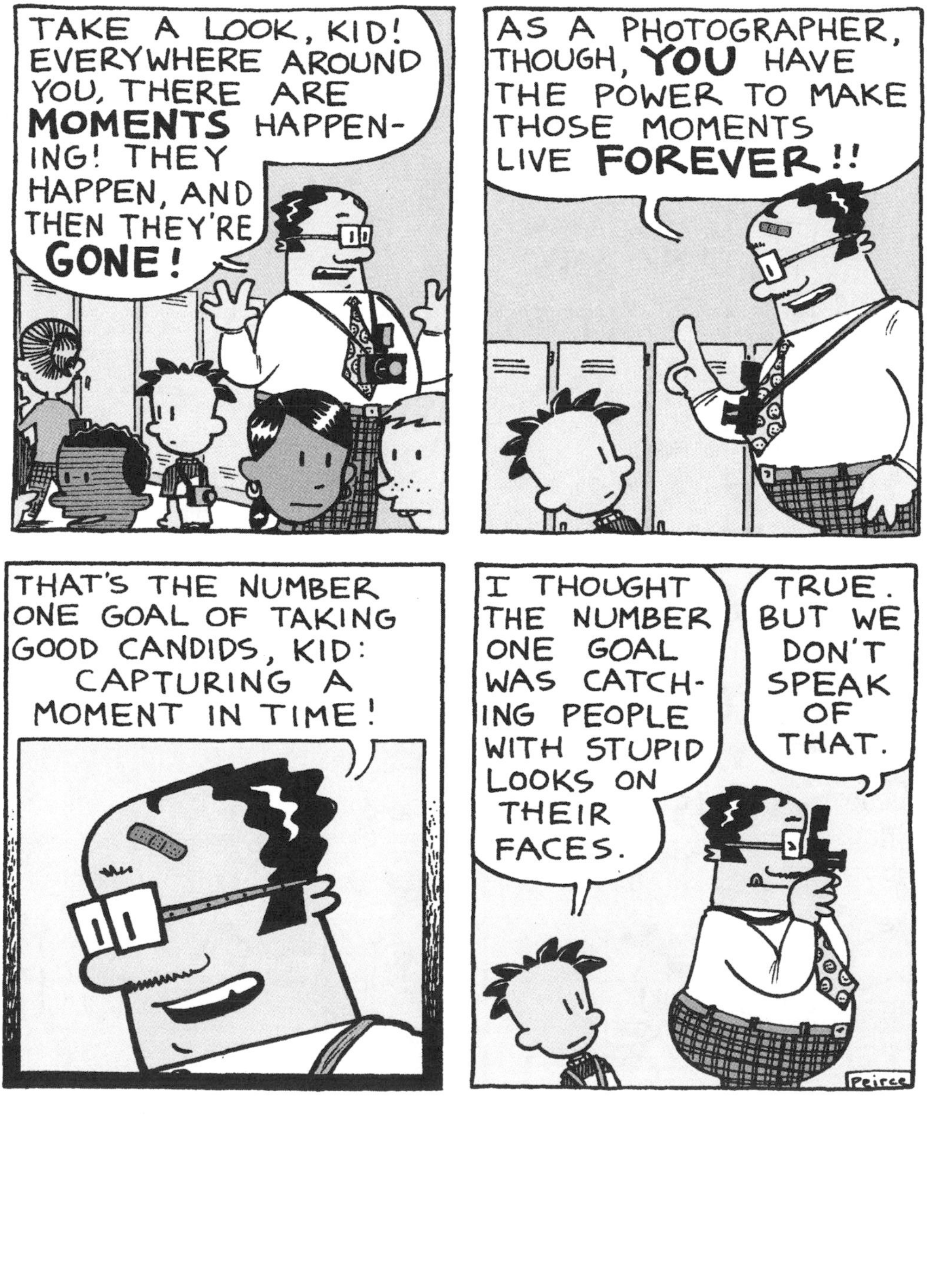
TAKE A LOOK, KID! EVERYWHERE AROUND YOU, THERE ARE **MOMENTS** HAPPENING! THEY HAPPEN, AND THEN THEY'RE **GONE**!
AS A PHOTOGRAPHER, THOUGH, **YOU** HAVE THE POWER TO MAKE THOSE MOMENTS LIVE **FOREVER**!!
THAT'S THE NUMBER ONE GOAL OF TAKING GOOD CANDIDS, KID: CAPTURING A MOMENT IN TIME!
I THOUGHT THE NUMBER ONE GOAL WAS CATCHING PEOPLE WITH STUPID LOOKS ON THEIR FACES.
TRUE. BUT WE DON'T SPEAK OF THAT.
Peirce

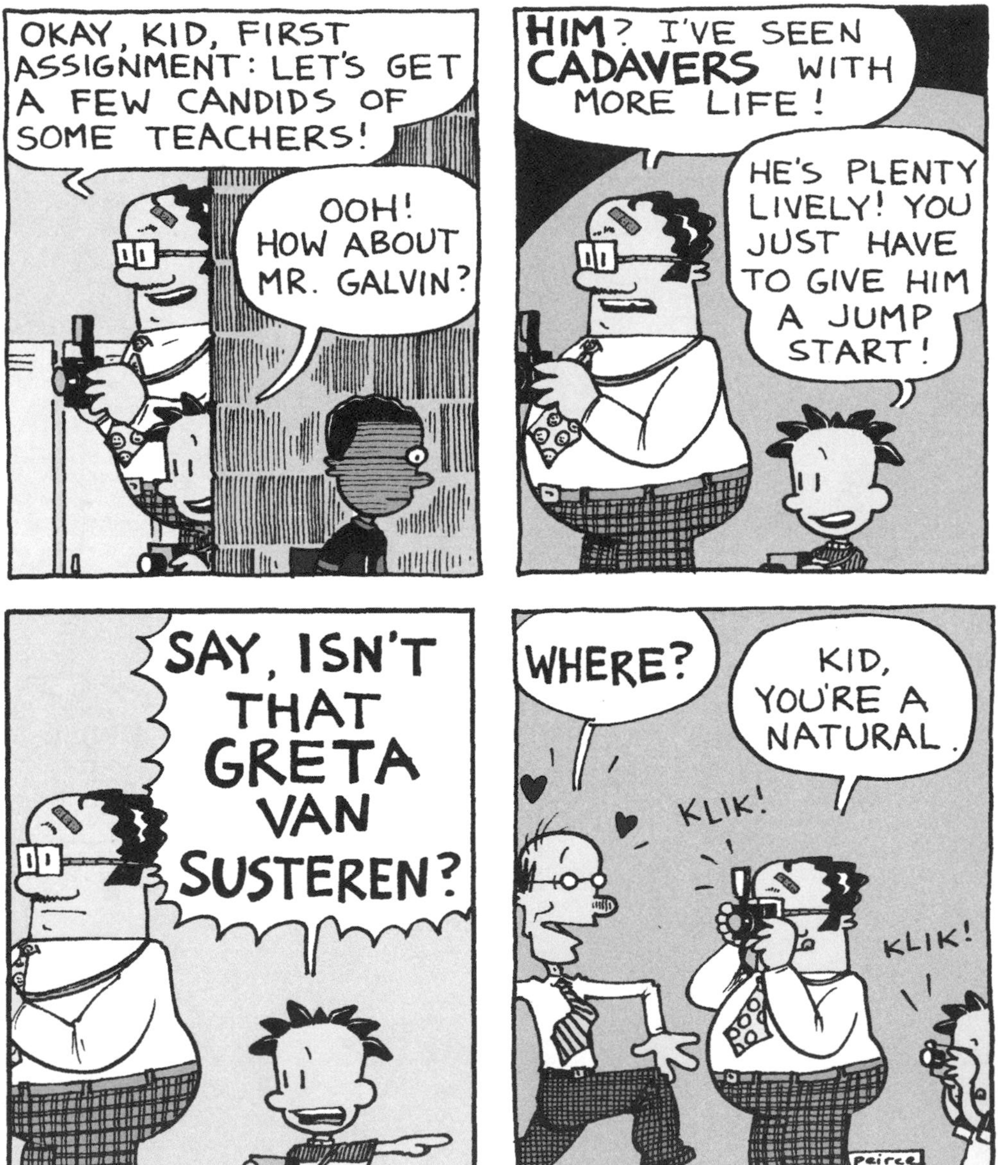
OKAY, KID, FIRST ASSIGNMENT: LET'S GET A FEW CANDIDS OF SOME TEACHERS!
OOH! HOW ABOUT MR. GALVIN?
HIM? I'VE SEEN CADAVERS WITH MORE LIFE!
HE'S PLENTY LIVELY! YOU JUST HAVE TO GIVE HIM A JUMP START!
SAY, ISN'T THAT GRETA VAN SUSTEREN?
WHERE?
KID, YOU'RE A NATURAL.
KLIK!
KLIK!
peirce

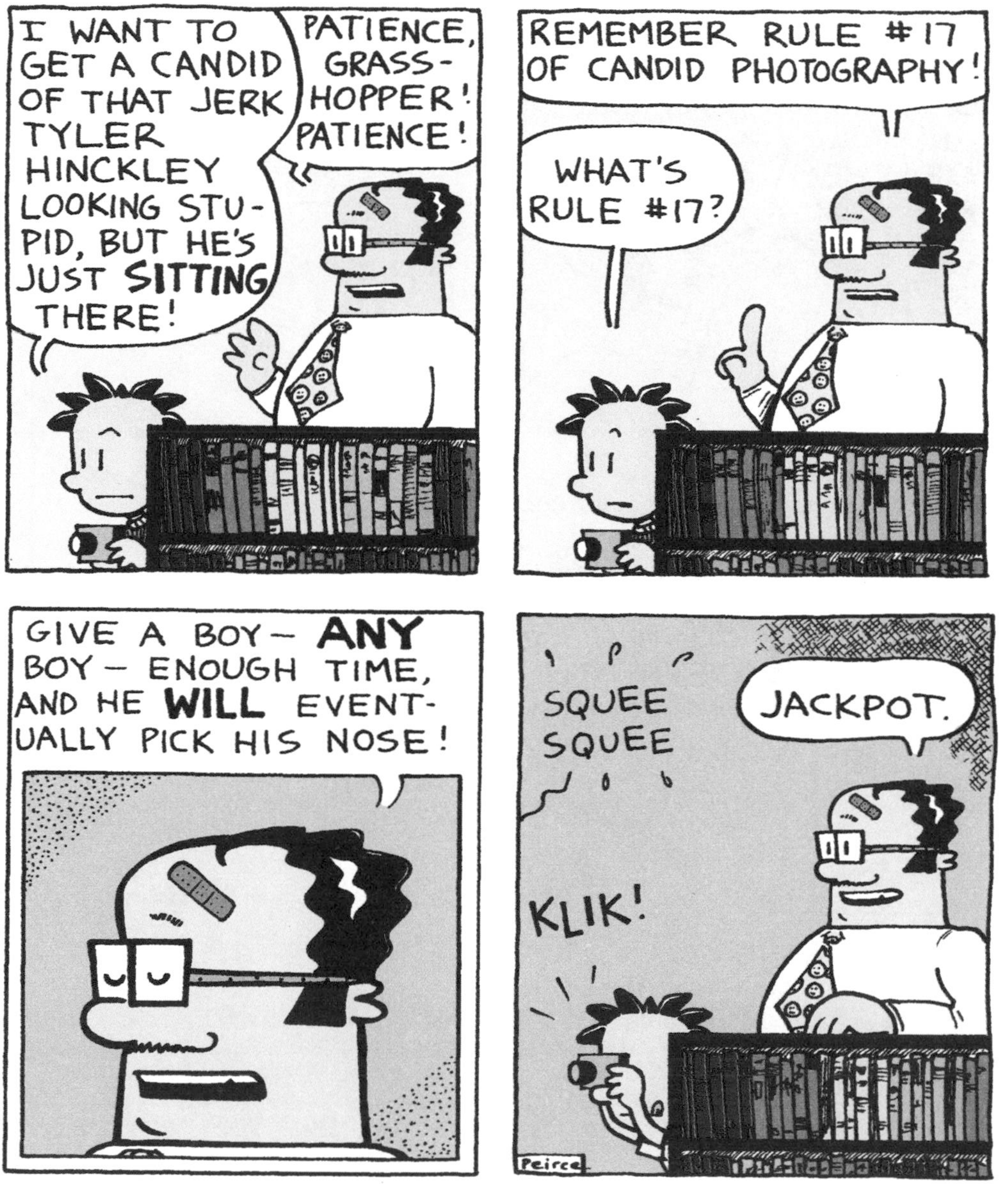
I WANT TO GET A CANDID OF THAT JERK TYLER HINCKLEY LOOKING STUPID, BUT HE'S JUST SITTING THERE!
PATIENCE, GRASSHOPPER! PATIENCE!
REMEMBER RULE #17 OF CANDID PHOTOGRAPHY!
WHAT'S RULE #17?
GIVE A BOY— ANY BOY— ENOUGH TIME, AND HE WILL EVENTUALLY PICK HIS NOSE!
SQUEE SQUEE
JACKPOT.
KLIK!
Peirce

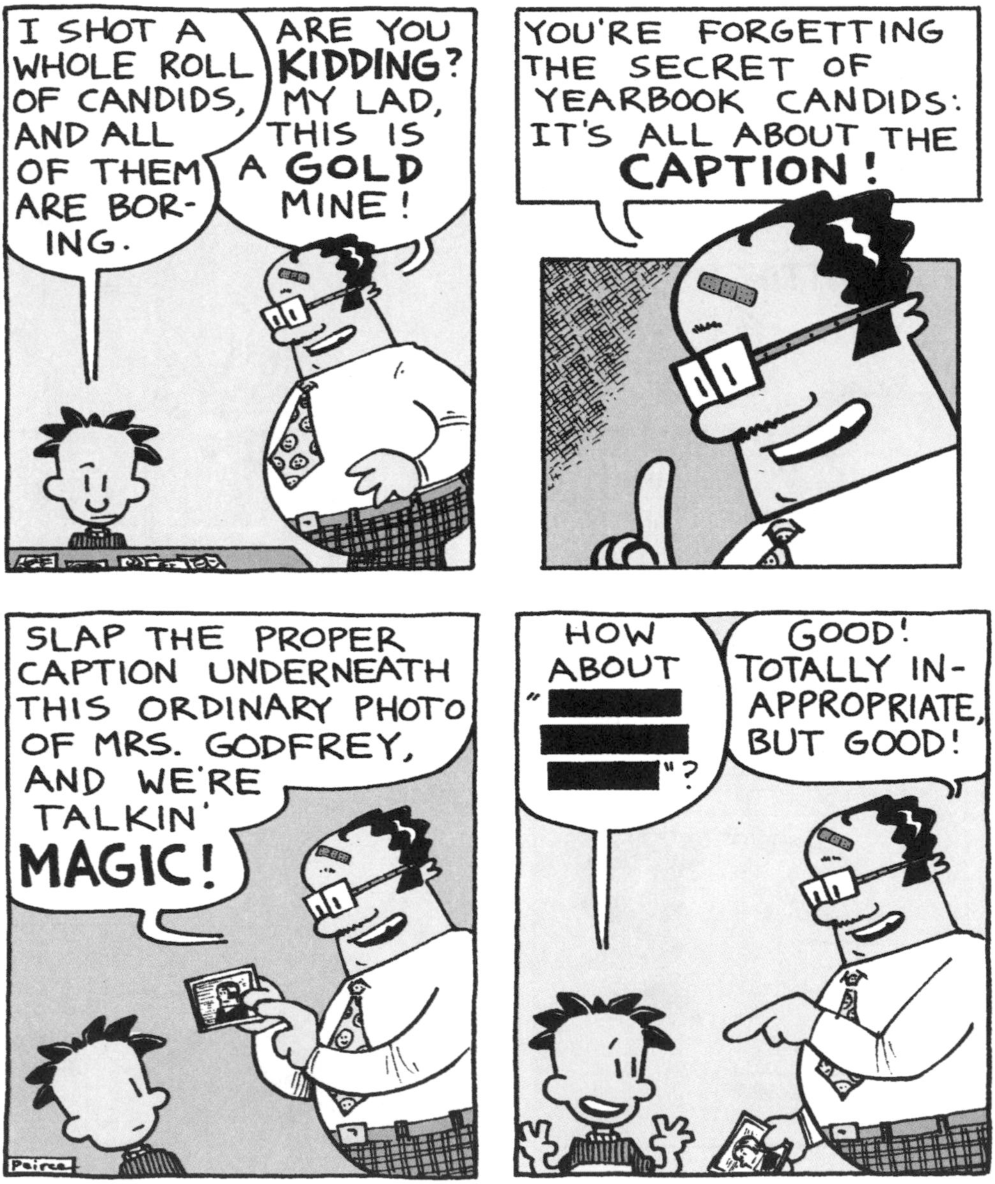
I SHOT A WHOLE ROLL OF CANDIDS, AND ALL OF THEM ARE BOR-ING.
ARE YOU **KIDDING**? MY LAD, THIS IS A **GOLD** MINE!
YOU'RE FORGETTING THE SECRET OF YEARBOOK CANDIDS: IT'S ALL ABOUT THE **CAPTION**!
SLAP THE PROPER CAPTION UNDERNEATH THIS ORDINARY PHOTO OF MRS. GODFREY, AND WE'RE TALKIN' **MAGIC**!
Peirce
HOW ABOUT "[redacted]"?
GOOD! TOTALLY IN-APPROPRIATE, BUT GOOD!

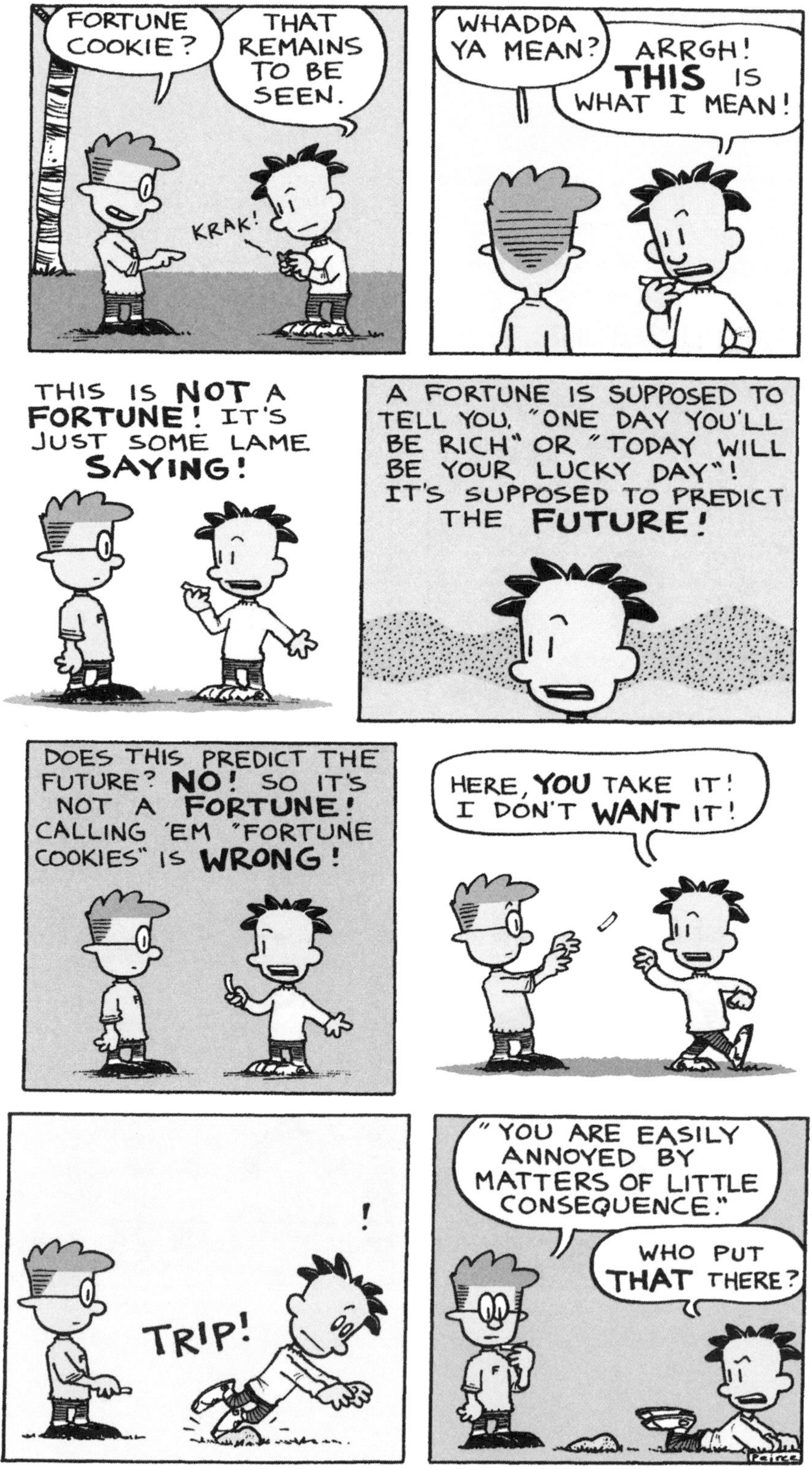
FORTUNE COOKIE?
THAT REMAINS TO BE SEEN.
KRAK!
WHADDA YA MEAN?
ARRGH! THIS IS WHAT I MEAN!
THIS IS NOT A FORTUNE! IT'S JUST SOME LAME SAYING!
A FORTUNE IS SUPPOSED TO TELL YOU, "ONE DAY YOU'LL BE RICH" OR "TODAY WILL BE YOUR LUCKY DAY"! IT'S SUPPOSED TO PREDICT THE FUTURE!
DOES THIS PREDICT THE FUTURE? NO! SO IT'S NOT A FORTUNE! CALLING 'EM "FORTUNE COOKIES" IS WRONG!
HERE, YOU TAKE IT! I DON'T WANT IT!
!
TRIP!
"YOU ARE EASILY ANNOYED BY MATTERS OF LITTLE CONSEQUENCE."
WHO PUT THAT THERE?
Peirce

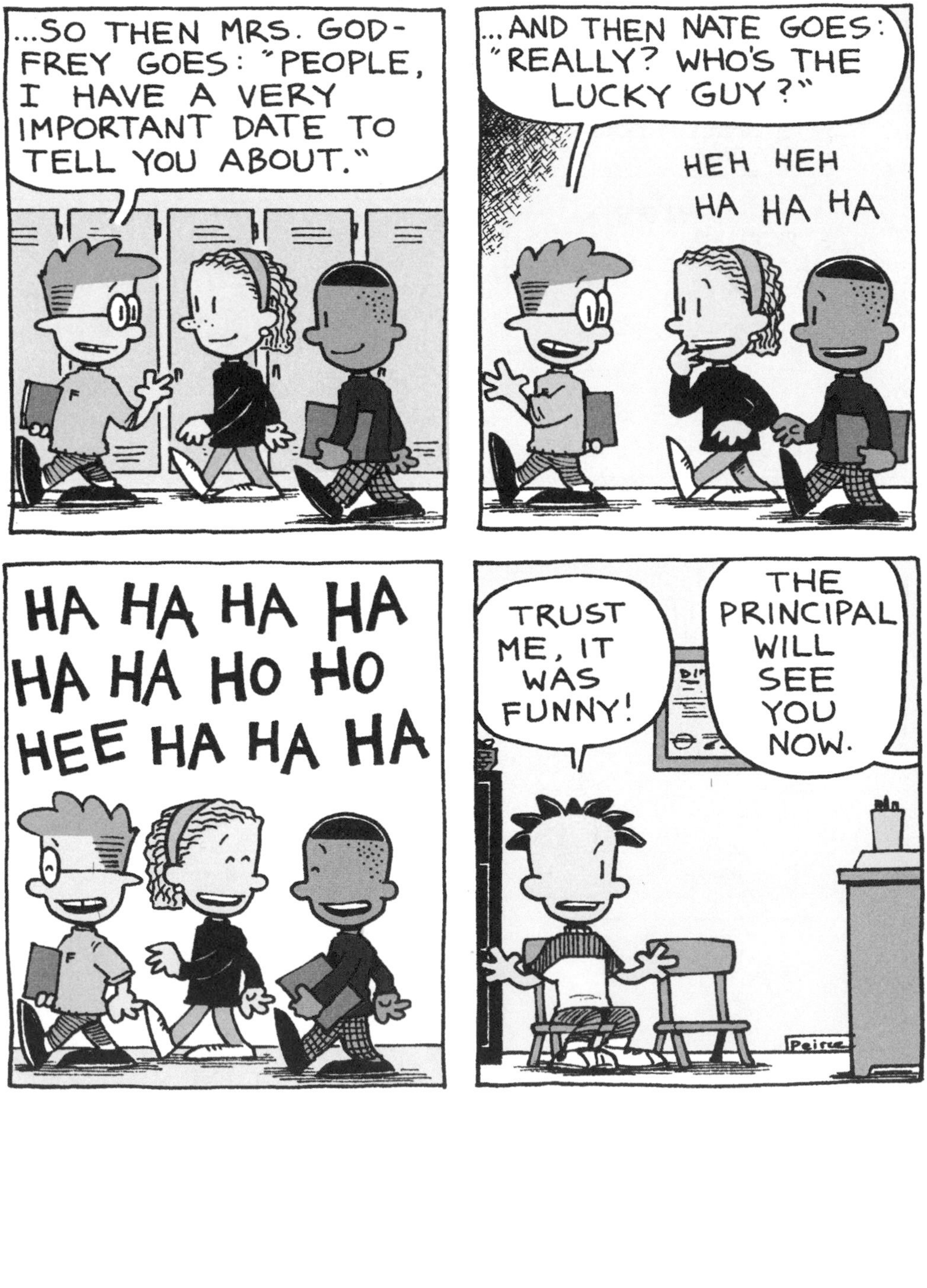
...SO THEN MRS. GODFREY GOES: "PEOPLE, I HAVE A VERY IMPORTANT DATE TO TELL YOU ABOUT."
...AND THEN NATE GOES: "REALLY? WHO'S THE LUCKY GUY?"
HEH HEH
HA HA HA
HA HA HA HA HA HA HO HO HEE HA HA HA
TRUST ME, IT WAS FUNNY!
THE PRINCIPAL WILL SEE YOU NOW.
Peirce

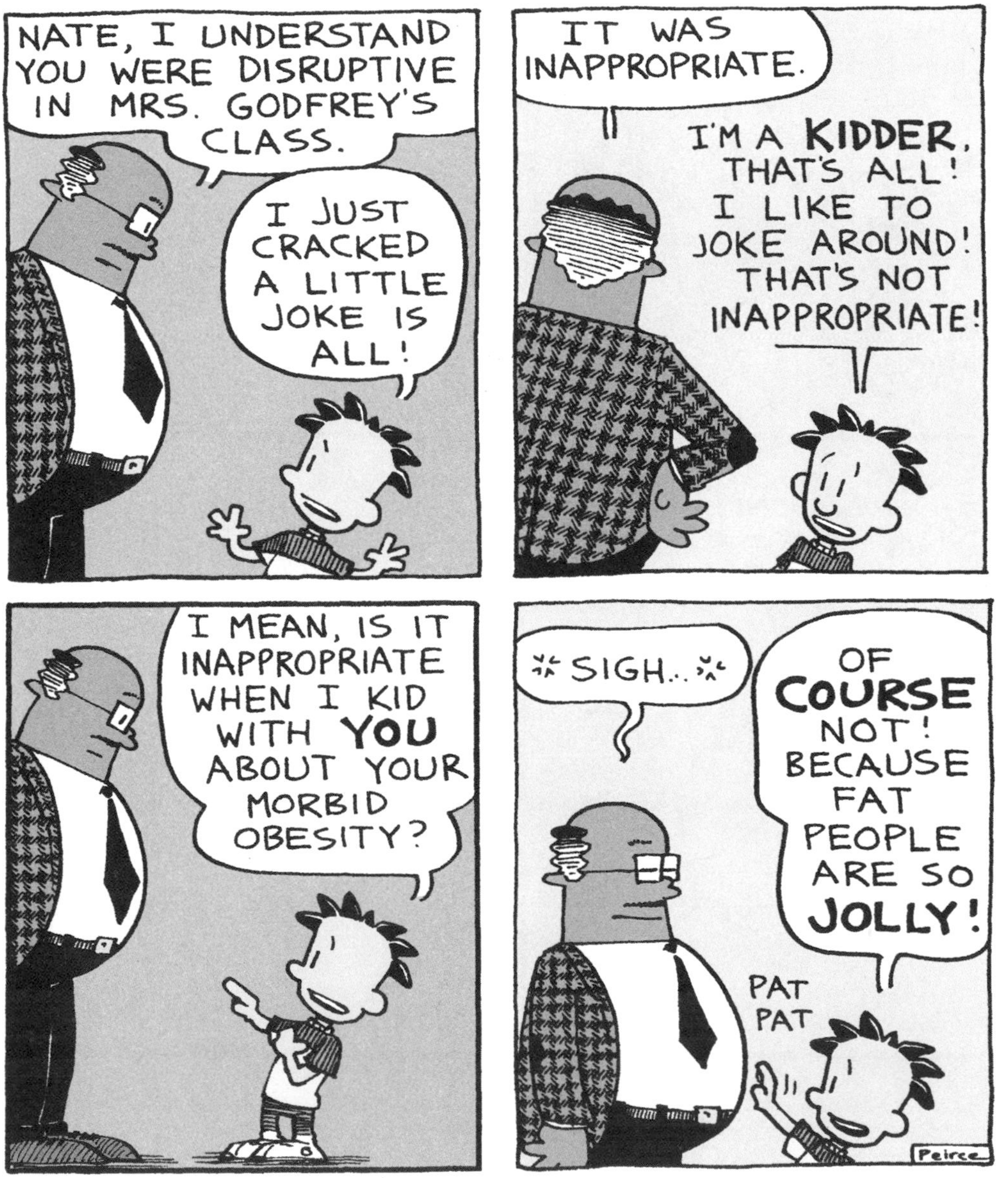
NATE, I UNDERSTAND YOU WERE DISRUPTIVE IN MRS. GODFREY'S CLASS.
I JUST CRACKED A LITTLE JOKE IS ALL!
IT WAS INAPPROPRIATE.
I'M A KIDDER. THAT'S ALL! I LIKE TO JOKE AROUND! THAT'S NOT INAPPROPRIATE!
I MEAN, IS IT INAPPROPRIATE WHEN I KID WITH YOU ABOUT YOUR MORBID OBESITY?
SIGH...
OF COURSE NOT! BECAUSE FAT PEOPLE ARE SO JOLLY!
PAT PAT
Peirce

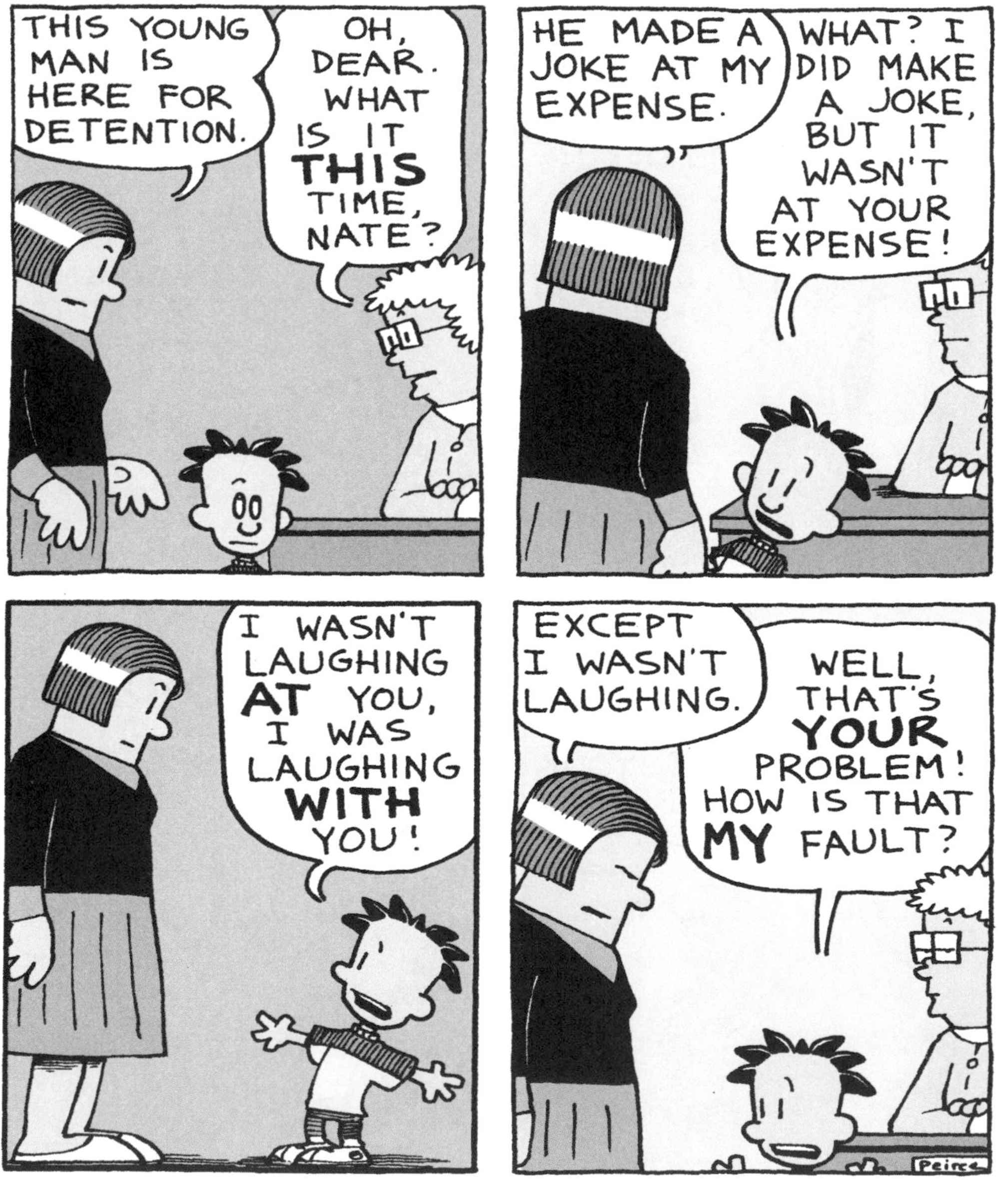
THIS YOUNG MAN IS HERE FOR DETENTION.
OH, DEAR. WHAT IS IT **THIS** TIME, NATE?
HE MADE A JOKE AT MY EXPENSE.
WHAT? I DID MAKE A JOKE, BUT IT WASN'T AT YOUR EXPENSE!
I WASN'T LAUGHING **AT** YOU, I WAS LAUGHING **WITH** YOU!
EXCEPT I WASN'T LAUGHING.
WELL, THAT'S **YOUR** PROBLEM! HOW IS THAT **MY** FAULT?
Peirce

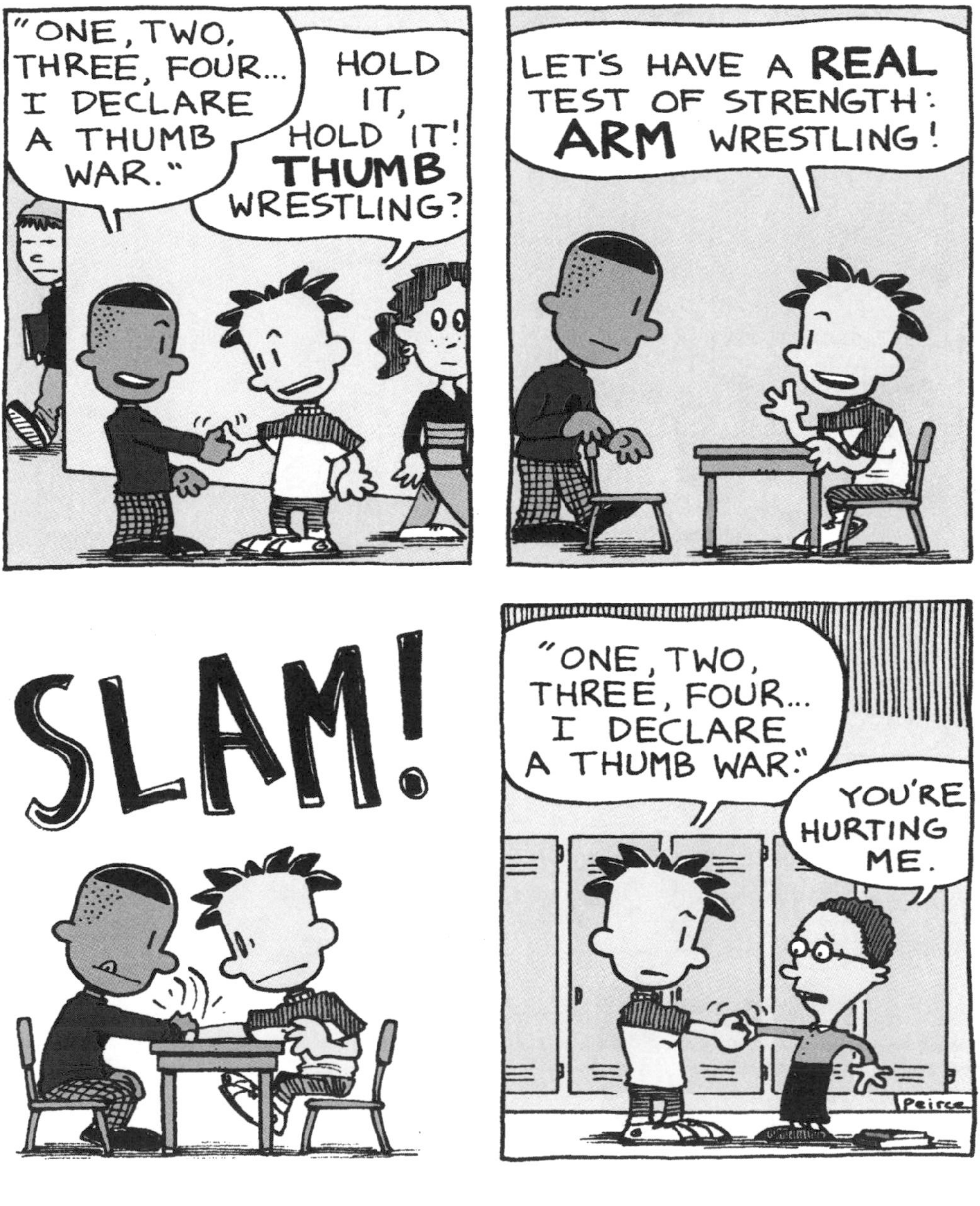
"ONE, TWO, THREE, FOUR... I DECLARE A THUMB WAR."
HOLD IT, HOLD IT! THUMB WRESTLING?
LET'S HAVE A REAL TEST OF STRENGTH: ARM WRESTLING!
SLAM!
"ONE, TWO, THREE, FOUR... I DECLARE A THUMB WAR."
YOU'RE HURTING ME.
Peirce

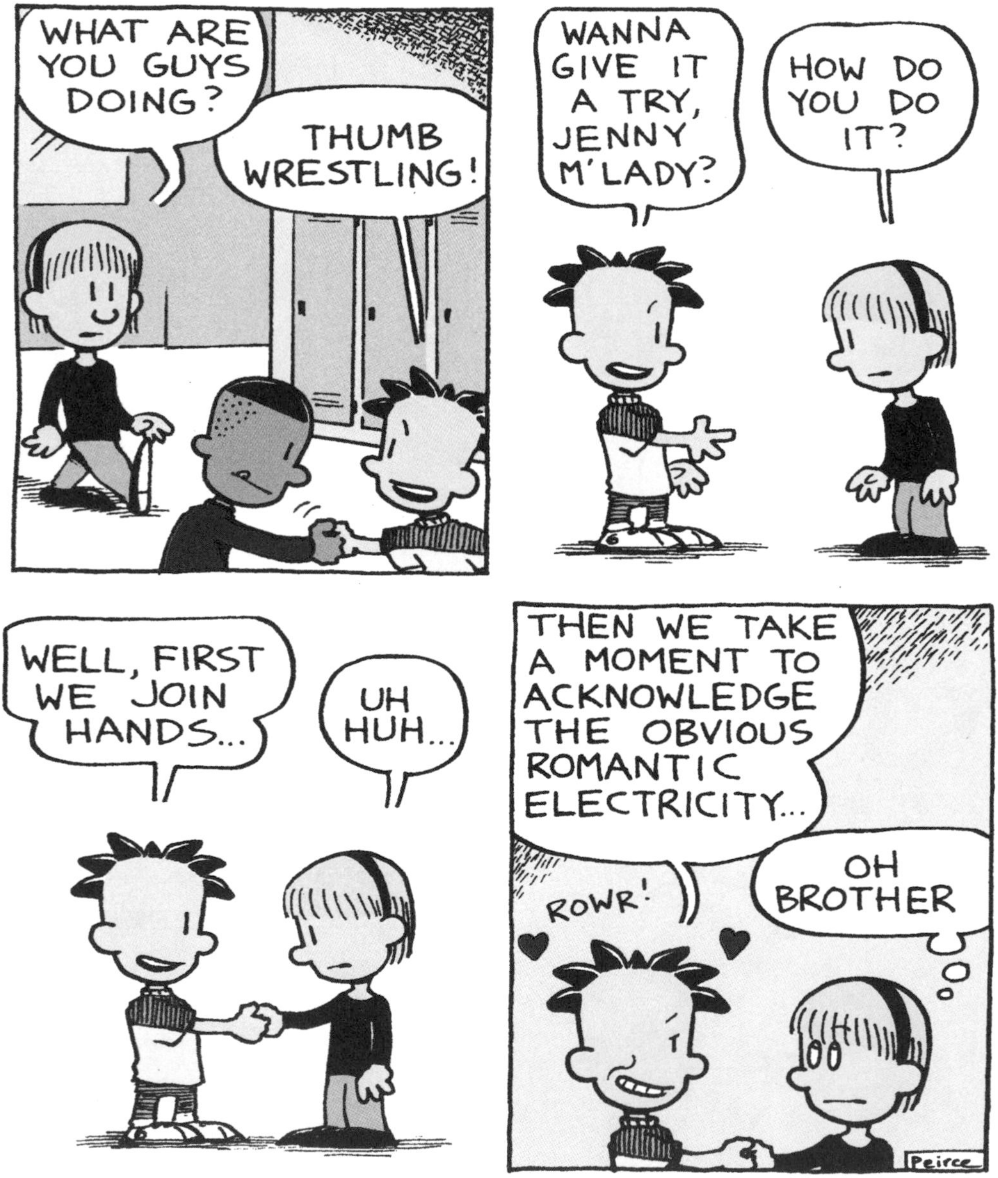
WHAT ARE YOU GUYS DOING?
THUMB WRESTLING!
WANNA GIVE IT A TRY, JENNY M'LADY?
HOW DO YOU DO IT?
WELL, FIRST WE JOIN HANDS...
UH HUH...
THEN WE TAKE A MOMENT TO ACKNOWLEDGE THE OBVIOUS ROMANTIC ELECTRICITY...
ROWR!
OH BROTHER
Peirce

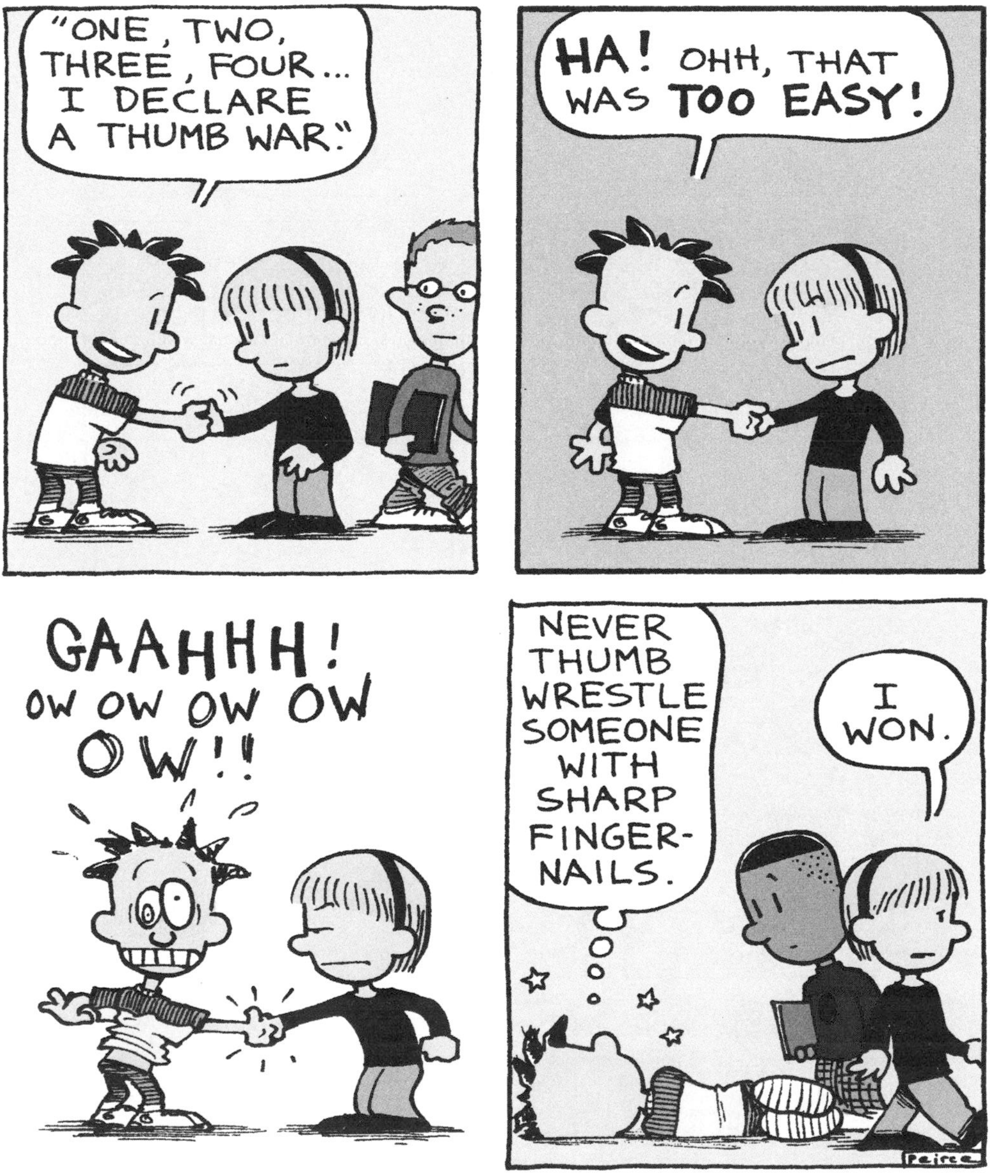
"ONE, TWO, THREE, FOUR... I DECLARE A THUMB WAR."
HA! OHH, THAT WAS TOO EASY!
GAAHHH! OW OW OW OW OW!!
NEVER THUMB WRESTLE SOMEONE WITH SHARP FINGER-NAILS.
I WON.
Peirce

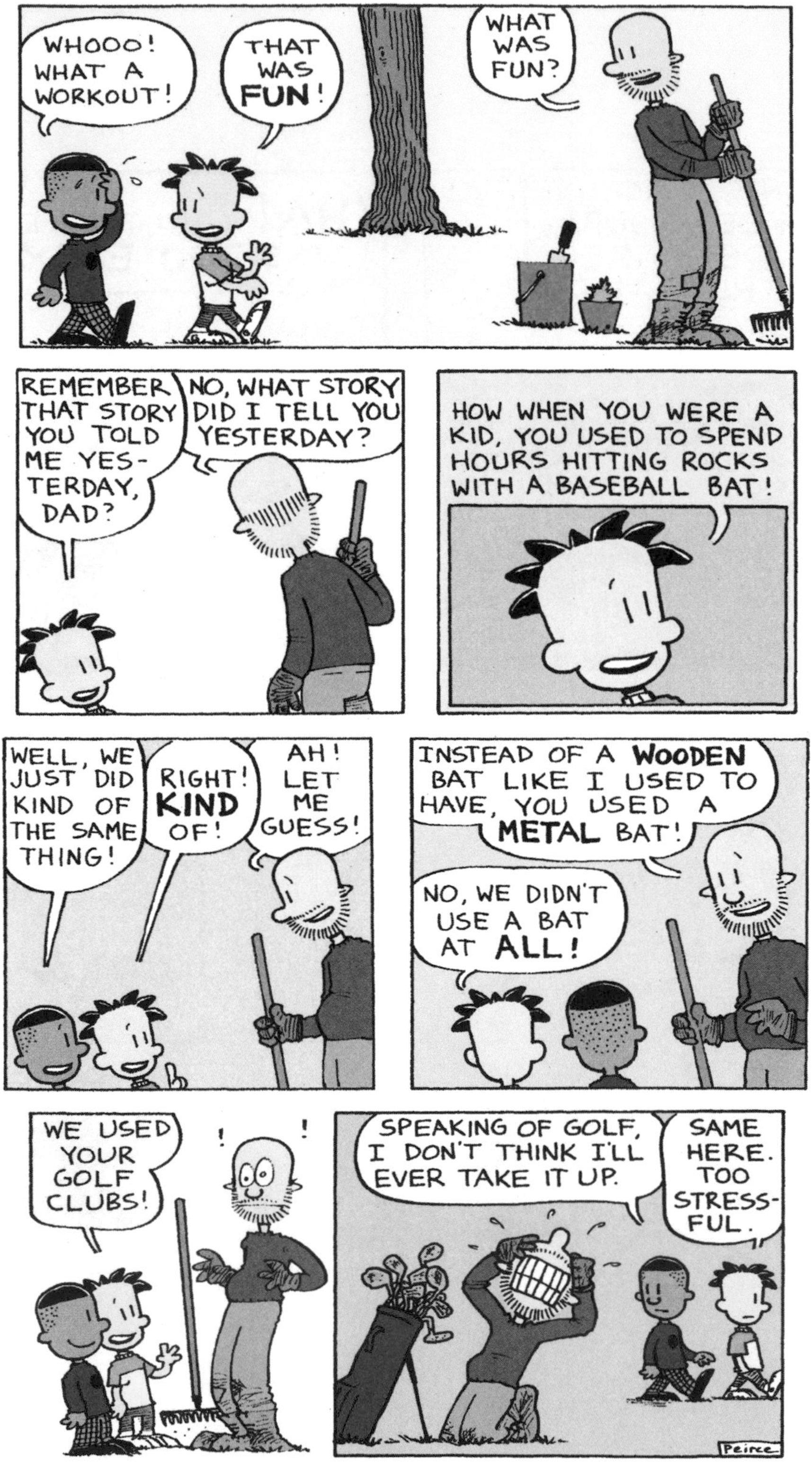
WHOOO! WHAT A WORKOUT!
THAT WAS FUN!
WHAT WAS FUN?
REMEMBER THAT STORY YOU TOLD ME YES-TERDAY, DAD?
NO, WHAT STORY DID I TELL YOU YESTERDAY?
HOW WHEN YOU WERE A KID, YOU USED TO SPEND HOURS HITTING ROCKS WITH A BASEBALL BAT!
WELL, WE JUST DID KIND OF THE SAME THING!
RIGHT! KIND OF!
AH! LET ME GUESS!
INSTEAD OF A WOODEN BAT LIKE I USED TO HAVE, YOU USED A METAL BAT!
NO, WE DIDN'T USE A BAT AT ALL!
WE USED YOUR GOLF CLUBS!
! !
SPEAKING OF GOLF, I DON'T THINK I'LL EVER TAKE IT UP.
SAME HERE. TOO STRESS-FUL.
Peirce

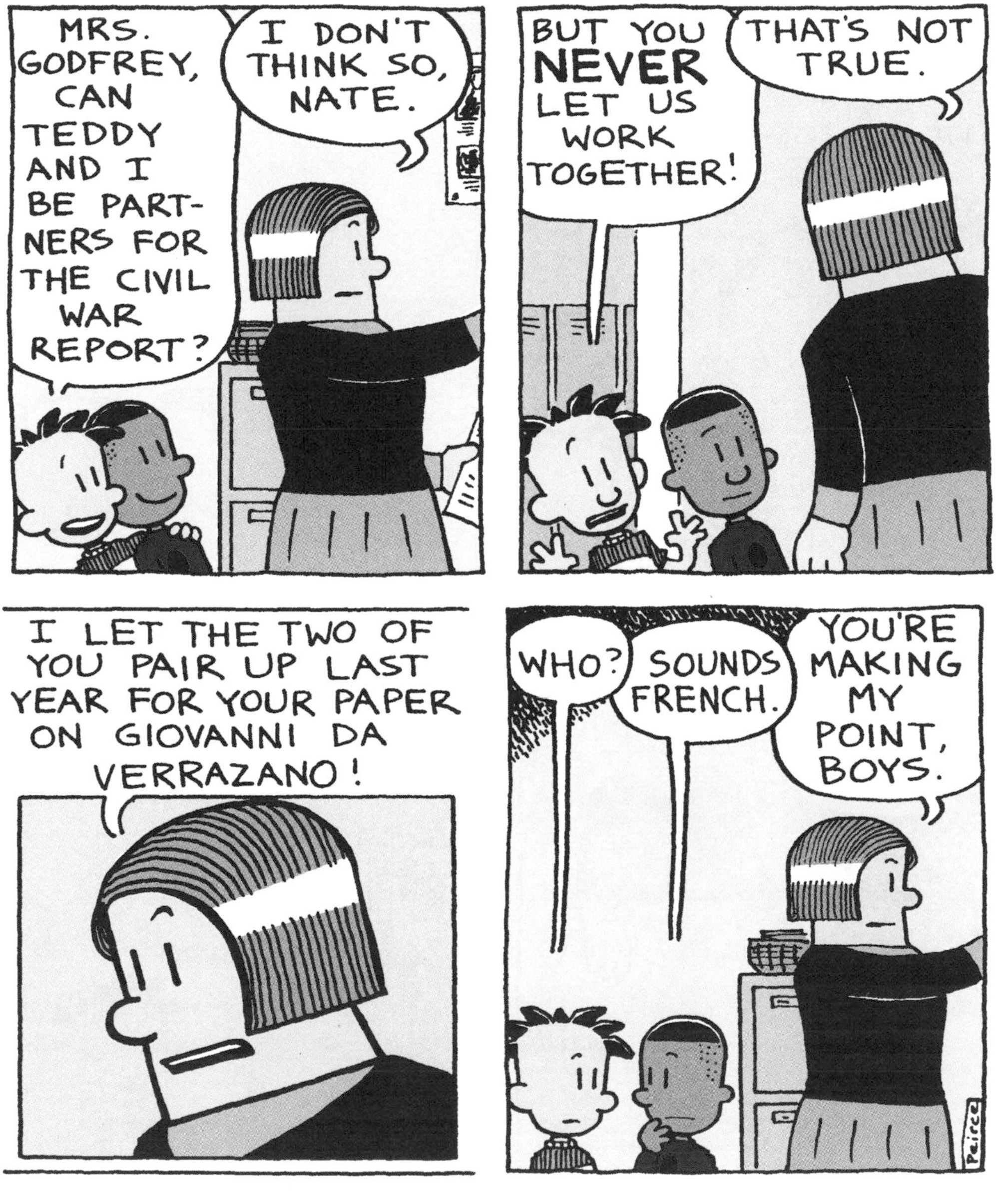
MRS. GODFREY, CAN TEDDY AND I BE PARTNERS FOR THE CIVIL WAR REPORT?
I DON'T THINK SO, NATE.
BUT YOU **NEVER** LET US WORK TOGETHER!
THAT'S NOT TRUE.
I LET THE TWO OF YOU PAIR UP LAST YEAR FOR YOUR PAPER ON GIOVANNI DA VERRAZANO!
WHO?
SOUNDS FRENCH.
YOU'RE MAKING MY POINT, BOYS.
Peirce

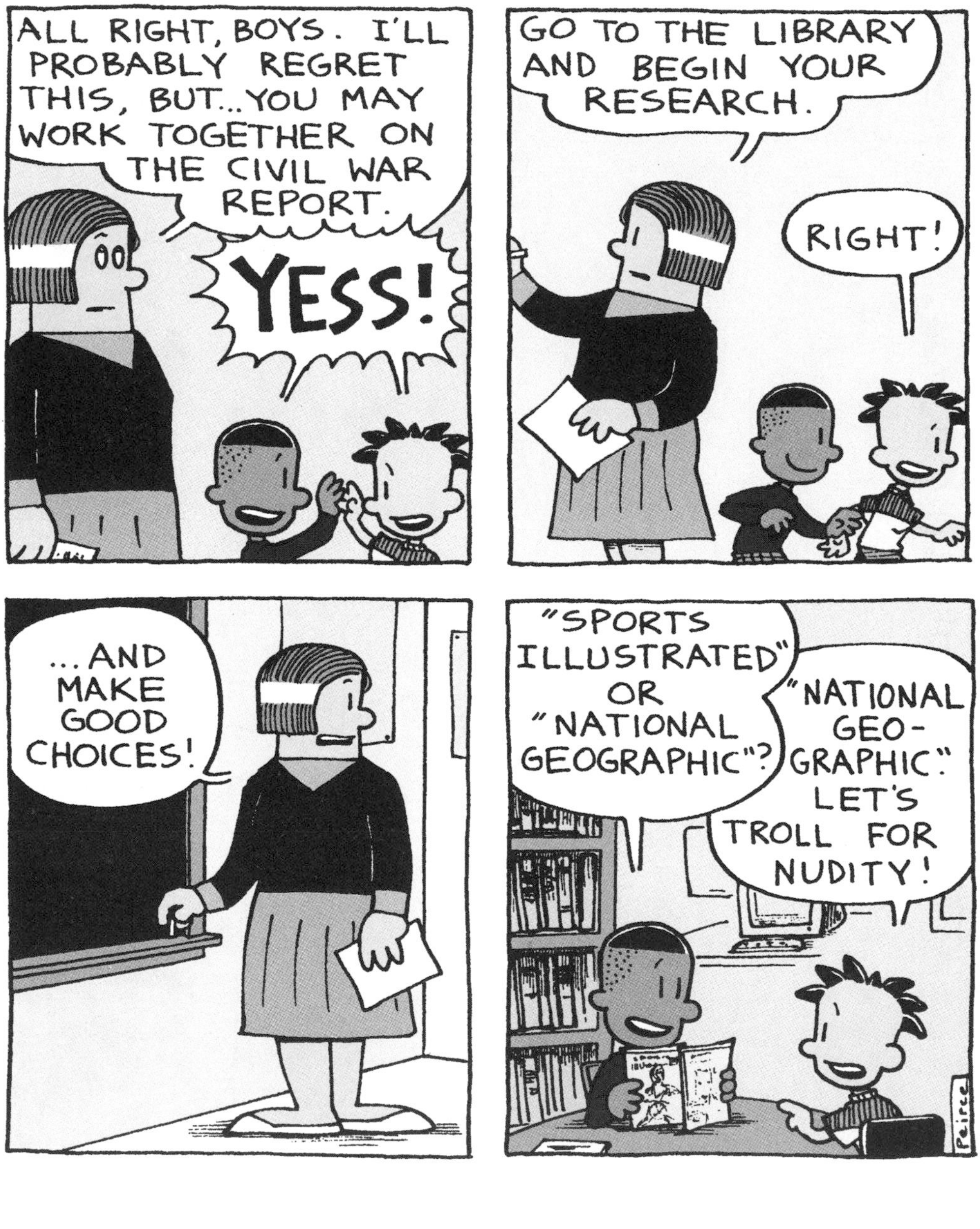
ALL RIGHT, BOYS. I'LL PROBABLY REGRET THIS, BUT...YOU MAY WORK TOGETHER ON THE CIVIL WAR REPORT.
YESS!
GO TO THE LIBRARY AND BEGIN YOUR RESEARCH.
RIGHT!
...AND MAKE GOOD CHOICES!
"SPORTS ILLUSTRATED" OR "NATIONAL GEOGRAPHIC"?
"NATIONAL GEO-GRAPHIC." LET'S TROLL FOR NUDITY!
Peirce

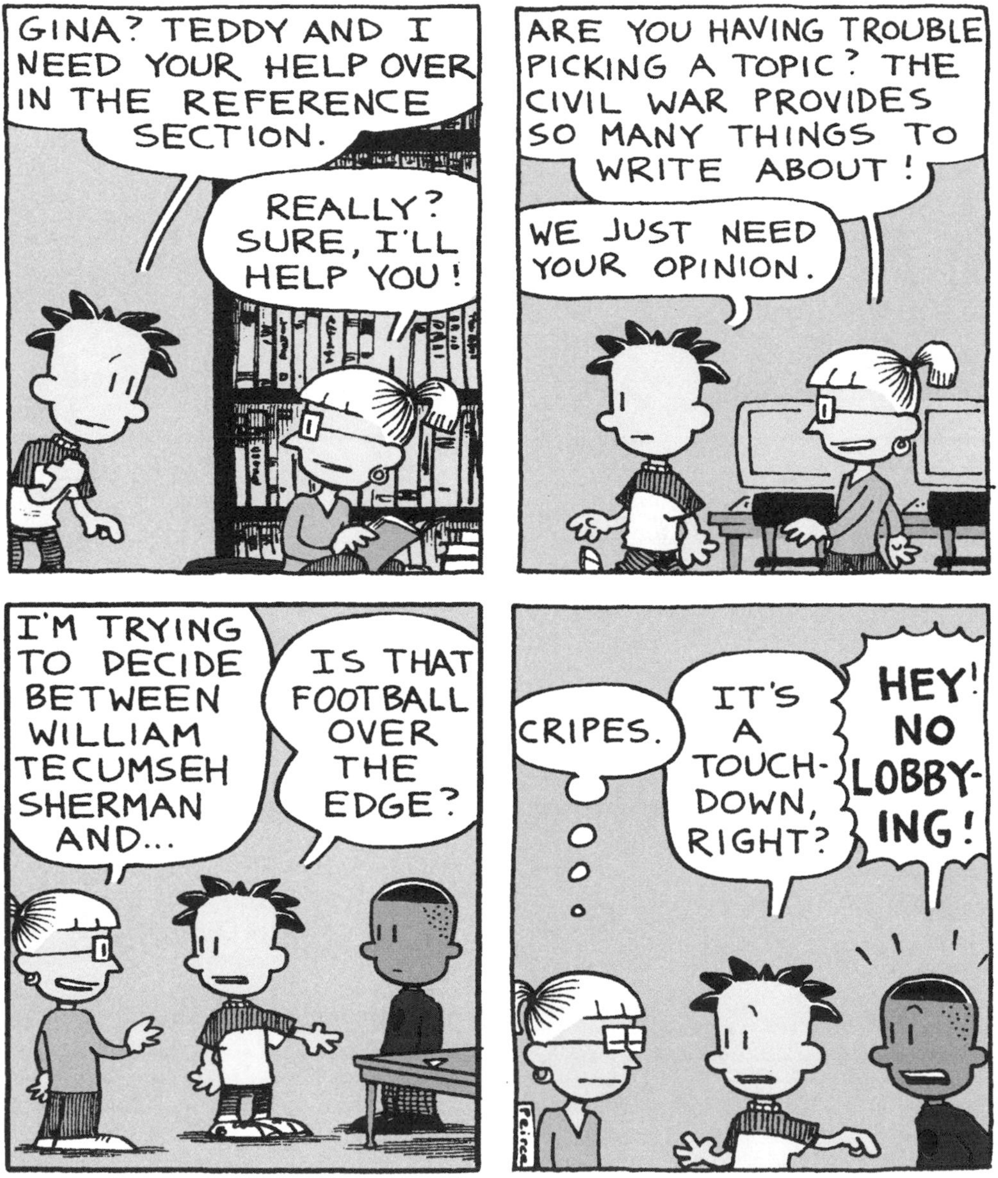
GINA? TEDDY AND I NEED YOUR HELP OVER IN THE REFERENCE SECTION.
REALLY? SURE, I'LL HELP YOU!
ARE YOU HAVING TROUBLE PICKING A TOPIC? THE CIVIL WAR PROVIDES SO MANY THINGS TO WRITE ABOUT!
WE JUST NEED YOUR OPINION.
I'M TRYING TO DECIDE BETWEEN WILLIAM TECUMSEH SHERMAN AND...
IS THAT FOOTBALL OVER THE EDGE?
CRIPES.
IT'S A TOUCH-DOWN, RIGHT?
HEY! NO LOBBY-ING!
PEIRCE

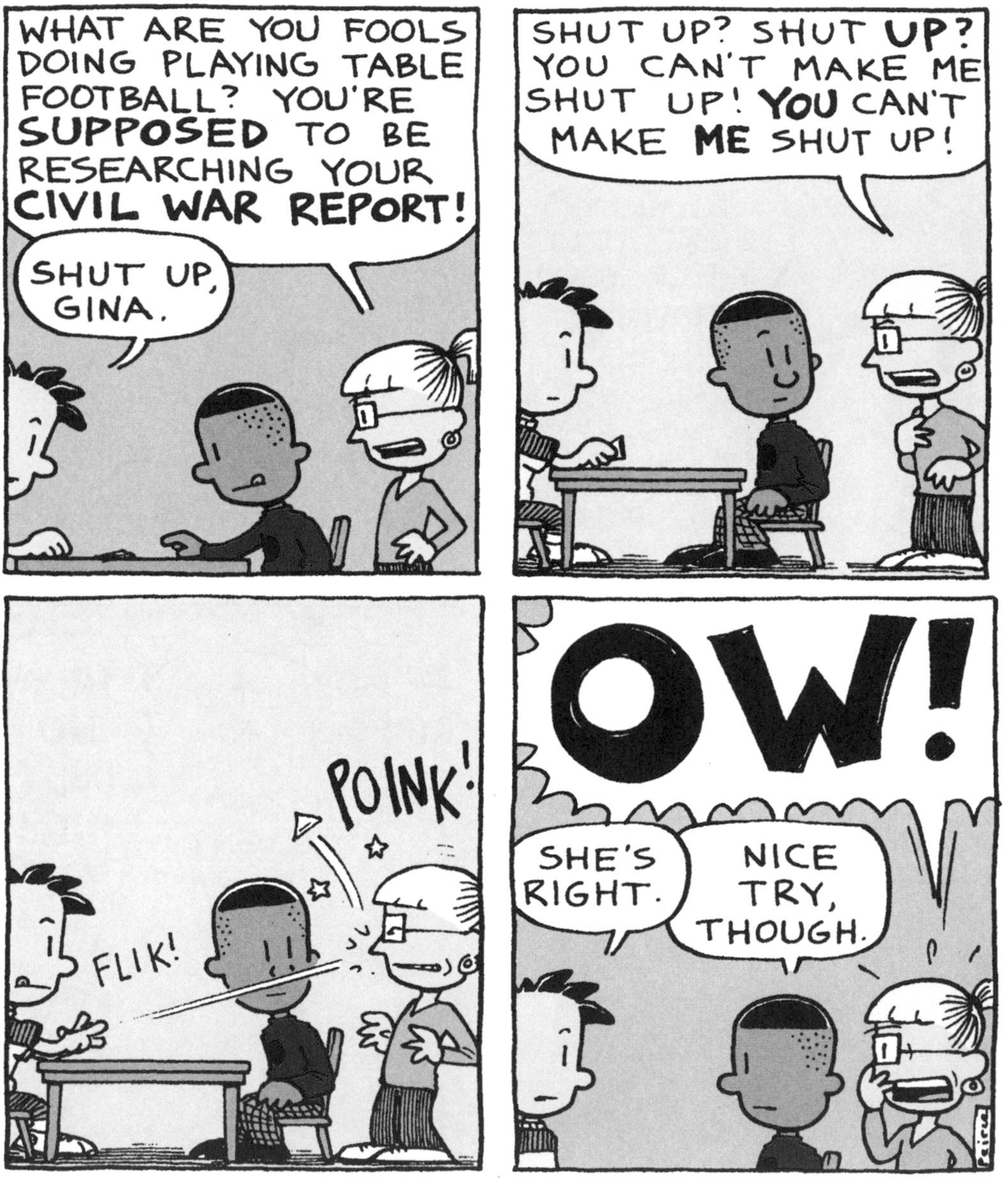
WHAT ARE YOU FOOLS DOING PLAYING TABLE FOOTBALL? YOU'RE **SUPPOSED** TO BE RESEARCHING YOUR **CIVIL WAR REPORT!**
SHUT UP, GINA.
SHUT UP? SHUT **UP**? YOU CAN'T MAKE ME SHUT UP! **YOU** CAN'T MAKE **ME** SHUT UP!
FLIK!
POINK!
OW!
SHE'S RIGHT.
NICE TRY, THOUGH.

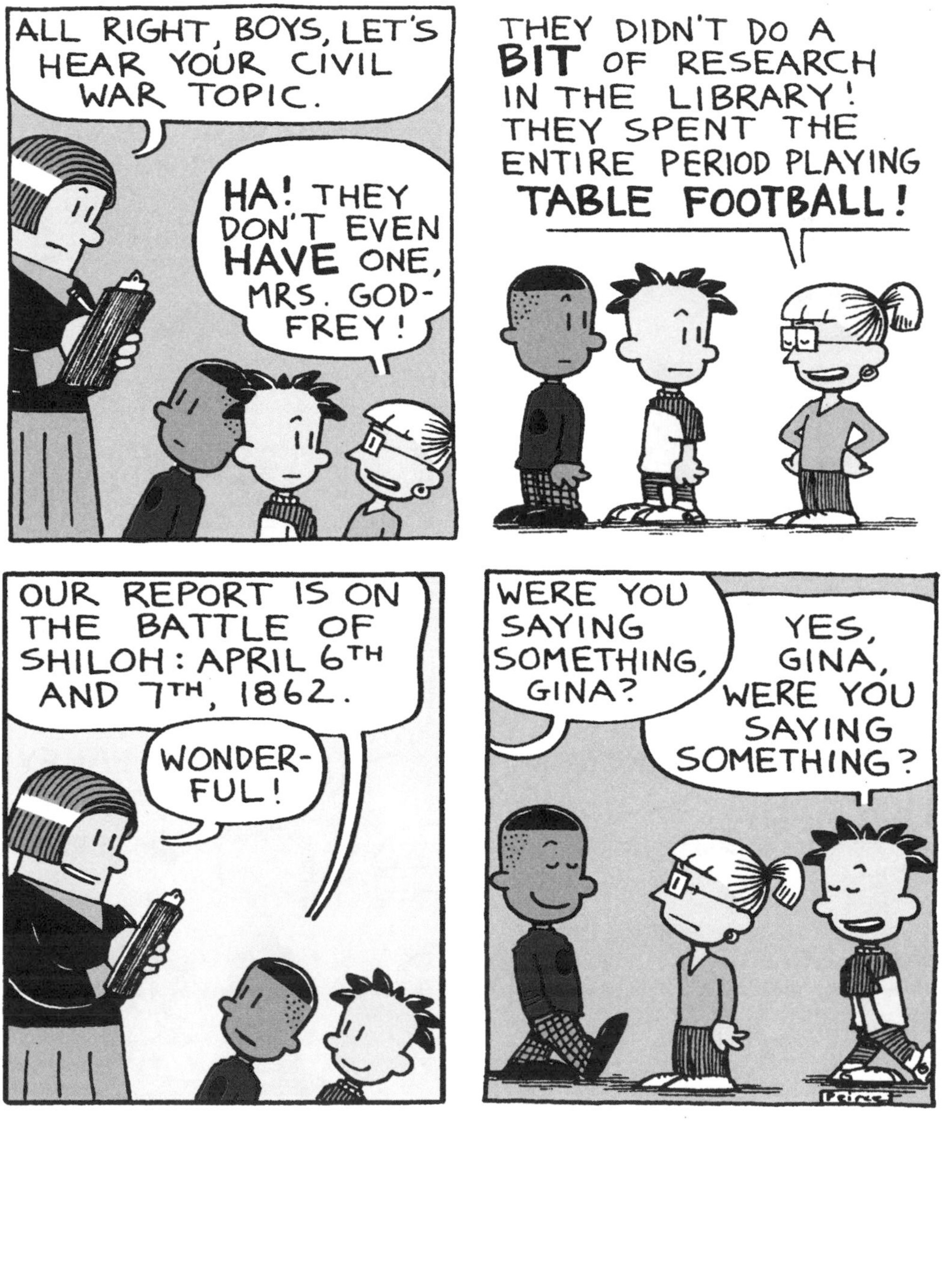
ALL RIGHT, BOYS, LET'S HEAR YOUR CIVIL WAR TOPIC.
HA! THEY DON'T EVEN HAVE ONE, MRS. GODFREY!
THEY DIDN'T DO A BIT OF RESEARCH IN THE LIBRARY! THEY SPENT THE ENTIRE PERIOD PLAYING TABLE FOOTBALL!
OUR REPORT IS ON THE BATTLE OF SHILOH: APRIL 6TH AND 7TH, 1862.
WONDERFUL!
WERE YOU SAYING SOMETHING, GINA?
YES, GINA, WERE YOU SAYING SOMETHING?

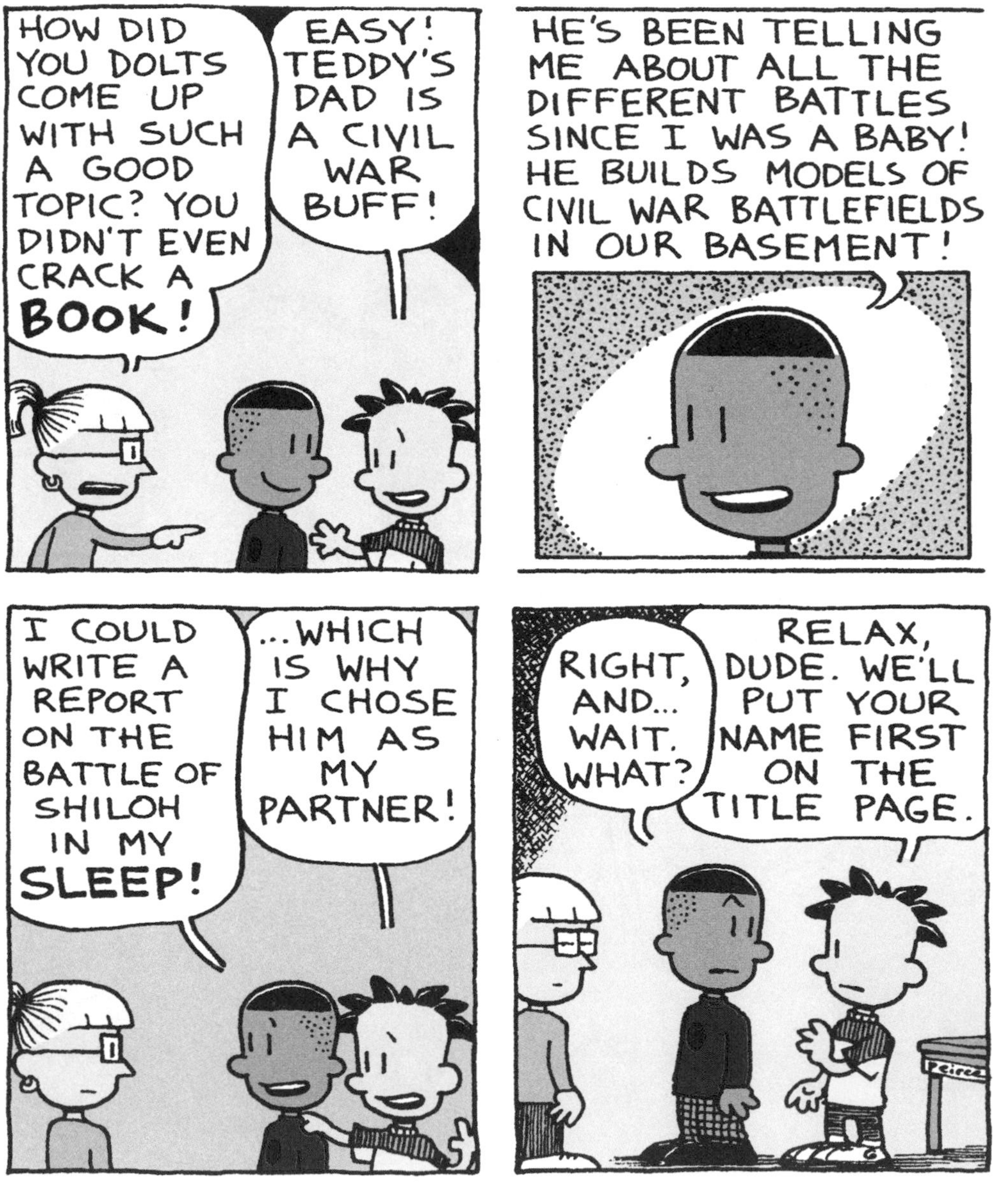
HOW DID YOU DOLTS COME UP WITH SUCH A GOOD TOPIC? YOU DIDN'T EVEN CRACK A BOOK!
EASY! TEDDY'S DAD IS A CIVIL WAR BUFF!
HE'S BEEN TELLING ME ABOUT ALL THE DIFFERENT BATTLES SINCE I WAS A BABY! HE BUILDS MODELS OF CIVIL WAR BATTLEFIELDS IN OUR BASEMENT!
I COULD WRITE A REPORT ON THE BATTLE OF SHILOH IN MY SLEEP!
...WHICH IS WHY I CHOSE HIM AS MY PARTNER!
RIGHT, AND... WAIT. WHAT?
RELAX, DUDE. WE'LL PUT YOUR NAME FIRST ON THE TITLE PAGE.

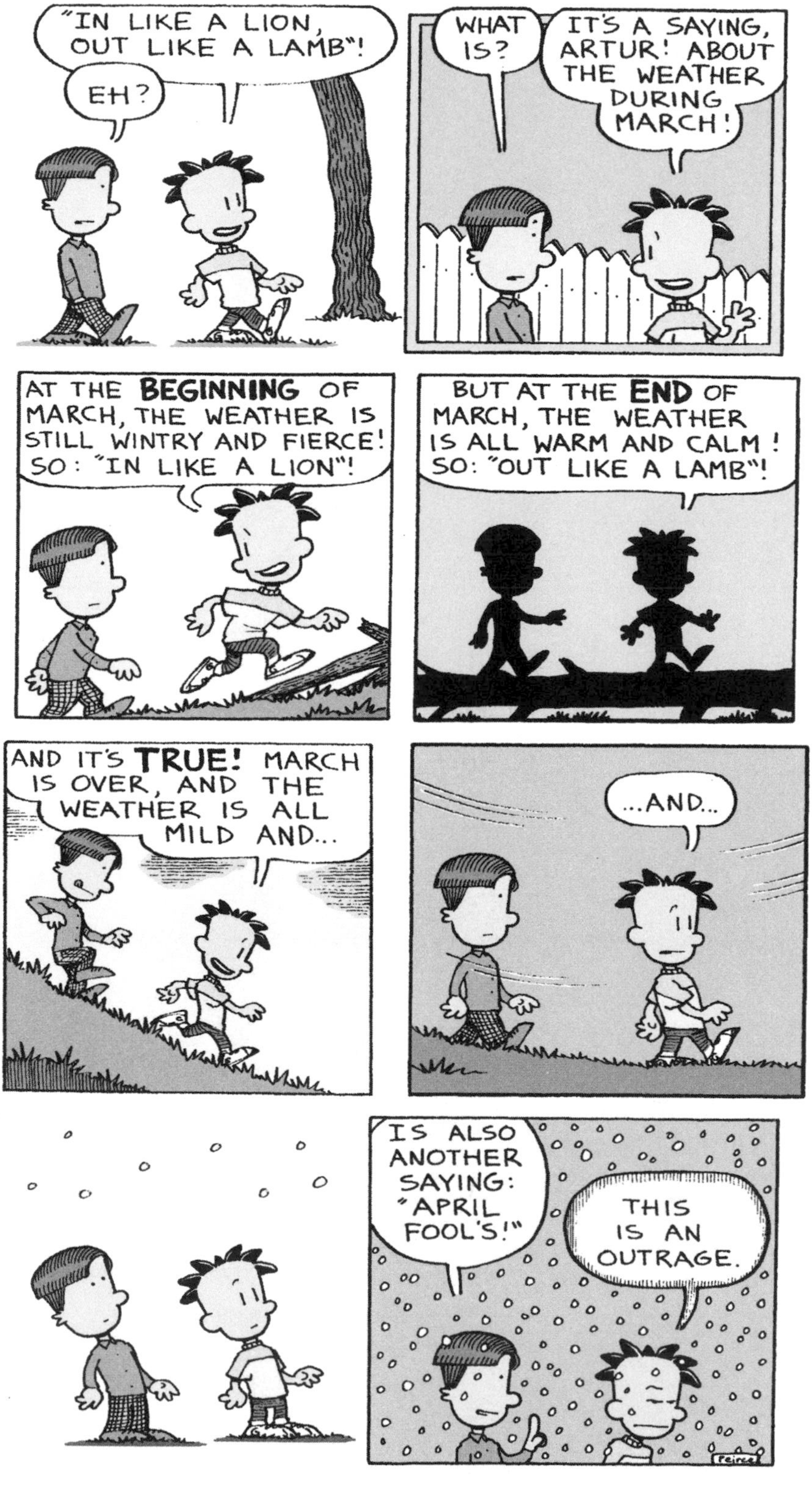
"IN LIKE A LION, OUT LIKE A LAMB"!
EH?
WHAT IS?
IT'S A SAYING, ARTUR! ABOUT THE WEATHER DURING MARCH!
AT THE BEGINNING OF MARCH, THE WEATHER IS STILL WINTRY AND FIERCE! SO: "IN LIKE A LION"!
BUT AT THE END OF MARCH, THE WEATHER IS ALL WARM AND CALM! SO: "OUT LIKE A LAMB"!
AND IT'S TRUE! MARCH IS OVER, AND THE WEATHER IS ALL MILD AND...
...AND...
IS ALSO ANOTHER SAYING: "APRIL FOOL'S!"
THIS IS AN OUTRAGE.
Peirce

big NATE

OUT LOUD

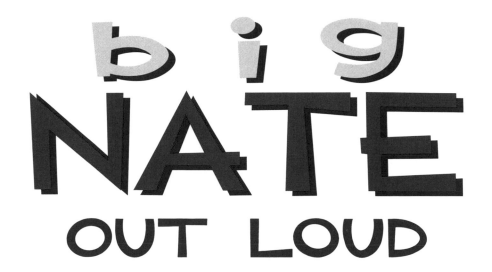

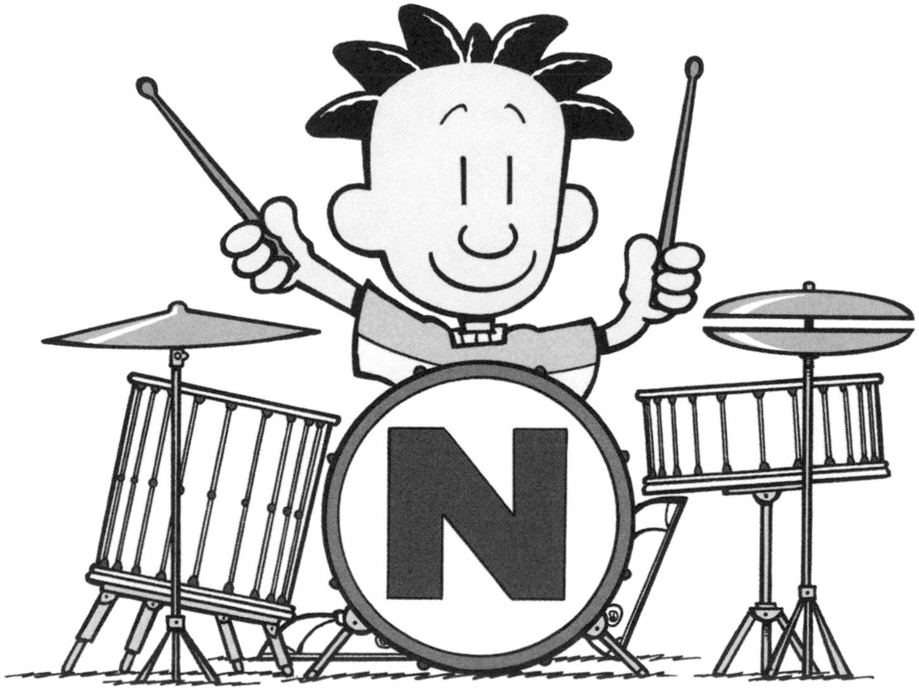
N

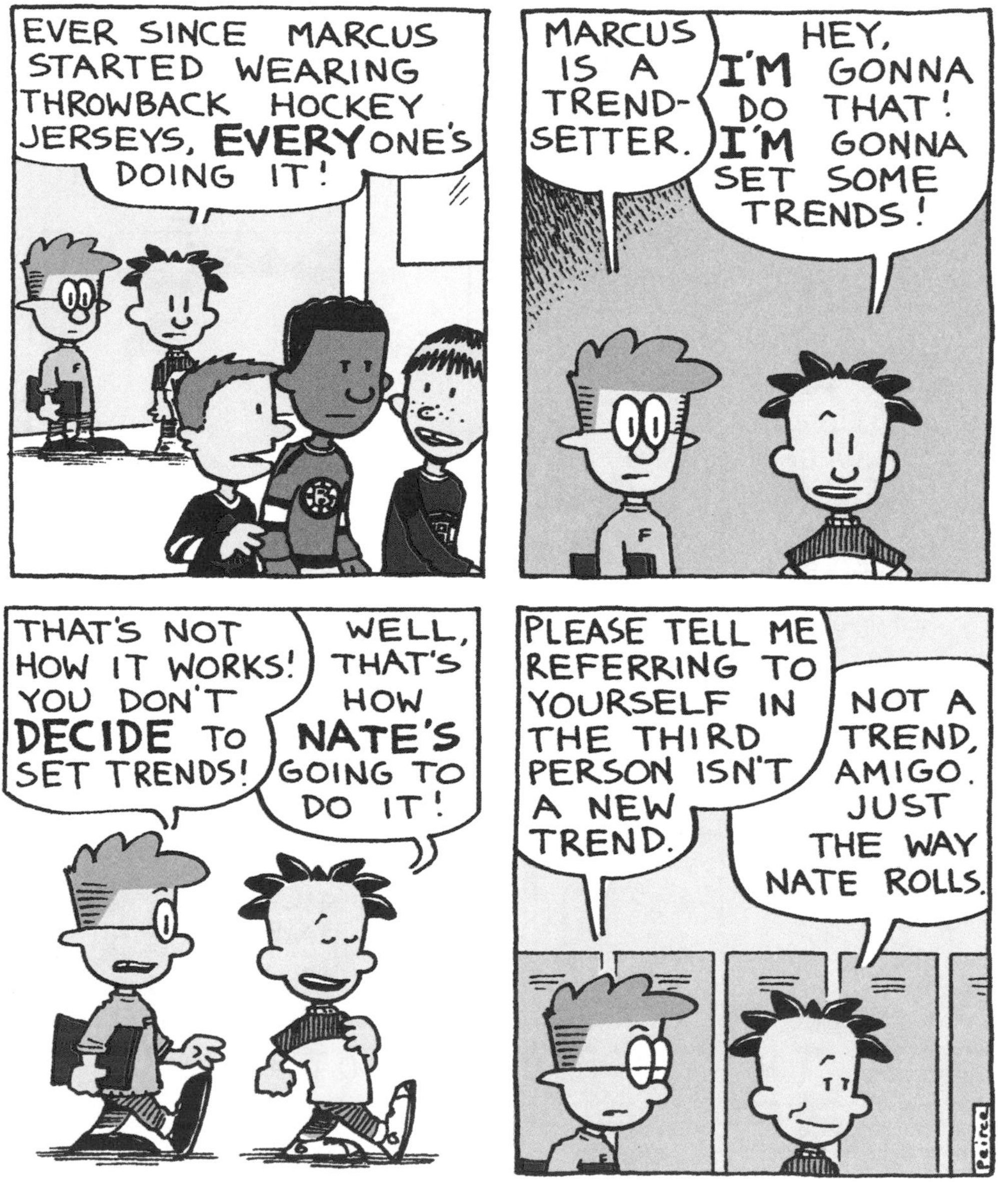
EVER SINCE MARCUS STARTED WEARING THROWBACK HOCKEY JERSEYS, EVERYONE'S DOING IT!
MARCUS IS A TREND-SETTER.
HEY, I'M GONNA DO THAT! I'M GONNA SET SOME TRENDS!
THAT'S NOT HOW IT WORKS! YOU DON'T DECIDE TO SET TRENDS!
WELL, THAT'S HOW NATE'S GOING TO DO IT!
PLEASE TELL ME REFERRING TO YOURSELF IN THE THIRD PERSON ISN'T A NEW TREND.
NOT A TREND, AMIGO. JUST THE WAY NATE ROLLS.
Peirce

IT'S OFFICIAL! I'VE DECIDED TO BECOME A TRENDSETTER!

WHAT'S THAT SUPPOSED TO MEAN?

IT MEANS I'M GOING TO **SET TRENDS**, OF COURSE! I'M GOING TO LIVE MY LIFE, AND PEOPLE ARE GOING TO **IMITATE** ME!

DUDE. PEOPLE AL**READY** IMITATE YOU.

THEY **DO**?

DOOYYY! GUESS WHO **I** AM!

SEE?

HA HA HA HA HEH HA HA HA NICE HAIR! HA HA

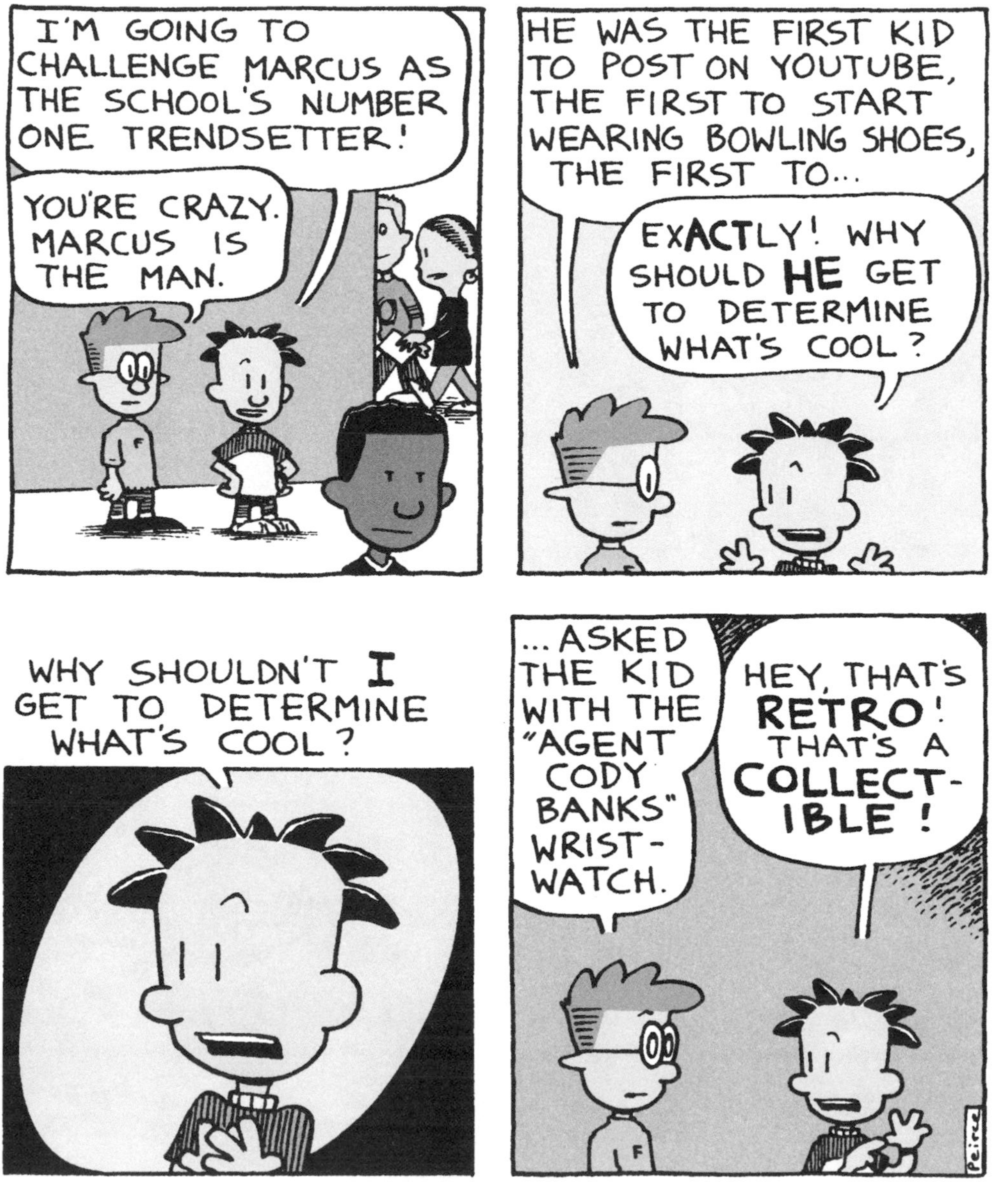
I'M GOING TO CHALLENGE MARCUS AS THE SCHOOL'S NUMBER ONE TRENDSETTER!
YOU'RE CRAZY. MARCUS IS THE MAN.
HE WAS THE FIRST KID TO POST ON YOUTUBE, THE FIRST TO START WEARING BOWLING SHOES, THE FIRST TO...
EXACTLY! WHY SHOULD HE GET TO DETERMINE WHAT'S COOL?
WHY SHOULDN'T I GET TO DETERMINE WHAT'S COOL?
...ASKED THE KID WITH THE "AGENT CODY BANKS" WRIST-WATCH.
HEY, THAT'S RETRO! THAT'S A COLLECT-IBLE!
Peirce

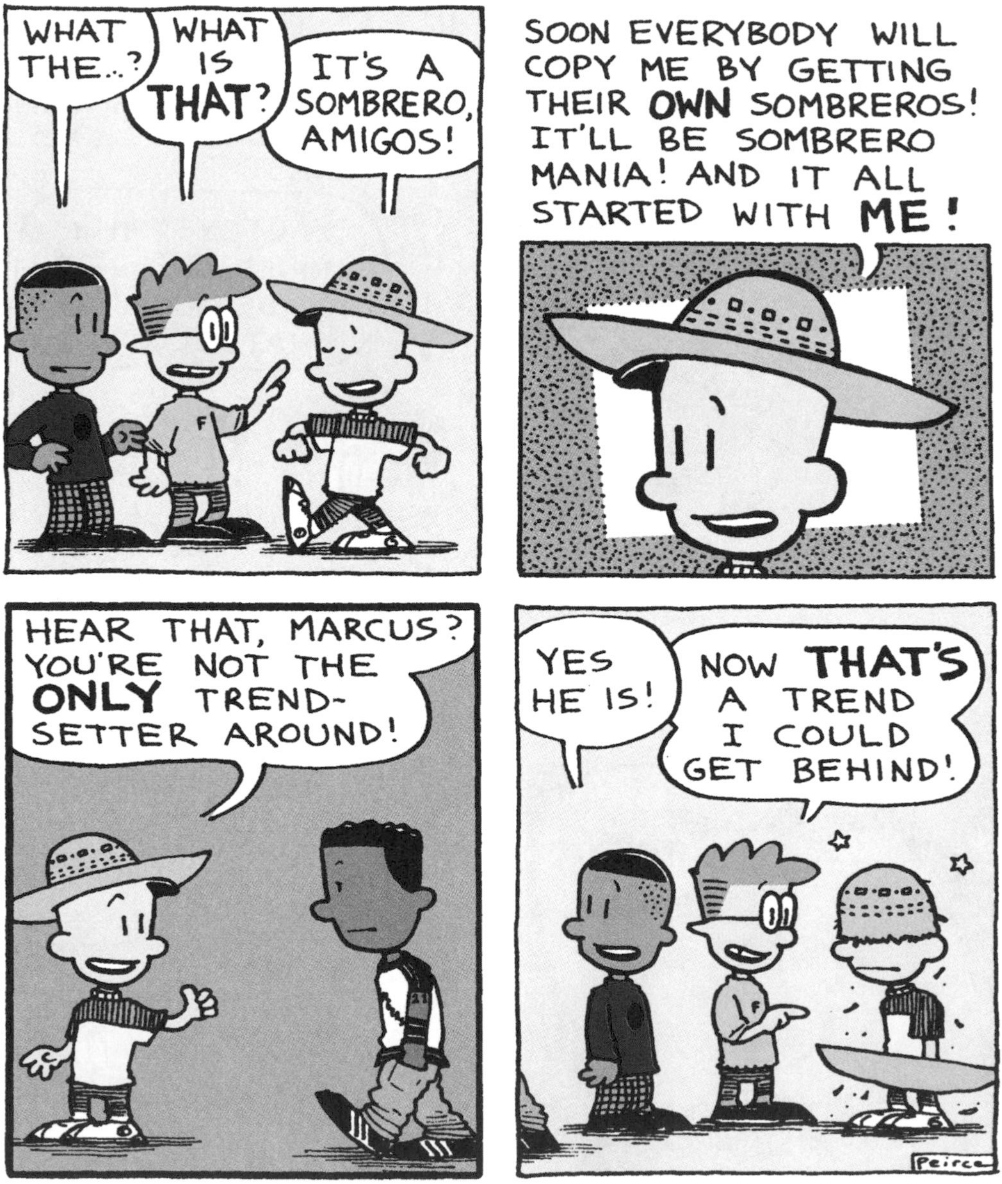
WHAT THE...?
WHAT IS THAT?
IT'S A SOMBRERO, AMIGOS!
SOON EVERYBODY WILL COPY ME BY GETTING THEIR OWN SOMBREROS! IT'LL BE SOMBRERO MANIA! AND IT ALL STARTED WITH ME!
HEAR THAT, MARCUS? YOU'RE NOT THE ONLY TREND-SETTER AROUND!
YES HE IS!
NOW THAT'S A TREND I COULD GET BEHIND!
Peirce

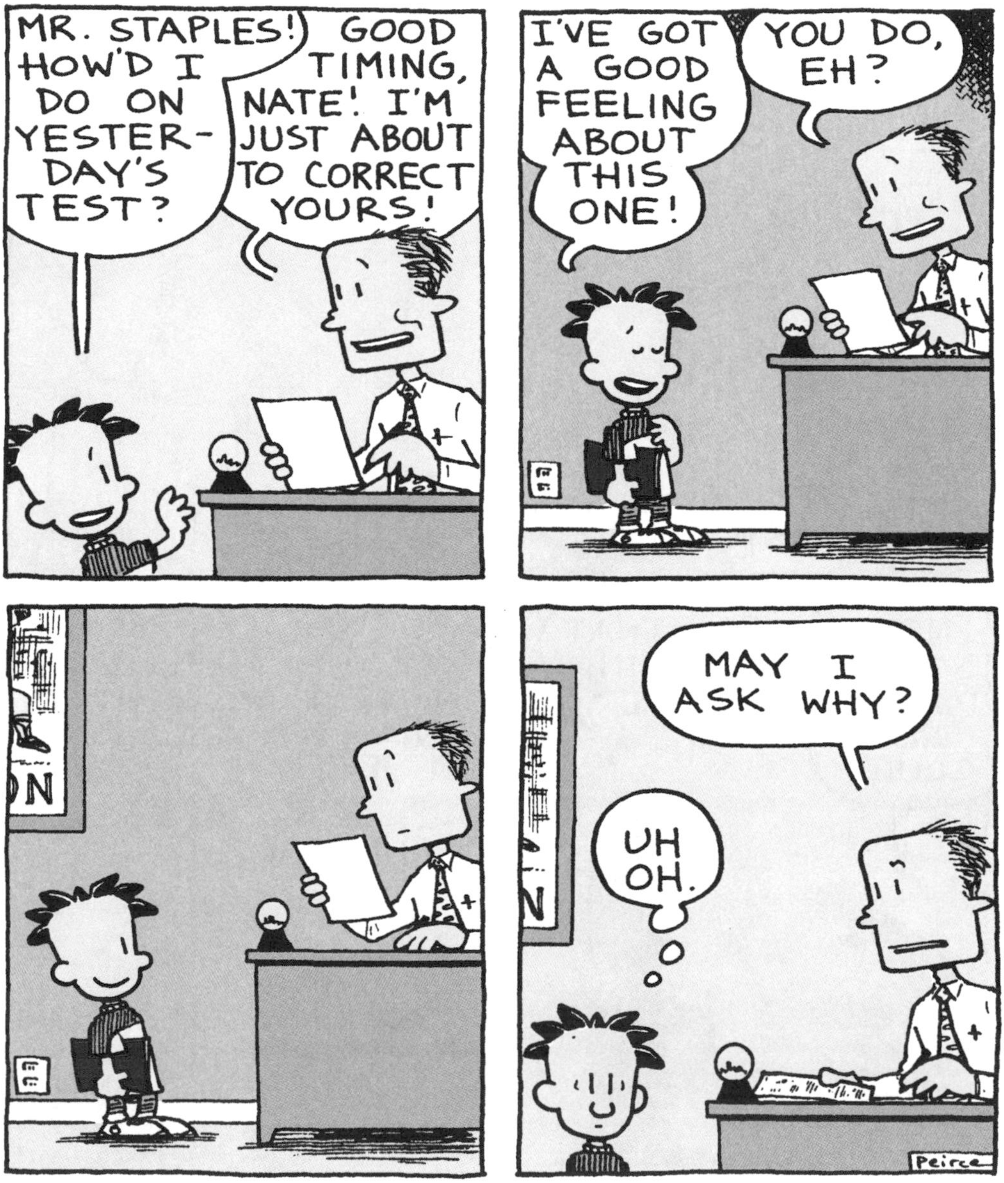
MR. STAPLES! HOW'D I DO ON YESTER-DAY'S TEST?
GOOD TIMING, NATE! I'M JUST ABOUT TO CORRECT YOURS!
I'VE GOT A GOOD FEELING ABOUT THIS ONE!
YOU DO, EH?
MAY I ASK WHY?
UH OH.
Peirce

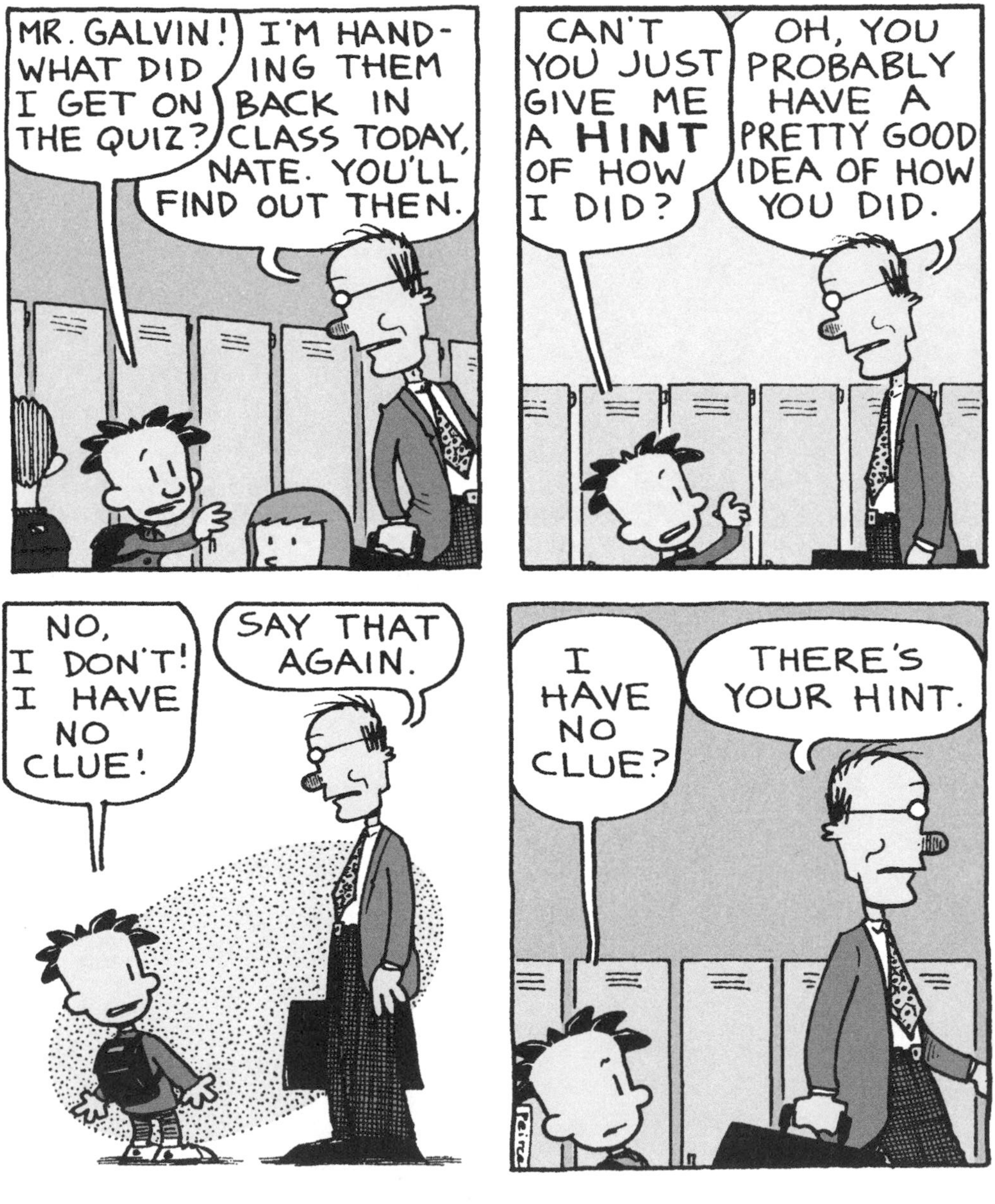
MR. GALVIN! WHAT DID I GET ON THE QUIZ?
I'M HANDING THEM BACK IN CLASS TODAY, NATE. YOU'LL FIND OUT THEN.
CAN'T YOU JUST GIVE ME A **HINT** OF HOW I DID?
OH, YOU PROBABLY HAVE A PRETTY GOOD IDEA OF HOW YOU DID.
NO, I DON'T! I HAVE NO CLUE!
SAY THAT AGAIN.
I HAVE NO CLUE?
THERE'S YOUR HINT.

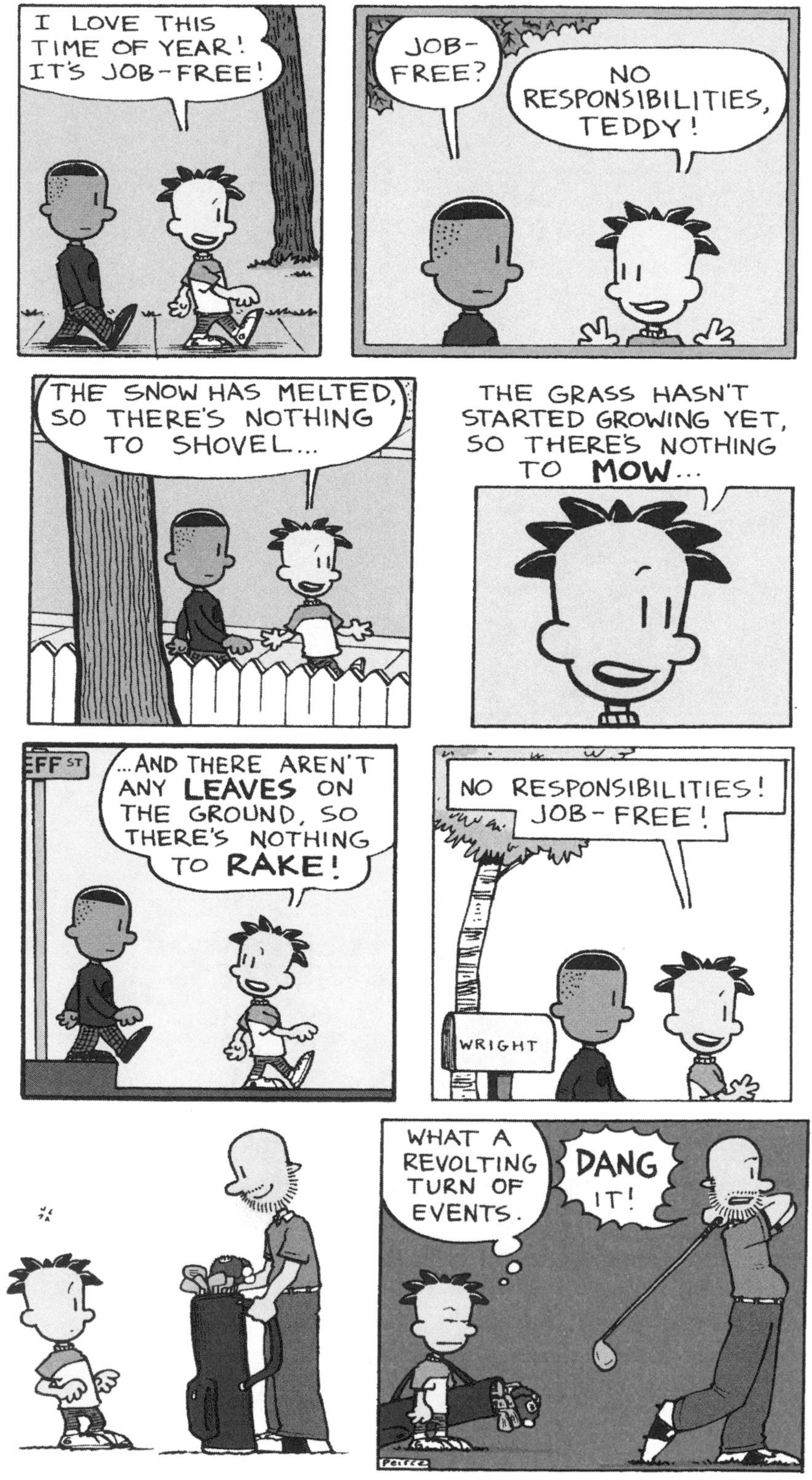
I LOVE THIS TIME OF YEAR! IT'S JOB-FREE!
JOB-FREE?
NO RESPONSIBILITIES, TEDDY!
THE SNOW HAS MELTED, SO THERE'S NOTHING TO SHOVEL...
THE GRASS HASN'T STARTED GROWING YET, SO THERE'S NOTHING TO MOW...
EFF ST
...AND THERE AREN'T ANY LEAVES ON THE GROUND, SO THERE'S NOTHING TO RAKE!
NO RESPONSIBILITIES! JOB-FREE!
WRIGHT
WHAT A REVOLTING TURN OF EVENTS.
DANG IT!
PEIRCE

THAT WAS COACH CALLING. PRACTICE IS CANCELED BECAUSE THE FIELD IS TOO WET.
THAT'S TOO BAD.
POST
BUT JUST BECAUSE THERE'S NO PRACTICE...
...DOESN'T MEAN THERE'S NO BASEBALL!
...AND JUST BECAUSE THERE'S BASE-BALL DOESN'T MEAN THERE'S ATHLETIC ABILITY.
WHOOPS. SORRY.
Peirce

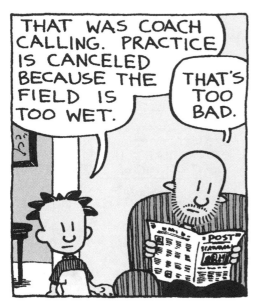

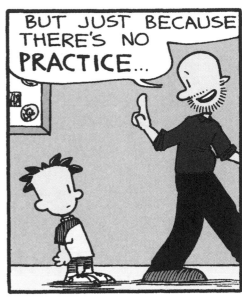

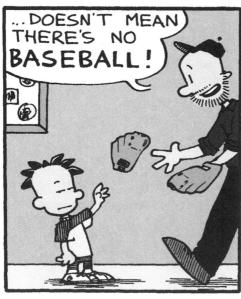

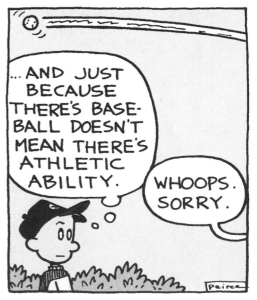

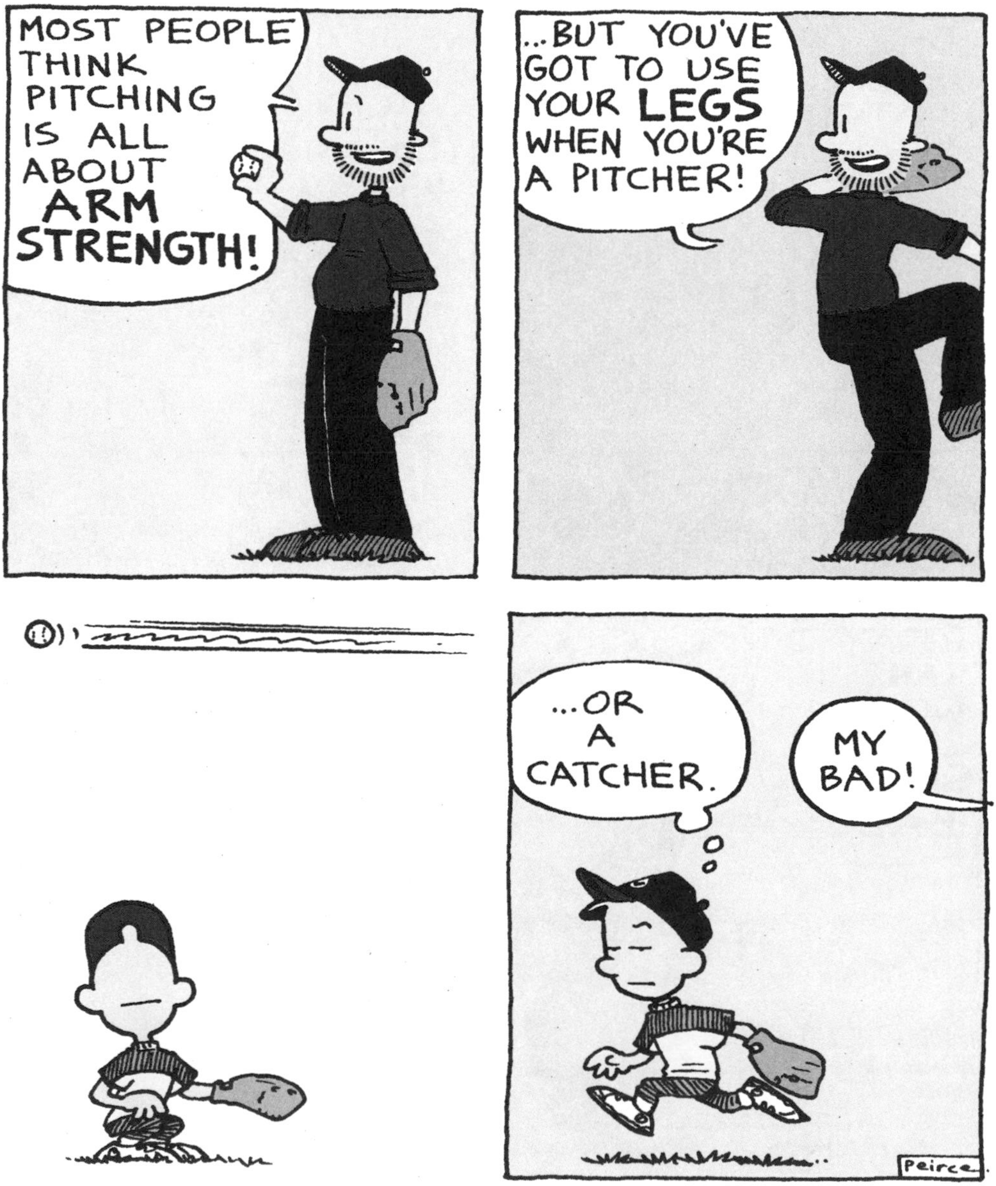
MOST PEOPLE THINK PITCHING IS ALL ABOUT ARM STRENGTH!
...BUT YOU'VE GOT TO USE YOUR LEGS WHEN YOU'RE A PITCHER!
...OR A CATCHER.
MY BAD!
Peirce

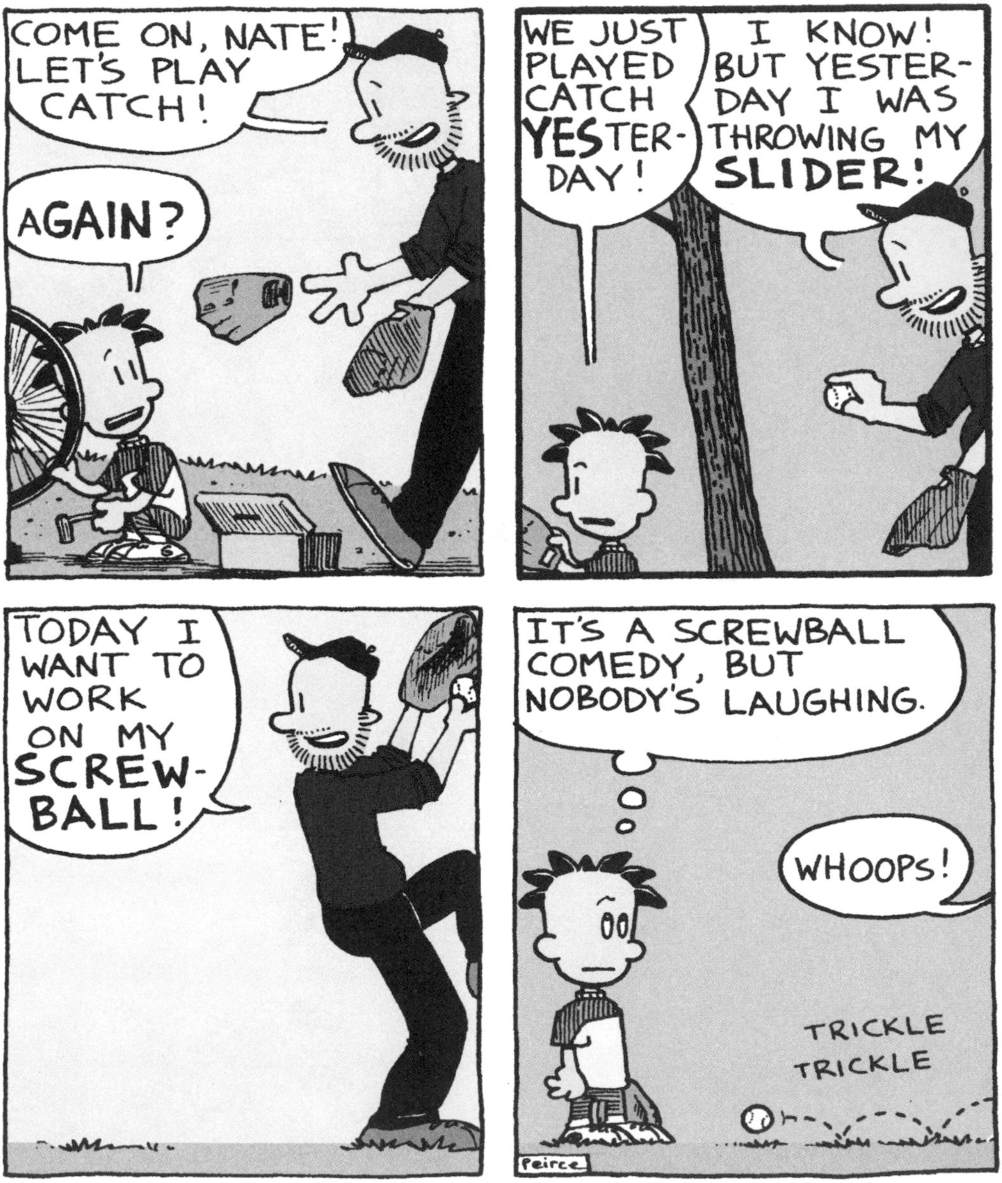
COME ON, NATE! LET'S PLAY CATCH!
AGAIN?
WE JUST PLAYED CATCH YESTERDAY!
I KNOW! BUT YESTERDAY I WAS THROWING MY SLIDER!
TODAY I WANT TO WORK ON MY SCREWBALL!
IT'S A SCREWBALL COMEDY, BUT NOBODY'S LAUGHING.
WHOOPS!
TRICKLE TRICKLE
Peirce

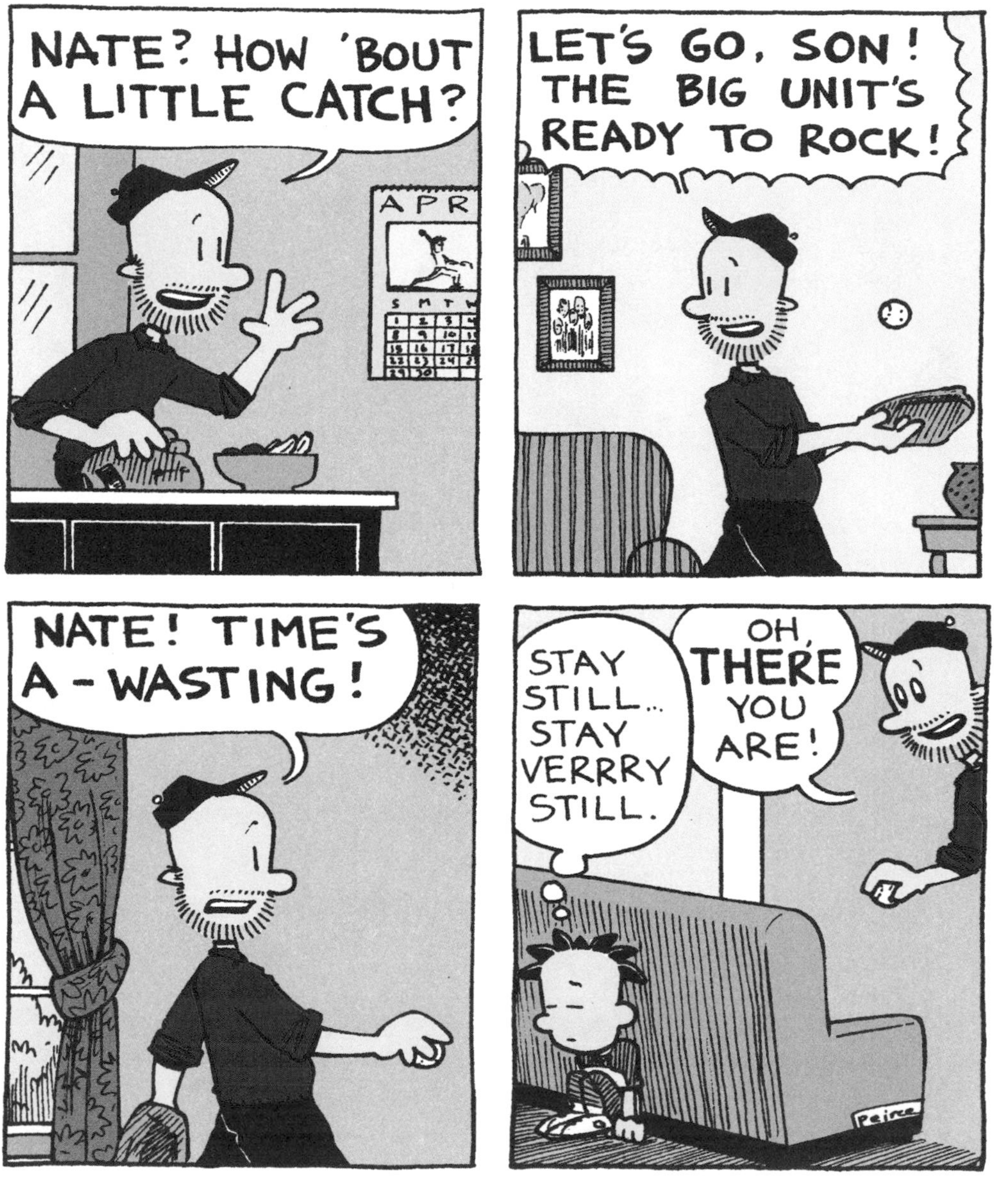
NATE? HOW 'BOUT A LITTLE CATCH?
APR
S M T W
LET'S GO, SON! THE BIG UNIT'S READY TO ROCK!
NATE! TIME'S A-WASTING!
STAY STILL... STAY VERRRY STILL.
OH, THERE YOU ARE!
Peirce

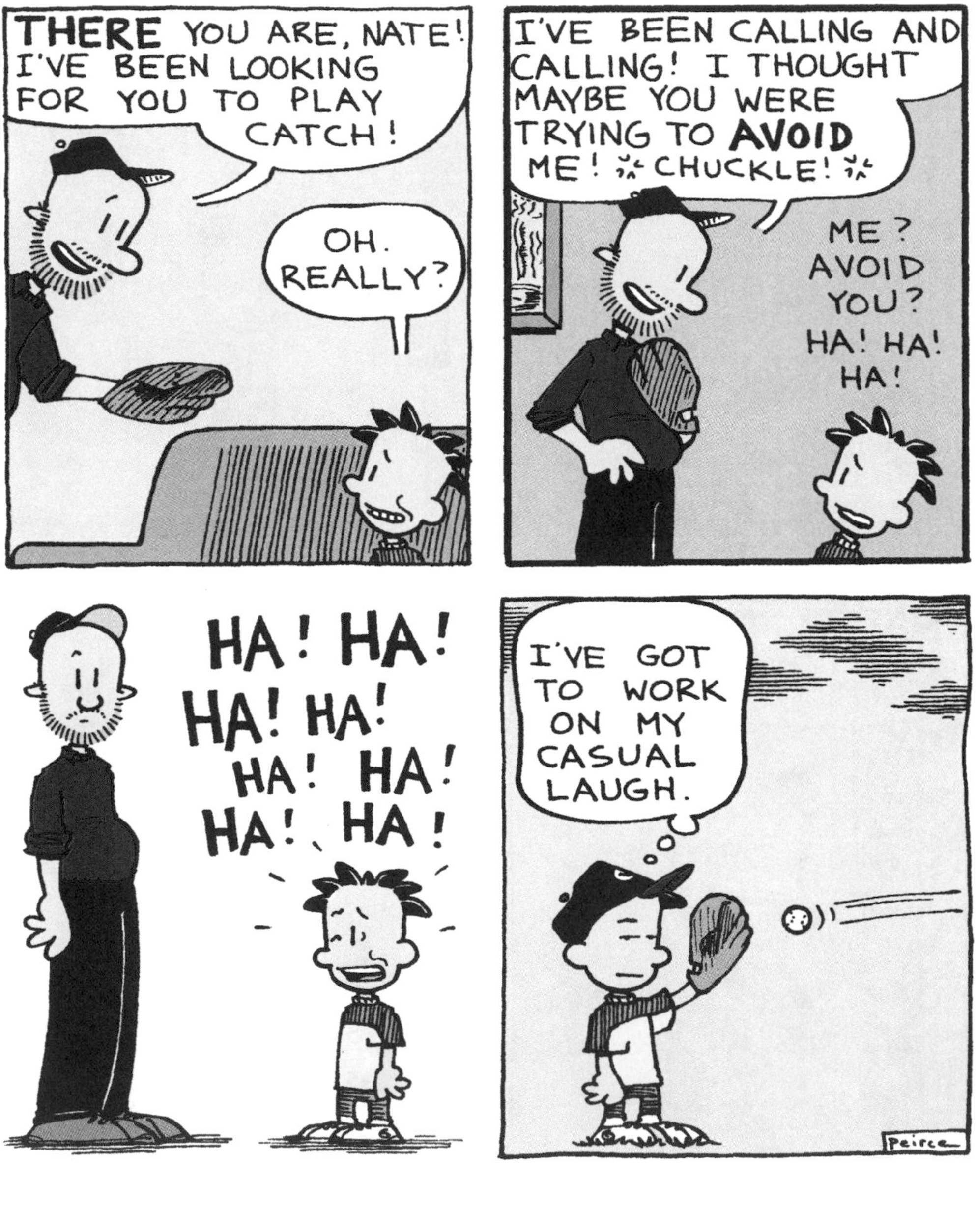
THERE YOU ARE, NATE! I'VE BEEN LOOKING FOR YOU TO PLAY CATCH!
OH. REALLY?
I'VE BEEN CALLING AND CALLING! I THOUGHT MAYBE YOU WERE TRYING TO AVOID ME! *CHUCKLE!*
ME? AVOID YOU? HA! HA! HA!
HA! HA! HA! HA! HA! HA! HA! HA!
I'VE GOT TO WORK ON MY CASUAL LAUGH.
Peirce

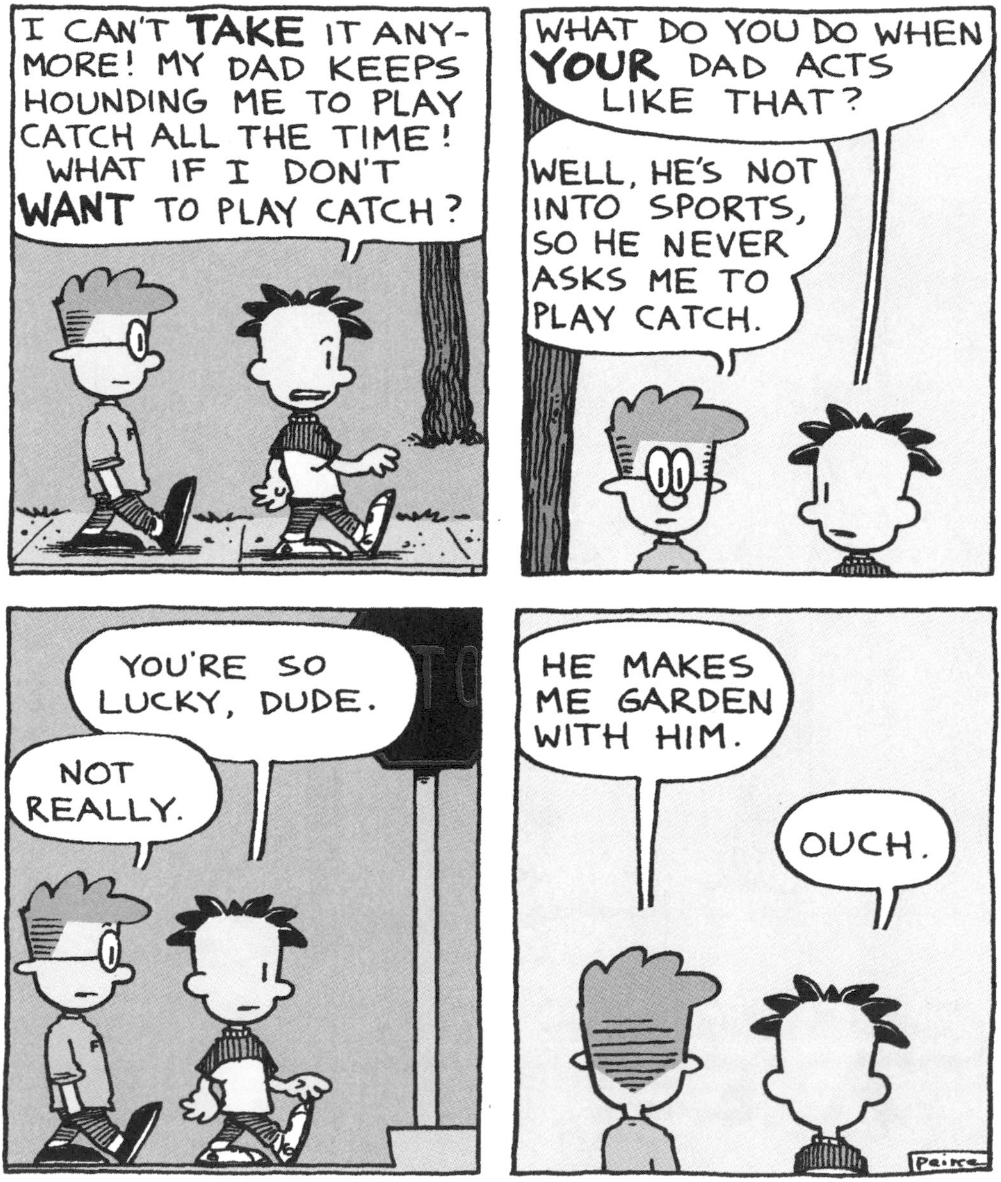
I CAN'T **TAKE** IT ANYMORE! MY DAD KEEPS HOUNDING ME TO PLAY CATCH ALL THE TIME! WHAT IF I DON'T **WANT** TO PLAY CATCH?
WHAT DO YOU DO WHEN **YOUR** DAD ACTS LIKE THAT?
WELL, HE'S NOT INTO SPORTS, SO HE NEVER ASKS ME TO PLAY CATCH.
YOU'RE SO LUCKY, DUDE.
NOT REALLY.
HE MAKES ME GARDEN WITH HIM.
OUCH.
Peirce

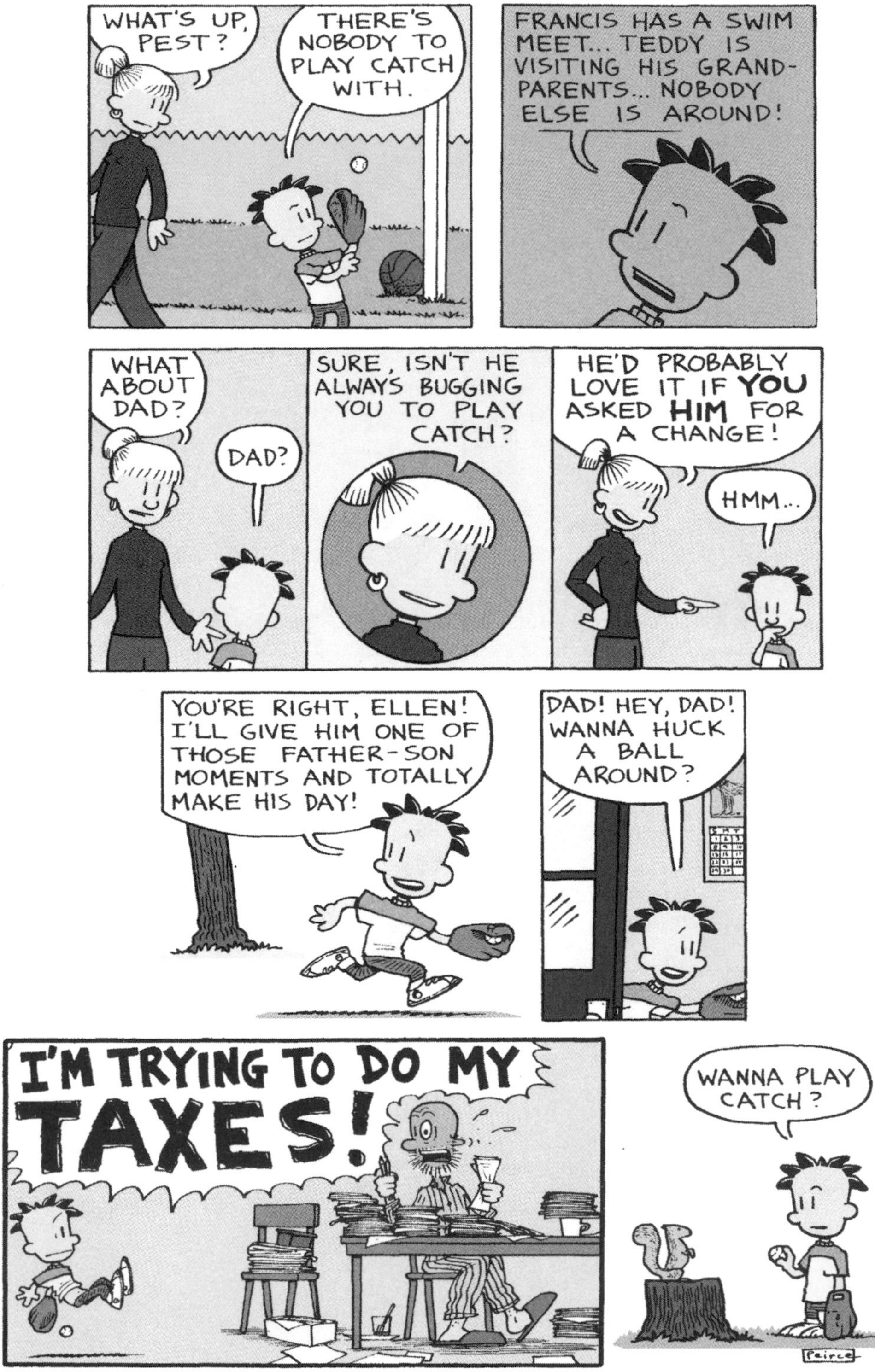
WHAT'S UP, PEST?
THERE'S NOBODY TO PLAY CATCH WITH.
FRANCIS HAS A SWIM MEET... TEDDY IS VISITING HIS GRAND-PARENTS... NOBODY ELSE IS AROUND!
WHAT ABOUT DAD?
DAD?
SURE, ISN'T HE ALWAYS BUGGING YOU TO PLAY CATCH?
HE'D PROBABLY LOVE IT IF **YOU** ASKED **HIM** FOR A CHANGE!
HMM...
YOU'RE RIGHT, ELLEN! I'LL GIVE HIM ONE OF THOSE FATHER-SON MOMENTS AND TOTALLY MAKE HIS DAY!
DAD! HEY, DAD! WANNA HUCK A BALL AROUND?
I'M TRYING TO DO MY TAXES!
WANNA PLAY CATCH?
Peirce

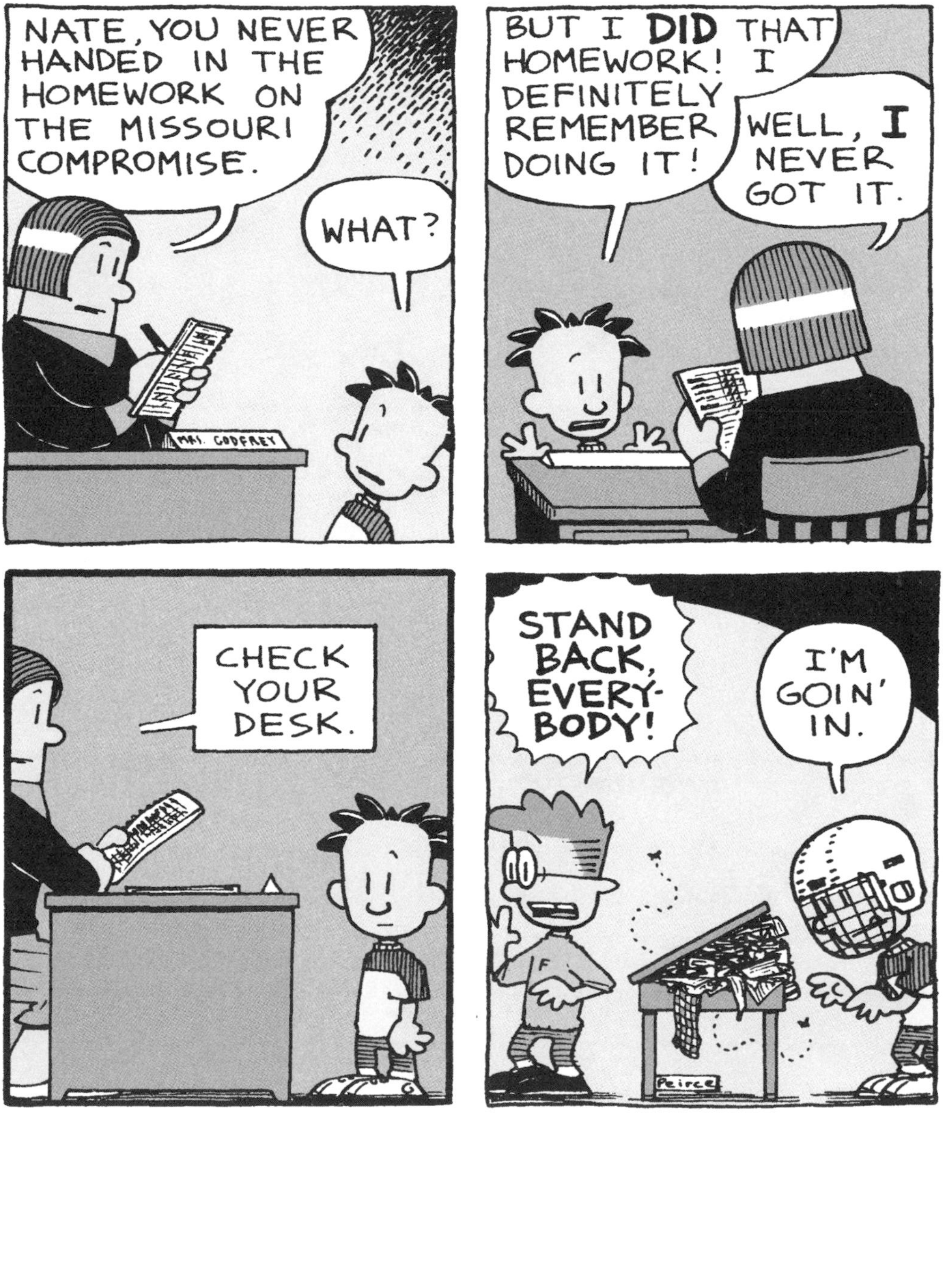
NATE, YOU NEVER HANDED IN THE HOMEWORK ON THE MISSOURI COMPROMISE.
WHAT?
MRS. GODFREY
BUT I **DID** THAT HOMEWORK! I DEFINITELY REMEMBER DOING IT!
WELL, **I** NEVER GOT IT.
CHECK YOUR DESK.
STAND BACK, EVERY-BODY!
I'M GOIN' IN.
Peirce

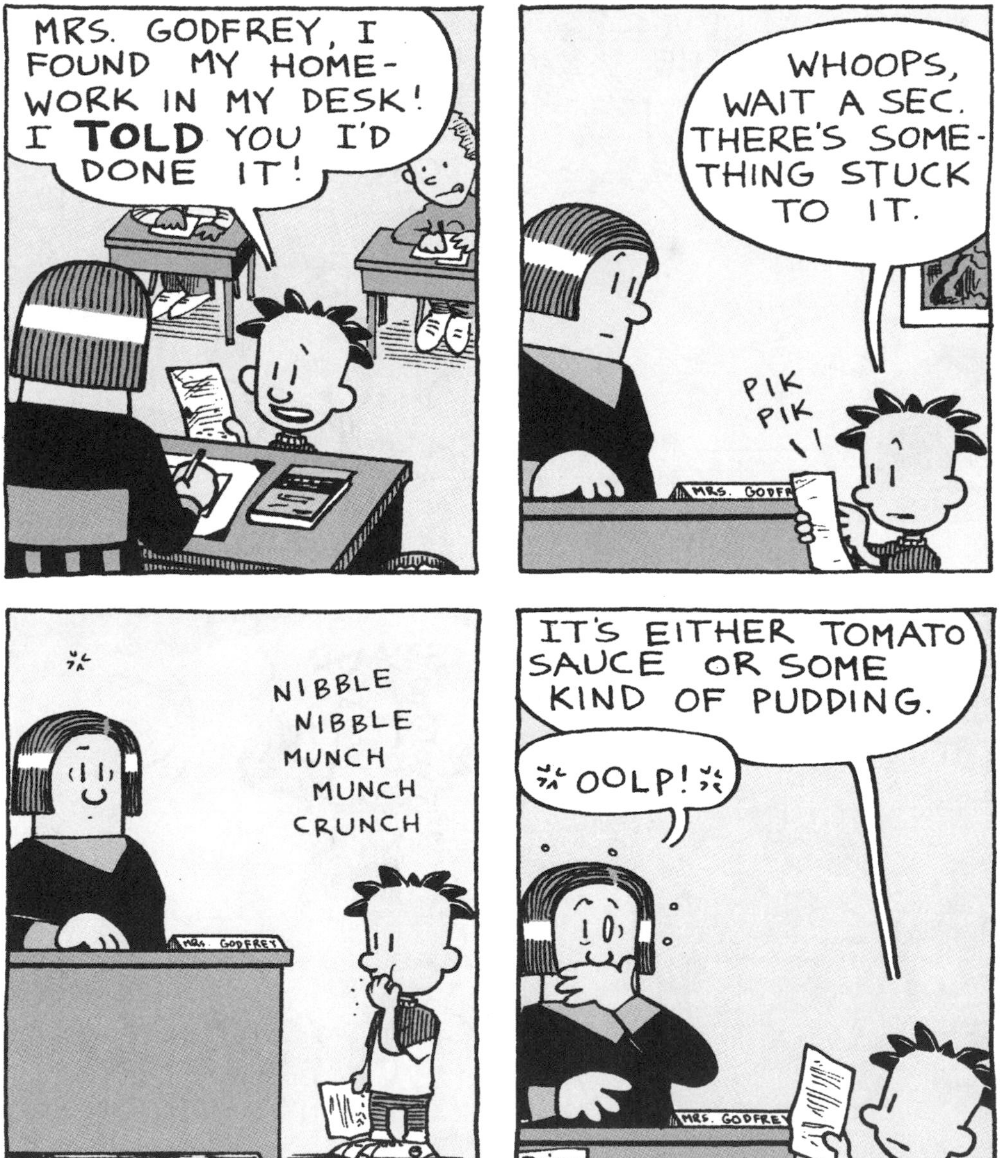
MRS. GODFREY, I FOUND MY HOME-WORK IN MY DESK! I TOLD YOU I'D DONE IT!
WHOOPS, WAIT A SEC. THERE'S SOME-THING STUCK TO IT.
PIK PIK
MRS. GODFR
NIBBLE NIBBLE MUNCH MUNCH CRUNCH
MRS. GODFREY
IT'S EITHER TOMATO SAUCE OR SOME KIND OF PUDDING.
OOLP!
MRS. GODFREY
Peirce

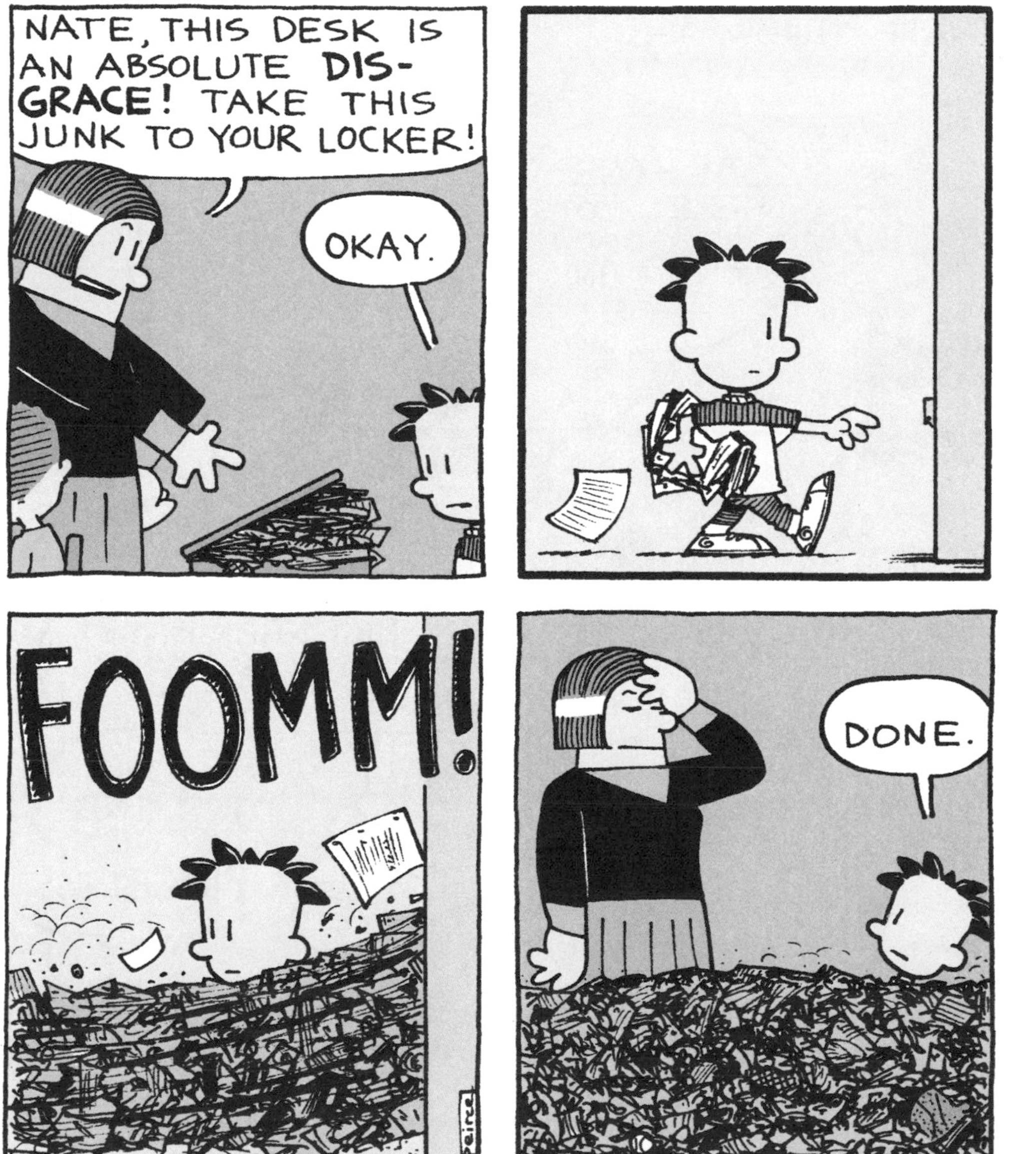
NATE, THIS DESK IS AN ABSOLUTE **DIS-GRACE!** TAKE THIS JUNK TO YOUR LOCKER!
OKAY.
FOOMM!
peirce
DONE.

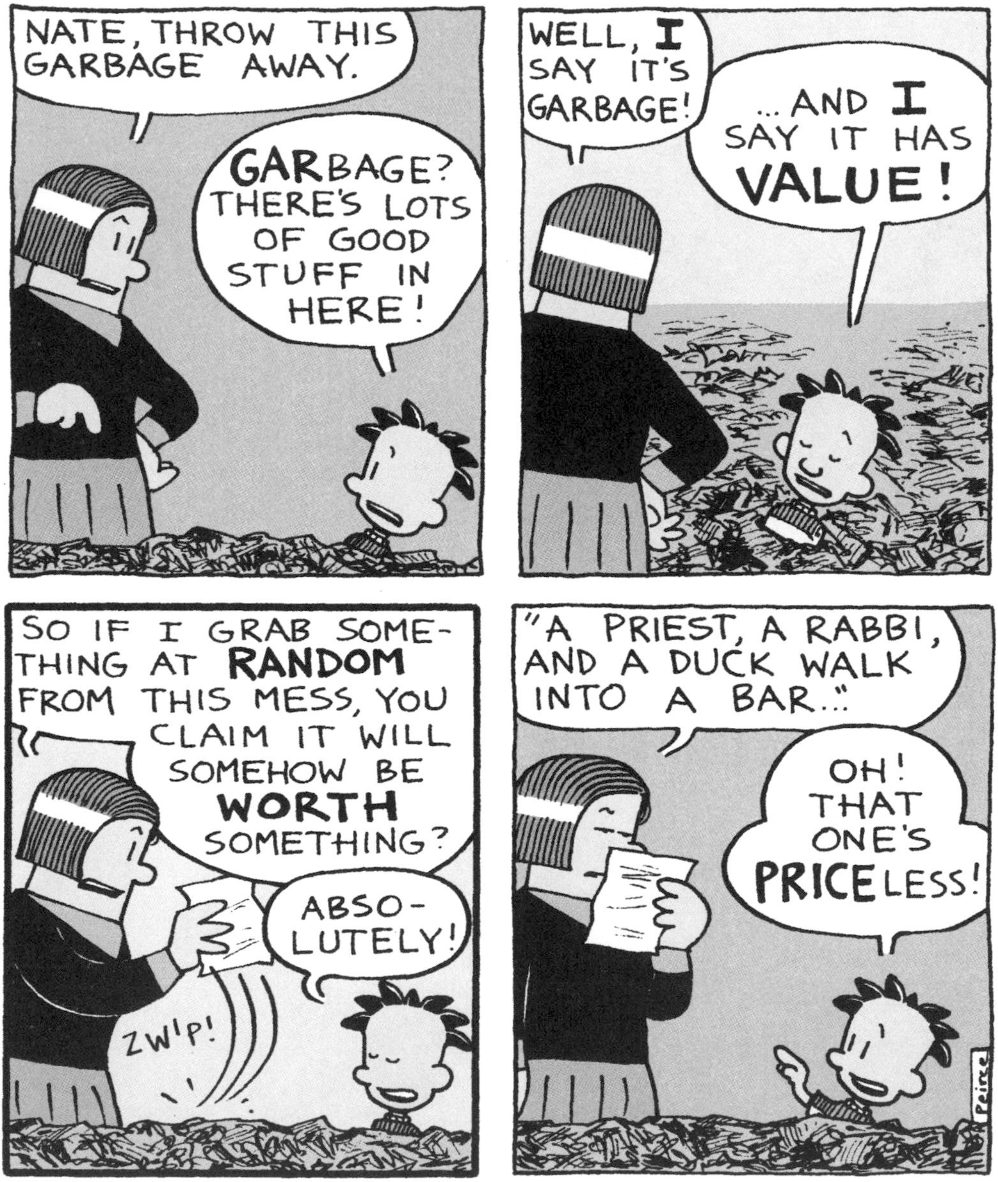
NATE, THROW THIS GARBAGE AWAY.
GARBAGE? THERE'S LOTS OF GOOD STUFF IN HERE!
WELL, I SAY IT'S GARBAGE!
...AND I SAY IT HAS VALUE!
SO IF I GRAB SOMETHING AT RANDOM FROM THIS MESS, YOU CLAIM IT WILL SOMEHOW BE WORTH SOMETHING?
ABSOLUTELY!
ZW'P!
"A PRIEST, A RABBI, AND A DUCK WALK INTO A BAR..."
OH! THAT ONE'S PRICELESS!
Peirce

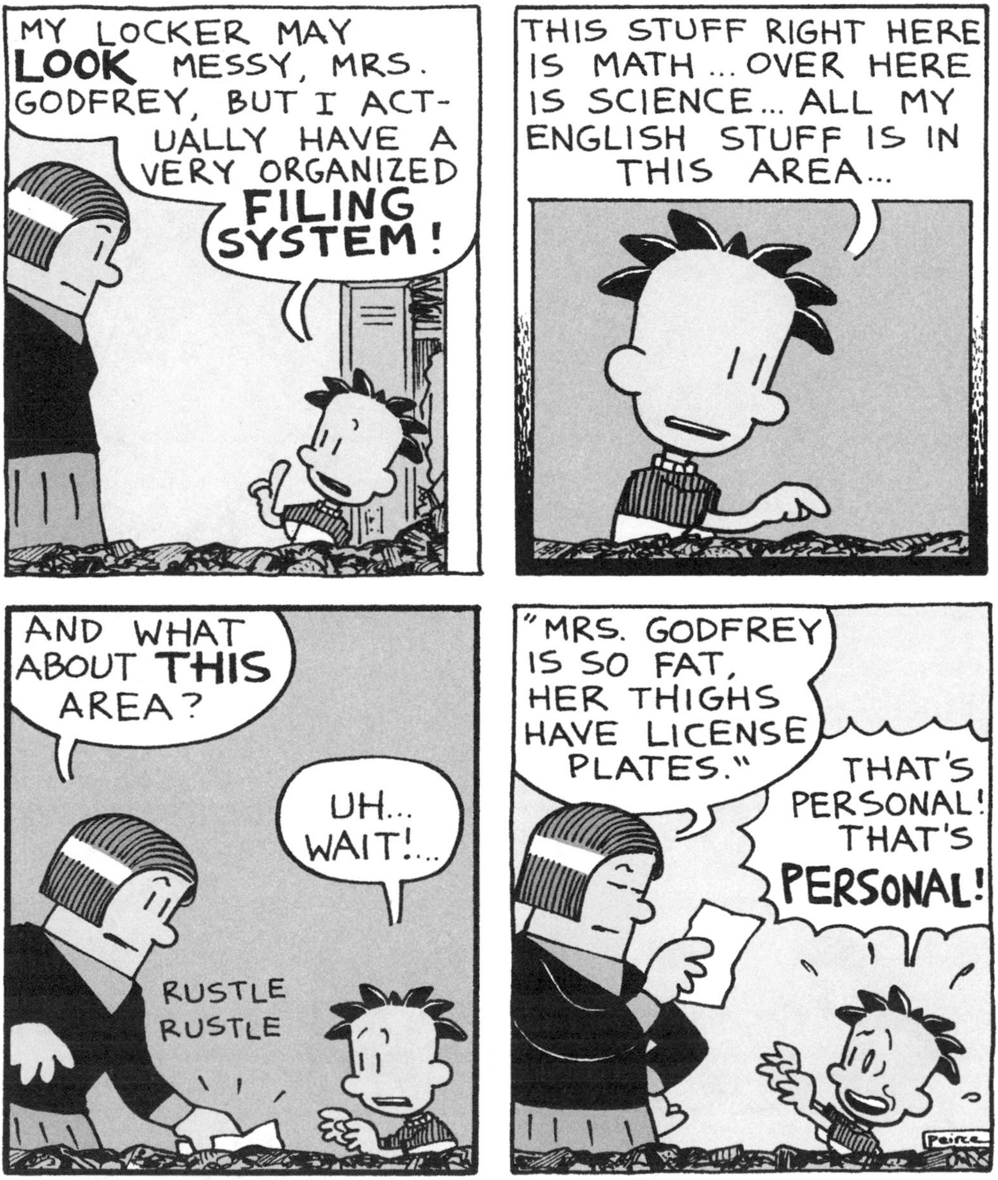
MY LOCKER MAY **LOOK** MESSY, MRS. GODFREY, BUT I ACTUALLY HAVE A VERY ORGANIZED **FILING SYSTEM!**
THIS STUFF RIGHT HERE IS MATH ... OVER HERE IS SCIENCE... ALL MY ENGLISH STUFF IS IN THIS AREA...
AND WHAT ABOUT **THIS** AREA?
UH... WAIT!...
RUSTLE RUSTLE
"MRS. GODFREY IS SO FAT, HER THIGHS HAVE LICENSE PLATES."
THAT'S PERSONAL! THAT'S **PERSONAL!**
Peirce

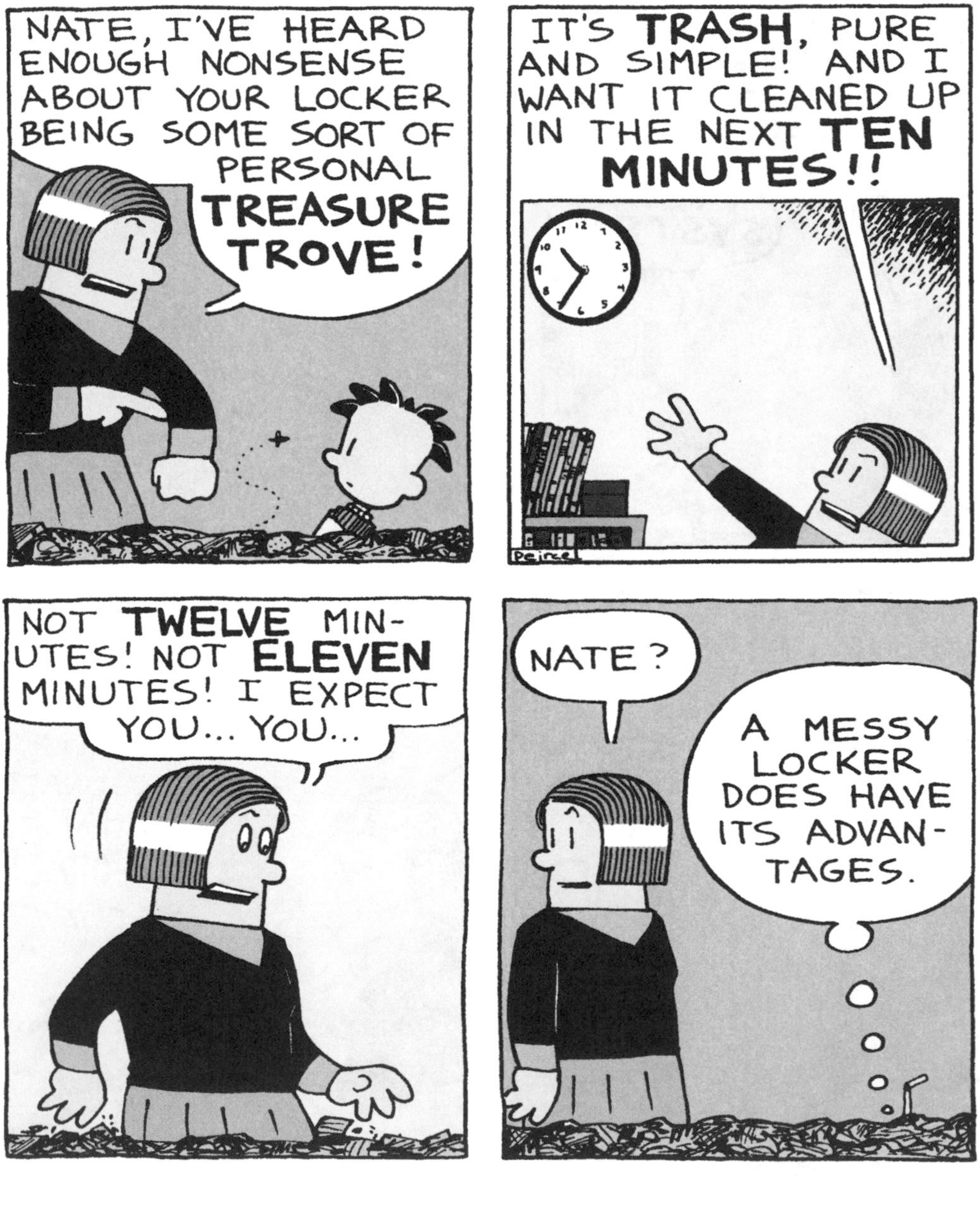
NATE, I'VE HEARD ENOUGH NONSENSE ABOUT YOUR LOCKER BEING SOME SORT OF PERSONAL **TREASURE TROVE**!
IT'S **TRASH**, PURE AND SIMPLE! AND I WANT IT CLEANED UP IN THE NEXT **TEN MINUTES**!!
Peirce
NOT **TWELVE** MINUTES! NOT **ELEVEN** MINUTES! I EXPECT YOU... YOU...
NATE?
A MESSY LOCKER DOES HAVE ITS ADVANTAGES.

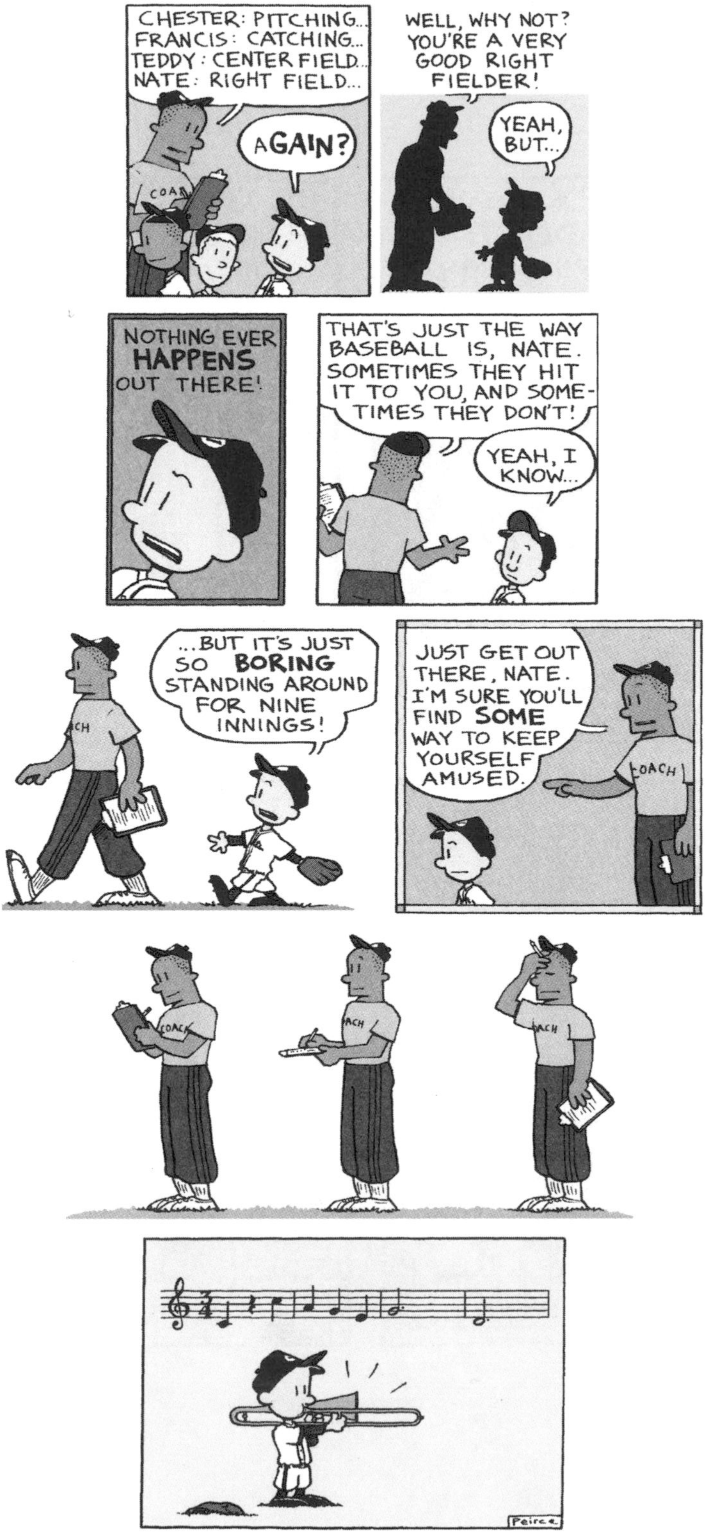
CHESTER: PITCHING... FRANCIS: CATCHING... TEDDY: CENTER FIELD... NATE: RIGHT FIELD...
AGAIN?
WELL, WHY NOT? YOU'RE A VERY GOOD RIGHT FIELDER!
YEAH, BUT...
NOTHING EVER HAPPENS OUT THERE!
THAT'S JUST THE WAY BASEBALL IS, NATE. SOMETIMES THEY HIT IT TO YOU, AND SOMETIMES THEY DON'T!
YEAH, I KNOW...
...BUT IT'S JUST SO BORING STANDING AROUND FOR NINE INNINGS!
JUST GET OUT THERE, NATE. I'M SURE YOU'LL FIND SOME WAY TO KEEP YOURSELF AMUSED.
Peirce

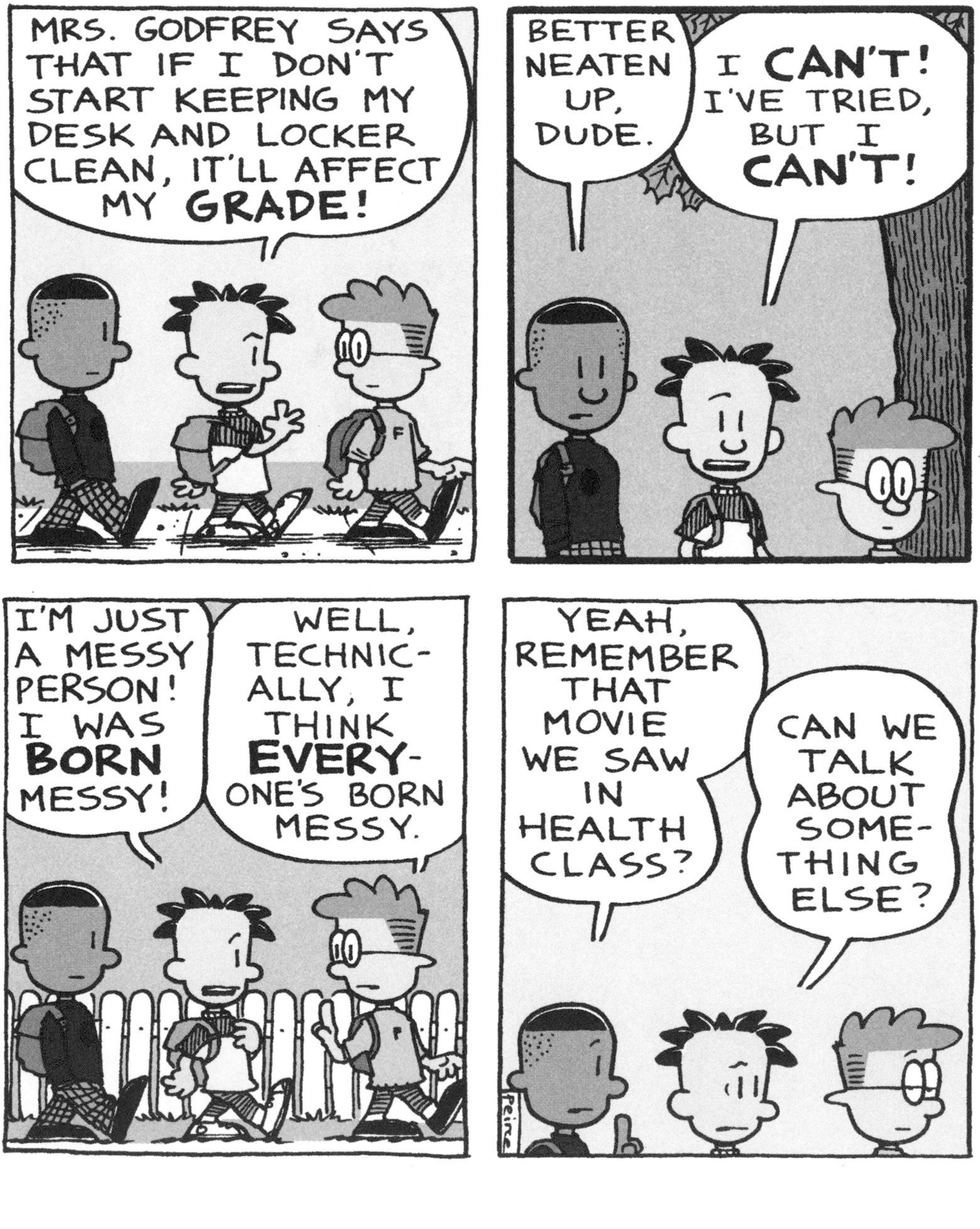
MRS. GODFREY SAYS THAT IF I DON'T START KEEPING MY DESK AND LOCKER CLEAN, IT'LL AFFECT MY **GRADE**!
BETTER NEATEN UP, DUDE.
I **CAN'T**! I'VE TRIED, BUT I **CAN'T**!
I'M JUST A MESSY PERSON! I WAS **BORN** MESSY!
WELL, TECHNIC-ALLY, I THINK **EVERY**-ONE'S BORN MESSY.
YEAH, REMEMBER THAT MOVIE WE SAW IN HEALTH CLASS?
CAN WE TALK ABOUT SOME-THING ELSE?
PEIRCE

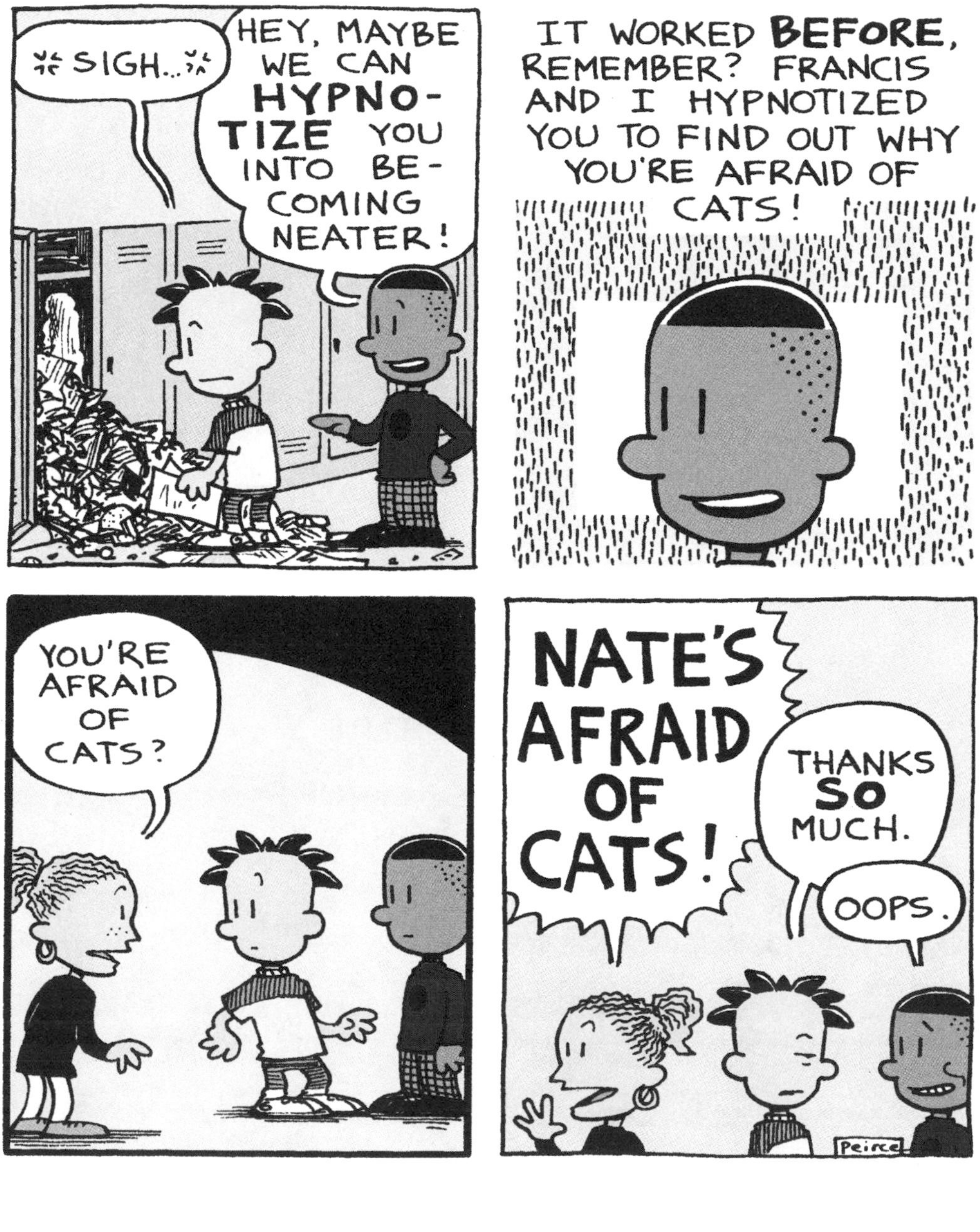
SIGH...
HEY, MAYBE WE CAN HYPNOTIZE YOU INTO BECOMING NEATER!
IT WORKED BEFORE, REMEMBER? FRANCIS AND I HYPNOTIZED YOU TO FIND OUT WHY YOU'RE AFRAID OF CATS!
YOU'RE AFRAID OF CATS?
NATE'S AFRAID OF CATS!
THANKS SO MUCH.
OOPS.
Peirce

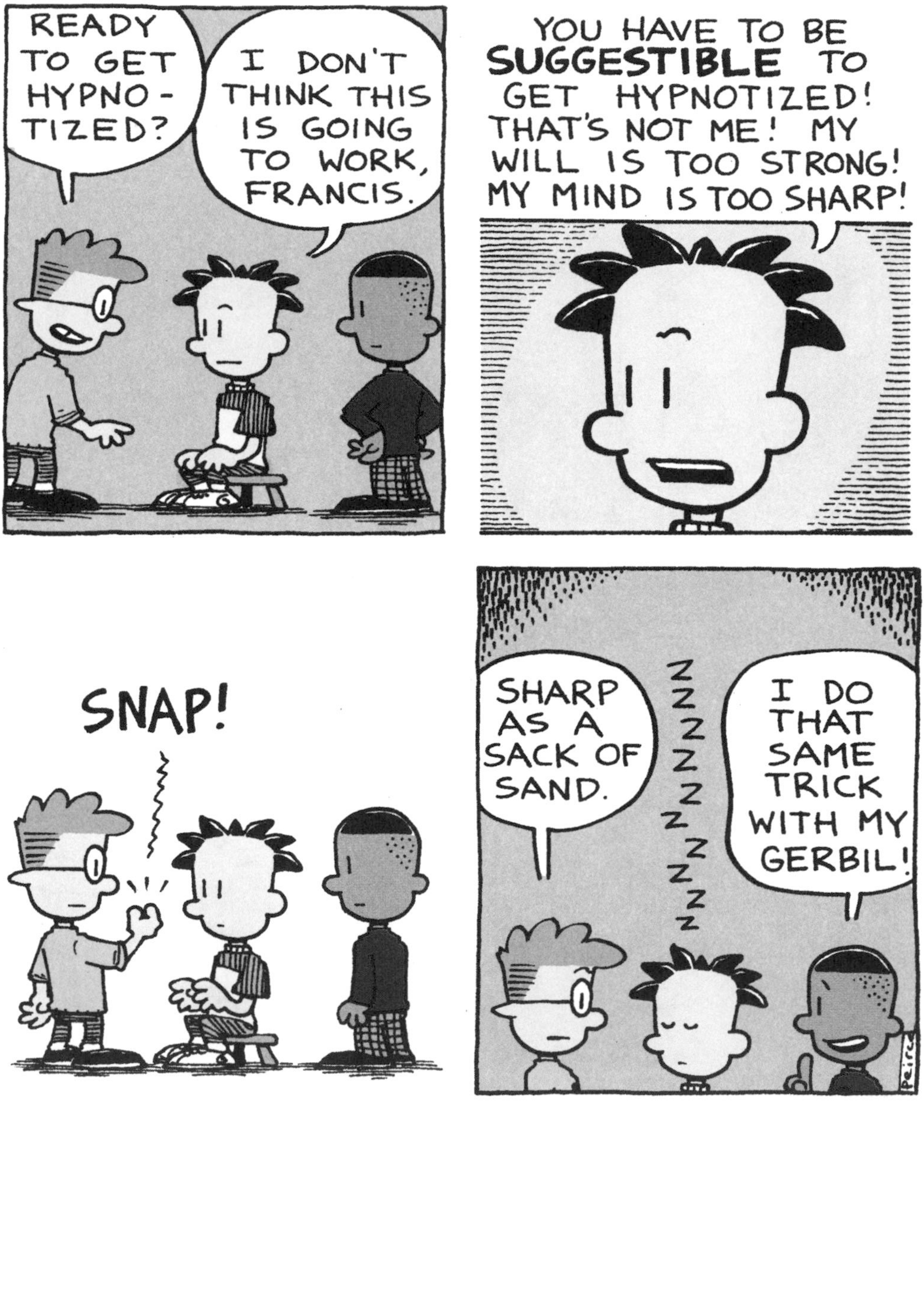
READY TO GET HYPNO-TIZED?
I DON'T THINK THIS IS GOING TO WORK, FRANCIS.
YOU HAVE TO BE **SUGGESTIBLE** TO GET HYPNOTIZED! THAT'S NOT ME! MY WILL IS TOO STRONG! MY MIND IS TOO SHARP!
SNAP!
SHARP AS A SACK OF SAND.
ZZZZZZZZZZ
I DO THAT SAME TRICK WITH MY GERBIL!

WHAT'S UP?
WE'RE HYPNOTIZING NATE!
HYPNO-TIZING HIM?
YUP! TO MAKE HIM LESS OF A SLOB!
MRS. GODFREY GAVE HIM AN ULTIMATUM, SO WE'RE GIVING HIM A POST-HYPNOTIC SUGGESTION TO BECOME NEATER!
CAN YOU ALSO MAKE HIM LESS ANNOY-ING?
HEY!
WE'RE HYPNO-TISTS, NOT MAGICIANS.
Peirce

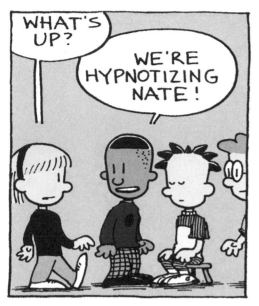

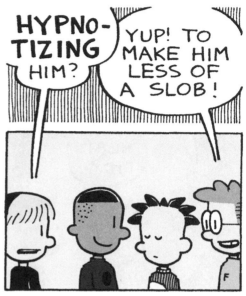

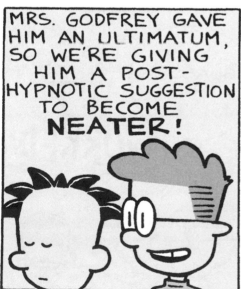

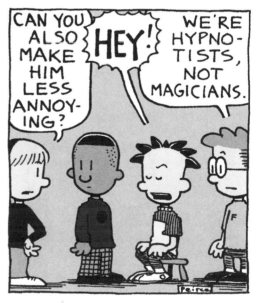

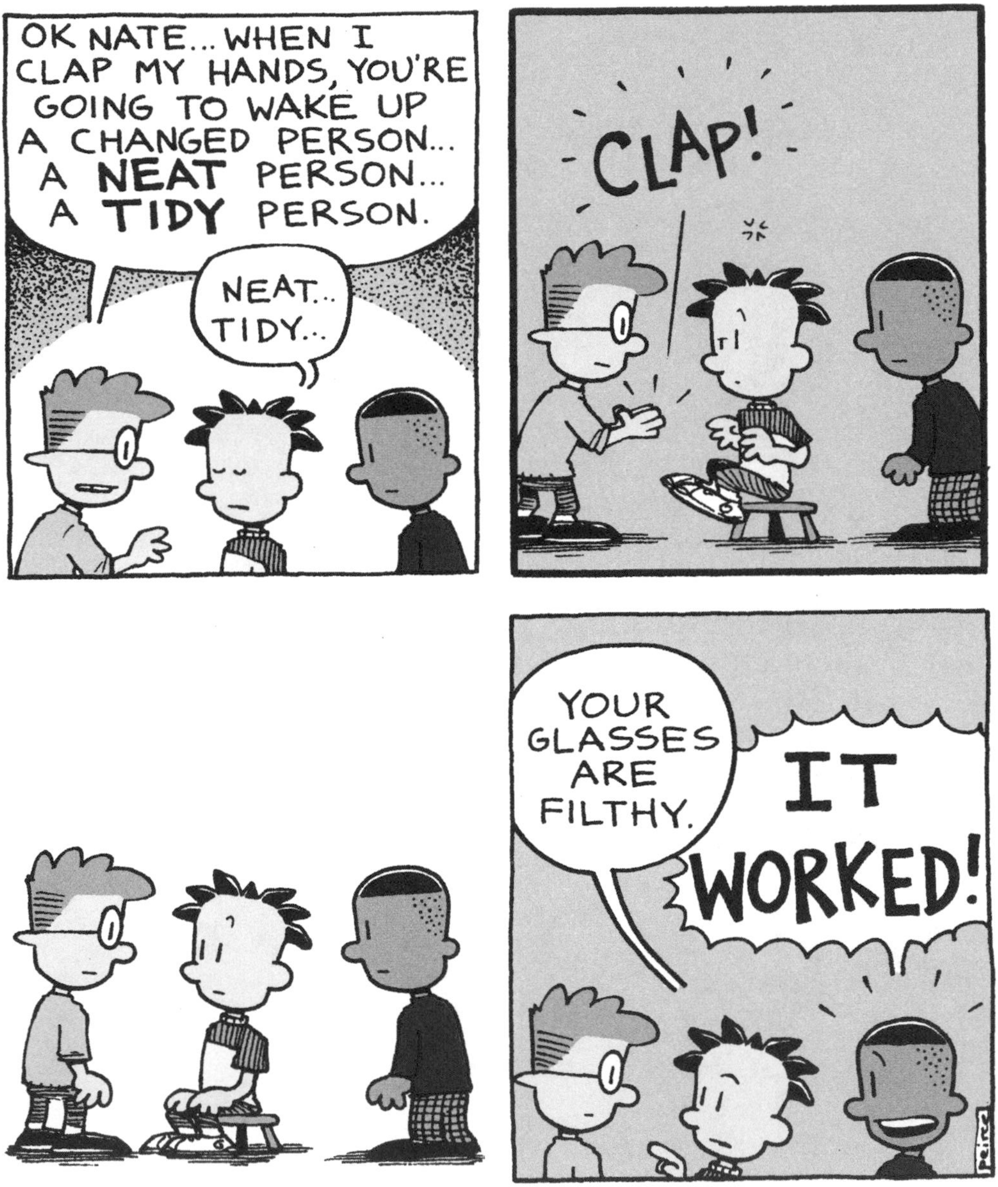
OK NATE... WHEN I CLAP MY HANDS, YOU'RE GOING TO WAKE UP A CHANGED PERSON... A NEAT PERSON... A TIDY PERSON.
NEAT... TIDY...
CLAP!
YOUR GLASSES ARE FILTHY.
IT WORKED!
peirce

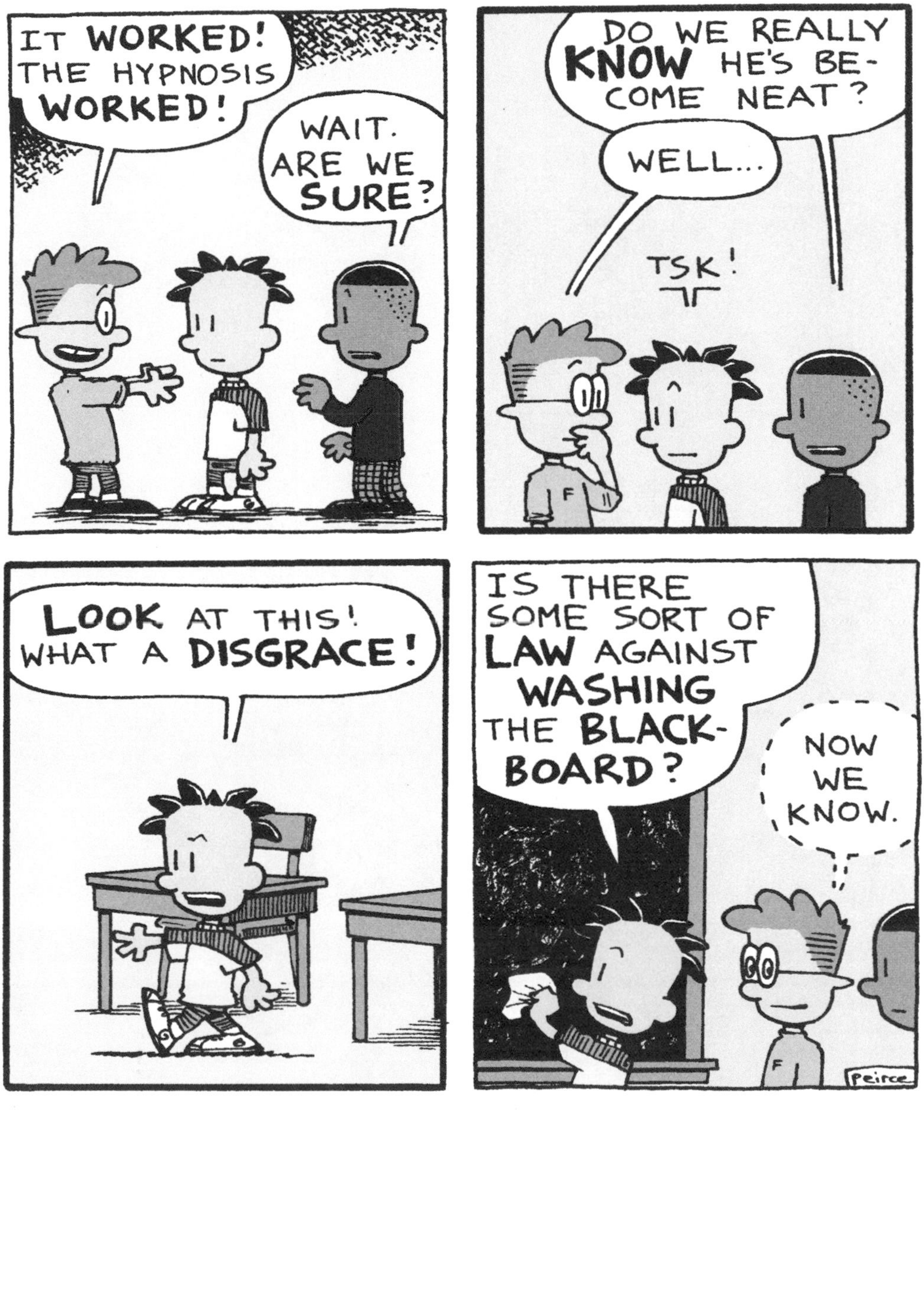
IT WORKED! THE HYPNOSIS WORKED!
WAIT. ARE WE SURE?
DO WE REALLY KNOW HE'S BE-COME NEAT?
WELL...
TSK!
LOOK AT THIS! WHAT A DISGRACE!
IS THERE SOME SORT OF LAW AGAINST WASHING THE BLACK-BOARD?
NOW WE KNOW.
Peirce

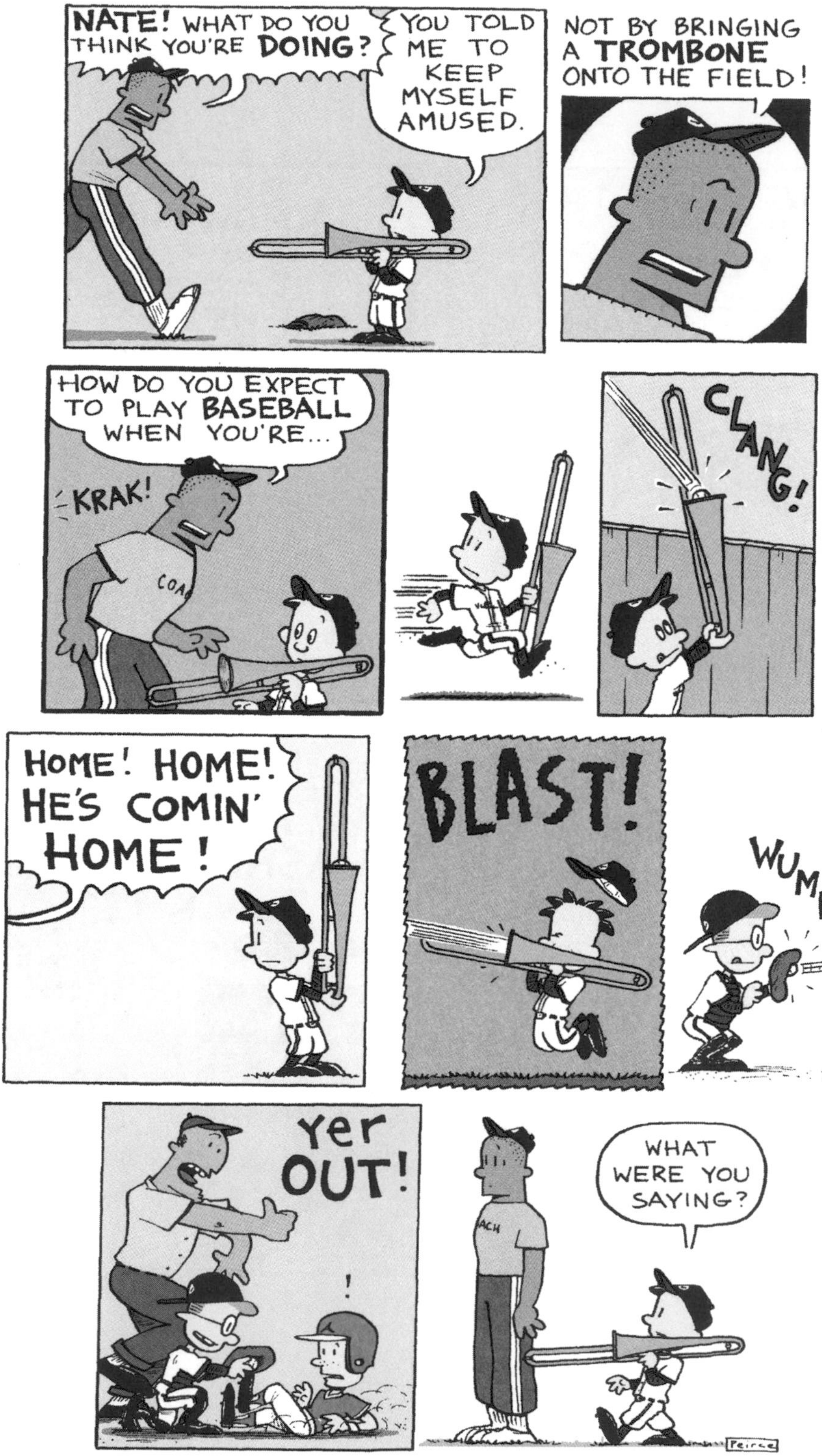
NATE! WHAT DO YOU THINK YOU'RE DOING?
YOU TOLD ME TO KEEP MYSELF AMUSED.
NOT BY BRINGING A TROMBONE ONTO THE FIELD!
HOW DO YOU EXPECT TO PLAY BASEBALL WHEN YOU'RE...
KRAK!
CLANG!
HOME! HOME! HE'S COMIN' HOME!
BLAST!
WUMP!
yer OUT!
!
WHAT WERE YOU SAYING?
Peirce

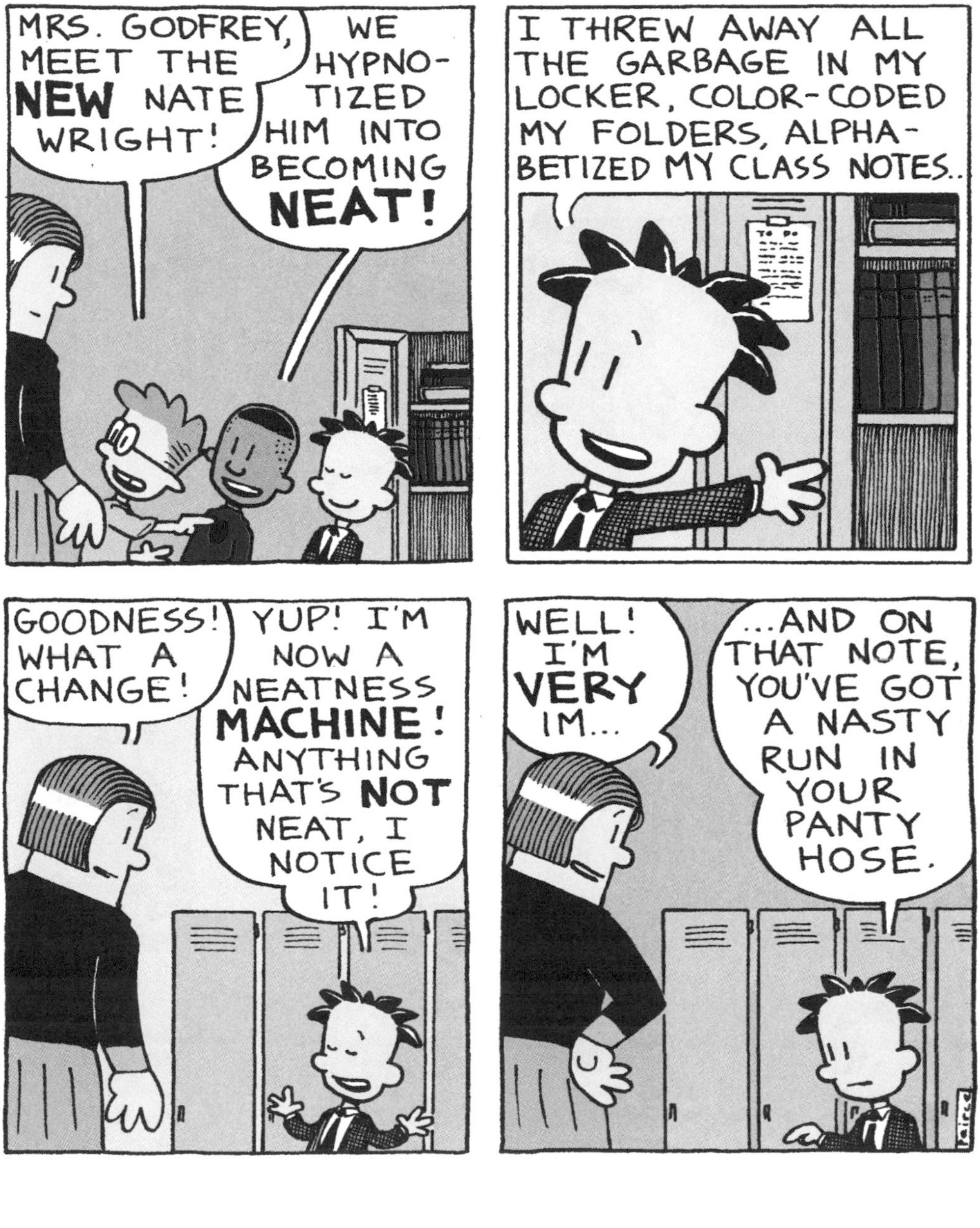
MRS. GODFREY, MEET THE NEW NATE WRIGHT!
WE HYPNO-TIZED HIM INTO BECOMING NEAT!
I THREW AWAY ALL THE GARBAGE IN MY LOCKER, COLOR-CODED MY FOLDERS, ALPHA-BETIZED MY CLASS NOTES..
GOODNESS! WHAT A CHANGE!
YUP! I'M NOW A NEATNESS MACHINE! ANYTHING THAT'S NOT NEAT, I NOTICE IT!
WELL! I'M VERY IM...
...AND ON THAT NOTE, YOU'VE GOT A NASTY RUN IN YOUR PANTY HOSE.

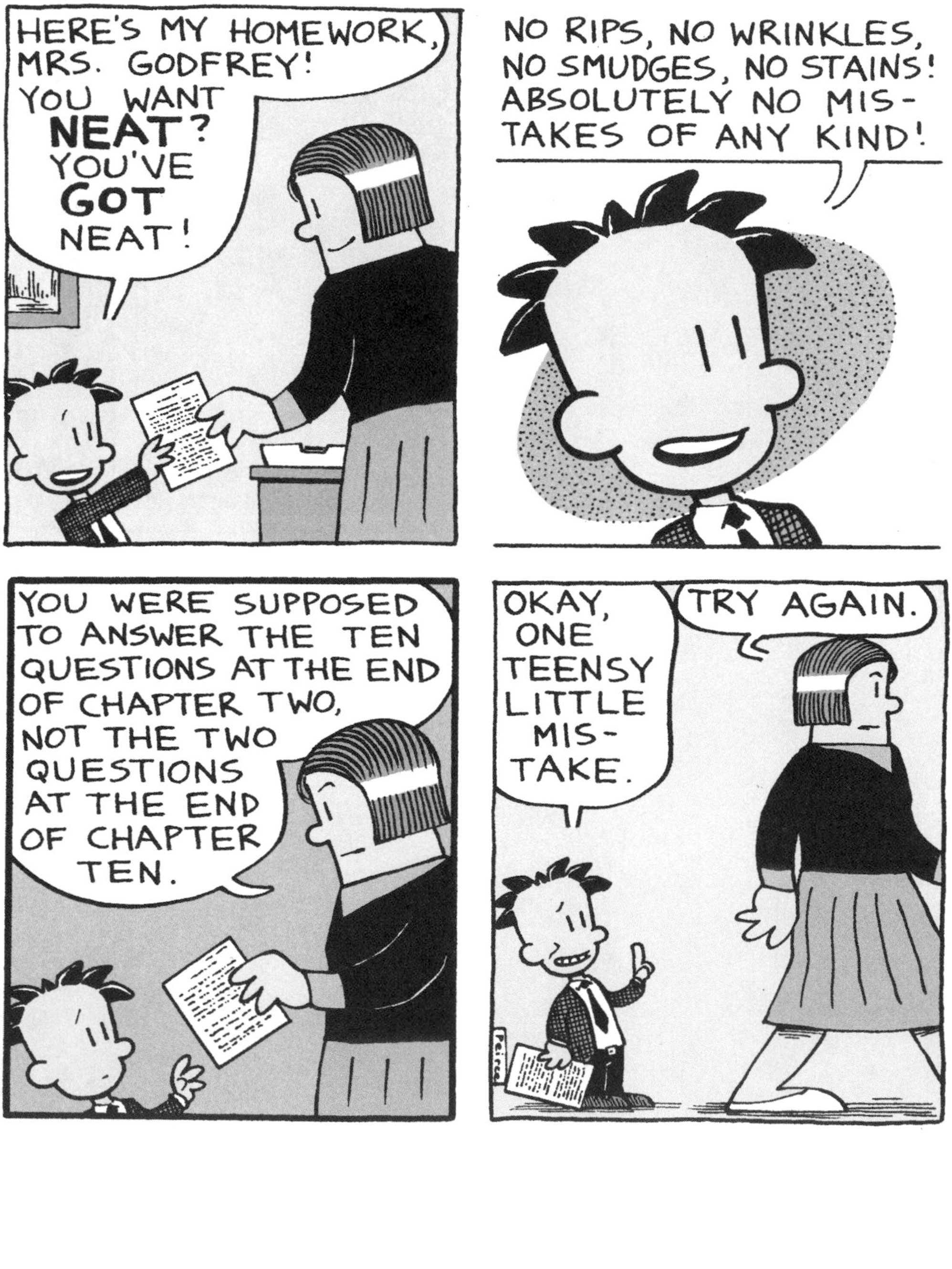
HERE'S MY HOMEWORK, MRS. GODFREY! YOU WANT NEAT? YOU'VE GOT NEAT!
NO RIPS, NO WRINKLES, NO SMUDGES, NO STAINS! ABSOLUTELY NO MIS-TAKES OF ANY KIND!
YOU WERE SUPPOSED TO ANSWER THE TEN QUESTIONS AT THE END OF CHAPTER TWO, NOT THE TWO QUESTIONS AT THE END OF CHAPTER TEN.
OKAY, ONE TEENSY LITTLE MIS-TAKE.
TRY AGAIN.
PEIRCE

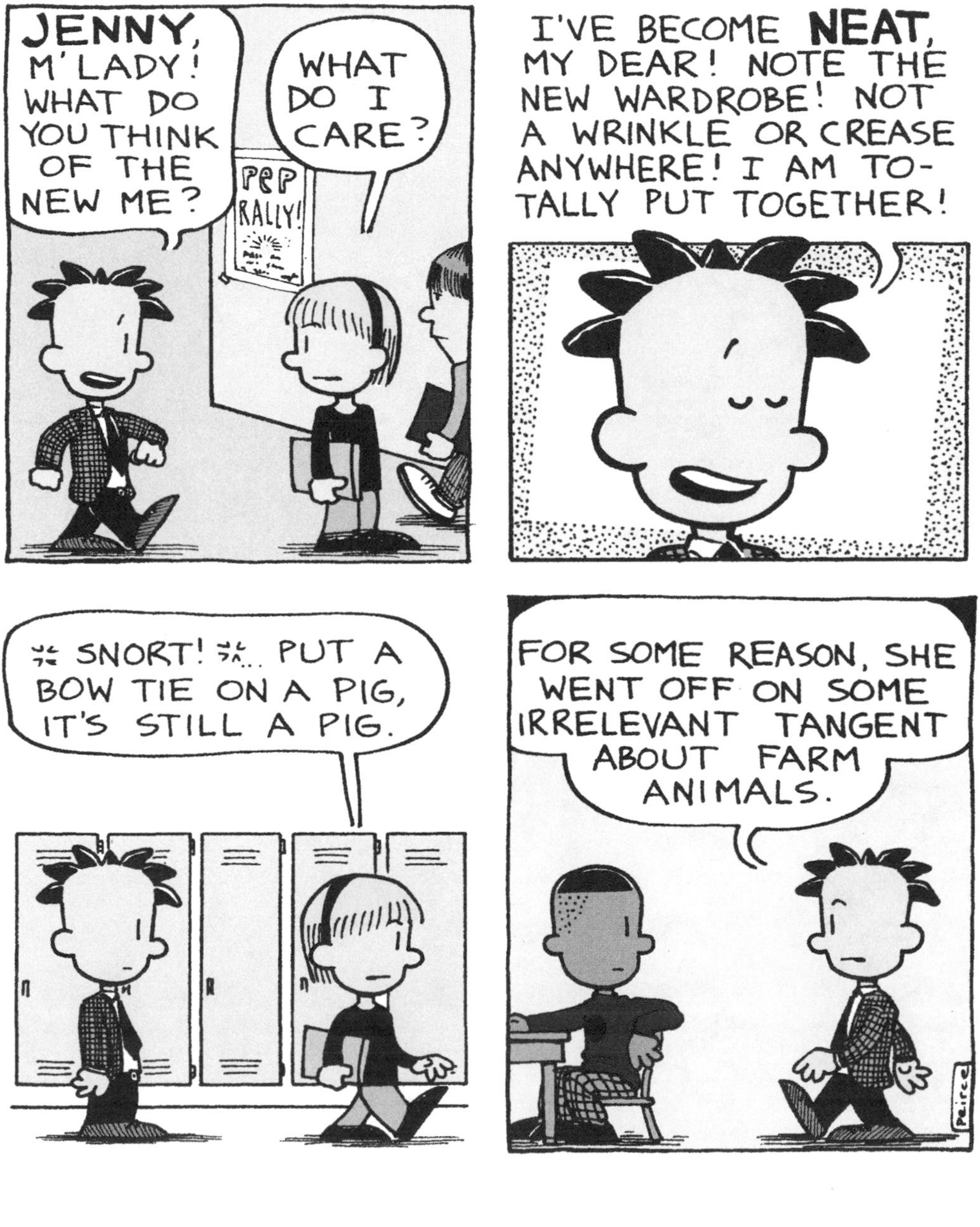
JENNY, M'LADY! WHAT DO YOU THINK OF THE NEW ME?
WHAT DO I CARE?
PEP RALLY!
I'VE BECOME NEAT, MY DEAR! NOTE THE NEW WARDROBE! NOT A WRINKLE OR CREASE ANYWHERE! I AM TOTALLY PUT TOGETHER!
SNORT! ... PUT A BOW TIE ON A PIG, IT'S STILL A PIG.
FOR SOME REASON, SHE WENT OFF ON SOME IRRELEVANT TANGENT ABOUT FARM ANIMALS.
Peirce

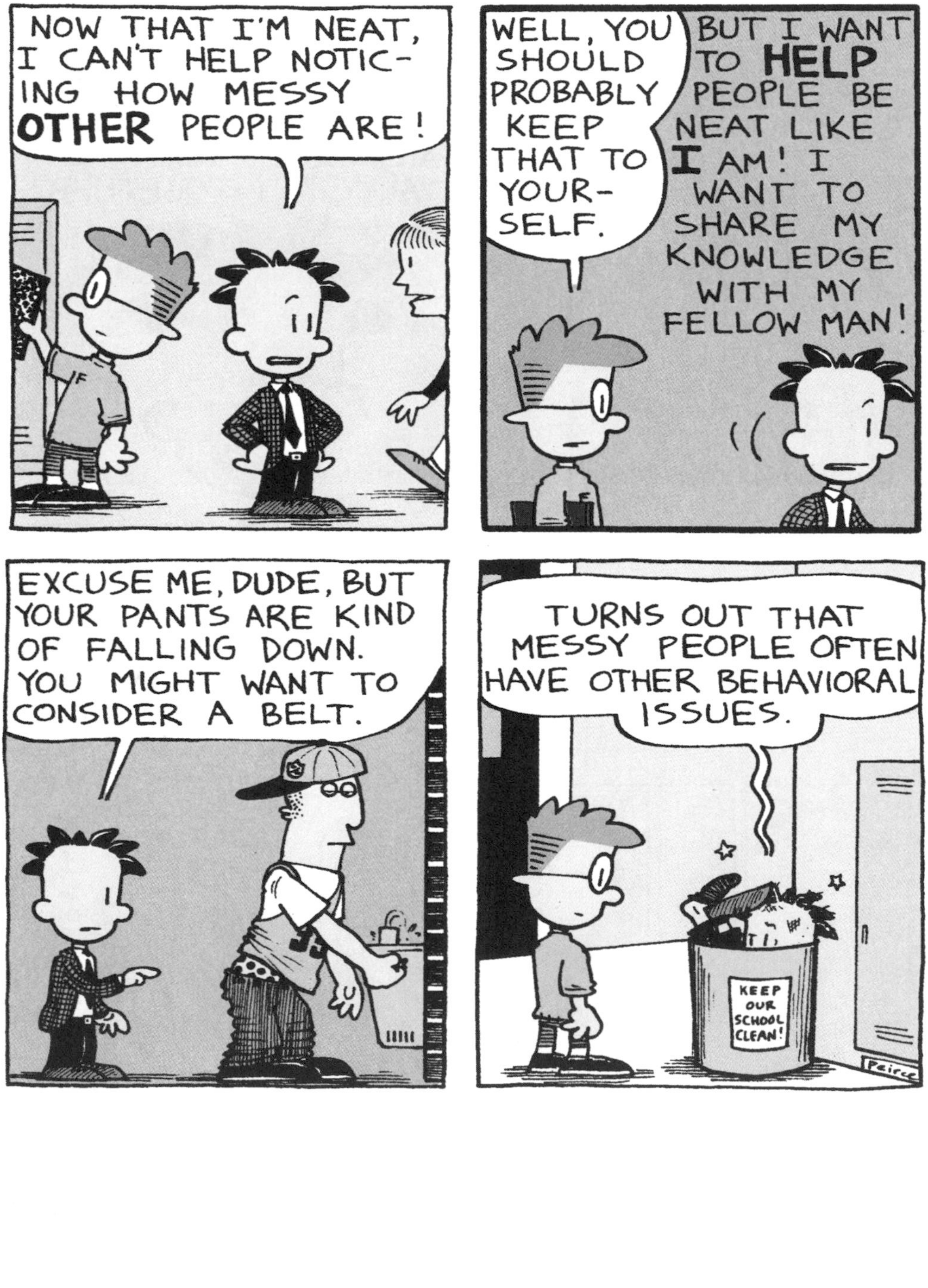

NOW THAT I'M NEAT, I CAN'T HELP NOTICING HOW MESSY **OTHER** PEOPLE ARE!
WELL, YOU SHOULD PROBABLY KEEP THAT TO YOURSELF.
BUT I WANT TO **HELP** PEOPLE BE NEAT LIKE **I** AM! I WANT TO SHARE MY KNOWLEDGE WITH MY FELLOW MAN!
EXCUSE ME, DUDE, BUT YOUR PANTS ARE KIND OF FALLING DOWN. YOU MIGHT WANT TO CONSIDER A BELT.
TURNS OUT THAT MESSY PEOPLE OFTEN HAVE OTHER BEHAVIORAL ISSUES.
KEEP OUR SCHOOL CLEAN!
Peirce

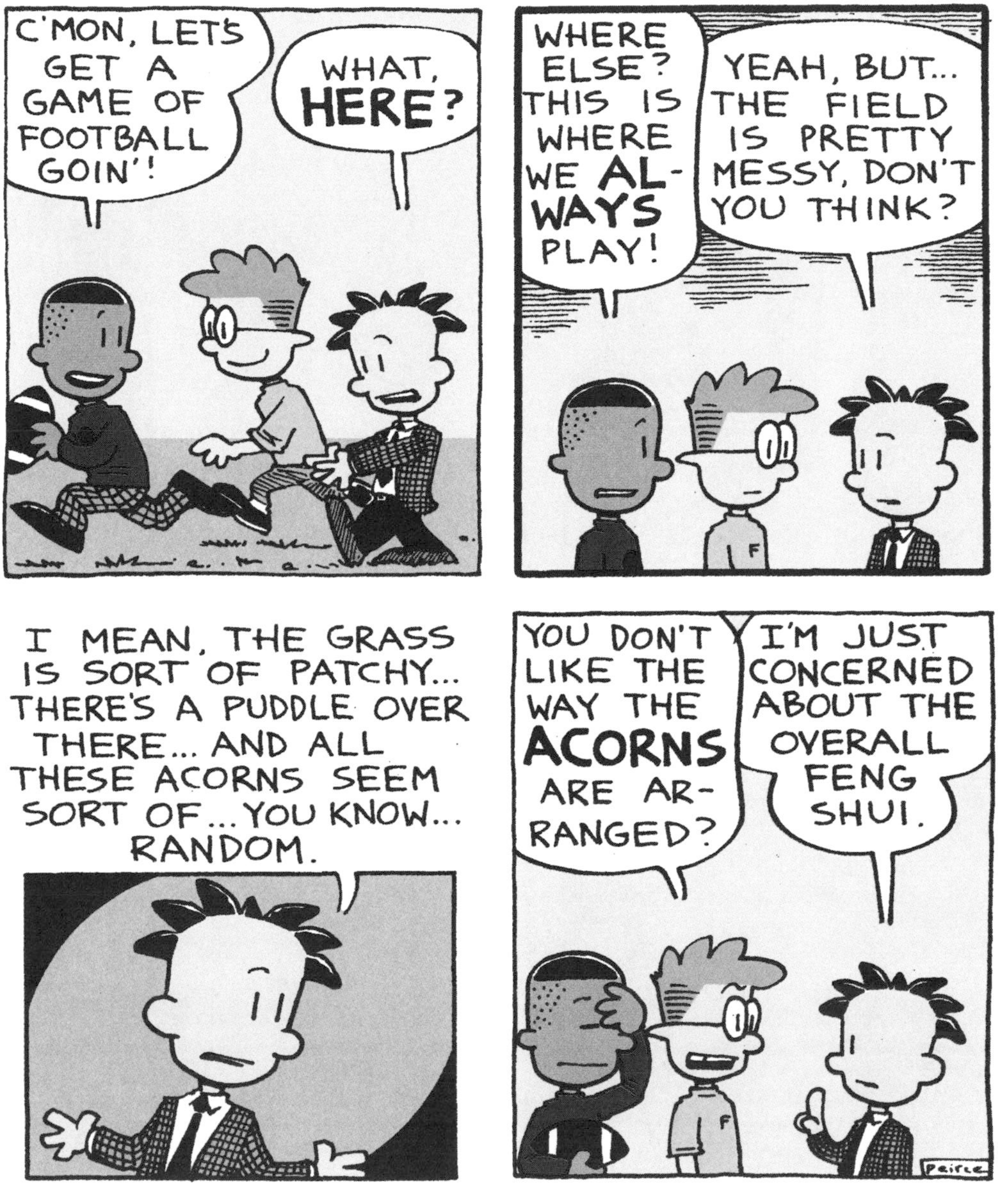
C'MON, LET'S GET A GAME OF FOOTBALL GOIN'!
WHAT, HERE?
WHERE ELSE? THIS IS WHERE WE AL-WAYS PLAY!
YEAH, BUT... THE FIELD IS PRETTY MESSY, DON'T YOU THINK?
I MEAN, THE GRASS IS SORT OF PATCHY... THERE'S A PUDDLE OVER THERE... AND ALL THESE ACORNS SEEM SORT OF... YOU KNOW... RANDOM.
YOU DON'T LIKE THE WAY THE ACORNS ARE AR-RANGED?
I'M JUST CONCERNED ABOUT THE OVERALL FENG SHUI.
PEIRCE

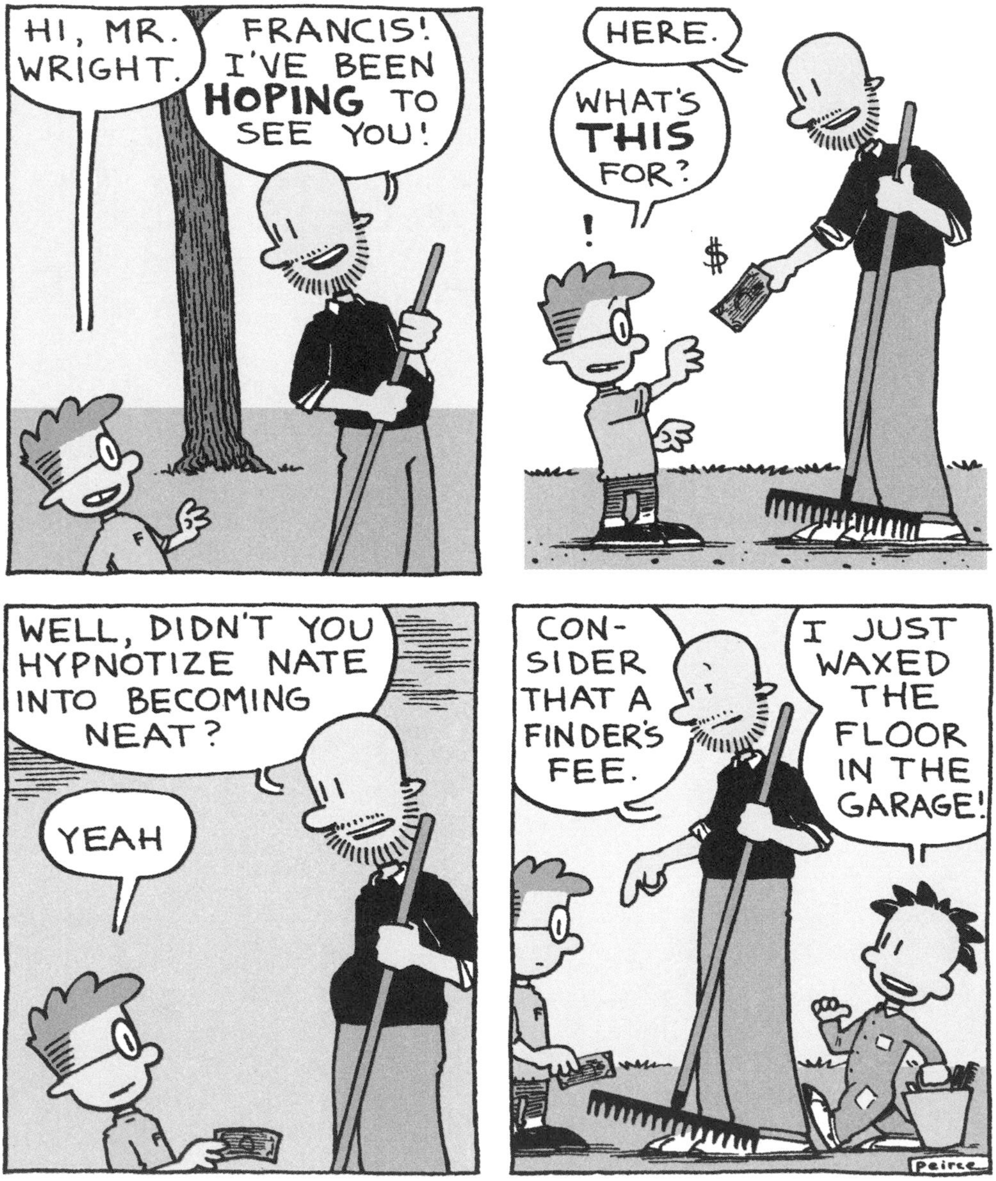
HI, MR. WRIGHT.
FRANCIS! I'VE BEEN HOPING TO SEE YOU!
HERE.
WHAT'S THIS FOR?
!
$
WELL, DIDN'T YOU HYPNOTIZE NATE INTO BECOMING NEAT?
YEAH
CONSIDER THAT A FINDER'S FEE.
I JUST WAXED THE FLOOR IN THE GARAGE!
peirce

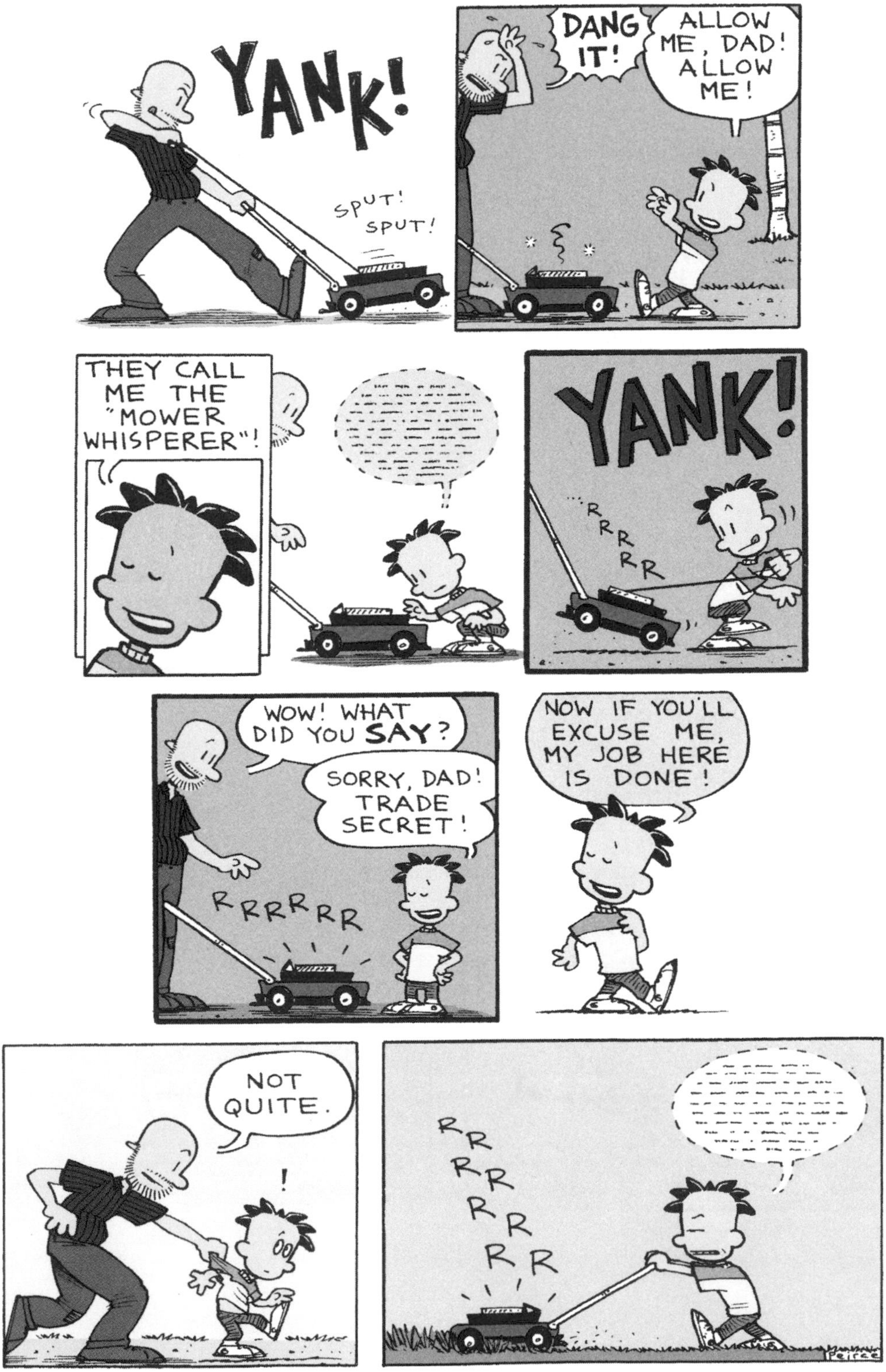
YANK!
SPUT! SPUT!
DANG IT!
ALLOW ME, DAD! ALLOW ME!
THEY CALL ME THE "MOWER WHISPERER"!
YANK!
RRRRR
WOW! WHAT DID YOU SAY?
SORRY, DAD! TRADE SECRET!
RRRRRR
NOW IF YOU'LL EXCUSE ME, MY JOB HERE IS DONE!
NOT QUITE.
!
RRRRRRRR
Peirce

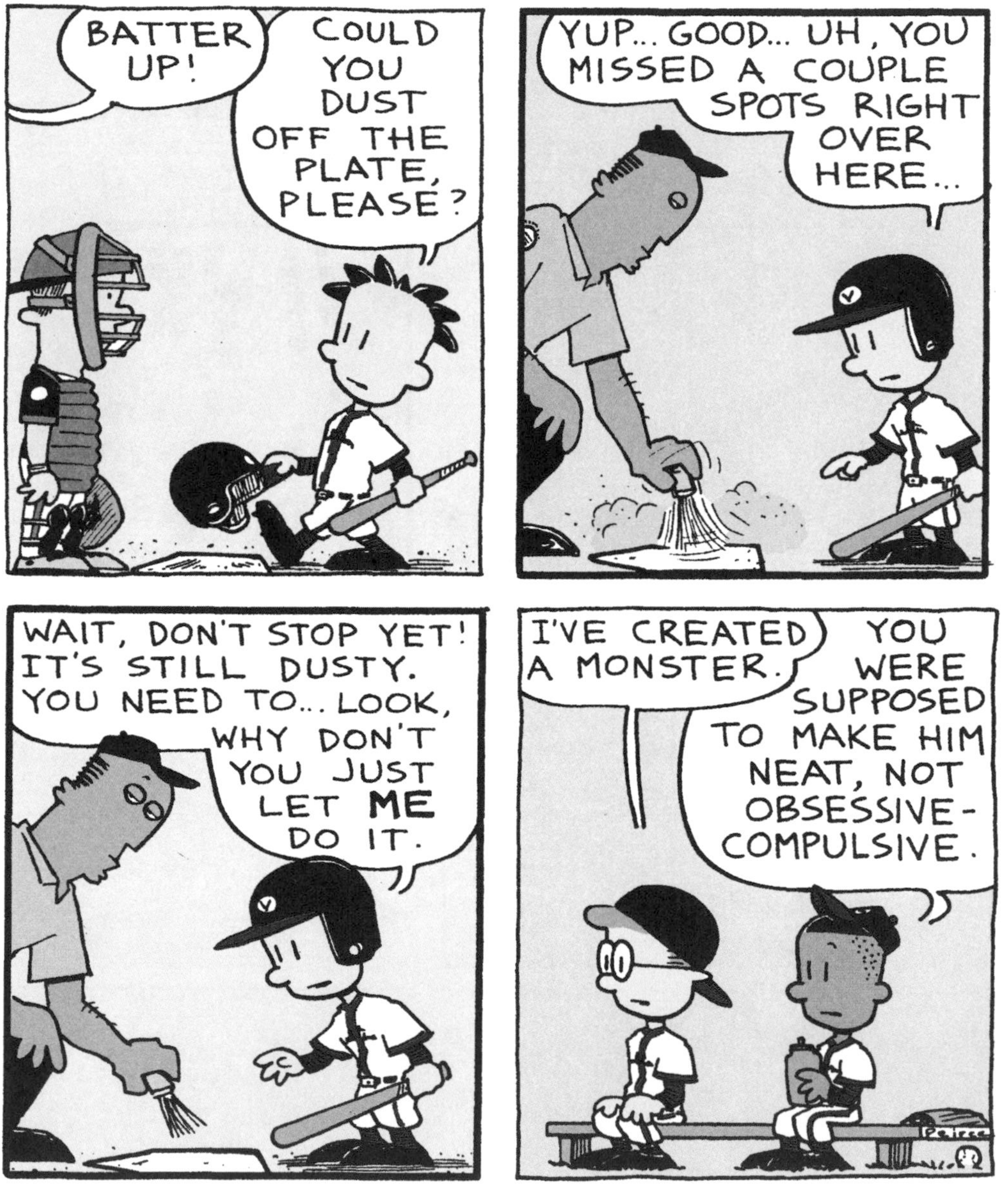
BATTER UP!
COULD YOU DUST OFF THE PLATE, PLEASE?
YUP... GOOD... UH, YOU MISSED A COUPLE SPOTS RIGHT OVER HERE...
WAIT, DON'T STOP YET! IT'S STILL DUSTY. YOU NEED TO... LOOK, WHY DON'T YOU JUST LET **ME** DO IT.
I'VE CREATED A MONSTER.
YOU WERE SUPPOSED TO MAKE HIM NEAT, NOT OBSESSIVE-COMPULSIVE.
Peirce

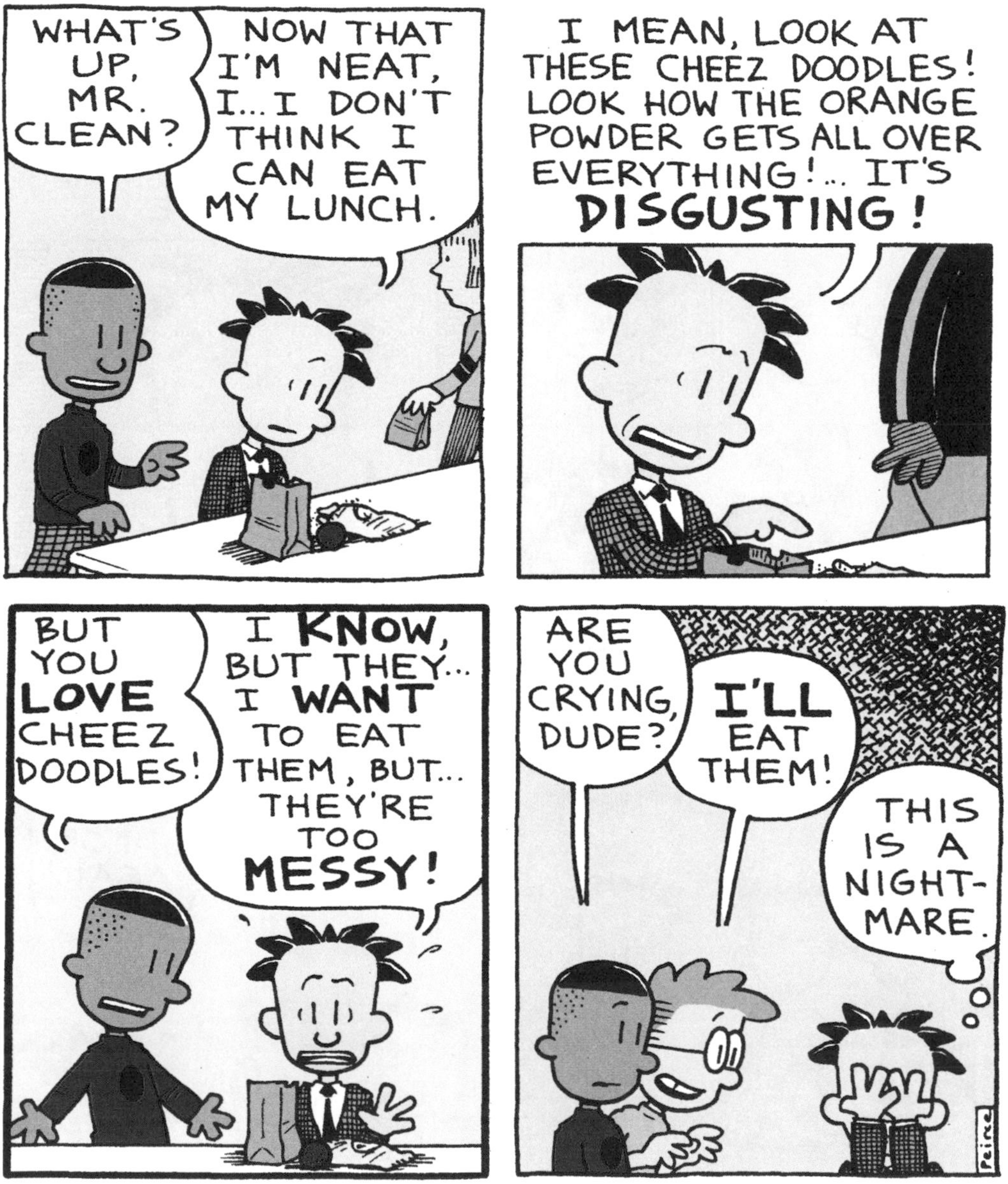
WHAT'S UP, MR. CLEAN?
NOW THAT I'M NEAT, I... I DON'T THINK I CAN EAT MY LUNCH.
I MEAN, LOOK AT THESE CHEEZ DOODLES! LOOK HOW THE ORANGE POWDER GETS ALL OVER EVERYTHING!... IT'S DISGUSTING!
BUT YOU LOVE CHEEZ DOODLES!
I KNOW, BUT THEY... I WANT TO EAT THEM, BUT... THEY'RE TOO MESSY!
ARE YOU CRYING, DUDE?
I'LL EAT THEM!
THIS IS A NIGHT-MARE.
Peirce

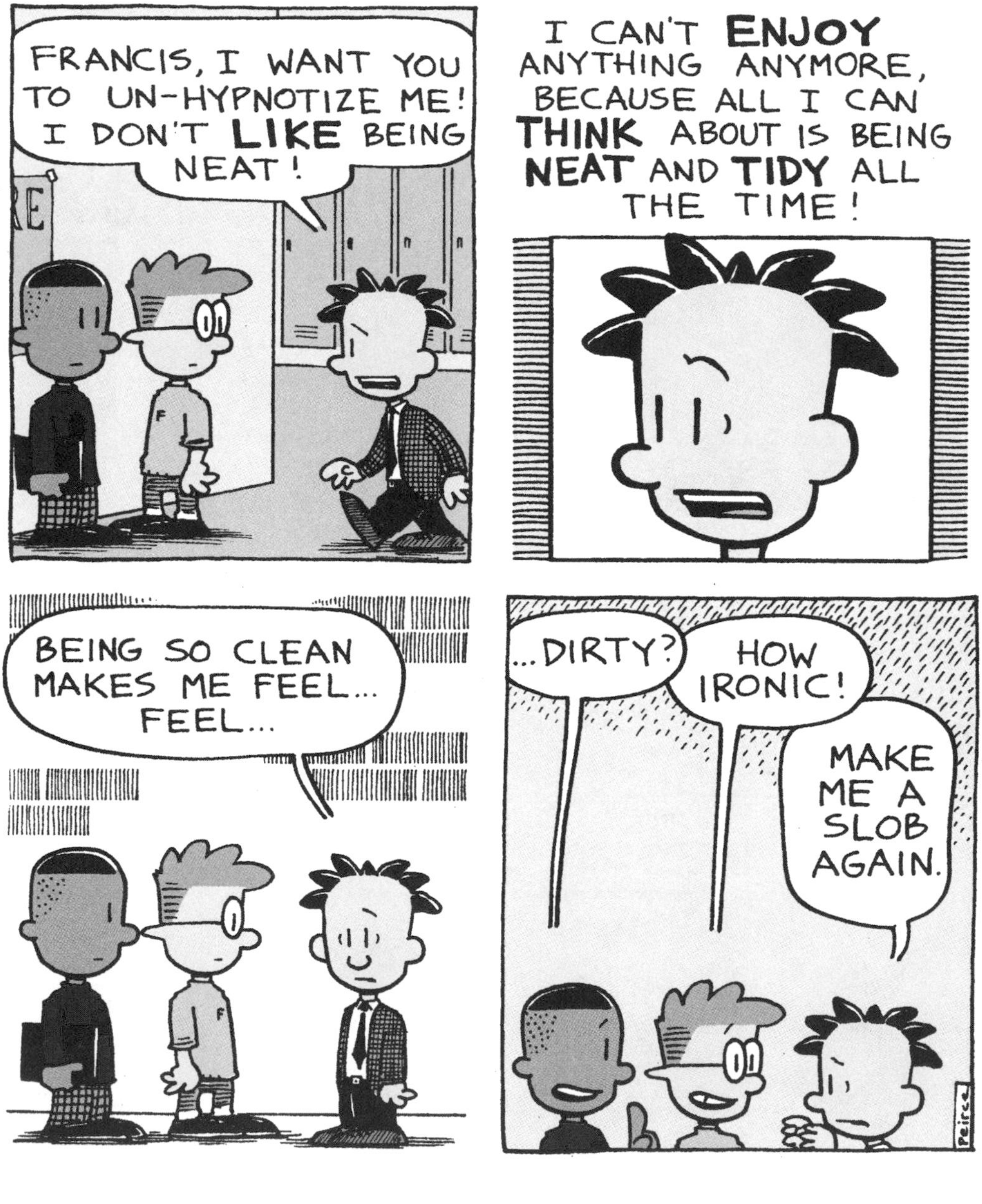
FRANCIS, I WANT YOU TO UN-HYPNOTIZE ME! I DON'T **LIKE** BEING NEAT!
I CAN'T **ENJOY** ANYTHING ANYMORE, BECAUSE ALL I CAN **THINK** ABOUT IS BEING **NEAT** AND **TIDY** ALL THE TIME!
BEING SO CLEAN MAKES ME FEEL... FEEL...
...DIRTY?
HOW IRONIC!
MAKE ME A SLOB AGAIN.
Peirce

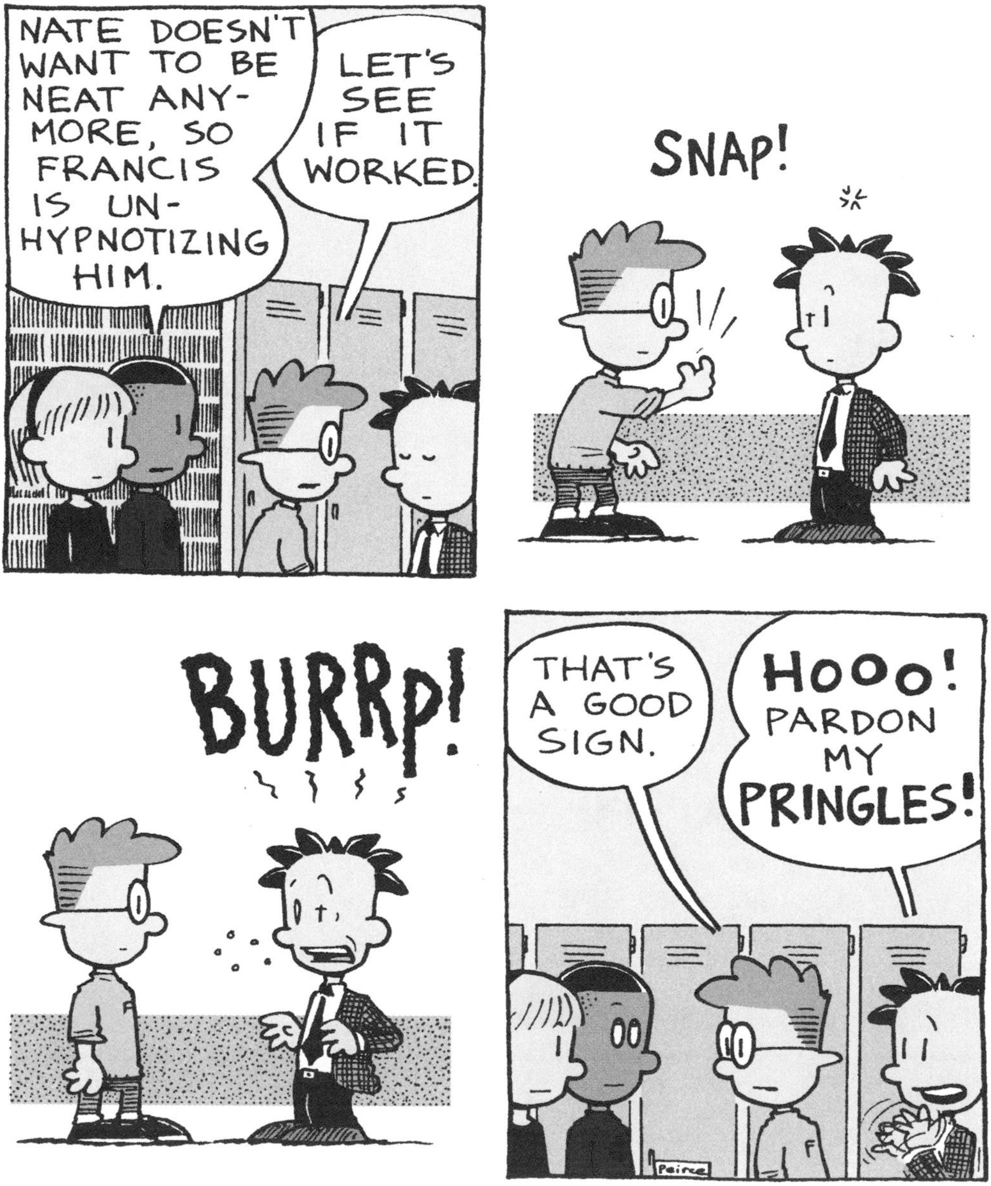
NATE DOESN'T WANT TO BE NEAT ANYMORE, SO FRANCIS IS UN-HYPNOTIZING HIM.
LET'S SEE IF IT WORKED.
SNAP!
BURRP!
THAT'S A GOOD SIGN.
HOOo! PARDON MY PRINGLES!
Peirce

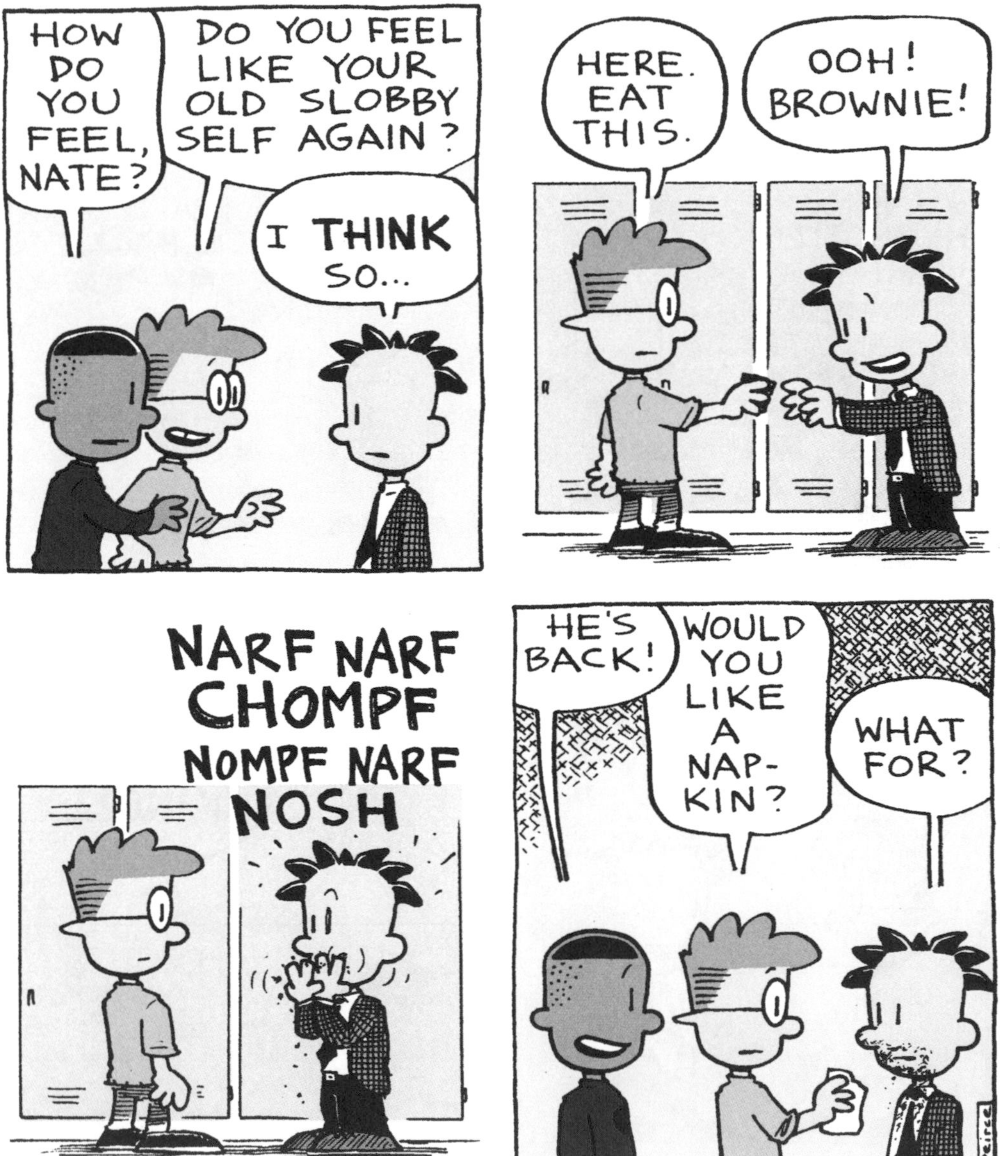
HOW DO YOU FEEL, NATE?
DO YOU FEEL LIKE YOUR OLD SLOBBY SELF AGAIN?
I **THINK** SO...
HERE. EAT THIS.
OOH! BROWNIE!
NARF NARF CHOMPF NOMPF NARF NOSH
HE'S BACK!
WOULD YOU LIKE A NAP-KIN?
WHAT FOR?

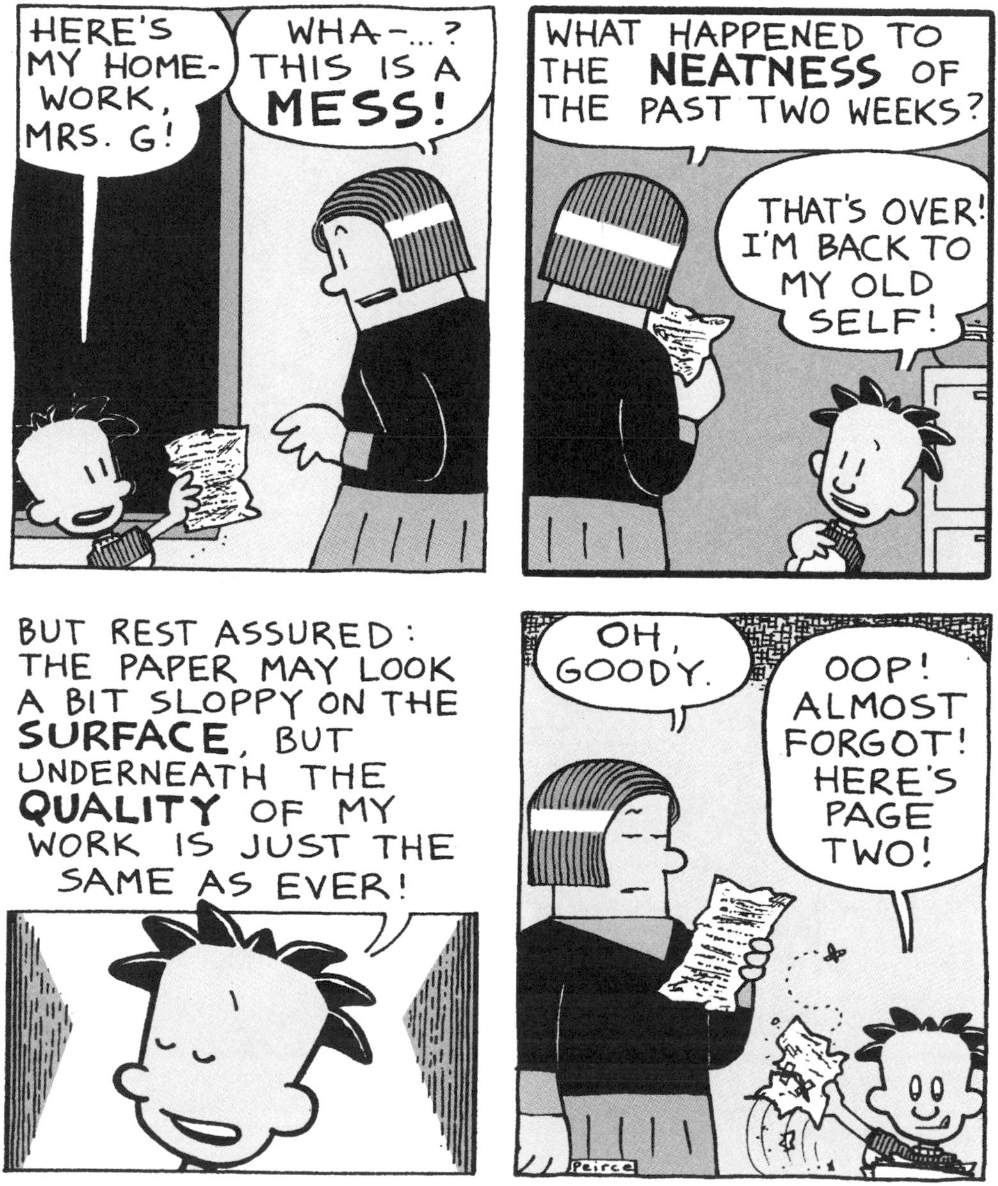
HERE'S MY HOME-WORK, MRS. G!
WHA-...? THIS IS A **MESS**!
WHAT HAPPENED TO THE **NEATNESS** OF THE PAST TWO WEEKS?
THAT'S OVER! I'M BACK TO MY OLD SELF!
BUT REST ASSURED: THE PAPER MAY LOOK A BIT SLOPPY ON THE **SURFACE**, BUT UNDERNEATH THE **QUALITY** OF MY WORK IS JUST THE SAME AS EVER!
OH, GOODY.
OOP! ALMOST FORGOT! HERE'S PAGE TWO!
Peirce

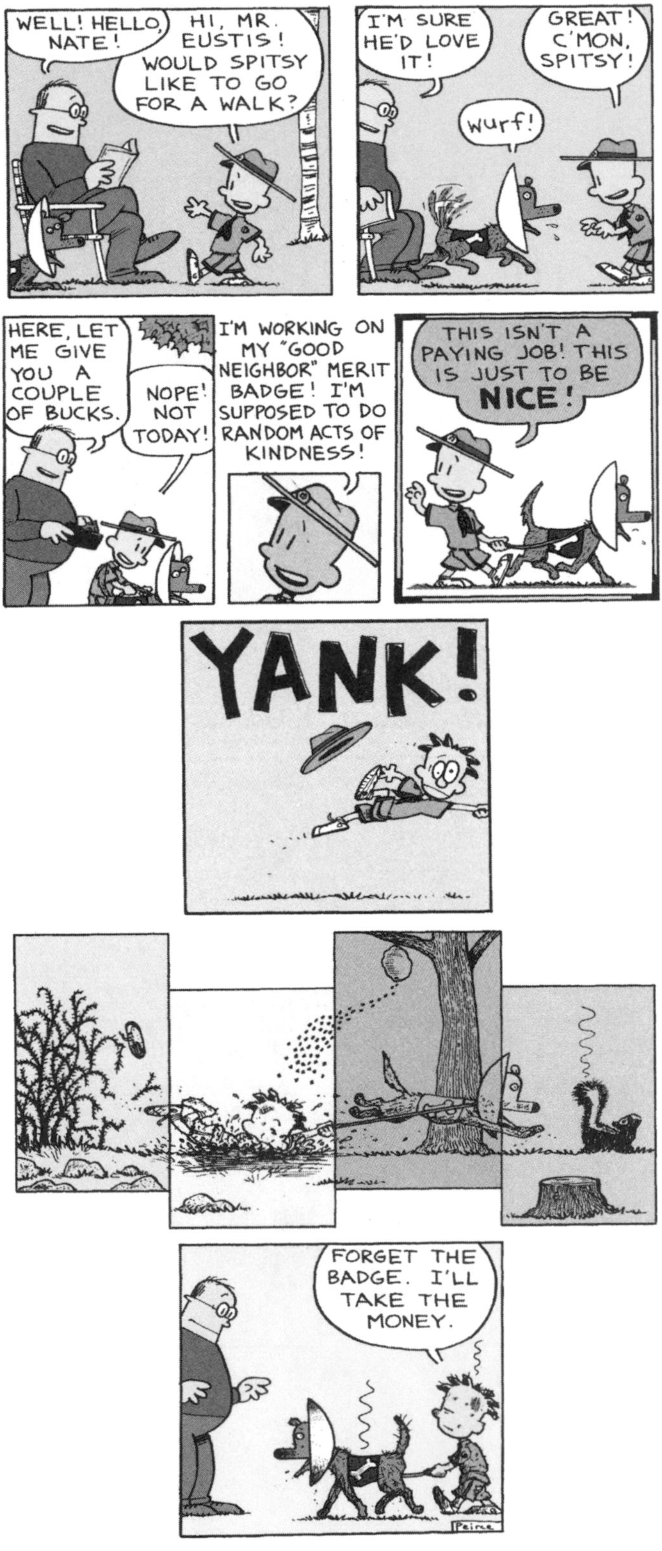
WELL! HELLO, NATE!
HI, MR. EUSTIS! WOULD SPITSY LIKE TO GO FOR A WALK?
I'M SURE HE'D LOVE IT!
GREAT! C'MON, SPITSY!
wurf!
HERE, LET ME GIVE YOU A COUPLE OF BUCKS.
NOPE! NOT TODAY!
I'M WORKING ON MY "GOOD NEIGHBOR" MERIT BADGE! I'M SUPPOSED TO DO RANDOM ACTS OF KINDNESS!
THIS ISN'T A PAYING JOB! THIS IS JUST TO BE NICE!
YANK!
FORGET THE BADGE. I'LL TAKE THE MONEY.
Peirce

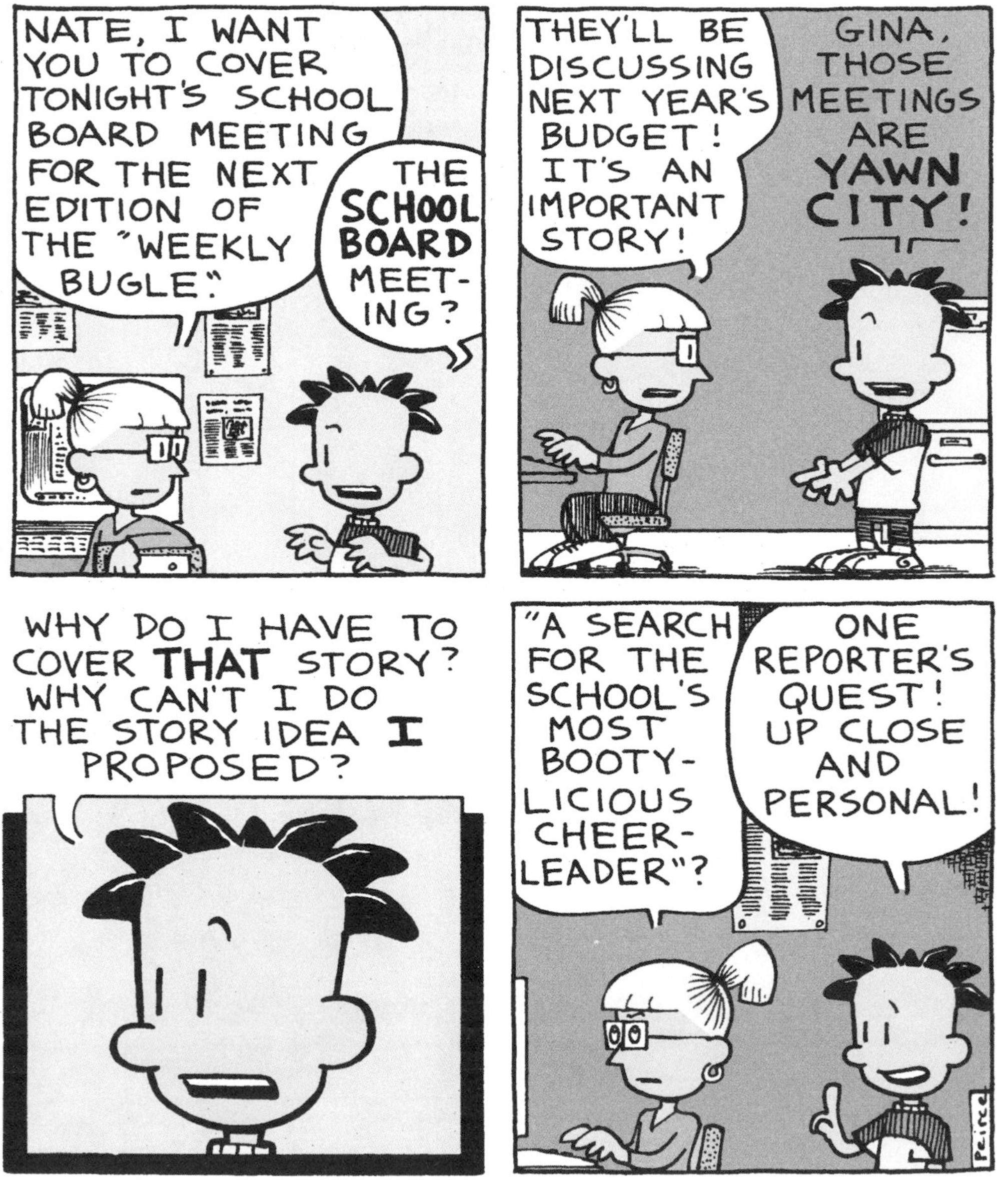
NATE, I WANT YOU TO COVER TONIGHT'S SCHOOL BOARD MEETING FOR THE NEXT EDITION OF THE "WEEKLY BUGLE."
THE SCHOOL BOARD MEETING?
THEY'LL BE DISCUSSING NEXT YEAR'S BUDGET! IT'S AN IMPORTANT STORY!
GINA, THOSE MEETINGS ARE YAWN CITY!
WHY DO I HAVE TO COVER THAT STORY? WHY CAN'T I DO THE STORY IDEA I PROPOSED?
"A SEARCH FOR THE SCHOOL'S MOST BOOTY-LICIOUS CHEER-LEADER"?
ONE REPORTER'S QUEST! UP CLOSE AND PERSONAL!
Peirce

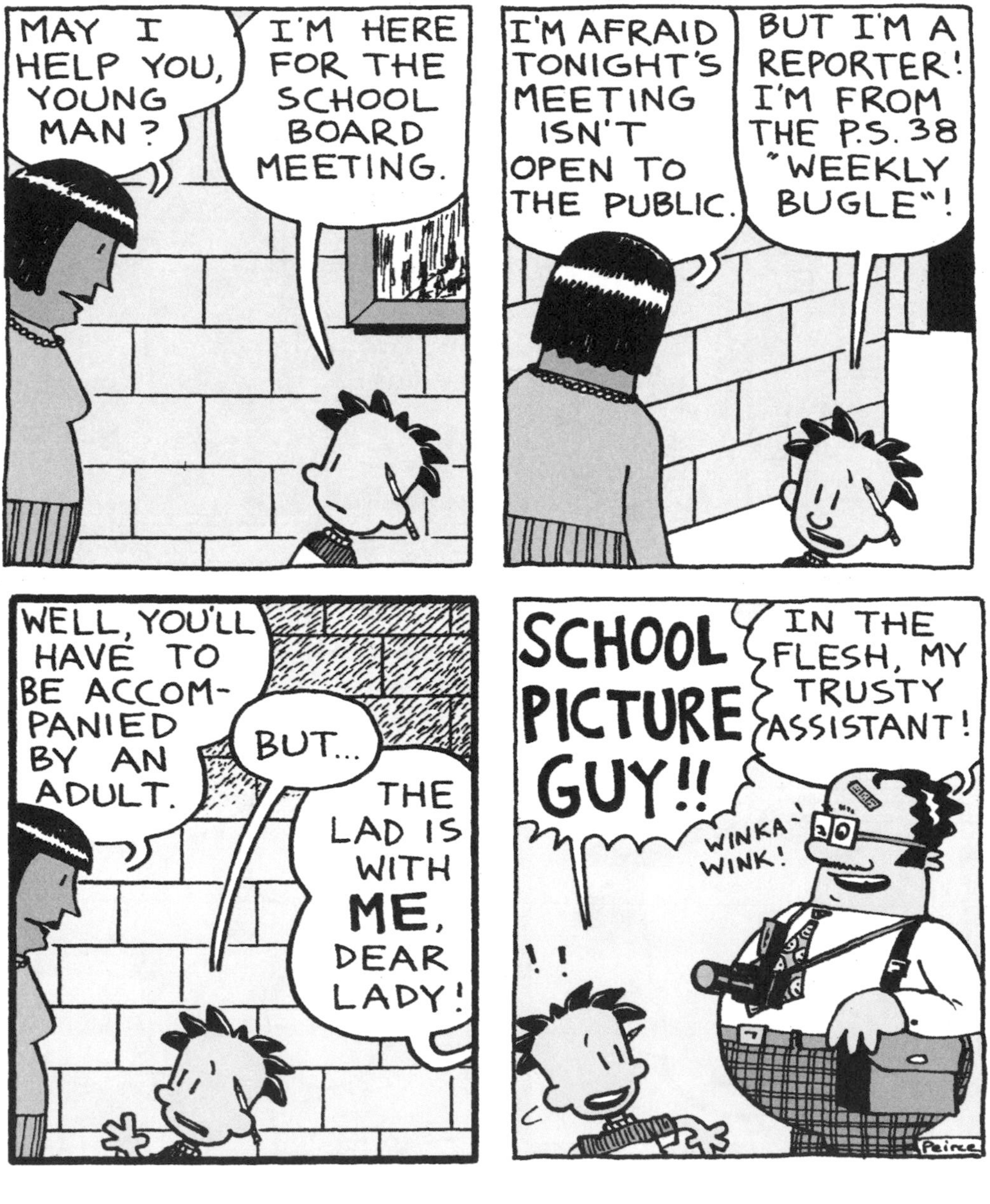
MAY I HELP YOU, YOUNG MAN?
I'M HERE FOR THE SCHOOL BOARD MEETING.
I'M AFRAID TONIGHT'S MEETING ISN'T OPEN TO THE PUBLIC.
BUT I'M A REPORTER! I'M FROM THE P.S. 38 "WEEKLY BUGLE"!
WELL, YOU'LL HAVE TO BE ACCOMPANIED BY AN ADULT.
BUT...
THE LAD IS WITH **ME**, DEAR LADY!
SCHOOL PICTURE GUY!!
IN THE FLESH, MY TRUSTY ASSISTANT!
WINKA WINK!
!!
Peirce

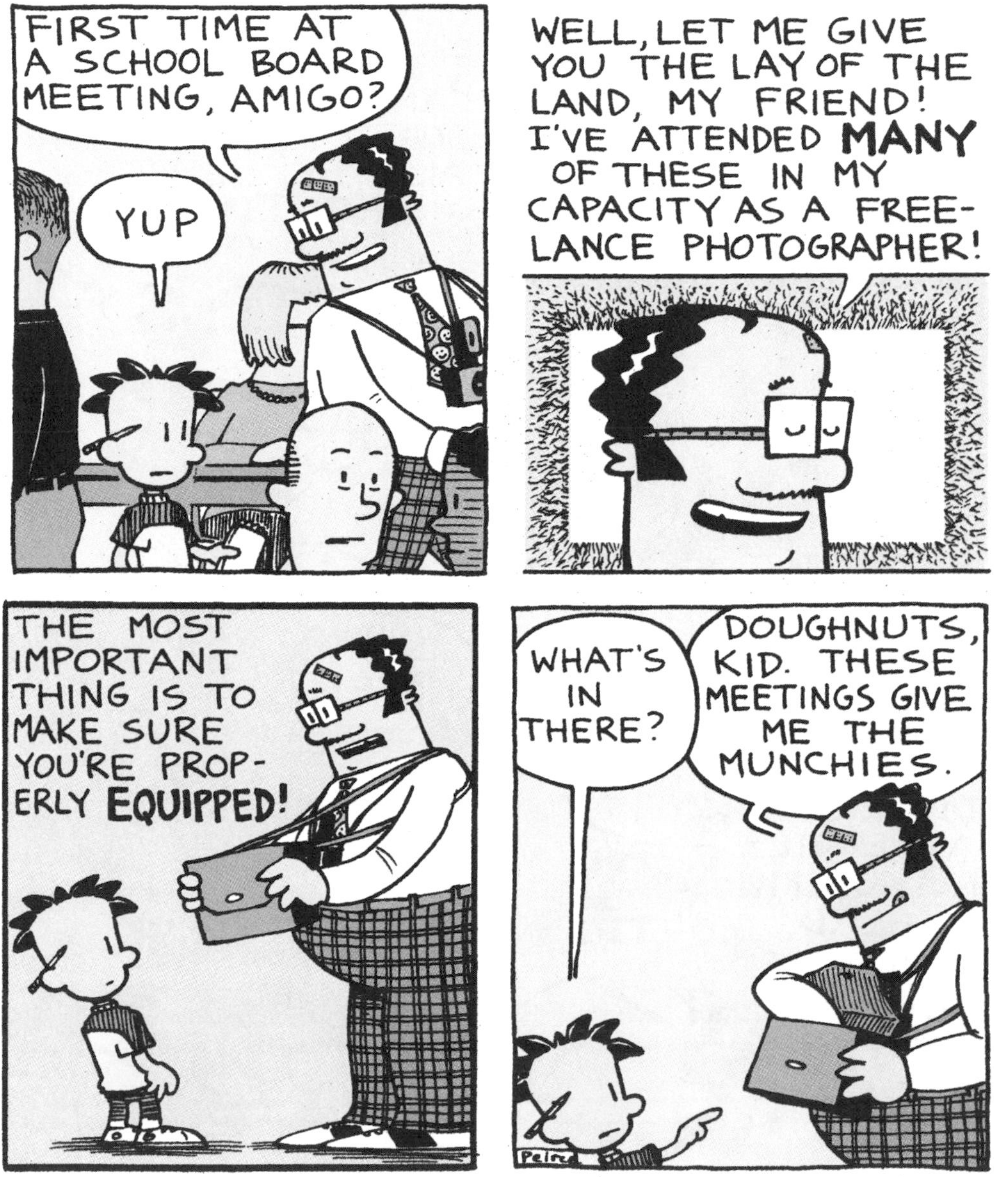
FIRST TIME AT A SCHOOL BOARD MEETING, AMIGO?
YUP
WELL, LET ME GIVE YOU THE LAY OF THE LAND, MY FRIEND! I'VE ATTENDED **MANY** OF THESE IN MY CAPACITY AS A FREE-LANCE PHOTOGRAPHER!
THE MOST IMPORTANT THING IS TO MAKE SURE YOU'RE PROPERLY **EQUIPPED**!
WHAT'S IN THERE?
DOUGHNUTS, KID. THESE MEETINGS GIVE ME THE MUNCHIES.
Peirce

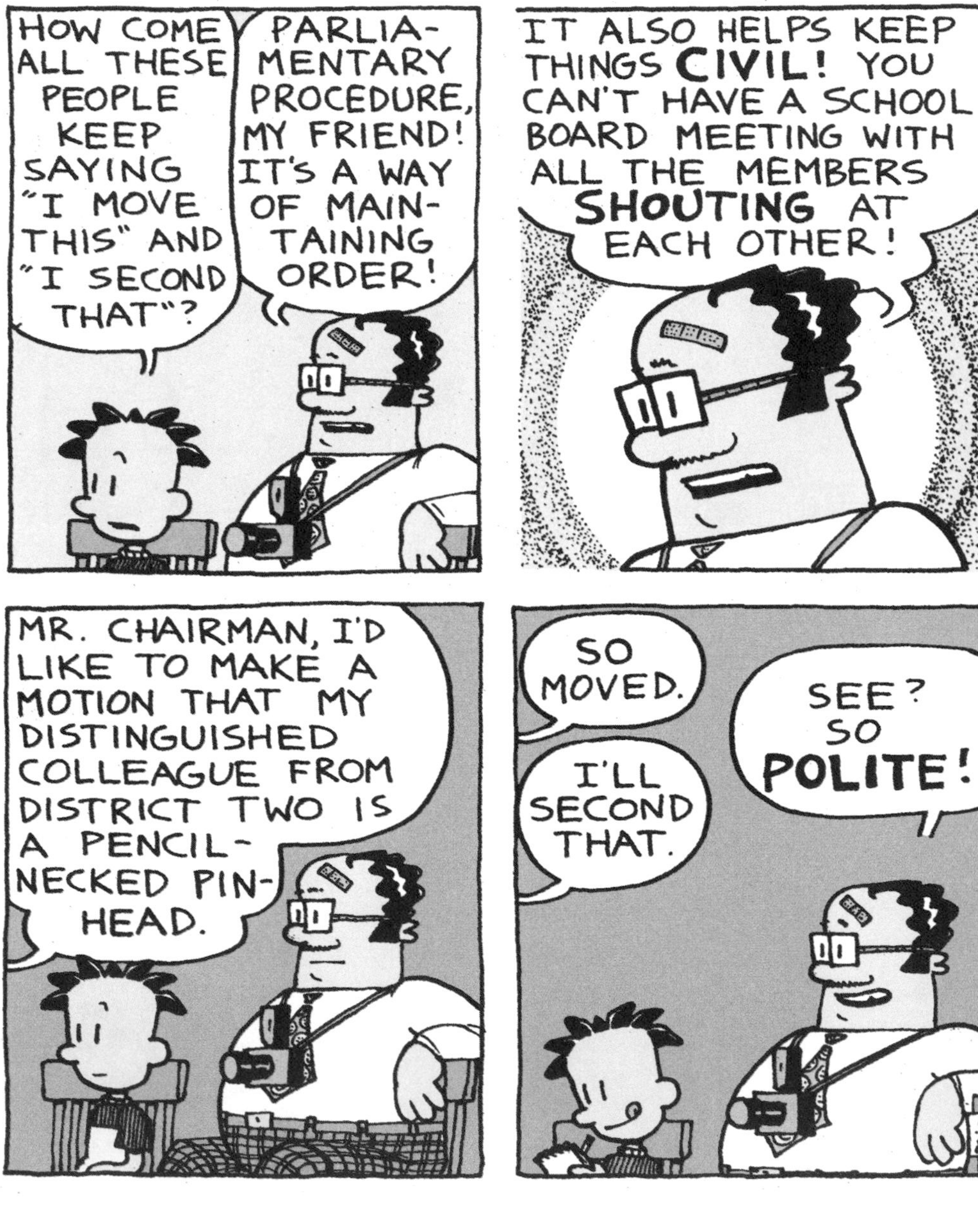
HOW COME ALL THESE PEOPLE KEEP SAYING "I MOVE THIS" AND "I SECOND THAT"?
PARLIAMENTARY PROCEDURE, MY FRIEND! IT'S A WAY OF MAINTAINING ORDER!
IT ALSO HELPS KEEP THINGS CIVIL! YOU CAN'T HAVE A SCHOOL BOARD MEETING WITH ALL THE MEMBERS SHOUTING AT EACH OTHER!
MR. CHAIRMAN, I'D LIKE TO MAKE A MOTION THAT MY DISTINGUISHED COLLEAGUE FROM DISTRICT TWO IS A PENCIL-NECKED PIN-HEAD.
SO MOVED.
I'LL SECOND THAT.
SEE? SO POLITE!

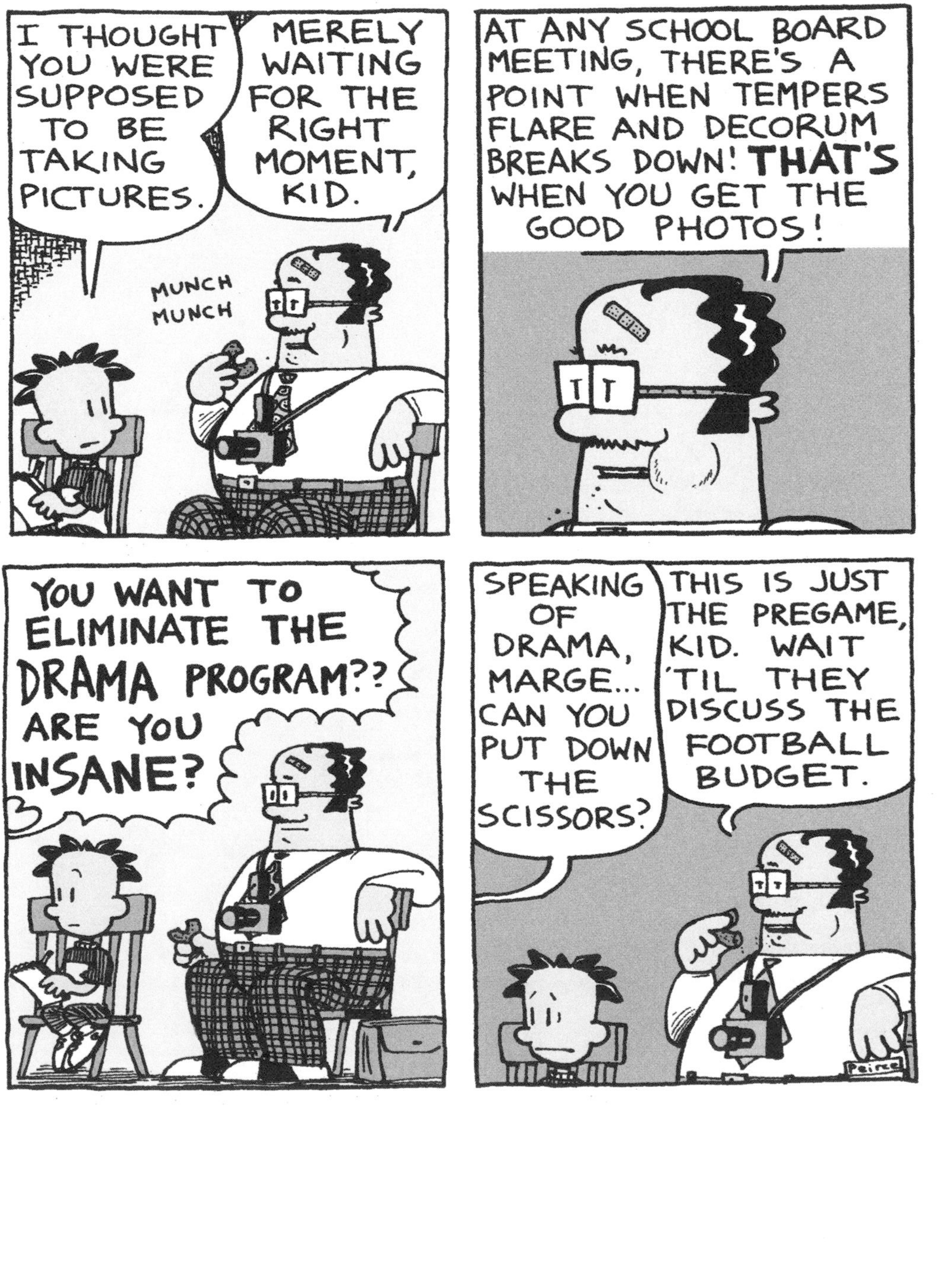
I THOUGHT YOU WERE SUPPOSED TO BE TAKING PICTURES.
MERELY WAITING FOR THE RIGHT MOMENT, KID.
MUNCH MUNCH
AT ANY SCHOOL BOARD MEETING, THERE'S A POINT WHEN TEMPERS FLARE AND DECORUM BREAKS DOWN! THAT'S WHEN YOU GET THE GOOD PHOTOS!
YOU WANT TO ELIMINATE THE DRAMA PROGRAM?? ARE YOU INSANE?
SPEAKING OF DRAMA, MARGE... CAN YOU PUT DOWN THE SCISSORS?
THIS IS JUST THE PREGAME, KID. WAIT 'TIL THEY DISCUSS THE FOOTBALL BUDGET.
Peirce

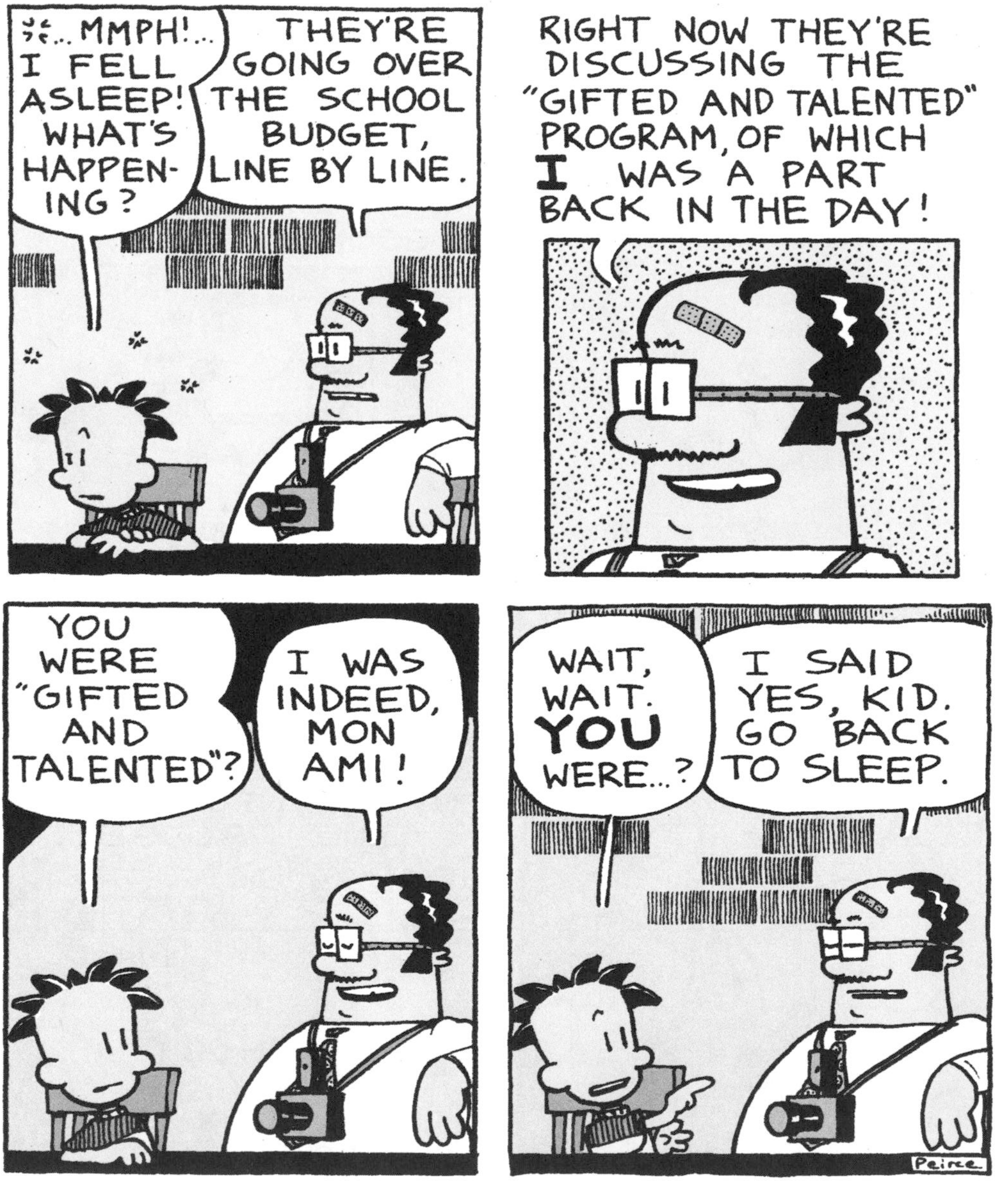
…MMPH!… I FELL ASLEEP! WHAT'S HAPPEN-ING?
THEY'RE GOING OVER THE SCHOOL BUDGET, LINE BY LINE.
RIGHT NOW THEY'RE DISCUSSING THE "GIFTED AND TALENTED" PROGRAM, OF WHICH I WAS A PART BACK IN THE DAY!
YOU WERE "GIFTED AND TALENTED"?
I WAS INDEED, MON AMI!
WAIT, WAIT. YOU WERE…?
I SAID YES, KID. GO BACK TO SLEEP.
Peirce

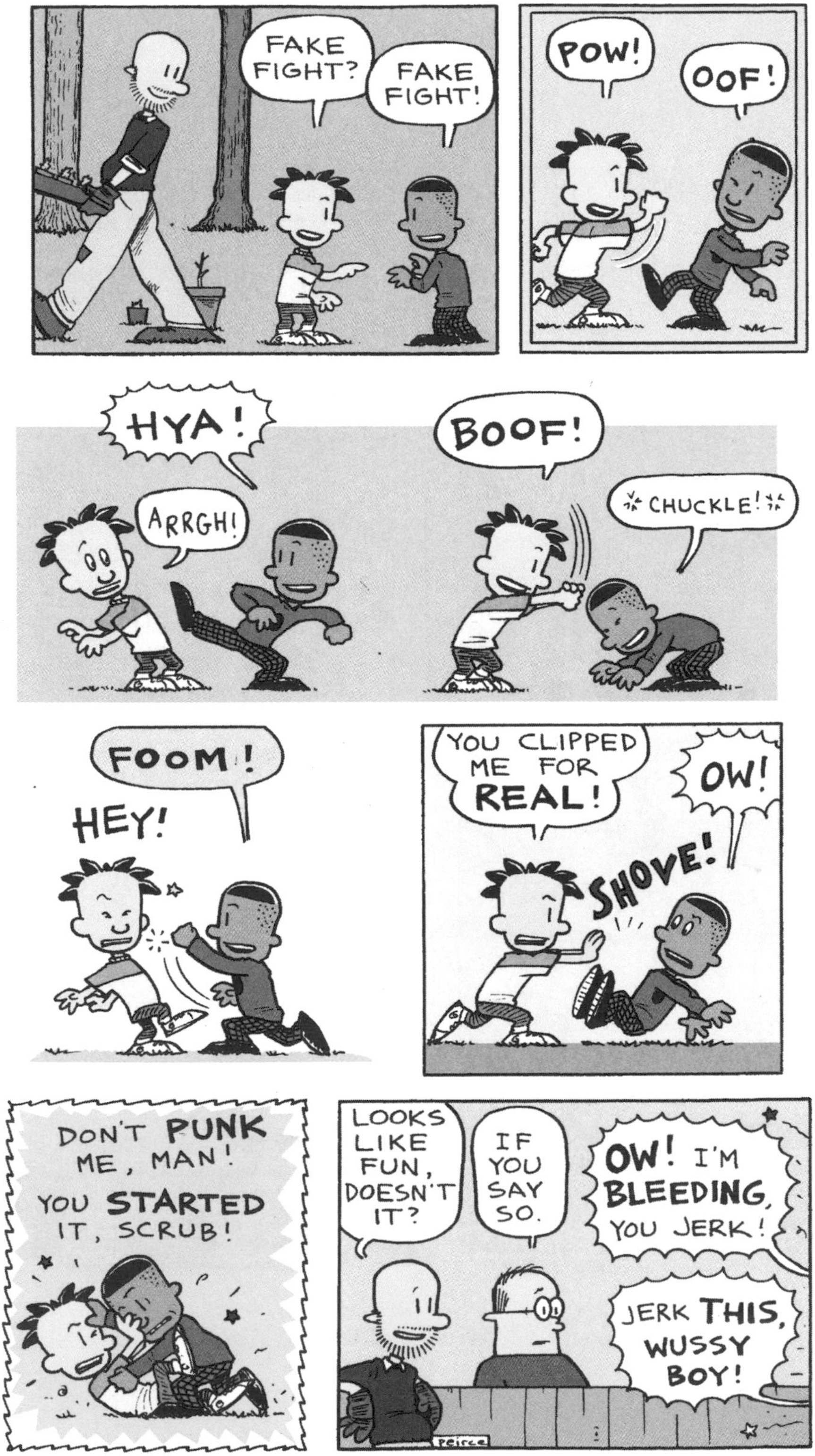
FAKE FIGHT?
FAKE FIGHT!
POW!
OOF!
HYA!
ARRGH!
BOOF!
CHUCKLE!
FOOM!
HEY!
YOU CLIPPED ME FOR REAL!
OW!
SHOVE!
DON'T PUNK ME, MAN!
YOU STARTED IT, SCRUB!
LOOKS LIKE FUN, DOESN'T IT?
IF YOU SAY SO.
OW! I'M BLEEDING, YOU JERK!
JERK THIS, WUSSY BOY!
peirce

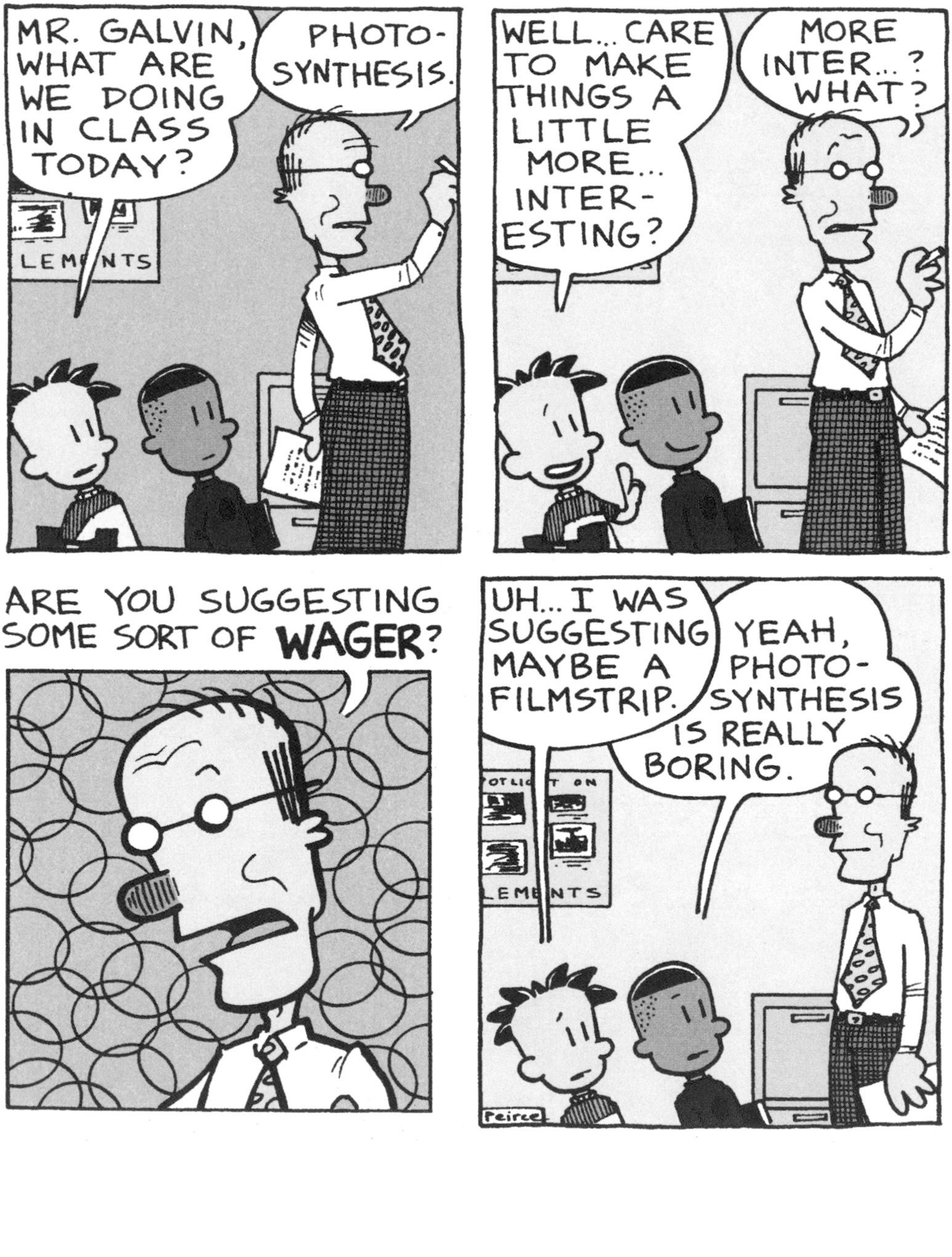
MR. GALVIN, WHAT ARE WE DOING IN CLASS TODAY?
PHOTO-SYNTHESIS.
WELL... CARE TO MAKE THINGS A LITTLE MORE... INTER-ESTING?
MORE INTER...? WHAT?
ARE YOU SUGGESTING SOME SORT OF **WAGER**?
UH... I WAS SUGGESTING MAYBE A FILMSTRIP.
YEAH, PHOTO-SYNTHESIS IS REALLY BORING.
LEMENTS
Peirce

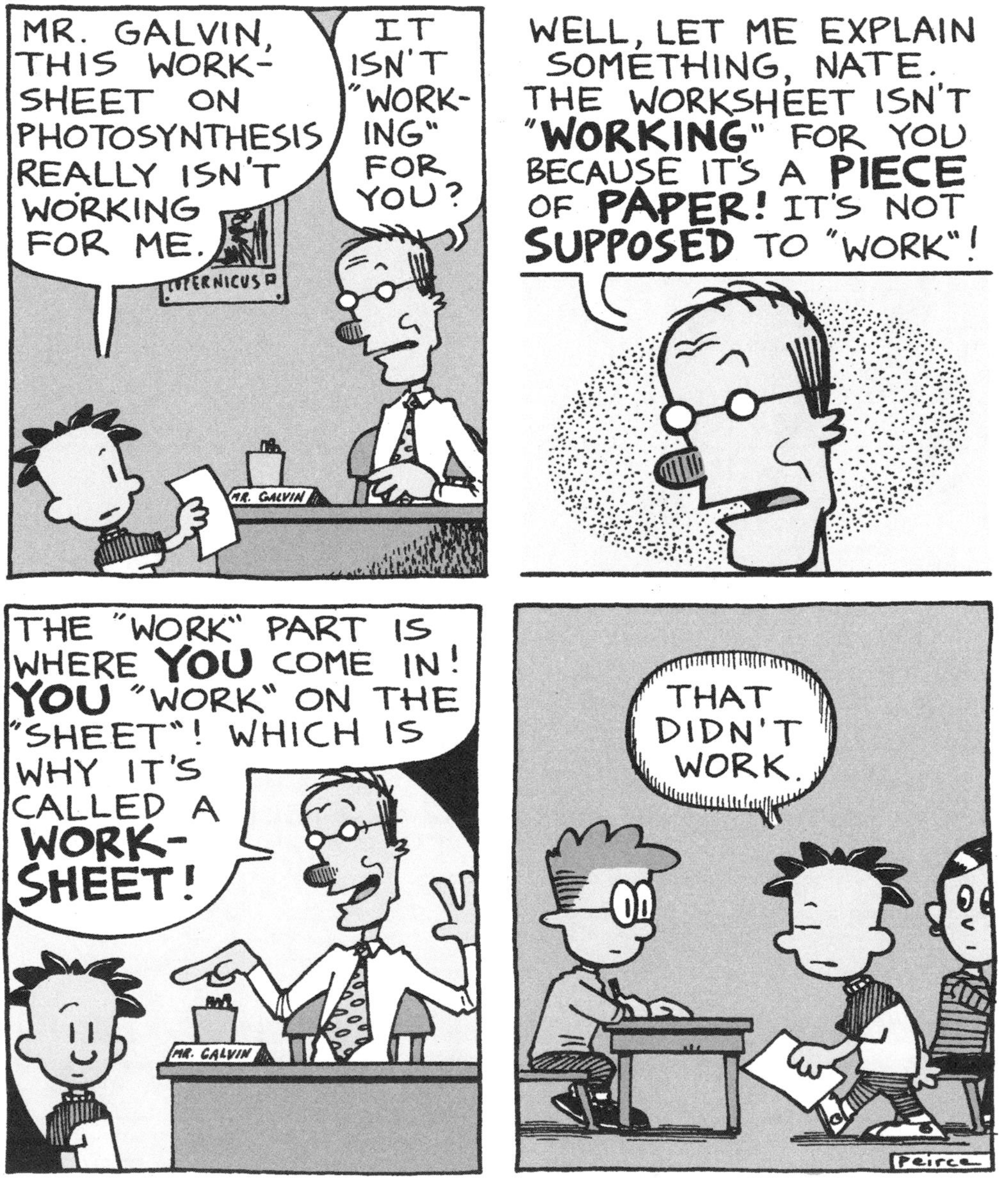
MR. GALVIN, THIS WORK-SHEET ON PHOTOSYNTHESIS REALLY ISN'T WORKING FOR ME.
IT ISN'T "WORKING" FOR YOU?
COPERNICUS
MR. GALVIN
WELL, LET ME EXPLAIN SOMETHING, NATE. THE WORKSHEET ISN'T "WORKING" FOR YOU BECAUSE IT'S A PIECE OF PAPER! IT'S NOT SUPPOSED TO "WORK"!
THE "WORK" PART IS WHERE YOU COME IN! YOU "WORK" ON THE "SHEET"! WHICH IS WHY IT'S CALLED A WORK-SHEET!
MR. GALVIN
THAT DIDN'T WORK.
Peirce

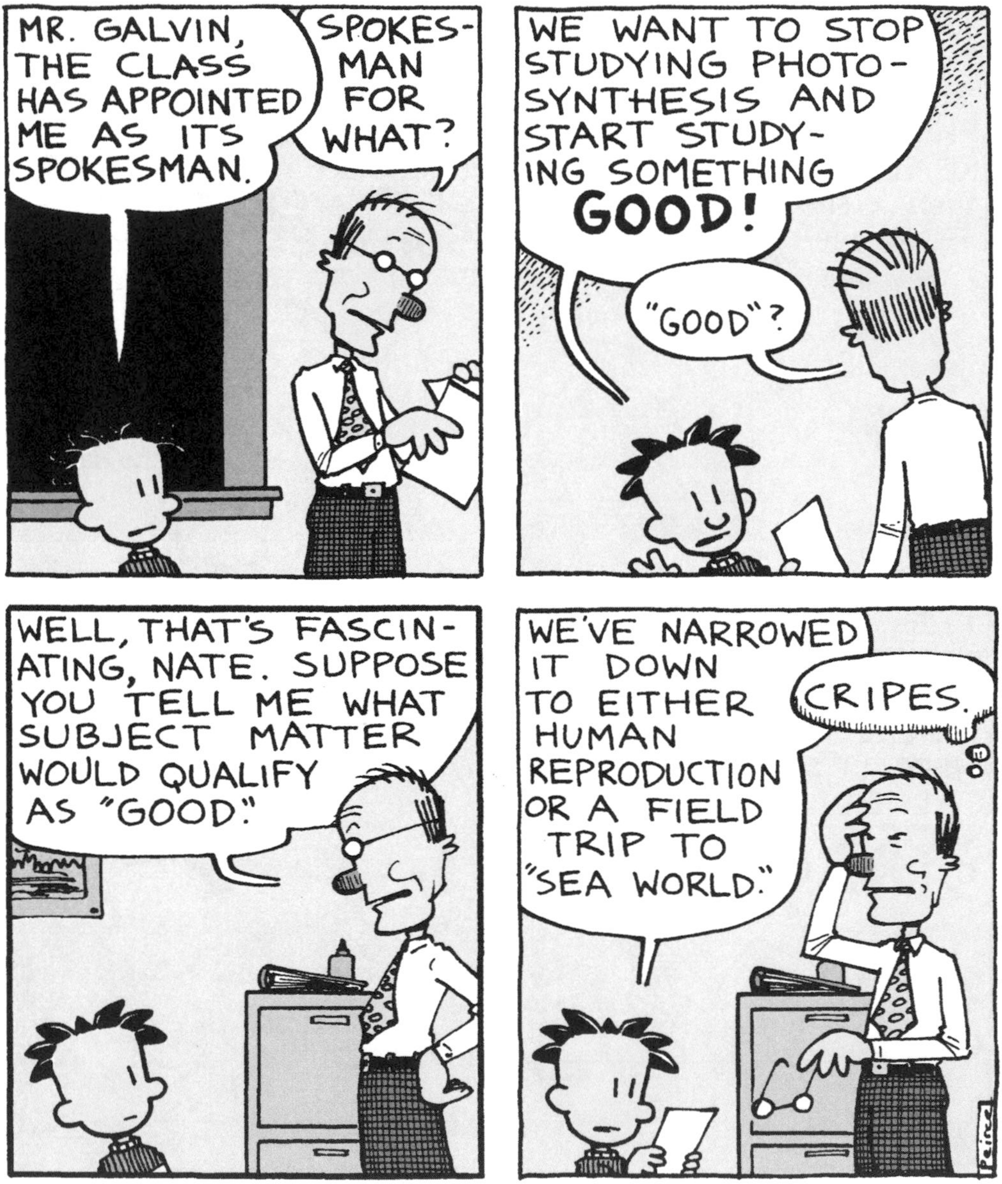
MR. GALVIN, THE CLASS HAS APPOINTED ME AS ITS SPOKESMAN.
SPOKES-MAN FOR WHAT?
WE WANT TO STOP STUDYING PHOTO-SYNTHESIS AND START STUDY-ING SOMETHING GOOD!
"GOOD"?
WELL, THAT'S FASCIN-ATING, NATE. SUPPOSE YOU TELL ME WHAT SUBJECT MATTER WOULD QUALIFY AS "GOOD."
WE'VE NARROWED IT DOWN TO EITHER HUMAN REPRODUCTION OR A FIELD TRIP TO "SEA WORLD."
CRIPES.
Peirce

MR. GALVIN NEEDS TO LIGHTEN UP.
HEY, THERE'S A NEWS FLASH.
I'M SERIOUS! HAVE YOU EVER SEEN THE MAN LAUGH?
LAUGH? I'VE NEVER EVEN SEEN HIM SMILE!
I'LL BET I COULD GET A CHUCKLE OUT OF HIM!
YOU? HOW?
HAVE YOU FORGOTTEN ABOUT MY LEGENDARY ARSENAL OF "KNOCK KNOCK" JOKES?
SADLY, NO.
"ARSENAL" IS RIGHT.

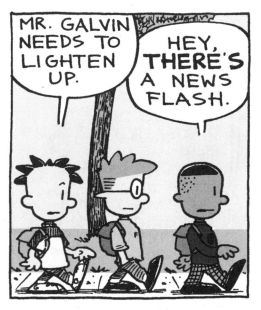

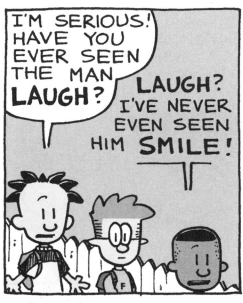

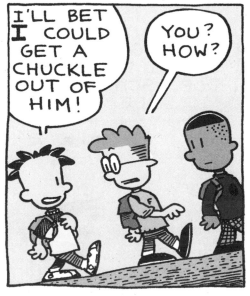

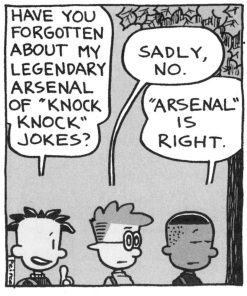

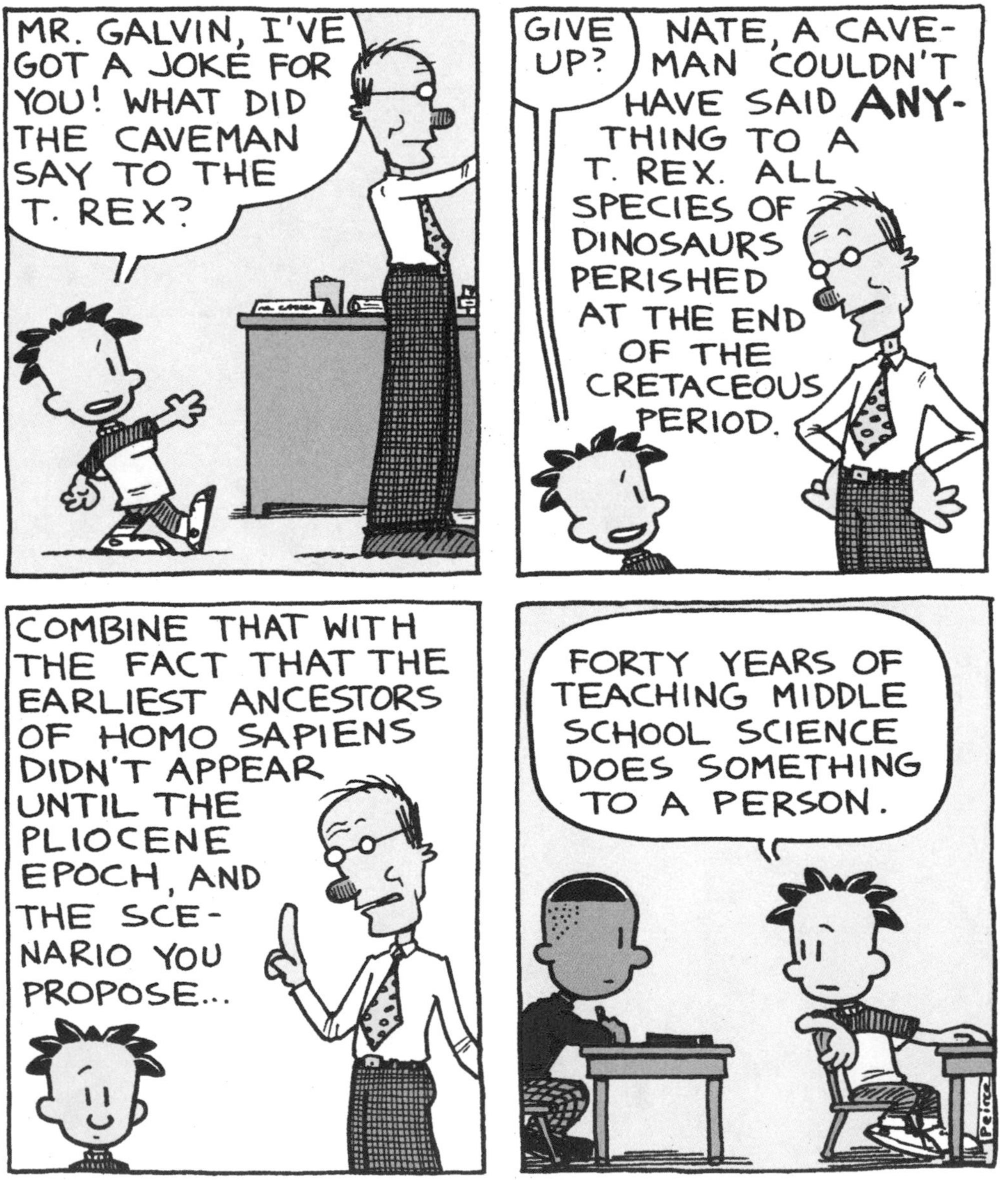
MR. GALVIN, I'VE GOT A JOKE FOR YOU! WHAT DID THE CAVEMAN SAY TO THE T. REX?
GIVE UP?
NATE, A CAVE-MAN COULDN'T HAVE SAID ANY-THING TO A T. REX. ALL SPECIES OF DINOSAURS PERISHED AT THE END OF THE CRETACEOUS PERIOD.
COMBINE THAT WITH THE FACT THAT THE EARLIEST ANCESTORS OF HOMO SAPIENS DIDN'T APPEAR UNTIL THE PLIOCENE EPOCH, AND THE SCE-NARIO YOU PROPOSE...
FORTY YEARS OF TEACHING MIDDLE SCHOOL SCIENCE DOES SOMETHING TO A PERSON.
PEIRCE

OKAY, MR. GALVIN... **HERE'S** A JOKE I THINK YOU'LL APPREC-IATE!

WHAT DID THE THEORETICAL PHYSICIST USE TO DRINK HIS BEER?

AN EIN-STEIN!

WA HA HA HA HA HO HO HA

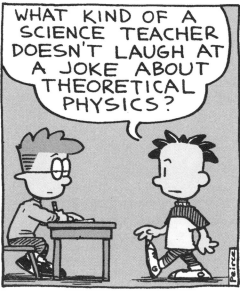

WHAT KIND OF A SCIENCE TEACHER DOESN'T LAUGH AT A JOKE ABOUT THEORETICAL PHYSICS?

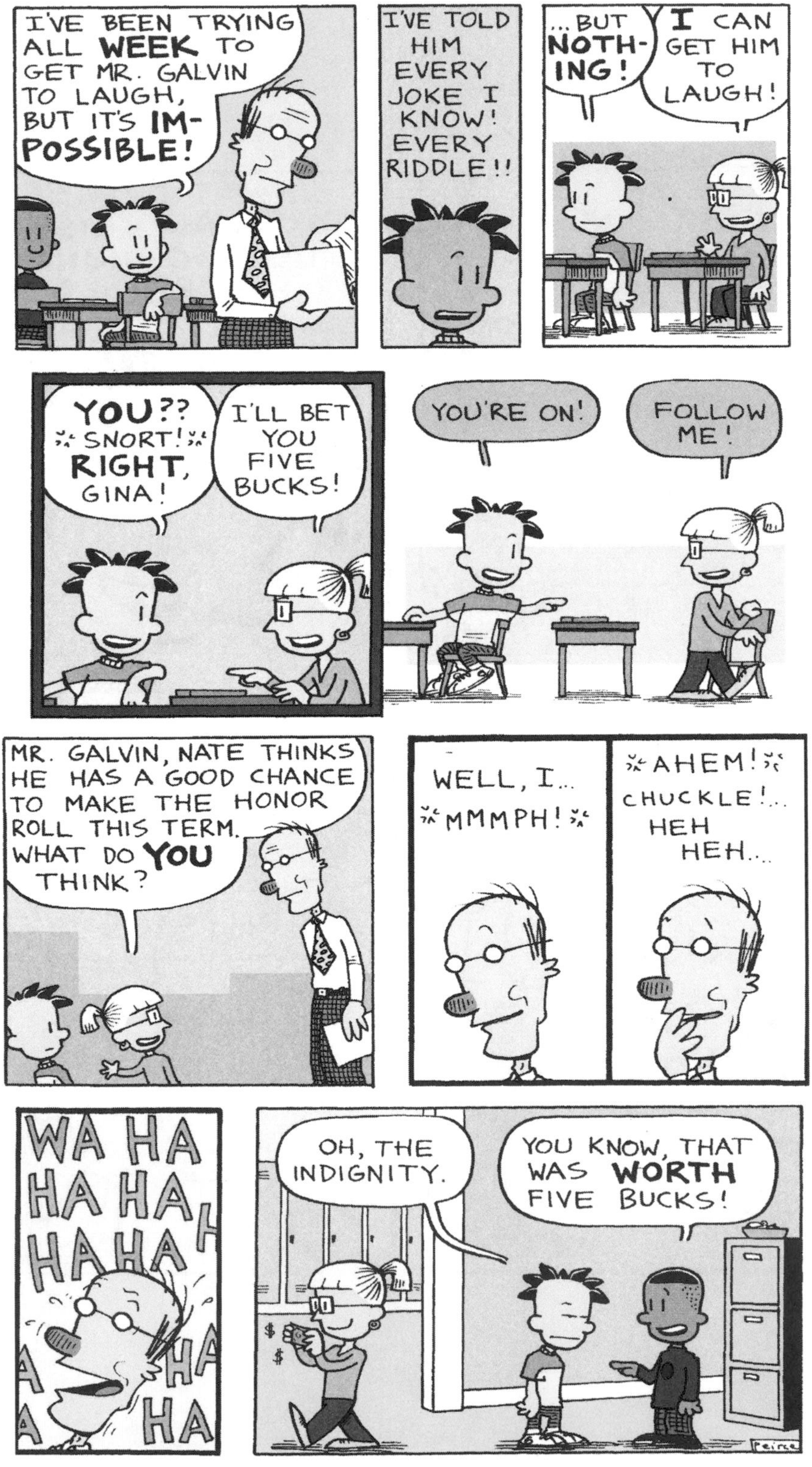
I'VE BEEN TRYING ALL **WEEK** TO GET MR. GALVIN TO LAUGH, BUT IT'S **IMPOSSIBLE!**
I'VE TOLD HIM EVERY JOKE I KNOW! EVERY RIDDLE!!
...BUT **NOTHING!**
I CAN GET HIM TO LAUGH!
YOU?? *SNORT!* **RIGHT,** GINA!
I'LL BET YOU FIVE BUCKS!
YOU'RE ON!
FOLLOW ME!
MR. GALVIN, NATE THINKS HE HAS A GOOD CHANCE TO MAKE THE HONOR ROLL THIS TERM. WHAT DO **YOU** THINK?
WELL, I... *MMMPH!*
AHEM! CHUCKLE!... HEH HEH...
WA HA HA HA HA HA HA HA HA HA HA
OH, THE INDIGNITY.
YOU KNOW, THAT WAS **WORTH** FIVE BUCKS!
peirce

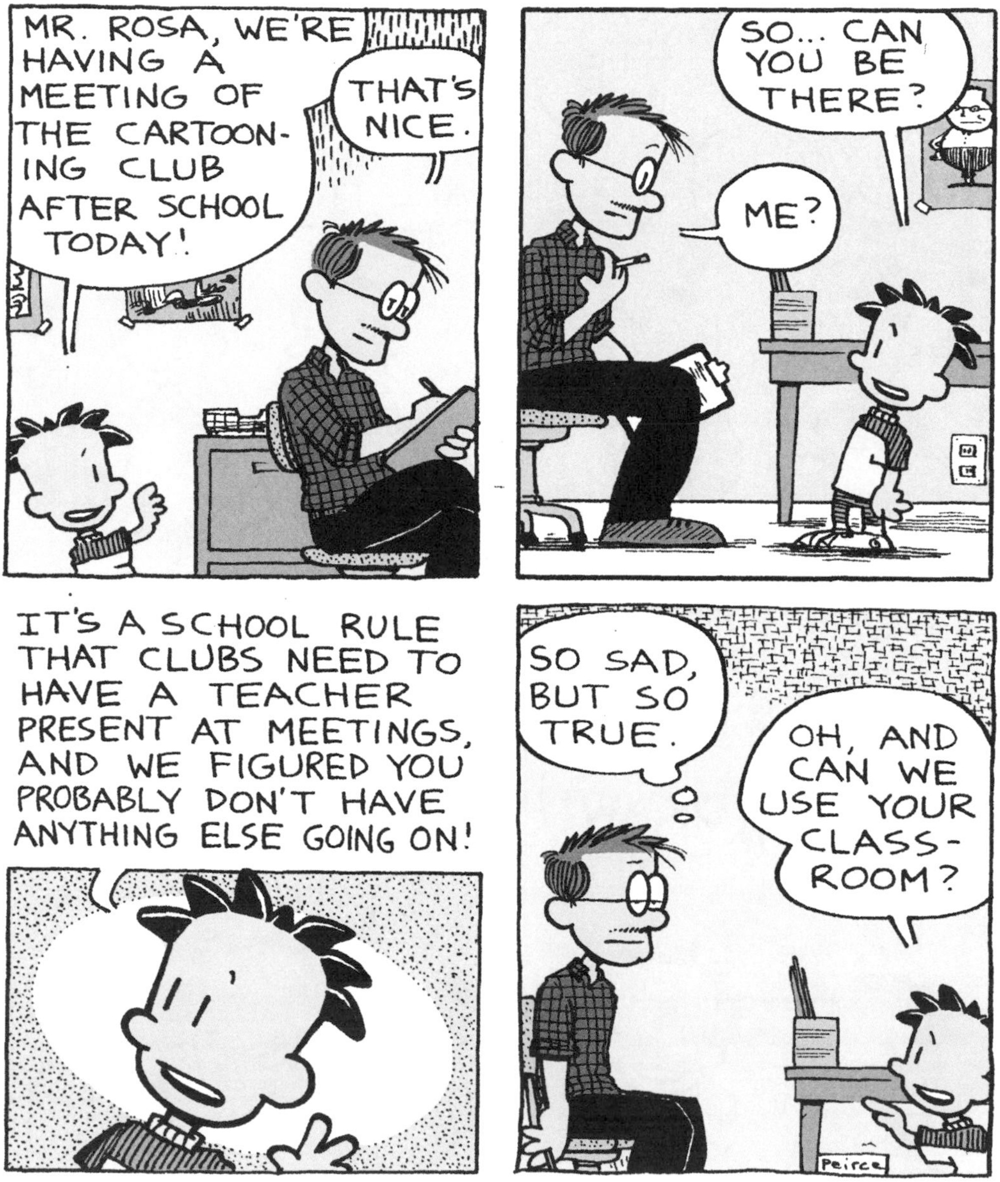
MR. ROSA, WE'RE HAVING A MEETING OF THE CARTOONING CLUB AFTER SCHOOL TODAY!
THAT'S NICE.
SO... CAN YOU BE THERE?
ME?
IT'S A SCHOOL RULE THAT CLUBS NEED TO HAVE A TEACHER PRESENT AT MEETINGS, AND WE FIGURED YOU PROBABLY DON'T HAVE ANYTHING ELSE GOING ON!
SO SAD, BUT SO TRUE.
OH, AND CAN WE USE YOUR CLASSROOM?
Peirce

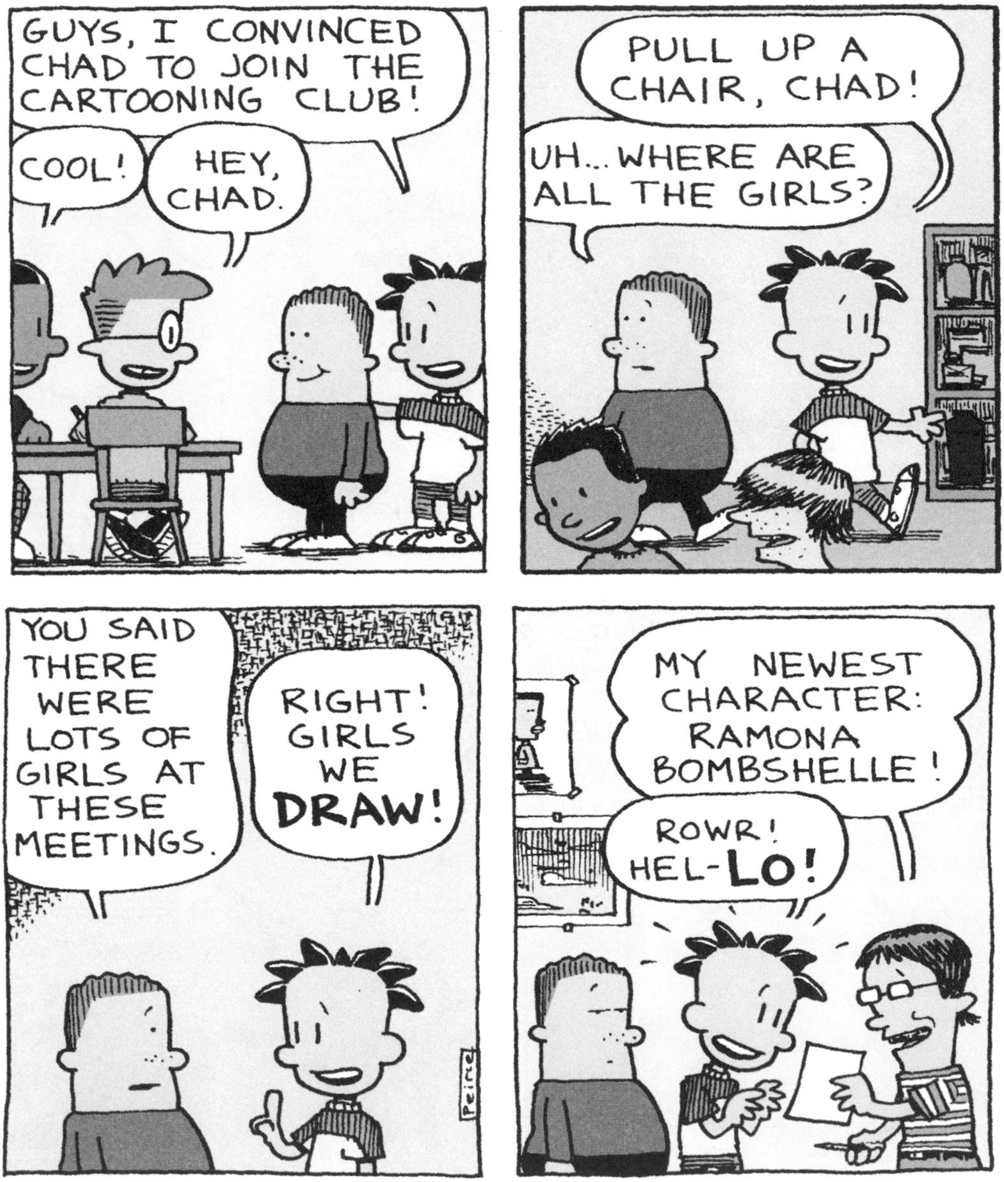
GUYS, I CONVINCED CHAD TO JOIN THE CARTOONING CLUB!
COOL!
HEY, CHAD.
PULL UP A CHAIR, CHAD!
UH... WHERE ARE ALL THE GIRLS?
YOU SAID THERE WERE LOTS OF GIRLS AT THESE MEETINGS.
RIGHT! GIRLS WE **DRAW**!
Peirce
MY NEWEST CHARACTER: RAMONA BOMBSHELLE!
ROWR! HEL-**LO**!

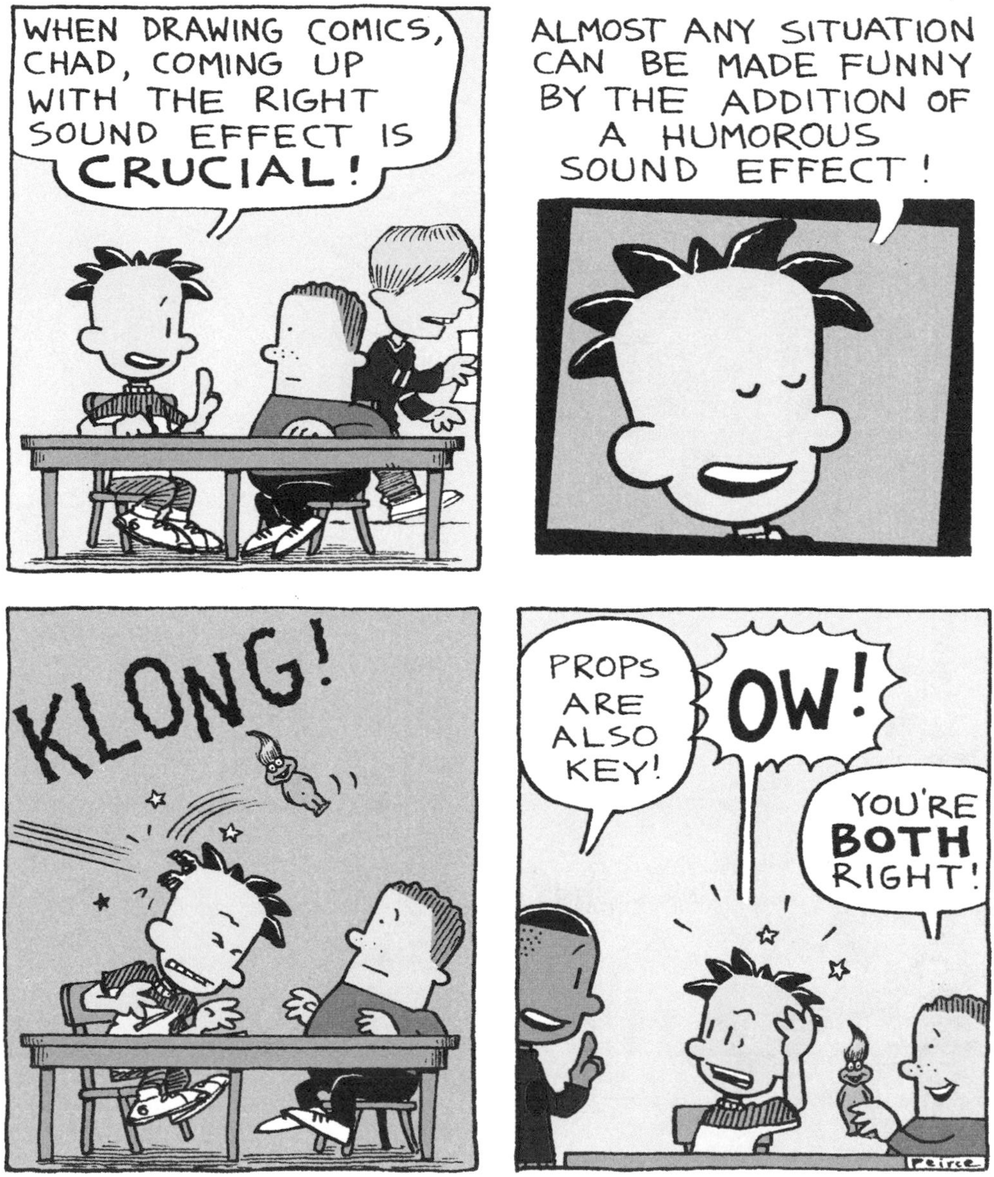
WHEN DRAWING COMICS, CHAD, COMING UP WITH THE RIGHT SOUND EFFECT IS CRUCIAL!
ALMOST ANY SITUATION CAN BE MADE FUNNY BY THE ADDITION OF A HUMOROUS SOUND EFFECT!
KLONG!
PROPS ARE ALSO KEY!
OW!
YOU'RE BOTH RIGHT!
Peirce

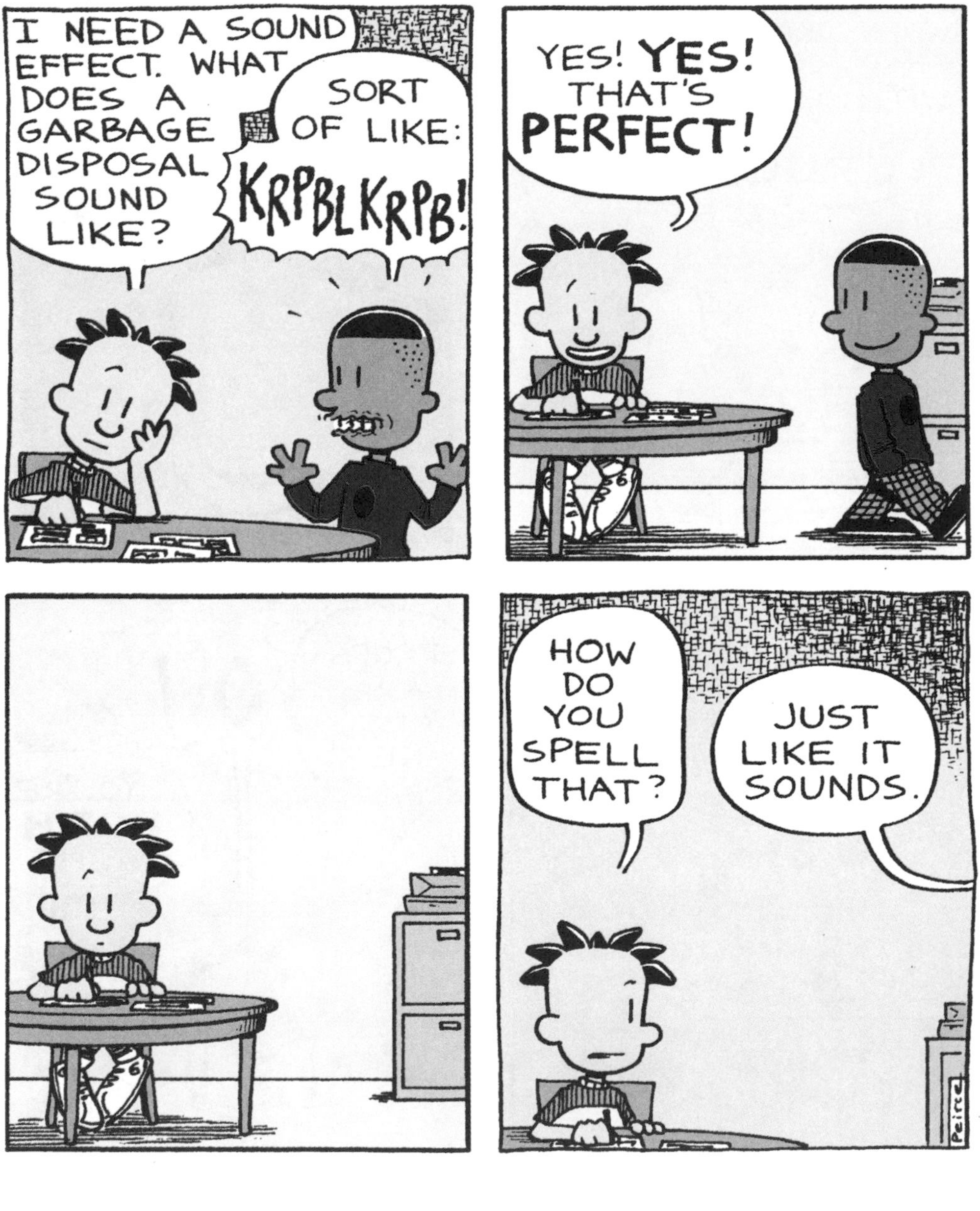
I NEED A SOUND EFFECT. WHAT DOES A GARBAGE DISPOSAL SOUND LIKE?
SORT OF LIKE: KRPBLKRPB!
YES! YES! THAT'S PERFECT!
HOW DO YOU SPELL THAT?
JUST LIKE IT SOUNDS.
Peirce

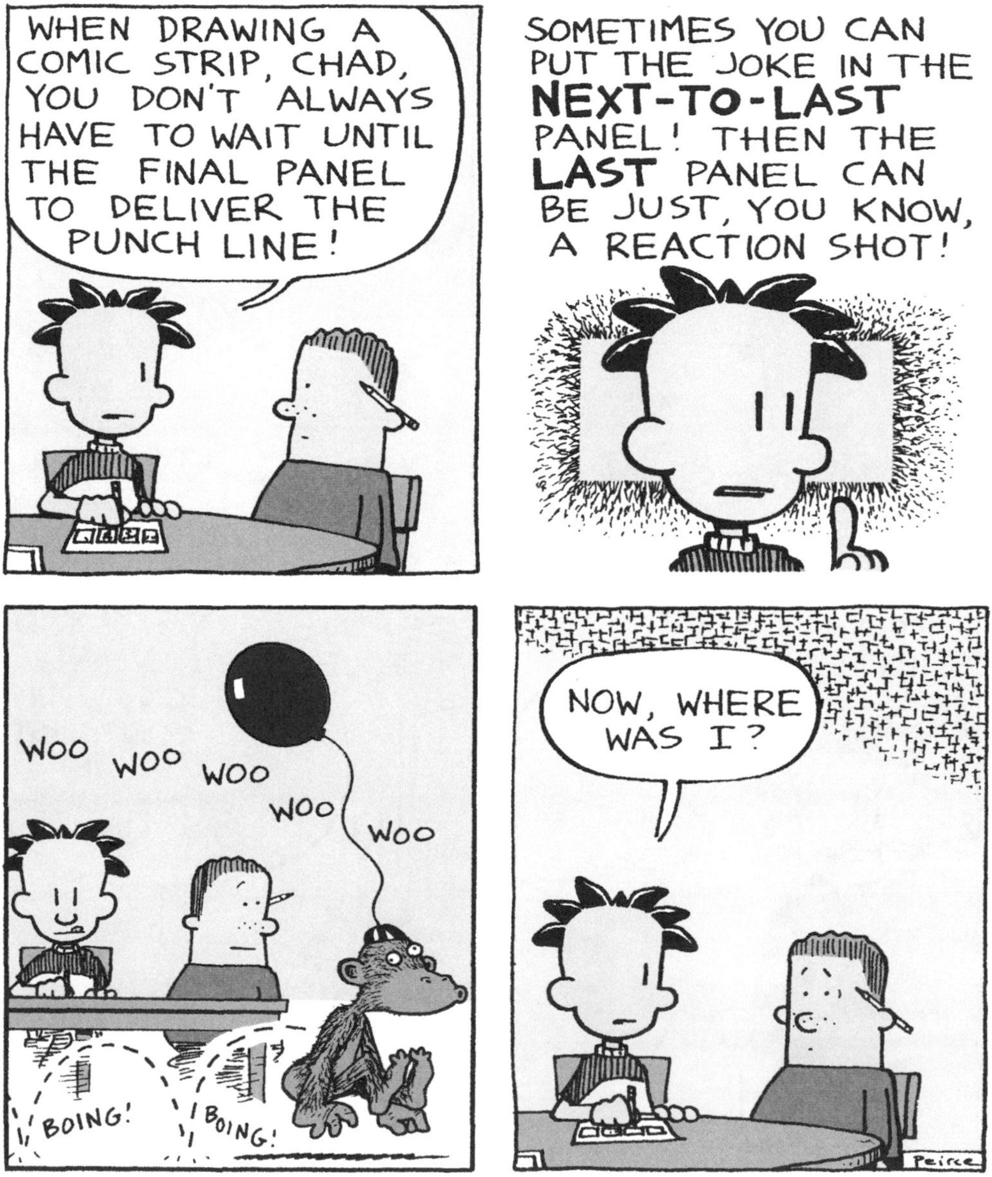
WHEN DRAWING A COMIC STRIP, CHAD, YOU DON'T ALWAYS HAVE TO WAIT UNTIL THE FINAL PANEL TO DELIVER THE PUNCH LINE!
SOMETIMES YOU CAN PUT THE JOKE IN THE NEXT-TO-LAST PANEL! THEN THE LAST PANEL CAN BE JUST, YOU KNOW, A REACTION SHOT!
WOO WOO WOO WOO WOO
BOING!
BOING!
NOW, WHERE WAS I?
Peirce

MR. ROSA, ARE WE ALLOWED TO DRAW COMICS ABOUT TEACHERS?
PROVIDED THEY'RE NOT IN-APPROPRIATE.
"INAPPROPRIATE"?
YOU KNOW... MEAN-SPIRITED.
"MEAN-SPIRITED"?
NEEDLESSLY CRUEL.
DEFINE "NEEDLESSLY."
TELL YOU WHAT, SON, WHY DON'T YOU JUST FOCUS ON SUPERHEROES FOR NOW.
PEIRCE

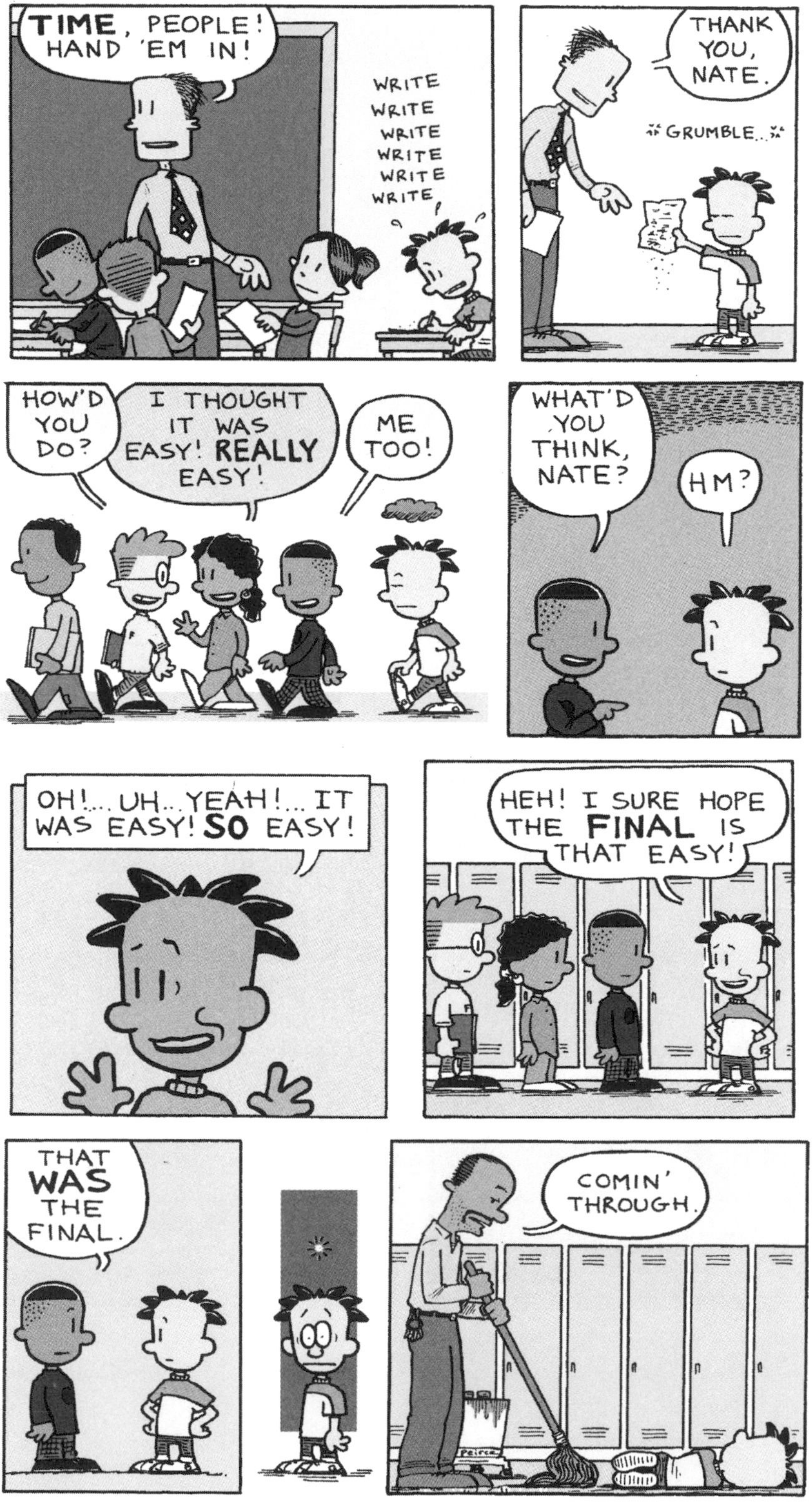
TIME, PEOPLE! HAND 'EM IN!
WRITE WRITE WRITE WRITE WRITE WRITE
THANK YOU, NATE.
GRUMBLE...
HOW'D YOU DO?
I THOUGHT IT WAS EASY! REALLY EASY!
ME TOO!
WHAT'D YOU THINK, NATE?
HM?
OH!... UH... YEAH!... IT WAS EASY! SO EASY!
HEH! I SURE HOPE THE FINAL IS THAT EASY!
THAT WAS THE FINAL.
COMIN' THROUGH.

I'M HERE FOR DETENTION, MRS. CZERWICKI.
AGAIN? NATE, WHY?
WELL... I MISSED YOU.
YOU... YOU MISSED ME?
!
COUNT TO TEN!
WHY, NATE, HOW VERY SWEET! I DON'T KNOW WHAT TO...
YEAH, I HUCKED A CUPCAKE AT YOU WHILE YOU WERE ON LUNCH DUTY...
... AND INSTEAD I HIT THAT SNITCH MIRANDA KILGORE.
GO SIT DOWN, SON.
Peirce

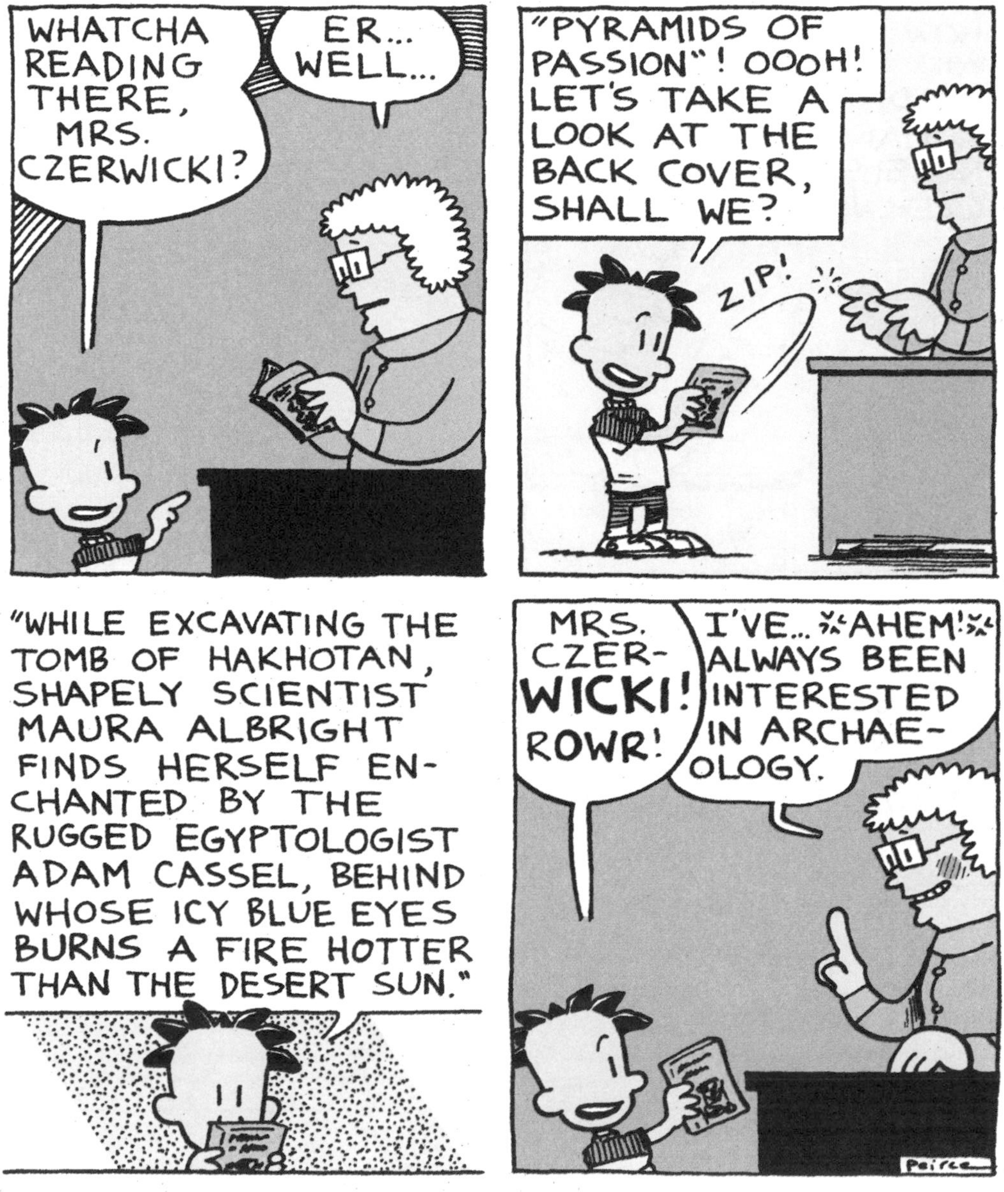
WHATCHA READING THERE, MRS. CZERWICKI?
ER... WELL...
"PYRAMIDS OF PASSION"! OOOH! LET'S TAKE A LOOK AT THE BACK COVER, SHALL WE?
ZIP!
"WHILE EXCAVATING THE TOMB OF HAKHOTAN, SHAPELY SCIENTIST MAURA ALBRIGHT FINDS HERSELF EN-CHANTED BY THE RUGGED EGYPTOLOGIST ADAM CASSEL, BEHIND WHOSE ICY BLUE EYES BURNS A FIRE HOTTER THAN THE DESERT SUN."
MRS. CZER-WICKI! ROWR!
I'VE... AHEM! ALWAYS BEEN INTERESTED IN ARCHAE-OLOGY.
Peirce

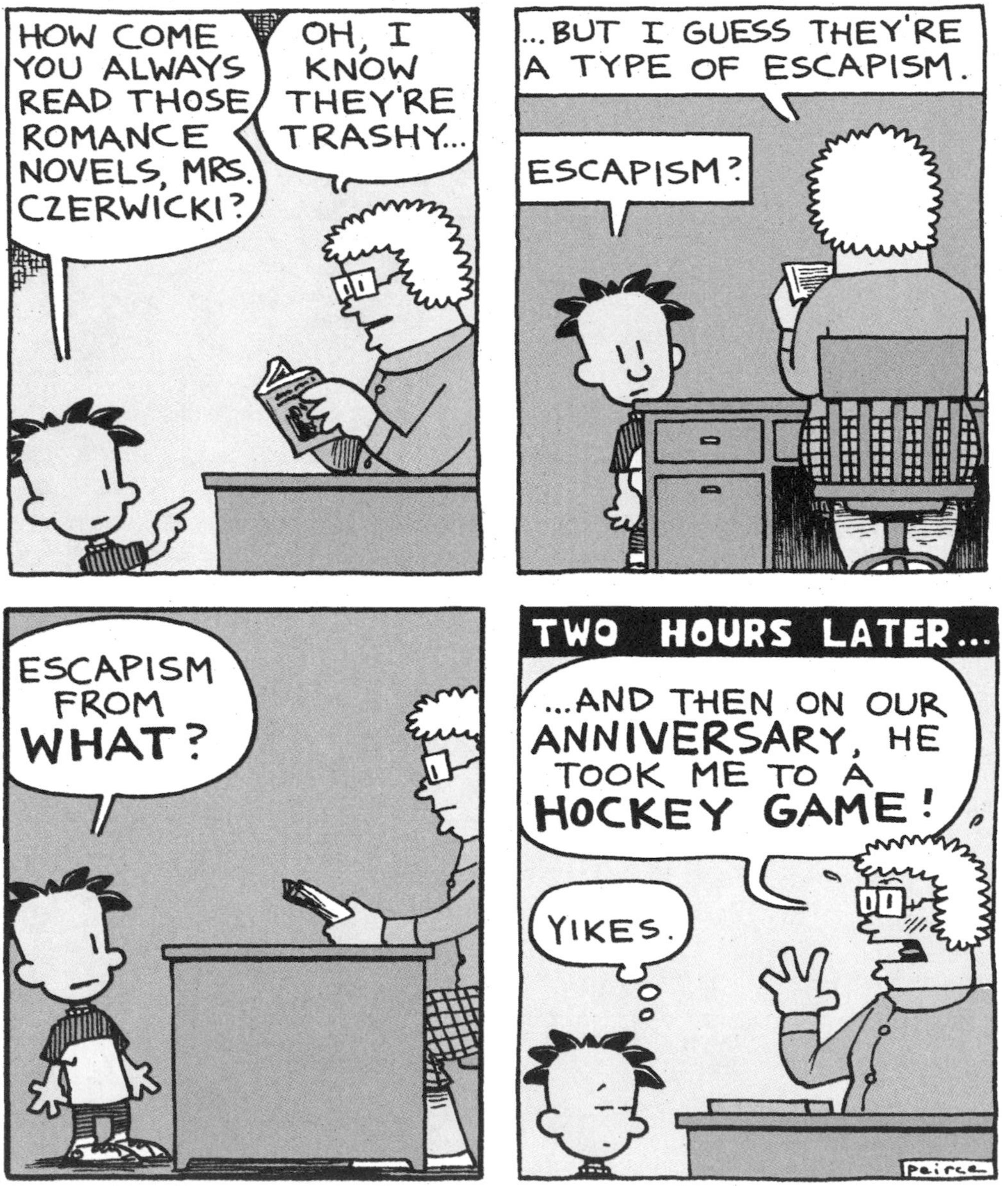
HOW COME YOU ALWAYS READ THOSE ROMANCE NOVELS, MRS. CZERWICKI?
OH, I KNOW THEY'RE TRASHY...
...BUT I GUESS THEY'RE A TYPE OF ESCAPISM.
ESCAPISM?
ESCAPISM FROM WHAT?
TWO HOURS LATER...
...AND THEN ON OUR ANNIVERSARY, HE TOOK ME TO A HOCKEY GAME!
YIKES.
peirce

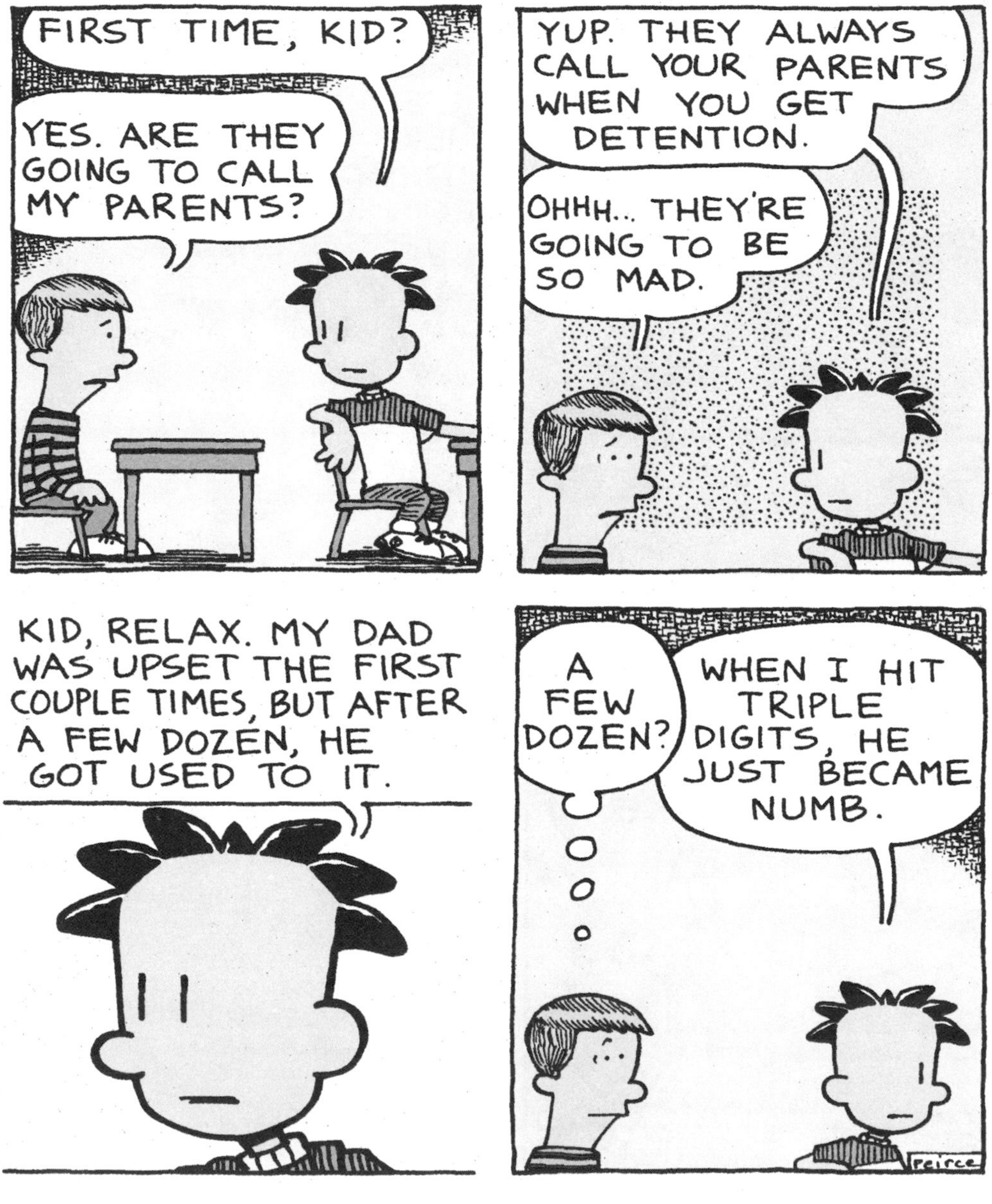
FIRST TIME, KID?
YES. ARE THEY GOING TO CALL MY PARENTS?
YUP. THEY ALWAYS CALL YOUR PARENTS WHEN YOU GET DETENTION.
OHHH... THEY'RE GOING TO BE SO MAD.
KID, RELAX. MY DAD WAS UPSET THE FIRST COUPLE TIMES, BUT AFTER A FEW DOZEN, HE GOT USED TO IT.
A FEW DOZEN?
WHEN I HIT TRIPLE DIGITS, HE JUST BECAME NUMB.
Peirce

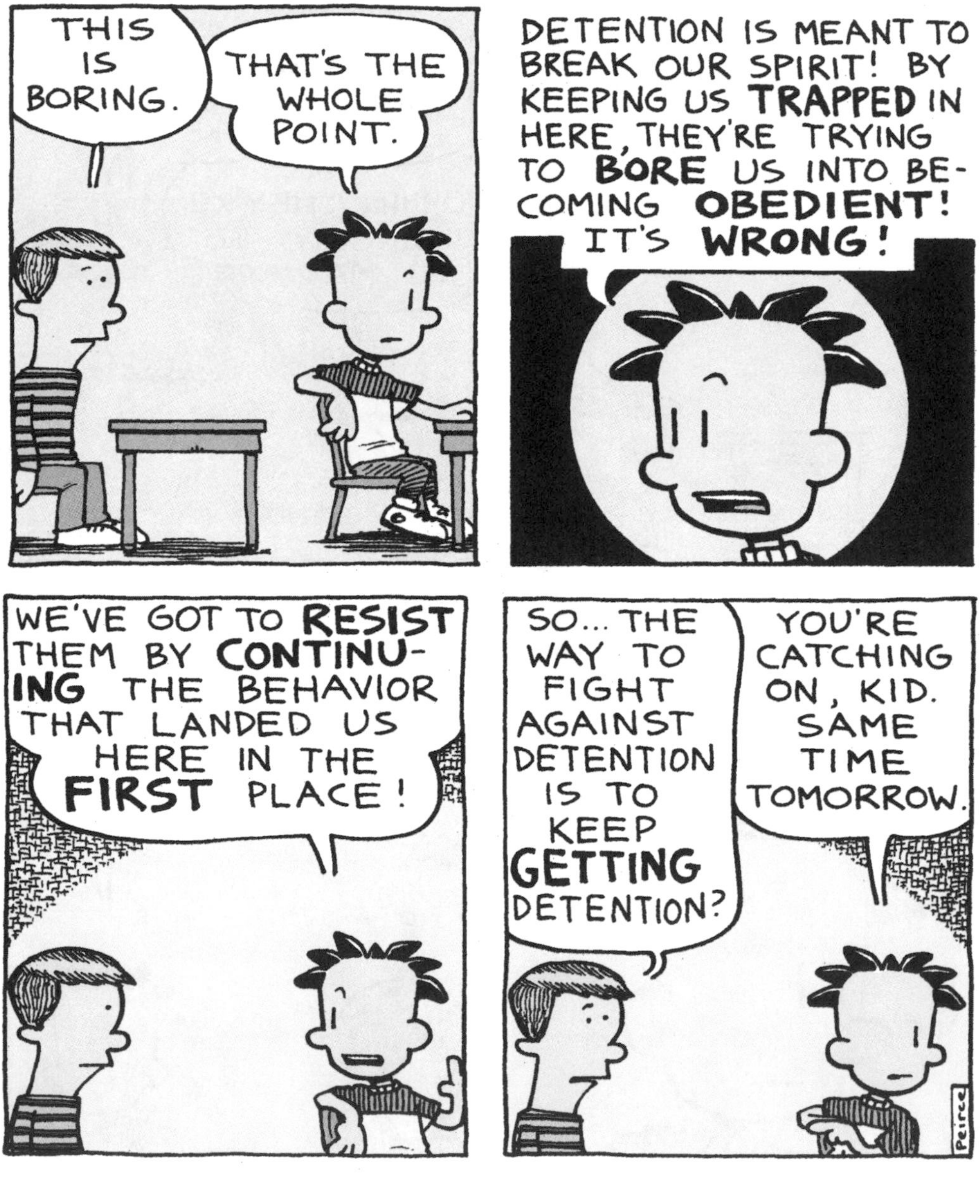
THIS IS BORING.
THAT'S THE WHOLE POINT.
DETENTION IS MEANT TO BREAK OUR SPIRIT! BY KEEPING US TRAPPED IN HERE, THEY'RE TRYING TO BORE US INTO BECOMING OBEDIENT! IT'S WRONG!
WE'VE GOT TO RESIST THEM BY CONTINUING THE BEHAVIOR THAT LANDED US HERE IN THE FIRST PLACE!
SO... THE WAY TO FIGHT AGAINST DETENTION IS TO KEEP GETTING DETENTION?
YOU'RE CATCHING ON, KID. SAME TIME TOMORROW.
Peirce

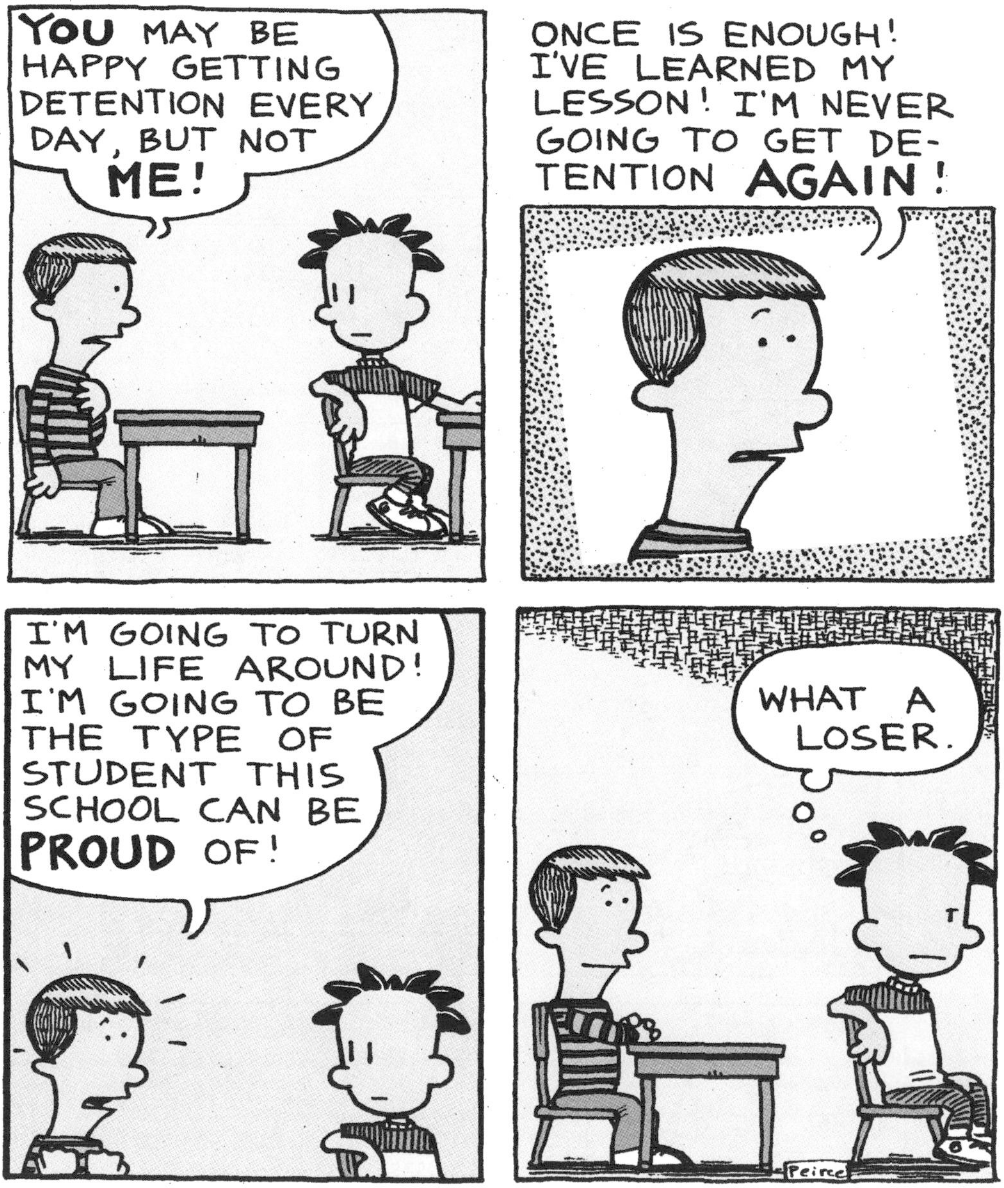
YOU MAY BE HAPPY GETTING DETENTION EVERY DAY, BUT NOT ME!
ONCE IS ENOUGH! I'VE LEARNED MY LESSON! I'M NEVER GOING TO GET DETENTION AGAIN!
I'M GOING TO TURN MY LIFE AROUND! I'M GOING TO BE THE TYPE OF STUDENT THIS SCHOOL CAN BE PROUD OF!
WHAT A LOSER.
Peirce

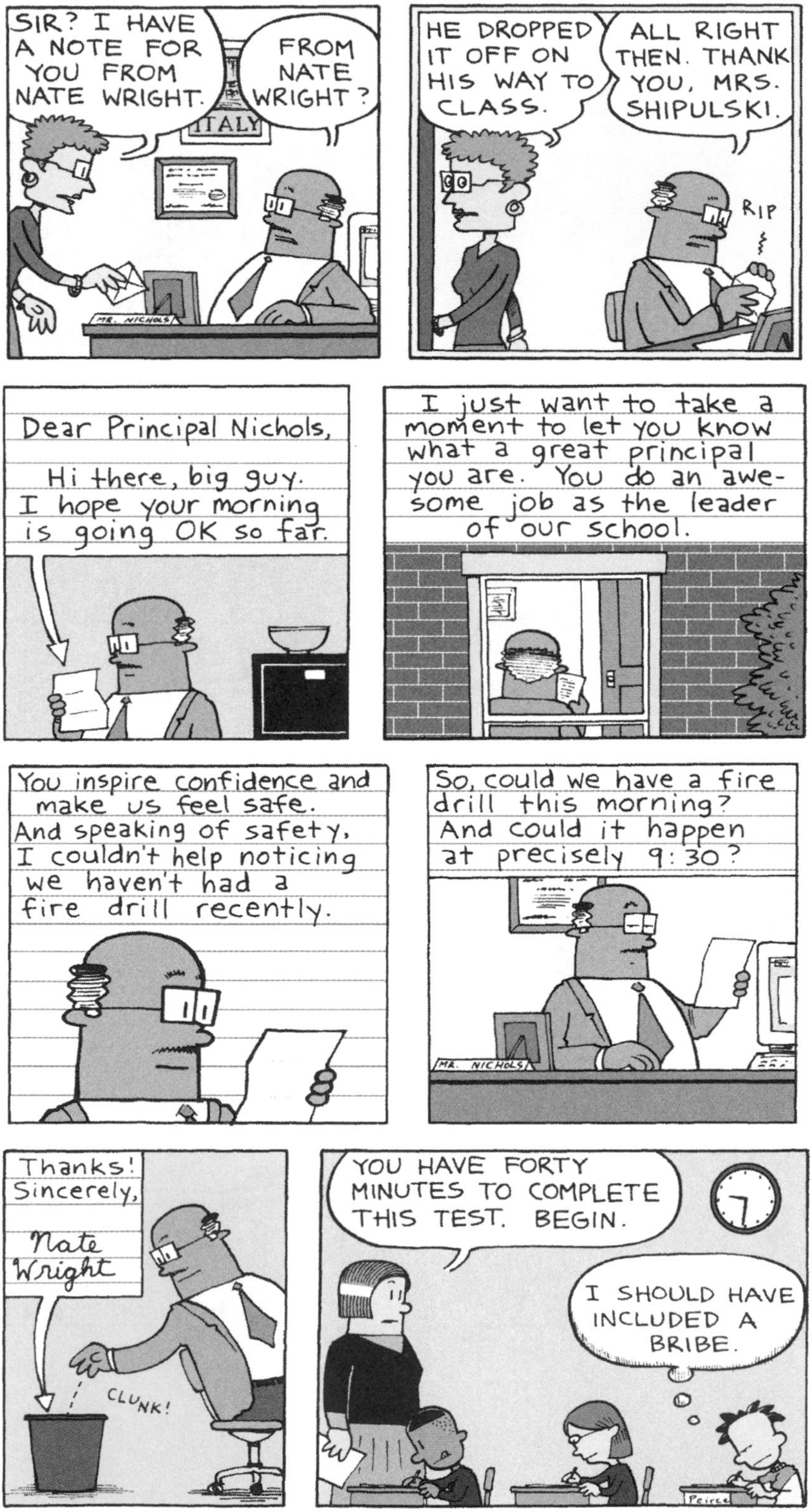
SIR? I HAVE A NOTE FOR YOU FROM NATE WRIGHT.
FROM NATE WRIGHT?
ITALY
MR. NICHOLS
HE DROPPED IT OFF ON HIS WAY TO CLASS.
ALL RIGHT THEN. THANK YOU, MRS. SHIPULSKI.
RIP
Dear Principal Nichols,
Hi there, big guy. I hope your morning is going OK so far.
I just want to take a moment to let you know what a great principal you are. You do an awe-some job as the leader of our school.
You inspire confidence and make us feel safe. And speaking of safety, I couldn't help noticing we haven't had a fire drill recently.
So, could we have a fire drill this morning? And could it happen at precisely 9:30?
MR. NICHOLS
Thanks! Sincerely, Nate Wright
CLUNK!
YOU HAVE FORTY MINUTES TO COMPLETE THIS TEST. BEGIN.
I SHOULD HAVE INCLUDED A BRIBE.
Peirce

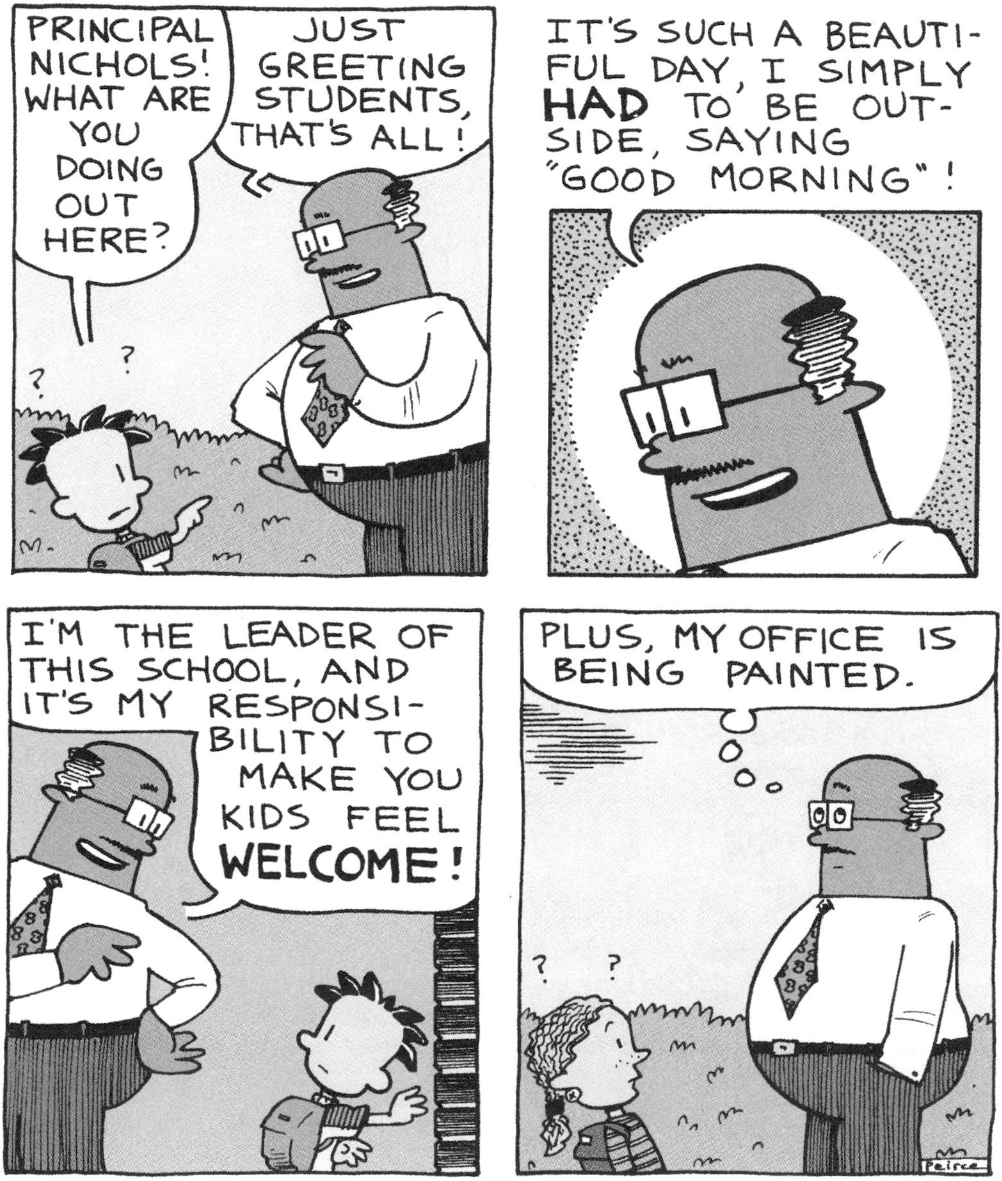
PRINCIPAL NICHOLS! WHAT ARE YOU DOING OUT HERE?
JUST GREETING STUDENTS, THAT'S ALL!
IT'S SUCH A BEAUTIFUL DAY, I SIMPLY HAD TO BE OUTSIDE, SAYING "GOOD MORNING"!
I'M THE LEADER OF THIS SCHOOL, AND IT'S MY RESPONSIBILITY TO MAKE YOU KIDS FEEL WELCOME!
PLUS, MY OFFICE IS BEING PAINTED.
Peirce

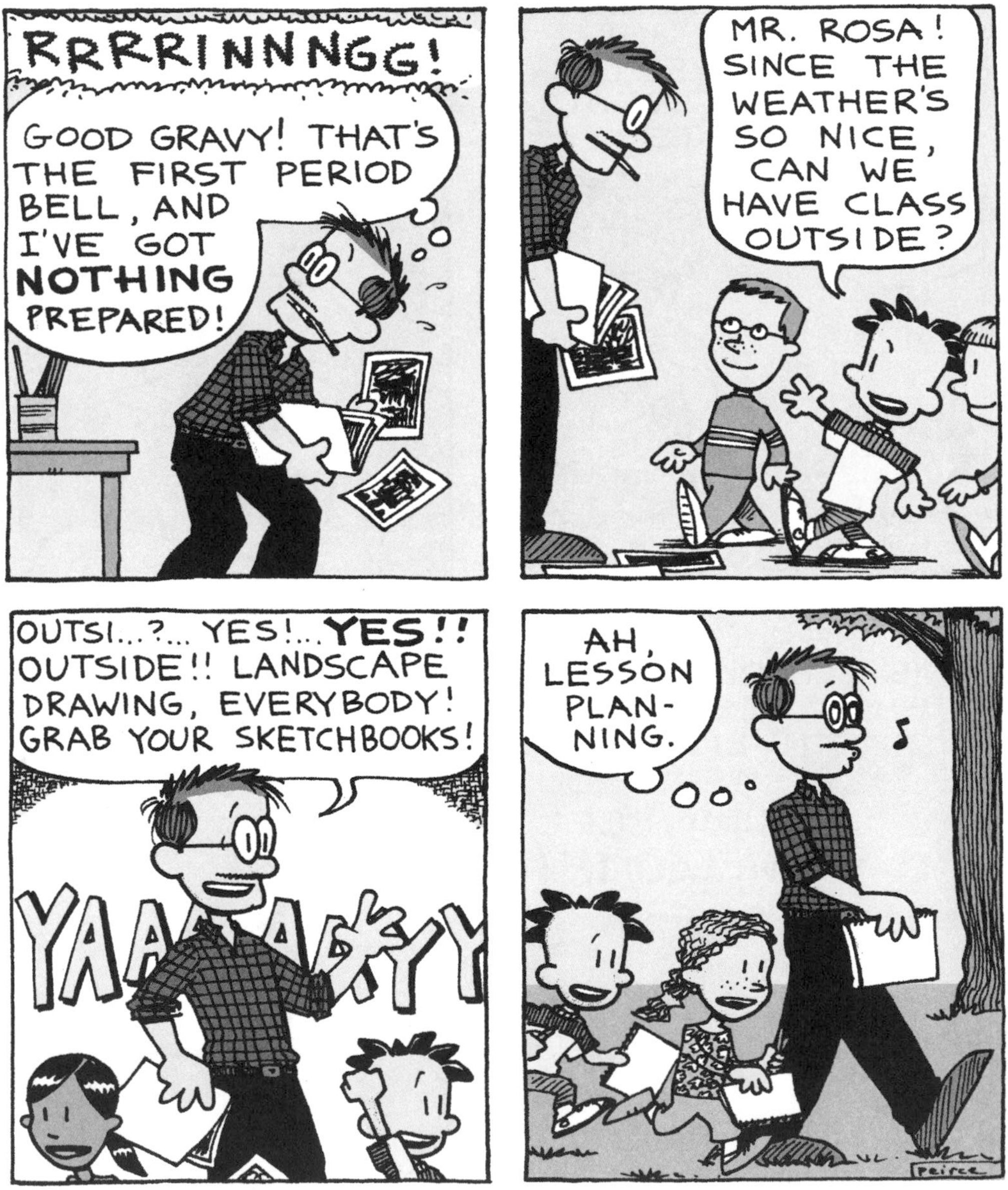
RRRRINNNGG!
GOOD GRAVY! THAT'S THE FIRST PERIOD BELL, AND I'VE GOT **NOTHING** PREPARED!
MR. ROSA! SINCE THE WEATHER'S SO NICE, CAN WE HAVE CLASS OUTSIDE?
OUTSI...?... YES!... **YES!!** OUTSIDE!! LANDSCAPE DRAWING, EVERYBODY! GRAB YOUR SKETCHBOOKS!
AH, LESSON PLAN-NING.
PEIRCE

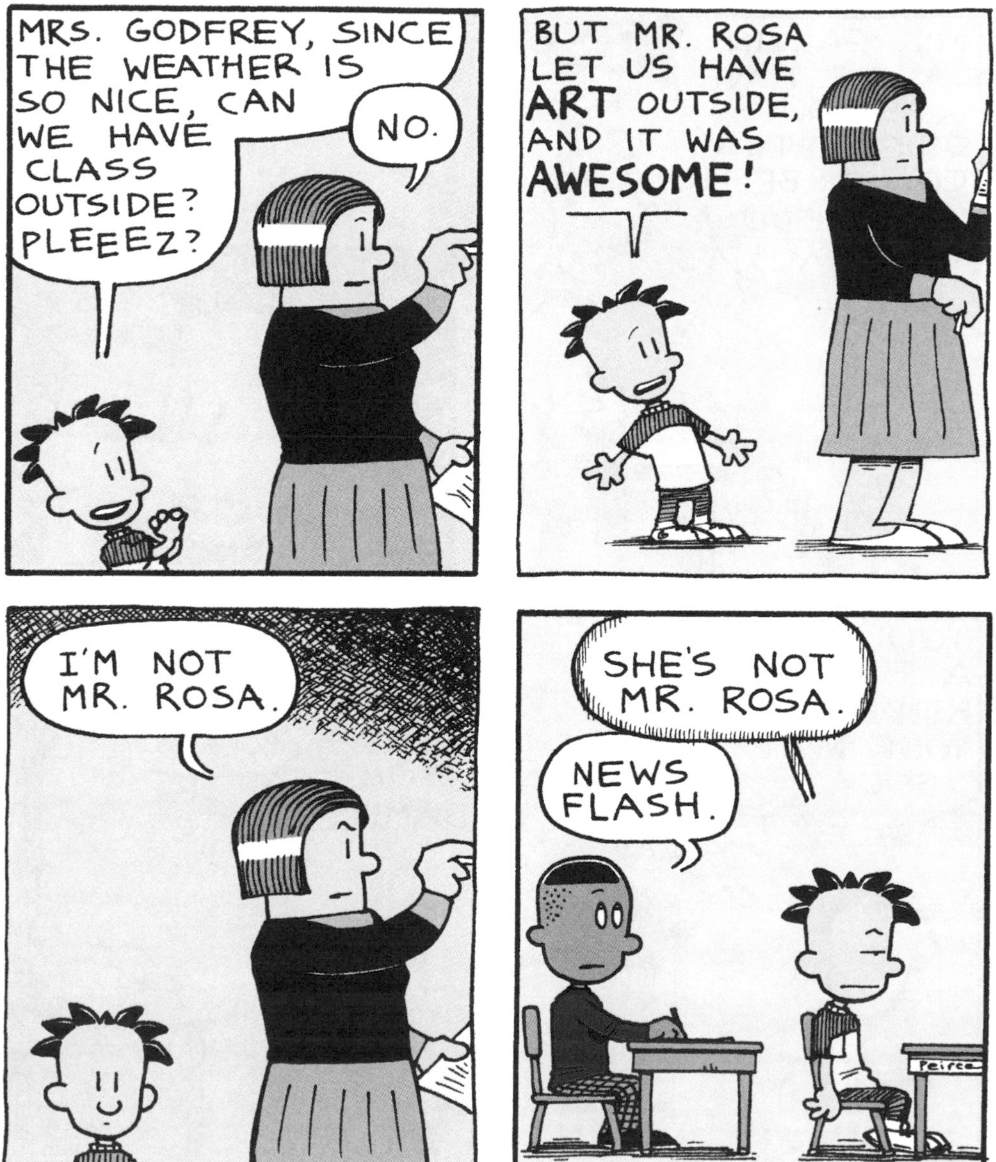
MRS. GODFREY, SINCE THE WEATHER IS SO NICE, CAN WE HAVE CLASS OUTSIDE? PLEEEZ?
NO.
BUT MR. ROSA LET US HAVE ART OUTSIDE, AND IT WAS AWESOME!
I'M NOT MR. ROSA.
SHE'S NOT MR. ROSA.
NEWS FLASH.
Peirce

MR. GALVIN, CAN WE HAVE CLASS OUTSIDE? IT COULD BE **VERY** EDUCATIONAL!

LET'S GET OUT IN THE FIELD LIKE REAL SCIENTISTS! WE'LL STUDY ECOSYSTEMS! WE'LL DO RESEARCH!

YOU HAVE A FRISBEE HIDDEN IN YOUR NOTEBOOK.

THAT'S FOR COLLECTING SOIL SAMPLES.

THERE'S A HACKY SACK IN YOUR POCKET.

Peirce

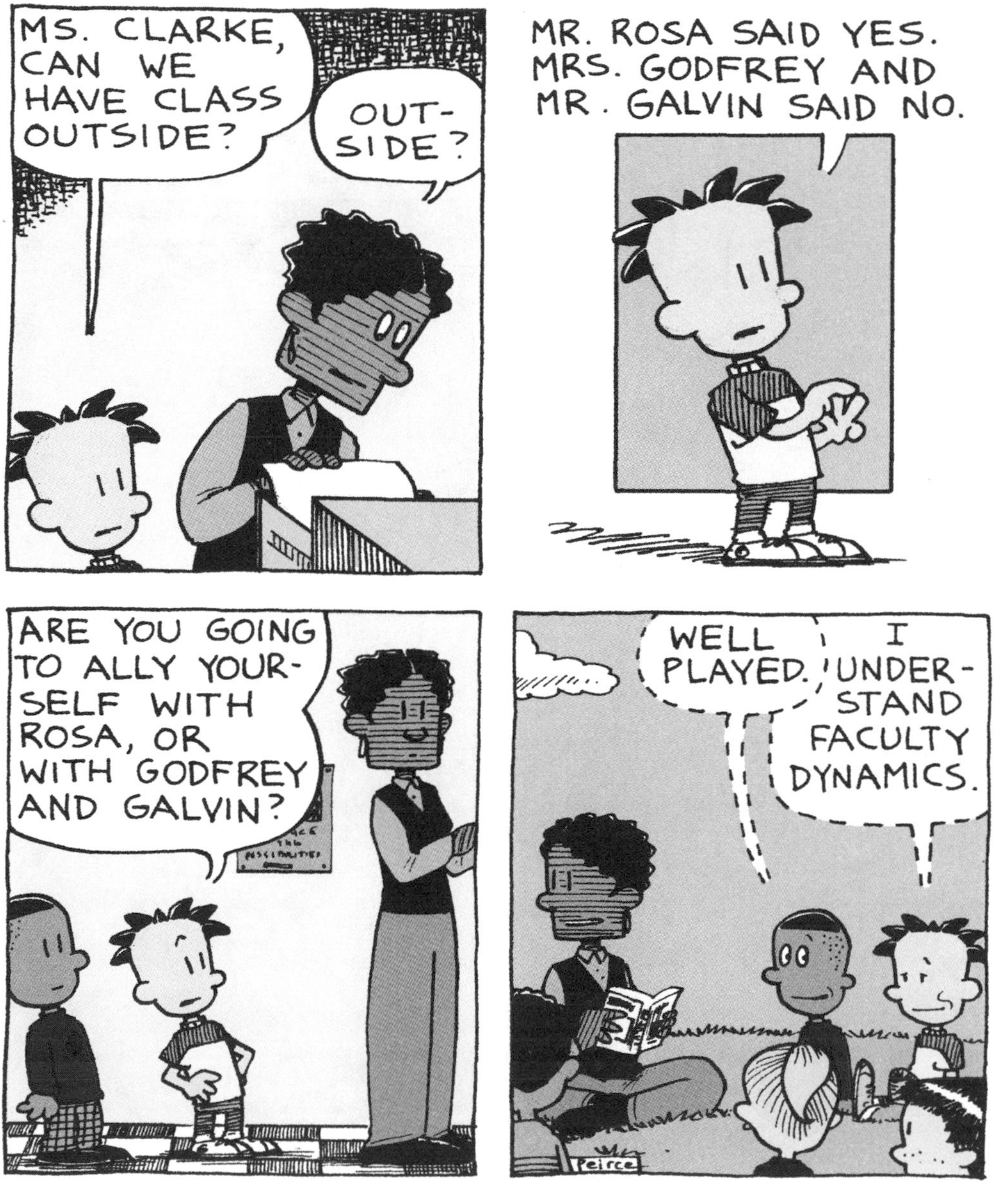
MS. CLARKE, CAN WE HAVE CLASS OUTSIDE?
OUT-SIDE?
MR. ROSA SAID YES. MRS. GODFREY AND MR. GALVIN SAID NO.
ARE YOU GOING TO ALLY YOUR-SELF WITH ROSA, OR WITH GODFREY AND GALVIN?
WELL PLAYED.
I UNDER-STAND FACULTY DYNAMICS.
Peirce

MR. STAPLES, IT'S SUCH A NICE DAY THAT WE'VE BEEN ASKING TEACHERS TO LET US HAVE CLASS OUTSIDE.

TWO TEACHERS HAVE SAID **YES**, TWO HAVE SAID **NO**. WE HAVE A **TIE**, AND ONLY **YOU** CAN BREAK IT!

THE CLOCK IS TICKING, MR. STAPLES.

IT'S HERO TIME.

SCORE! I HAPPEN TO KNOW THE MAN PLAYED DIVISION 3 BASKETBALL!

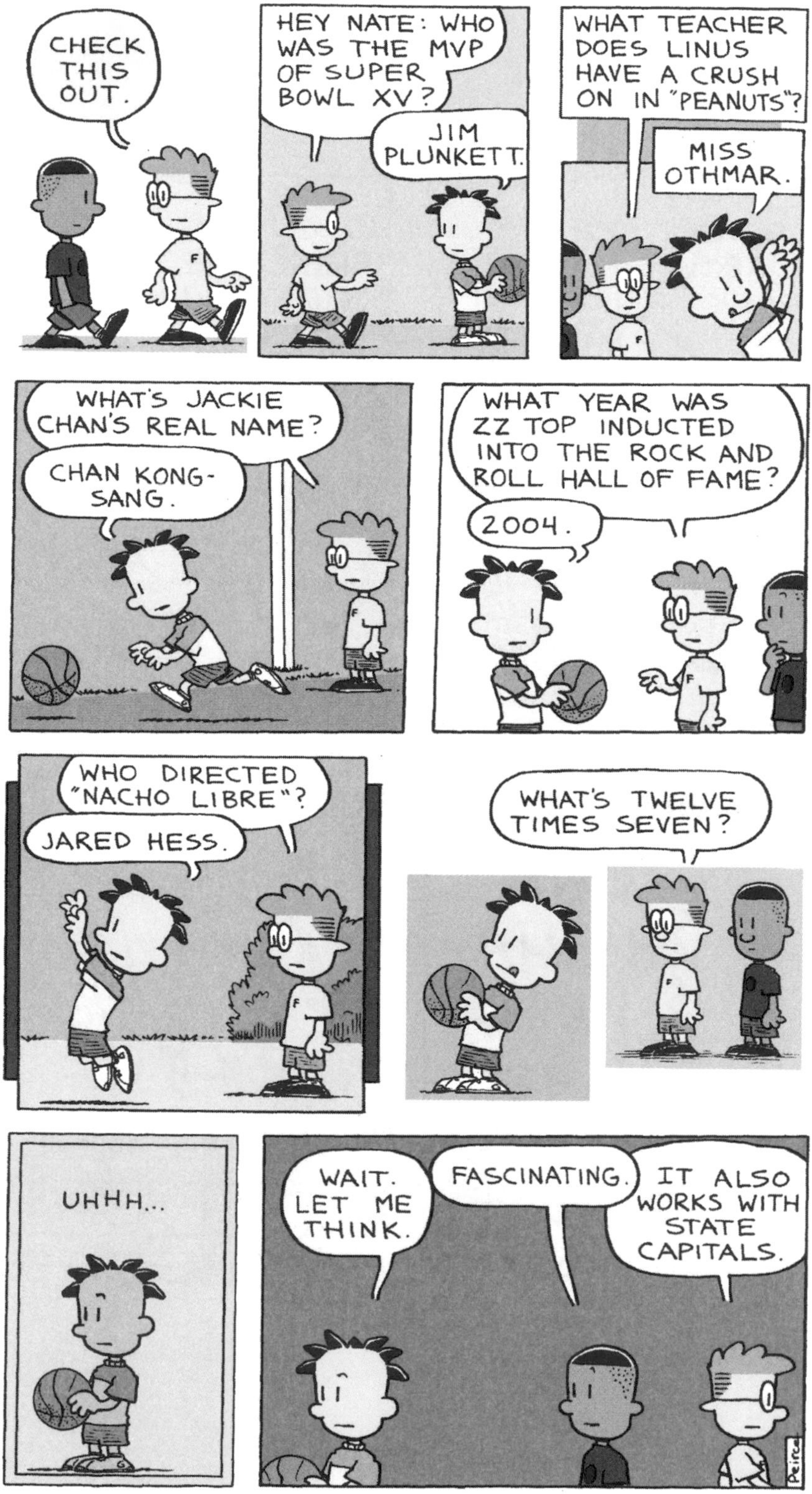
CHECK THIS OUT.
HEY NATE: WHO WAS THE MVP OF SUPER BOWL XV?
JIM PLUNKETT.
WHAT TEACHER DOES LINUS HAVE A CRUSH ON IN "PEANUTS"?
MISS OTHMAR.
WHAT'S JACKIE CHAN'S REAL NAME?
CHAN KONG-SANG.
WHAT YEAR WAS ZZ TOP INDUCTED INTO THE ROCK AND ROLL HALL OF FAME?
2004.
WHO DIRECTED "NACHO LIBRE"?
JARED HESS.
WHAT'S TWELVE TIMES SEVEN?
UHHH...
WAIT. LET ME THINK.
FASCINATING.
IT ALSO WORKS WITH STATE CAPITALS.
Peirce

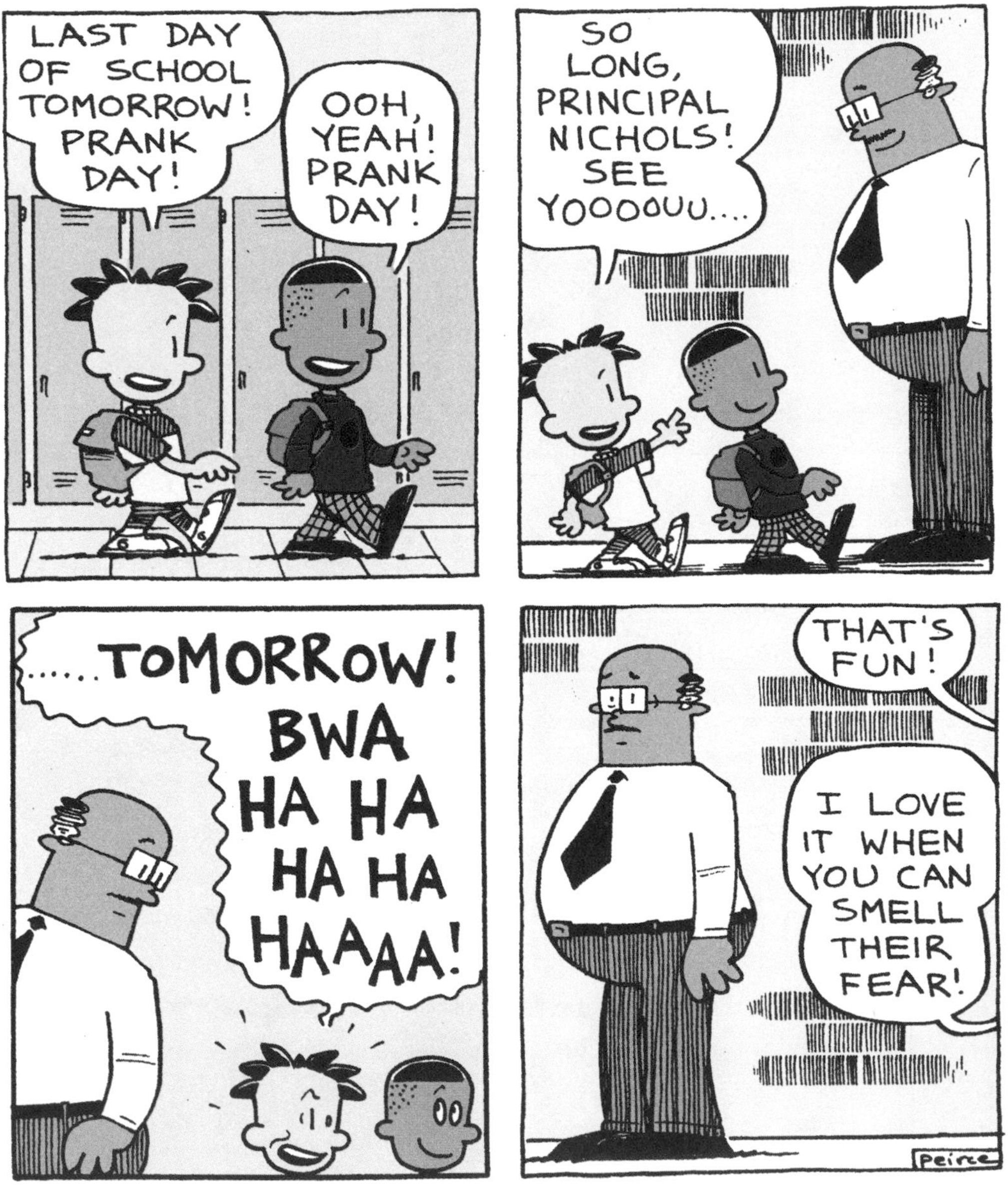

LAST DAY OF SCHOOL TOMORROW! PRANK DAY!
OOH, YEAH! PRANK DAY!
SO LONG, PRINCIPAL NICHOLS! SEE YOOOOUU....
......TOMORROW! BWA HA HA HA HA HAAAA!
THAT'S FUN!
I LOVE IT WHEN YOU CAN SMELL THEIR FEAR!
Peirce

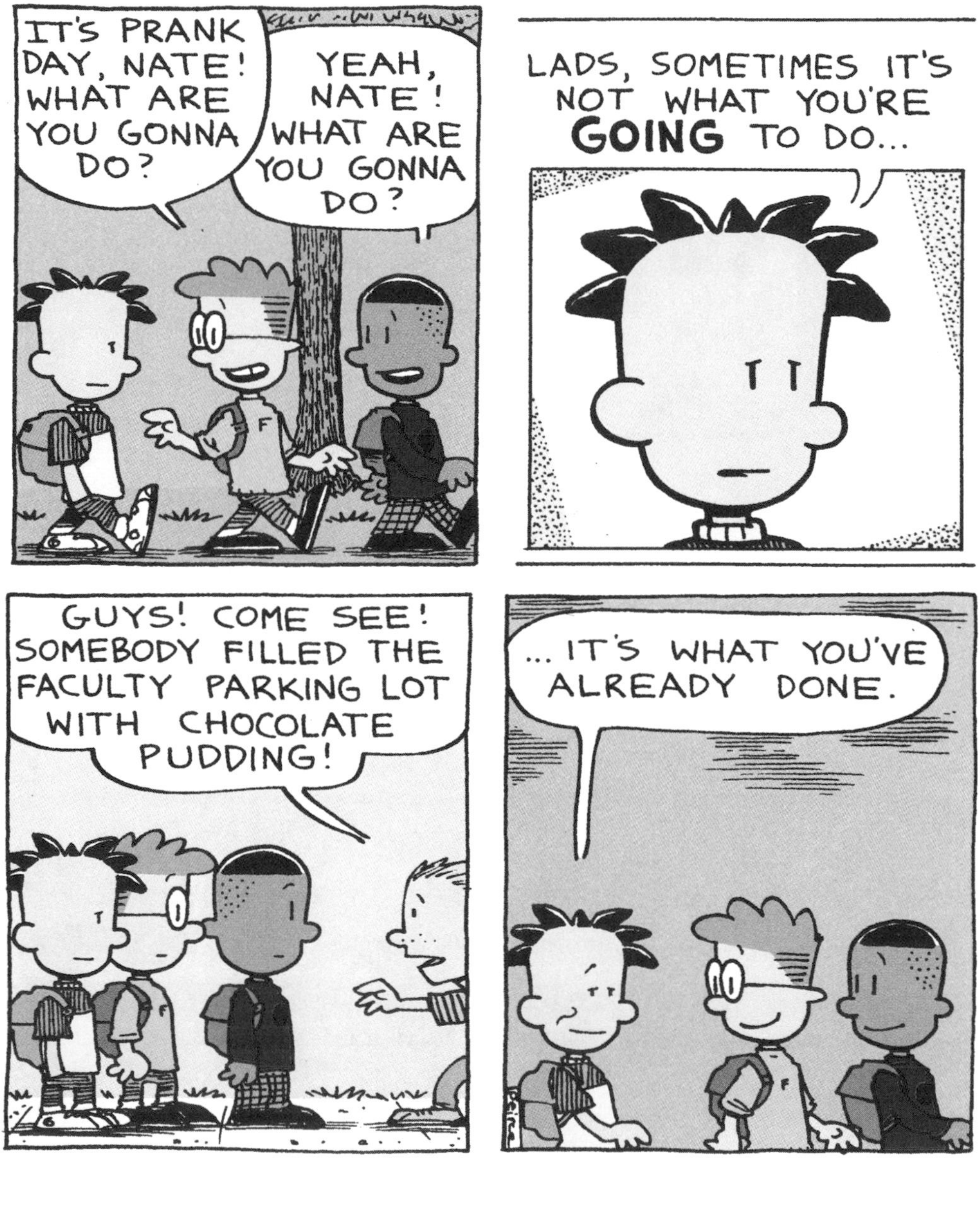
IT'S PRANK DAY, NATE! WHAT ARE YOU GONNA DO?
YEAH, NATE! WHAT ARE YOU GONNA DO?
LADS, SOMETIMES IT'S NOT WHAT YOU'RE **GOING** TO DO...
GUYS! COME SEE! SOMEBODY FILLED THE FACULTY PARKING LOT WITH CHOCOLATE PUDDING!
... IT'S WHAT YOU'VE ALREADY DONE.

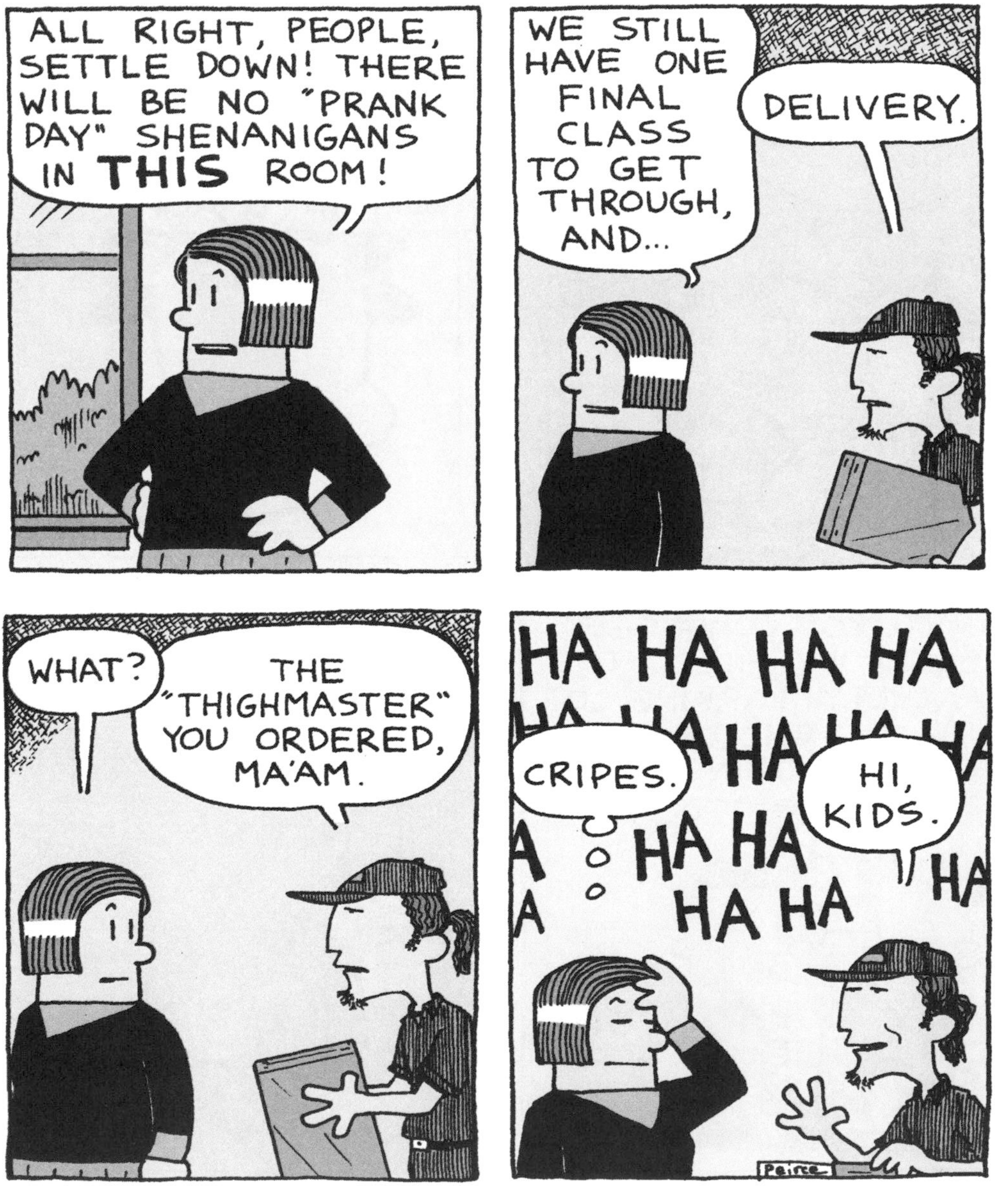
ALL RIGHT, PEOPLE, SETTLE DOWN! THERE WILL BE NO "PRANK DAY" SHENANIGANS IN THIS ROOM!
WE STILL HAVE ONE FINAL CLASS TO GET THROUGH, AND...
DELIVERY.
WHAT?
THE "THIGHMASTER" YOU ORDERED, MA'AM.
HA HA HA HA
HA HA HA HA HA HA
CRIPES.
HI, KIDS.
HA HA HA HA
HA HA
Peirce

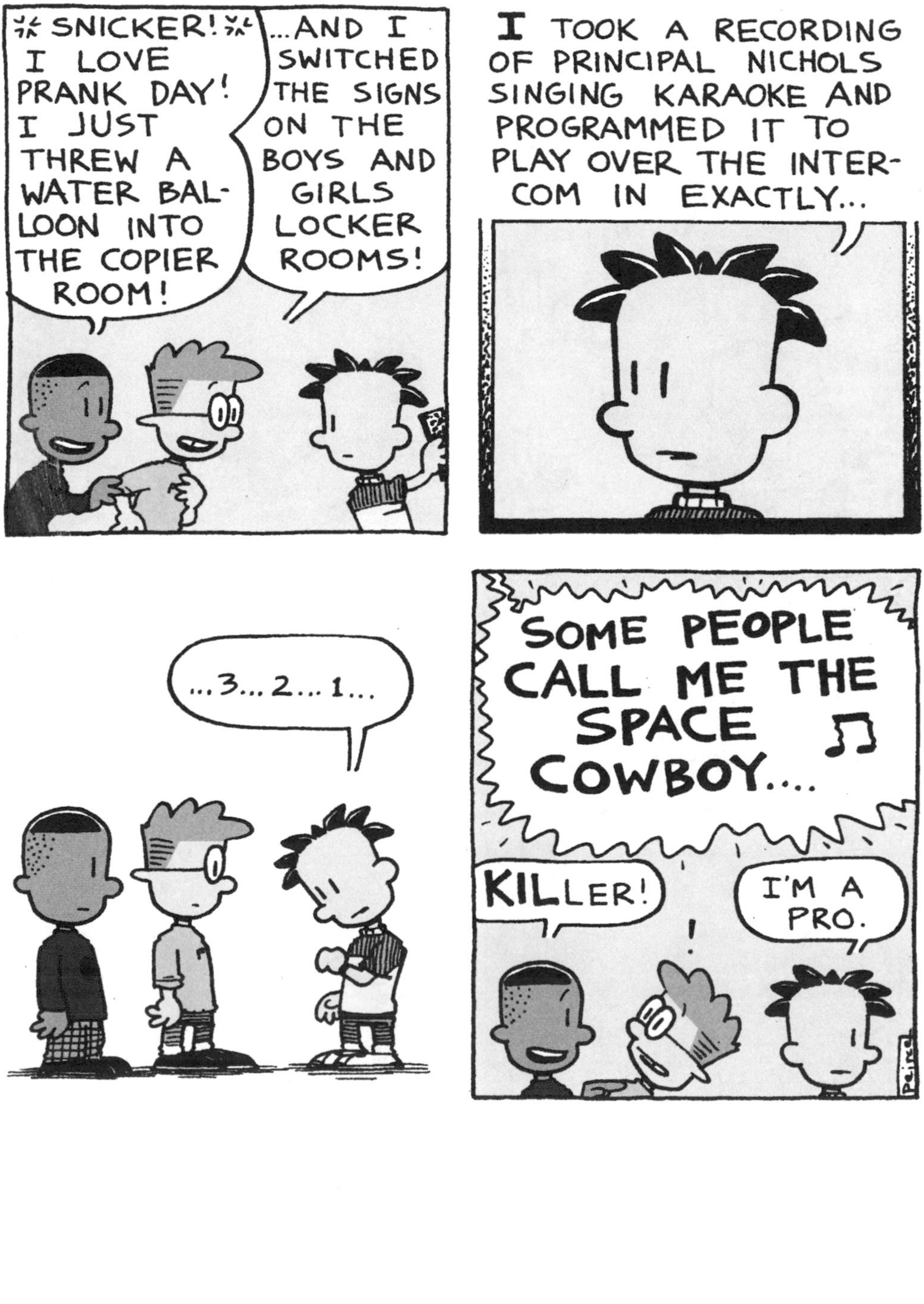
SNICKER! I LOVE PRANK DAY! I JUST THREW A WATER BALLOON INTO THE COPIER ROOM!
...AND I SWITCHED THE SIGNS ON THE BOYS AND GIRLS LOCKER ROOMS!
I TOOK A RECORDING OF PRINCIPAL NICHOLS SINGING KARAOKE AND PROGRAMMED IT TO PLAY OVER THE INTERCOM IN EXACTLY...
...3...2...1...
SOME PEOPLE CALL ME THE SPACE COWBOY....
KILLER!
!
I'M A PRO.

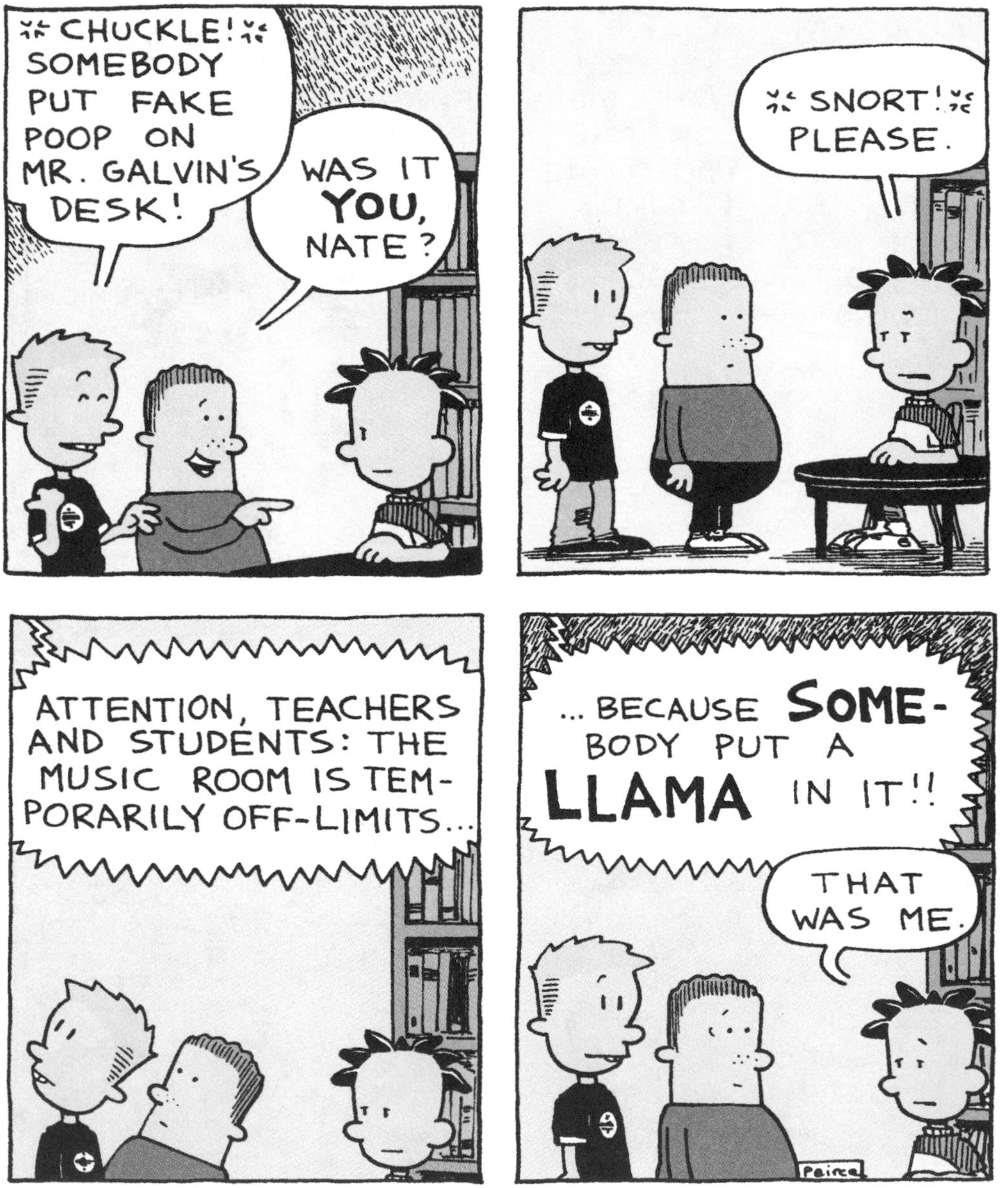
CHUCKLE! SOMEBODY PUT FAKE POOP ON MR. GALVIN'S DESK!
WAS IT YOU, NATE?
SNORT! PLEASE.
ATTENTION, TEACHERS AND STUDENTS: THE MUSIC ROOM IS TEMPORARILY OFF-LIMITS...
... BECAUSE SOMEBODY PUT A LLAMA IN IT!!
THAT WAS ME.
Peirce

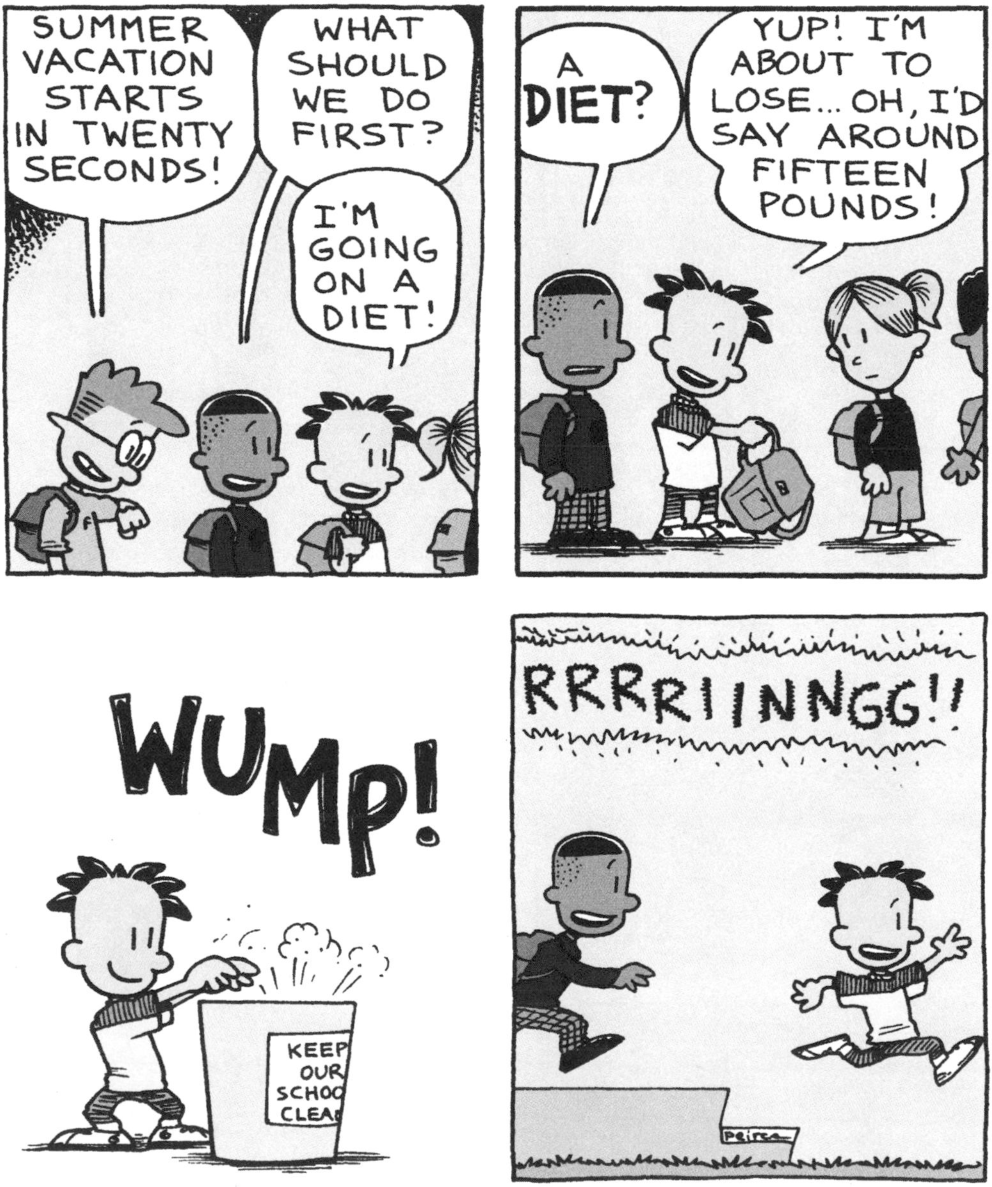
SUMMER VACATION STARTS IN TWENTY SECONDS!
WHAT SHOULD WE DO FIRST?
I'M GOING ON A DIET!
A DIET?
YUP! I'M ABOUT TO LOSE... OH, I'D SAY AROUND FIFTEEN POUNDS!
WUMP!
KEEP OUR SCHOO CLEA
RRRRIINNGG!!
Peirce

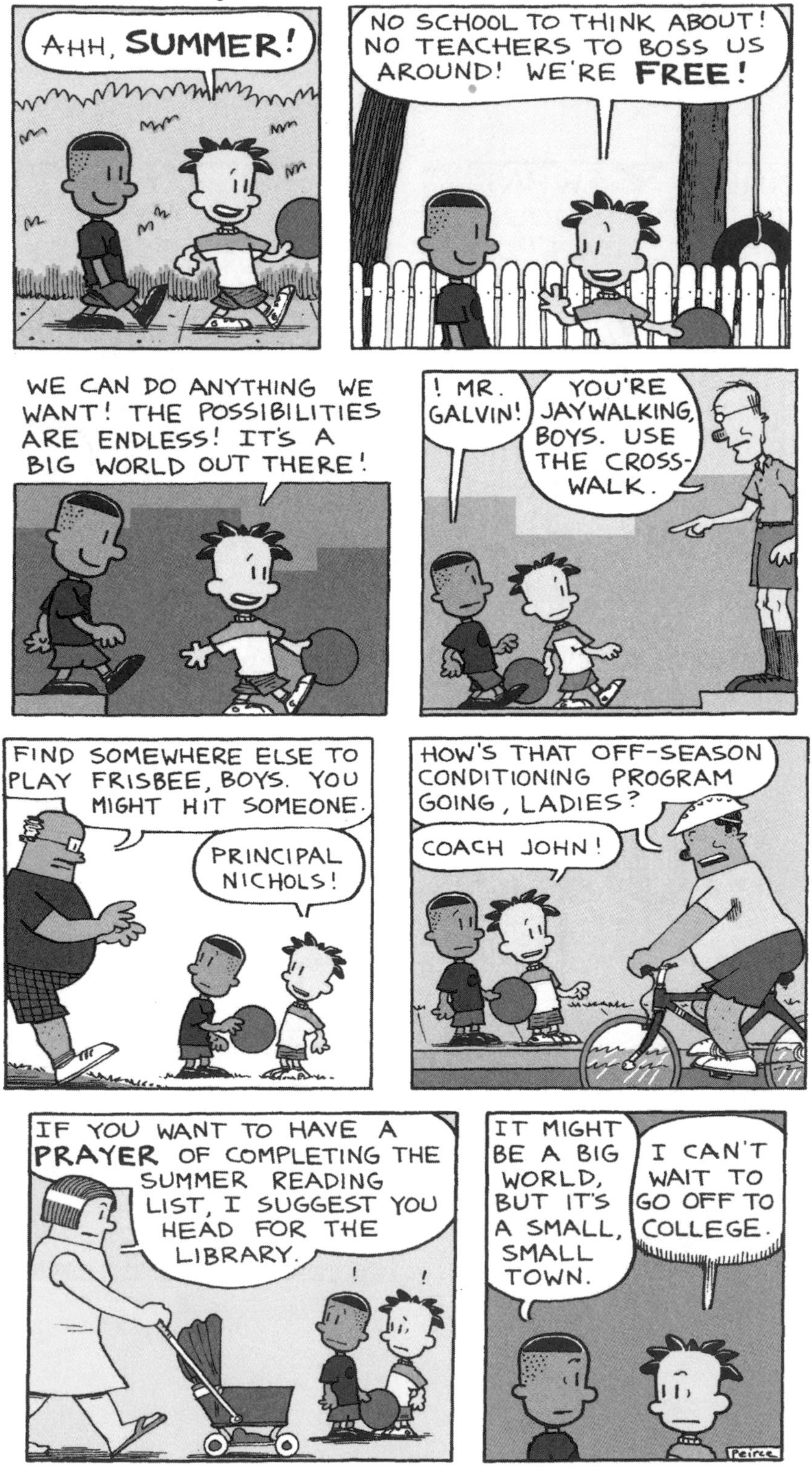
AHH, SUMMER!
NO SCHOOL TO THINK ABOUT! NO TEACHERS TO BOSS US AROUND! WE'RE FREE!
WE CAN DO ANYTHING WE WANT! THE POSSIBILITIES ARE ENDLESS! IT'S A BIG WORLD OUT THERE!
! MR. GALVIN!
YOU'RE JAYWALKING, BOYS. USE THE CROSS-WALK.
FIND SOMEWHERE ELSE TO PLAY FRISBEE, BOYS. YOU MIGHT HIT SOMEONE.
PRINCIPAL NICHOLS!
HOW'S THAT OFF-SEASON CONDITIONING PROGRAM GOING, LADIES?
COACH JOHN!
IF YOU WANT TO HAVE A PRAYER OF COMPLETING THE SUMMER READING LIST, I SUGGEST YOU HEAD FOR THE LIBRARY.
!
!
IT MIGHT BE A BIG WORLD, BUT IT'S A SMALL, SMALL TOWN.
I CAN'T WAIT TO GO OFF TO COLLEGE.
Peirce

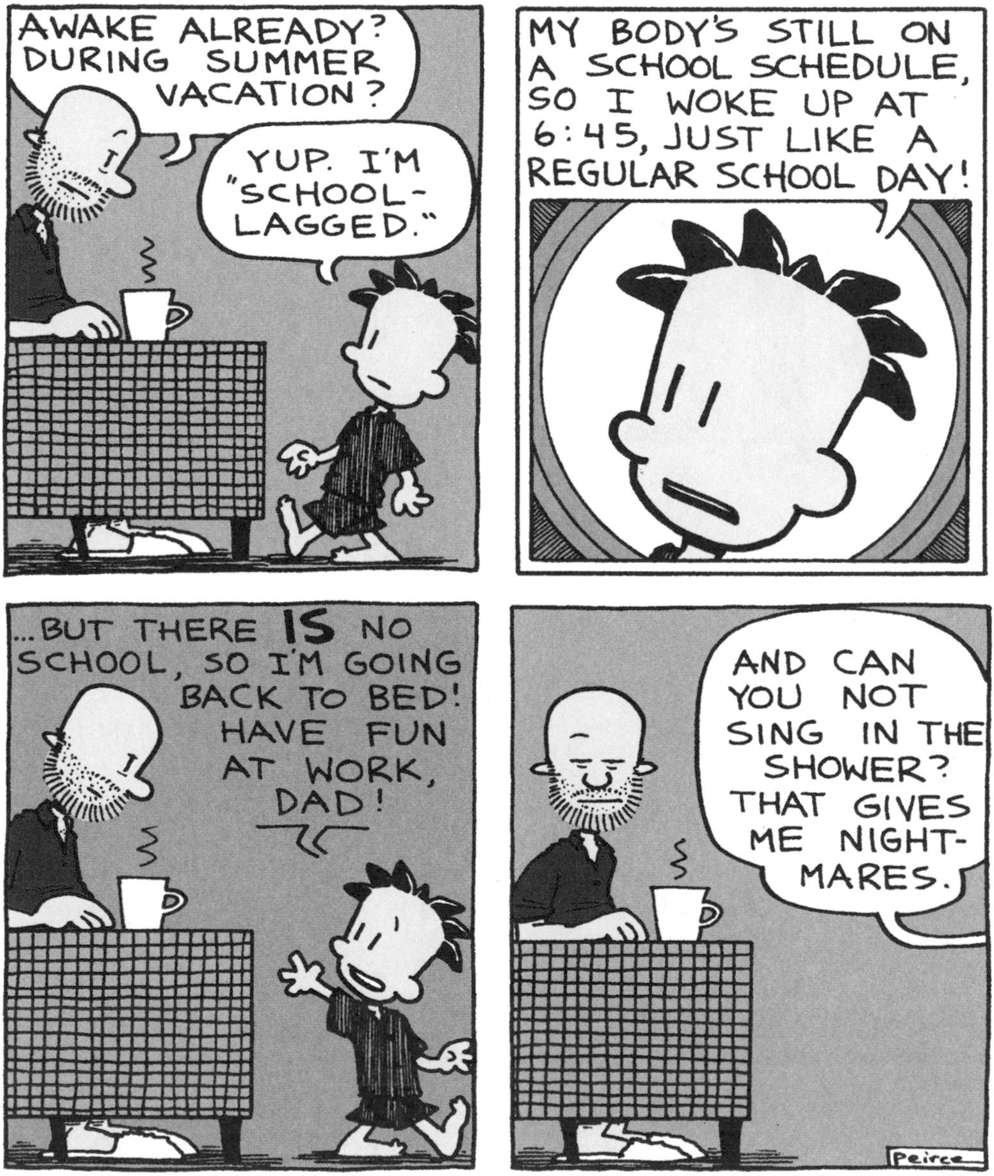
AWAKE ALREADY? DURING SUMMER VACATION?
YUP. I'M "SCHOOL-LAGGED."
MY BODY'S STILL ON A SCHOOL SCHEDULE, SO I WOKE UP AT 6:45, JUST LIKE A REGULAR SCHOOL DAY!
...BUT THERE **IS** NO SCHOOL, SO I'M GOING BACK TO BED! HAVE FUN AT WORK, DAD!
AND CAN YOU NOT SING IN THE SHOWER? THAT GIVES ME NIGHTMARES.
Peirce

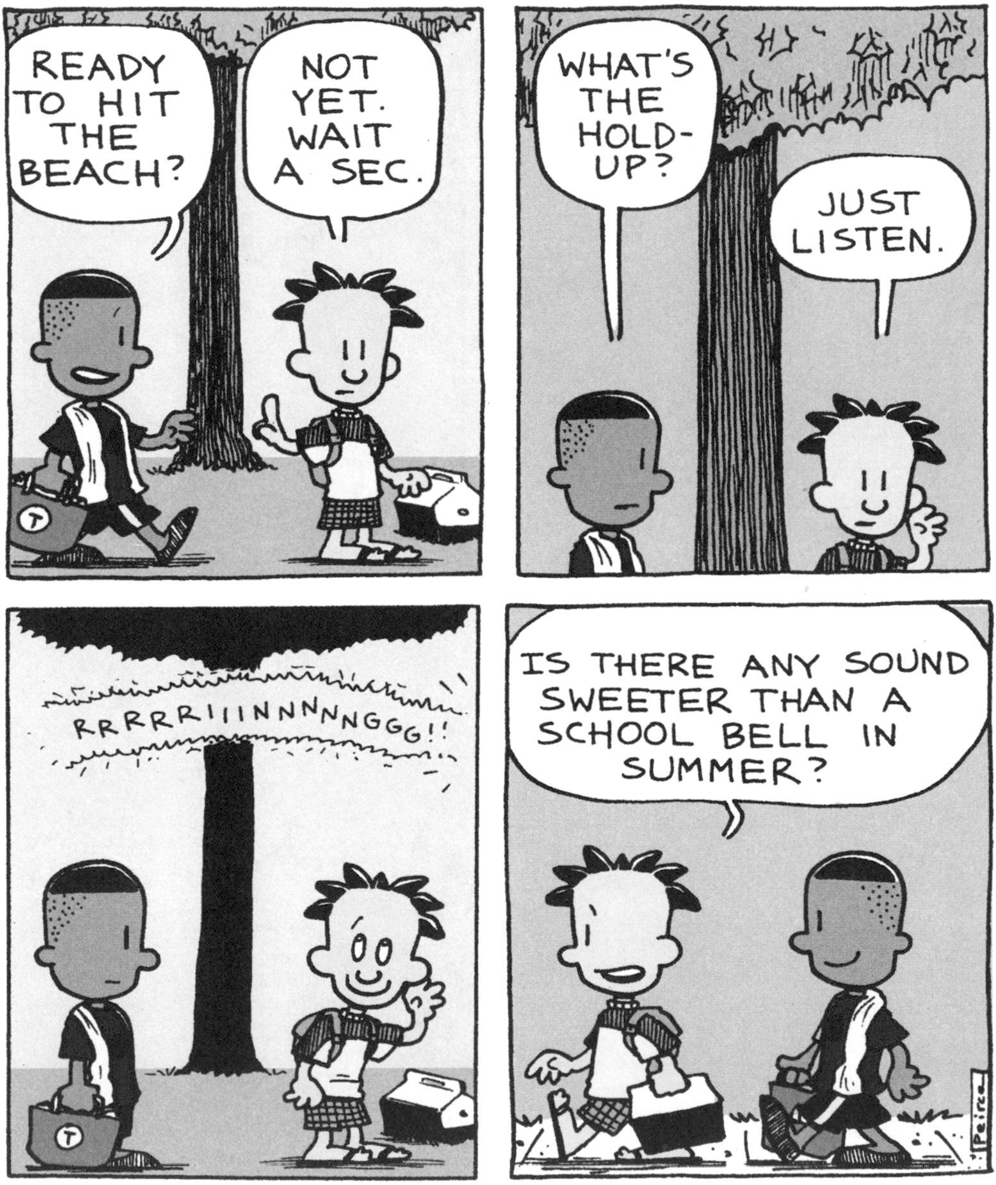
READY TO HIT THE BEACH?
NOT YET. WAIT A SEC.
WHAT'S THE HOLD-UP?
JUST LISTEN.
RRRRRIIINNNNNGGG!!
IS THERE ANY SOUND SWEETER THAN A SCHOOL BELL IN SUMMER?
Peirce

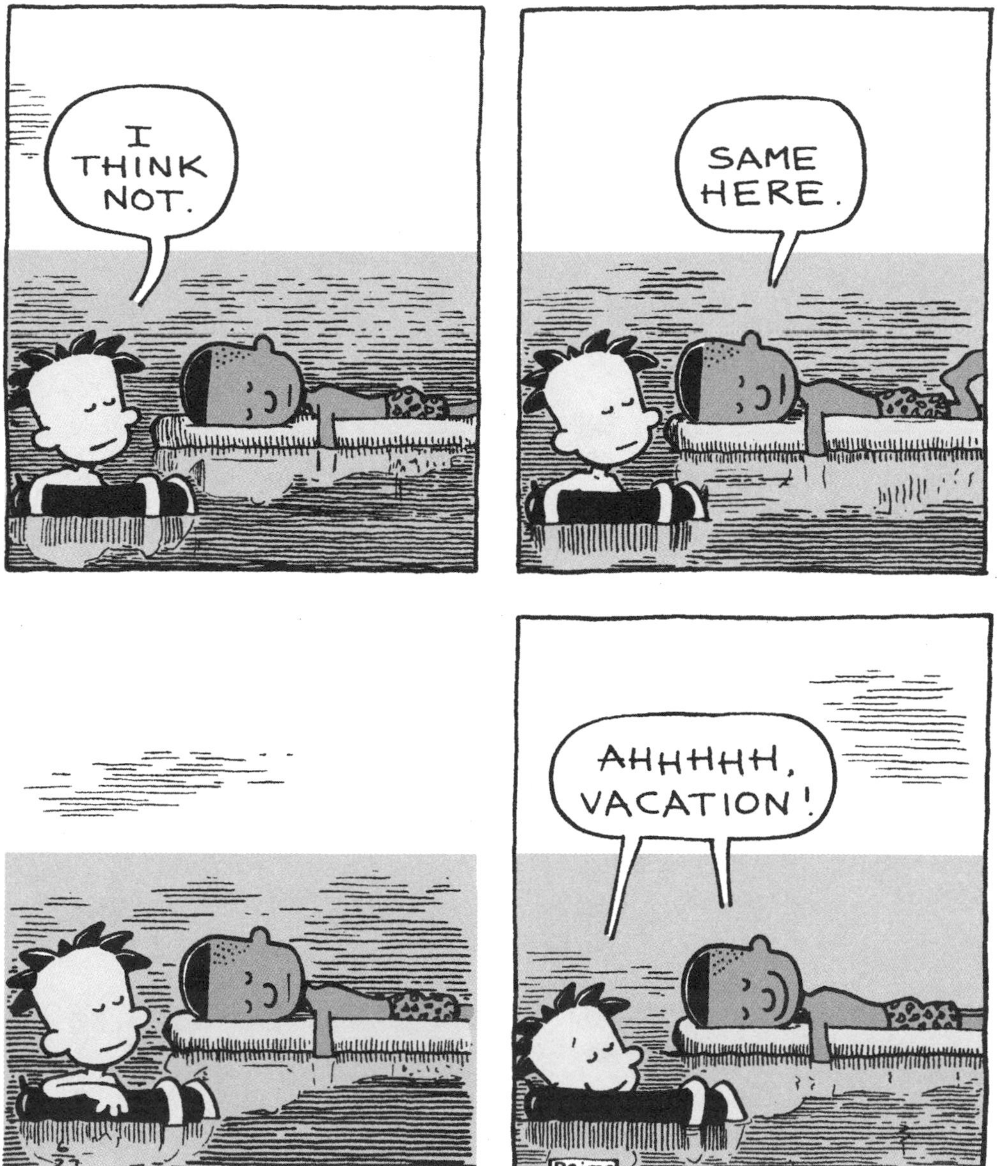
I THINK NOT.
SAME HERE.
AHHHHH, VACATION!
Peirce

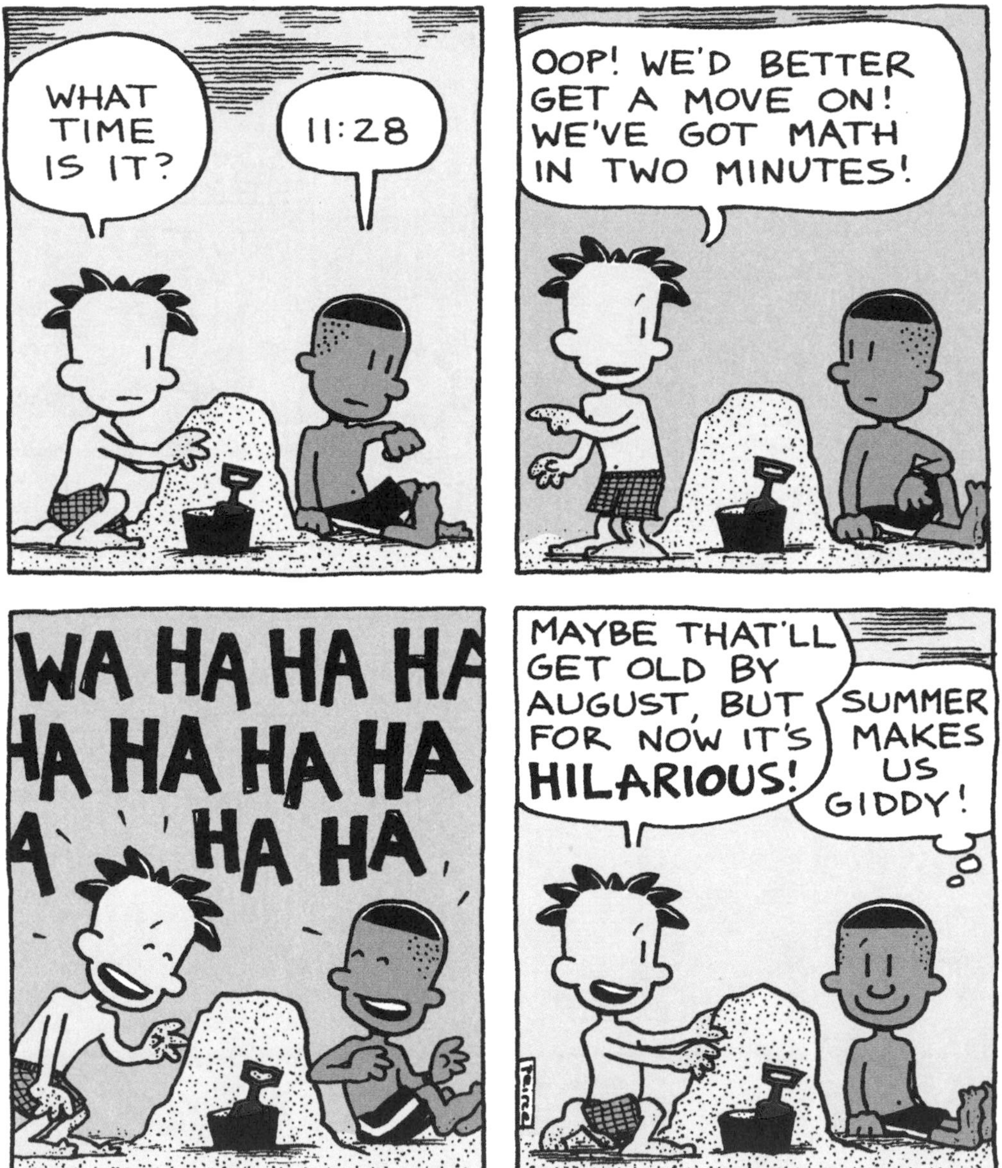
WHAT TIME IS IT?
11:28
OOP! WE'D BETTER GET A MOVE ON! WE'VE GOT MATH IN TWO MINUTES!
WA HA HA HA HA HA HA HA HA HA A HA HA
MAYBE THAT'LL GET OLD BY AUGUST, BUT FOR NOW IT'S **HILARIOUS!**
SUMMER MAKES US GIDDY!

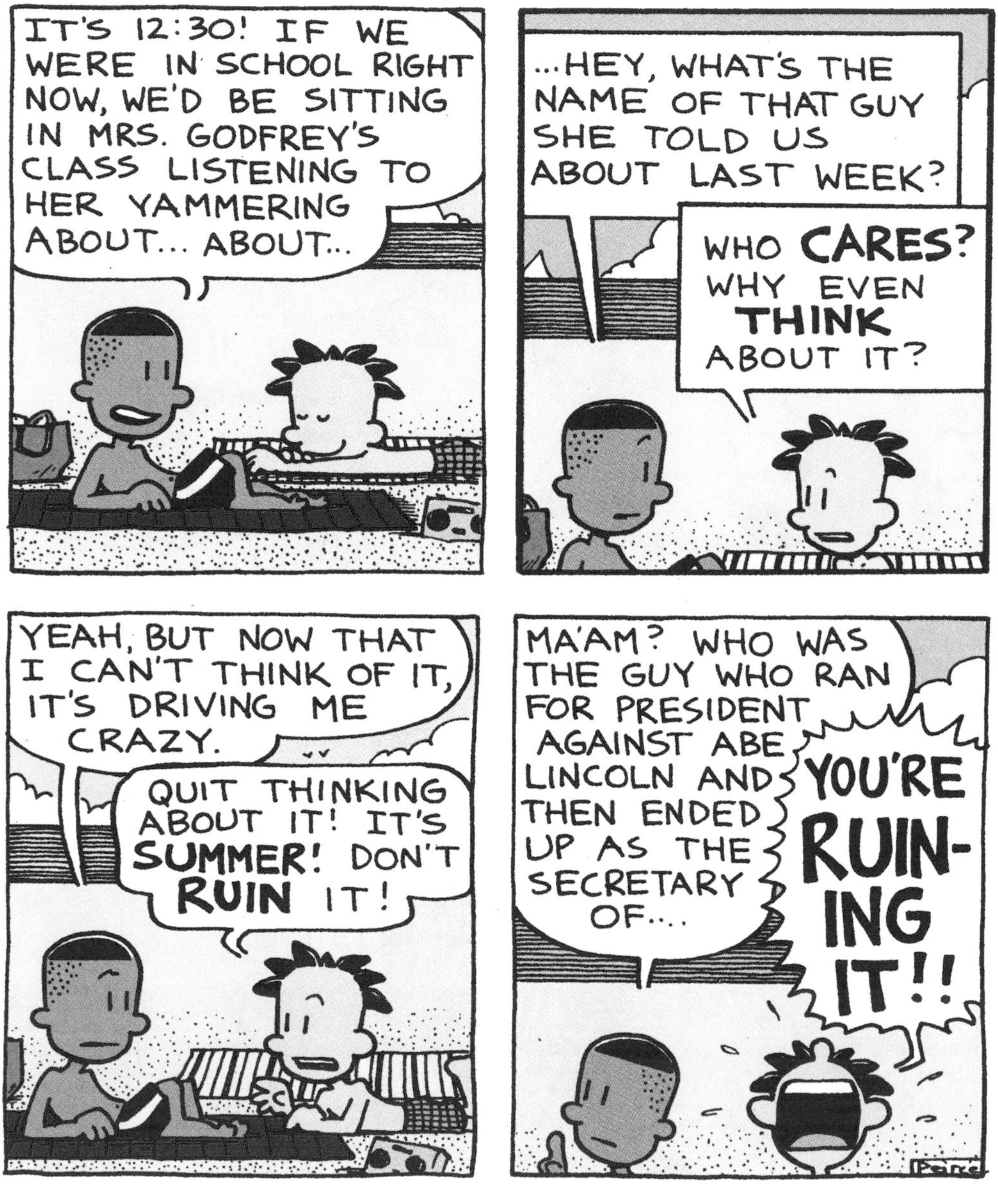
IT'S 12:30! IF WE WERE IN SCHOOL RIGHT NOW, WE'D BE SITTING IN MRS. GODFREY'S CLASS LISTENING TO HER YAMMERING ABOUT... ABOUT...
...HEY, WHAT'S THE NAME OF THAT GUY SHE TOLD US ABOUT LAST WEEK?
WHO CARES? WHY EVEN THINK ABOUT IT?
YEAH, BUT NOW THAT I CAN'T THINK OF IT, IT'S DRIVING ME CRAZY.
QUIT THINKING ABOUT IT! IT'S SUMMER! DON'T RUIN IT!
MA'AM? WHO WAS THE GUY WHO RAN FOR PRESIDENT AGAINST ABE LINCOLN AND THEN ENDED UP AS THE SECRETARY OF....
YOU'RE RUIN-ING IT!!
Peirce

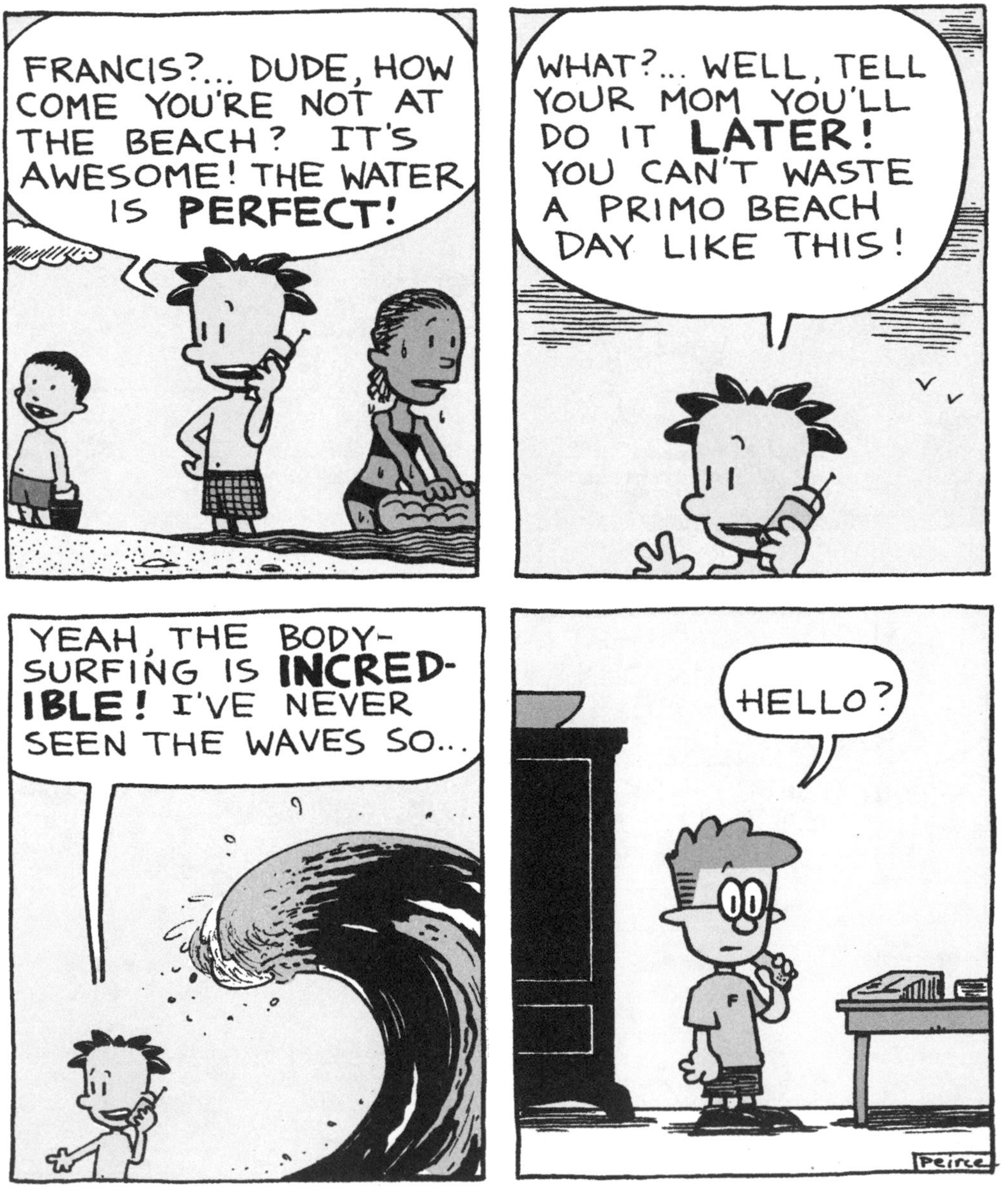
FRANCIS?... DUDE, HOW COME YOU'RE NOT AT THE BEACH? IT'S AWESOME! THE WATER IS PERFECT!
WHAT?... WELL, TELL YOUR MOM YOU'LL DO IT LATER! YOU CAN'T WASTE A PRIMO BEACH DAY LIKE THIS!
YEAH, THE BODY-SURFING IS INCREDIBLE! I'VE NEVER SEEN THE WAVES SO...
HELLO?
F
PEIRCE

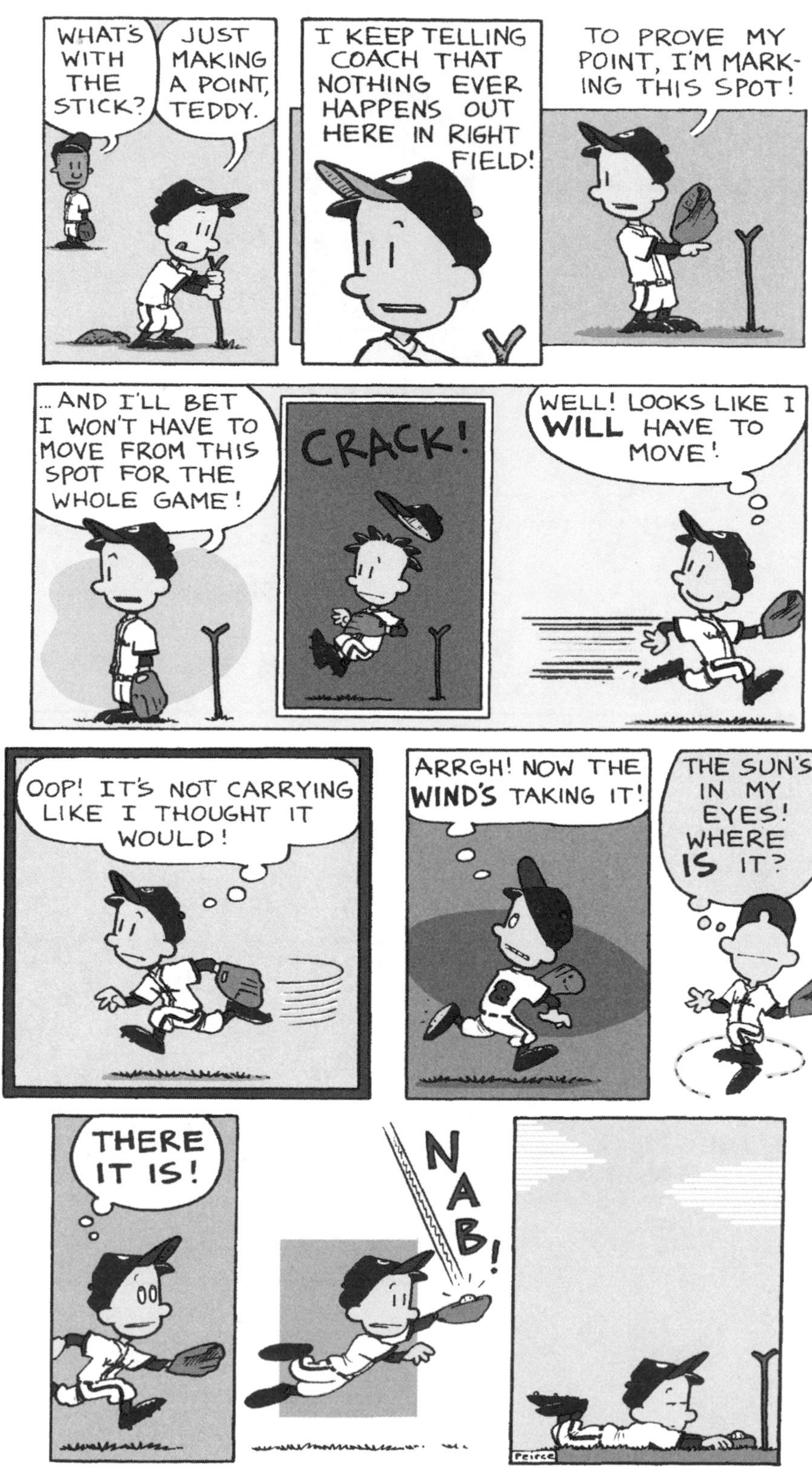
WHAT'S WITH THE STICK?
JUST MAKING A POINT, TEDDY.
I KEEP TELLING COACH THAT NOTHING EVER HAPPENS OUT HERE IN RIGHT FIELD!
TO PROVE MY POINT, I'M MARKING THIS SPOT!
...AND I'LL BET I WON'T HAVE TO MOVE FROM THIS SPOT FOR THE WHOLE GAME!
CRACK!
WELL! LOOKS LIKE I WILL HAVE TO MOVE!
OOP! IT'S NOT CARRYING LIKE I THOUGHT IT WOULD!
ARRGH! NOW THE WIND'S TAKING IT!
THE SUN'S IN MY EYES! WHERE IS IT?
THERE IT IS!
NAB!
PEIRCE

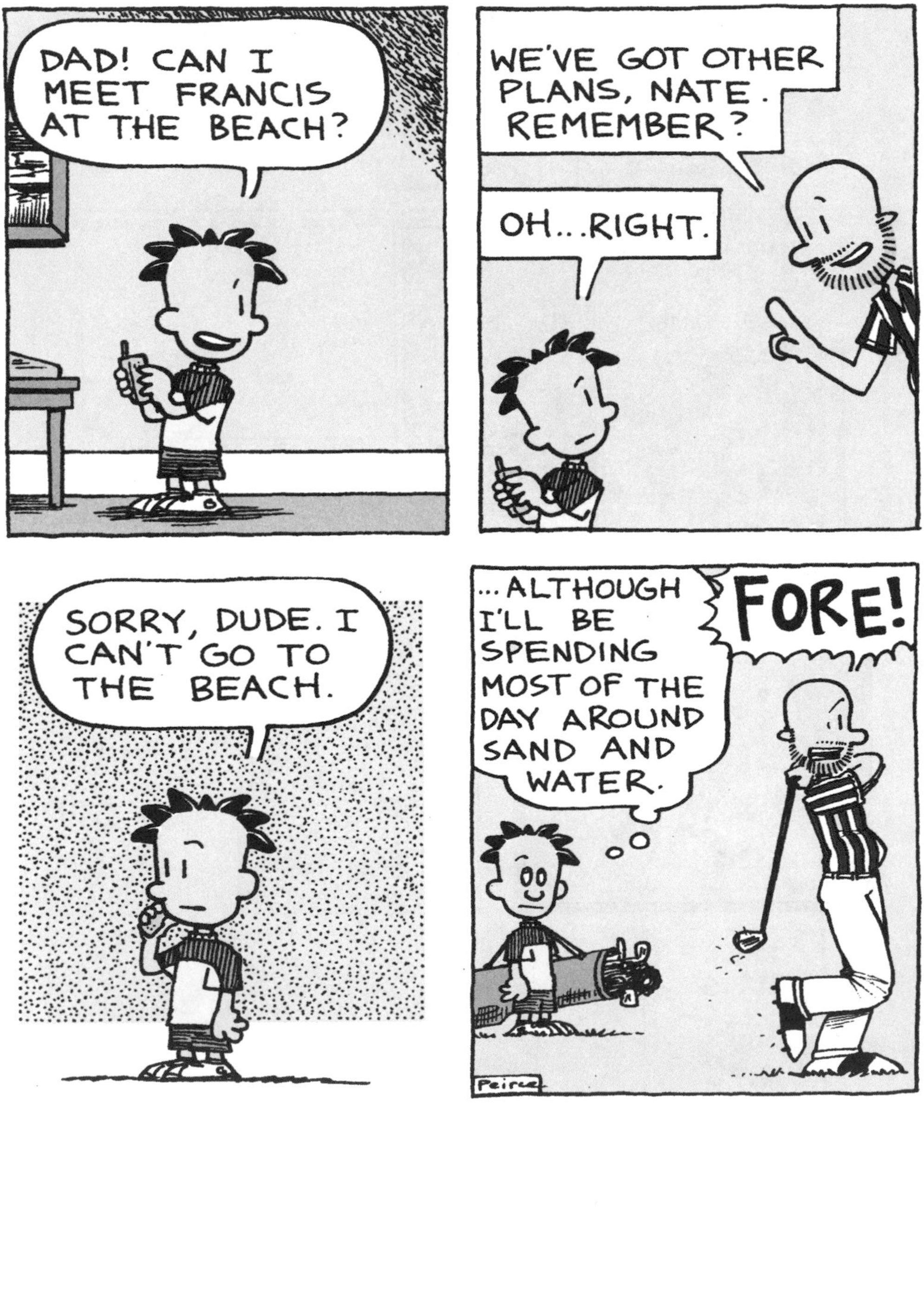
DAD! CAN I MEET FRANCIS AT THE BEACH?
WE'VE GOT OTHER PLANS, NATE. REMEMBER?
OH...RIGHT.
SORRY, DUDE. I CAN'T GO TO THE BEACH.
...ALTHOUGH I'LL BE SPENDING MOST OF THE DAY AROUND SAND AND WATER.
FORE!
Peirce

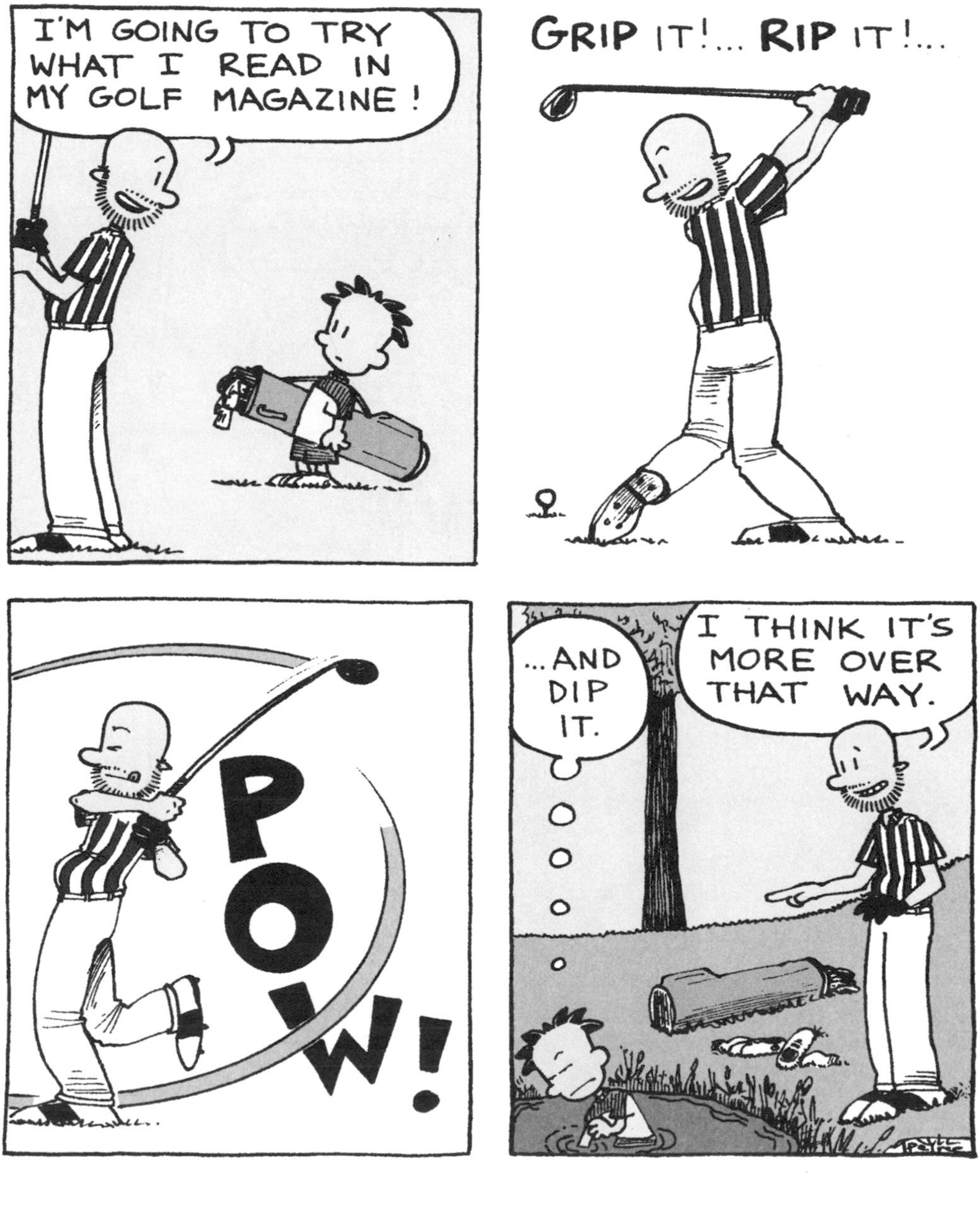
I'M GOING TO TRY WHAT I READ IN MY GOLF MAGAZINE!
GRIP IT!... RIP IT!...
POW!
...AND DIP IT.
I THINK IT'S MORE OVER THAT WAY.

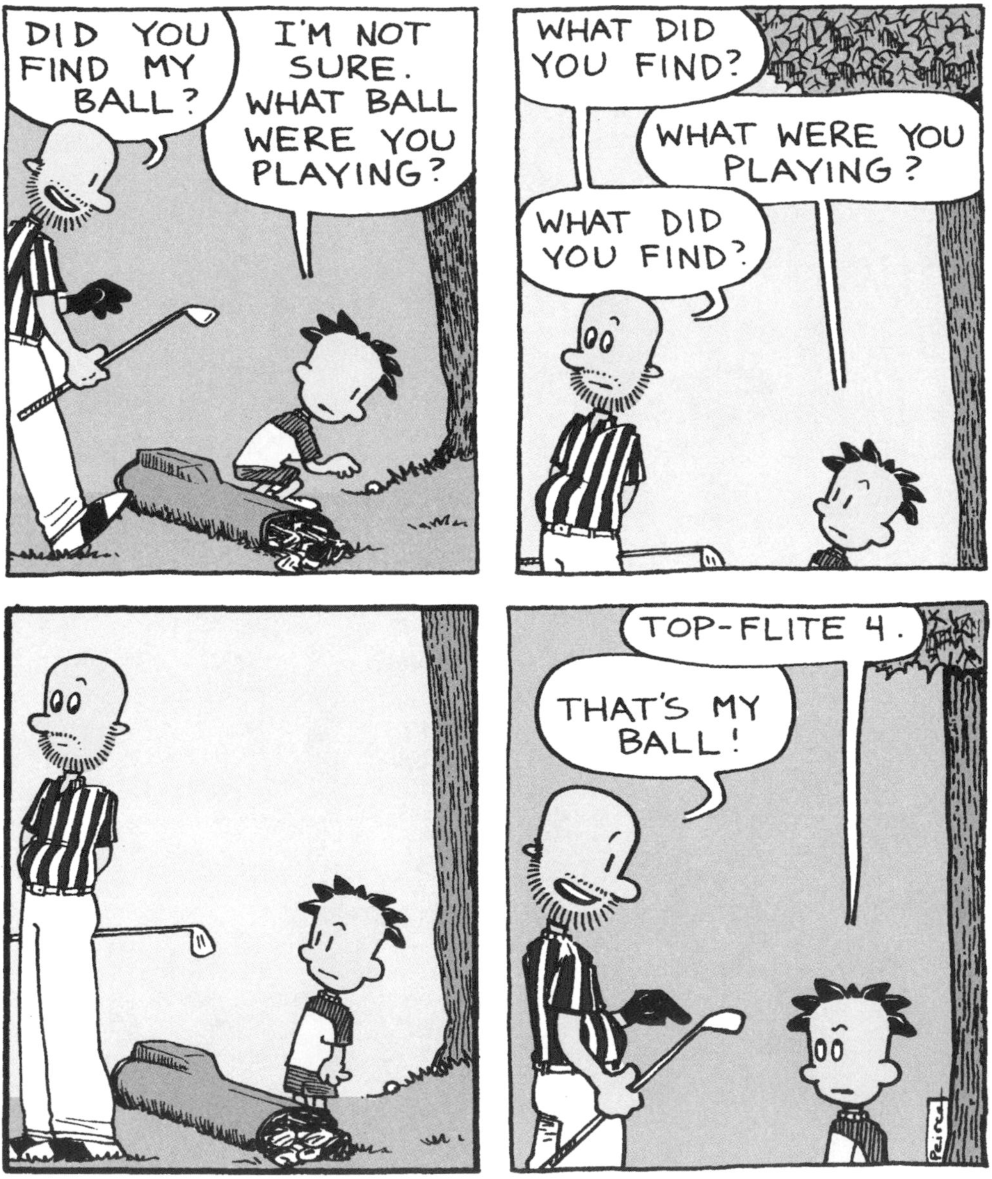
DID YOU FIND MY BALL?
I'M NOT SURE. WHAT BALL WERE YOU PLAYING?
WHAT DID YOU FIND?
WHAT WERE YOU PLAYING?
WHAT DID YOU FIND?
TOP-FLITE 4.
THAT'S MY BALL!
Peirce

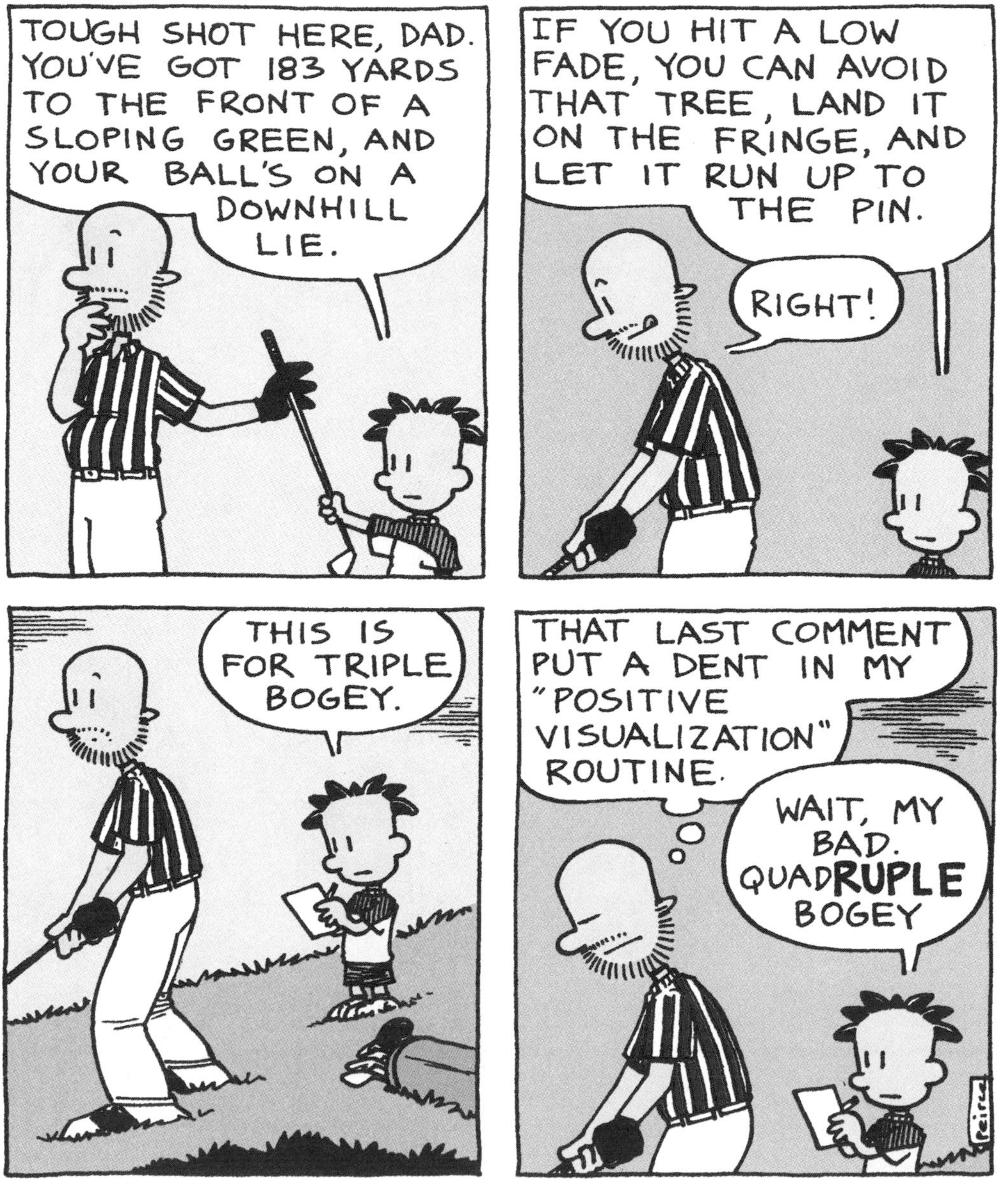
TOUGH SHOT HERE, DAD. YOU'VE GOT 183 YARDS TO THE FRONT OF A SLOPING GREEN, AND YOUR BALL'S ON A DOWNHILL LIE.
IF YOU HIT A LOW FADE, YOU CAN AVOID THAT TREE, LAND IT ON THE FRINGE, AND LET IT RUN UP TO THE PIN.
RIGHT!
THIS IS FOR TRIPLE BOGEY.
THAT LAST COMMENT PUT A DENT IN MY "POSITIVE VISUALIZATION" ROUTINE.
WAIT, MY BAD. QUADRUPLE BOGEY
PEIRCE

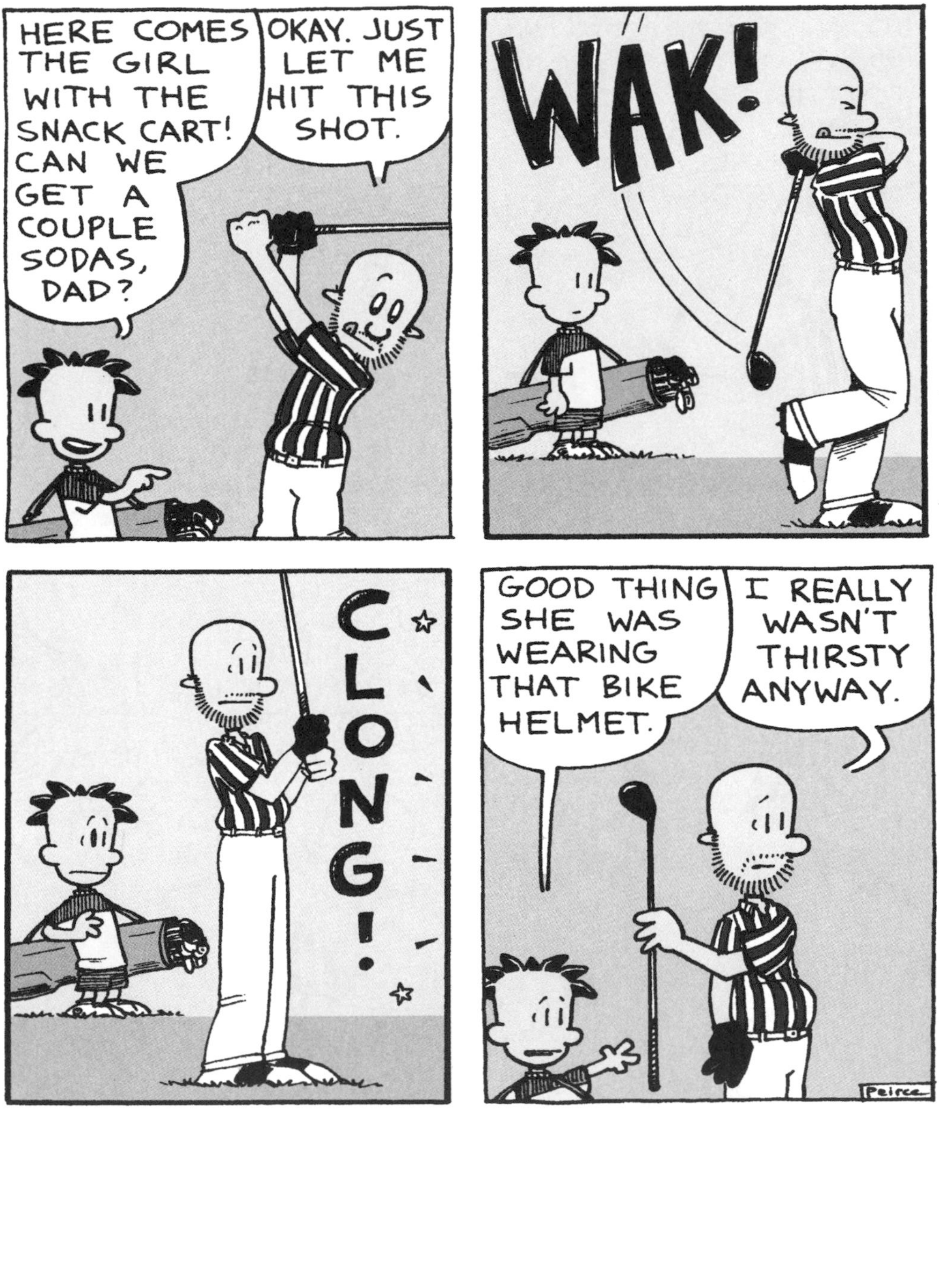
HERE COMES THE GIRL WITH THE SNACK CART! CAN WE GET A COUPLE SODAS, DAD?
OKAY. JUST LET ME HIT THIS SHOT.
WAK!
CLONG!
GOOD THING SHE WAS WEARING THAT BIKE HELMET.
I REALLY WASN'T THIRSTY ANYWAY.
Peirce

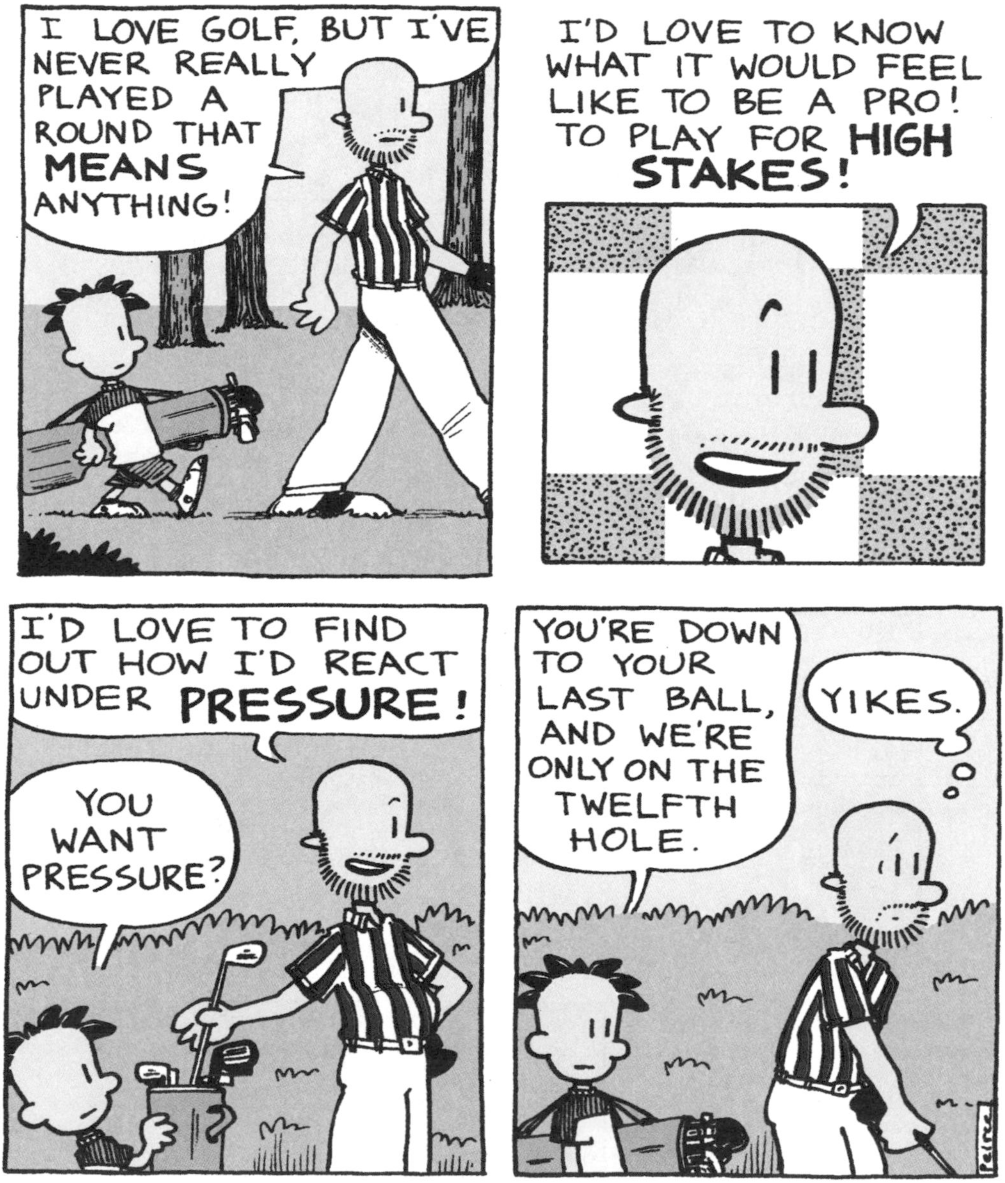
I LOVE GOLF, BUT I'VE NEVER REALLY PLAYED A ROUND THAT **MEANS** ANYTHING!
I'D LOVE TO KNOW WHAT IT WOULD FEEL LIKE TO BE A PRO! TO PLAY FOR **HIGH STAKES!**
I'D LOVE TO FIND OUT HOW I'D REACT UNDER **PRESSURE!**
YOU WANT PRESSURE?
YOU'RE DOWN TO YOUR LAST BALL, AND WE'RE ONLY ON THE TWELFTH HOLE.
YIKES.
PEIRCE

"POOR NATE'S ALMANAC"? WHAT'S THIS?

I'M FOLLOWING IN THE FOOTSTEPS OF BEN FRANKLIN, BOYS!

POOR NATE'S ALMANAC $2

BACK IN THE 1700s, OL' BEN PUBLISHED "POOR RICHARD'S ALMANACK"!

IT WAS FILLED WITH ALL SORTS OF WISE SAYINGS LIKE "THE EARLY BIRD GETS THE WORM" AND "A PENNY SAVED IS A PENNY EARNED"!

"POOR NATE'S ALMANAC" IS THE SAME THING, ONLY **BETTER!** YOU WON'T BELIEVE ALL THE WISDOM IN HERE!

POOR NATE'S

AND THESE ARE MY LAST TWO COPIES! A BARGAIN AT TWO BUCKS EACH!

OKAY, I'LL TAKE ONE.

ME TOO!

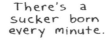

HEY! THIS THING'S **BLANK!**

WAIT, THERE'S SOMETHING WRITTEN ON THE LAST PAGE.

FLIP FLIP FLIP

There's a sucker born every minute.

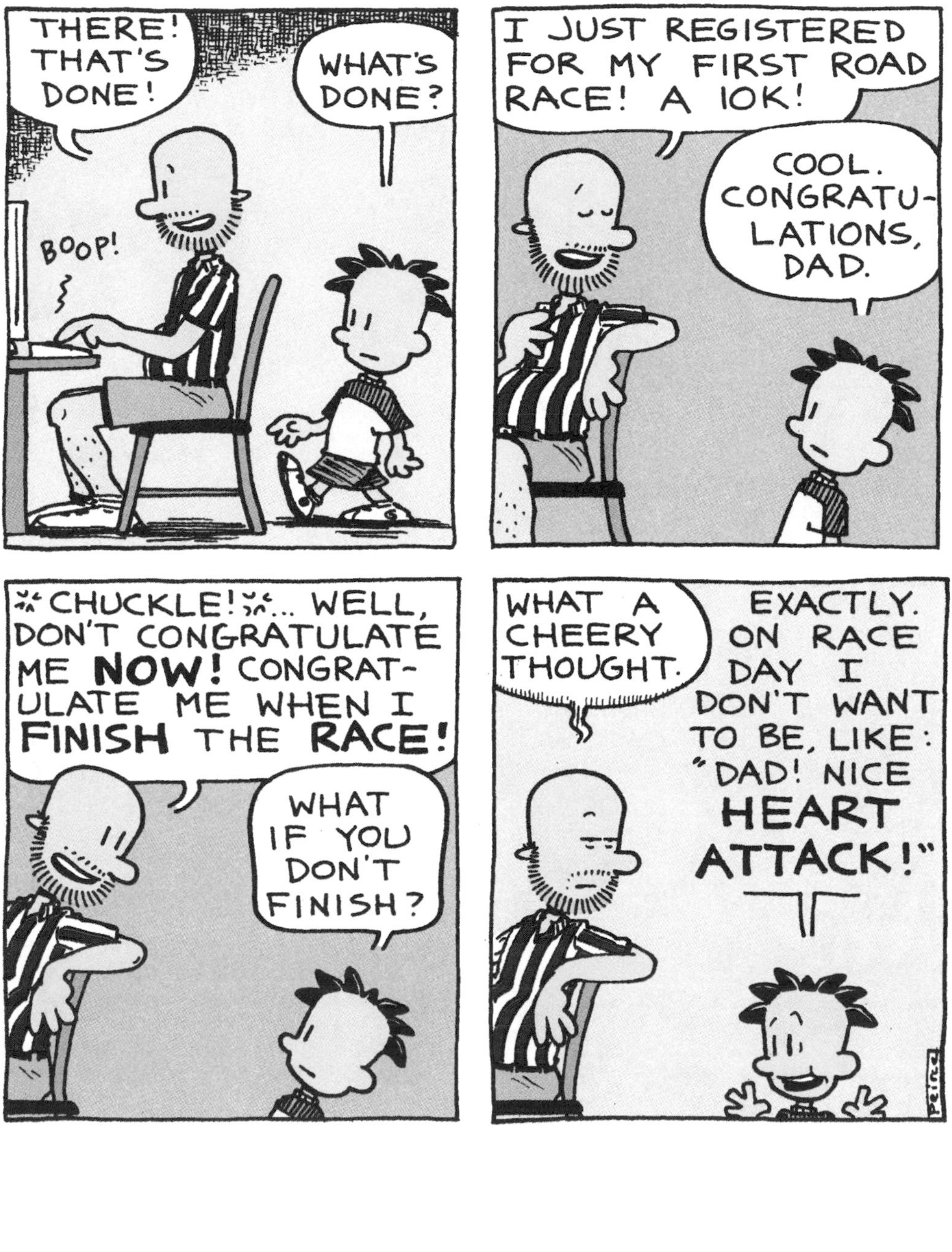
THERE! THAT'S DONE!
WHAT'S DONE?
BOOP!
I JUST REGISTERED FOR MY FIRST ROAD RACE! A 10K!
COOL. CONGRATULATIONS, DAD.
CHUCKLE! ... WELL, DON'T CONGRATULATE ME NOW! CONGRATULATE ME WHEN I FINISH THE RACE!
WHAT IF YOU DON'T FINISH?
WHAT A CHEERY THOUGHT.
EXACTLY. ON RACE DAY I DON'T WANT TO BE, LIKE: "DAD! NICE HEART ATTACK!"
PEIRCE

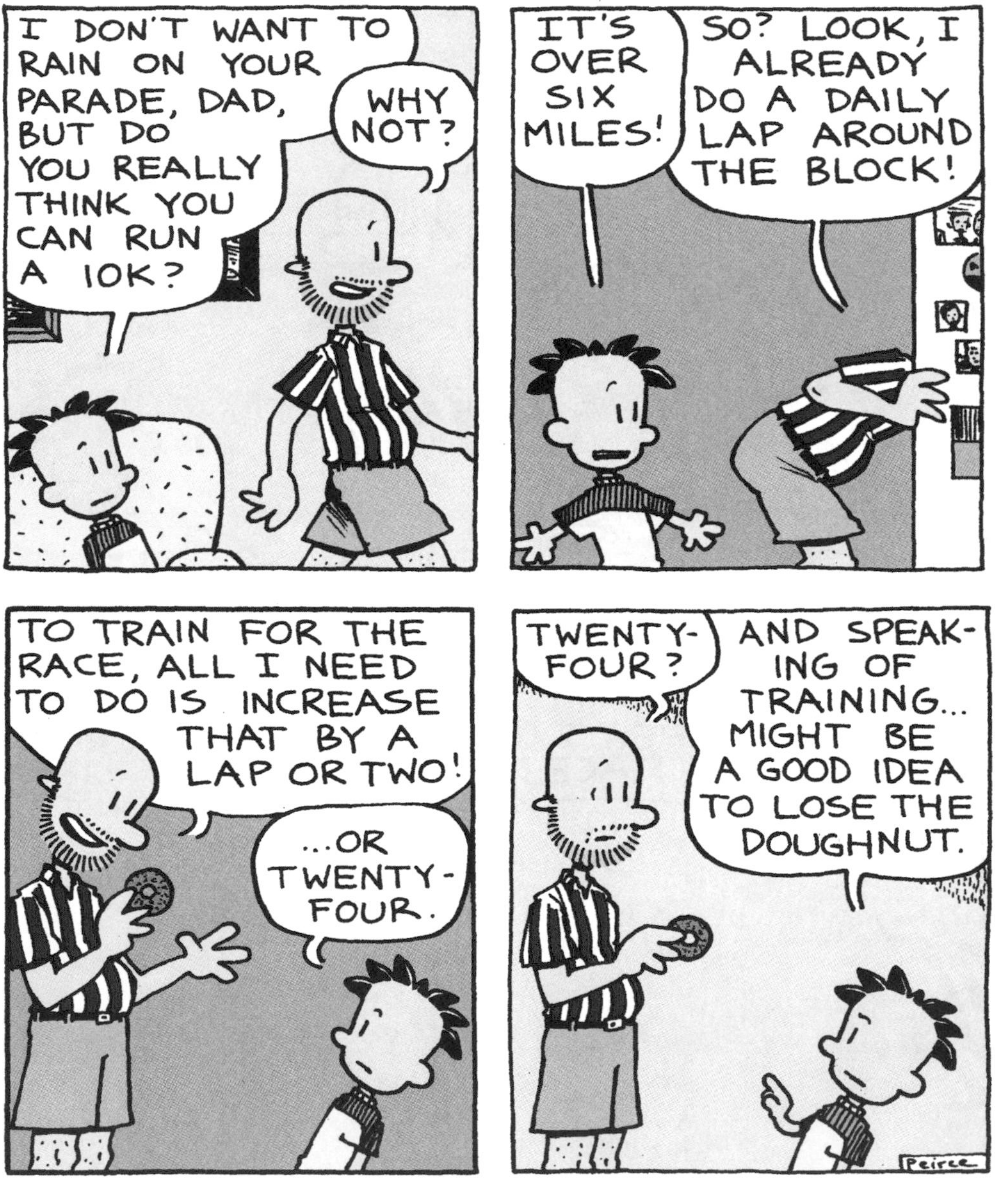
I DON'T WANT TO RAIN ON YOUR PARADE, DAD, BUT DO YOU REALLY THINK YOU CAN RUN A 10K?
WHY NOT?
IT'S OVER SIX MILES!
SO? LOOK, I ALREADY DO A DAILY LAP AROUND THE BLOCK!
TO TRAIN FOR THE RACE, ALL I NEED TO DO IS INCREASE THAT BY A LAP OR TWO!
...OR TWENTY-FOUR.
TWENTY-FOUR?
AND SPEAKING OF TRAINING... MIGHT BE A GOOD IDEA TO LOSE THE DOUGHNUT.
Peirce

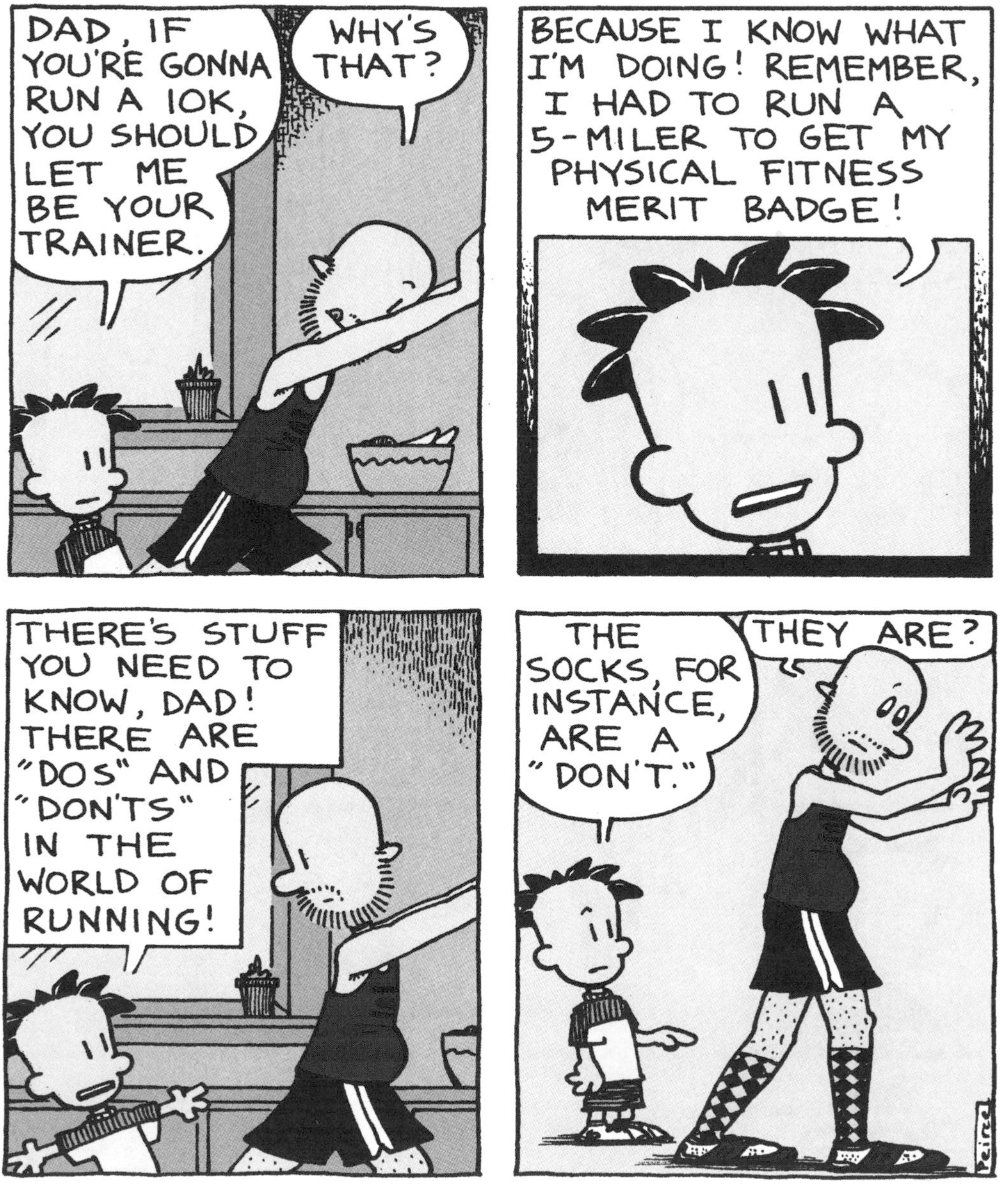
DAD, IF YOU'RE GONNA RUN A 10K, YOU SHOULD LET ME BE YOUR TRAINER.
WHY'S THAT?
BECAUSE I KNOW WHAT I'M DOING! REMEMBER, I HAD TO RUN A 5-MILER TO GET MY PHYSICAL FITNESS MERIT BADGE!
THERE'S STUFF YOU NEED TO KNOW, DAD! THERE ARE "DOS" AND "DON'TS" IN THE WORLD OF RUNNING!
THE SOCKS, FOR INSTANCE, ARE A "DON'T."
THEY ARE?
PEIRCE

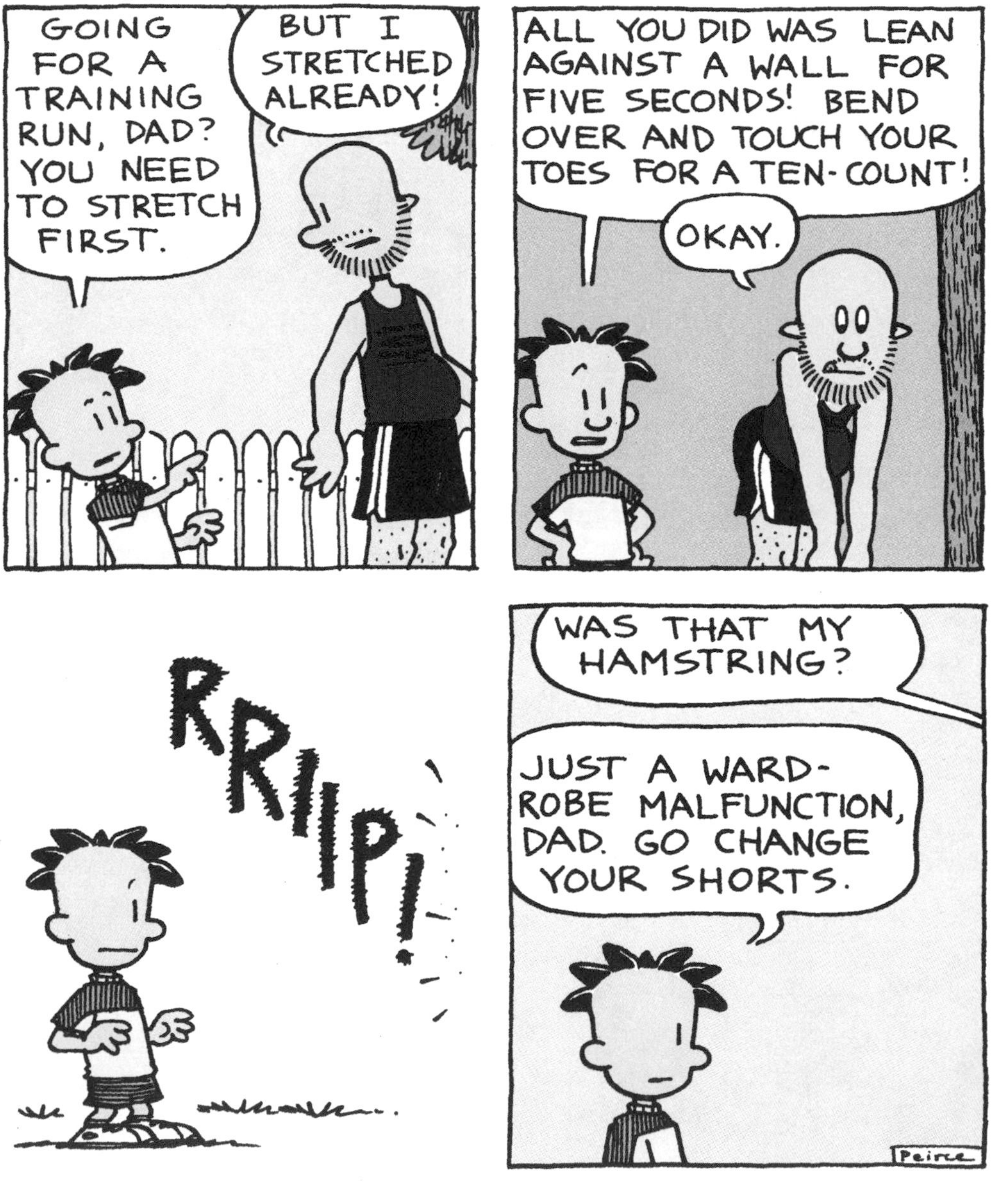
GOING FOR A TRAINING RUN, DAD? YOU NEED TO STRETCH FIRST.
BUT I STRETCHED ALREADY!
ALL YOU DID WAS LEAN AGAINST A WALL FOR FIVE SECONDS! BEND OVER AND TOUCH YOUR TOES FOR A TEN-COUNT!
OKAY.
RRIIP!
WAS THAT MY HAMSTRING?
JUST A WARD-ROBE MALFUNCTION, DAD. GO CHANGE YOUR SHORTS.
Peirce

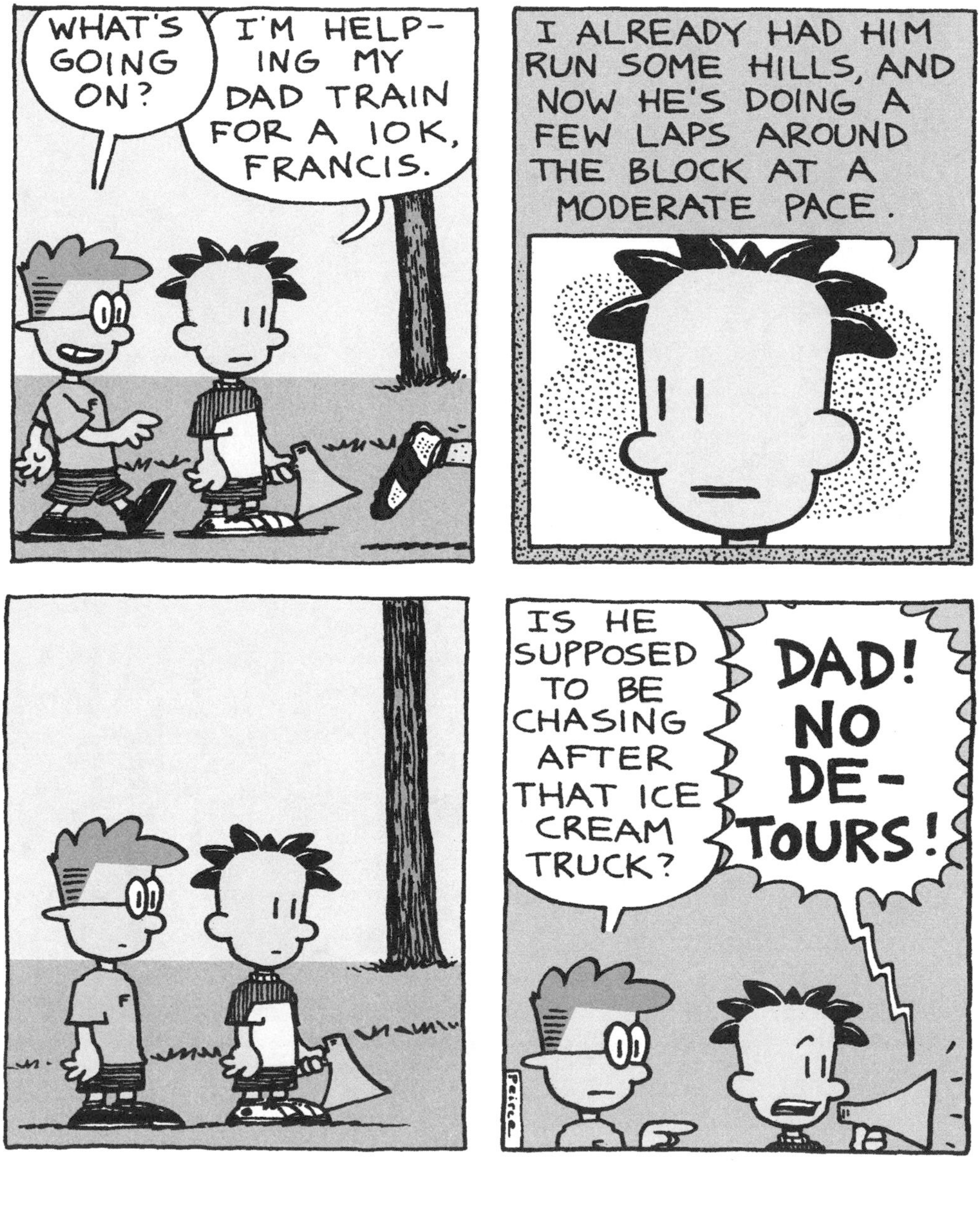
WHAT'S GOING ON?
I'M HELPING MY DAD TRAIN FOR A 10K, FRANCIS.
I ALREADY HAD HIM RUN SOME HILLS, AND NOW HE'S DOING A FEW LAPS AROUND THE BLOCK AT A MODERATE PACE.
IS HE SUPPOSED TO BE CHASING AFTER THAT ICE CREAM TRUCK?
DAD! NO DE-TOURS!
PEIRCE

HAS YOUR DAD EVER RUN A 10K BEFORE?
NOPE. FIRST TIME.
AND WHEN'S THE RACE?
IN FOUR WEEKS.
SHOULD BE AN ENTER-TAINING MONTH!
DAD! GET UP!
Peirce

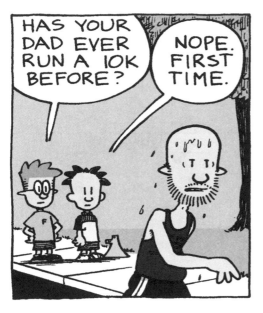

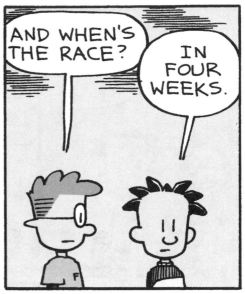

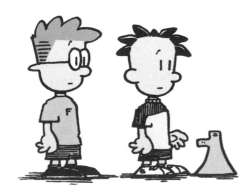

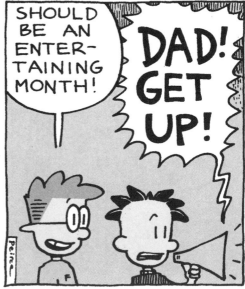

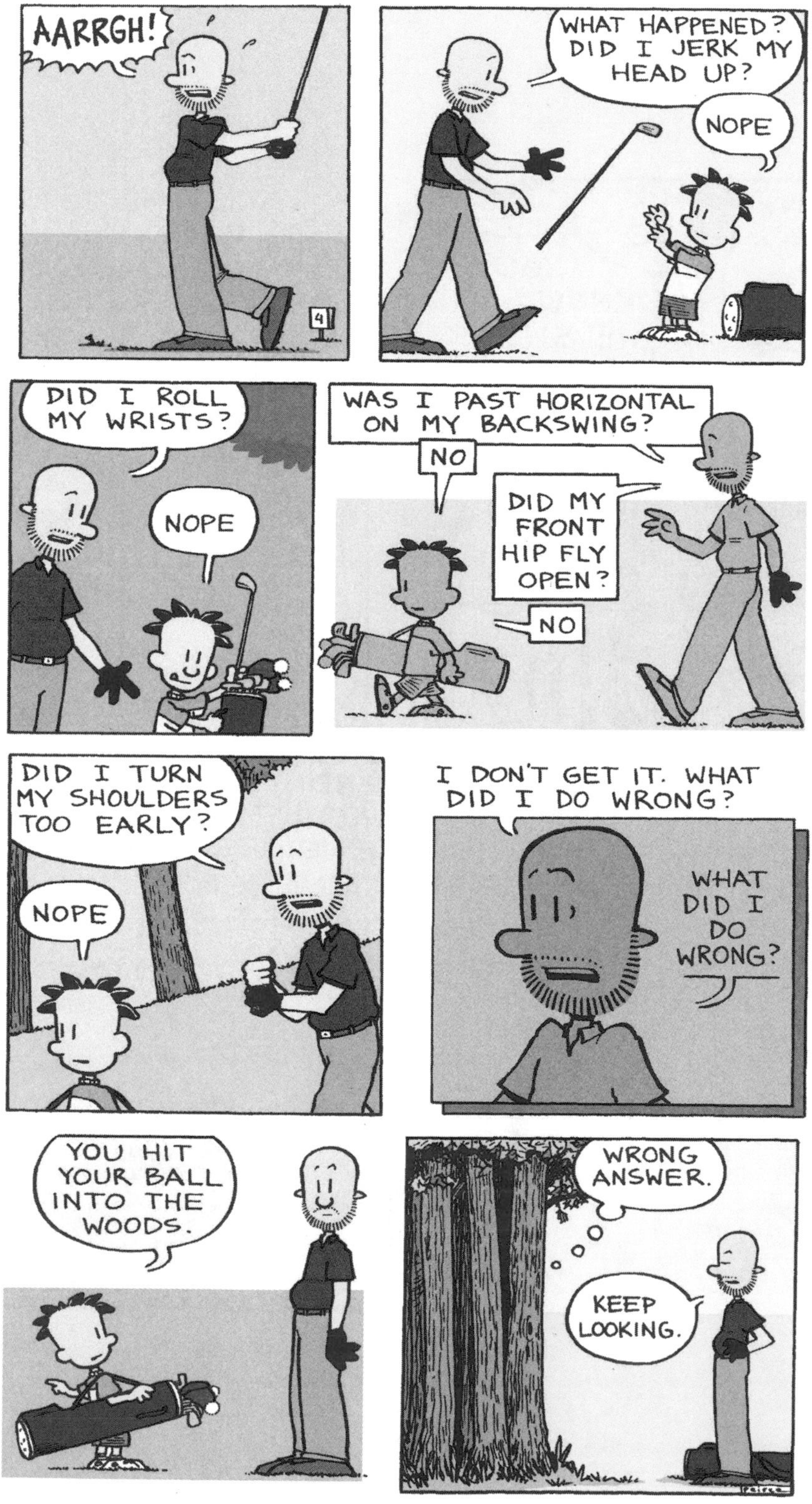
AARRGH!
WHAT HAPPENED? DID I JERK MY HEAD UP?
NOPE
DID I ROLL MY WRISTS?
NOPE
WAS I PAST HORIZONTAL ON MY BACKSWING?
NO
DID MY FRONT HIP FLY OPEN?
NO
DID I TURN MY SHOULDERS TOO EARLY?
NOPE
I DON'T GET IT. WHAT DID I DO WRONG?
WHAT DID I DO WRONG?
YOU HIT YOUR BALL INTO THE WOODS.
WRONG ANSWER.
KEEP LOOKING.

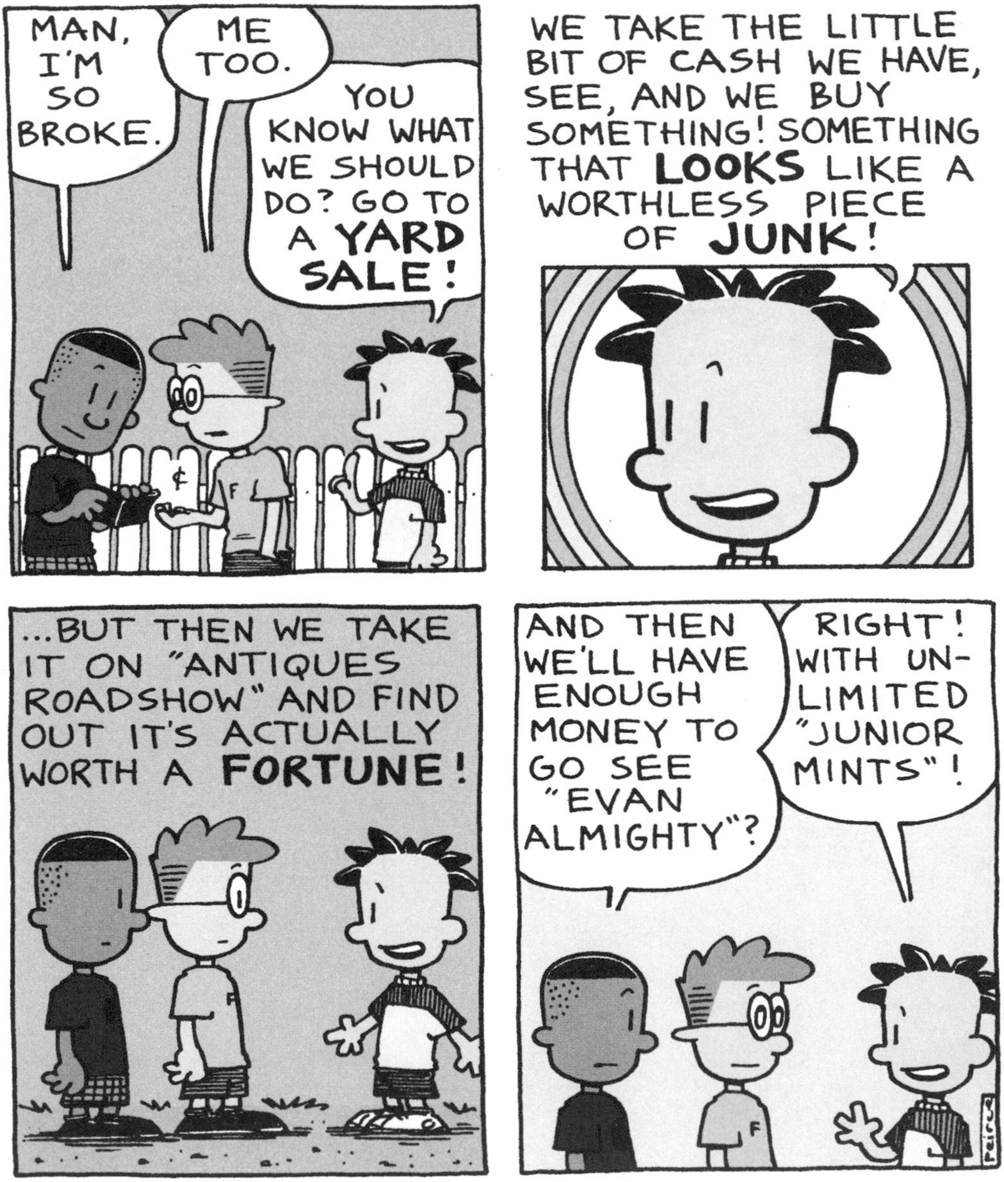
MAN, I'M SO BROKE.
ME TOO.
YOU KNOW WHAT WE SHOULD DO? GO TO A YARD SALE!
WE TAKE THE LITTLE BIT OF CASH WE HAVE, SEE, AND WE BUY SOMETHING! SOMETHING THAT LOOKS LIKE A WORTHLESS PIECE OF JUNK!
...BUT THEN WE TAKE IT ON "ANTIQUES ROADSHOW" AND FIND OUT IT'S ACTUALLY WORTH A FORTUNE!
AND THEN WE'LL HAVE ENOUGH MONEY TO GO SEE "EVAN ALMIGHTY"?
RIGHT! WITH UNLIMITED "JUNIOR MINTS"!

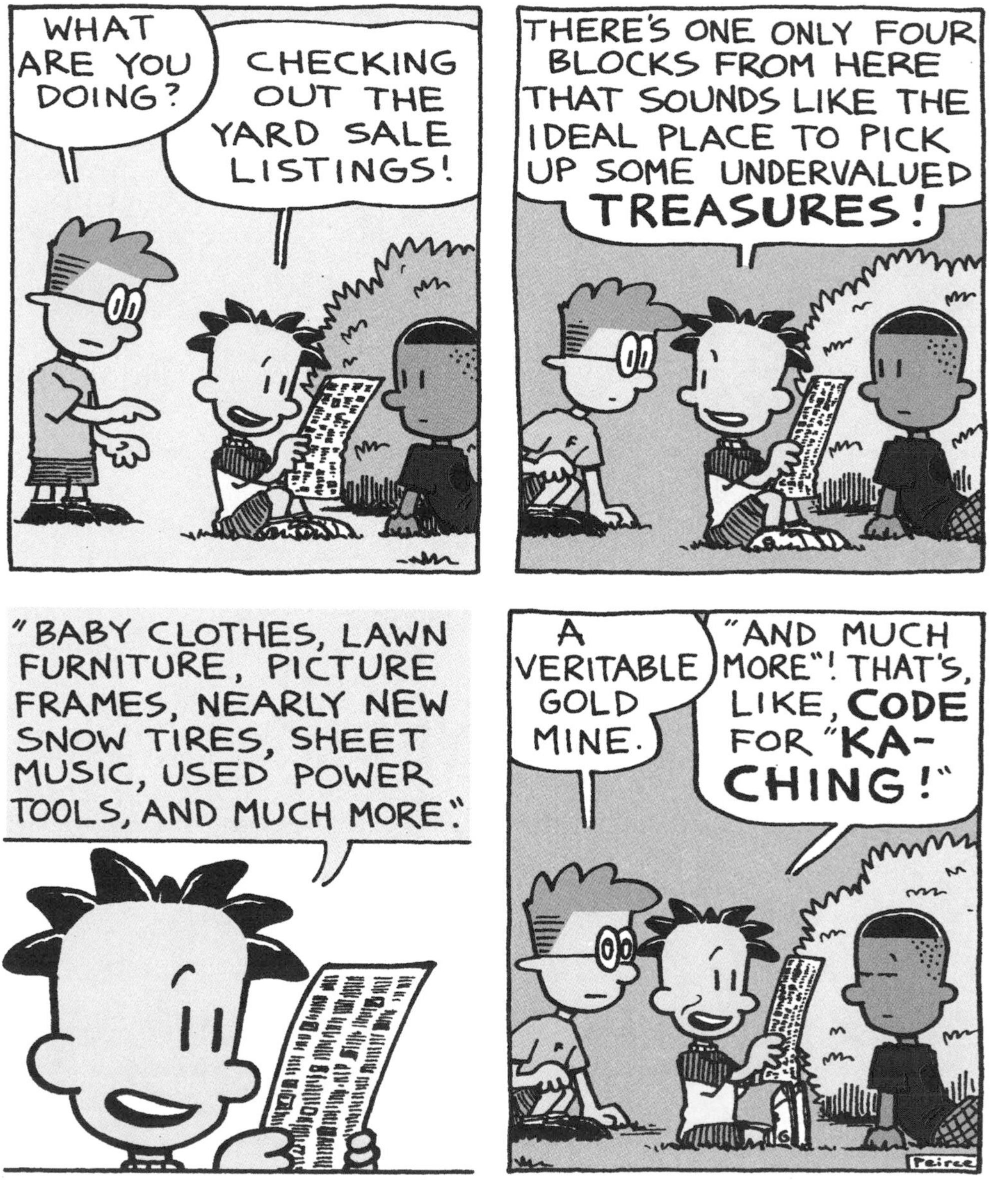
WHAT ARE YOU DOING?
CHECKING OUT THE YARD SALE LISTINGS!
THERE'S ONE ONLY FOUR BLOCKS FROM HERE THAT SOUNDS LIKE THE IDEAL PLACE TO PICK UP SOME UNDERVALUED **TREASURES!**
"BABY CLOTHES, LAWN FURNITURE, PICTURE FRAMES, NEARLY NEW SNOW TIRES, SHEET MUSIC, USED POWER TOOLS, AND MUCH MORE."
A VERITABLE GOLD MINE.
"AND MUCH MORE"! THAT'S, LIKE, **CODE** FOR "**KA-CHING!**"
Peirce

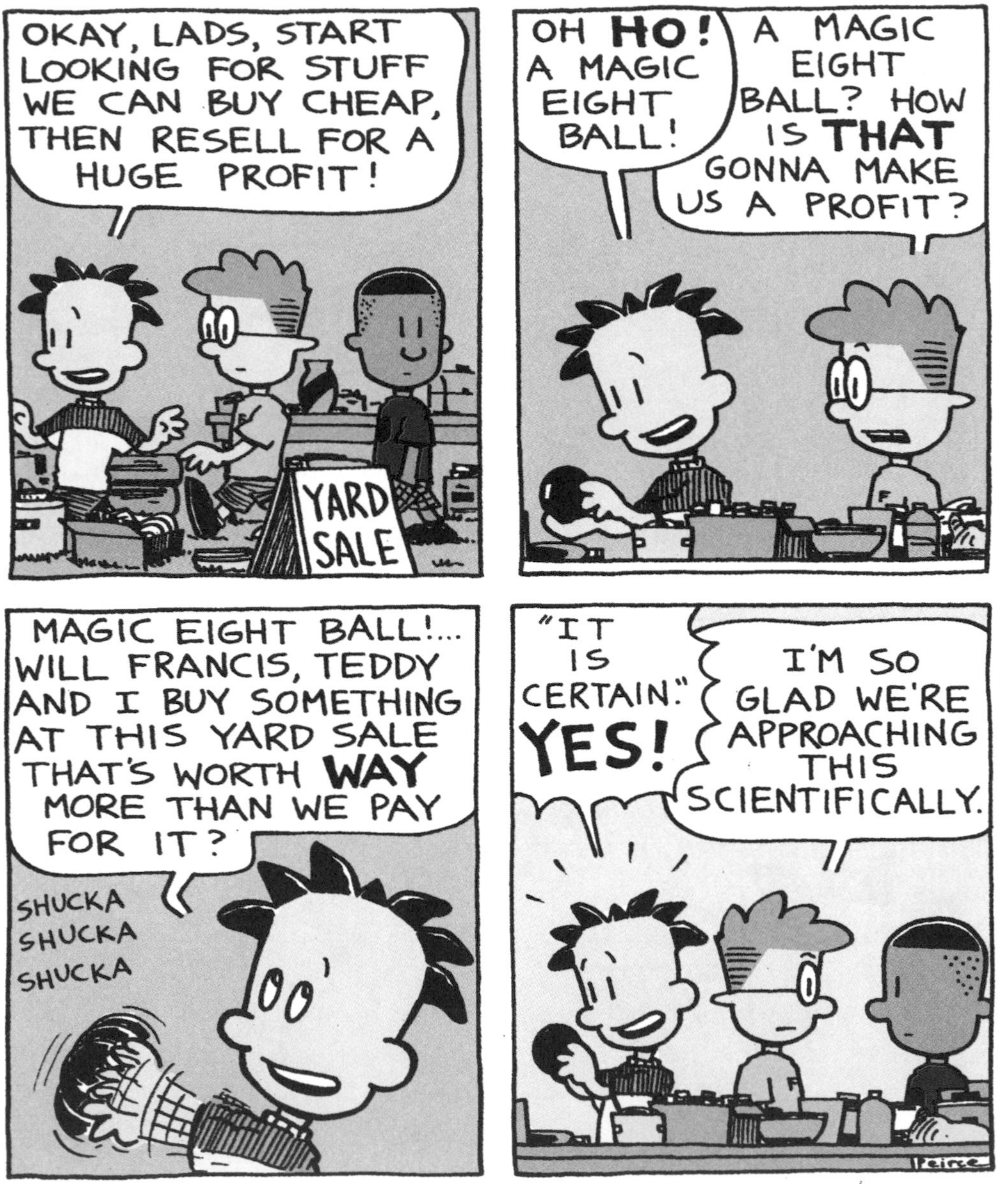
OKAY, LADS, START LOOKING FOR STUFF WE CAN BUY CHEAP, THEN RESELL FOR A HUGE PROFIT!
YARD SALE
OH HO! A MAGIC EIGHT BALL!
A MAGIC EIGHT BALL? HOW IS THAT GONNA MAKE US A PROFIT?
MAGIC EIGHT BALL!... WILL FRANCIS, TEDDY AND I BUY SOMETHING AT THIS YARD SALE THAT'S WORTH WAY MORE THAN WE PAY FOR IT?
SHUCKA SHUCKA SHUCKA
"IT IS CERTAIN." YES!
I'M SO GLAD WE'RE APPROACHING THIS SCIENTIFICALLY.
Peirce

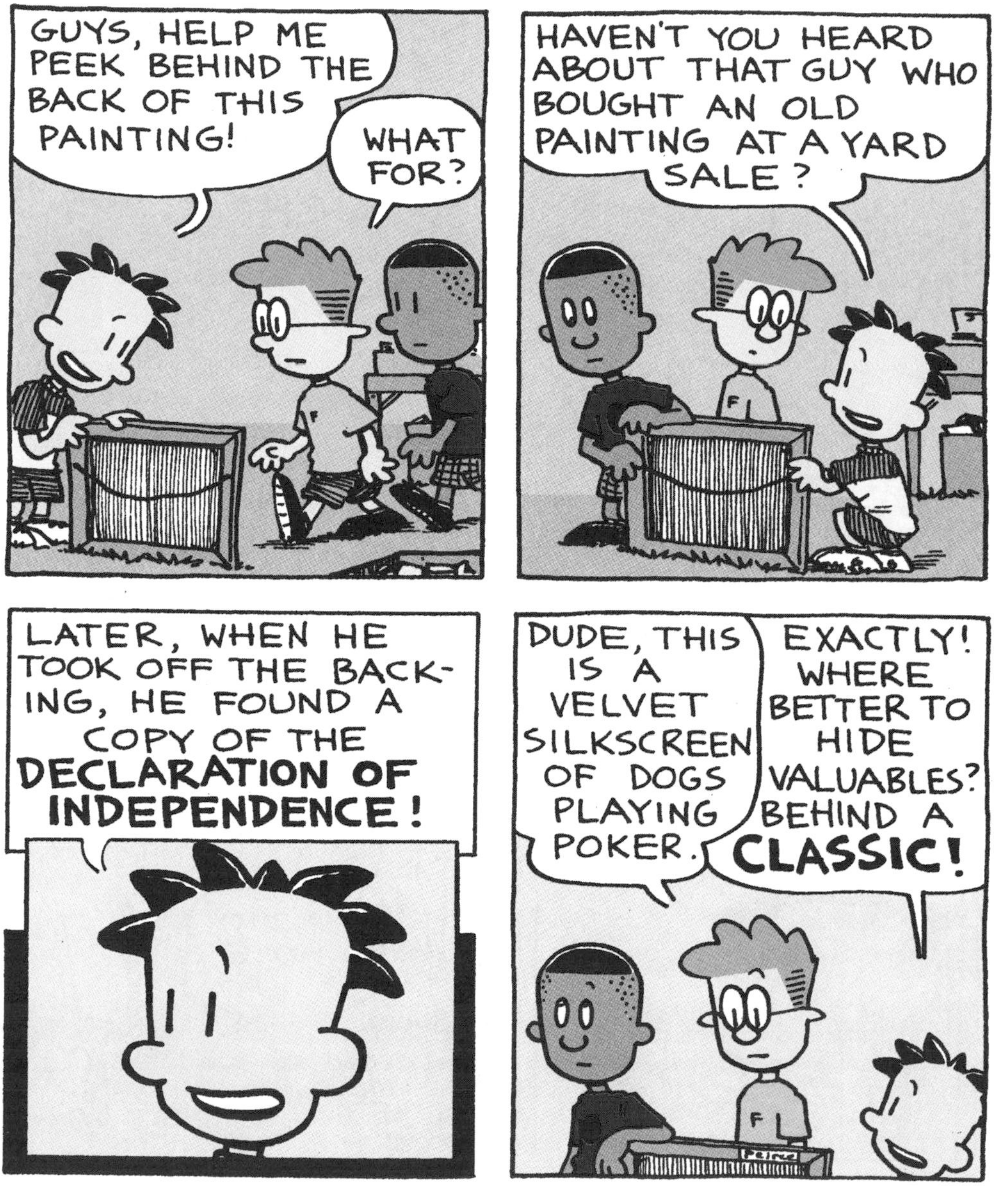
GUYS, HELP ME PEEK BEHIND THE BACK OF THIS PAINTING!
WHAT FOR?
HAVEN'T YOU HEARD ABOUT THAT GUY WHO BOUGHT AN OLD PAINTING AT A YARD SALE?
LATER, WHEN HE TOOK OFF THE BACK-ING, HE FOUND A COPY OF THE **DECLARATION OF INDEPENDENCE!**
DUDE, THIS IS A VELVET SILKSCREEN OF DOGS PLAYING POKER.
EXACTLY! WHERE BETTER TO HIDE VALUABLES? BEHIND A **CLASSIC!**

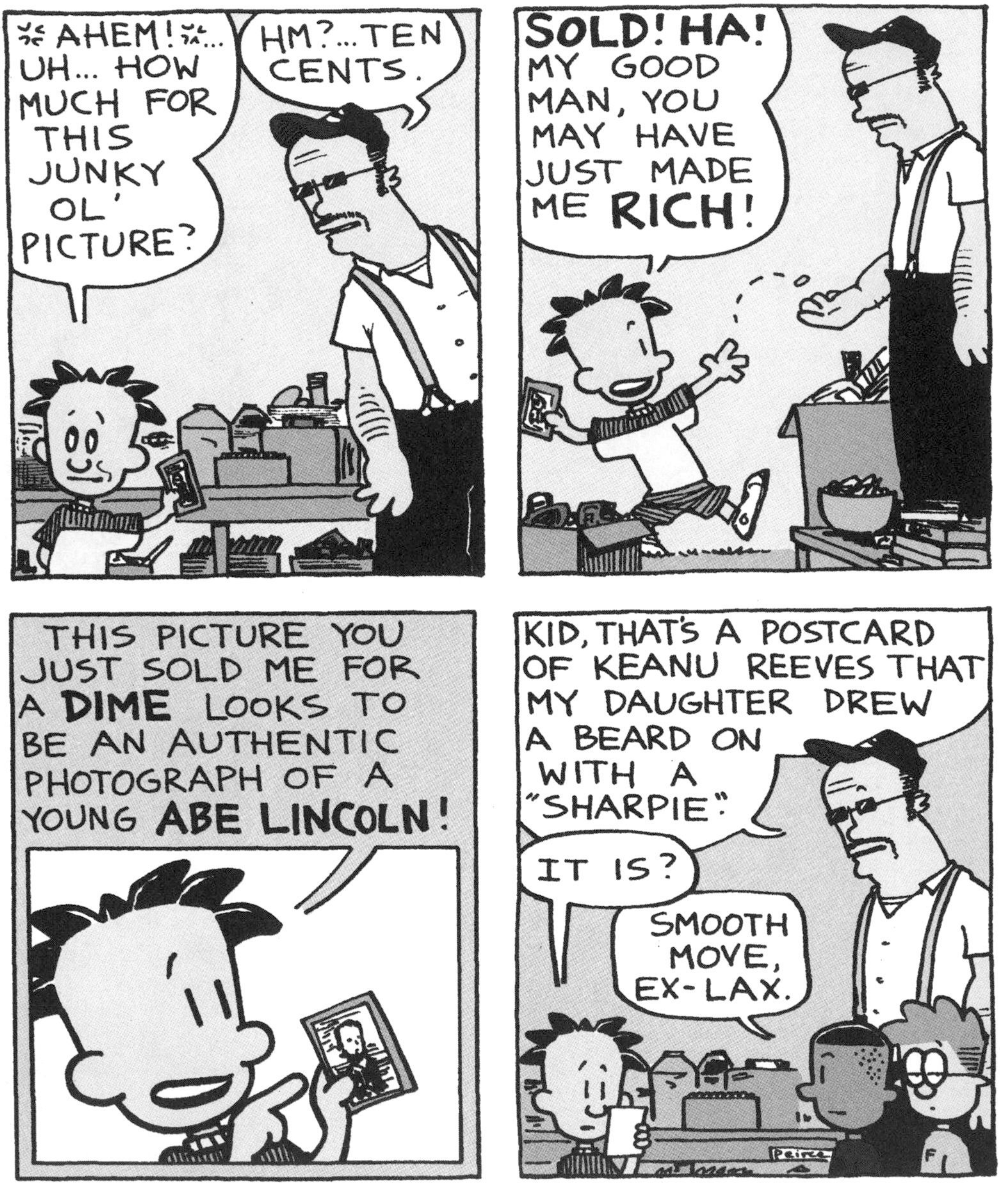
AHEM! ... UH... HOW MUCH FOR THIS JUNKY OL' PICTURE?
HM?...TEN CENTS.
SOLD! HA! MY GOOD MAN, YOU MAY HAVE JUST MADE ME RICH!
THIS PICTURE YOU JUST SOLD ME FOR A DIME LOOKS TO BE AN AUTHENTIC PHOTOGRAPH OF A YOUNG ABE LINCOLN!
KID, THAT'S A POSTCARD OF KEANU REEVES THAT MY DAUGHTER DREW A BEARD ON WITH A "SHARPIE."
IT IS?
SMOOTH MOVE, EX-LAX.
Peirce

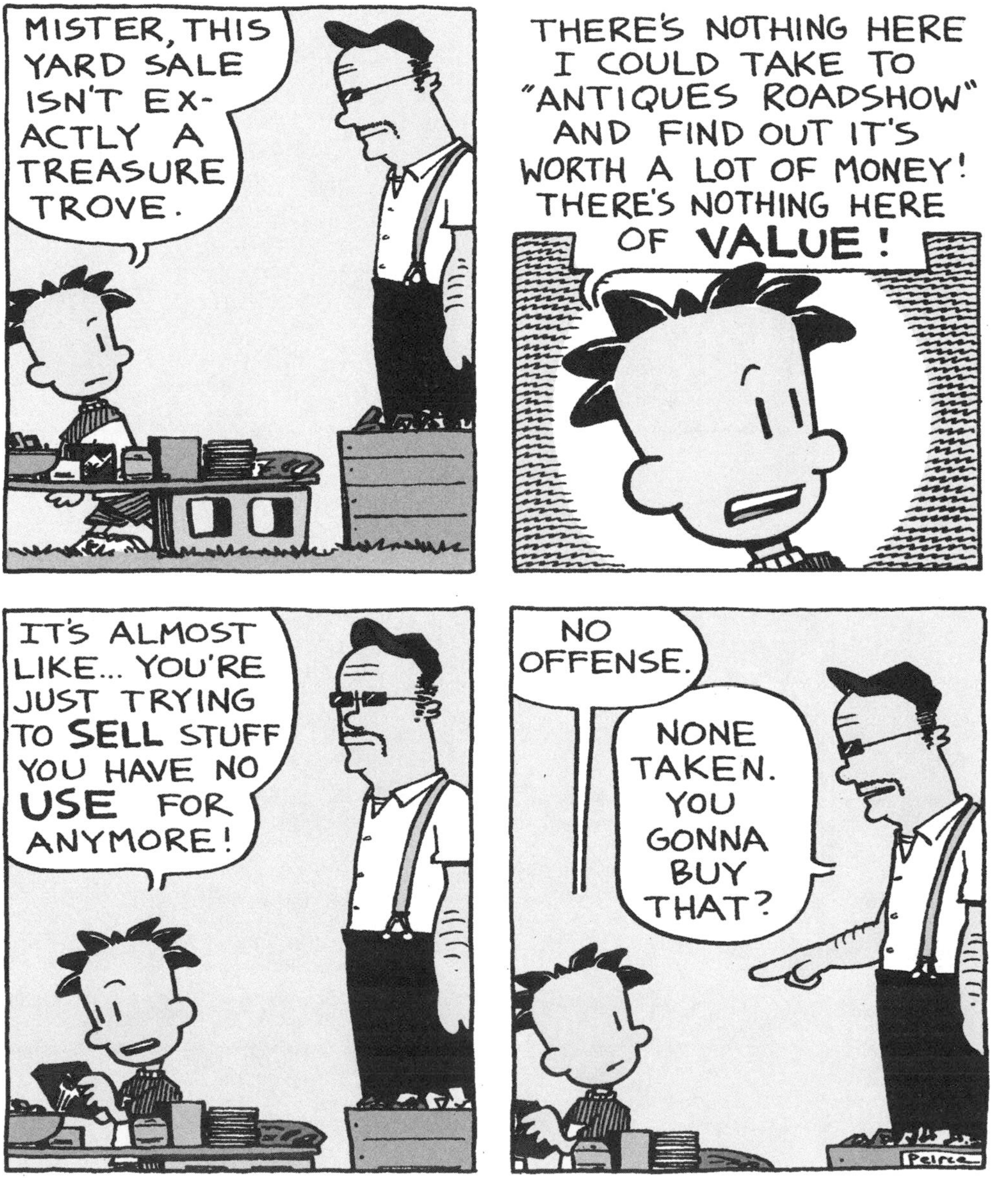

MISTER, THIS YARD SALE ISN'T EX-ACTLY A TREASURE TROVE.
THERE'S NOTHING HERE I COULD TAKE TO "ANTIQUES ROADSHOW" AND FIND OUT IT'S WORTH A LOT OF MONEY! THERE'S NOTHING HERE OF VALUE!
IT'S ALMOST LIKE... YOU'RE JUST TRYING TO SELL STUFF YOU HAVE NO USE FOR ANYMORE!
NO OFFENSE.
NONE TAKEN. YOU GONNA BUY THAT?
Peirce

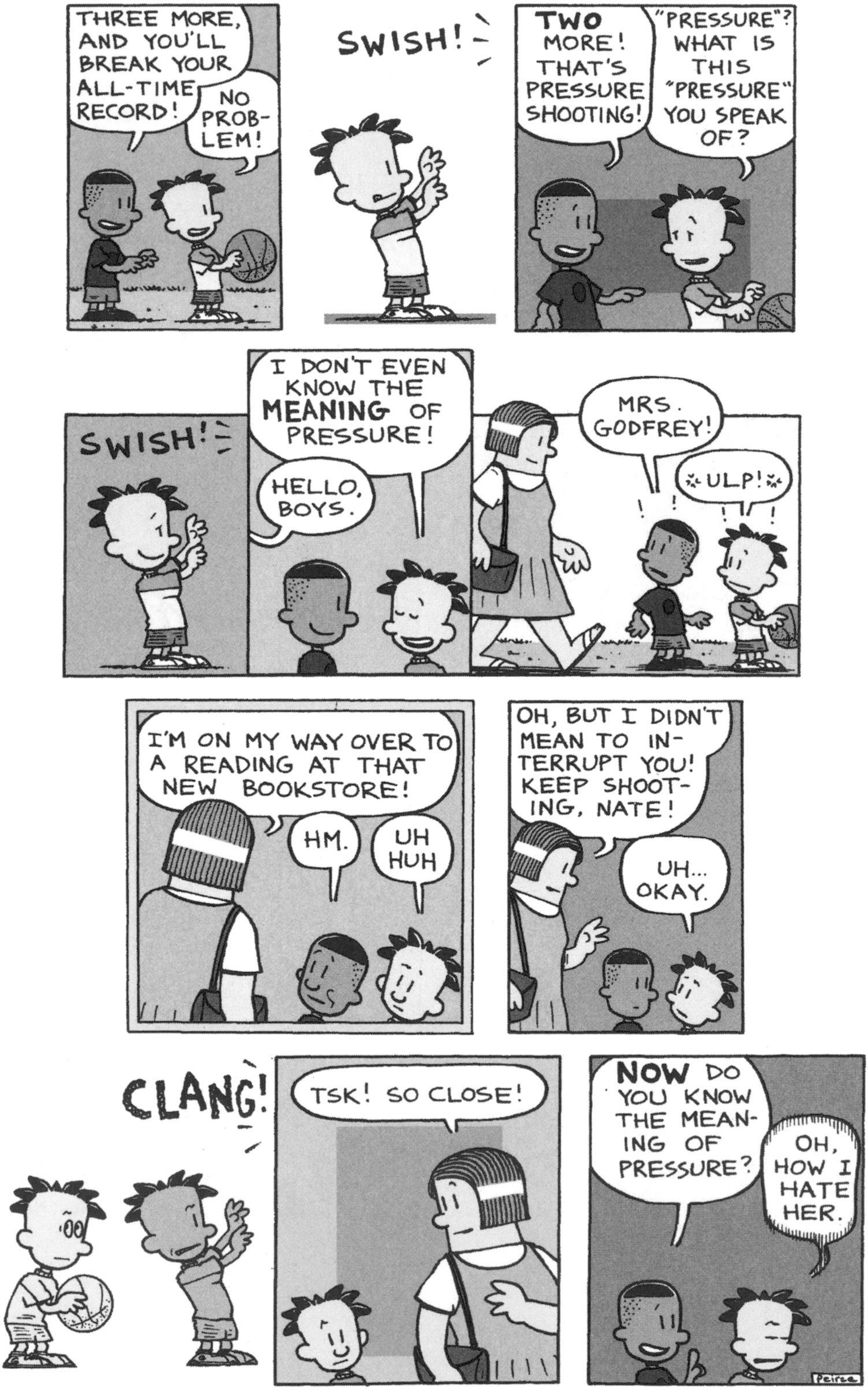
THREE MORE, AND YOU'LL BREAK YOUR ALL-TIME RECORD!
NO PROB-LEM!
SWISH!
TWO MORE! THAT'S PRESSURE SHOOTING!
"PRESSURE"? WHAT IS THIS "PRESSURE" YOU SPEAK OF?
SWISH!
I DON'T EVEN KNOW THE MEANING OF PRESSURE!
HELLO, BOYS.
MRS. GODFREY!
ULP!
I'M ON MY WAY OVER TO A READING AT THAT NEW BOOKSTORE!
HM.
UH HUH
OH, BUT I DIDN'T MEAN TO IN-TERRUPT YOU! KEEP SHOOT-ING, NATE!
UH... OKAY.
CLANG!
TSK! SO CLOSE!
NOW DO YOU KNOW THE MEAN-ING OF PRESSURE?
OH, HOW I HATE HER.
Peirce

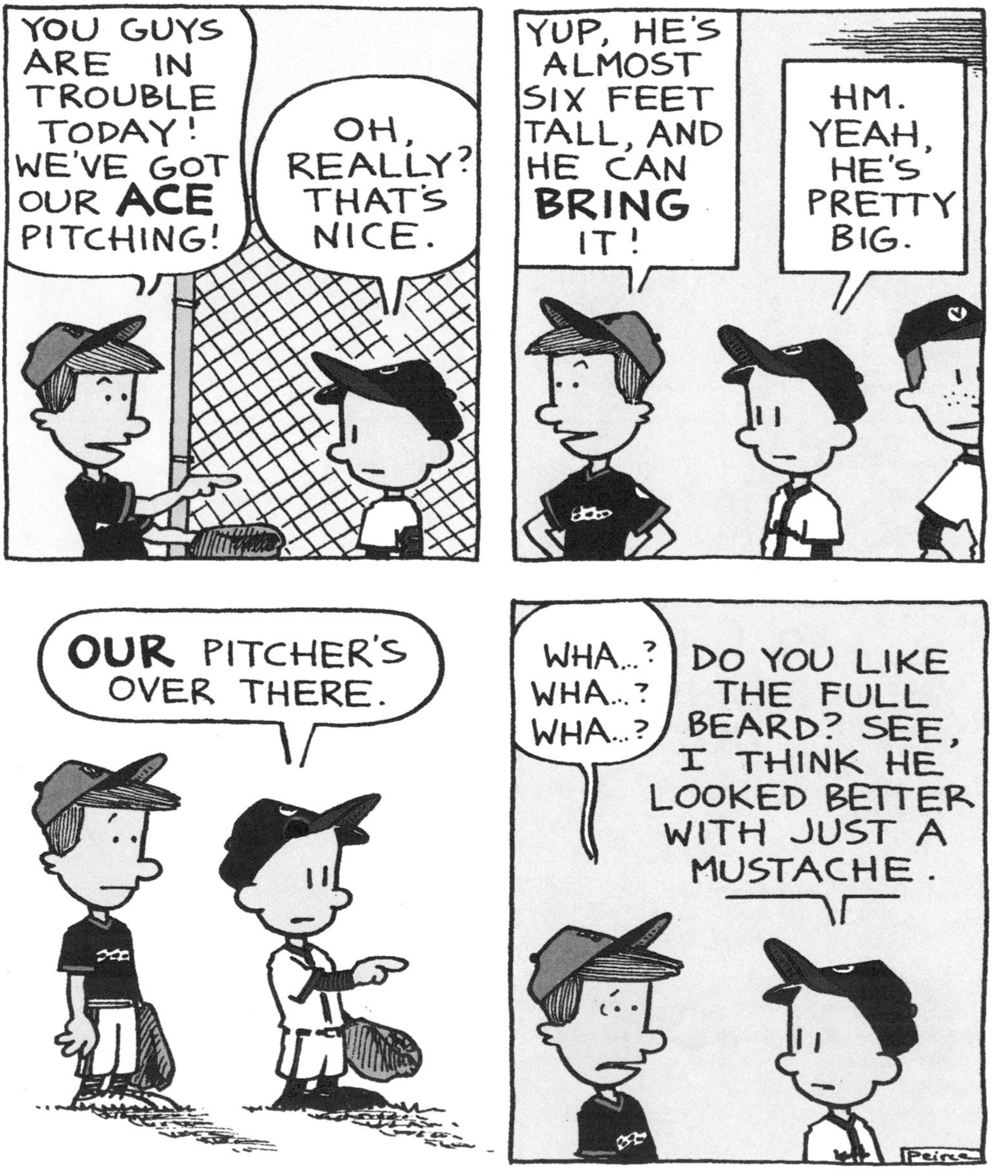
YOU GUYS ARE IN TROUBLE TODAY! WE'VE GOT OUR **ACE** PITCHING!
OH, REALLY? THAT'S NICE.
YUP, HE'S ALMOST SIX FEET TALL, AND HE CAN **BRING** IT!
HM. YEAH, HE'S PRETTY BIG.
OUR PITCHER'S OVER THERE.
WHA...? WHA...? WHA...?
DO YOU LIKE THE FULL BEARD? SEE, I THINK HE LOOKED BETTER WITH JUST A MUSTACHE.
Peirce

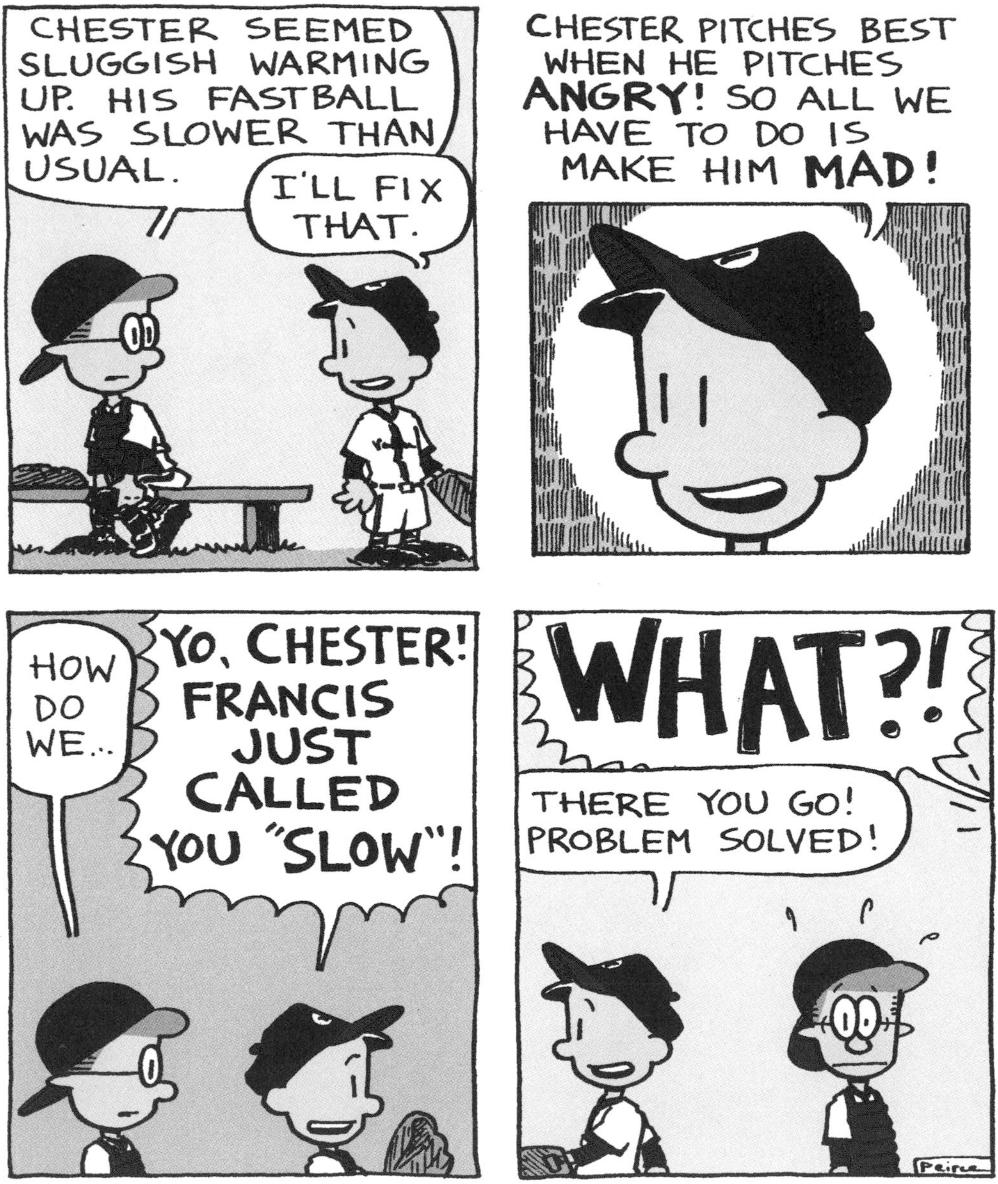
CHESTER SEEMED SLUGGISH WARMING UP. HIS FASTBALL WAS SLOWER THAN USUAL.
I'LL FIX THAT.
CHESTER PITCHES BEST WHEN HE PITCHES ANGRY! SO ALL WE HAVE TO DO IS MAKE HIM MAD!
HOW DO WE...
YO, CHESTER! FRANCIS JUST CALLED YOU "SLOW"!
WHAT?!
THERE YOU GO! PROBLEM SOLVED!
Peirce

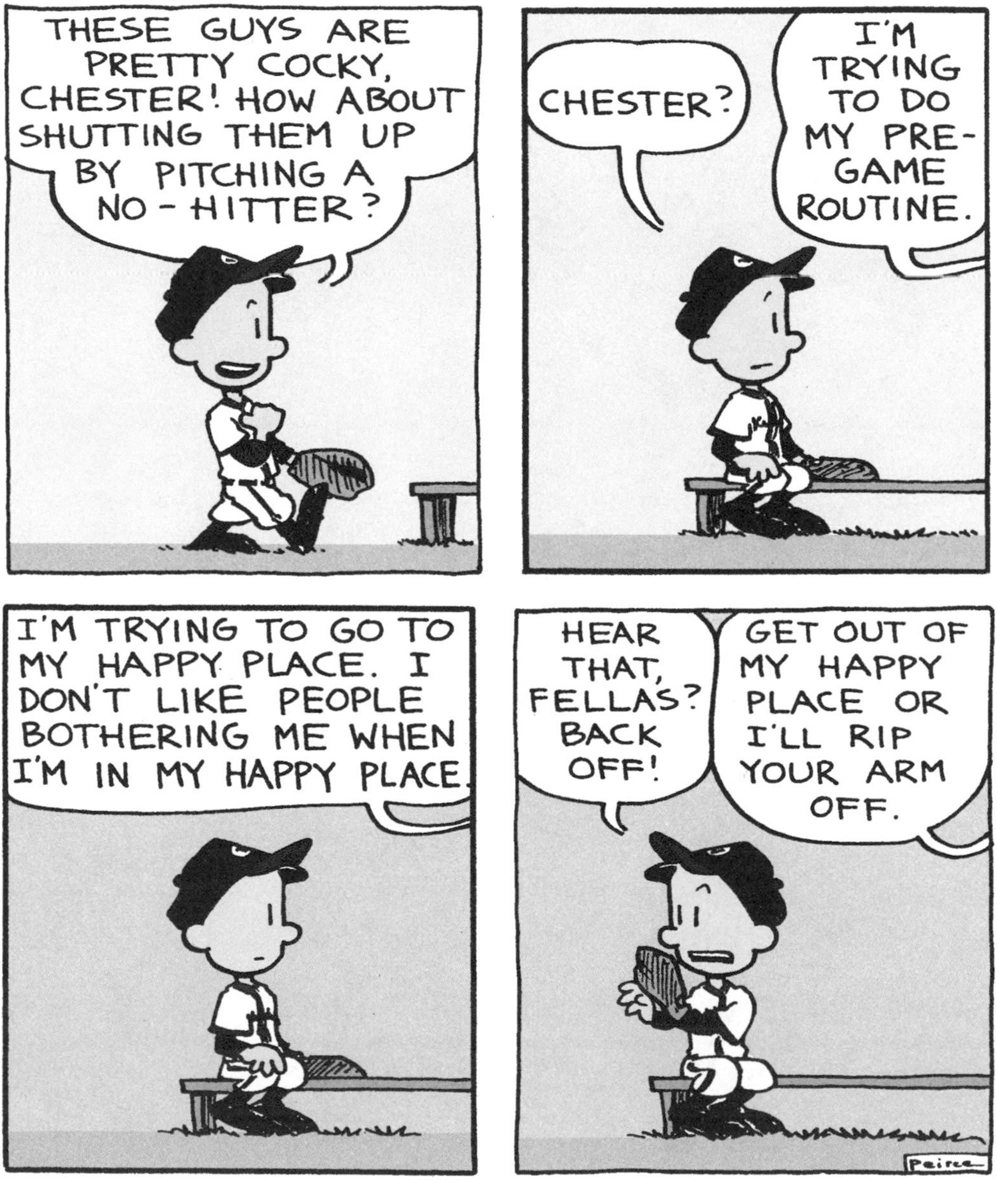
THESE GUYS ARE PRETTY COCKY, CHESTER! HOW ABOUT SHUTTING THEM UP BY PITCHING A NO-HITTER?
CHESTER?
I'M TRYING TO DO MY PRE-GAME ROUTINE.
I'M TRYING TO GO TO MY HAPPY PLACE. I DON'T LIKE PEOPLE BOTHERING ME WHEN I'M IN MY HAPPY PLACE.
HEAR THAT, FELLAS? BACK OFF!
GET OUT OF MY HAPPY PLACE OR I'LL RIP YOUR ARM OFF.
Peirce

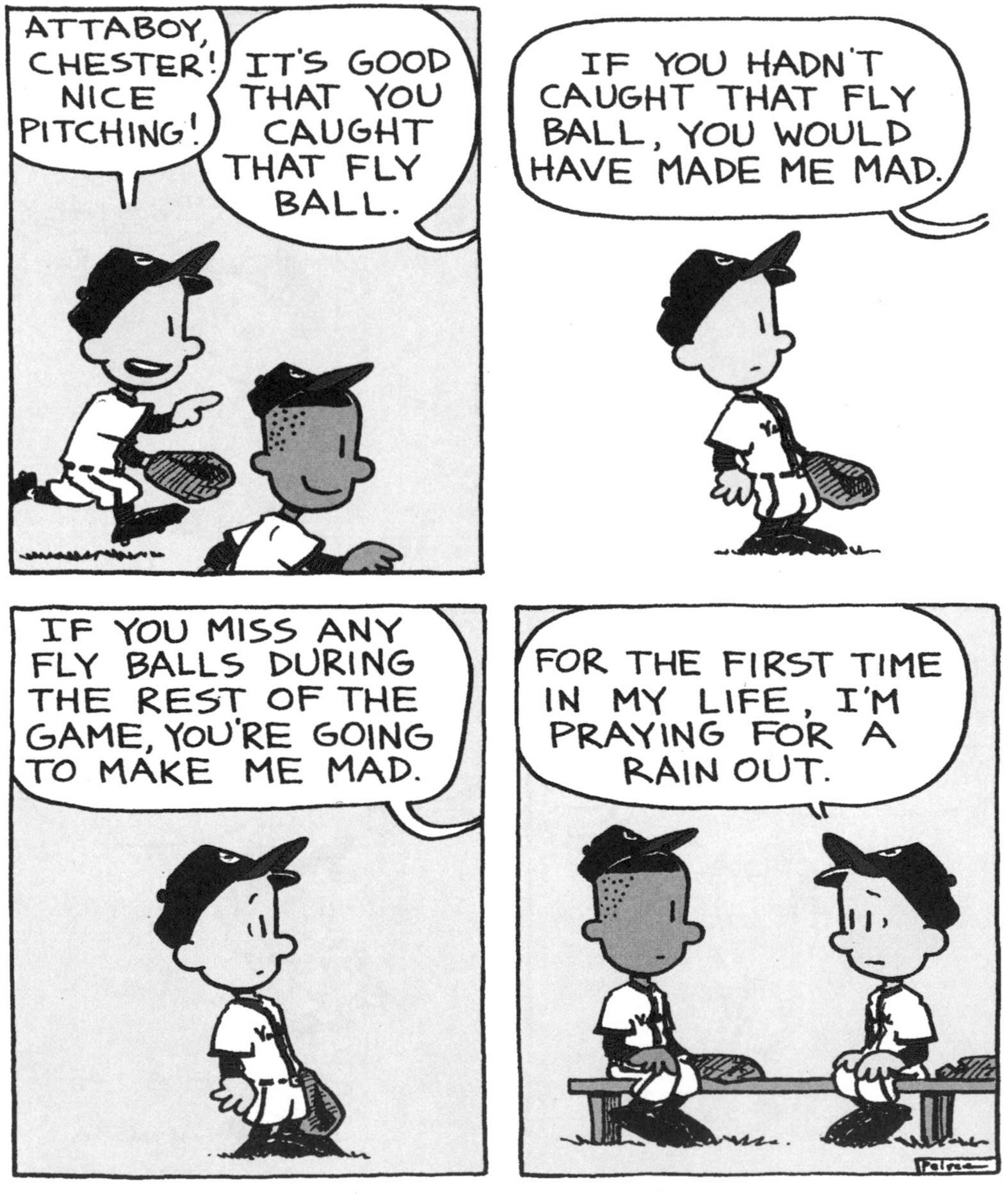
ATTABOY, CHESTER! NICE PITCHING!
IT'S GOOD THAT YOU CAUGHT THAT FLY BALL.
IF YOU HADN'T CAUGHT THAT FLY BALL, YOU WOULD HAVE MADE ME MAD.
IF YOU MISS ANY FLY BALLS DURING THE REST OF THE GAME, YOU'RE GOING TO MAKE ME MAD.
FOR THE FIRST TIME IN MY LIFE, I'M PRAYING FOR A RAIN OUT.

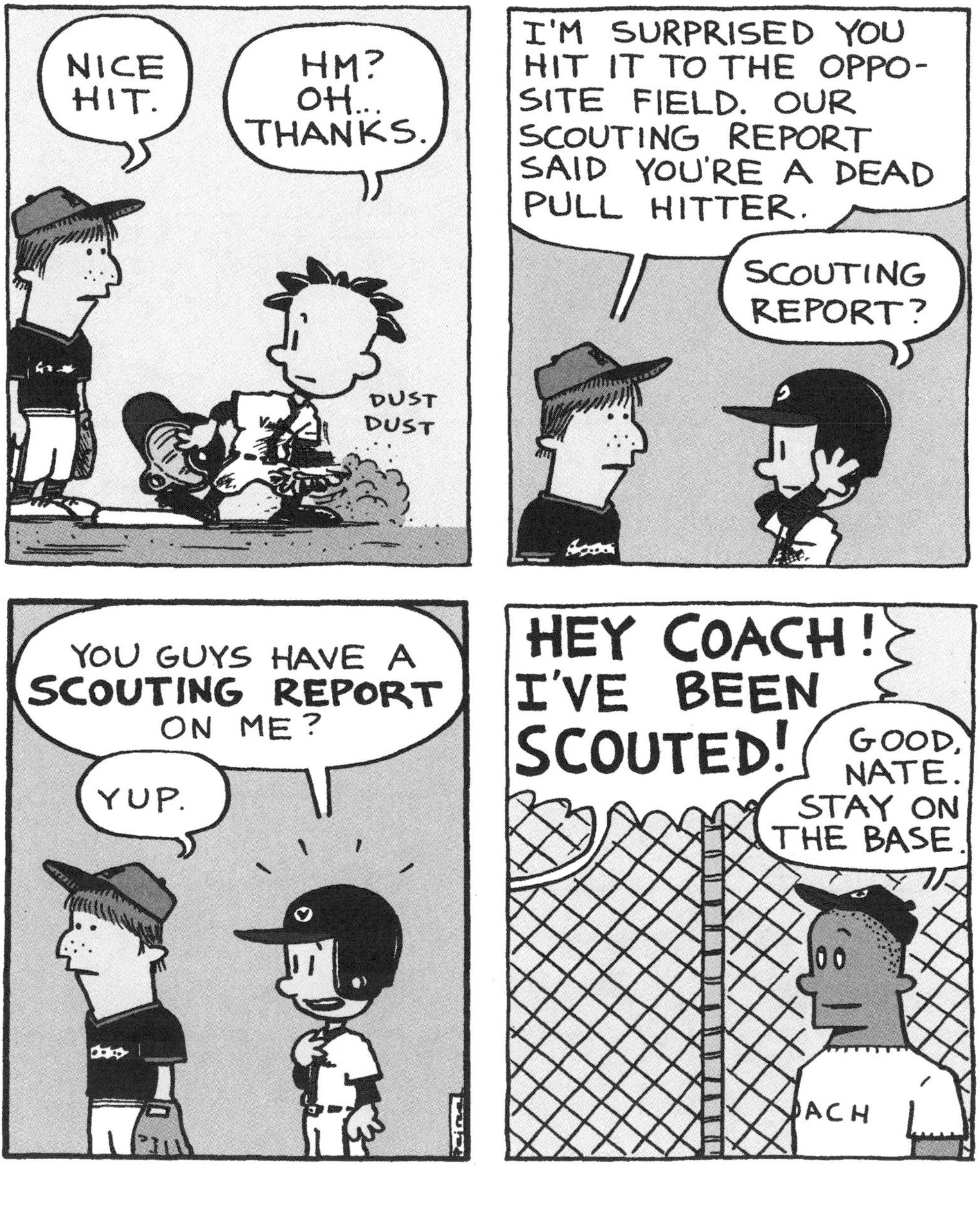
NICE HIT.
HM? OH... THANKS.
DUST DUST
I'M SURPRISED YOU HIT IT TO THE OPPO-SITE FIELD. OUR SCOUTING REPORT SAID YOU'RE A DEAD PULL HITTER.
SCOUTING REPORT?
YOU GUYS HAVE A SCOUTING REPORT ON ME?
YUP.
HEY COACH! I'VE BEEN SCOUTED!
GOOD, NATE. STAY ON THE BASE.
ACH

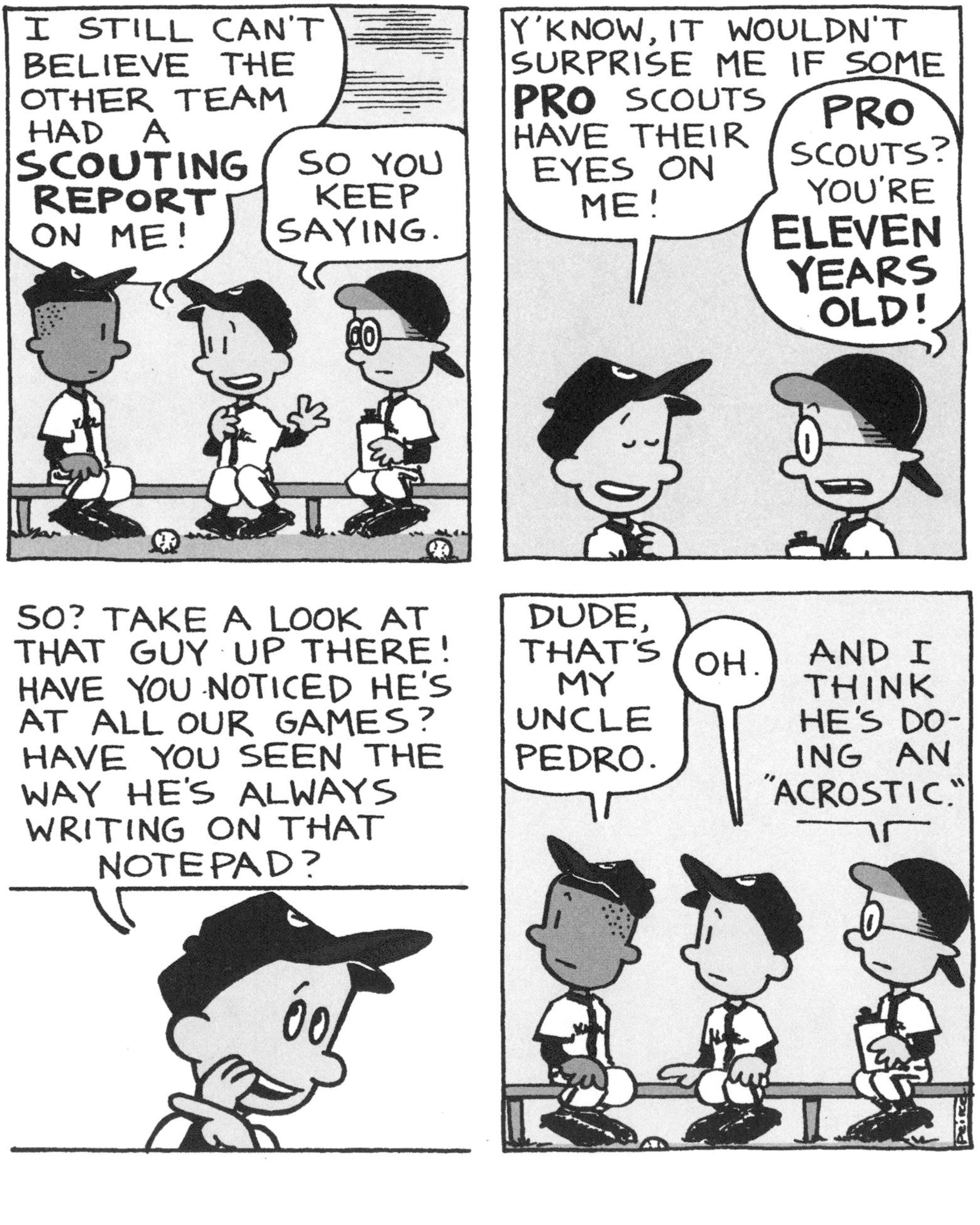

I STILL CAN'T BELIEVE THE OTHER TEAM HAD A **SCOUTING REPORT** ON ME!
SO YOU KEEP SAYING.
Y'KNOW, IT WOULDN'T SURPRISE ME IF SOME **PRO** SCOUTS HAVE THEIR EYES ON ME!
PRO SCOUTS? YOU'RE **ELEVEN YEARS OLD!**
SO? TAKE A LOOK AT THAT GUY UP THERE! HAVE YOU NOTICED HE'S AT ALL OUR GAMES? HAVE YOU SEEN THE WAY HE'S ALWAYS WRITING ON THAT NOTEPAD?
DUDE, THAT'S MY UNCLE PEDRO.
OH.
AND I THINK HE'S DOING AN "ACROSTIC."

FRANCIS! DO YOU BELIEVE IN OMENS?

I GUESS SO.

WELL, IF I MAKE THIS SHOT, IT'S AN OMEN THAT I'M GOING TO BE RICH!

IF I MAKE IT WITHOUT HITTING THE BACKBOARD, IT MEANS I'M GOING TO BE FAMOUS!

...AND IF I MAKE IT WITHOUT HITTING THE BACKBOARD **OR** THE RIM, IT MEANS I'M GOING TO MARRY A SUPER-MODEL!

FLing!

CLANG!

CRASH!

MYOWR!

!

Screeee...

THUMP!

WHAT IF YOU MISS, AND THEN THE BALL BREAKS A WINDOW, HITS A CAT, ROLLS INTO THE STREET, AND GETS RUN OVER BY A DUMP TRUCK?

THEN IT'S A PRACTICE SHOT.

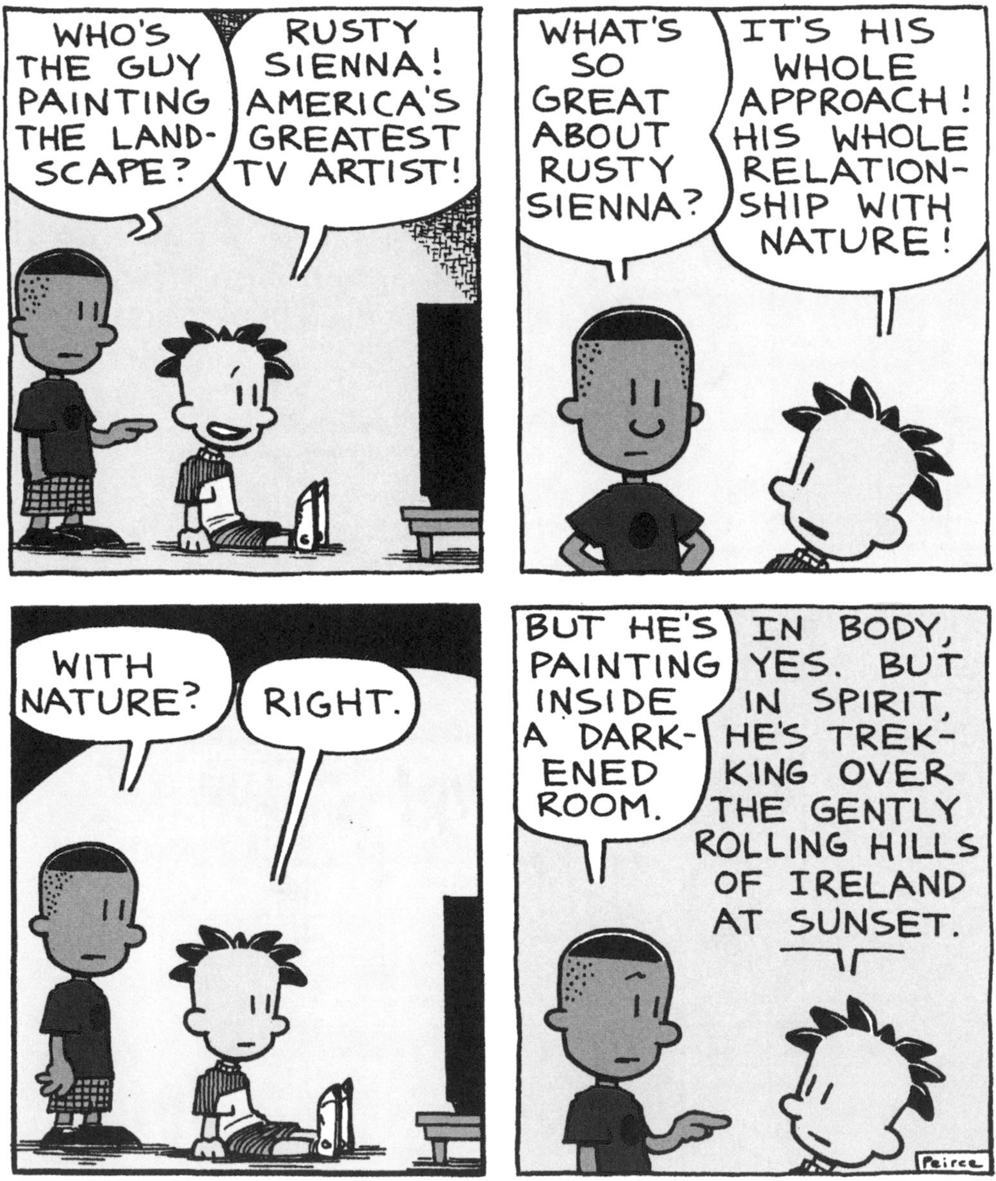
WHO'S THE GUY PAINTING THE LAND-SCAPE?
RUSTY SIENNA! AMERICA'S GREATEST TV ARTIST!
WHAT'S SO GREAT ABOUT RUSTY SIENNA?
IT'S HIS WHOLE APPROACH! HIS WHOLE RELATION-SHIP WITH NATURE!
WITH NATURE?
RIGHT.
BUT HE'S PAINTING INSIDE A DARK-ENED ROOM.
IN BODY, YES. BUT IN SPIRIT, HE'S TREK-KING OVER THE GENTLY ROLLING HILLS OF IRELAND AT SUNSET.
Peirce

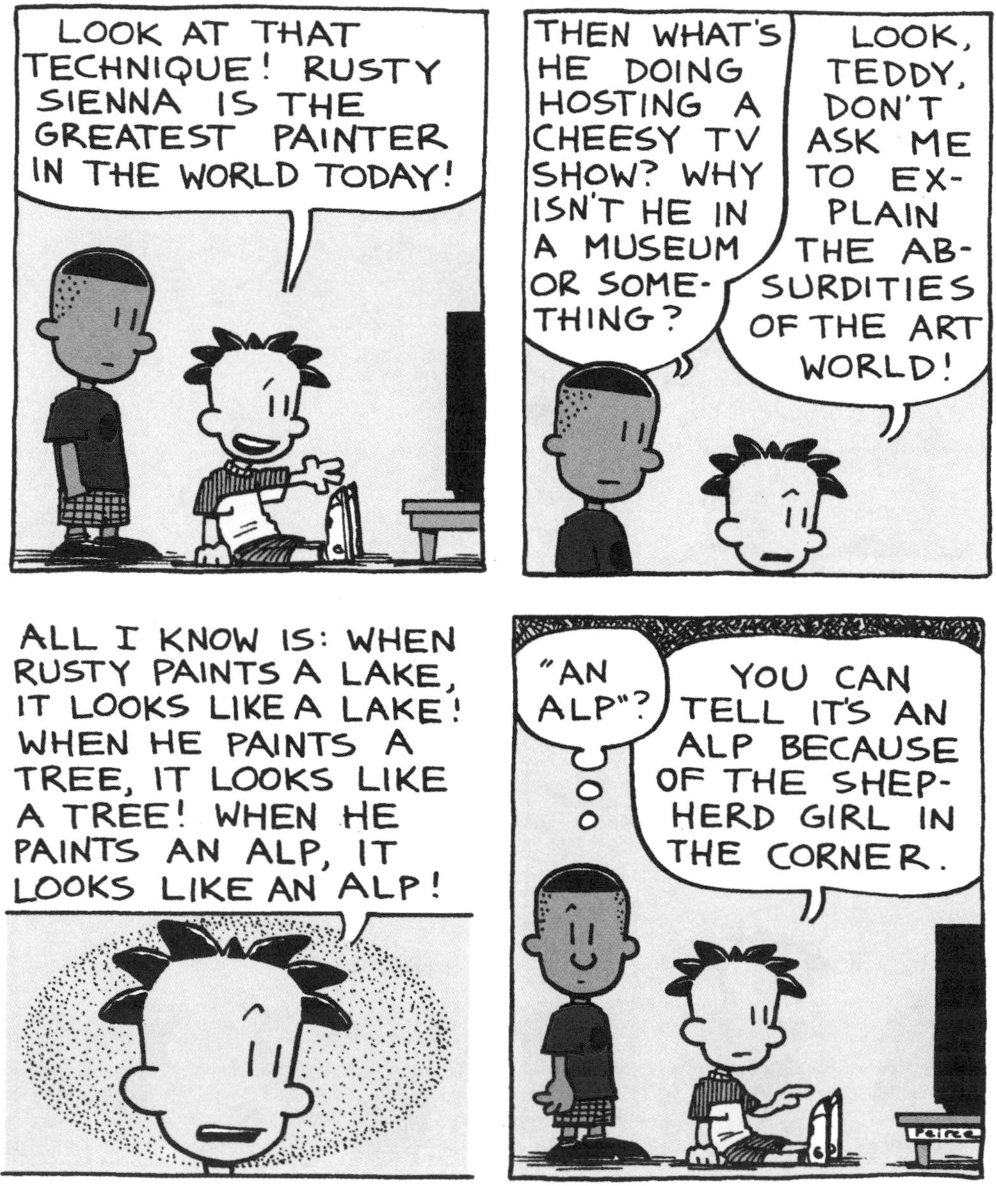
LOOK AT THAT TECHNIQUE! RUSTY SIENNA IS THE GREATEST PAINTER IN THE WORLD TODAY!
THEN WHAT'S HE DOING HOSTING A CHEESY TV SHOW? WHY ISN'T HE IN A MUSEUM OR SOMETHING?
LOOK, TEDDY, DON'T ASK ME TO EXPLAIN THE ABSURDITIES OF THE ART WORLD!
ALL I KNOW IS: WHEN RUSTY PAINTS A LAKE, IT LOOKS LIKE A LAKE! WHEN HE PAINTS A TREE, IT LOOKS LIKE A TREE! WHEN HE PAINTS AN ALP, IT LOOKS LIKE AN ALP!
"AN ALP"?
YOU CAN TELL IT'S AN ALP BECAUSE OF THE SHEPHERD GIRL IN THE CORNER.
Peirce

C'MON, NATE, LET'S SHOOT SOME HOOPS.
NOT YET. RUSTY HASN'T FINISHED THE PAINTING YET.
THE SHOW ENDS IN TWO MINUTES, DUDE. HE LOOKS DONE TO ME.
NO, NO... THE PART THAT SHOWS WHAT A GENIUS HE IS COMES AT THE END.
...AND HEY, KNOW WHAT I'M GOING TO DO NEXT, JUST FOR FUN? I'M GOING TO ADD A COUPLE OF DUCKS!
SEE?
I KNOW, I KNOW! CALL ME ZANY!
Peirce

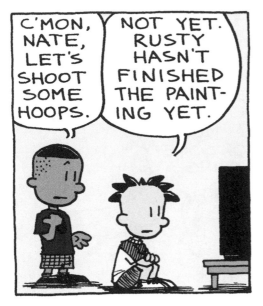

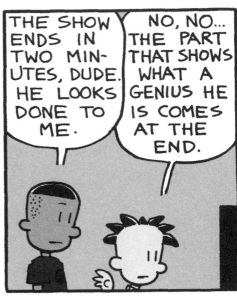

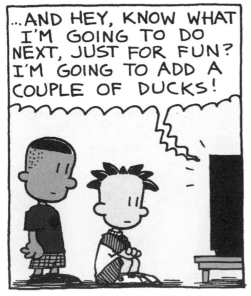

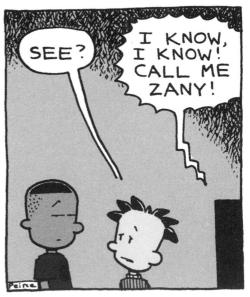

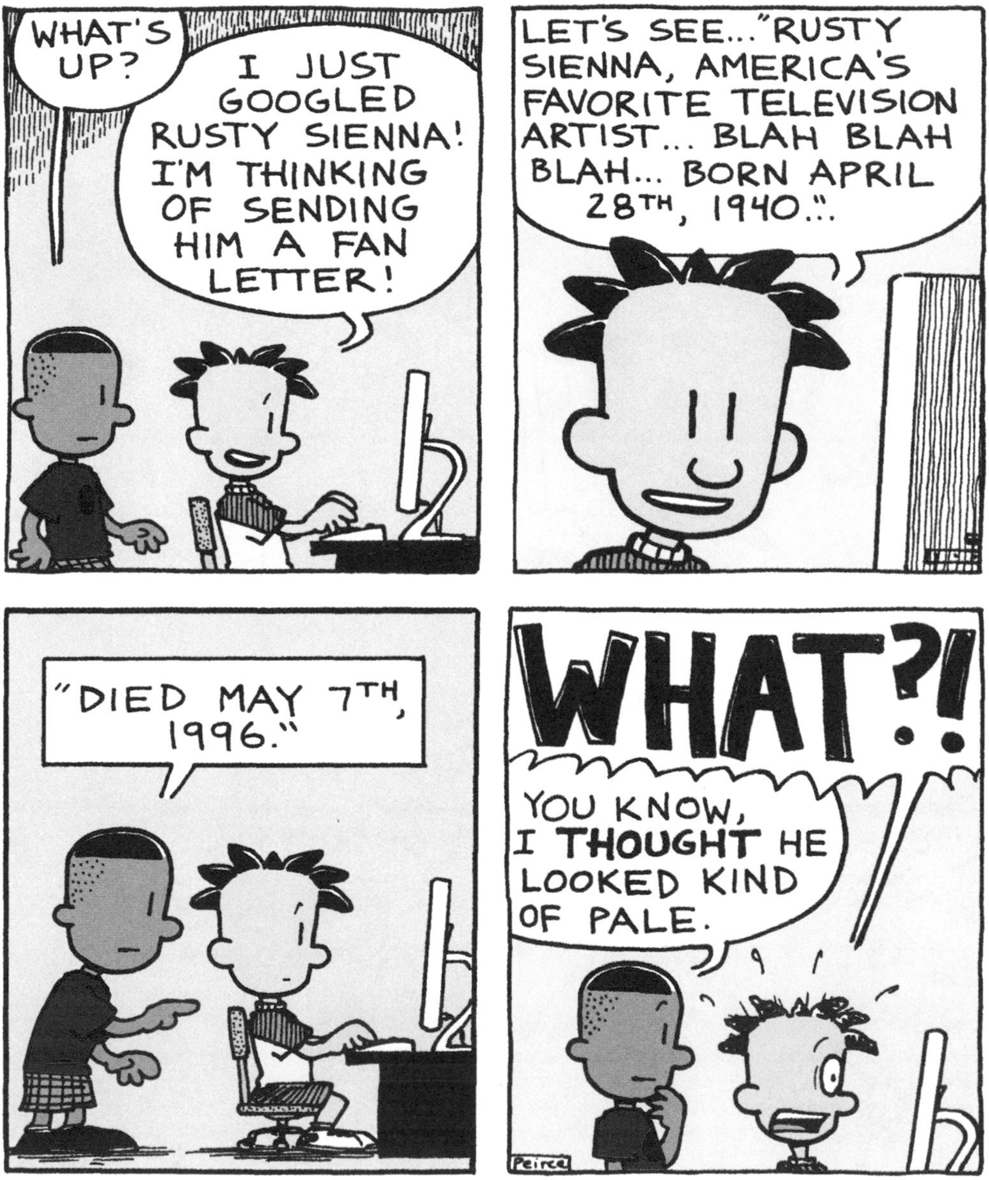
WHAT'S UP?
I JUST GOOGLED RUSTY SIENNA! I'M THINKING OF SENDING HIM A FAN LETTER!
LET'S SEE..."RUSTY SIENNA, AMERICA'S FAVORITE TELEVISION ARTIST... BLAH BLAH BLAH... BORN APRIL 28TH, 1940..."
"DIED MAY 7TH, 1996."
WHAT?!
YOU KNOW, I THOUGHT HE LOOKED KIND OF PALE.
Peirce

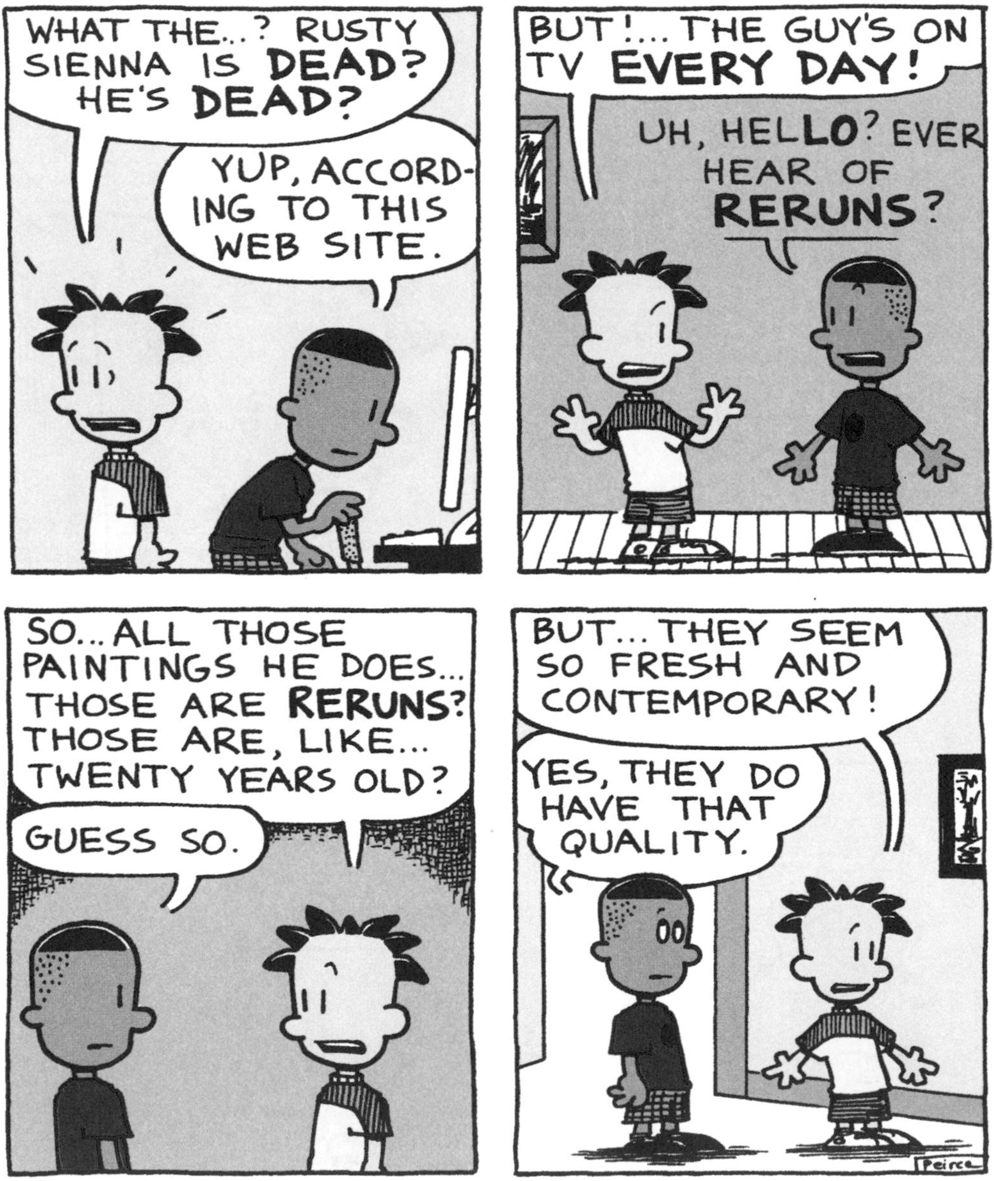

WHAT THE...? RUSTY SIENNA IS DEAD? HE'S DEAD?
YUP, ACCORDING TO THIS WEB SITE.
BUT!... THE GUY'S ON TV EVERY DAY!
UH, HELLO? EVER HEAR OF RERUNS?
SO... ALL THOSE PAINTINGS HE DOES... THOSE ARE RERUNS? THOSE ARE, LIKE... TWENTY YEARS OLD?
GUESS SO.
BUT... THEY SEEM SO FRESH AND CONTEMPORARY!
YES, THEY DO HAVE THAT QUALITY.
Peirce

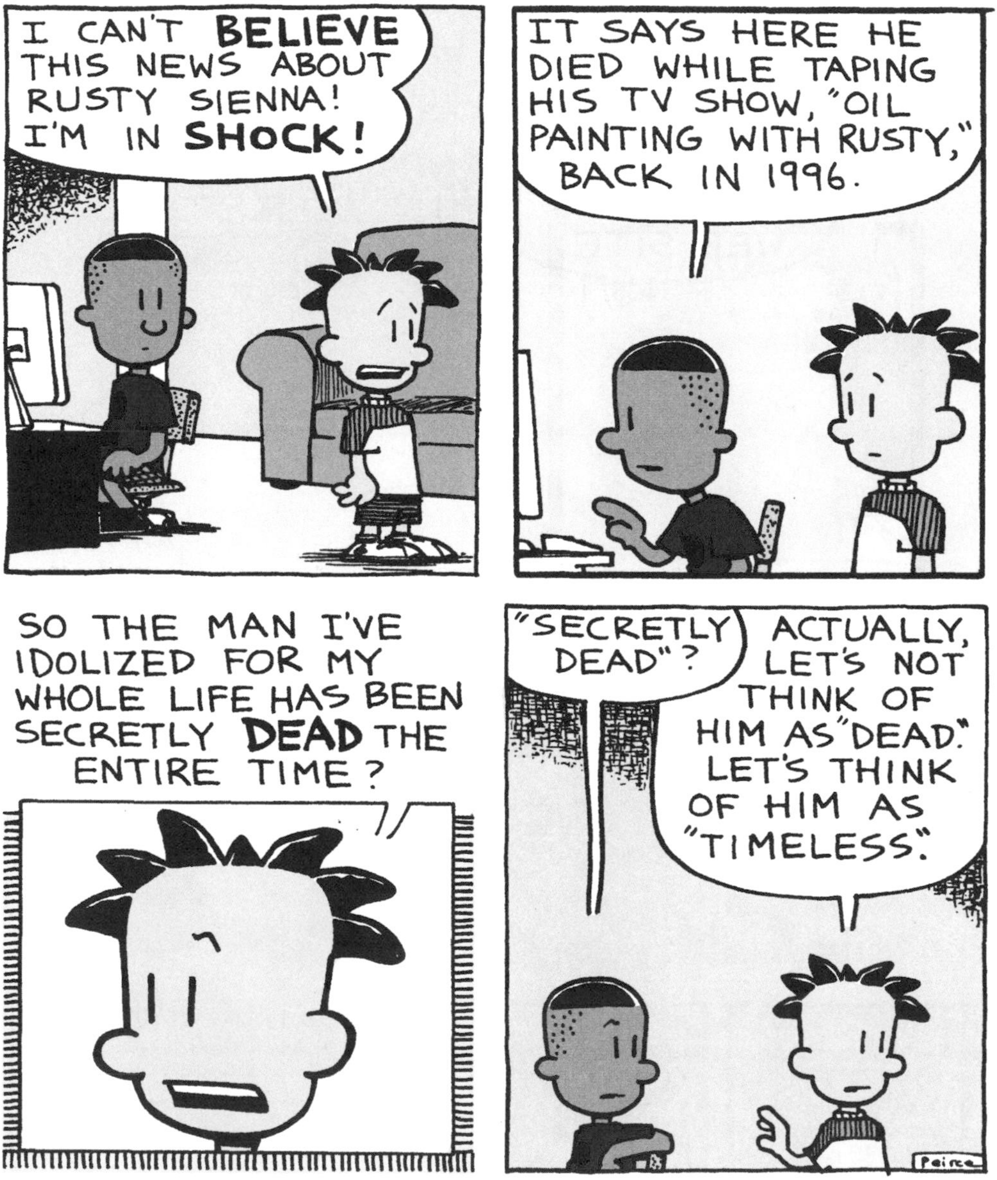

I CAN'T **BELIEVE** THIS NEWS ABOUT RUSTY SIENNA! I'M IN **SHOCK**!
IT SAYS HERE HE DIED WHILE TAPING HIS TV SHOW, "OIL PAINTING WITH RUSTY," BACK IN 1996.
SO THE MAN I'VE IDOLIZED FOR MY WHOLE LIFE HAS BEEN SECRETLY **DEAD** THE ENTIRE TIME?
"SECRETLY DEAD"?
ACTUALLY, LET'S NOT THINK OF HIM AS "DEAD." LET'S THINK OF HIM AS "TIMELESS."
Peirce

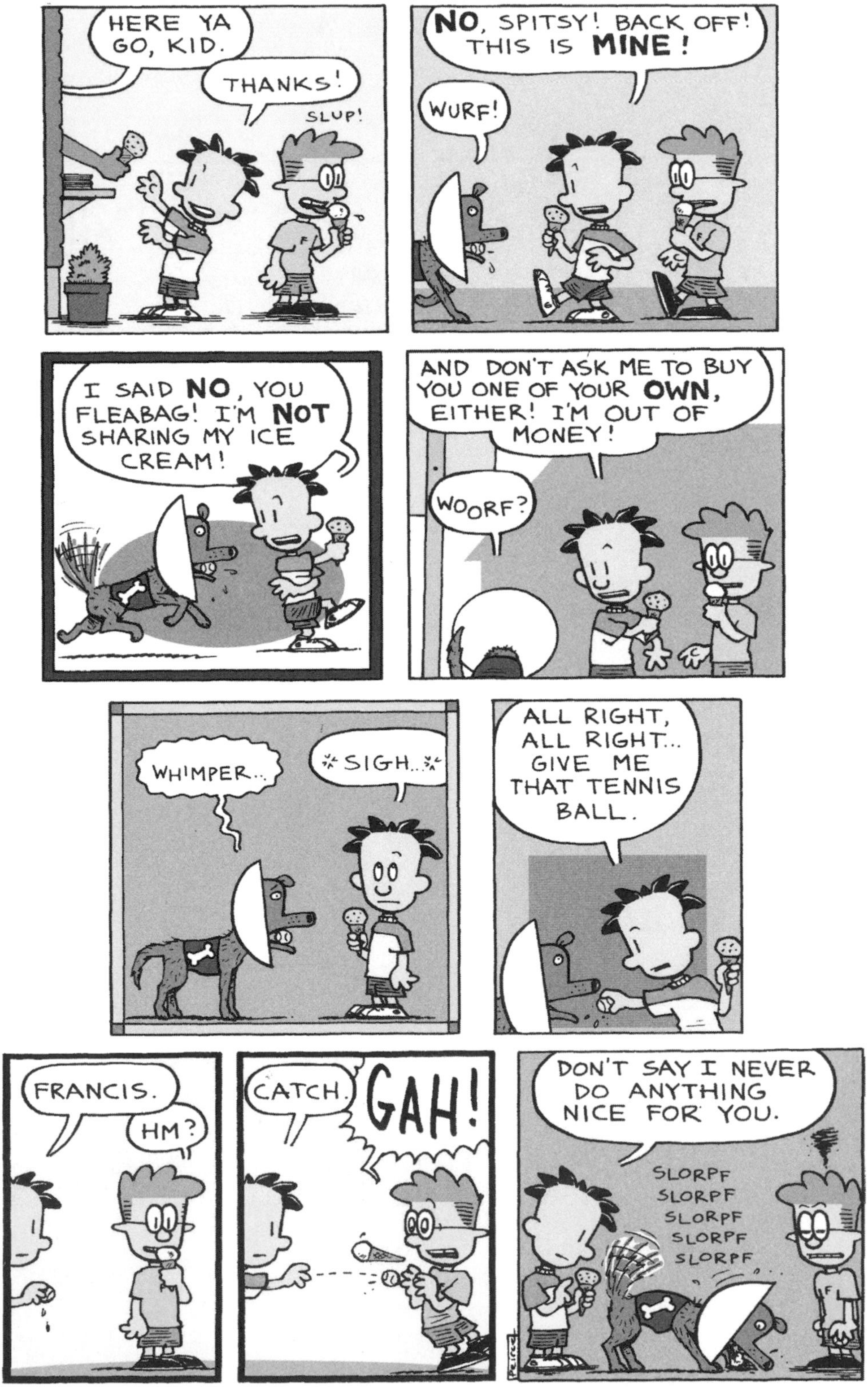
HERE YA GO, KID.
THANKS!
SLUP!
NO, SPITSY! BACK OFF! THIS IS MINE!
WURF!
I SAID NO, YOU FLEABAG! I'M NOT SHARING MY ICE CREAM!
AND DON'T ASK ME TO BUY YOU ONE OF YOUR OWN, EITHER! I'M OUT OF MONEY!
WOORF?
WHIMPER...
SIGH...
ALL RIGHT, ALL RIGHT... GIVE ME THAT TENNIS BALL.
FRANCIS.
HM?
CATCH.
GAH!
DON'T SAY I NEVER DO ANYTHING NICE FOR YOU.
SLORPF
SLORPF
SLORPF
SLORPF
SLORPF

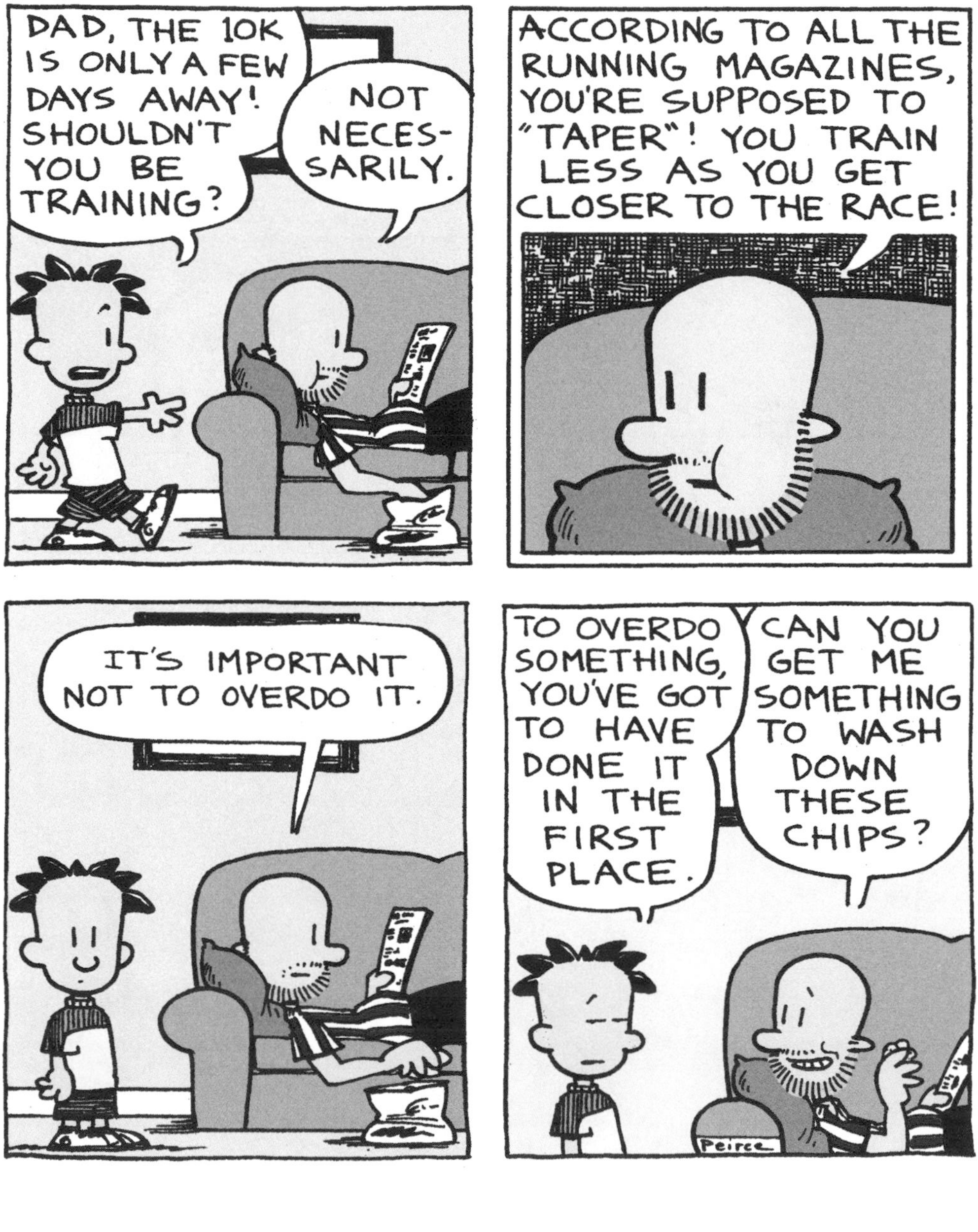
DAD, THE 10K IS ONLY A FEW DAYS AWAY! SHOULDN'T YOU BE TRAINING?
NOT NECES-SARILY.
ACCORDING TO ALL THE RUNNING MAGAZINES, YOU'RE SUPPOSED TO "TAPER"! YOU TRAIN LESS AS YOU GET CLOSER TO THE RACE!
IT'S IMPORTANT NOT TO OVERDO IT.
TO OVERDO SOMETHING, YOU'VE GOT TO HAVE DONE IT IN THE FIRST PLACE.
CAN YOU GET ME SOMETHING TO WASH DOWN THESE CHIPS?
Peirce

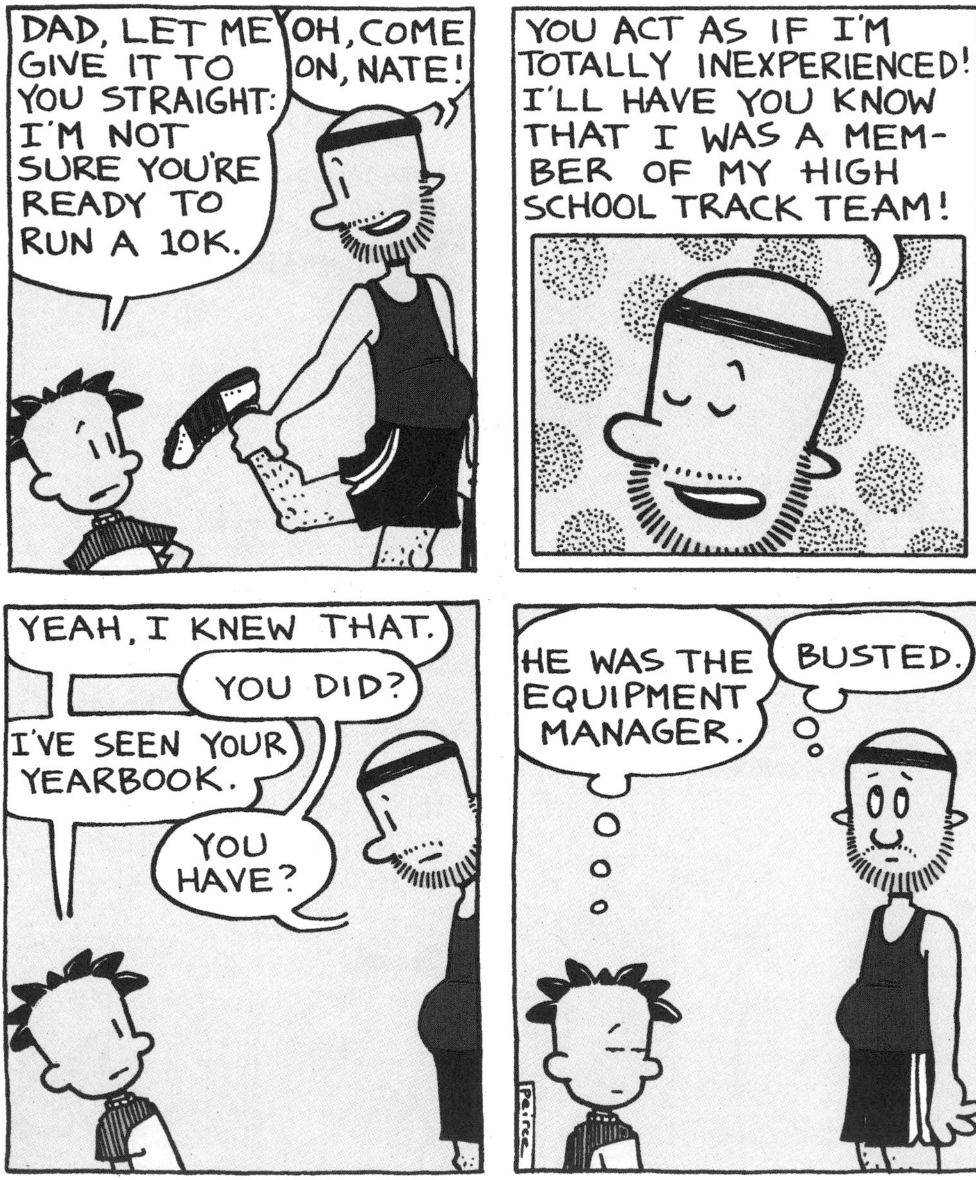
DAD, LET ME GIVE IT TO YOU STRAIGHT: I'M NOT SURE YOU'RE READY TO RUN A 10K.
OH, COME ON, NATE!
YOU ACT AS IF I'M TOTALLY INEXPERIENCED! I'LL HAVE YOU KNOW THAT I WAS A MEMBER OF MY HIGH SCHOOL TRACK TEAM!
YEAH, I KNEW THAT.
YOU DID?
I'VE SEEN YOUR YEARBOOK.
YOU HAVE?
HE WAS THE EQUIPMENT MANAGER.
BUSTED.
PEIRCE

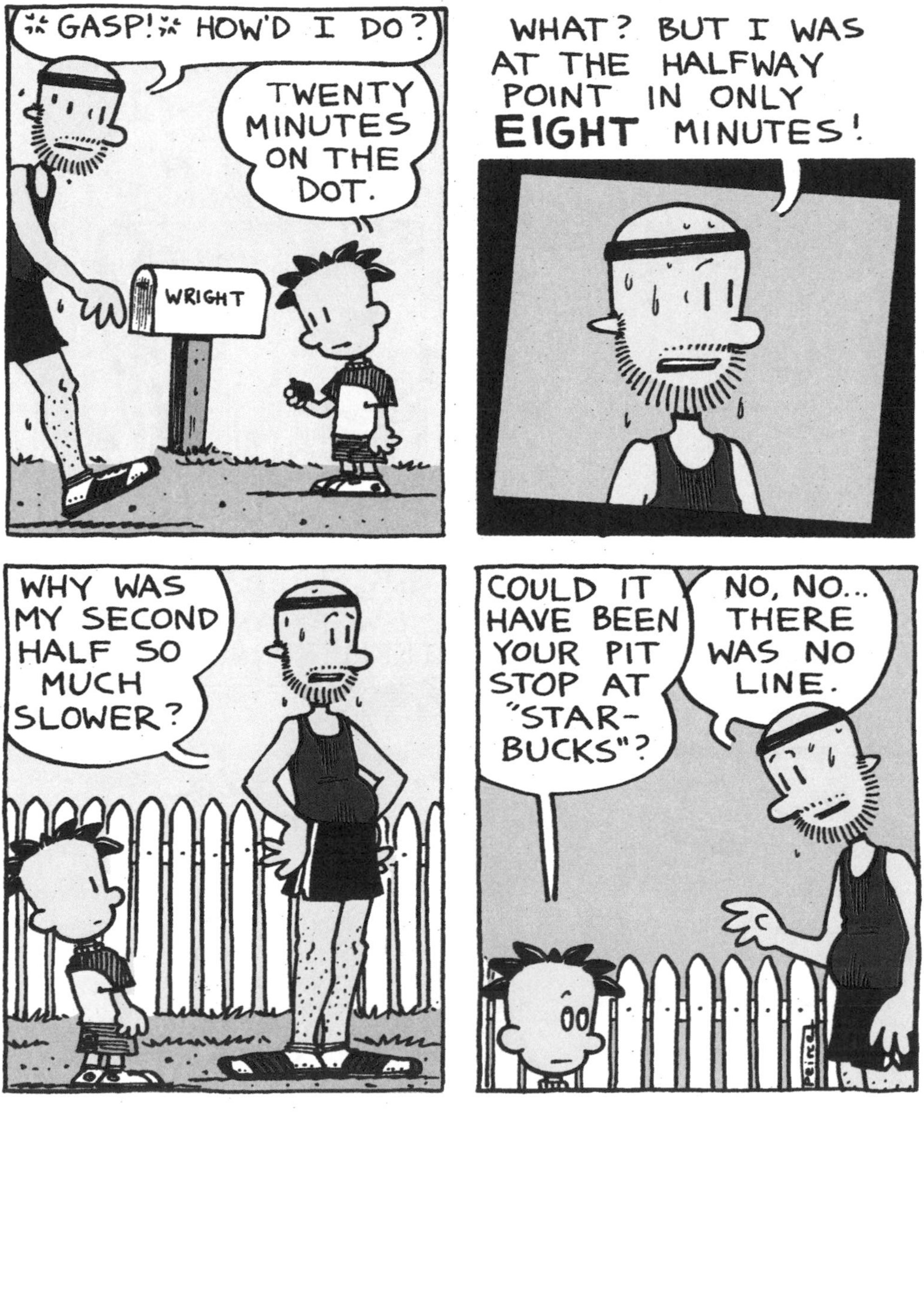
GASP! HOW'D I DO?
TWENTY MINUTES ON THE DOT.
WRIGHT
WHAT? BUT I WAS AT THE HALFWAY POINT IN ONLY **EIGHT** MINUTES!
WHY WAS MY SECOND HALF SO MUCH SLOWER?
COULD IT HAVE BEEN YOUR PIT STOP AT "STAR-BUCKS"?
NO, NO... THERE WAS NO LINE.

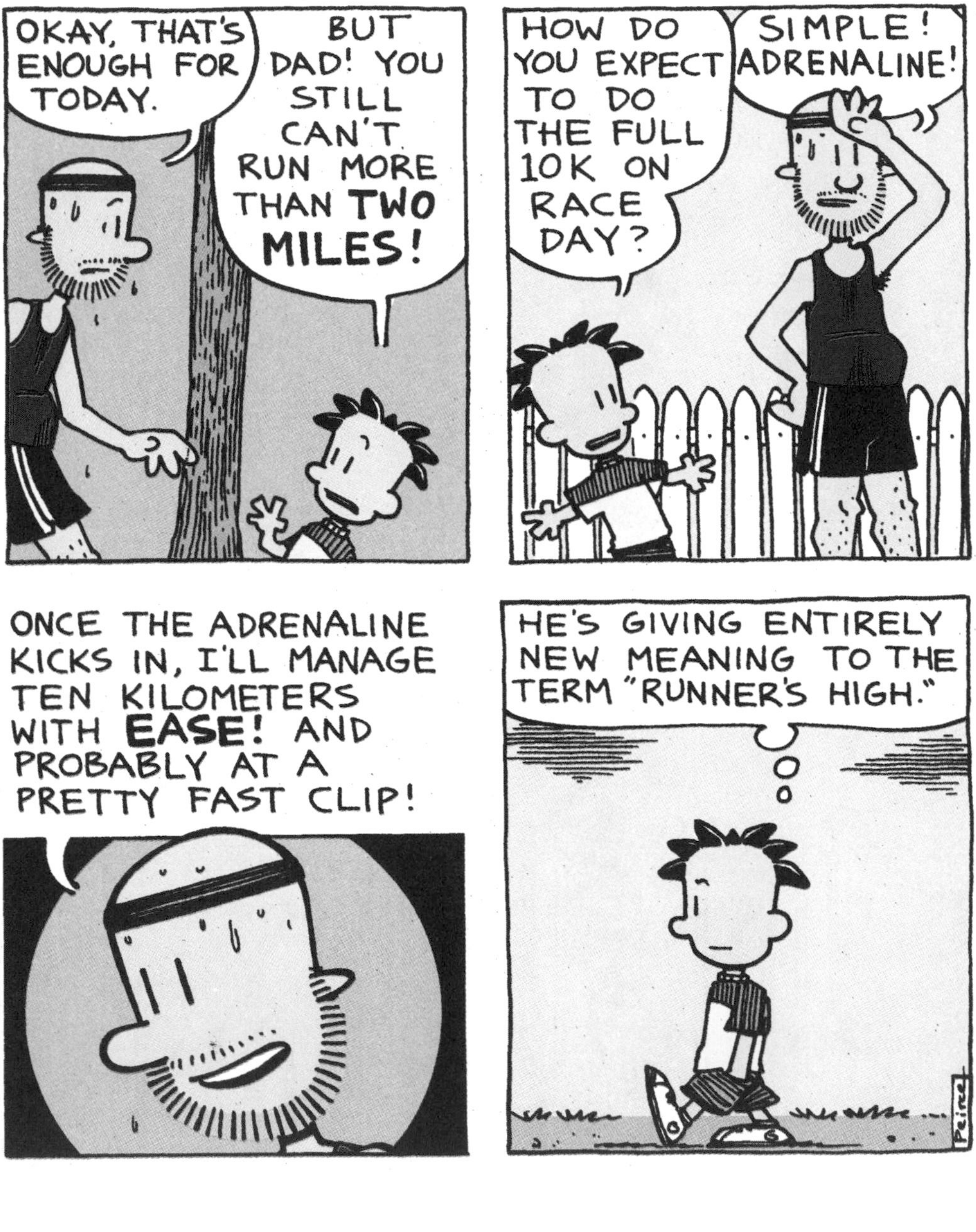
OKAY, THAT'S ENOUGH FOR TODAY.
BUT DAD! YOU STILL CAN'T RUN MORE THAN **TWO MILES!**
HOW DO YOU EXPECT TO DO THE FULL 10K ON RACE DAY?
SIMPLE! ADRENALINE!
ONCE THE ADRENALINE KICKS IN, I'LL MANAGE TEN KILOMETERS WITH **EASE!** AND PROBABLY AT A PRETTY FAST CLIP!
HE'S GIVING ENTIRELY NEW MEANING TO THE TERM "RUNNER'S HIGH."
Peirce

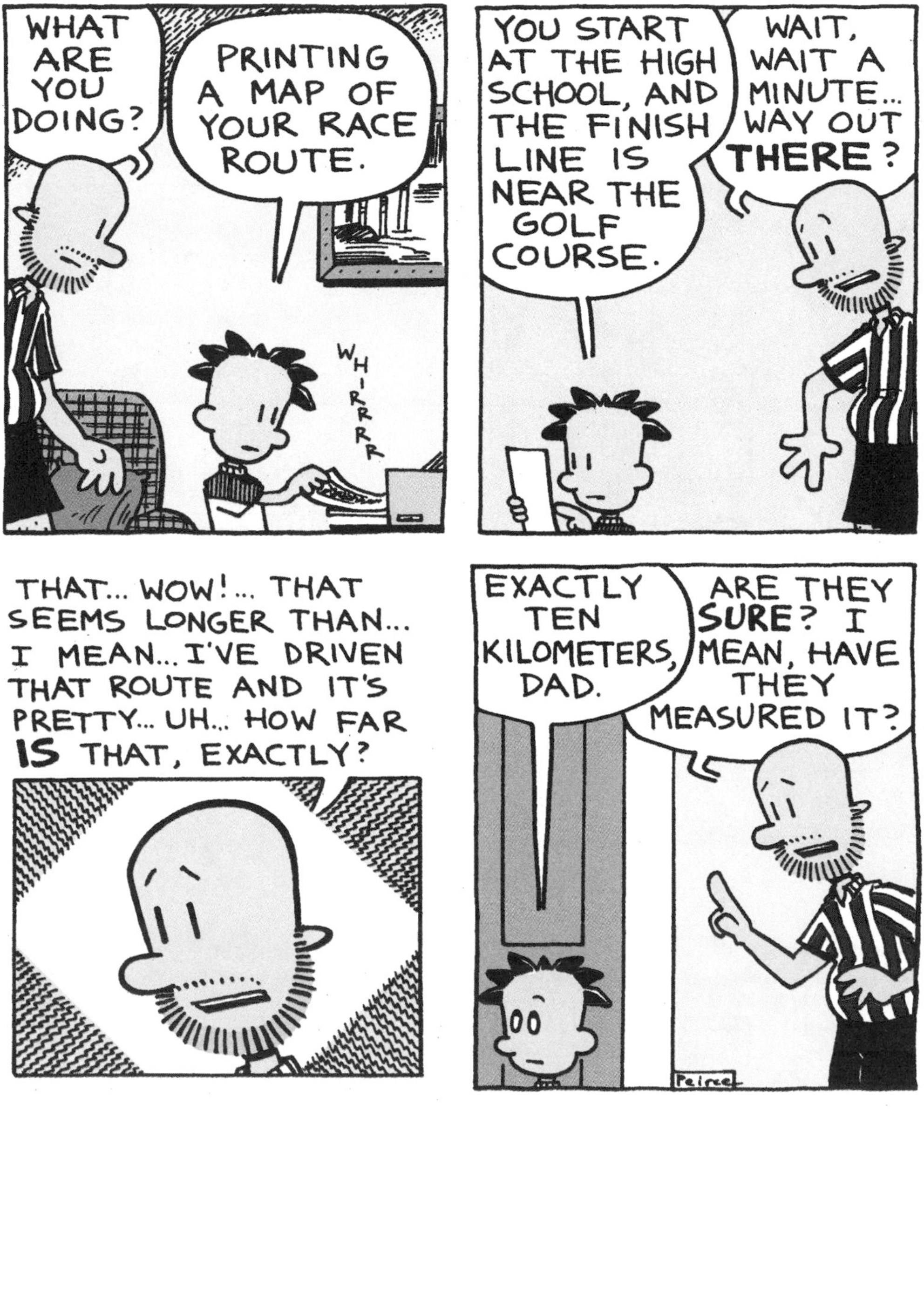
WHAT ARE YOU DOING?
PRINTING A MAP OF YOUR RACE ROUTE.
WHIRRRR
YOU START AT THE HIGH SCHOOL, AND THE FINISH LINE IS NEAR THE GOLF COURSE.
WAIT, WAIT A MINUTE... WAY OUT THERE?
THAT... WOW!... THAT SEEMS LONGER THAN... I MEAN... I'VE DRIVEN THAT ROUTE AND IT'S PRETTY... UH... HOW FAR IS THAT, EXACTLY?
EXACTLY TEN KILOMETERS, DAD.
ARE THEY SURE? I MEAN, HAVE THEY MEASURED IT?
Peirce

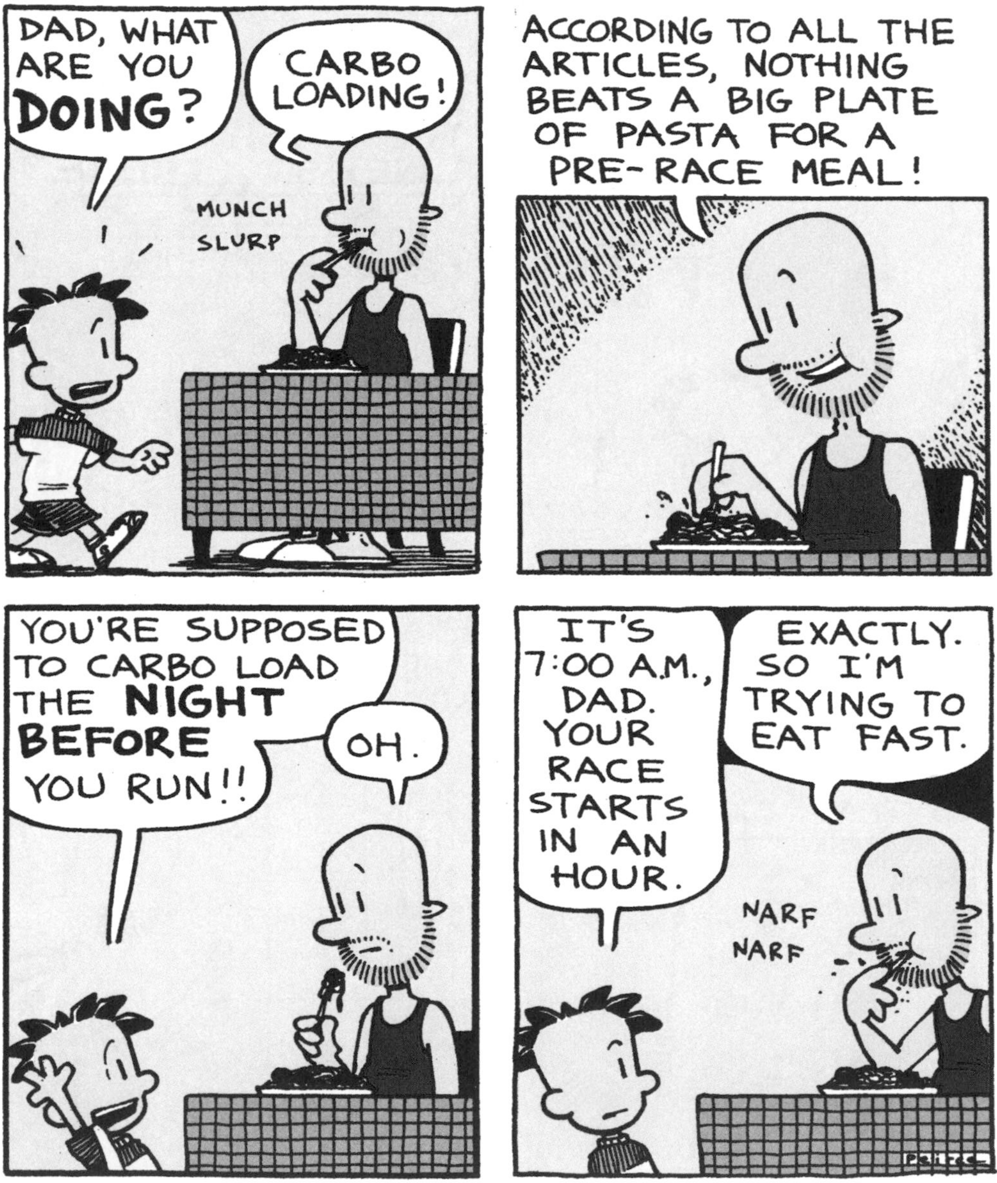
DAD, WHAT ARE YOU DOING?
CARBO LOADING!
MUNCH
SLURP
ACCORDING TO ALL THE ARTICLES, NOTHING BEATS A BIG PLATE OF PASTA FOR A PRE-RACE MEAL!
YOU'RE SUPPOSED TO CARBO LOAD THE NIGHT BEFORE YOU RUN!!
OH.
IT'S 7:00 A.M., DAD. YOUR RACE STARTS IN AN HOUR.
EXACTLY. SO I'M TRYING TO EAT FAST.
NARF
NARF

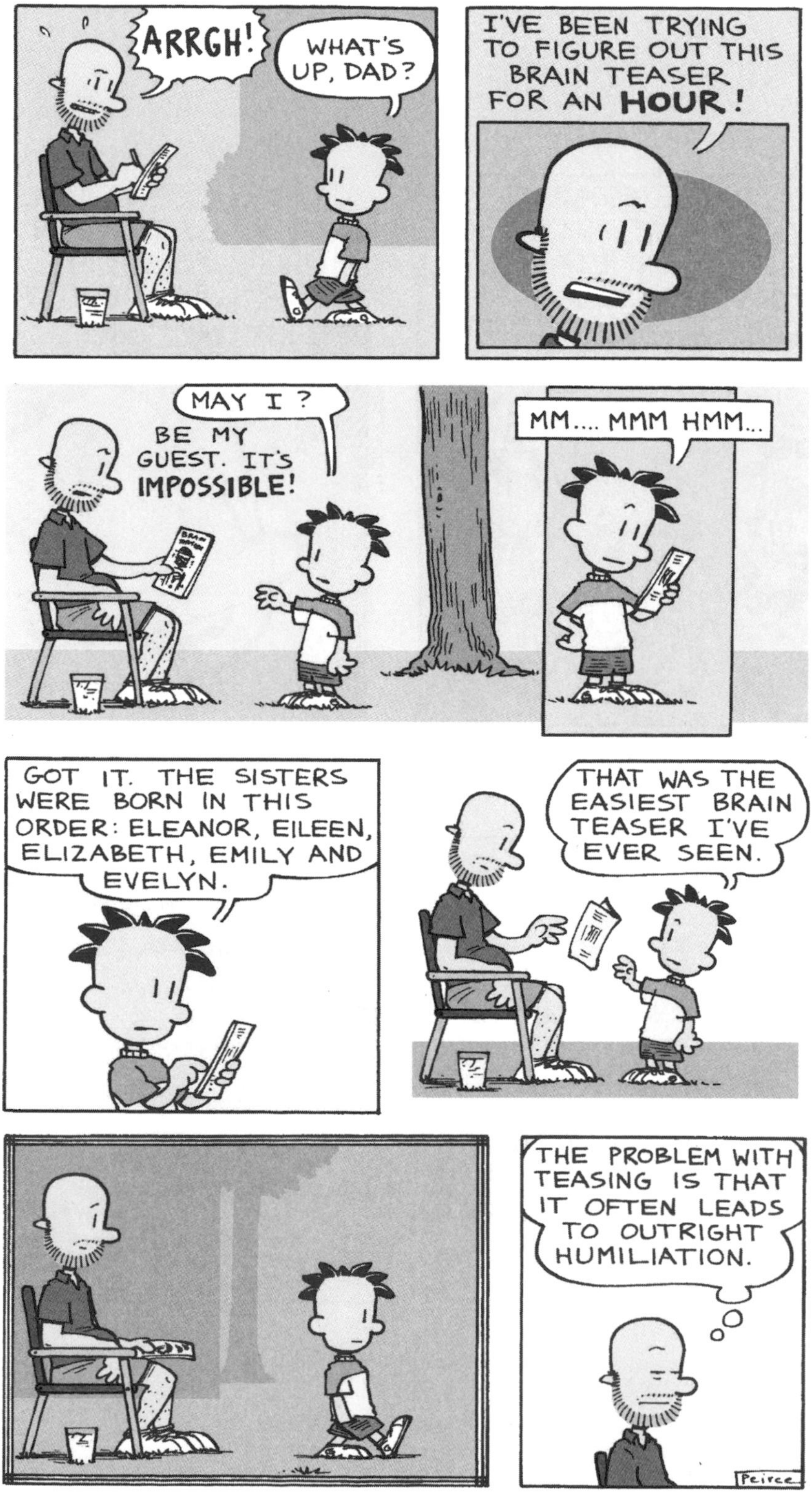
ARRGH!
WHAT'S UP, DAD?
I'VE BEEN TRYING TO FIGURE OUT THIS BRAIN TEASER FOR AN HOUR!
MAY I?
BE MY GUEST. IT'S IMPOSSIBLE!
MM.... MMM HMM...
GOT IT. THE SISTERS WERE BORN IN THIS ORDER: ELEANOR, EILEEN, ELIZABETH, EMILY AND EVELYN.
THAT WAS THE EASIEST BRAIN TEASER I'VE EVER SEEN.
THE PROBLEM WITH TEASING IS THAT IT OFTEN LEADS TO OUTRIGHT HUMILIATION.
Peirce

THE RACE STARTS IN FIVE MINUTES!... I'M GETTING A LITTLE NERVOUS.

DAD, **DAD!** RE**LAX**!

REMEMBER: IT'LL ONLY LAST AN HOUR, AND THEN IT'LL BE OVER!

ACTUALLY, YOU'RE PRETTY SLOW... SO MAYBE IT'LL LAST AN HOUR AND A HALF.

YOU KNOW WHAT? TO BE SAFE, LET'S SAY TWO HOURS.

THANKS FOR YOUR SUPPORT.

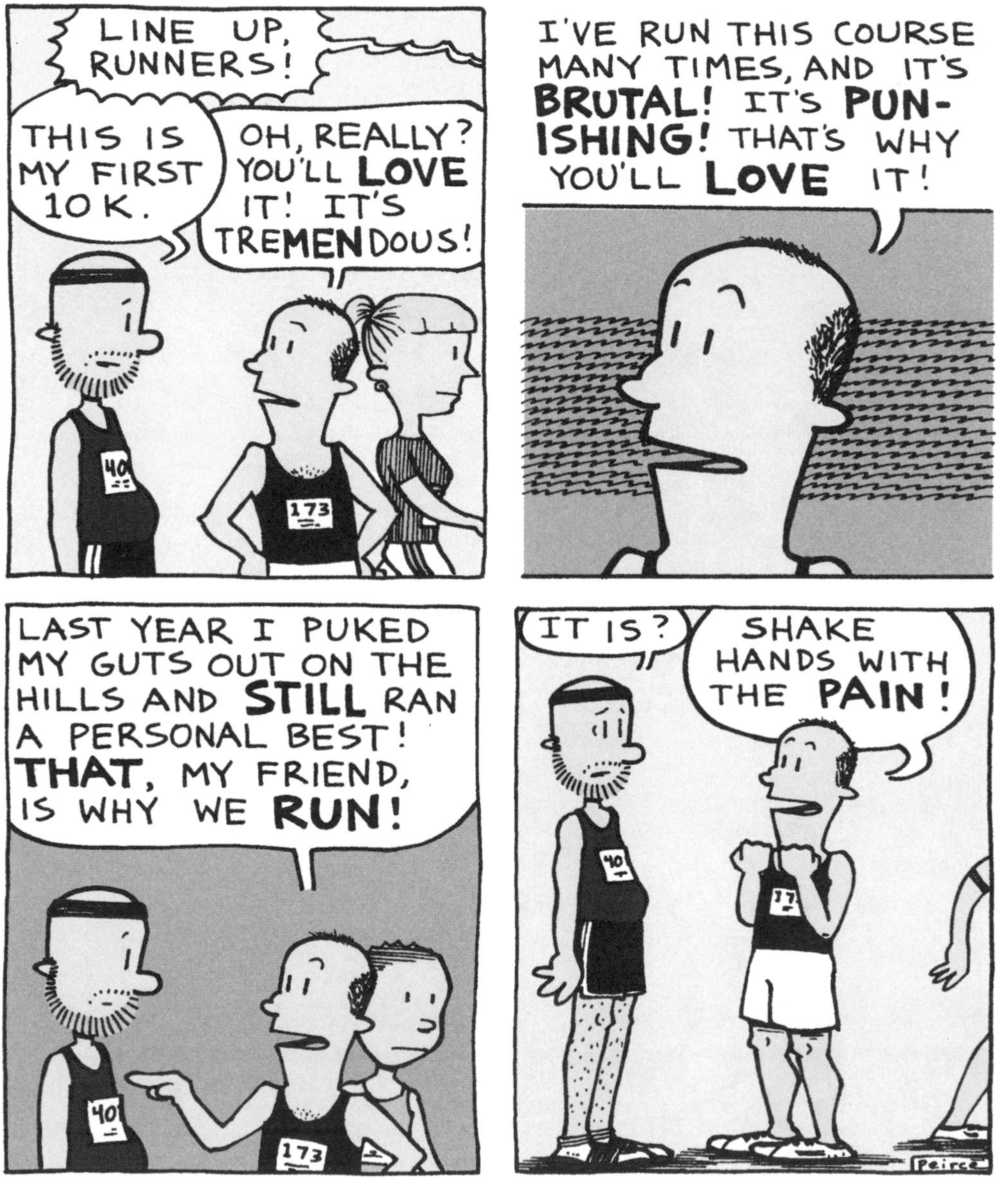
LINE UP, RUNNERS!
THIS IS MY FIRST 10 K.
OH, REALLY? YOU'LL **LOVE** IT! IT'S TRE**MEN**DOUS!
I'VE RUN THIS COURSE MANY TIMES, AND IT'S **BRUTAL!** IT'S **PUN-ISHING!** THAT'S WHY YOU'LL **LOVE** IT!
LAST YEAR I PUKED MY GUTS OUT ON THE HILLS AND **STILL** RAN A PERSONAL BEST! **THAT**, MY FRIEND, IS WHY WE **RUN**!
IT IS?
SHAKE HANDS WITH THE **PAIN**!
Peirce

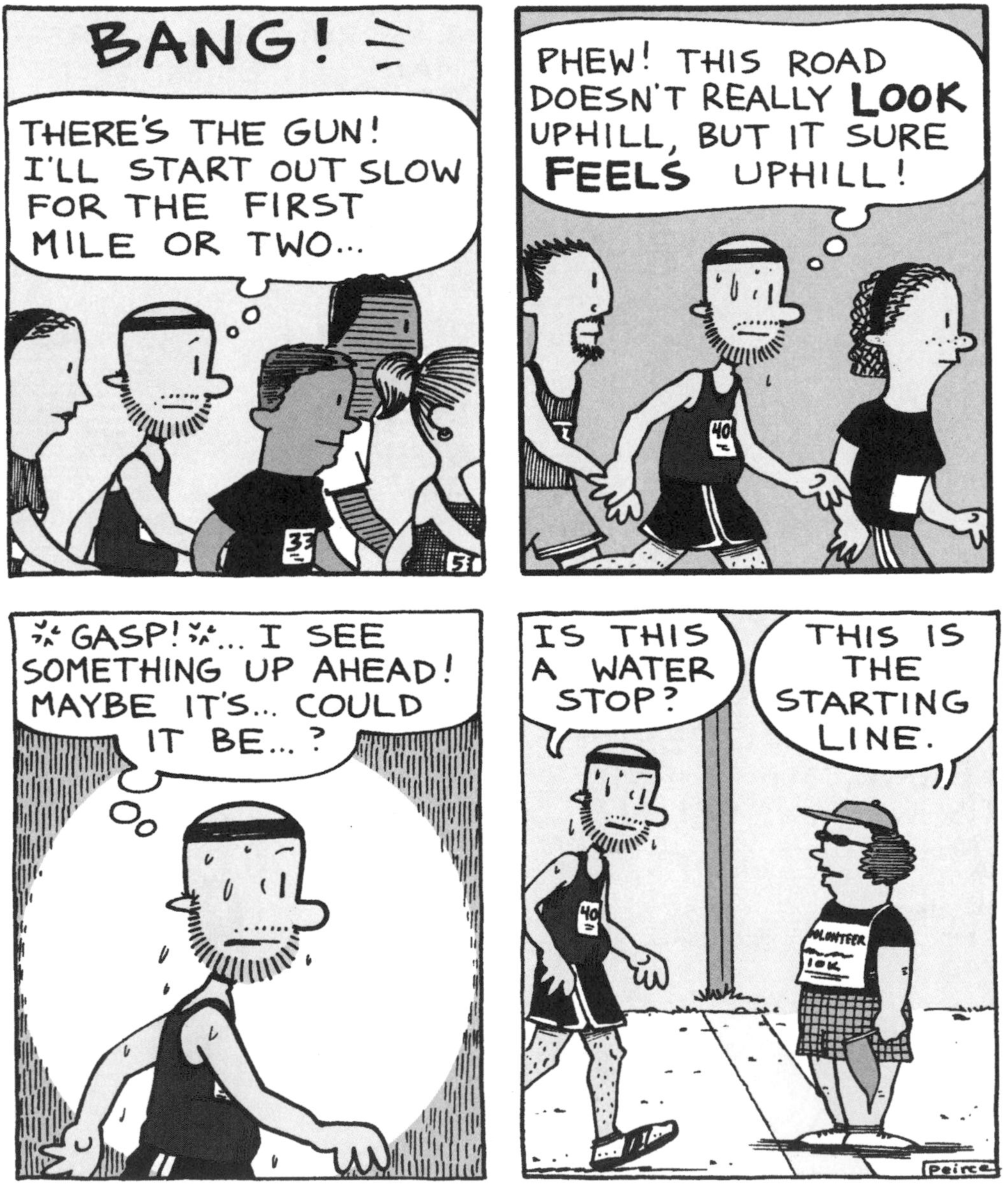
BANG!
THERE'S THE GUN! I'LL START OUT SLOW FOR THE FIRST MILE OR TWO...
PHEW! THIS ROAD DOESN'T REALLY **LOOK** UPHILL, BUT IT SURE **FEELS** UPHILL!
GASP! ... I SEE SOMETHING UP AHEAD! MAYBE IT'S... COULD IT BE...?
IS THIS A WATER STOP?
THIS IS THE STARTING LINE.
VOLUNTEER 10K
Peirce

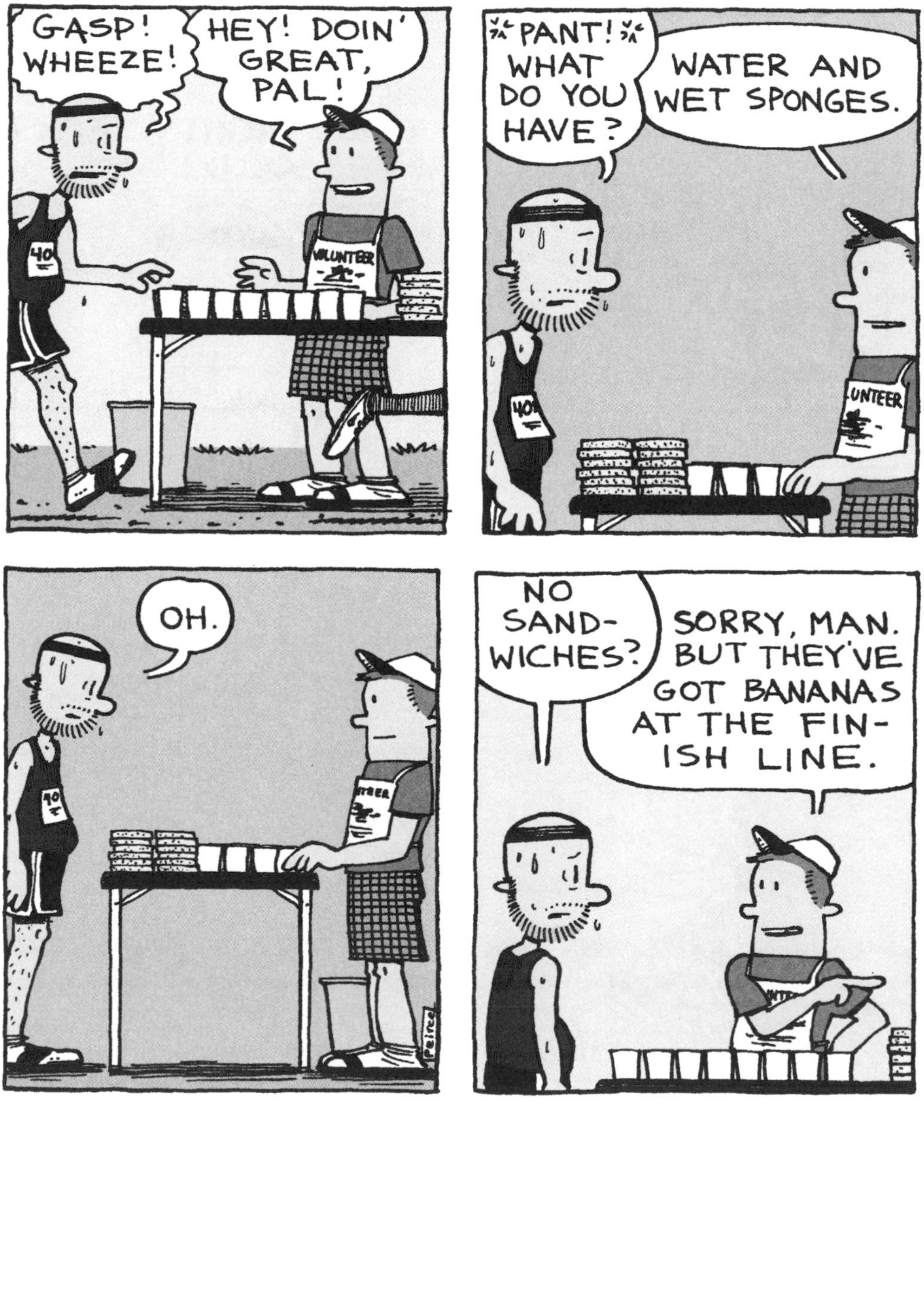
GASP! WHEEZE!
HEY! DOIN' GREAT, PAL!
VOLUNTEER
PANT! WHAT DO YOU HAVE?
WATER AND WET SPONGES.
OH.
NO SAND-WICHES?
SORRY, MAN. BUT THEY'VE GOT BANANAS AT THE FIN-ISH LINE.

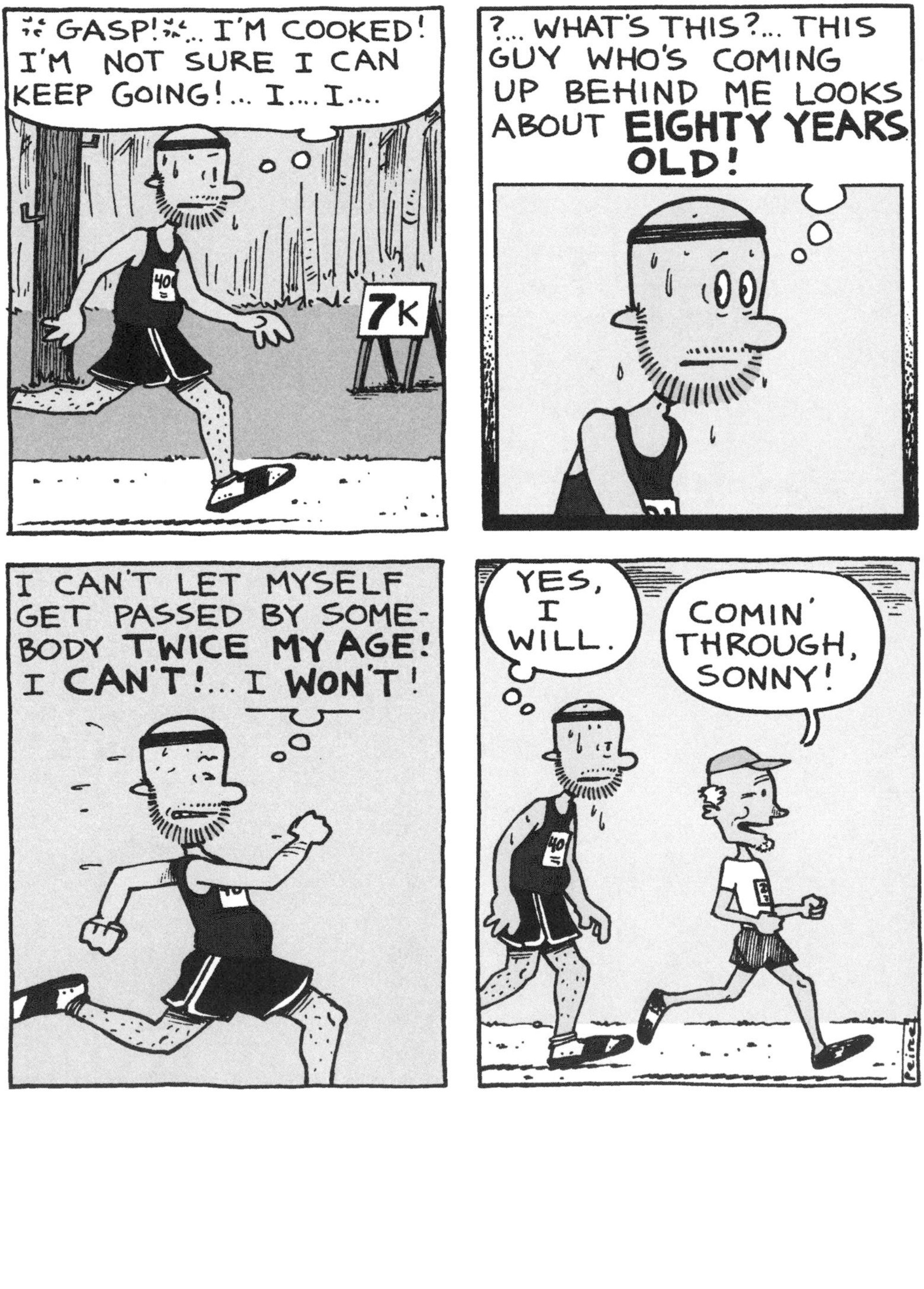

GASP! ... I'M COOKED! I'M NOT SURE I CAN KEEP GOING! ... I.... I....
7K
?... WHAT'S THIS?... THIS GUY WHO'S COMING UP BEHIND ME LOOKS ABOUT EIGHTY YEARS OLD!
I CAN'T LET MYSELF GET PASSED BY SOMEBODY TWICE MY AGE! I CAN'T!... I WON'T!
YES, I WILL.
COMIN' THROUGH, SONNY!

GO, DAD, GO! FINISH STRONG! YES!!

I MADE IT! ☆GASP!☆.. I DID IT!

GREAT JOB, DAD!

...AND I DIDN'T FINISH **LAST!** DID YOU SEE ME PASS THOSE TWO LADIES IN THE HOME STRETCH?

UH... YEAH! YES!

THEY WEREN'T IN THE RACE, WERE THEY?

NO, THEY WERE WALK-ING THEIR DOGS. BUT YOU **BLEW** BY THEM!

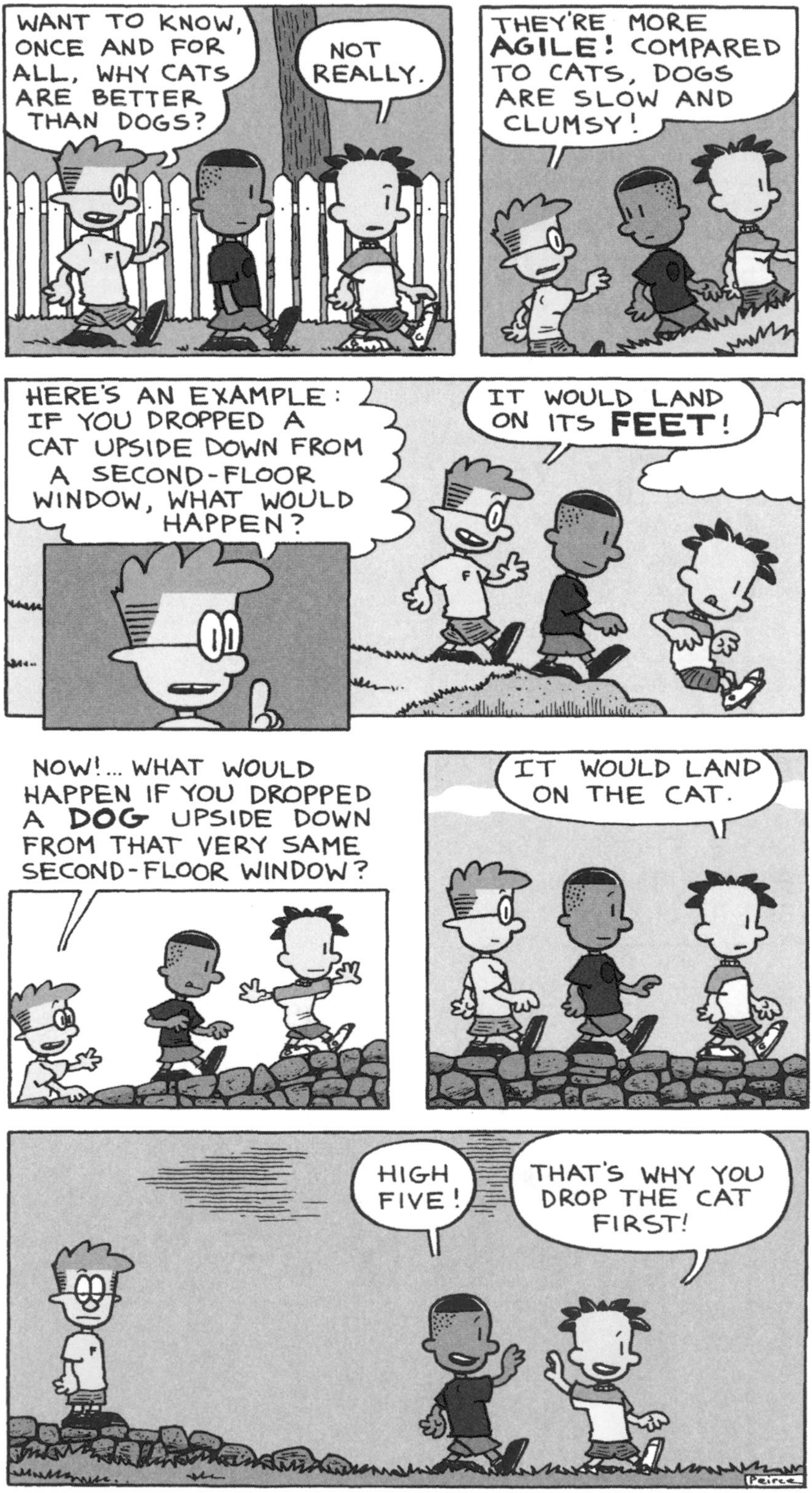
WANT TO KNOW, ONCE AND FOR ALL, WHY CATS ARE BETTER THAN DOGS?
NOT REALLY.
THEY'RE MORE **AGILE!** COMPARED TO CATS, DOGS ARE SLOW AND CLUMSY!
HERE'S AN EXAMPLE: IF YOU DROPPED A CAT UPSIDE DOWN FROM A SECOND-FLOOR WINDOW, WHAT WOULD HAPPEN?
IT WOULD LAND ON ITS **FEET**!
NOW!... WHAT WOULD HAPPEN IF YOU DROPPED A **DOG** UPSIDE DOWN FROM THAT VERY SAME SECOND-FLOOR WINDOW?
IT WOULD LAND ON THE CAT.
HIGH FIVE!
THAT'S WHY YOU DROP THE CAT FIRST!
Peirce

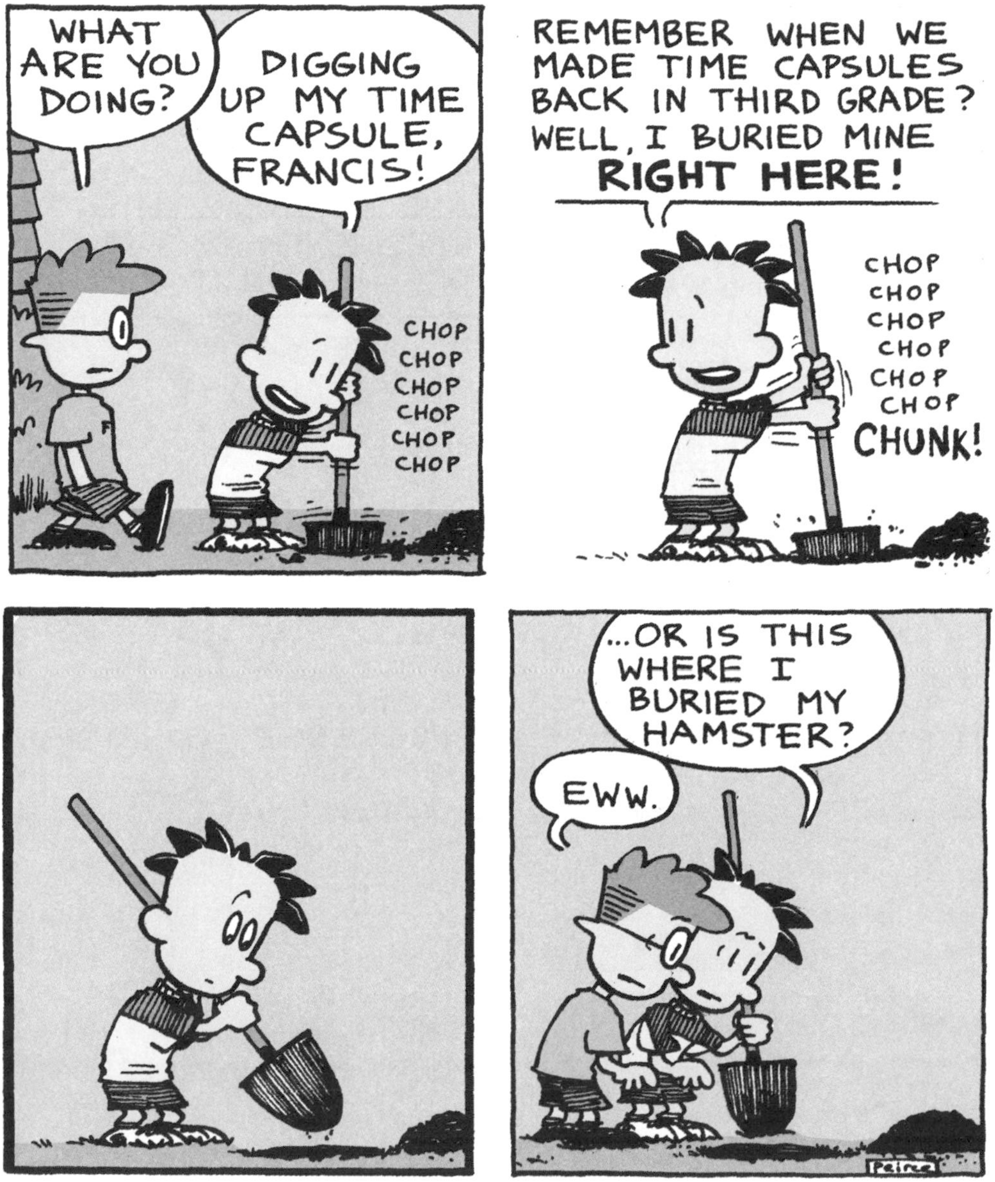

WHAT ARE YOU DOING?
DIGGING UP MY TIME CAPSULE, FRANCIS!
CHOP CHOP CHOP CHOP CHOP CHOP
REMEMBER WHEN WE MADE TIME CAPSULES BACK IN THIRD GRADE? WELL, I BURIED MINE **RIGHT HERE!**
CHOP CHOP CHOP CHOP CHOP CHOP
CHUNK!
...OR IS THIS WHERE I BURIED MY HAMSTER?
EWW.
Peirce

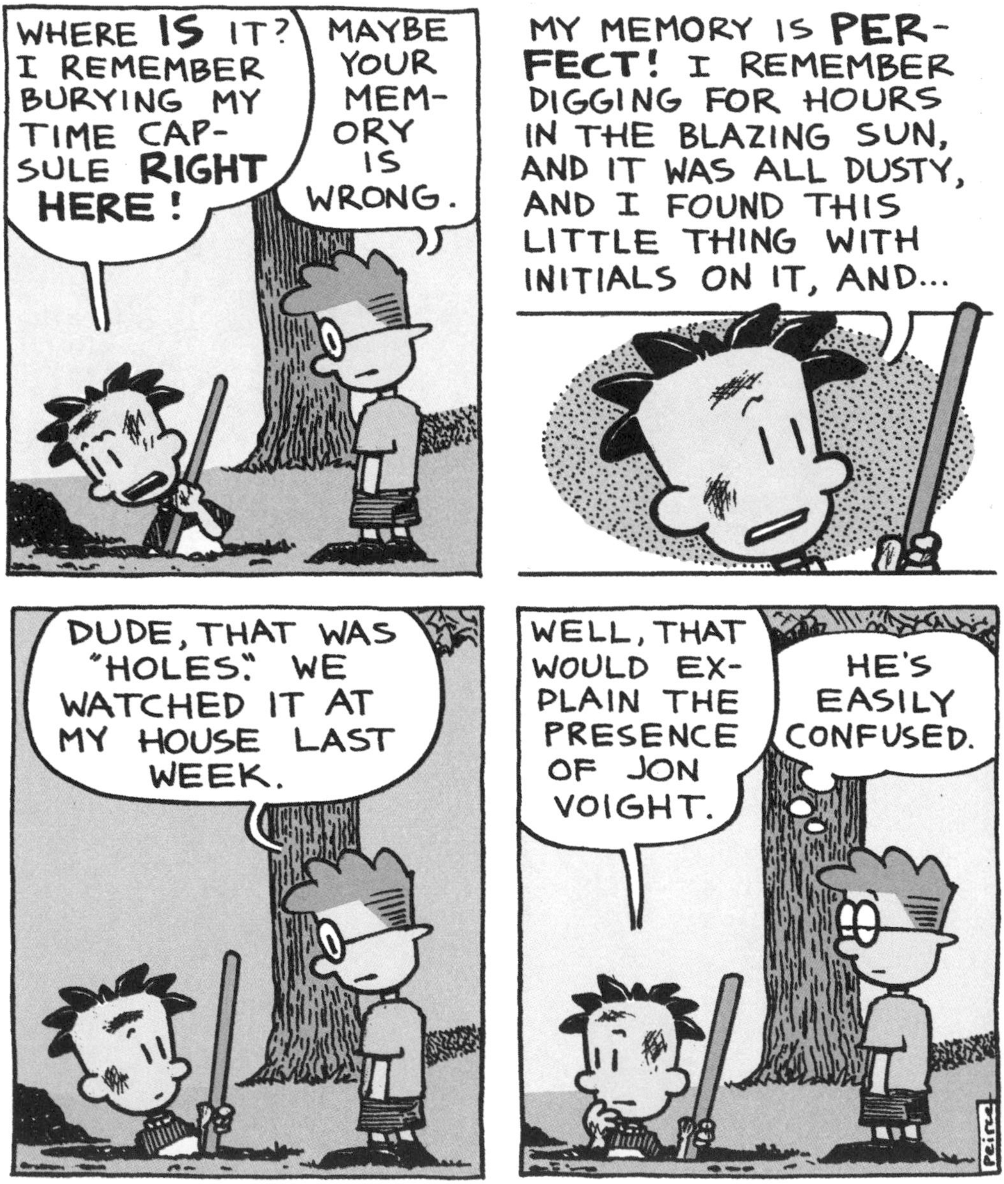
WHERE IS IT? I REMEMBER BURYING MY TIME CAP-SULE RIGHT HERE!
MAYBE YOUR MEM-ORY IS WRONG.
MY MEMORY IS PER-FECT! I REMEMBER DIGGING FOR HOURS IN THE BLAZING SUN, AND IT WAS ALL DUSTY, AND I FOUND THIS LITTLE THING WITH INITIALS ON IT, AND...
DUDE, THAT WAS "HOLES." WE WATCHED IT AT MY HOUSE LAST WEEK.
WELL, THAT WOULD EX-PLAIN THE PRESENCE OF JON VOIGHT.
HE'S EASILY CONFUSED.
Peirce

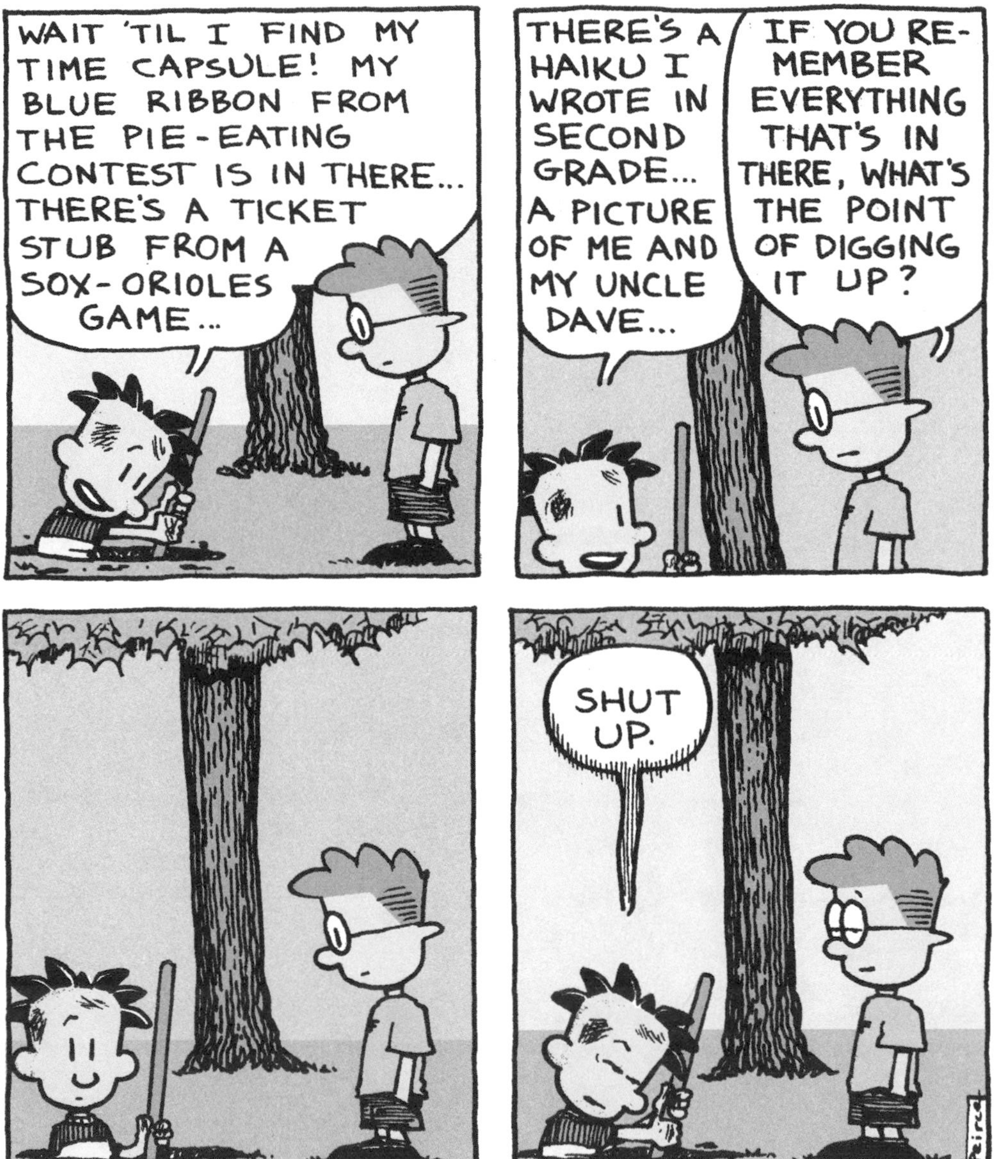
WAIT 'TIL I FIND MY TIME CAPSULE! MY BLUE RIBBON FROM THE PIE-EATING CONTEST IS IN THERE... THERE'S A TICKET STUB FROM A SOX-ORIOLES GAME...
THERE'S A HAIKU I WROTE IN SECOND GRADE... A PICTURE OF ME AND MY UNCLE DAVE...
IF YOU REMEMBER EVERYTHING THAT'S IN THERE, WHAT'S THE POINT OF DIGGING IT UP?
SHUT UP.
Peirce

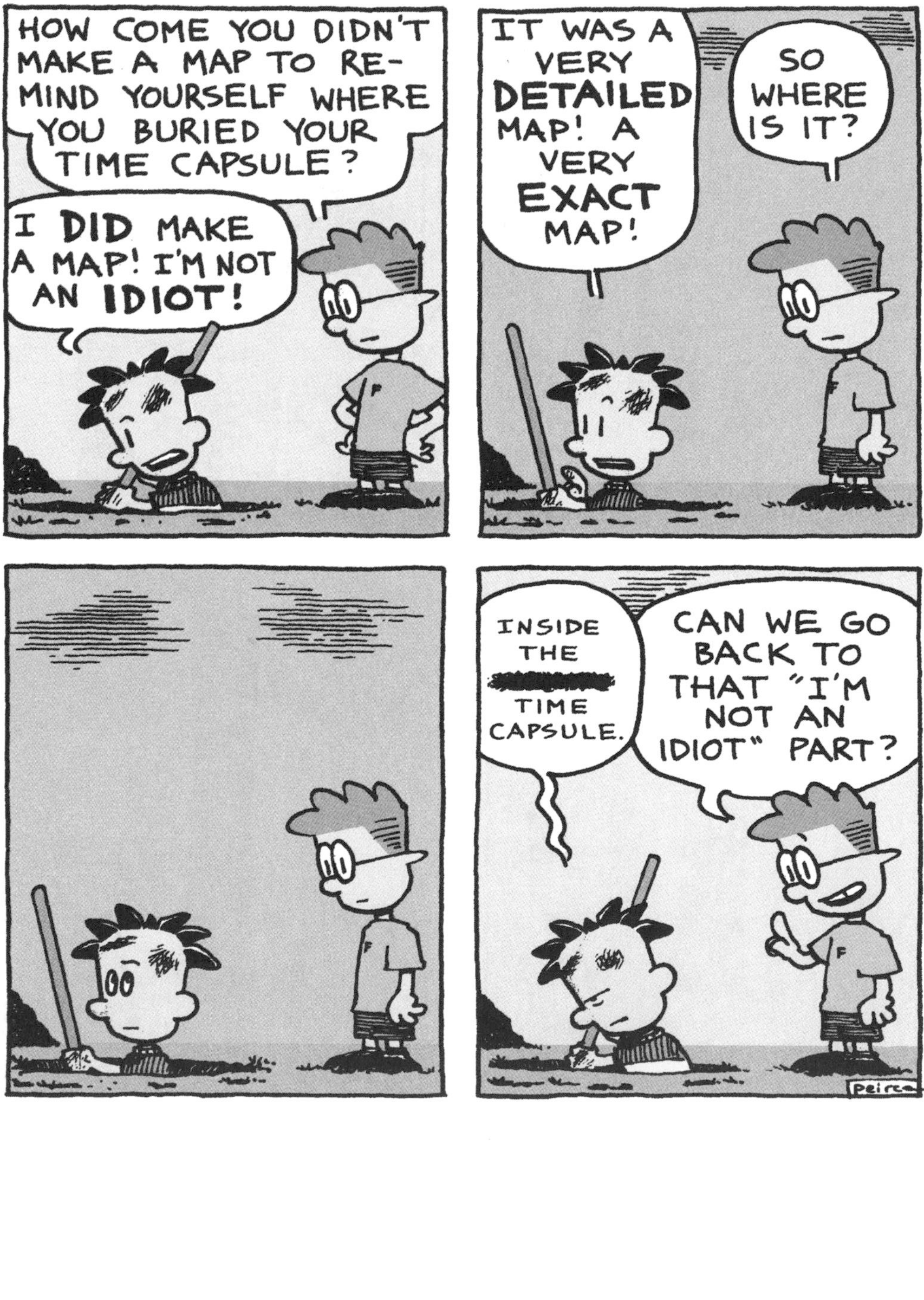
HOW COME YOU DIDN'T MAKE A MAP TO RE-MIND YOURSELF WHERE YOU BURIED YOUR TIME CAPSULE?
I DID MAKE A MAP! I'M NOT AN IDIOT!
IT WAS A VERY DETAILED MAP! A VERY EXACT MAP!
SO WHERE IS IT?
INSIDE THE [redacted] TIME CAPSULE.
CAN WE GO BACK TO THAT "I'M NOT AN IDIOT" PART?
Peirce

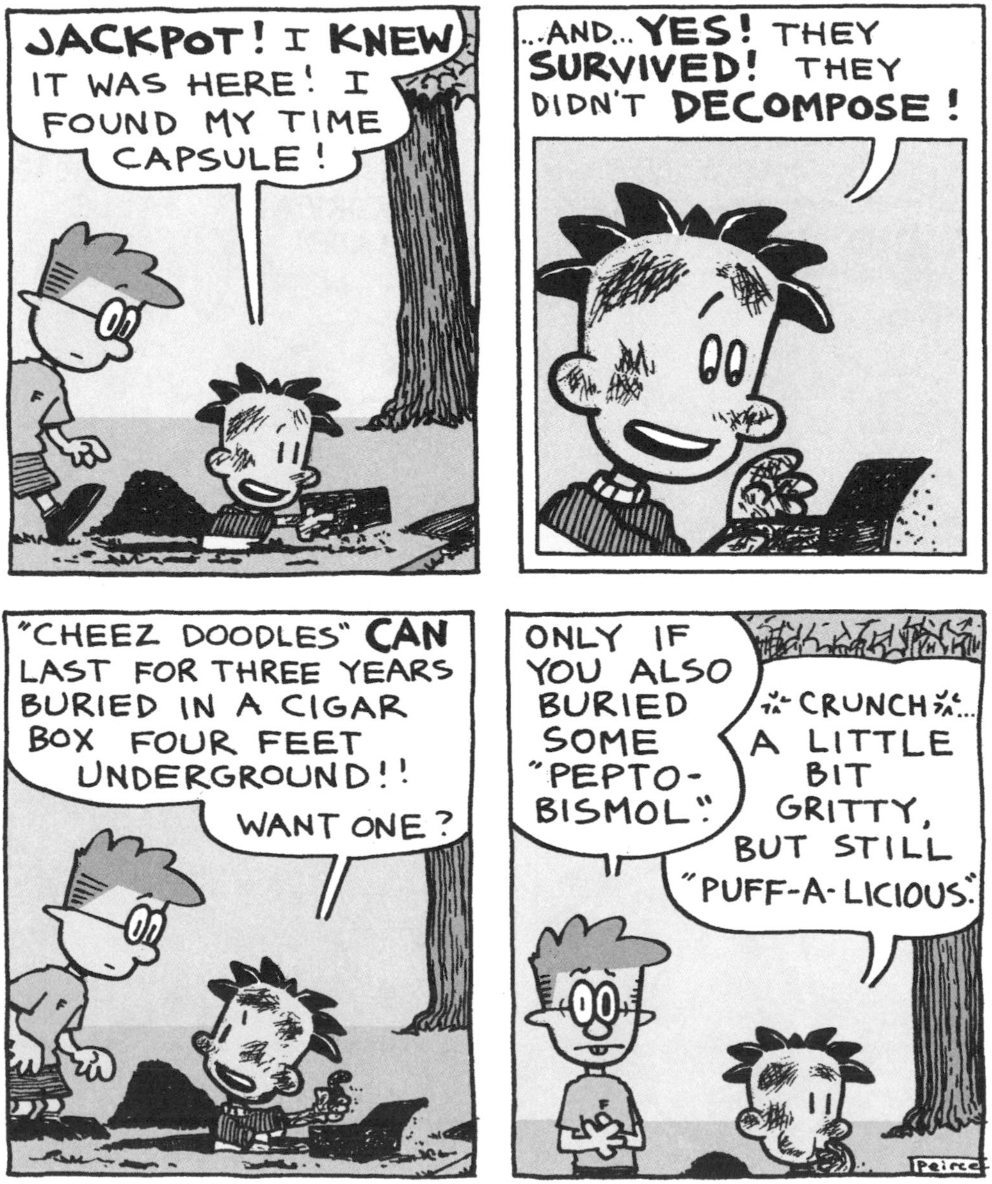
JACKPOT! I KNEW IT WAS HERE! I FOUND MY TIME CAPSULE!
...AND... YES! THEY SURVIVED! THEY DIDN'T DECOMPOSE!
"CHEEZ DOODLES" CAN LAST FOR THREE YEARS BURIED IN A CIGAR BOX FOUR FEET UNDERGROUND!!
WANT ONE?
ONLY IF YOU ALSO BURIED SOME "PEPTO-BISMOL."
CRUNCH... A LITTLE BIT GRITTY, BUT STILL "PUFF-A-LICIOUS."
Peirce

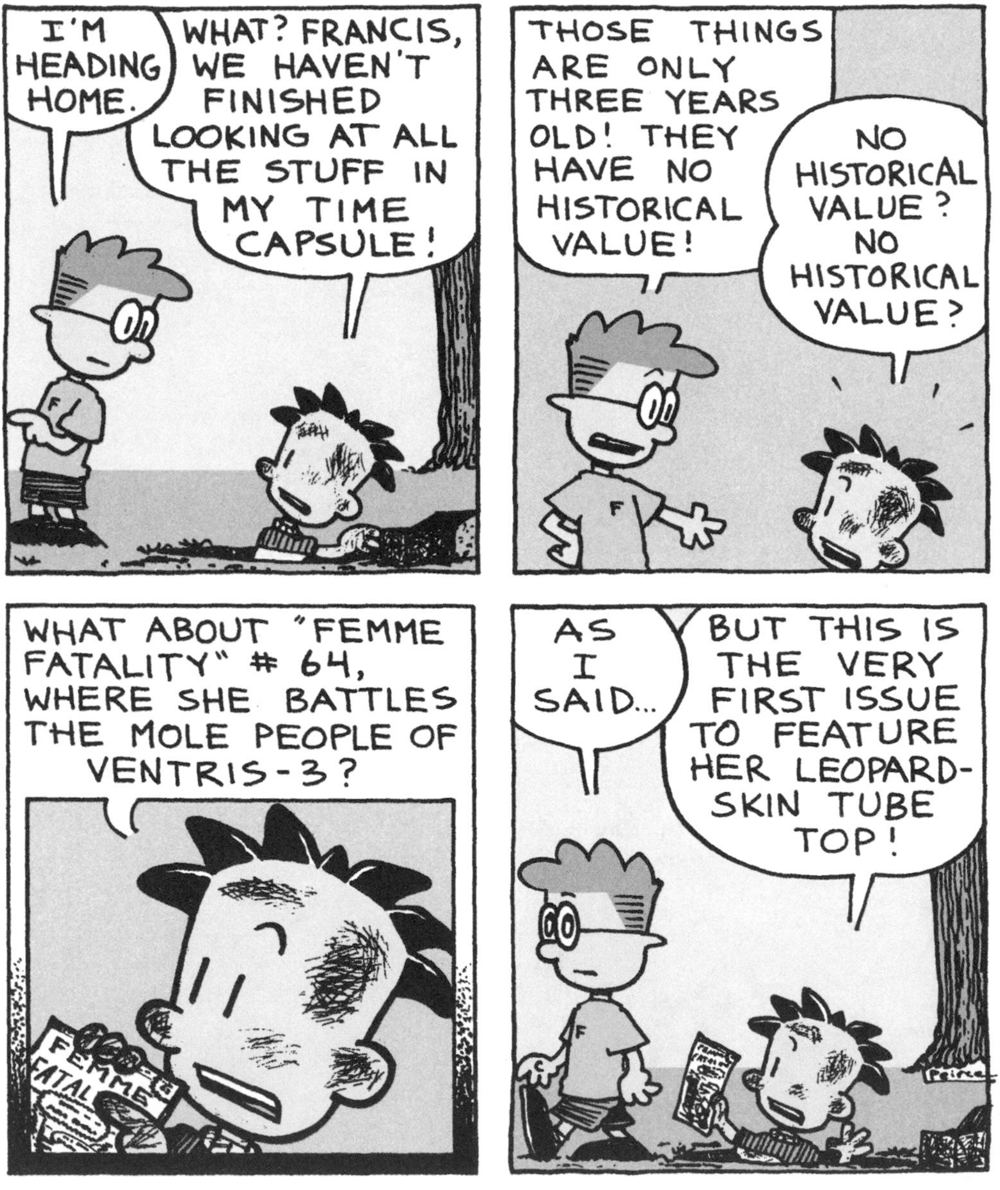
I'M HEADING HOME.
WHAT? FRANCIS, WE HAVEN'T FINISHED LOOKING AT ALL THE STUFF IN MY TIME CAPSULE!
THOSE THINGS ARE ONLY THREE YEARS OLD! THEY HAVE NO HISTORICAL VALUE!
NO HISTORICAL VALUE? NO HISTORICAL VALUE?
WHAT ABOUT "FEMME FATALITY" # 64, WHERE SHE BATTLES THE MOLE PEOPLE OF VENTRIS-3?
FEMME FATAL
AS I SAID...
BUT THIS IS THE VERY FIRST ISSUE TO FEATURE HER LEOPARD-SKIN TUBE TOP!
Peirce

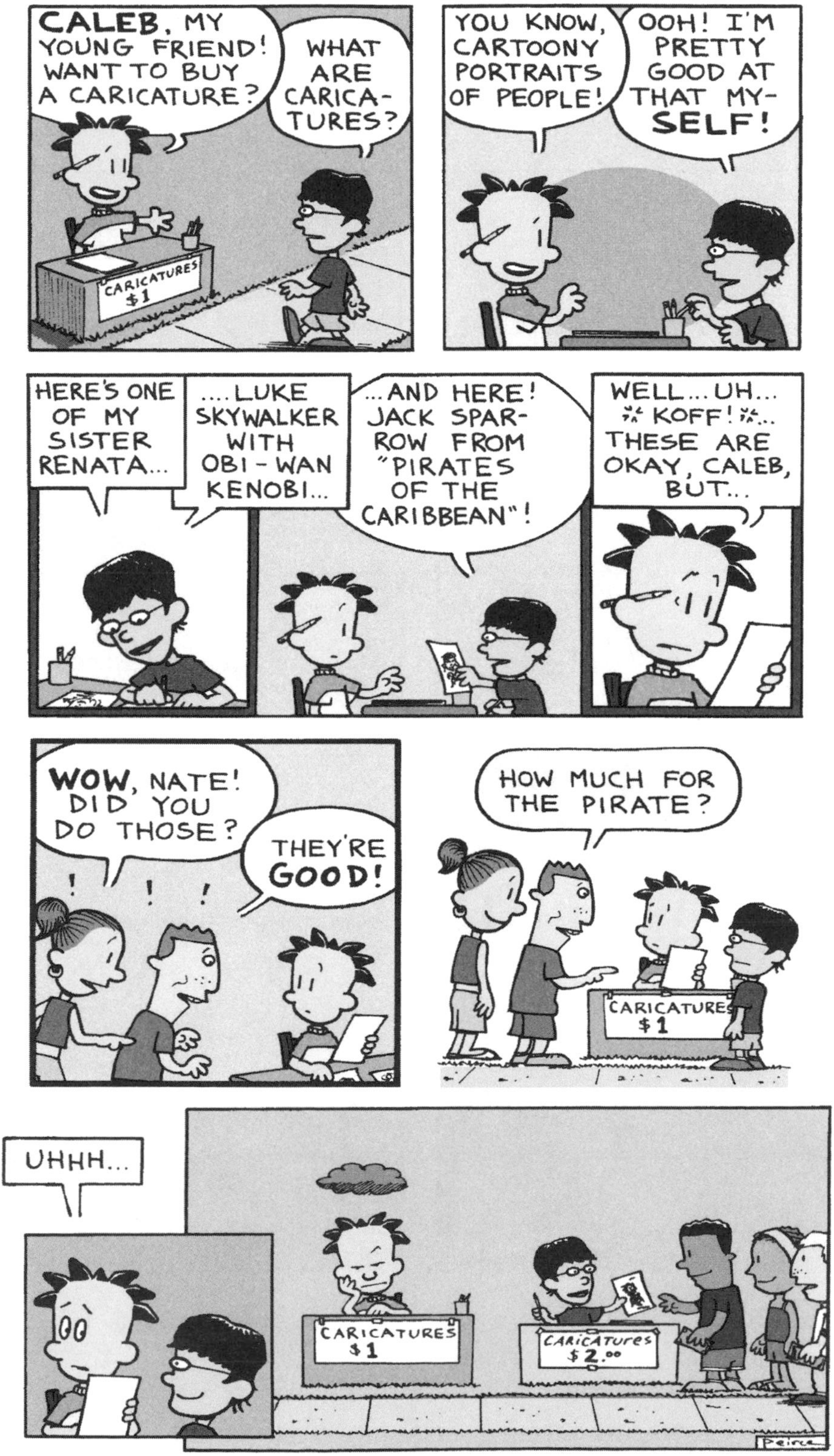
CALEB, MY YOUNG FRIEND! WANT TO BUY A CARICATURE?
WHAT ARE CARICATURES?
CARICATURES $1
YOU KNOW, CARTOONY PORTRAITS OF PEOPLE!
OOH! I'M PRETTY GOOD AT THAT MYSELF!
HERE'S ONE OF MY SISTER RENATA...
....LUKE SKYWALKER WITH OBI-WAN KENOBI...
...AND HERE! JACK SPARROW FROM "PIRATES OF THE CARIBBEAN"!
WELL... UH... KOFF!... THESE ARE OKAY, CALEB, BUT...
WOW, NATE! DID YOU DO THOSE?
! ! !
THEY'RE GOOD!
HOW MUCH FOR THE PIRATE?
CARICATURES $1
UHHH...
CARICATURES $1
CARICATURES $2.00
Peirce

SCHOOL STARTS IN EIGHT DAYS.
NO.
YEAH, IT DOES. ON SEPTEMBER 4TH.
NO. NO. NO.
YES, IT...
NO! NO! NO! NO! NO! NO! NO!
THIS IS A NEW STRATEGY FOR YOU, ISN'T IT?
NO.
Peirce

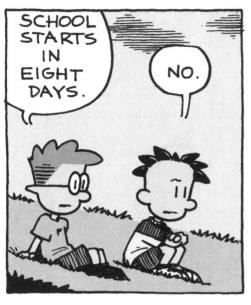

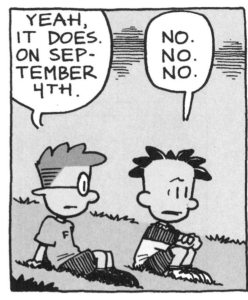

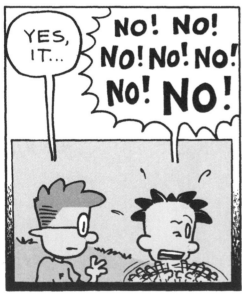

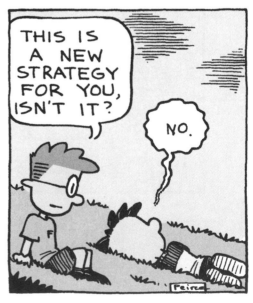

HOWDY, GENTS!
HEY TEDDY.
NO.
"NO"?
HE'S UPSET ABOUT SOME-THING, AND HE'S HAVING SOME KIND OF BRAIN CRAMP. ALL HE CAN SAY IS "NO."
NO.
WHAT'S HE UPSET ABOUT?
I DON'T WANT TO SAY. I DON'T WANT HIM TO GET MORE FREAKED OUT.
DOES IT HAVE ANY-THING TO DO WITH SCHOO—
SSH!
NO! NO! NO! NO!

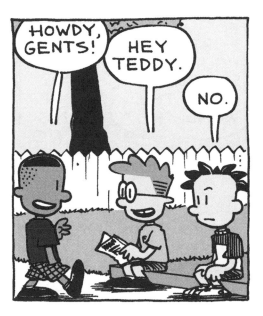

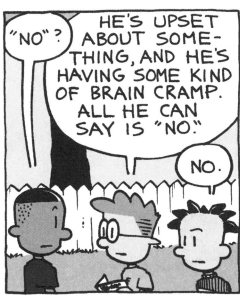

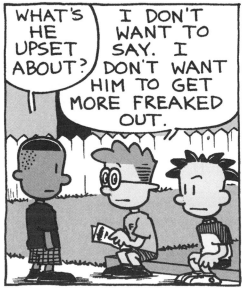

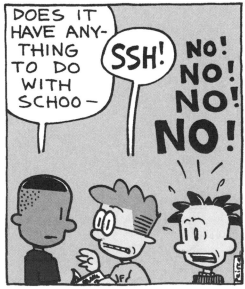

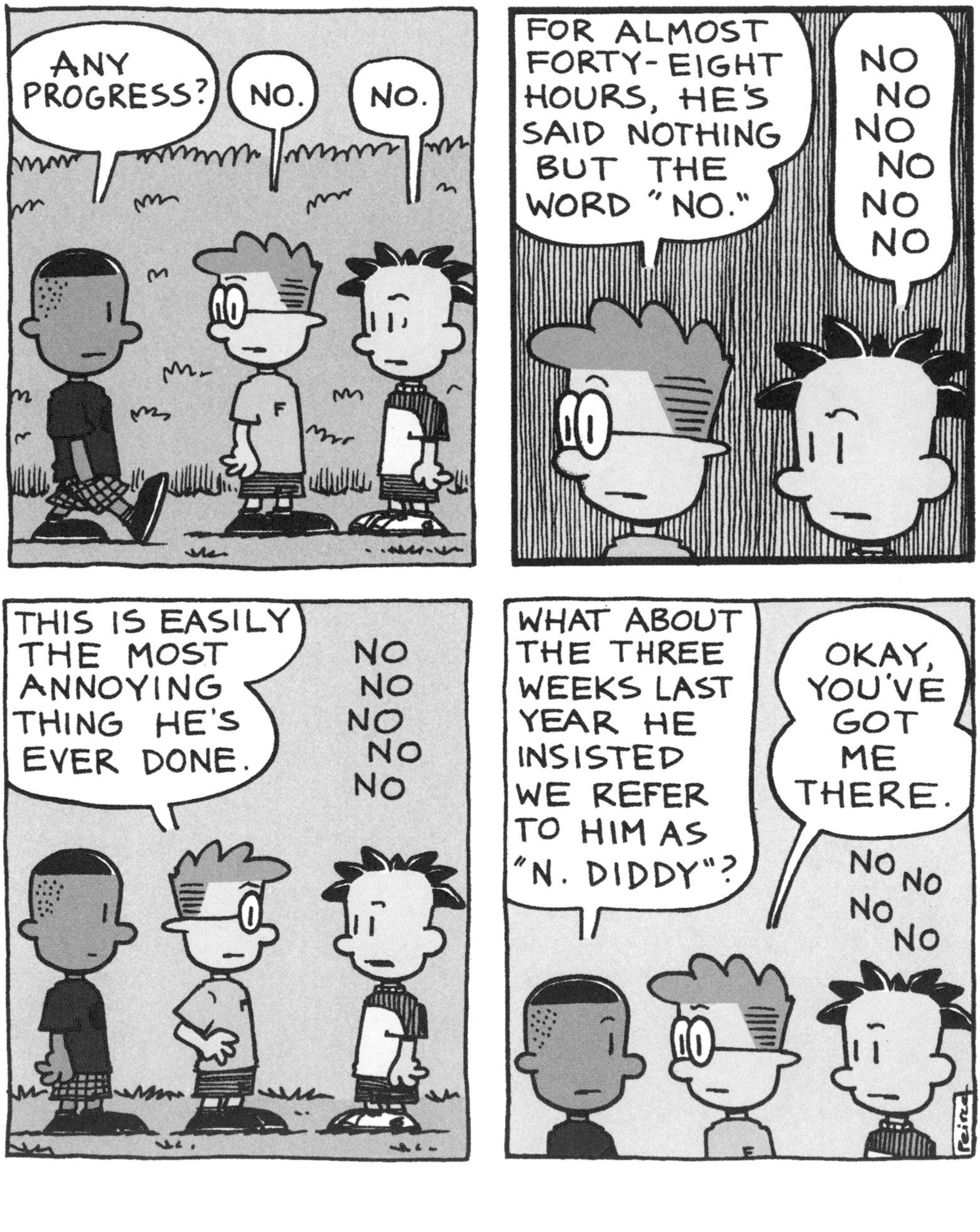
ANY PROGRESS?
NO.
NO.
FOR ALMOST FORTY-EIGHT HOURS, HE'S SAID NOTHING BUT THE WORD "NO."
NO NO NO NO NO NO
THIS IS EASILY THE MOST ANNOYING THING HE'S EVER DONE.
NO NO NO NO NO
WHAT ABOUT THE THREE WEEKS LAST YEAR HE INSISTED WE REFER TO HIM AS "N. DIDDY"?
OKAY, YOU'VE GOT ME THERE.
NO NO NO NO
Peirce

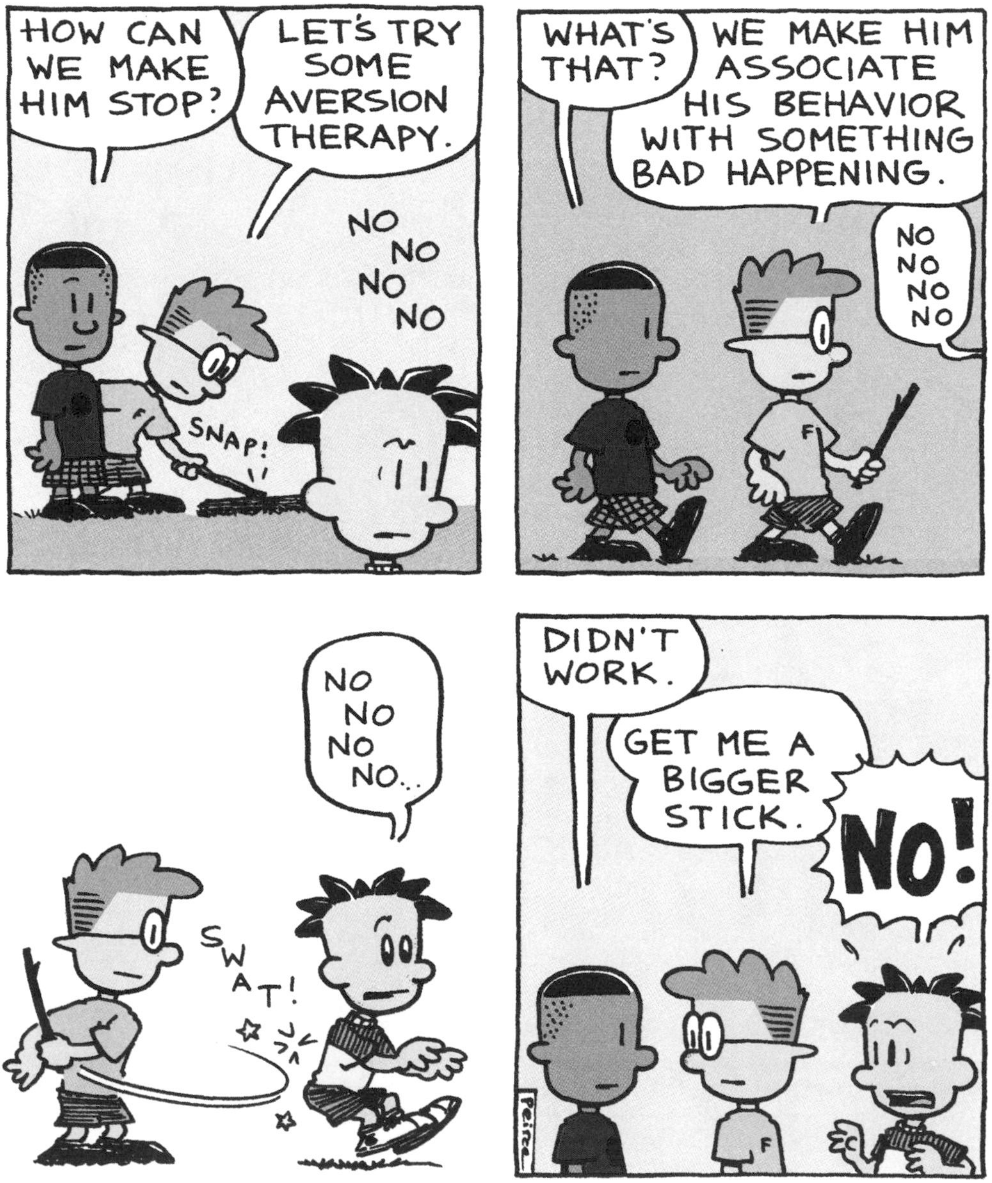
HOW CAN WE MAKE HIM STOP?
LET'S TRY SOME AVERSION THERAPY.
NO NO NO NO
SNAP!
WHAT'S THAT?
WE MAKE HIM ASSOCIATE HIS BEHAVIOR WITH SOMETHING BAD HAPPENING.
NO NO NO NO
NO NO NO NO...
SWAT!
DIDN'T WORK.
GET ME A BIGGER STICK.
NO!
Peirce

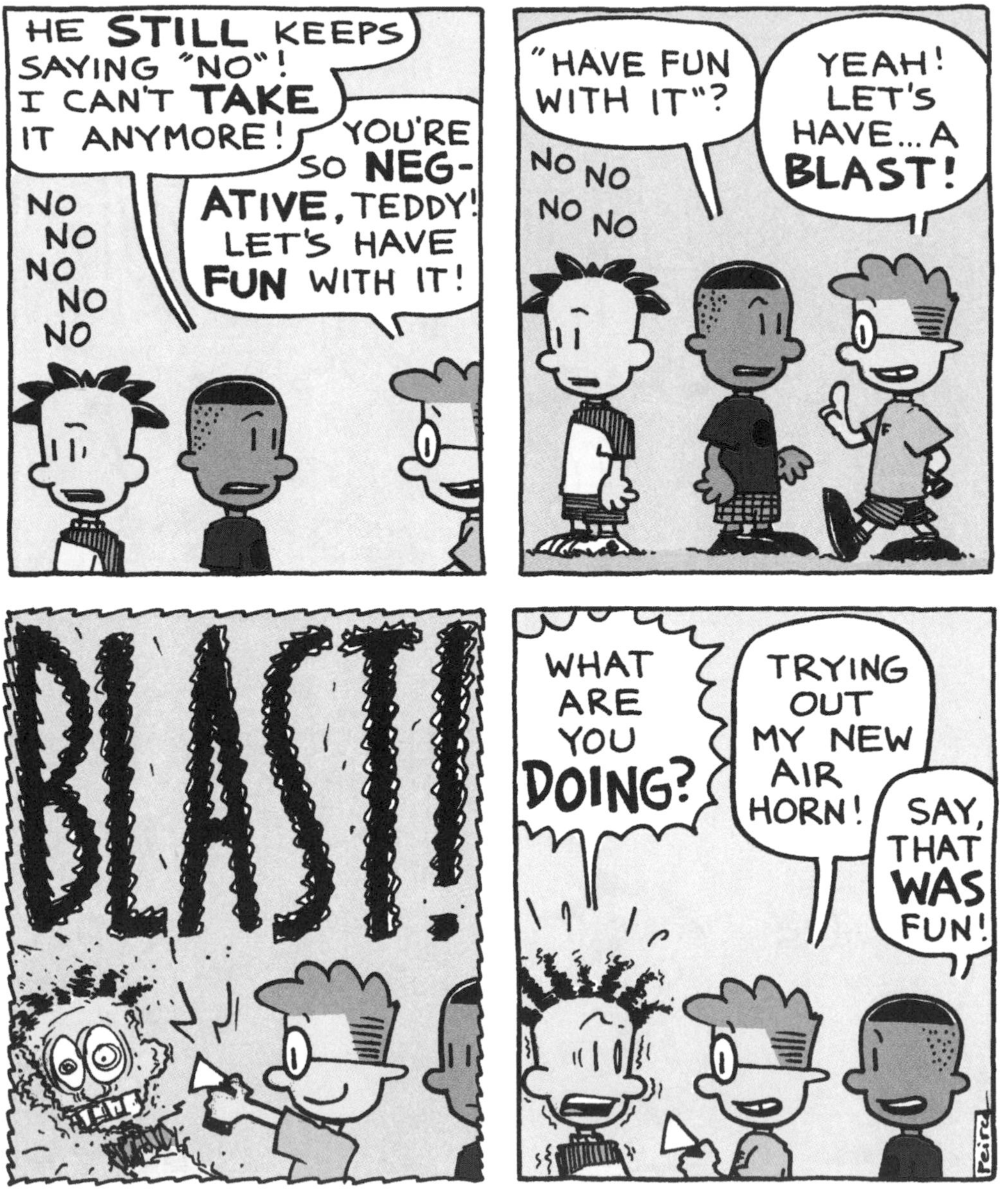
HE STILL KEEPS SAYING "NO"! I CAN'T TAKE IT ANYMORE!
NO NO NO NO NO
YOU'RE SO NEG-ATIVE, TEDDY! LET'S HAVE FUN WITH IT!
"HAVE FUN WITH IT"?
NO NO NO NO
YEAH! LET'S HAVE... A BLAST!
BLAST!
WHAT ARE YOU DOING?
TRYING OUT MY NEW AIR HORN!
SAY, THAT WAS FUN!
Peirce

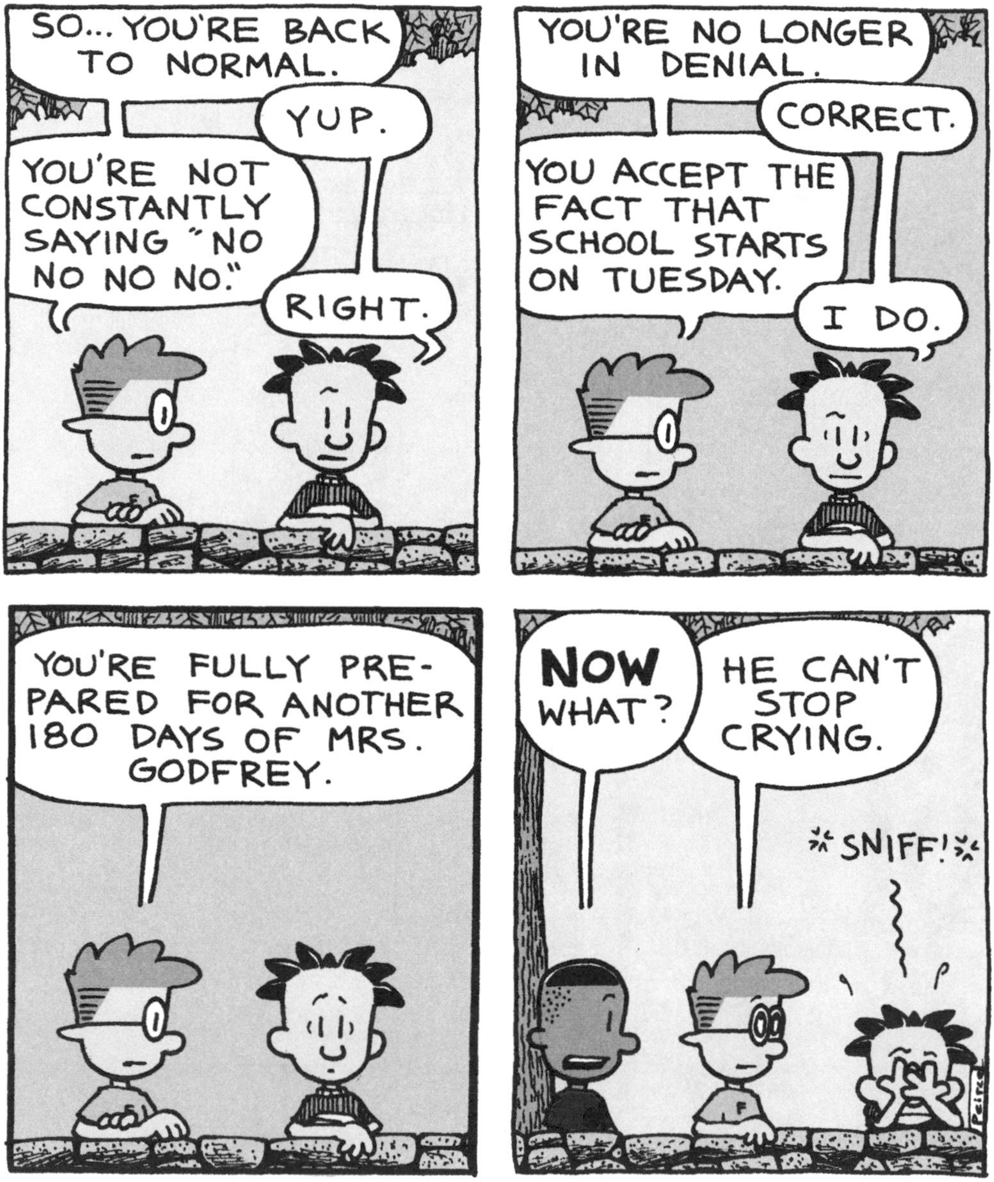
SO... YOU'RE BACK TO NORMAL.
YUP.
YOU'RE NOT CONSTANTLY SAYING "NO NO NO NO."
RIGHT.
YOU'RE NO LONGER IN DENIAL.
CORRECT.
YOU ACCEPT THE FACT THAT SCHOOL STARTS ON TUESDAY.
I DO.
YOU'RE FULLY PRE-PARED FOR ANOTHER 180 DAYS OF MRS. GODFREY.
NOW WHAT?
HE CAN'T STOP CRYING.
SNIFF!

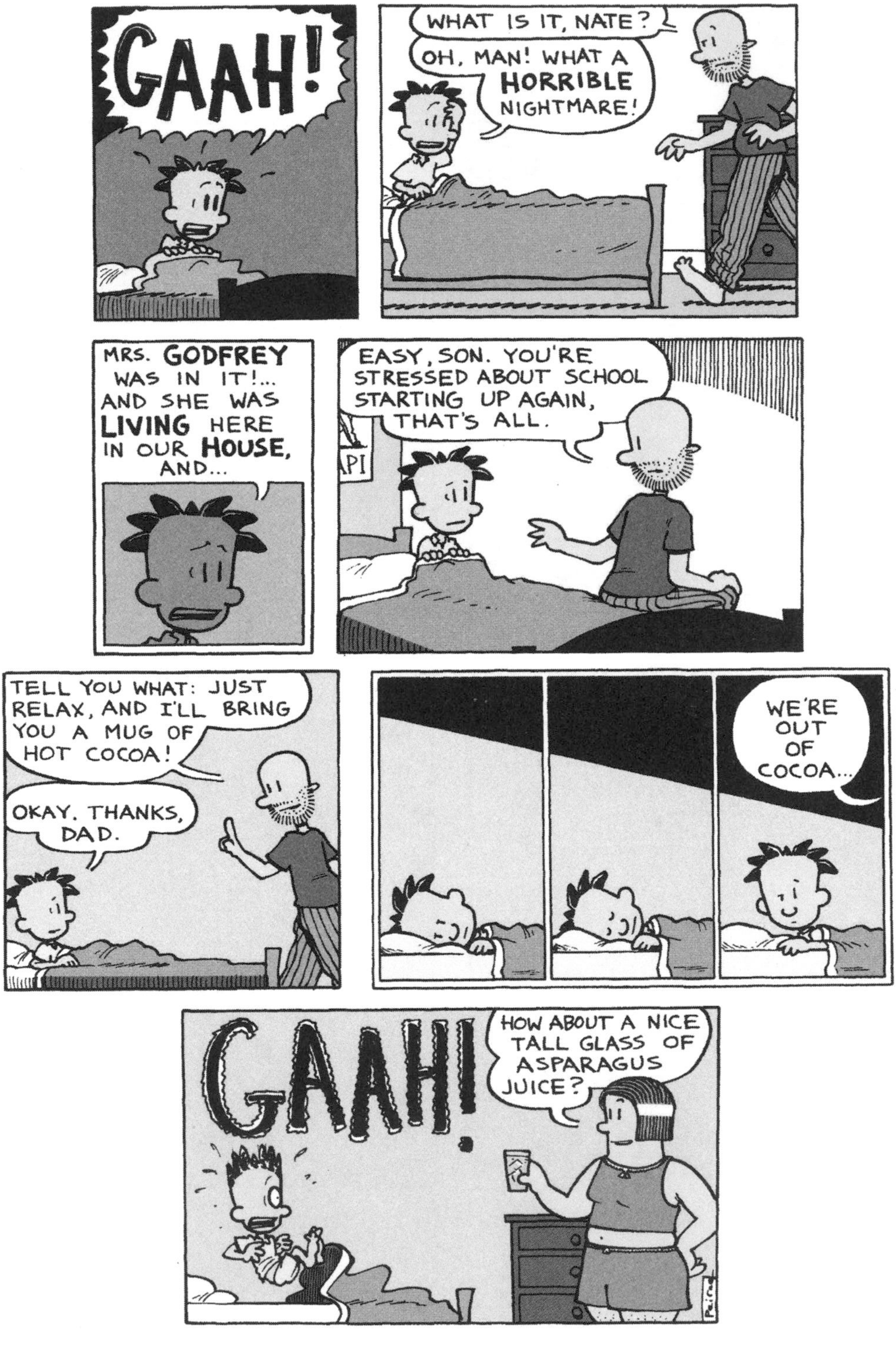
GAAH!
WHAT IS IT, NATE?
OH, MAN! WHAT A HORRIBLE NIGHTMARE!
MRS. GODFREY WAS IN IT!... AND SHE WAS LIVING HERE IN OUR HOUSE, AND...
EASY, SON. YOU'RE STRESSED ABOUT SCHOOL STARTING UP AGAIN, THAT'S ALL.
TELL YOU WHAT: JUST RELAX, AND I'LL BRING YOU A MUG OF HOT COCOA!
OKAY. THANKS, DAD.
WE'RE OUT OF COCOA...
GAAH!
HOW ABOUT A NICE TALL GLASS OF ASPARAGUS JUICE?

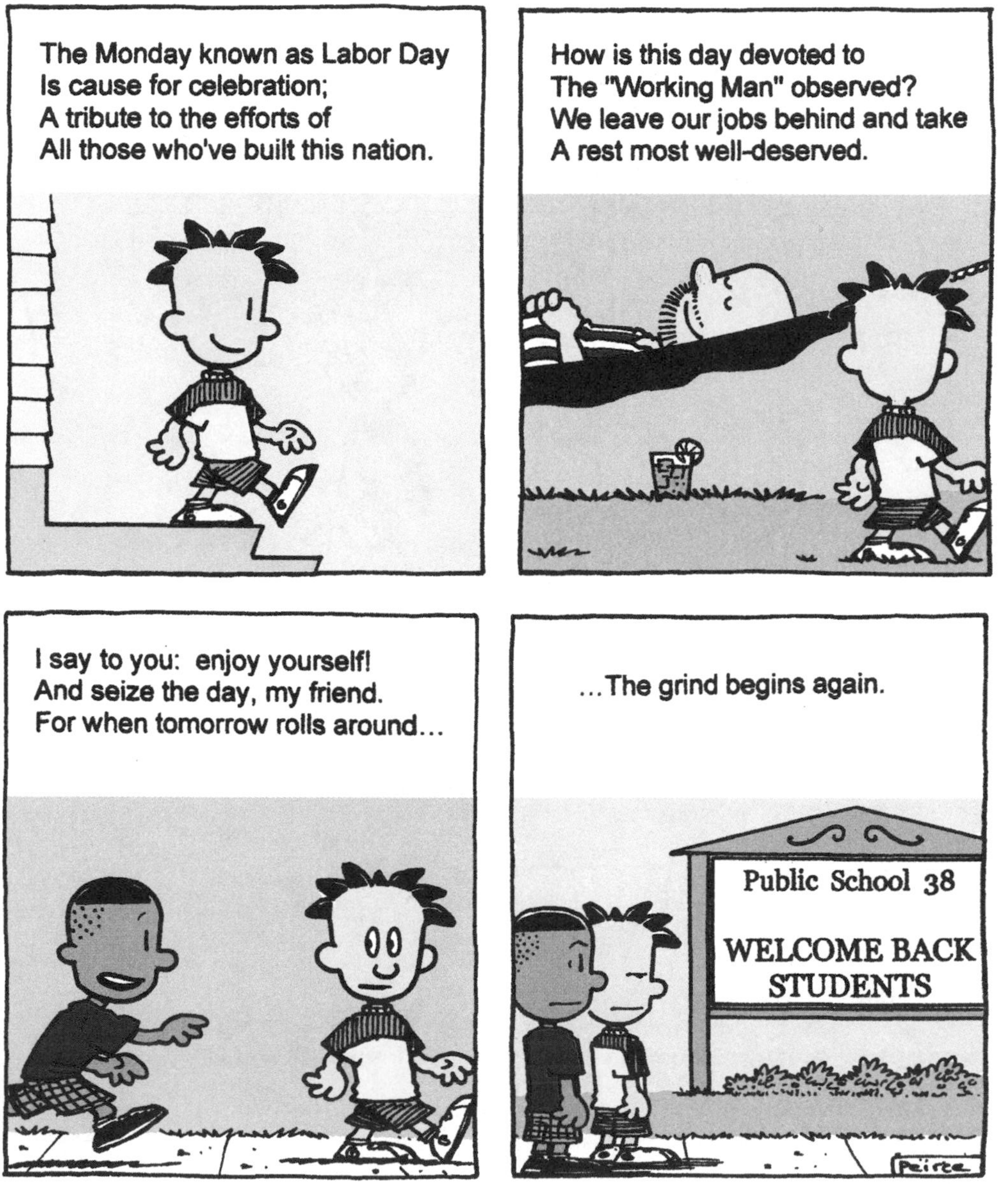
The Monday known as Labor Day
Is cause for celebration;
A tribute to the efforts of
All those who've built this nation.
How is this day devoted to
The "Working Man" observed?
We leave our jobs behind and take
A rest most well-deserved.
I say to you: enjoy yourself!
And seize the day, my friend.
For when tomorrow rolls around...
...The grind begins again.
Public School 38
WELCOME BACK
STUDENTS
Peirce

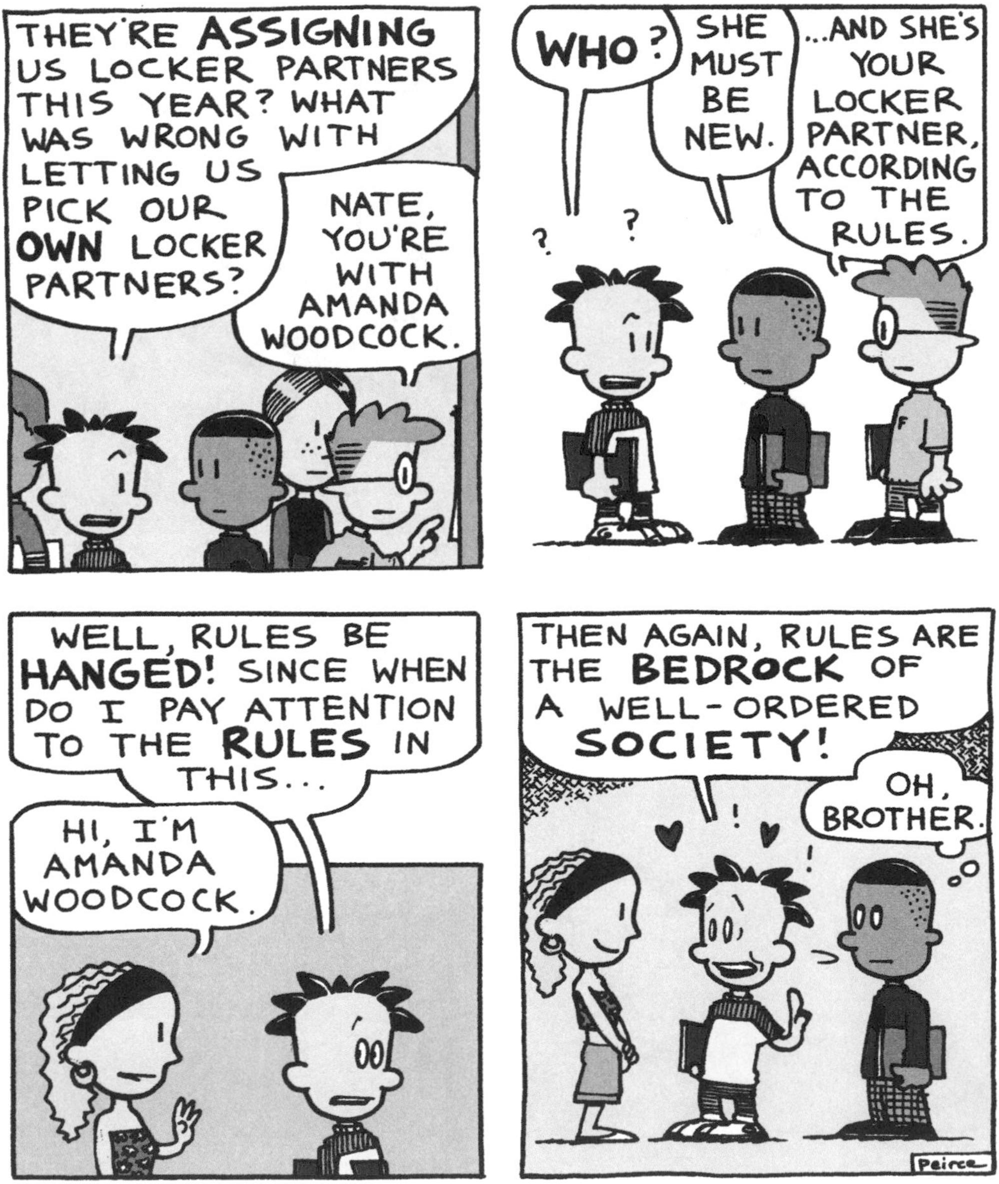
THEY'RE ASSIGNING US LOCKER PARTNERS THIS YEAR? WHAT WAS WRONG WITH LETTING US PICK OUR OWN LOCKER PARTNERS?
NATE, YOU'RE WITH AMANDA WOODCOCK.
WHO?
SHE MUST BE NEW.
...AND SHE'S YOUR LOCKER PARTNER, ACCORDING TO THE RULES.
WELL, RULES BE HANGED! SINCE WHEN DO I PAY ATTENTION TO THE RULES IN THIS...
HI, I'M AMANDA WOODCOCK.
THEN AGAIN, RULES ARE THE BEDROCK OF A WELL-ORDERED SOCIETY!
OH, BROTHER.
Peirce

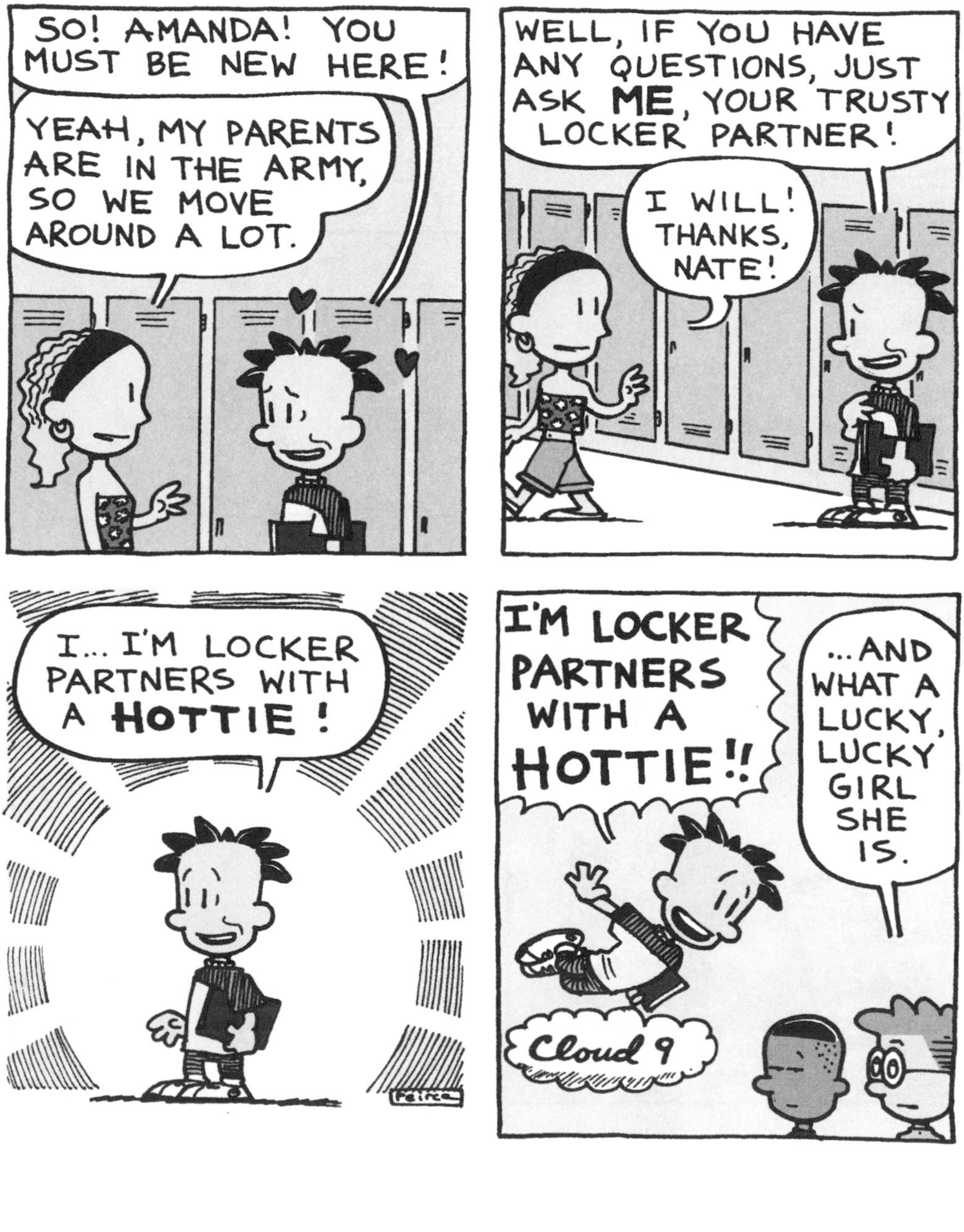
SO! AMANDA! YOU MUST BE NEW HERE!
YEAH, MY PARENTS ARE IN THE ARMY, SO WE MOVE AROUND A LOT.
WELL, IF YOU HAVE ANY QUESTIONS, JUST ASK **ME**, YOUR TRUSTY LOCKER PARTNER!
I WILL! THANKS, NATE!
I... I'M LOCKER PARTNERS WITH A **HOTTIE**!
I'M LOCKER PARTNERS WITH A HOTTIE!!
...AND WHAT A LUCKY, LUCKY GIRL SHE IS.
Cloud 9

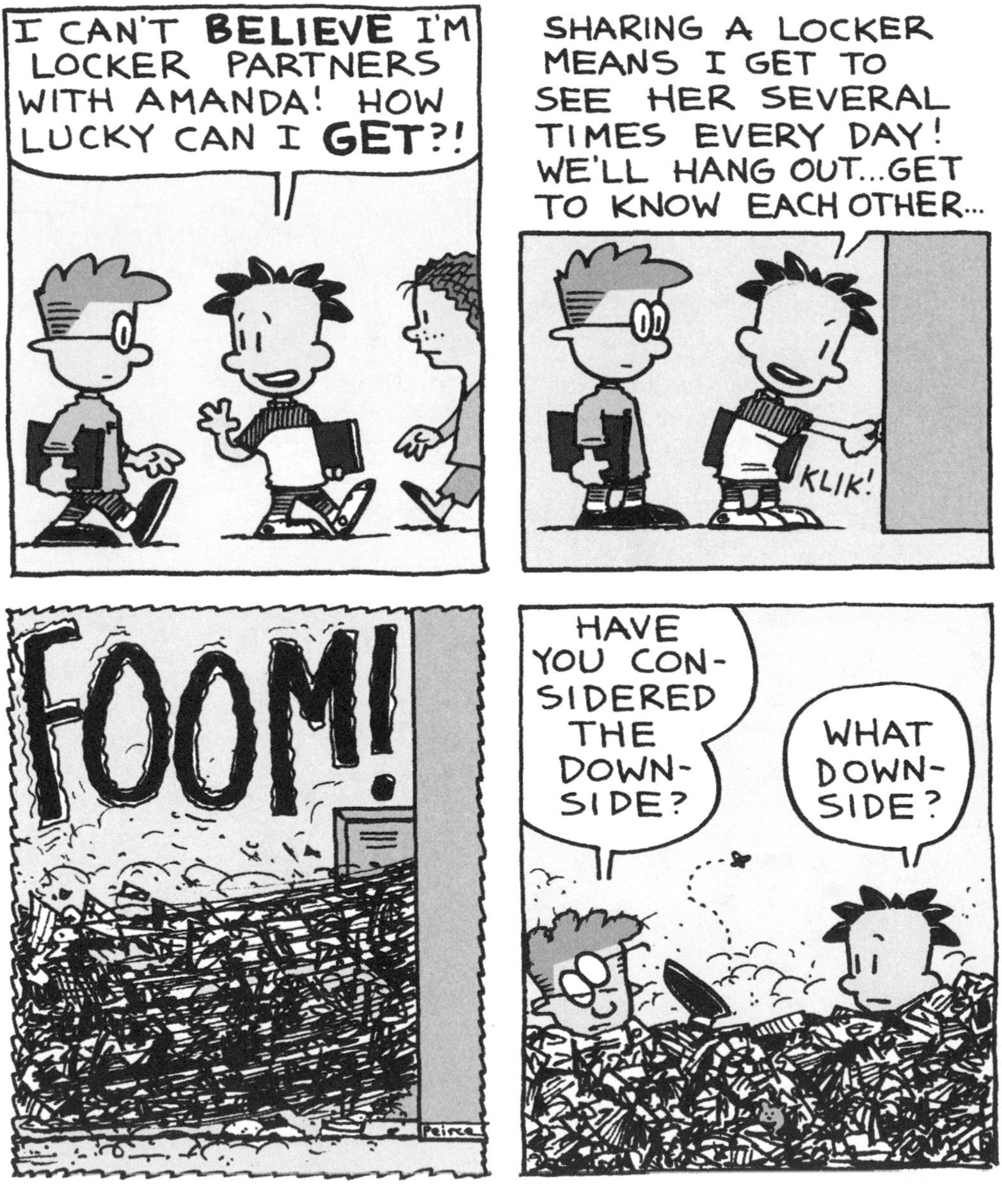
I CAN'T BELIEVE I'M LOCKER PARTNERS WITH AMANDA! HOW LUCKY CAN I GET?!
SHARING A LOCKER MEANS I GET TO SEE HER SEVERAL TIMES EVERY DAY! WE'LL HANG OUT...GET TO KNOW EACH OTHER...
KLIK!
FOOM!
HAVE YOU CONSIDERED THE DOWNSIDE?
WHAT DOWNSIDE?

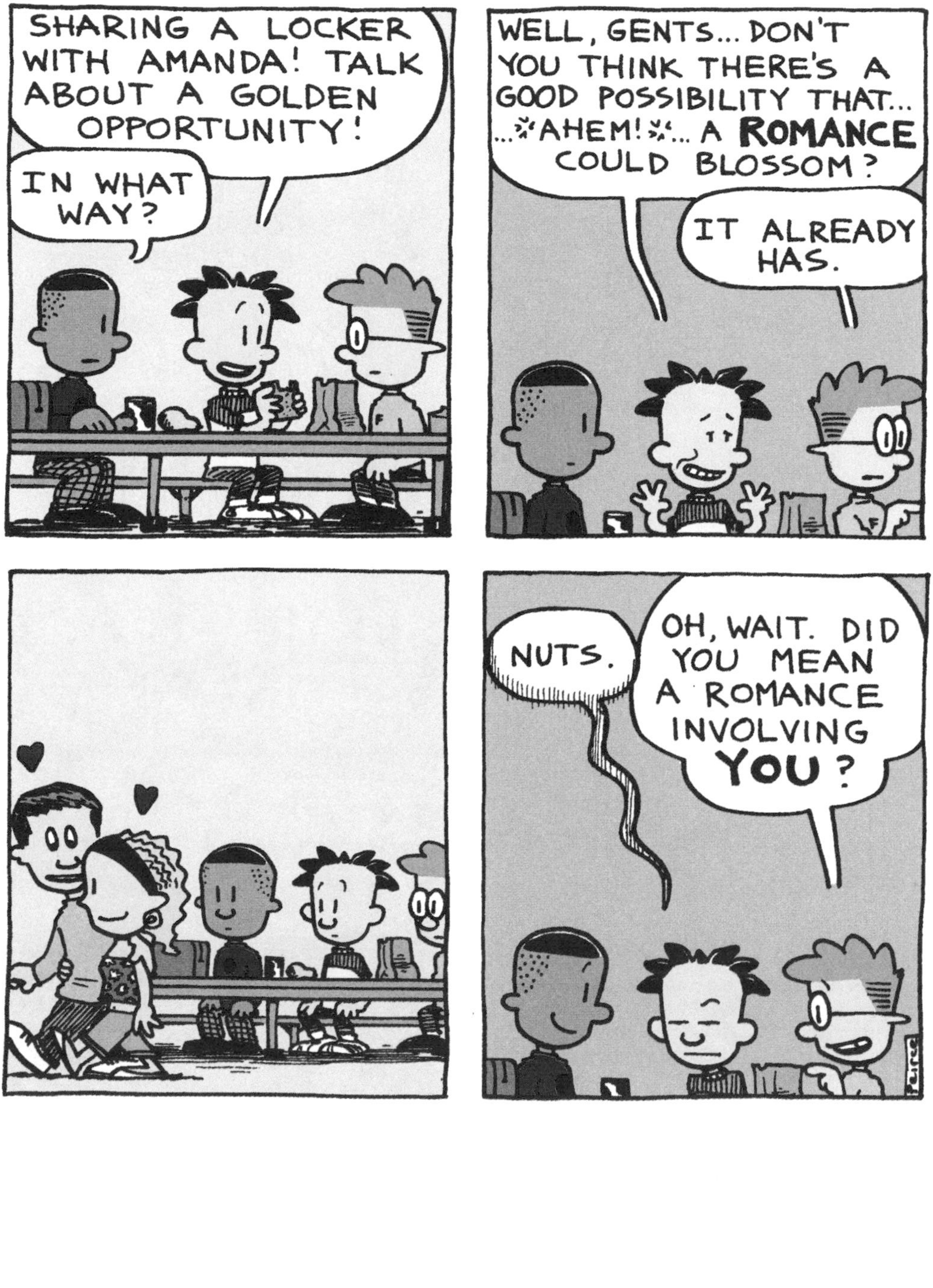
SHARING A LOCKER WITH AMANDA! TALK ABOUT A GOLDEN OPPORTUNITY!
IN WHAT WAY?
WELL, GENTS... DON'T YOU THINK THERE'S A GOOD POSSIBILITY THAT... ...AHEM!... A ROMANCE COULD BLOSSOM?
IT ALREADY HAS.
NUTS.
OH, WAIT. DID YOU MEAN A ROMANCE INVOLVING YOU?
PEIRCE

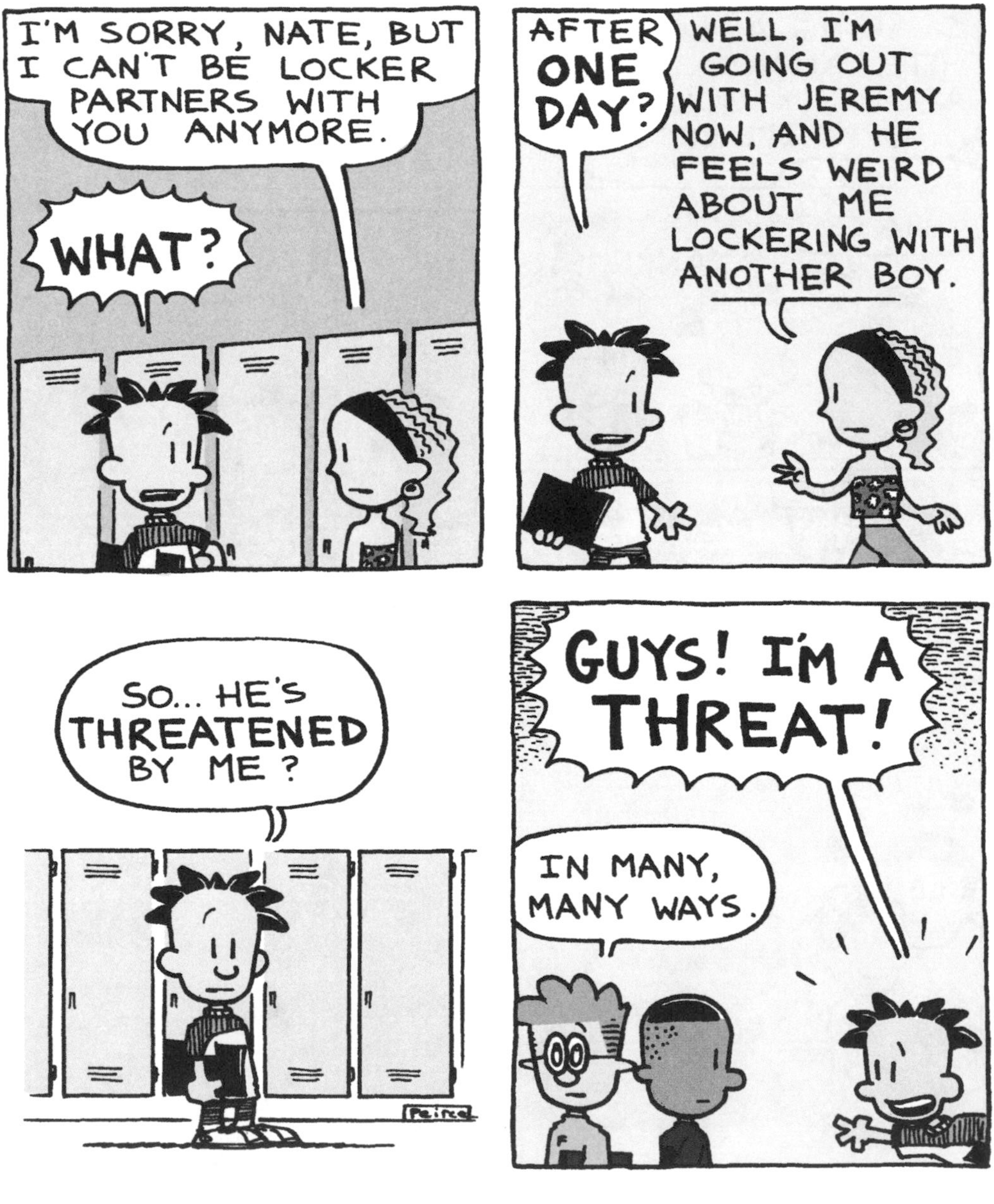
I'M SORRY, NATE, BUT I CAN'T BE LOCKER PARTNERS WITH YOU ANYMORE.
WHAT?
AFTER ONE DAY?
WELL, I'M GOING OUT WITH JEREMY NOW, AND HE FEELS WEIRD ABOUT ME LOCKERING WITH ANOTHER BOY.
SO... HE'S THREATENED BY ME?
Peirce
GUYS! I'M A THREAT!
IN MANY, MANY WAYS.

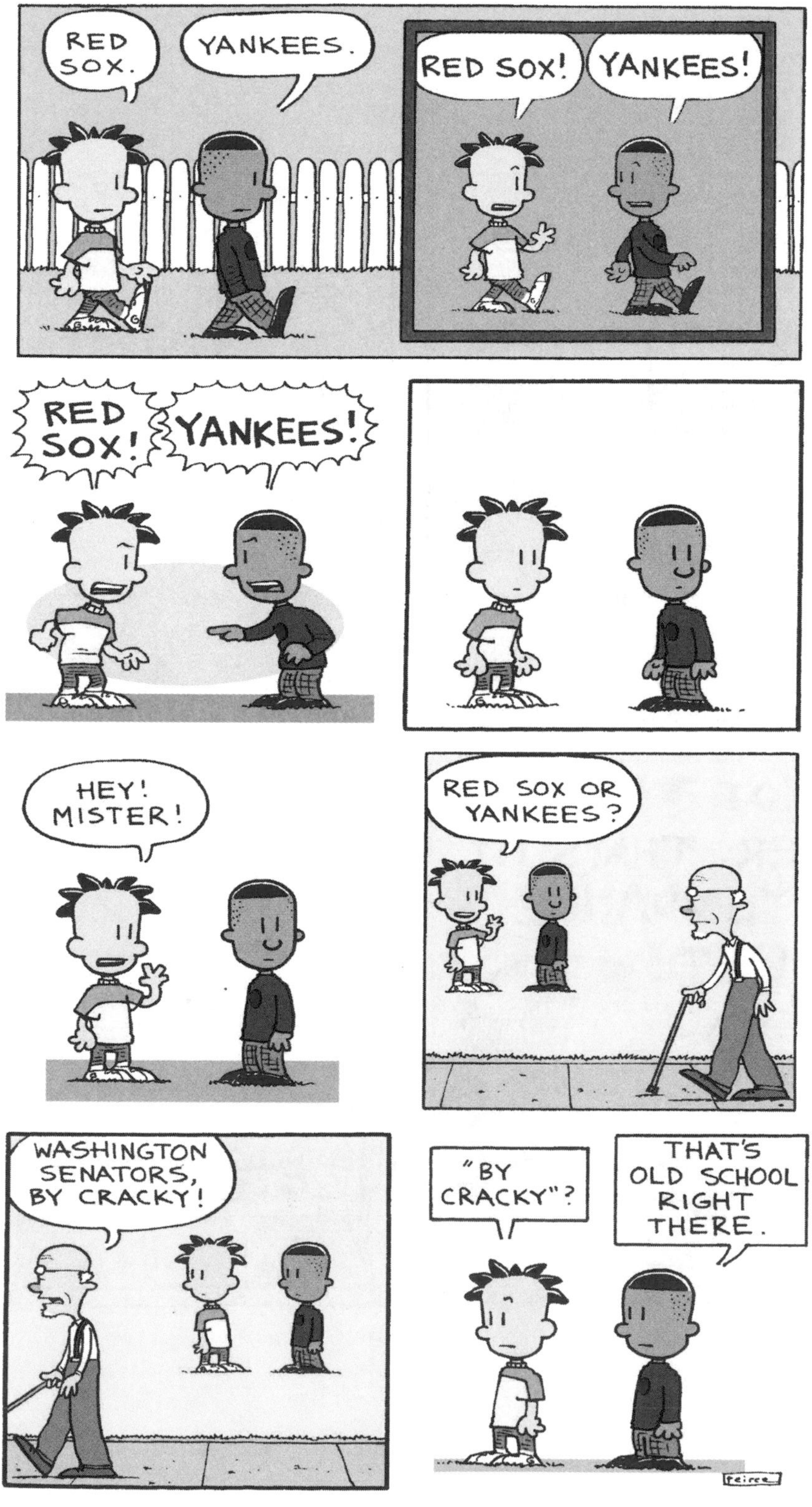
RED SOX.
YANKEES.
RED SOX!
YANKEES!
RED SOX!
YANKEES!
HEY! MISTER!
RED SOX OR YANKEES?
WASHINGTON SENATORS, BY CRACKY!
"BY CRACKY"?
THAT'S OLD SCHOOL RIGHT THERE.
peirce

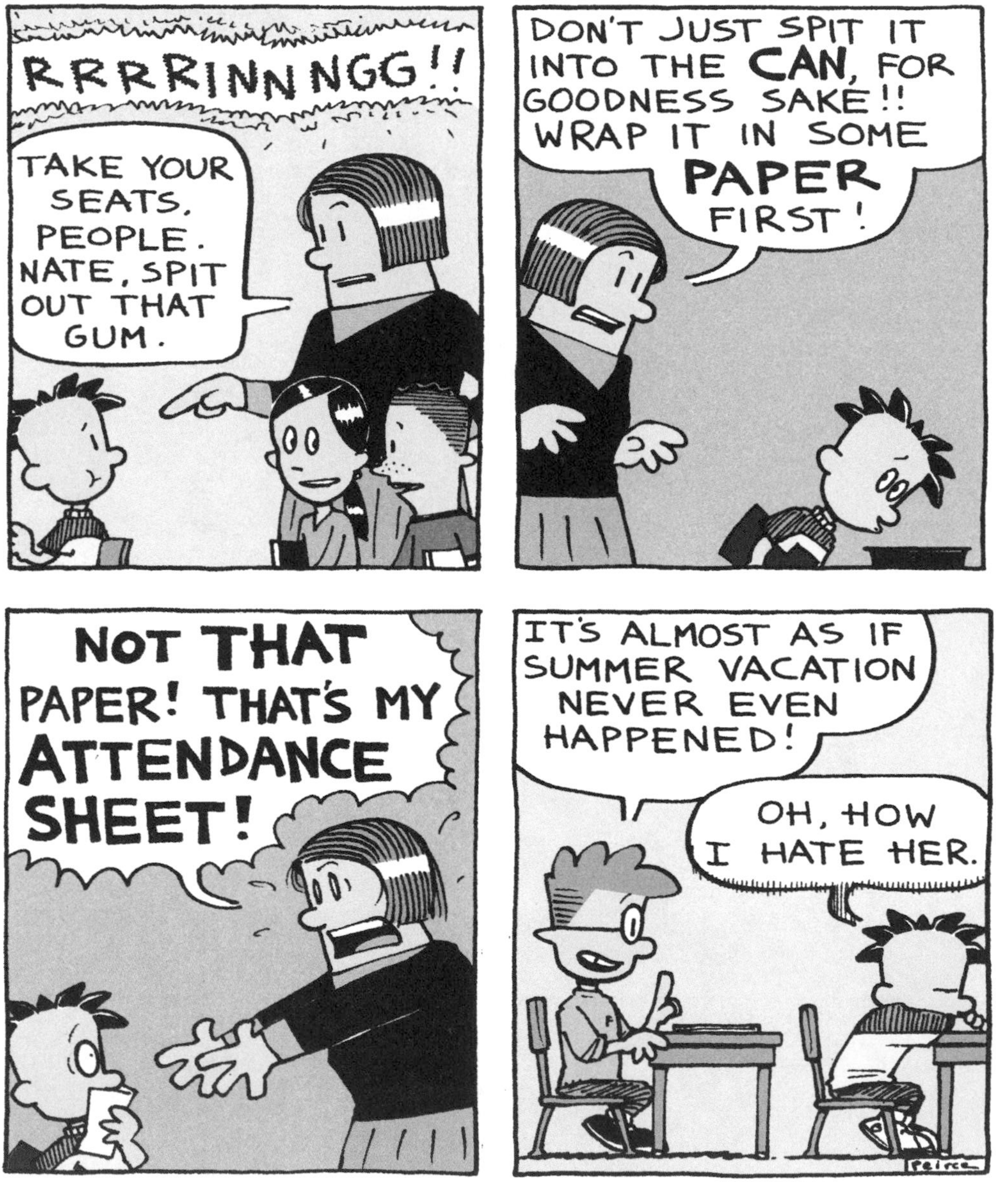
RRRRINNNGG!!
TAKE YOUR SEATS, PEOPLE. NATE, SPIT OUT THAT GUM.
DON'T JUST SPIT IT INTO THE CAN, FOR GOODNESS SAKE!! WRAP IT IN SOME PAPER FIRST!
NOT THAT PAPER! THAT'S MY ATTENDANCE SHEET!
IT'S ALMOST AS IF SUMMER VACATION NEVER EVEN HAPPENED!
OH, HOW I HATE HER.
Peirce

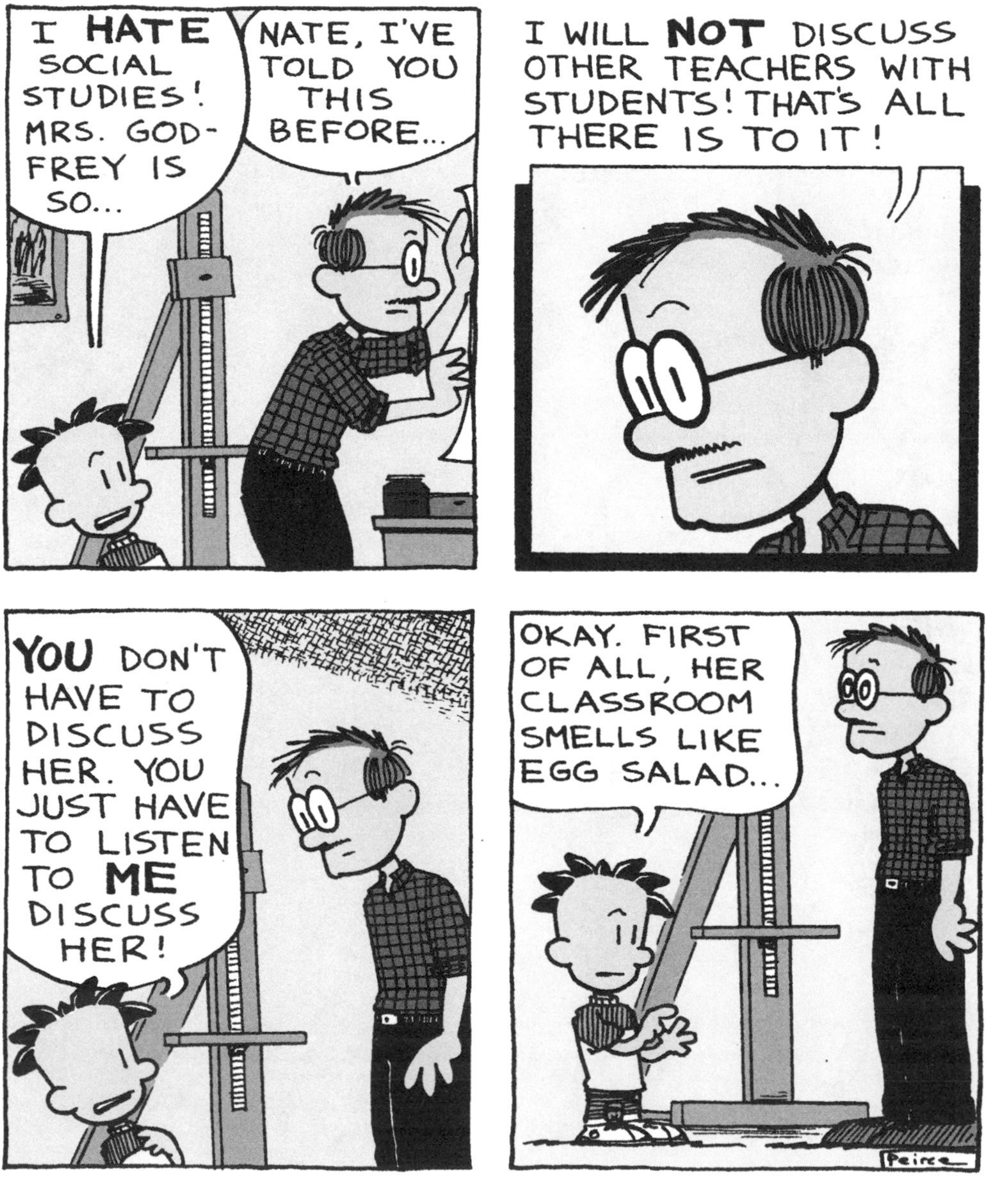
I HATE SOCIAL STUDIES! MRS. GODFREY IS SO...
NATE, I'VE TOLD YOU THIS BEFORE...
I WILL NOT DISCUSS OTHER TEACHERS WITH STUDENTS! THAT'S ALL THERE IS TO IT!
YOU DON'T HAVE TO DISCUSS HER. YOU JUST HAVE TO LISTEN TO ME DISCUSS HER!
OKAY. FIRST OF ALL, HER CLASSROOM SMELLS LIKE EGG SALAD...
Peirce

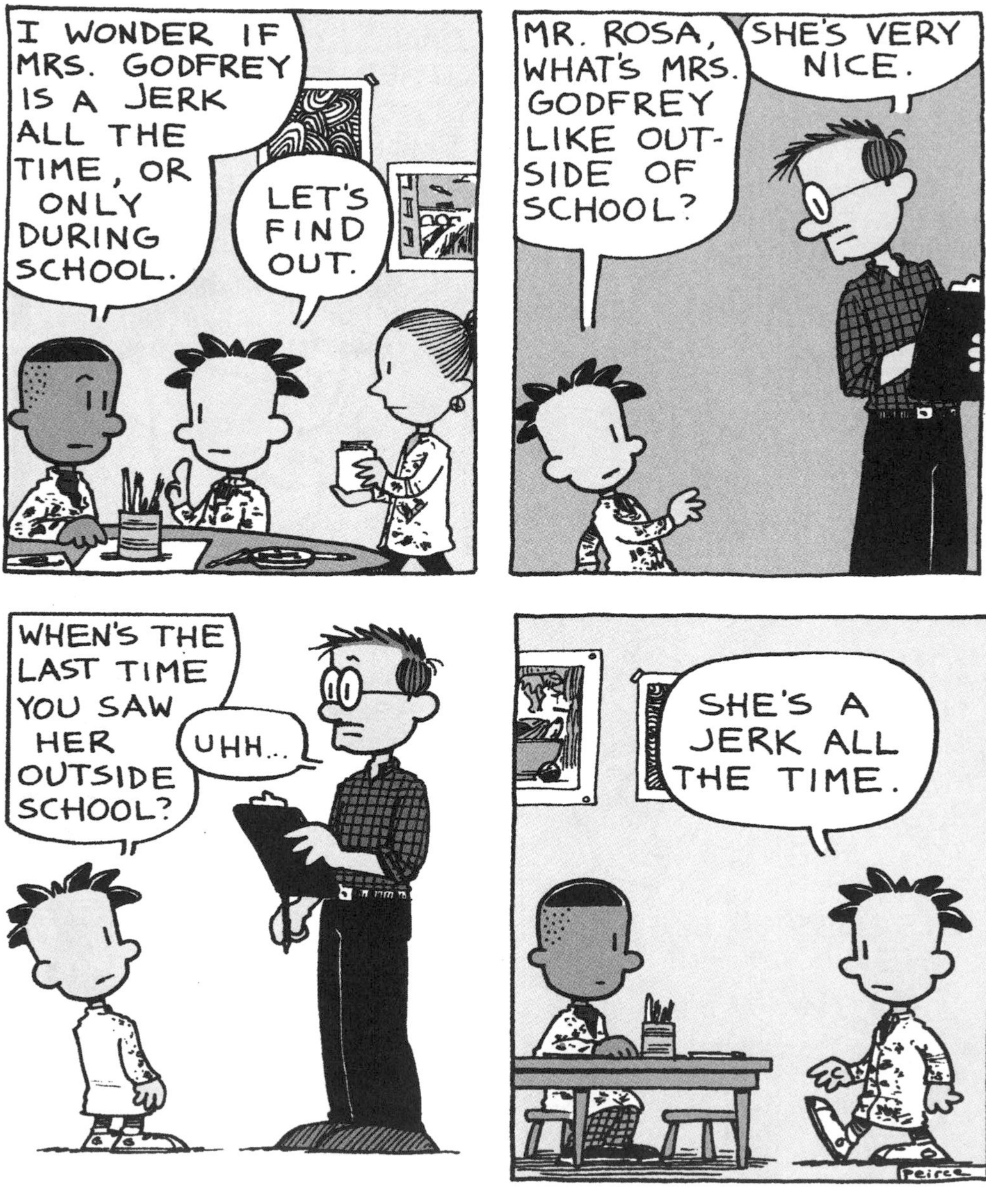
I WONDER IF MRS. GODFREY IS A JERK ALL THE TIME, OR ONLY DURING SCHOOL.
LET'S FIND OUT.
MR. ROSA, WHAT'S MRS. GODFREY LIKE OUTSIDE OF SCHOOL?
SHE'S VERY NICE.
WHEN'S THE LAST TIME YOU SAW HER OUTSIDE SCHOOL?
UHH...
SHE'S A JERK ALL THE TIME.
Peirce

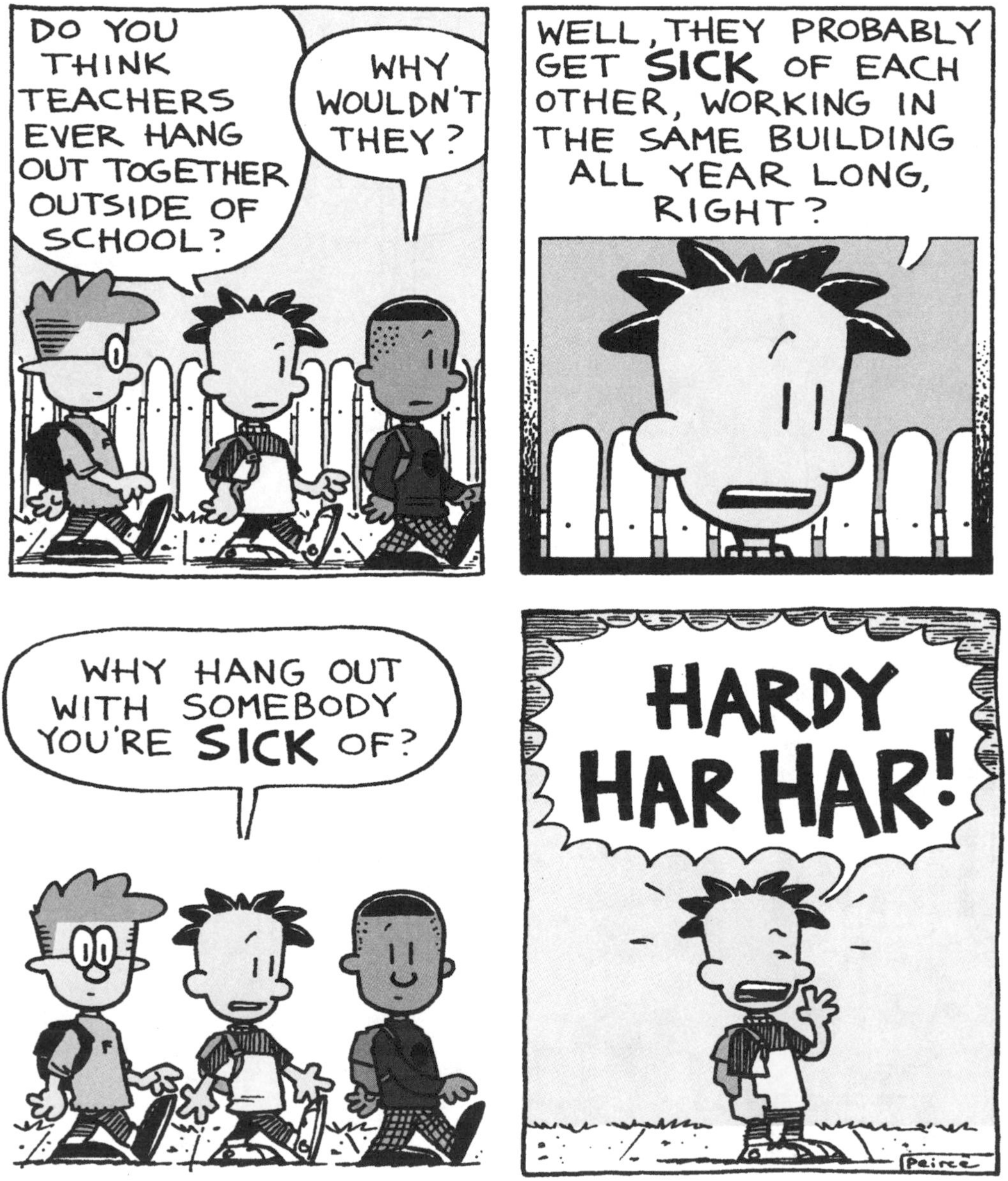
DO YOU THINK TEACHERS EVER HANG OUT TOGETHER OUTSIDE OF SCHOOL?
WHY WOULDN'T THEY?
WELL, THEY PROBABLY GET SICK OF EACH OTHER, WORKING IN THE SAME BUILDING ALL YEAR LONG, RIGHT?
WHY HANG OUT WITH SOMEBODY YOU'RE SICK OF?
HARDY HAR HAR!
Peirce

MS. CLARKE, DO TEACHERS EVER HANG OUT TOGETHER AWAY FROM SCHOOL?
SURE! I DO, ANYWAY!
REALLY? WITH WHO?
MRS. GODFREY, MOSTLY. SHE'S MY BEST FRIEND.
HA HA HA HA HA HA HA HA HA
TURNS OUT SHE WAS SERIOUS.
Peirce

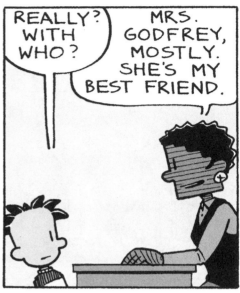

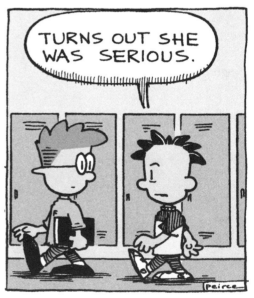

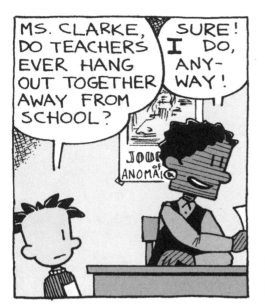

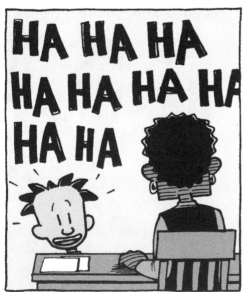

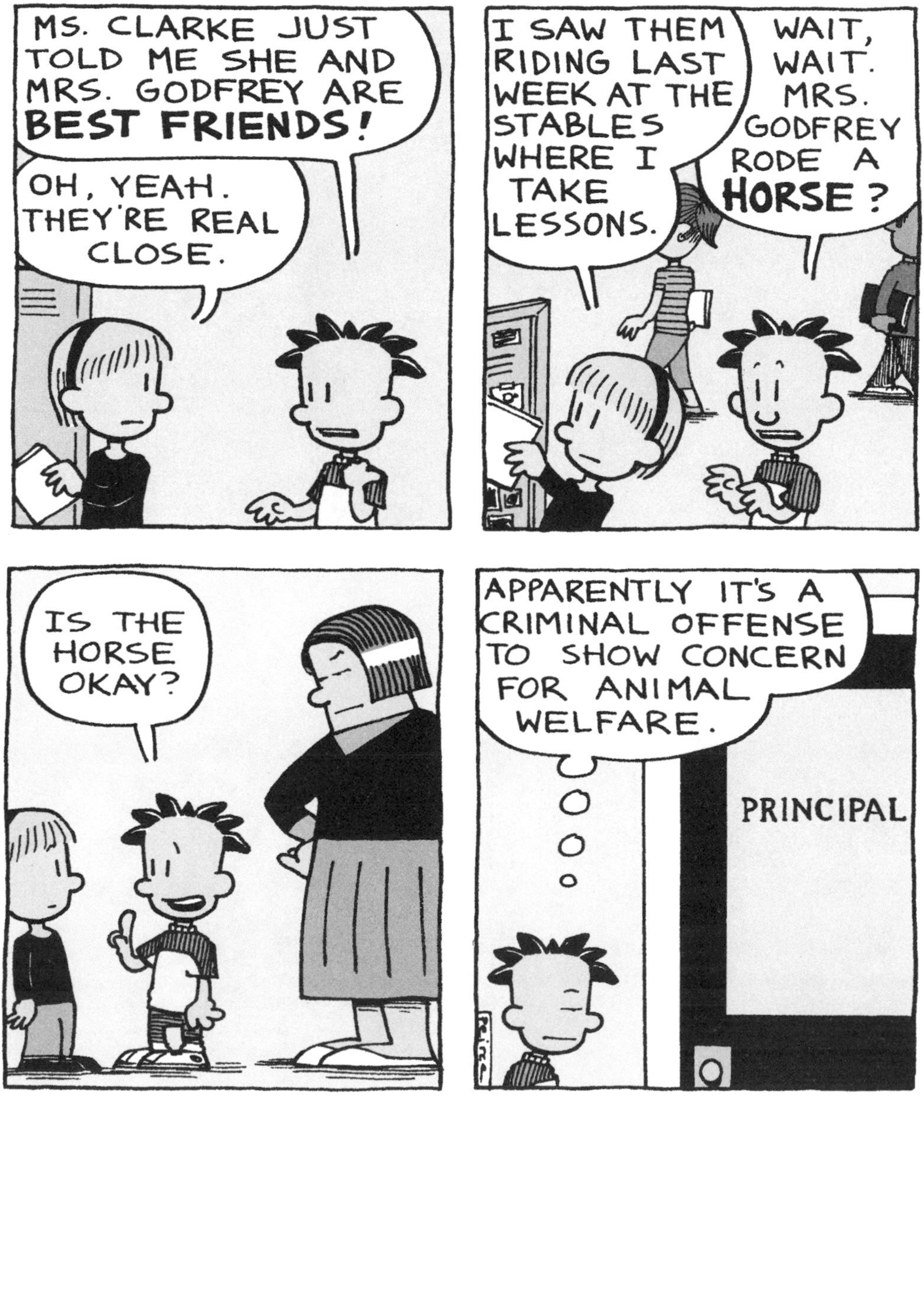
MS. CLARKE JUST TOLD ME SHE AND MRS. GODFREY ARE **BEST FRIENDS!**
OH, YEAH. THEY'RE REAL CLOSE.
I SAW THEM RIDING LAST WEEK AT THE STABLES WHERE I TAKE LESSONS.
WAIT, WAIT. MRS. GODFREY RODE A **HORSE**?
IS THE HORSE OKAY?
APPARENTLY IT'S A CRIMINAL OFFENSE TO SHOW CONCERN FOR ANIMAL WELFARE.
PRINCIPAL

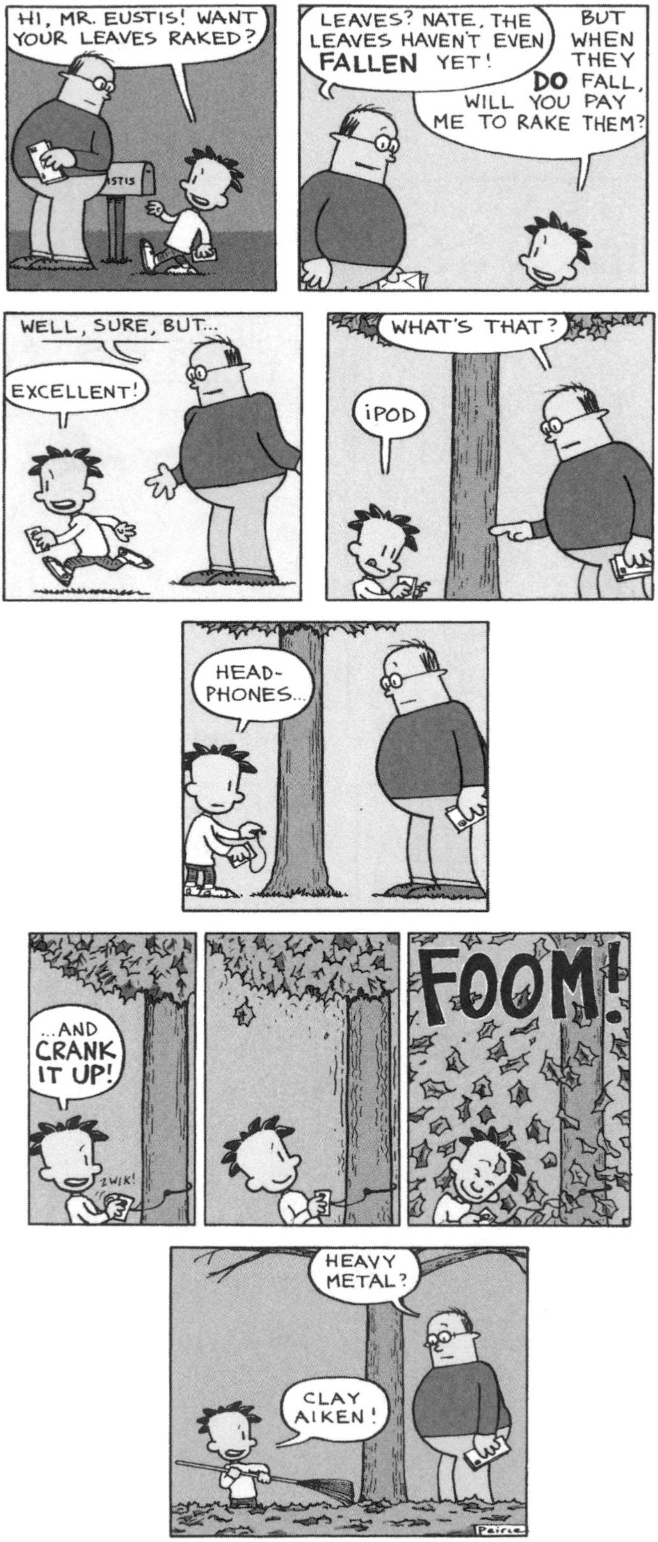

HI, MR. EUSTIS! WANT YOUR LEAVES RAKED?
LEAVES? NATE, THE LEAVES HAVEN'T EVEN FALLEN YET!
BUT WHEN THEY DO FALL, WILL YOU PAY ME TO RAKE THEM?
WELL, SURE, BUT...
EXCELLENT!
WHAT'S THAT?
iPOD
HEAD-PHONES...
...AND CRANK IT UP!
ZWIK!
FOOM!
HEAVY METAL?
CLAY AIKEN!
Peirce

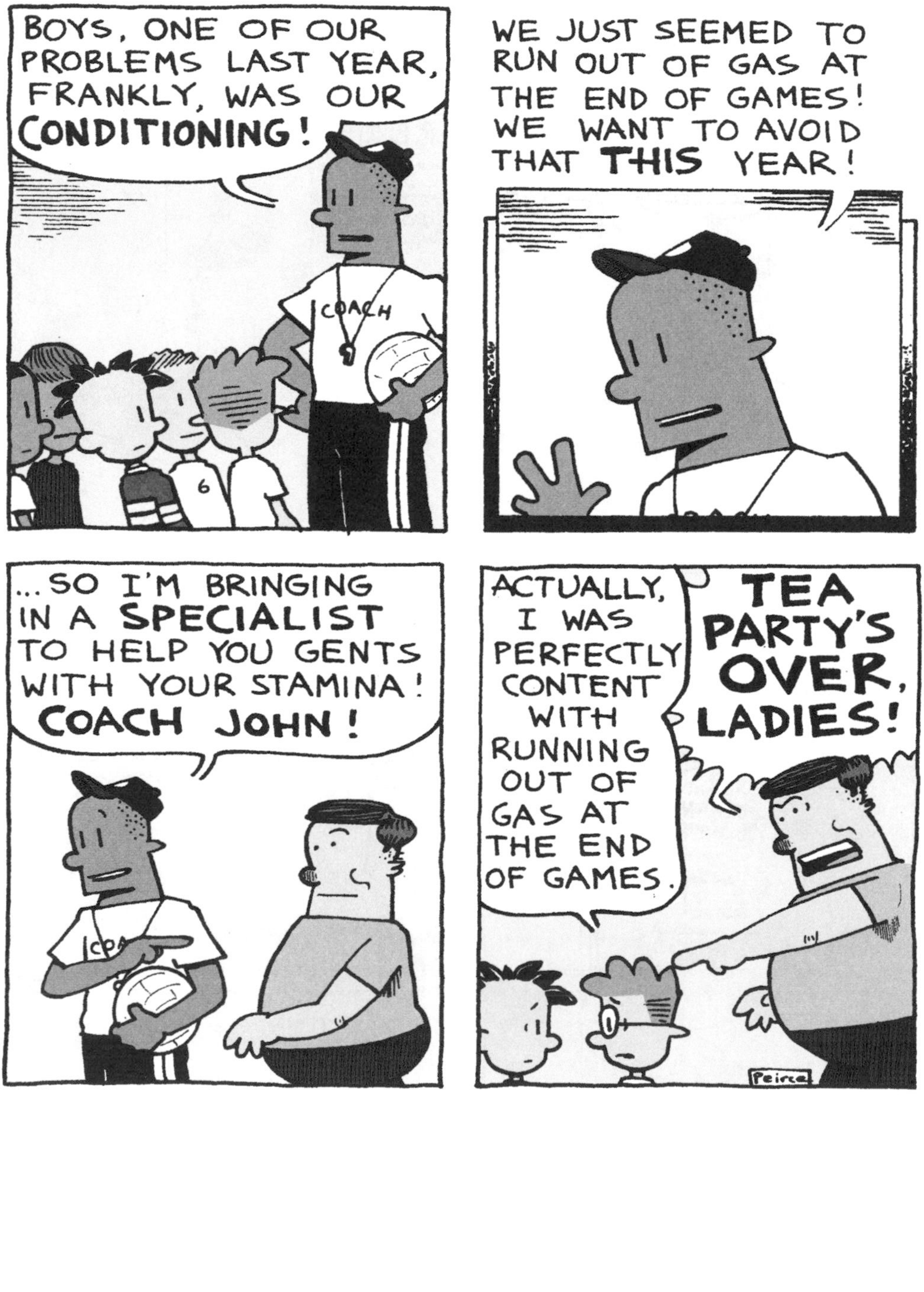
BOYS, ONE OF OUR PROBLEMS LAST YEAR, FRANKLY, WAS OUR CONDITIONING!
COACH
6
WE JUST SEEMED TO RUN OUT OF GAS AT THE END OF GAMES! WE WANT TO AVOID THAT THIS YEAR!
...SO I'M BRINGING IN A SPECIALIST TO HELP YOU GENTS WITH YOUR STAMINA! COACH JOHN!
ACTUALLY, I WAS PERFECTLY CONTENT WITH RUNNING OUT OF GAS AT THE END OF GAMES.
TEA PARTY'S OVER, LADIES!
Peirce

SO! THE TASK AT HAND, AS I UNDER-STAND IT, IS TO WHIP YOU MARSHMALLOWS INTO SHAPE!
THAT'LL TAKE WORK, SOLDIERS! LOTS OF WORK! BUT JUST REMEMBER THIS:
"THAT WHICH DOES NOT KILL ME MAKES ME STRONGER"!!
SO HE'S ONLY GOING TO ALMOST KILL US?
GULP!
FIRST RULE: IF YOU'RE GOING TO TOSS YOUR COOKIES, DO IT ON THE SIDE-LINES!
Peirce

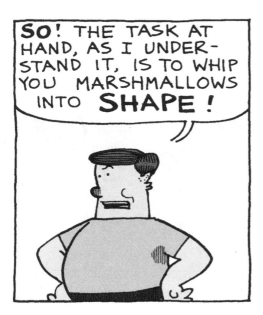

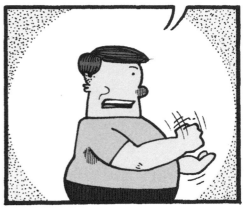

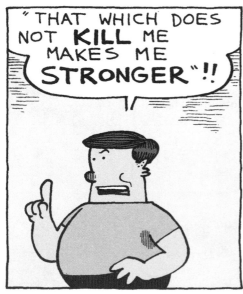

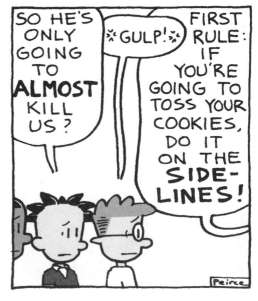

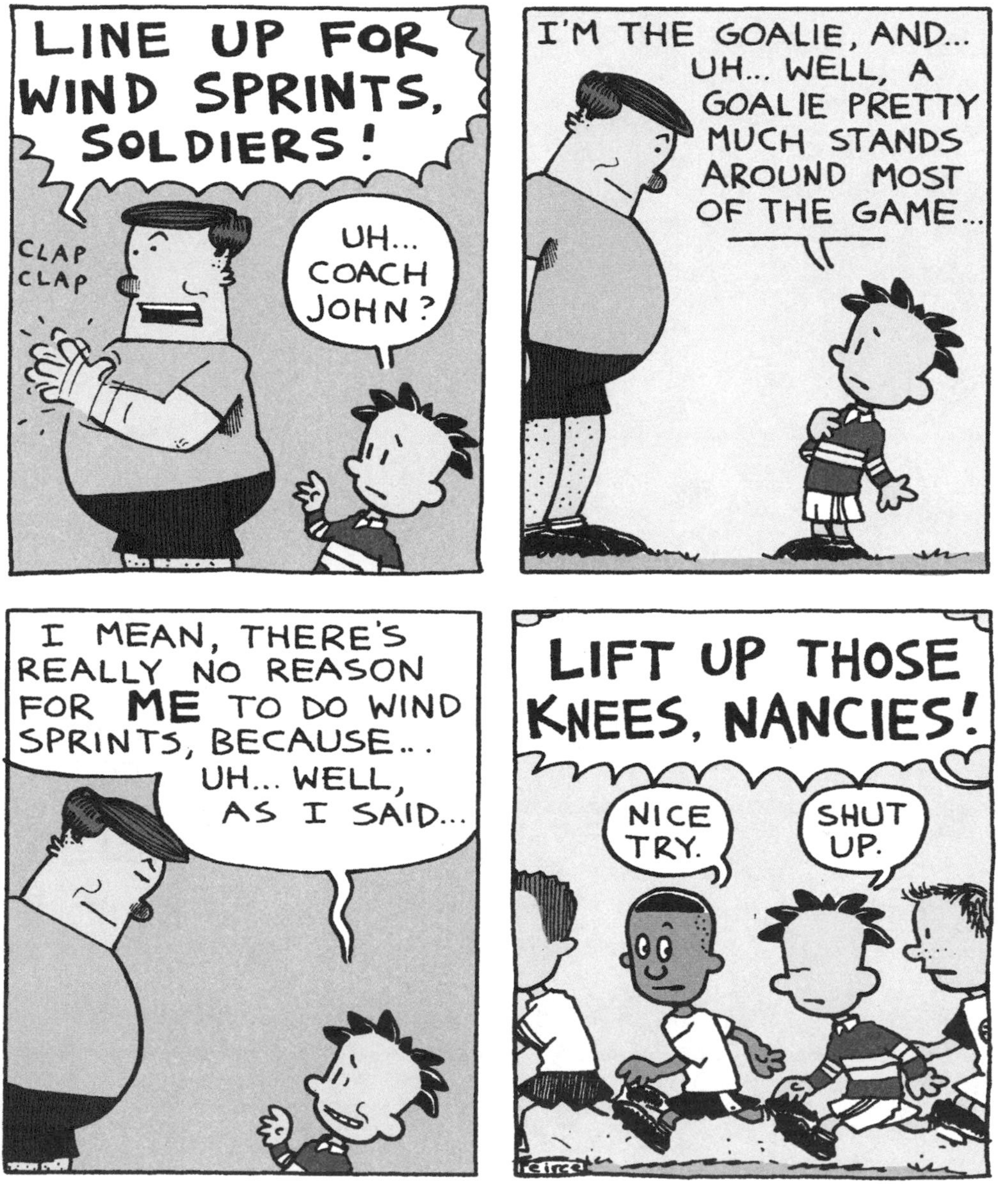
LINE UP FOR WIND SPRINTS, SOLDIERS!
CLAP CLAP
UH... COACH JOHN?
I'M THE GOALIE, AND... UH... WELL, A GOALIE PRETTY MUCH STANDS AROUND MOST OF THE GAME...
I MEAN, THERE'S REALLY NO REASON FOR ME TO DO WIND SPRINTS, BECAUSE... UH... WELL, AS I SAID...
LIFT UP THOSE KNEES, NANCIES!
NICE TRY.
SHUT UP.
Peirce

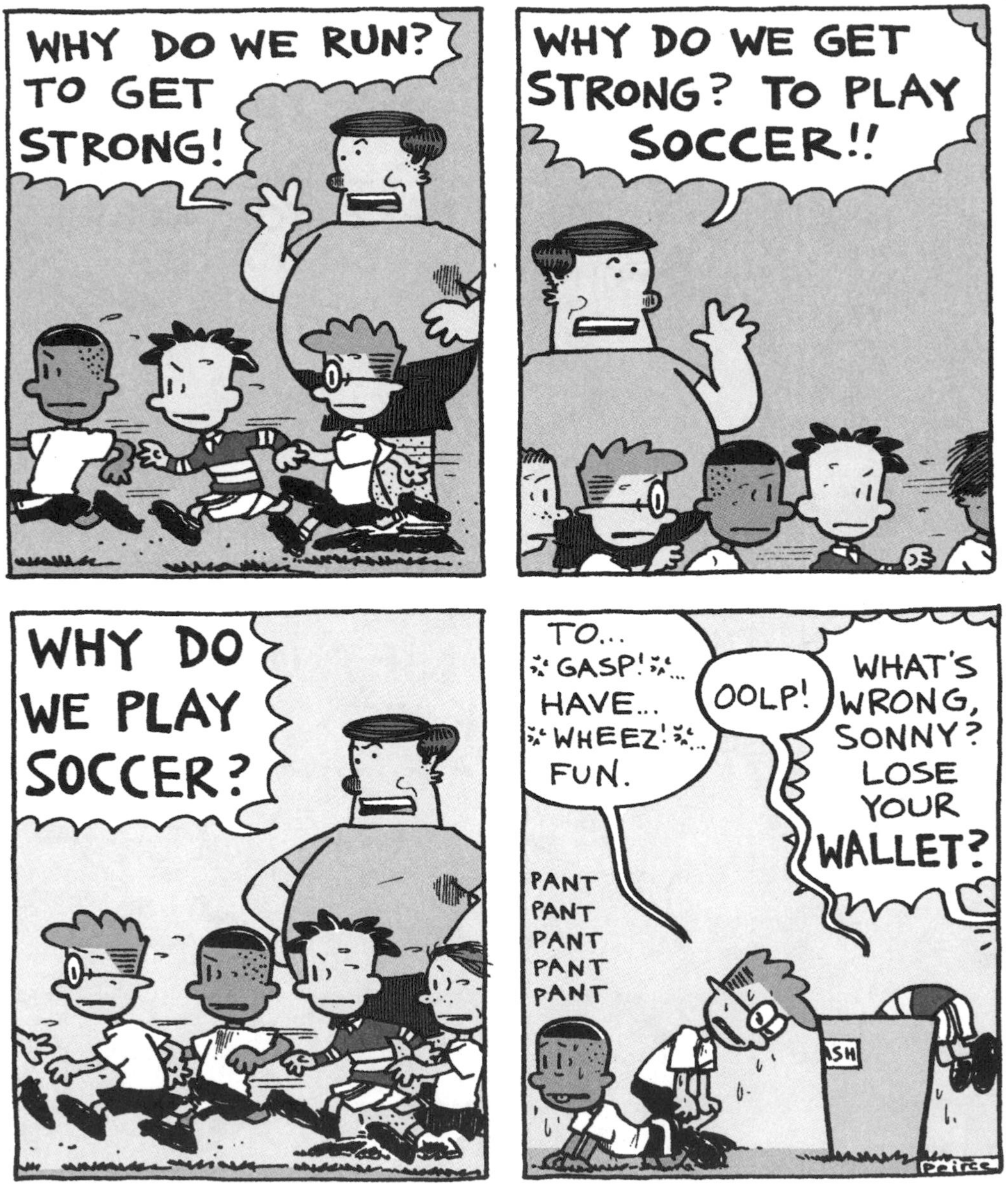
WHY DO WE RUN? TO GET STRONG!
WHY DO WE GET STRONG? TO PLAY SOCCER!!
WHY DO WE PLAY SOCCER?
TO... GASP! HAVE... WHEEZ! FUN.
OOLP!
WHAT'S WRONG, SONNY? LOSE YOUR WALLET?
PANT PANT PANT PANT PANT
ASH
peirce

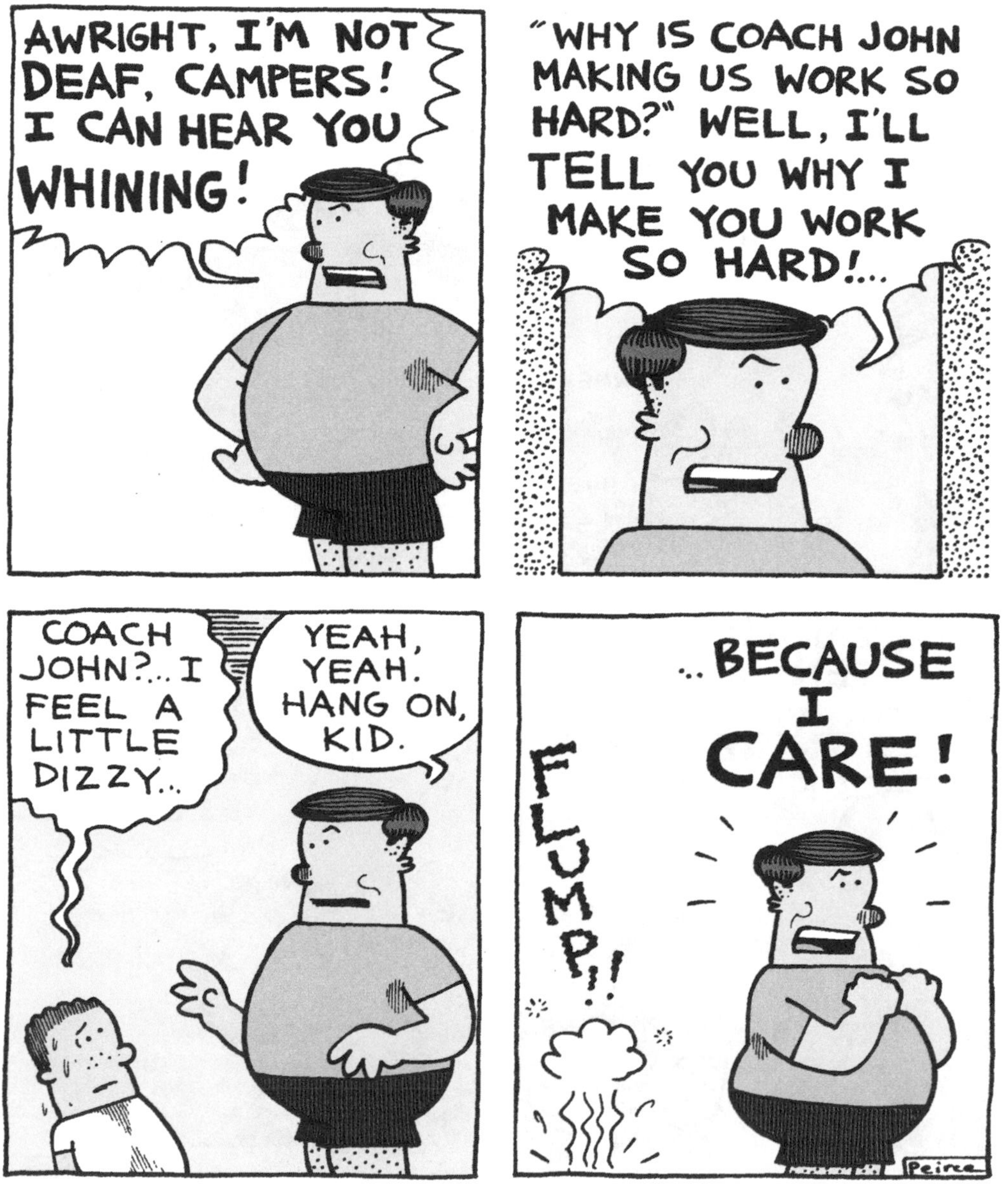
AWRIGHT, I'M NOT DEAF, CAMPERS! I CAN HEAR YOU WHINING!
"WHY IS COACH JOHN MAKING US WORK SO HARD?" WELL, I'LL TELL YOU WHY I MAKE YOU WORK SO HARD!...
COACH JOHN?... I FEEL A LITTLE DIZZY...
YEAH, YEAH. HANG ON, KID.
...BECAUSE I CARE!
FLUMP!!
Peirce

HANG IN THERE, GUYS! I KNOW COACH JOHN IS A BIT OF A TASKMASTER, BUT HAVING HIM HELP OUT WILL PAY BIG DIVIDENDS!

GASP!

WHEW!

DID I EVER TELL YOU HE WAS **MY** COACH BACK IN HIGH SCHOOL? HE WAS HIRED RIGHT BEFORE MY SENIOR YEAR, AND WHAT A YEAR THAT WAS!

INSTEAD OF LOSING ALL **TEN** OF OUR GAMES, WE ONLY LOST **NINE!**

THAT'S LAMETASTIC!

OUR WIN WAS A FORFEIT, BUT WE FELT **GOOD** ABOUT OURSELVES!

Peirce

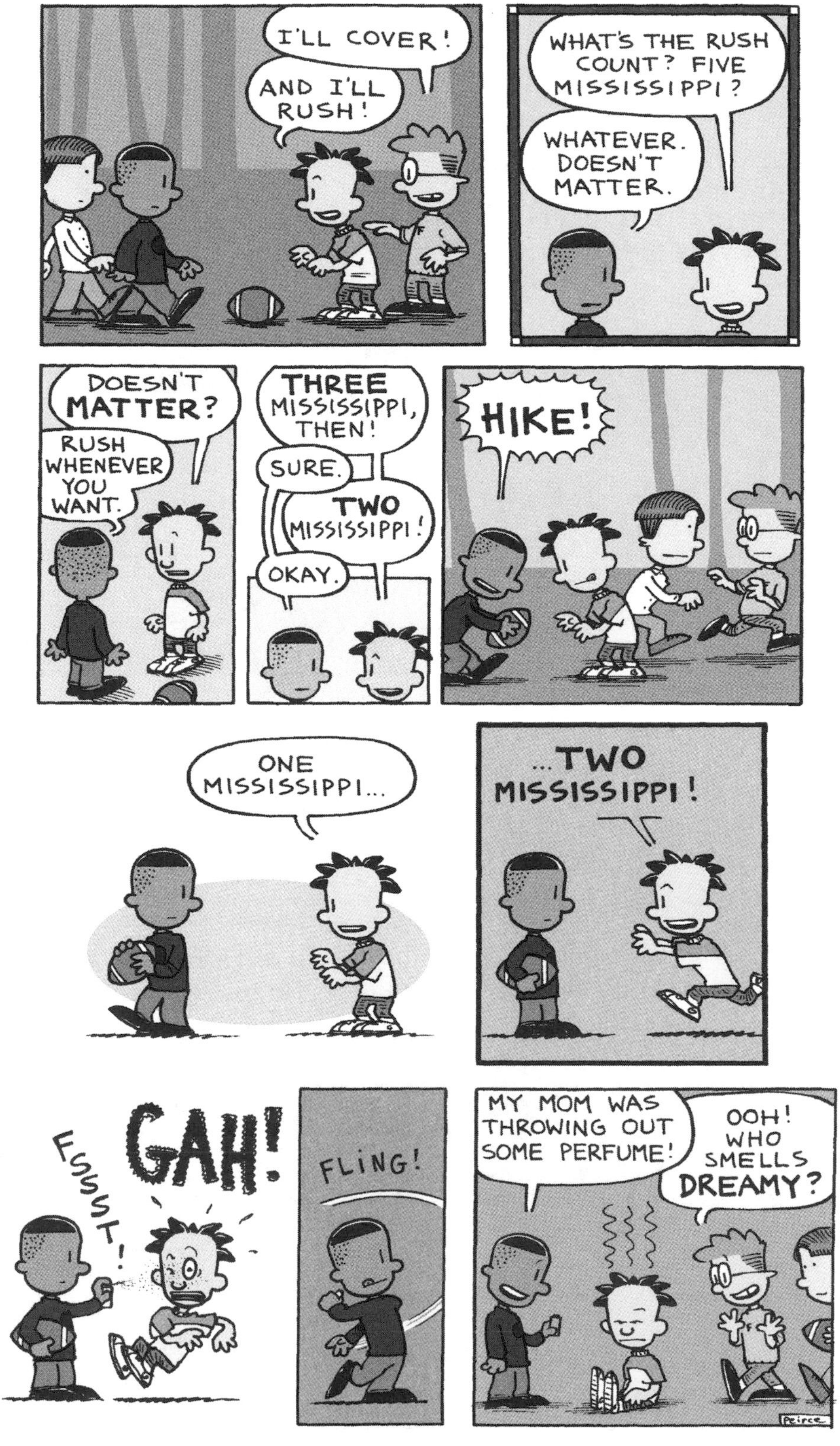
I'LL COVER!
AND I'LL RUSH!
WHAT'S THE RUSH COUNT? FIVE MISSISSIPPI?
WHATEVER. DOESN'T MATTER.
DOESN'T MATTER?
RUSH WHENEVER YOU WANT.
THREE MISSISSIPPI, THEN!
SURE.
TWO MISSISSIPPI!
OKAY.
HIKE!
ONE MISSISSIPPI...
...TWO MISSISSIPPI!
FSSST!
GAH!
FLING!
MY MOM WAS THROWING OUT SOME PERFUME!
OOH! WHO SMELLS DREAMY?
Peirce

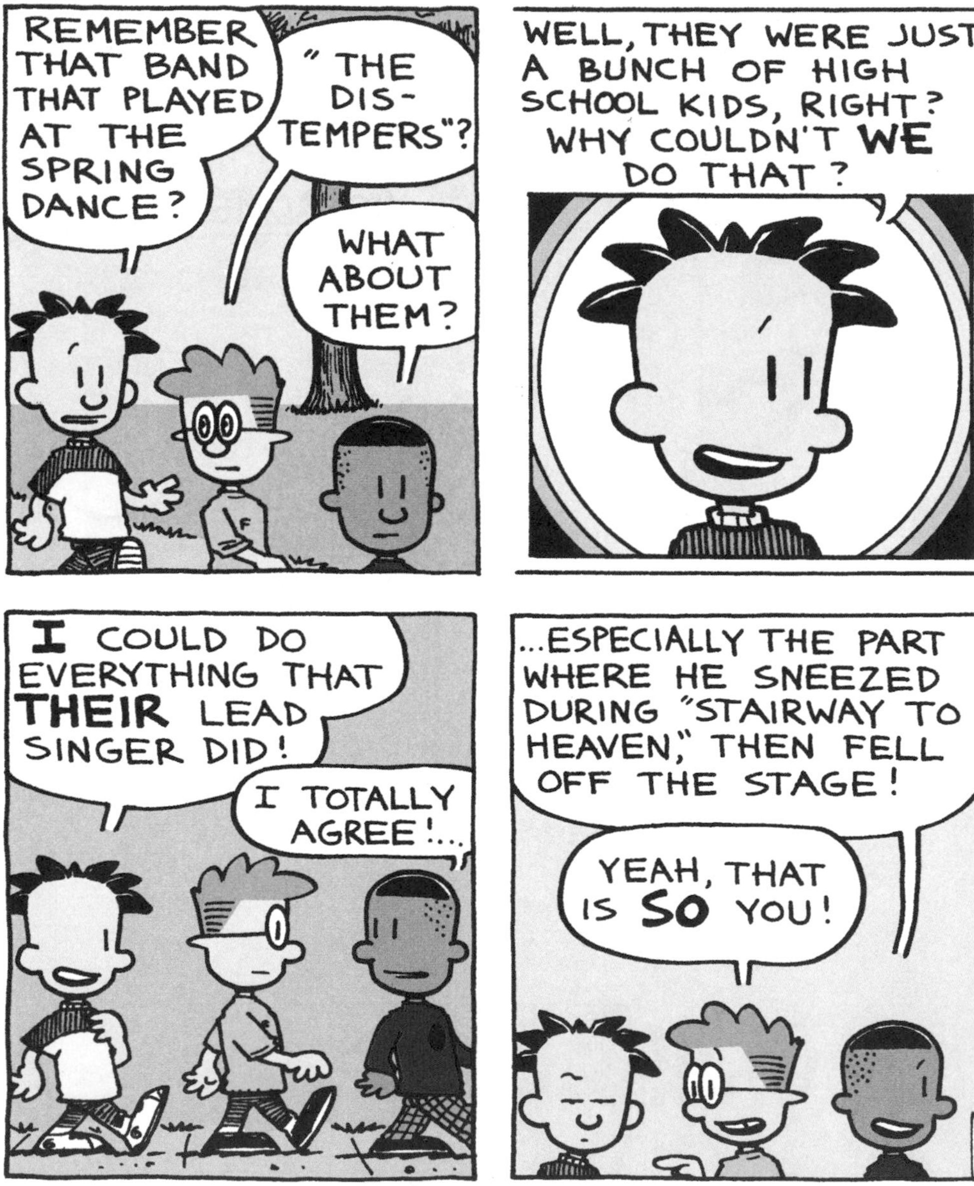
REMEMBER THAT BAND THAT PLAYED AT THE SPRING DANCE?
"THE DIS-TEMPERS"?
WHAT ABOUT THEM?
WELL, THEY WERE JUST A BUNCH OF HIGH SCHOOL KIDS, RIGHT? WHY COULDN'T WE DO THAT?
I COULD DO EVERYTHING THAT THEIR LEAD SINGER DID!
I TOTALLY AGREE!...
...ESPECIALLY THE PART WHERE HE SNEEZED DURING "STAIRWAY TO HEAVEN," THEN FELL OFF THE STAGE!
YEAH, THAT IS SO YOU!
PEIRCE

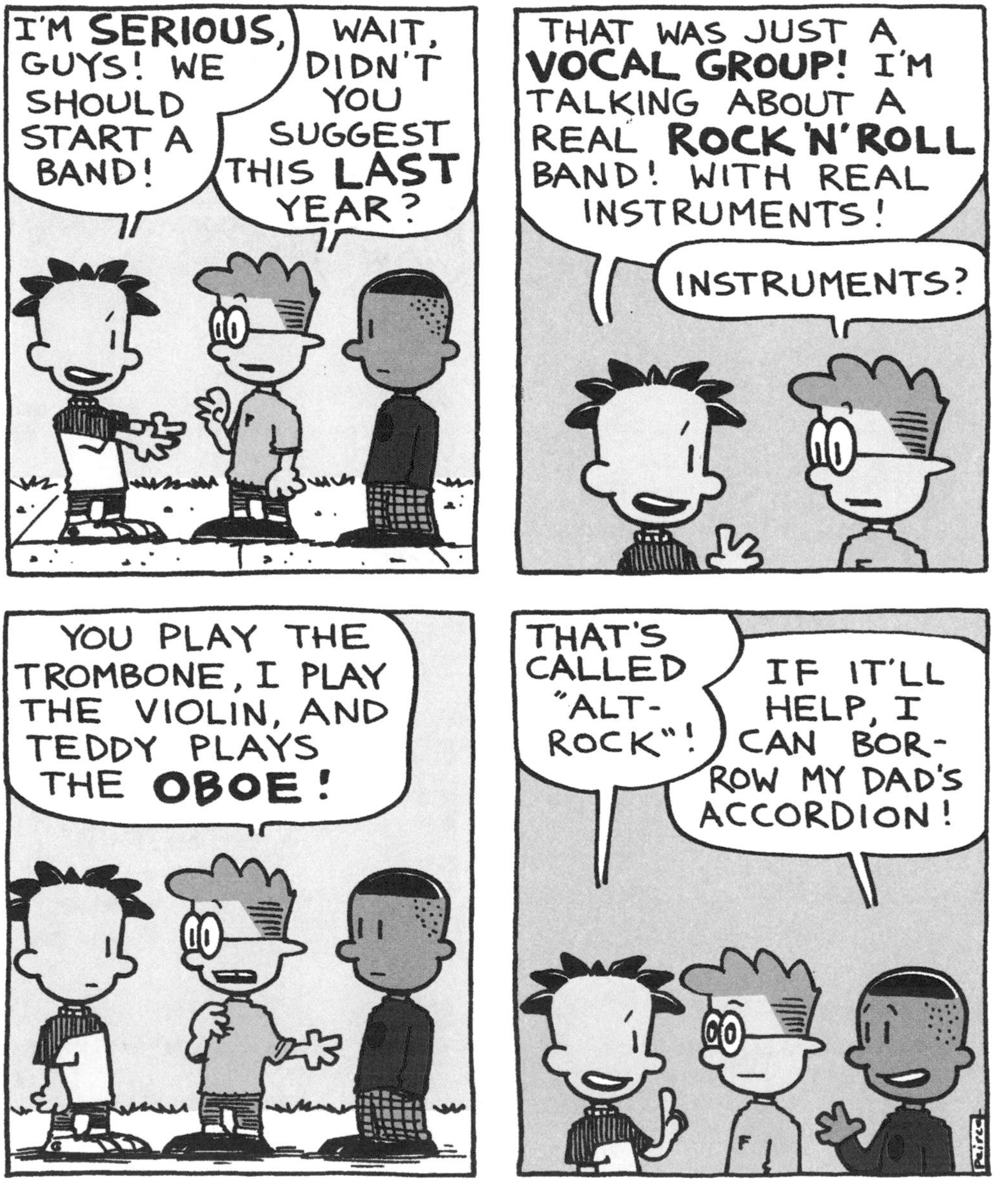
I'M SERIOUS, GUYS! WE SHOULD START A BAND!
WAIT, DIDN'T YOU SUGGEST THIS LAST YEAR?
THAT WAS JUST A VOCAL GROUP! I'M TALKING ABOUT A REAL ROCK 'N' ROLL BAND! WITH REAL INSTRUMENTS!
INSTRUMENTS?
YOU PLAY THE TROMBONE, I PLAY THE VIOLIN, AND TEDDY PLAYS THE OBOE!
THAT'S CALLED "ALT-ROCK"!
IF IT'LL HELP, I CAN BORROW MY DAD'S ACCORDION!

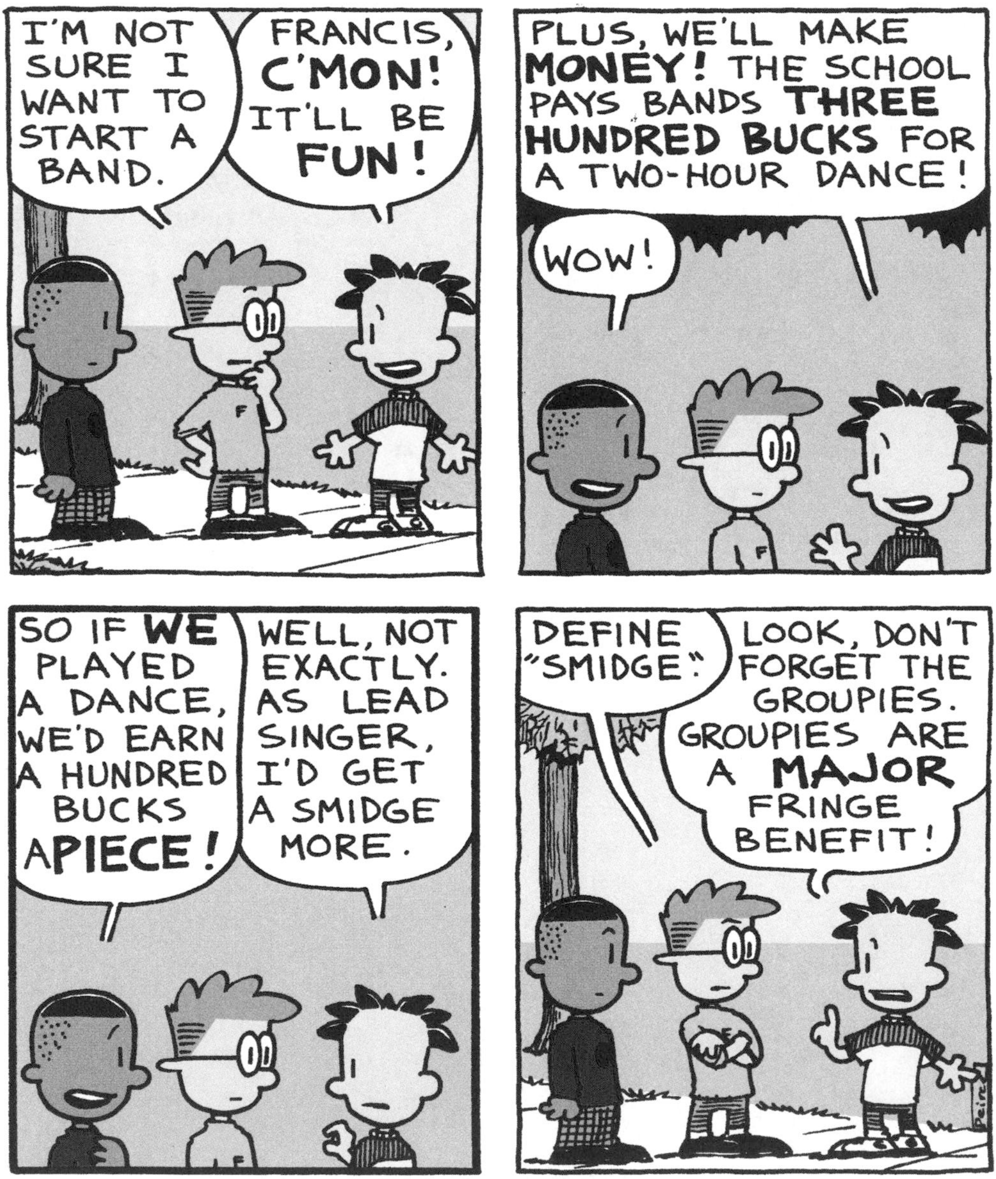
I'M NOT SURE I WANT TO START A BAND.
FRANCIS, C'MON! IT'LL BE FUN!
PLUS, WE'LL MAKE MONEY! THE SCHOOL PAYS BANDS THREE HUNDRED BUCKS FOR A TWO-HOUR DANCE!
WOW!
SO IF WE PLAYED A DANCE, WE'D EARN A HUNDRED BUCKS APIECE!
WELL, NOT EXACTLY. AS LEAD SINGER, I'D GET A SMIDGE MORE.
DEFINE "SMIDGE."
LOOK, DON'T FORGET THE GROUPIES. GROUPIES ARE A MAJOR FRINGE BENEFIT!
Peirce

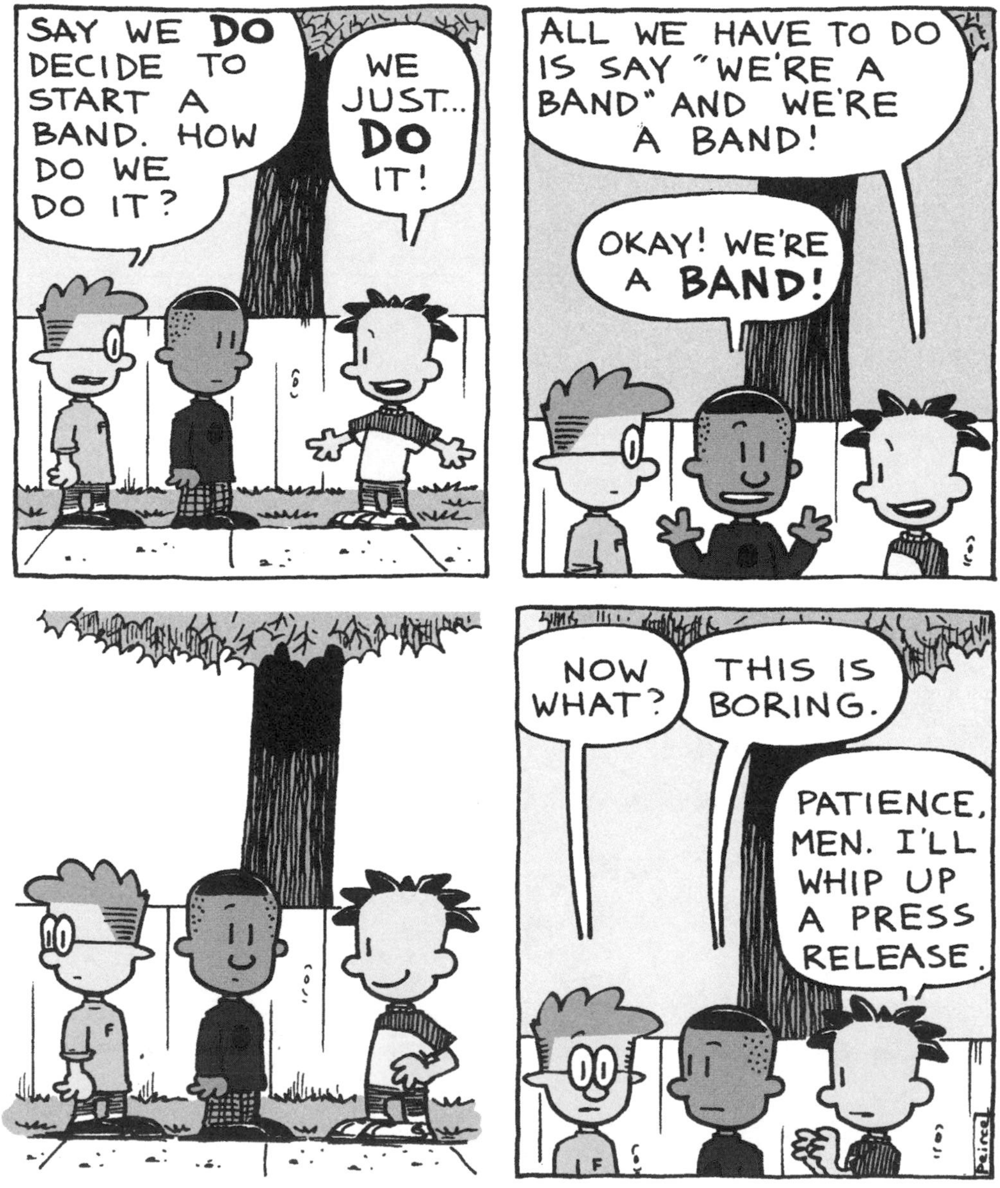
SAY WE DO DECIDE TO START A BAND. HOW DO WE DO IT?
WE JUST... DO IT!
ALL WE HAVE TO DO IS SAY "WE'RE A BAND" AND WE'RE A BAND!
OKAY! WE'RE A BAND!
NOW WHAT?
THIS IS BORING.
PATIENCE, MEN. I'LL WHIP UP A PRESS RELEASE.
Peirce

NOW THAT WE'RE A BAND, WHAT SHOULD WE DO FIRST?
LET'S THINK UP A NAME!
HOLD ON, LADS.
AS LEAD SINGER, **I** GET TO THINK UP A NAME FOR OUR BAND, AND I'VE ALREADY COME UP WITH A **GREAT** ONE!
ENSLAVE THE MOLLUSK!
"ENSLAVE THE MOLLUSK"?
HOW COME **YOU** GET TO BE THE LEAD SINGER?
I'VE GOT THE BEST HAIR.
Peirce

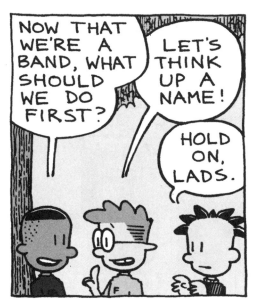

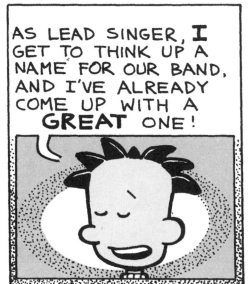

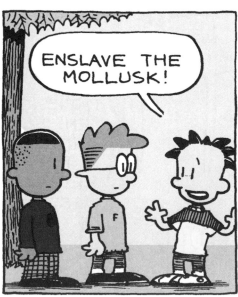

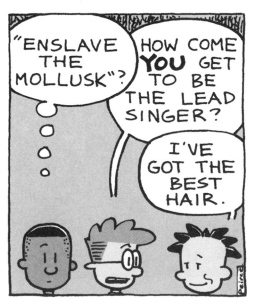

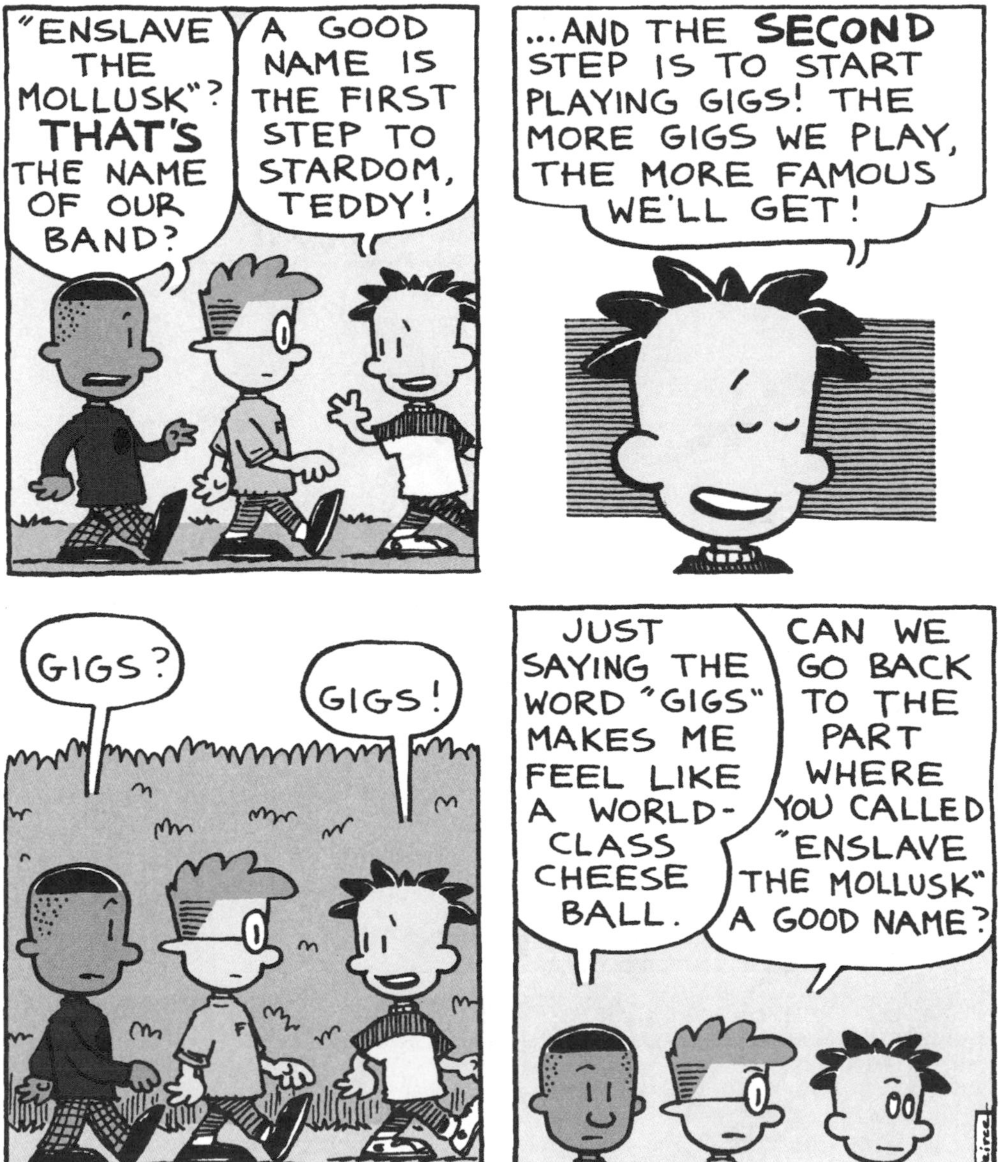
"ENSLAVE THE MOLLUSK"? THAT'S THE NAME OF OUR BAND?
A GOOD NAME IS THE FIRST STEP TO STARDOM, TEDDY!
...AND THE SECOND STEP IS TO START PLAYING GIGS! THE MORE GIGS WE PLAY, THE MORE FAMOUS WE'LL GET!
GIGS?
GIGS!
JUST SAYING THE WORD "GIGS" MAKES ME FEEL LIKE A WORLD-CLASS CHEESE BALL.
CAN WE GO BACK TO THE PART WHERE YOU CALLED "ENSLAVE THE MOLLUSK" A GOOD NAME?
Peirce

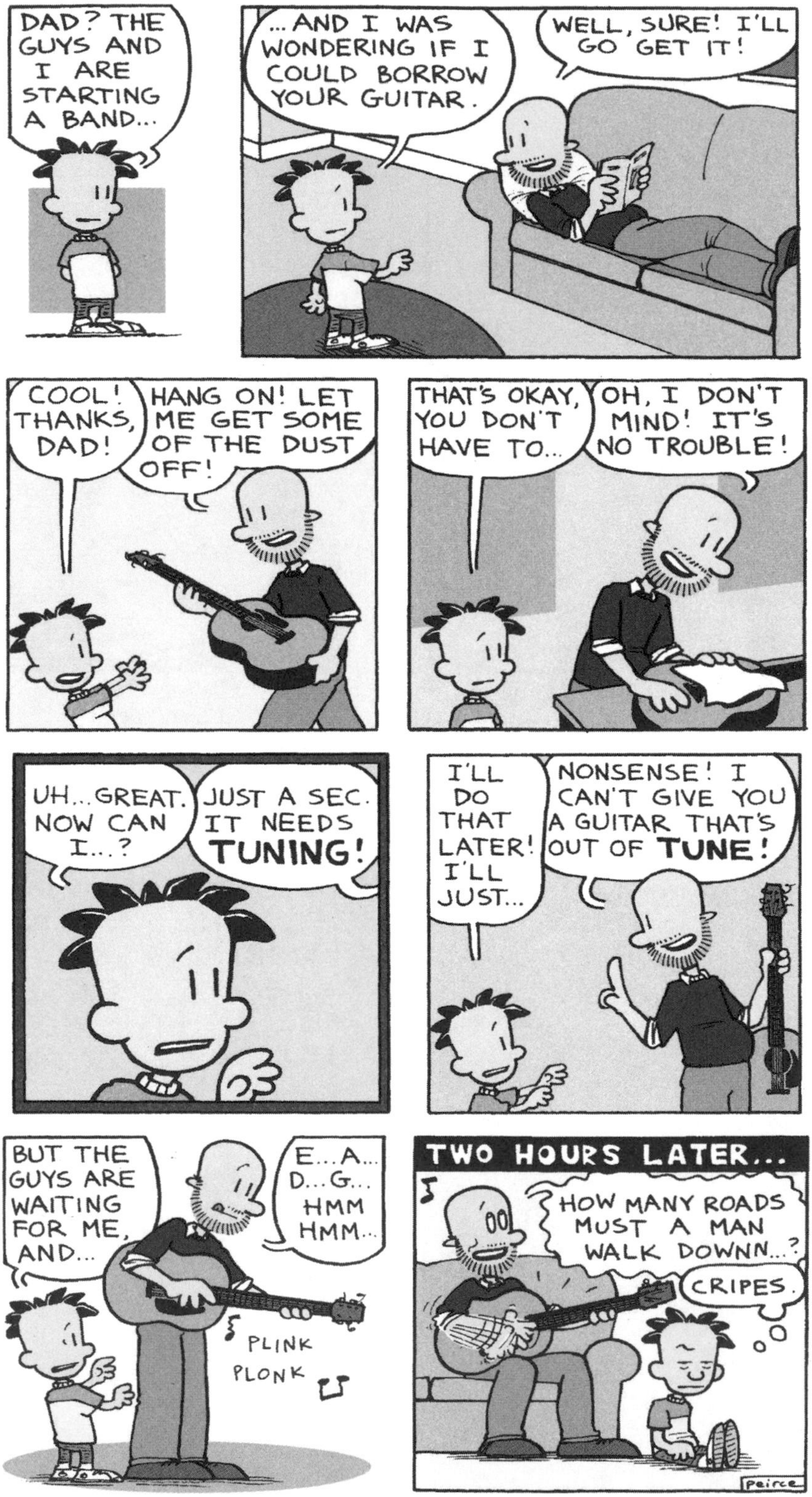
DAD? THE GUYS AND I ARE STARTING A BAND...
...AND I WAS WONDERING IF I COULD BORROW YOUR GUITAR.
WELL, SURE! I'LL GO GET IT!
COOL! THANKS, DAD!
HANG ON! LET ME GET SOME OF THE DUST OFF!
THAT'S OKAY, YOU DON'T HAVE TO...
OH, I DON'T MIND! IT'S NO TROUBLE!
UH... GREAT. NOW CAN I...?
JUST A SEC. IT NEEDS **TUNING**!
I'LL DO THAT LATER! I'LL JUST...
NONSENSE! I CAN'T GIVE YOU A GUITAR THAT'S OUT OF **TUNE**!
BUT THE GUYS ARE WAITING FOR ME, AND...
E...A... D...G... HMM HMM...
PLINK
PLONK
TWO HOURS LATER...
HOW MANY ROADS MUST A MAN WALK DOWNN...?
CRIPES.
Peirce

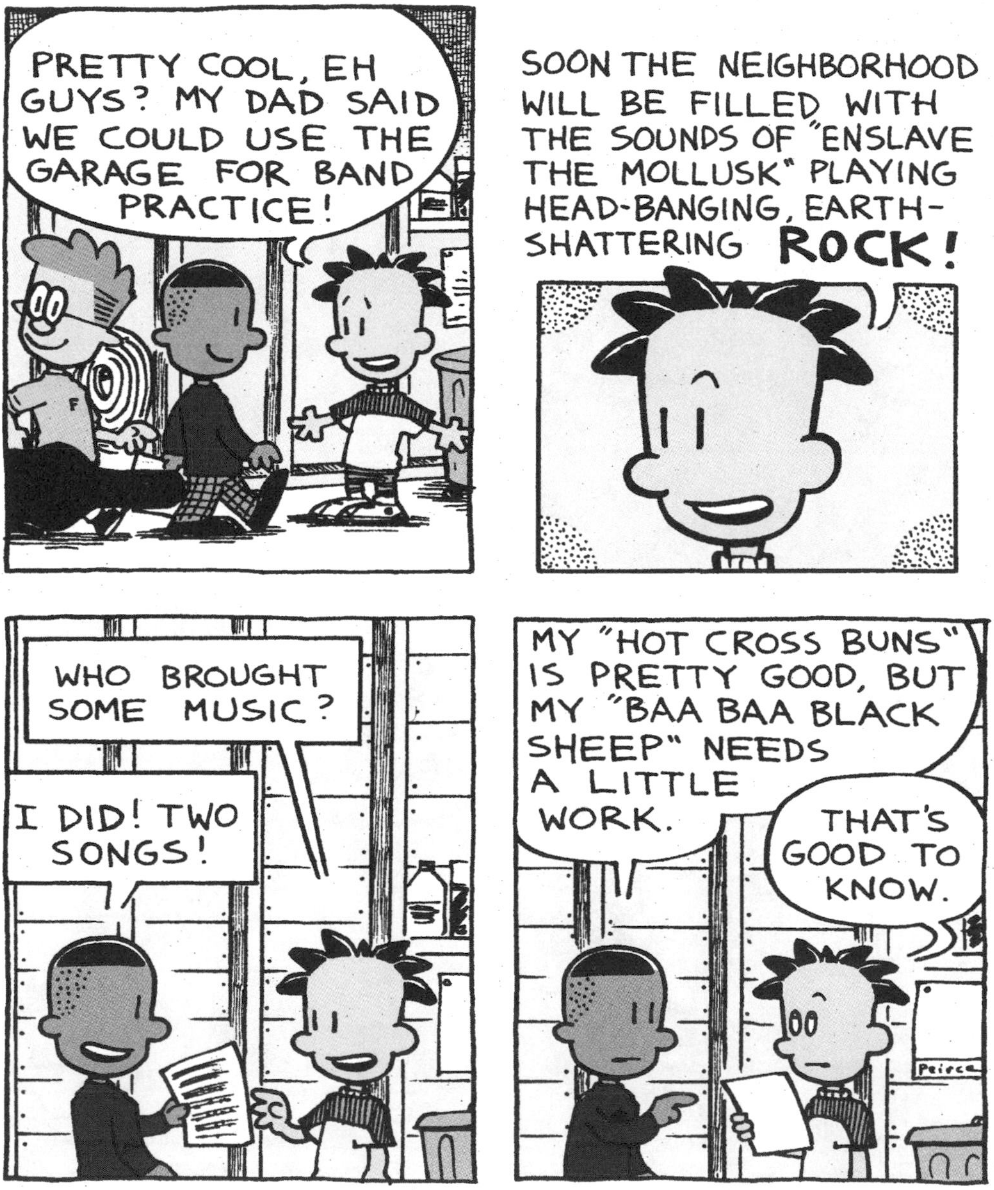
PRETTY COOL, EH GUYS? MY DAD SAID WE COULD USE THE GARAGE FOR BAND PRACTICE!
SOON THE NEIGHBORHOOD WILL BE FILLED WITH THE SOUNDS OF "ENSLAVE THE MOLLUSK" PLAYING HEAD-BANGING, EARTH-SHATTERING ROCK!
WHO BROUGHT SOME MUSIC?
I DID! TWO SONGS!
MY "HOT CROSS BUNS" IS PRETTY GOOD, BUT MY "BAA BAA BLACK SHEEP" NEEDS A LITTLE WORK.
THAT'S GOOD TO KNOW.
Peirce

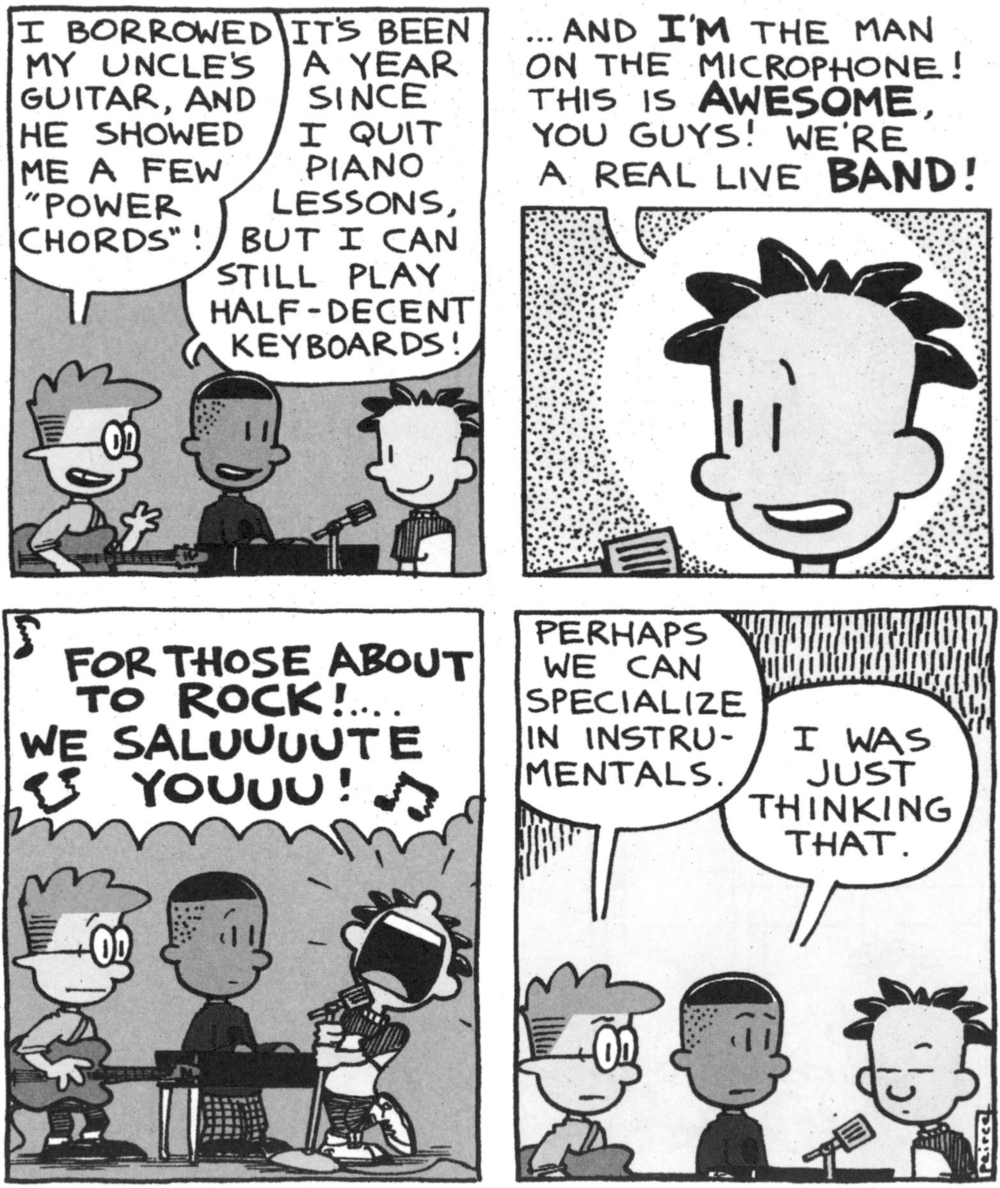
I BORROWED MY UNCLE'S GUITAR, AND HE SHOWED ME A FEW "POWER CHORDS"!
IT'S BEEN A YEAR SINCE I QUIT PIANO LESSONS, BUT I CAN STILL PLAY HALF-DECENT KEYBOARDS!
...AND I'M THE MAN ON THE MICROPHONE! THIS IS AWESOME, YOU GUYS! WE'RE A REAL LIVE BAND!
FOR THOSE ABOUT TO ROCK!.... WE SALUUUUTE YOUUU!
PERHAPS WE CAN SPECIALIZE IN INSTRU-MENTALS.
I WAS JUST THINKING THAT.
PEIRCE

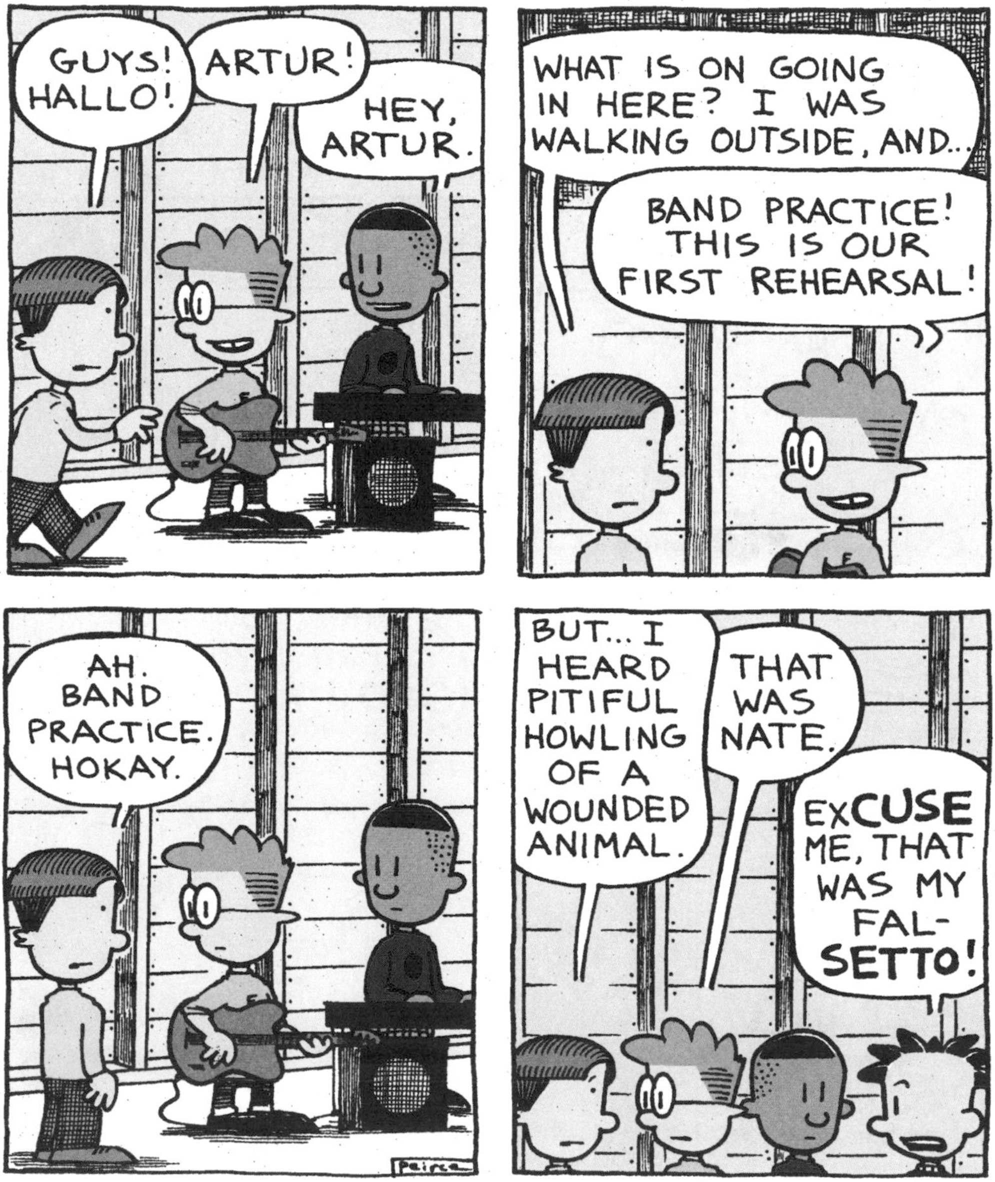
GUYS! HALLO!
ARTUR!
HEY, ARTUR.
WHAT IS ON GOING IN HERE? I WAS WALKING OUTSIDE, AND...
BAND PRACTICE! THIS IS OUR FIRST REHEARSAL!
AH. BAND PRACTICE. HOKAY.
Peirce
BUT... I HEARD PITIFUL HOWLING OF A WOUNDED ANIMAL.
THAT WAS NATE.
EXCUSE ME, THAT WAS MY FAL-SETTO!

SO! I WAS NOT KNOW YOU FELLOWS ARE A BAND!
"ENSLAVE THE MOLLUSK," ARTUR! WE'RE GOING TO BE FAMOUS!
WE'RE TRYING TO LEARN "I FOUGHT THE LAW."
AH! YES, THAT IS GOOD SONG!
BREAKIN' ROCKS IN THE HOT SUN... I FOUGHT THE LAW AND THE LAW WON...
YOU'RE GOOD!
YOU'RE FIRED.
WHAT?
Peirce

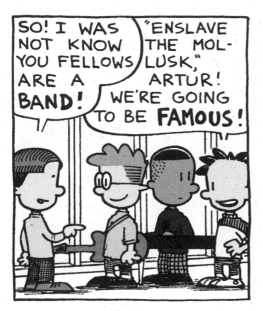

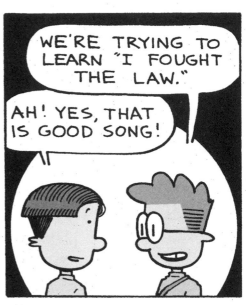

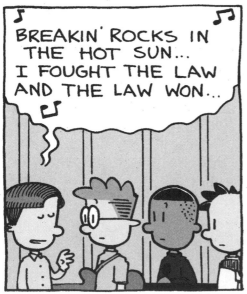

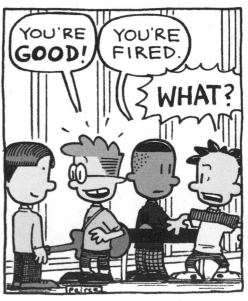

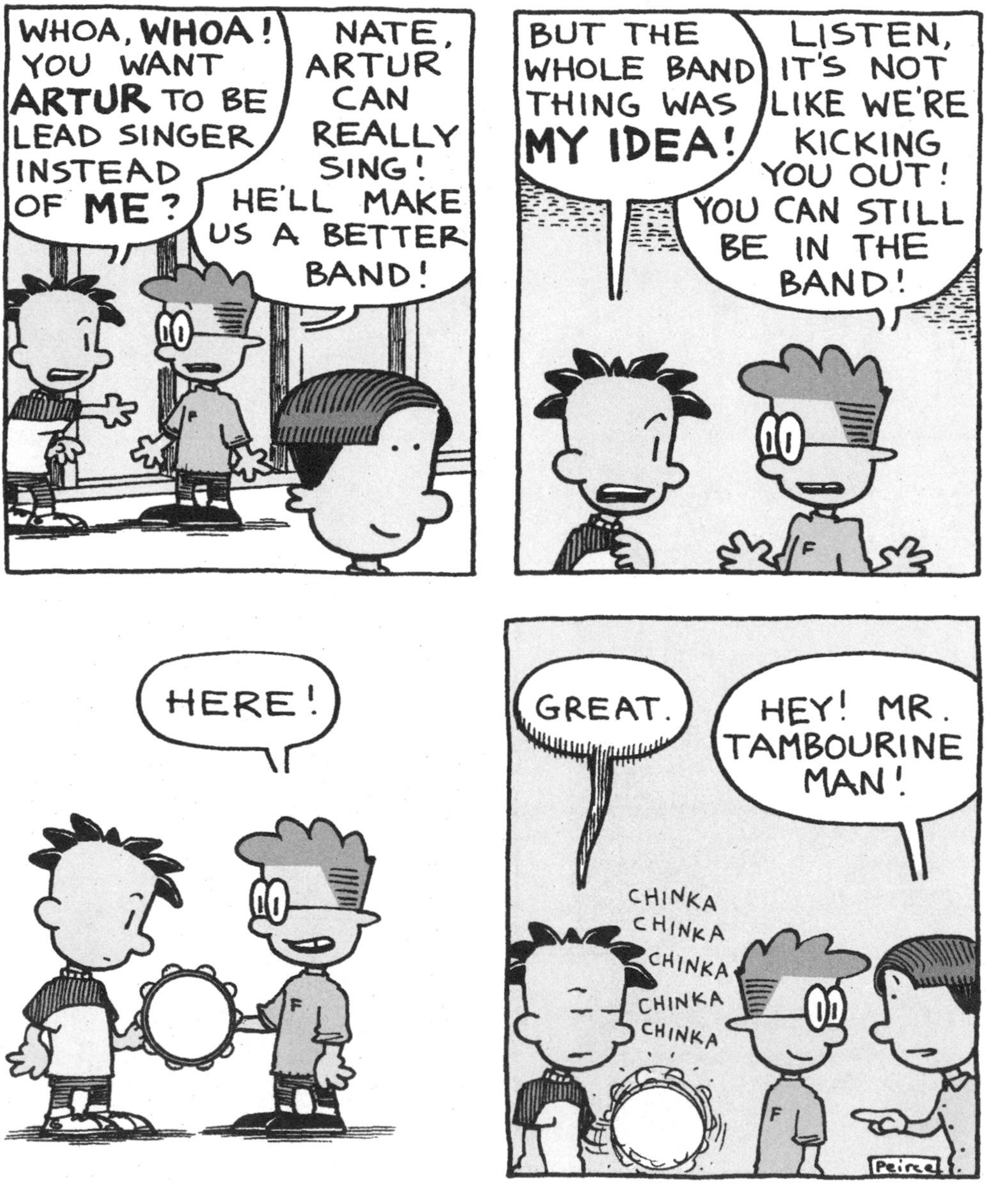
WHOA, WHOA! YOU WANT ARTUR TO BE LEAD SINGER INSTEAD OF ME?
NATE, ARTUR CAN REALLY SING! HE'LL MAKE US A BETTER BAND!
BUT THE WHOLE BAND THING WAS MY IDEA!
LISTEN, IT'S NOT LIKE WE'RE KICKING YOU OUT! YOU CAN STILL BE IN THE BAND!
HERE!
GREAT.
HEY! MR. TAMBOURINE MAN!
CHINKA CHINKA CHINKA CHINKA CHINKA
Peirce

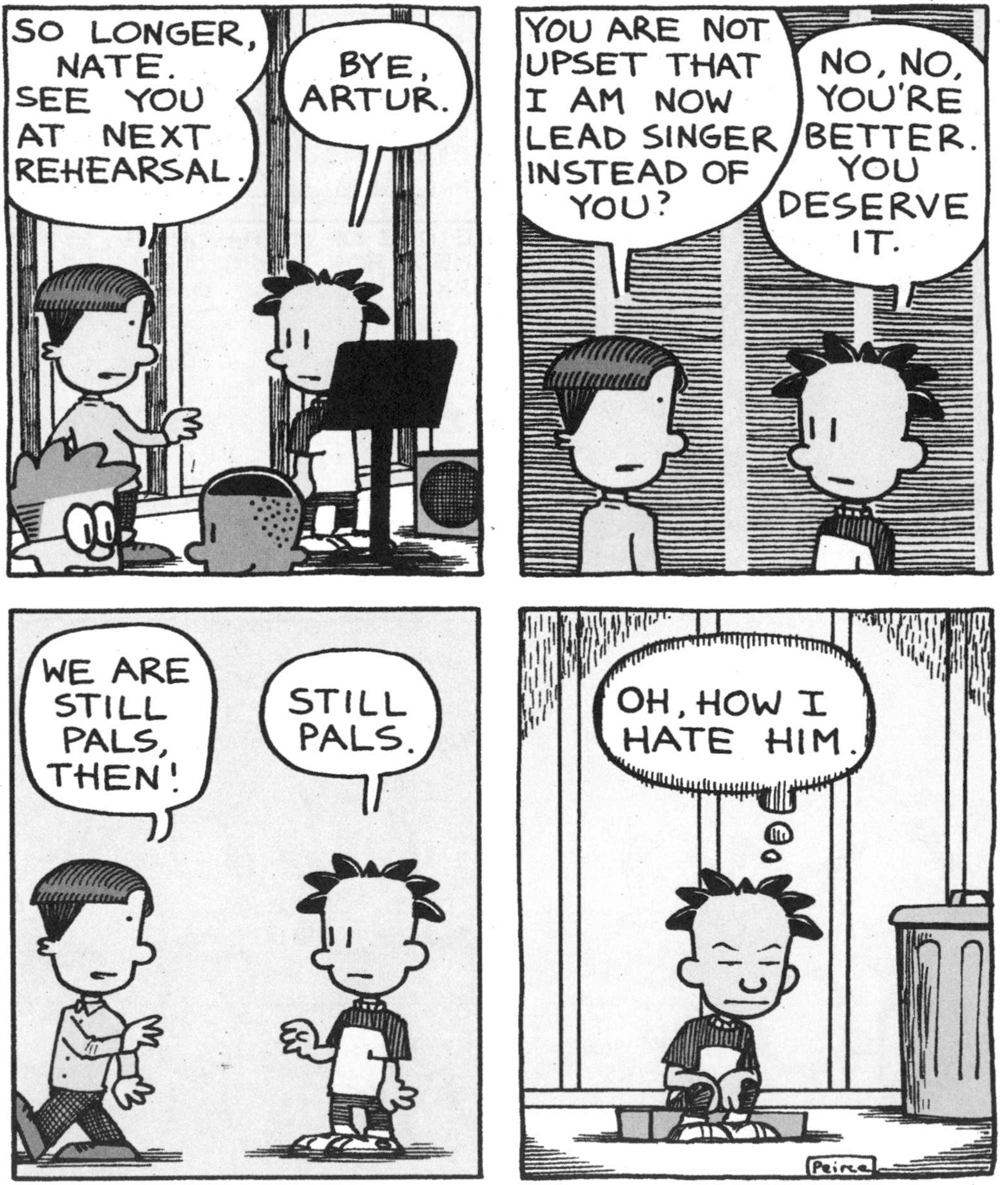
SO LONGER, NATE. SEE YOU AT NEXT REHEARSAL.
BYE, ARTUR.
YOU ARE NOT UPSET THAT I AM NOW LEAD SINGER INSTEAD OF YOU?
NO, NO, YOU'RE BETTER. YOU DESERVE IT.
WE ARE STILL PALS, THEN!
STILL PALS.
OH, HOW I HATE HIM.
Peirce

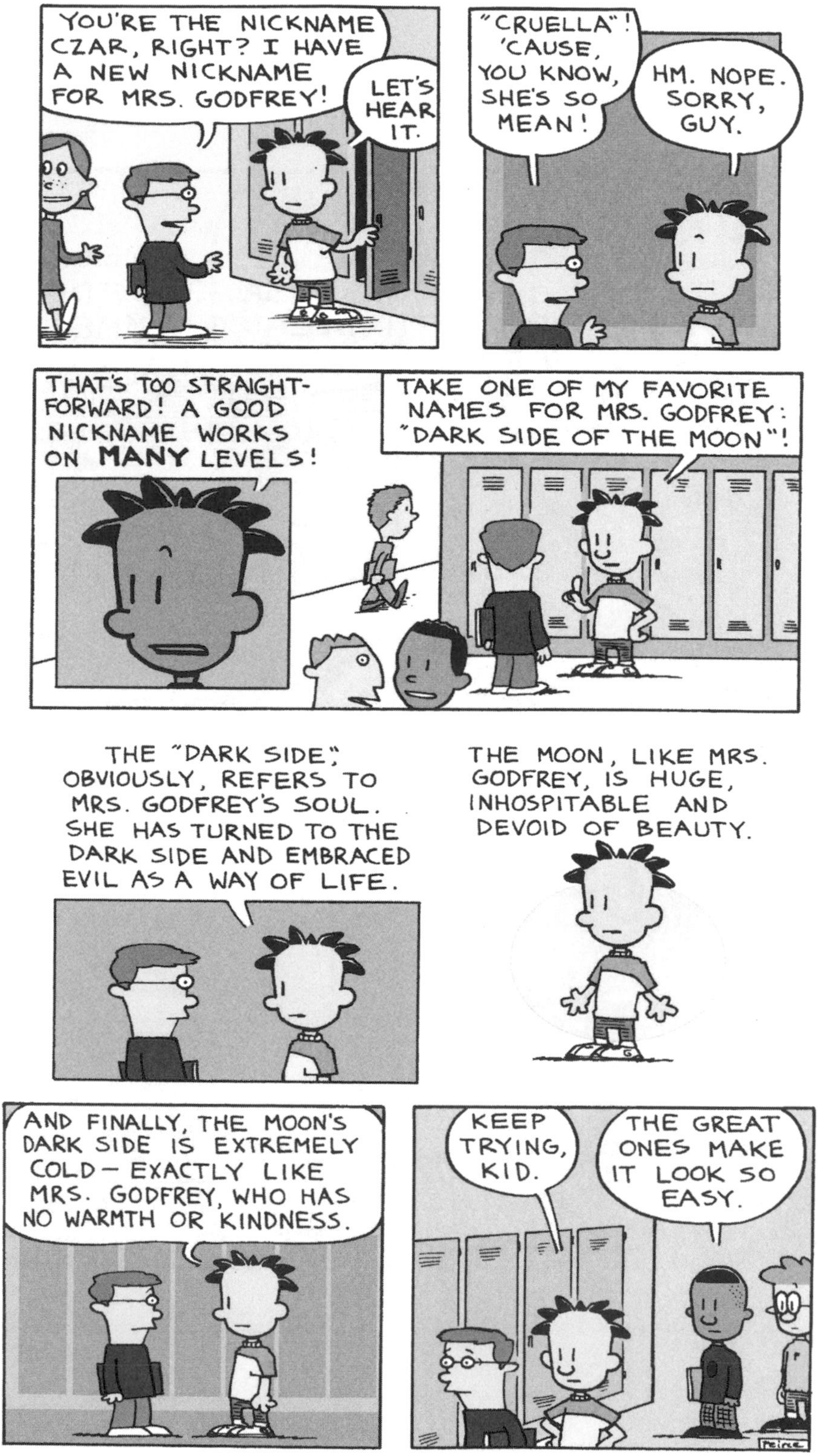
YOU'RE THE NICKNAME CZAR, RIGHT? I HAVE A NEW NICKNAME FOR MRS. GODFREY!
LET'S HEAR IT.
"CRUELLA"! 'CAUSE, YOU KNOW, SHE'S SO MEAN!
HM. NOPE. SORRY, GUY.
THAT'S TOO STRAIGHT-FORWARD! A GOOD NICKNAME WORKS ON **MANY** LEVELS!
TAKE ONE OF MY FAVORITE NAMES FOR MRS. GODFREY: "DARK SIDE OF THE MOON"!
THE "DARK SIDE," OBVIOUSLY, REFERS TO MRS. GODFREY'S SOUL. SHE HAS TURNED TO THE DARK SIDE AND EMBRACED EVIL AS A WAY OF LIFE.
THE MOON, LIKE MRS. GODFREY, IS HUGE, INHOSPITABLE AND DEVOID OF BEAUTY.
AND FINALLY, THE MOON'S DARK SIDE IS EXTREMELY COLD — EXACTLY LIKE MRS. GODFREY, WHO HAS NO WARMTH OR KINDNESS.
KEEP TRYING, KID.
THE GREAT ONES MAKE IT LOOK SO EASY.
PEIRCE

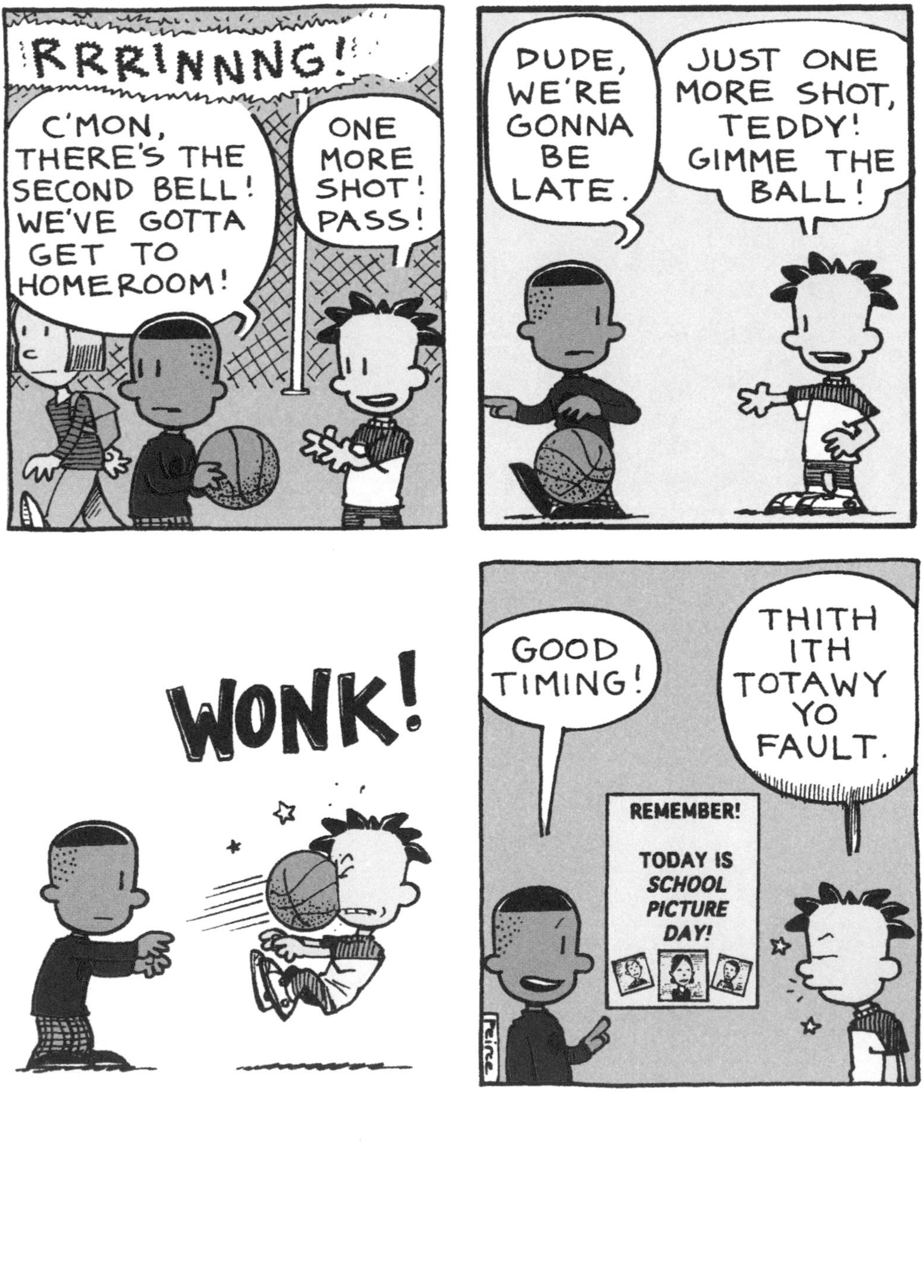
RRRINNNG!
C'MON, THERE'S THE SECOND BELL! WE'VE GOTTA GET TO HOMEROOM!
ONE MORE SHOT! PASS!
DUDE, WE'RE GONNA BE LATE.
JUST ONE MORE SHOT, TEDDY! GIMME THE BALL!
WONK!
GOOD TIMING!
THITH ITH TOTAWY YO FAULT.
REMEMBER!
TODAY IS SCHOOL PICTURE DAY!
Peirce

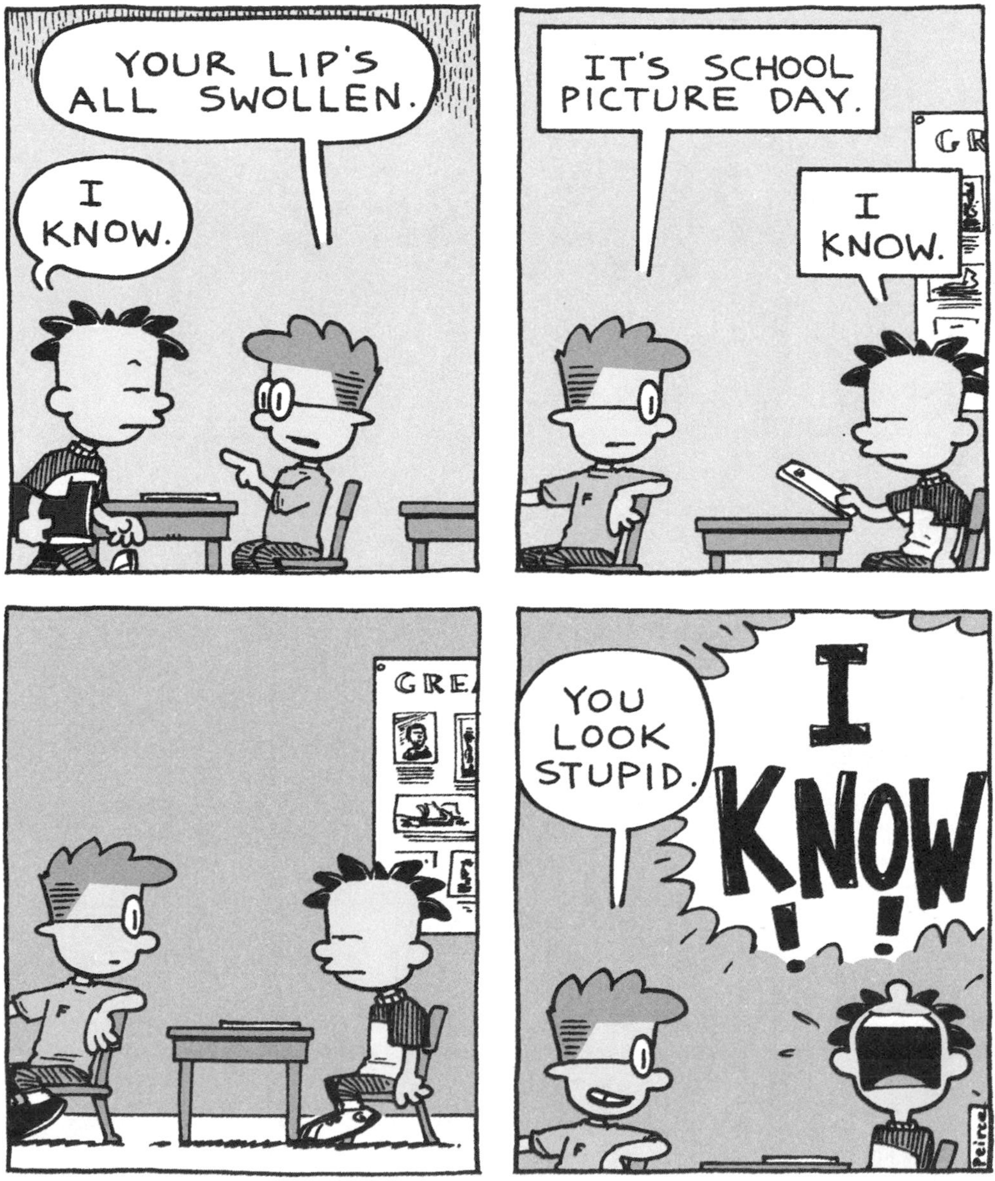
YOUR LIP'S ALL SWOLLEN.
I KNOW.
IT'S SCHOOL PICTURE DAY.
I KNOW.
YOU LOOK STUPID.
I KNOW!!
Peirce

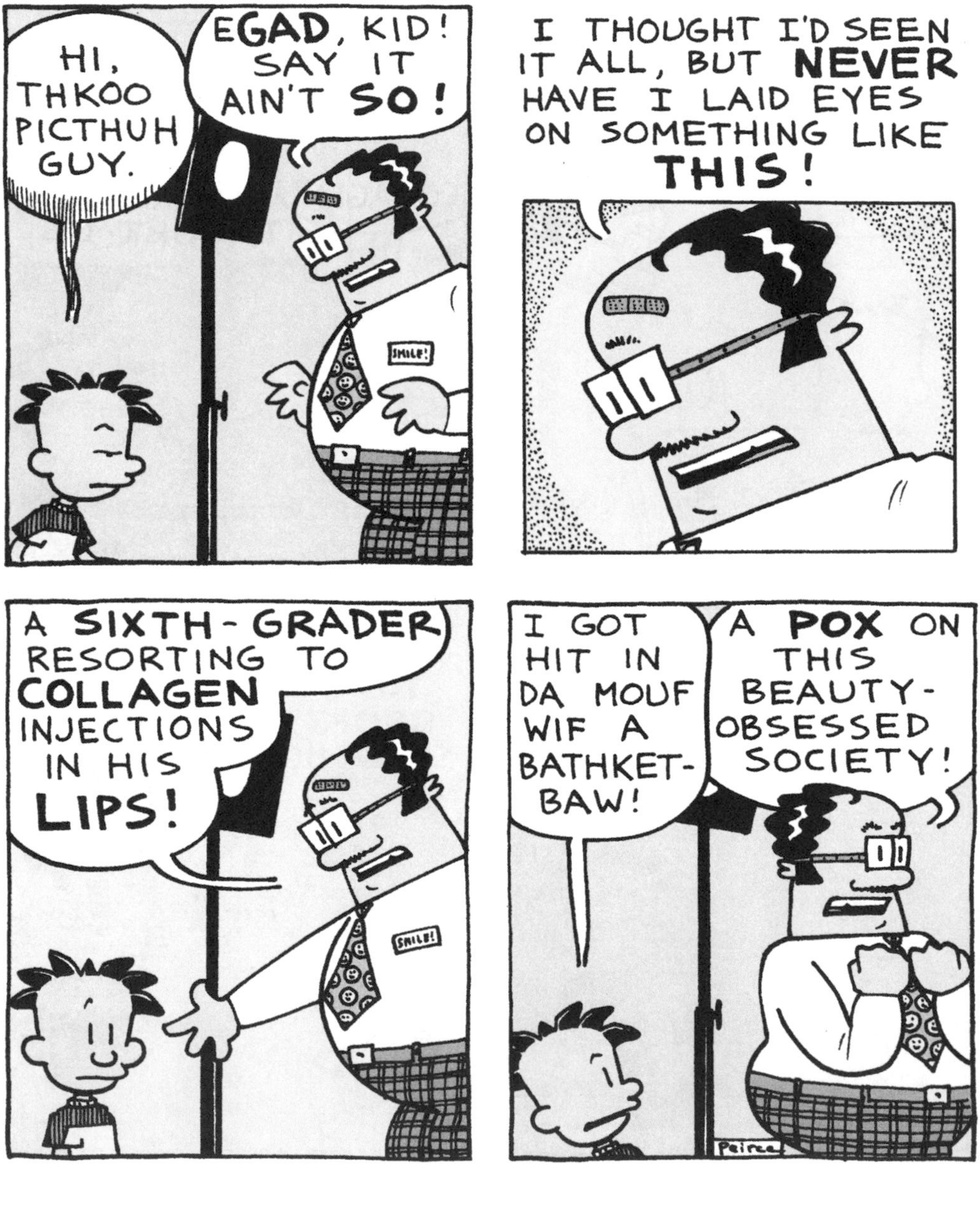
HI, THKOO PICTHUH GUY.
EGAD, KID! SAY IT AIN'T SO!
I THOUGHT I'D SEEN IT ALL, BUT NEVER HAVE I LAID EYES ON SOMETHING LIKE THIS!
SMILE!
A SIXTH-GRADER RESORTING TO COLLAGEN INJECTIONS IN HIS LIPS!
I GOT HIT IN DA MOUF WIF A BATHKET-BAW!
A POX ON THIS BEAUTY-OBSESSED SOCIETY!
Peirce

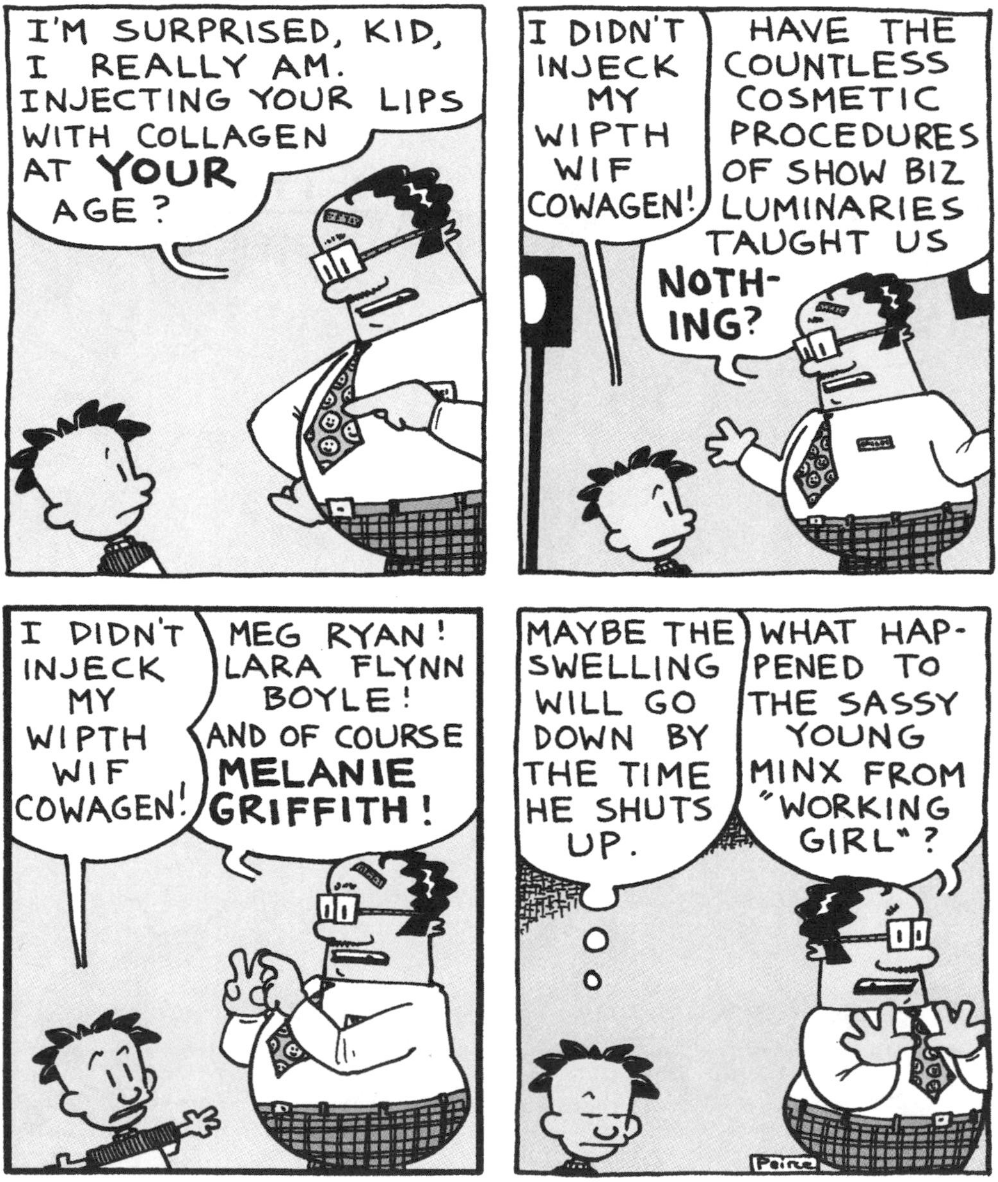
I'M SURPRISED, KID, I REALLY AM. INJECTING YOUR LIPS WITH COLLAGEN AT YOUR AGE?
I DIDN'T INJECK MY WIPTH WIF COWAGEN!
HAVE THE COUNTLESS COSMETIC PROCEDURES OF SHOW BIZ LUMINARIES TAUGHT US NOTH-ING?
I DIDN'T INJECK MY WIPTH WIF COWAGEN!
MEG RYAN! LARA FLYNN BOYLE! AND OF COURSE MELANIE GRIFFITH!
MAYBE THE SWELLING WILL GO DOWN BY THE TIME HE SHUTS UP.
WHAT HAPPENED TO THE SASSY YOUNG MINX FROM "WORKING GIRL"?
Peirce

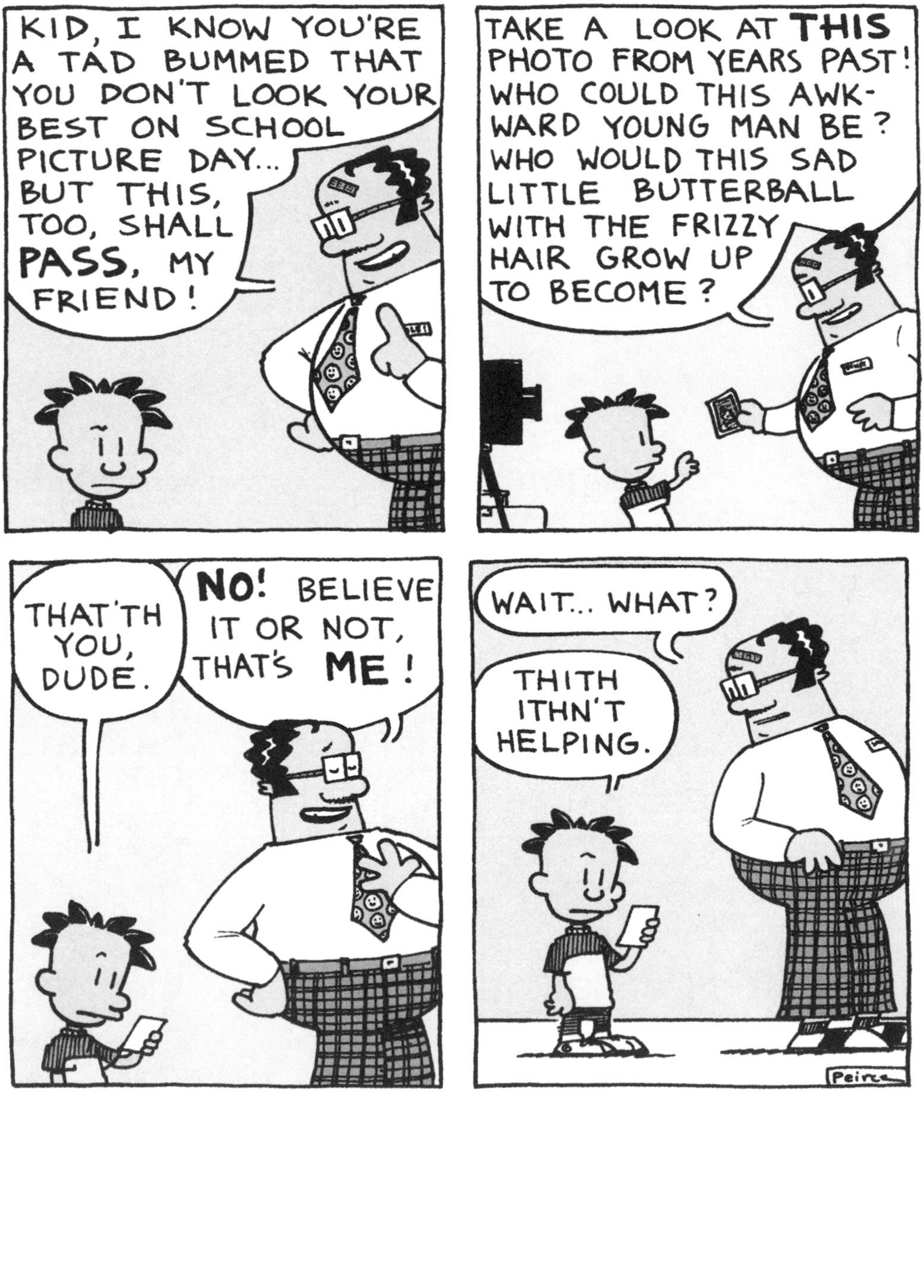
KID, I KNOW YOU'RE A TAD BUMMED THAT YOU DON'T LOOK YOUR BEST ON SCHOOL PICTURE DAY... BUT THIS, TOO, SHALL PASS, MY FRIEND!
TAKE A LOOK AT THIS PHOTO FROM YEARS PAST! WHO COULD THIS AWK-WARD YOUNG MAN BE? WHO WOULD THIS SAD LITTLE BUTTERBALL WITH THE FRIZZY HAIR GROW UP TO BECOME?
THAT'TH YOU, DUDE.
NO! BELIEVE IT OR NOT, THAT'S ME!
WAIT... WHAT?
THITH ITHN'T HELPING.
Peirce

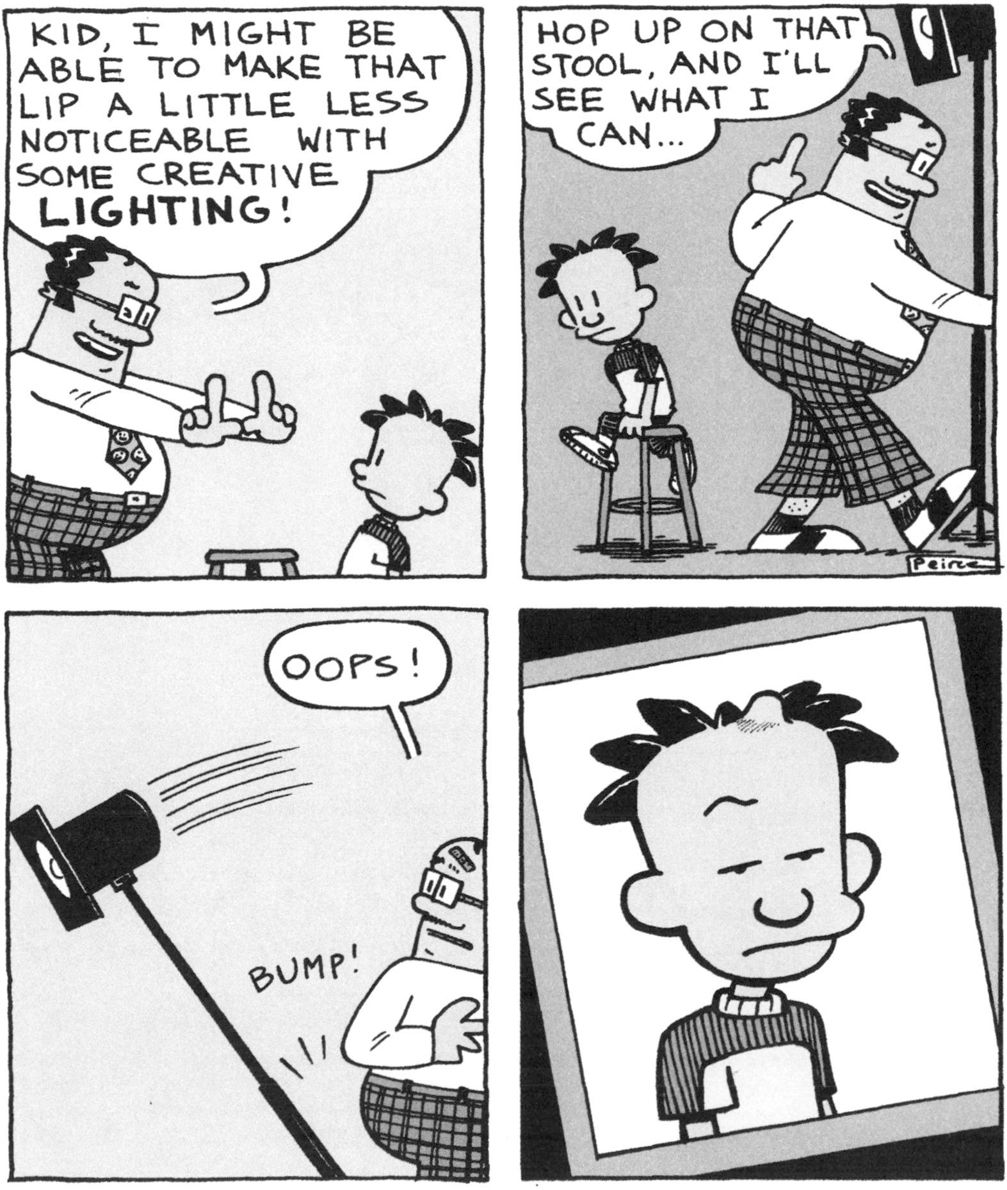
KID, I MIGHT BE ABLE TO MAKE THAT LIP A LITTLE LESS NOTICEABLE WITH SOME CREATIVE **LIGHTING**!
HOP UP ON THAT STOOL, AND I'LL SEE WHAT I CAN...
Peirce
OOPS!
BUMP!

HOW COME **YOU** GET TO BE NICKNAME CZAR?

HM?

I'M CHALLENGING YOU, NATE! **I** CAN COME UP WITH BETTER NICKNAMES THAN **YOU** CAN!

WE'LL HAVE A CONTEST!

EACH OF YOU HAS TO COME UP WITH A NICKNAME **ON THE SPOT** FOR THE FIRST TEACHER WHO WALKS BY!

TEDDY AND I WILL JUDGE!

AND REMEMBER: A GOOD NICKNAME WORKS ON **MANY** LEVELS!

GUYS! COACH JOHN!

UMM... LET'S SEE HERE...

"FAST BREAK."

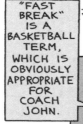

"FAST BREAK" IS A BASKETBALL TERM, WHICH IS OBVIOUSLY APPROPRIATE FOR COACH JOHN.

...BUT THE WORD "FAST" IS IRONIC, BECAUSE COACH JOHN IS SO SLOW.

ALSO, "FAST BREAK" IS A PLAY ON WORDS. WHEN YOU BREAK A FAST, YOU **EAT.** CLEARLY, COACH JOHN HAS BROKEN A FEW FASTS IN HIS DAY.

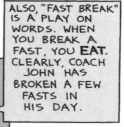

I KNOW WHEN I'M BEATEN.

LONG LIVE THE CZAR!

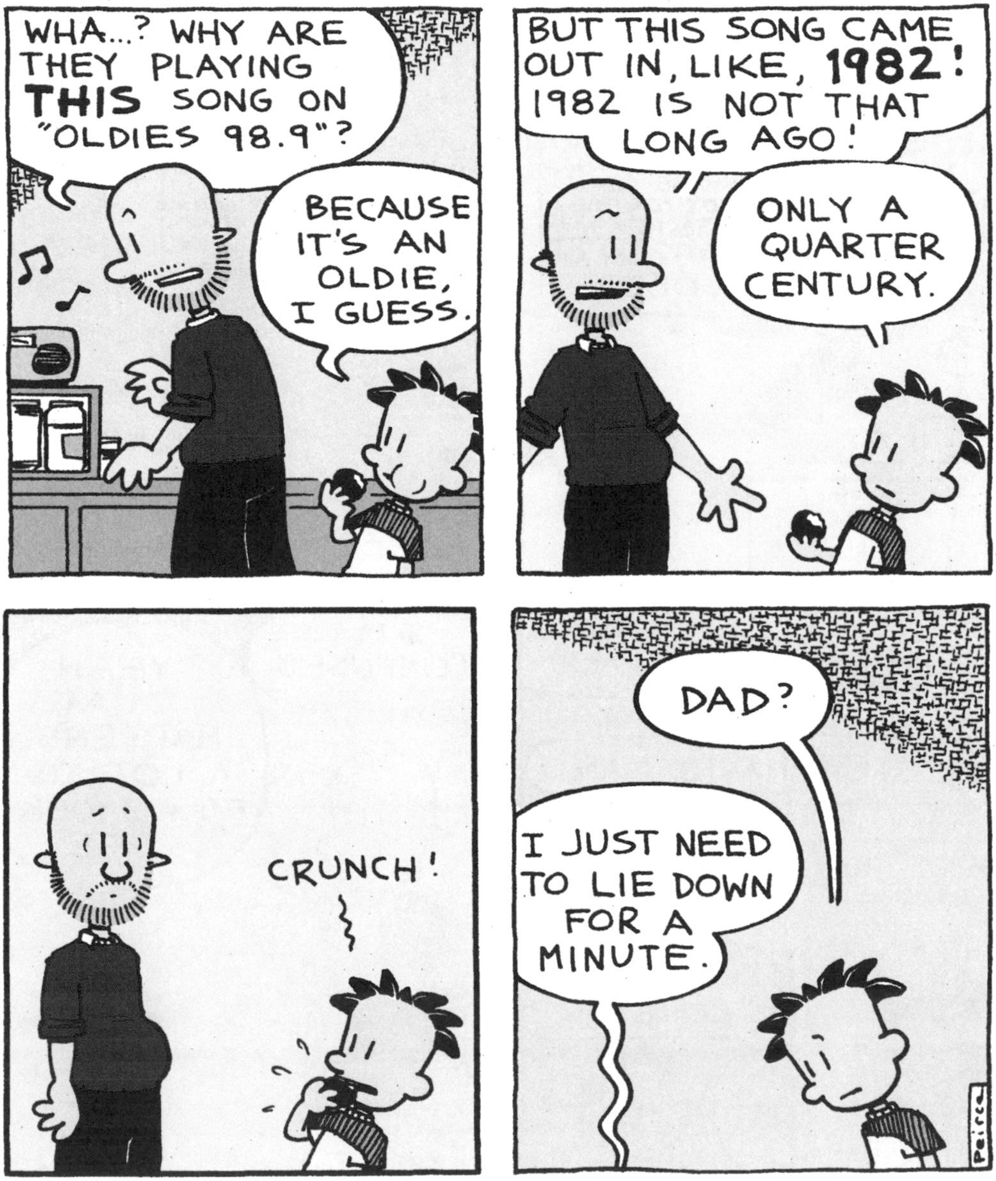
WHA...? WHY ARE THEY PLAYING **THIS** SONG ON "OLDIES 98.9"?
BECAUSE IT'S AN OLDIE, I GUESS.
BUT THIS SONG CAME OUT IN, LIKE, **1982**! 1982 IS NOT THAT LONG AGO!
ONLY A QUARTER CENTURY.
CRUNCH!
DAD?
I JUST NEED TO LIE DOWN FOR A MINUTE.
Peirce

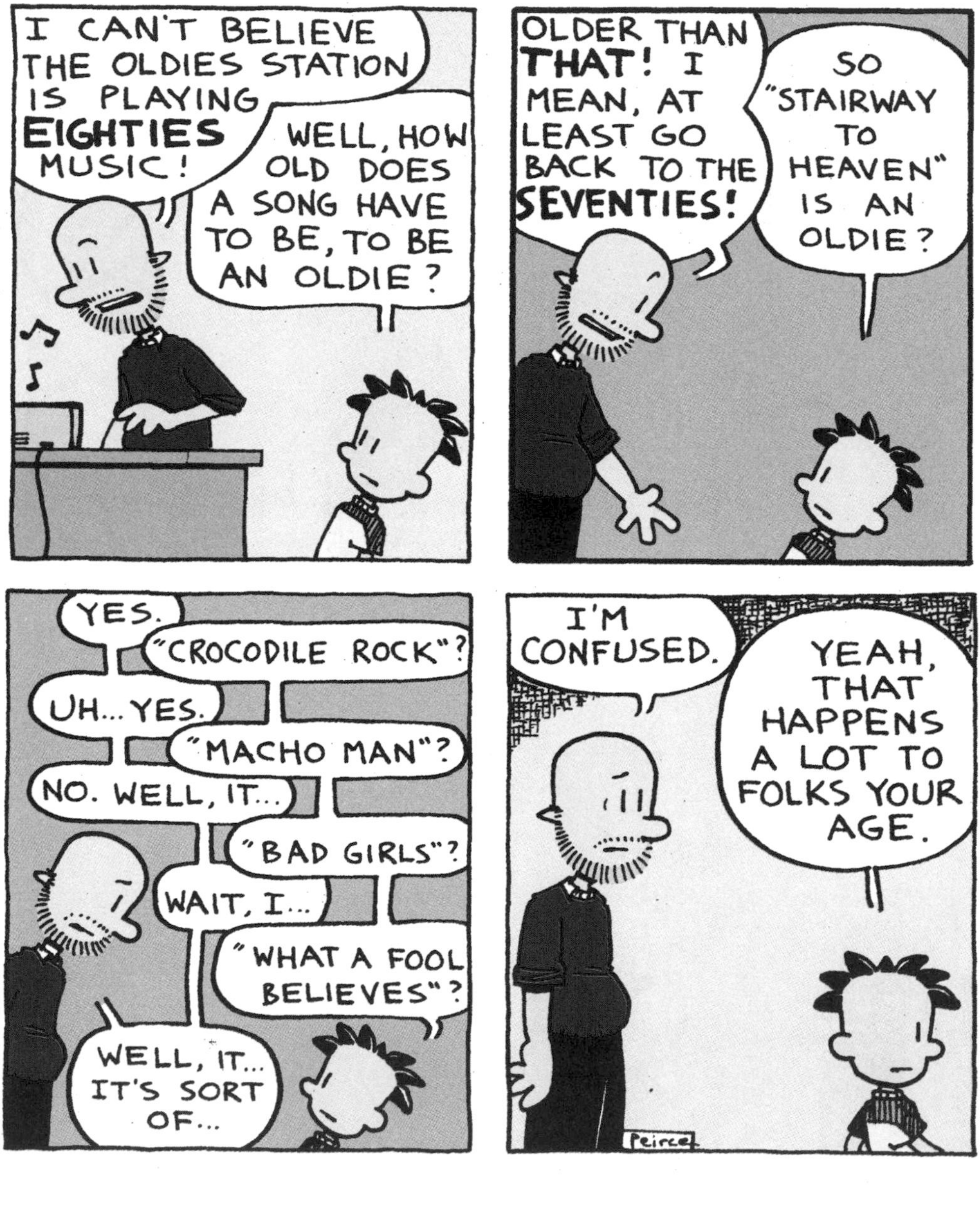
I CAN'T BELIEVE THE OLDIES STATION IS PLAYING **EIGHTIES** MUSIC!
WELL, HOW OLD DOES A SONG HAVE TO BE, TO BE AN OLDIE?
OLDER THAN **THAT!** I MEAN, AT LEAST GO BACK TO THE **SEVENTIES!**
SO "STAIRWAY TO HEAVEN" IS AN OLDIE?
YES.
"CROCODILE ROCK"?
UH... YES.
"MACHO MAN"?
NO. WELL, IT...
"BAD GIRLS"?
WAIT, I...
"WHAT A FOOL BELIEVES"?
WELL, IT... IT'S SORT OF...
I'M CONFUSED.
YEAH, THAT HAPPENS A LOT TO FOLKS YOUR AGE.
Peirce

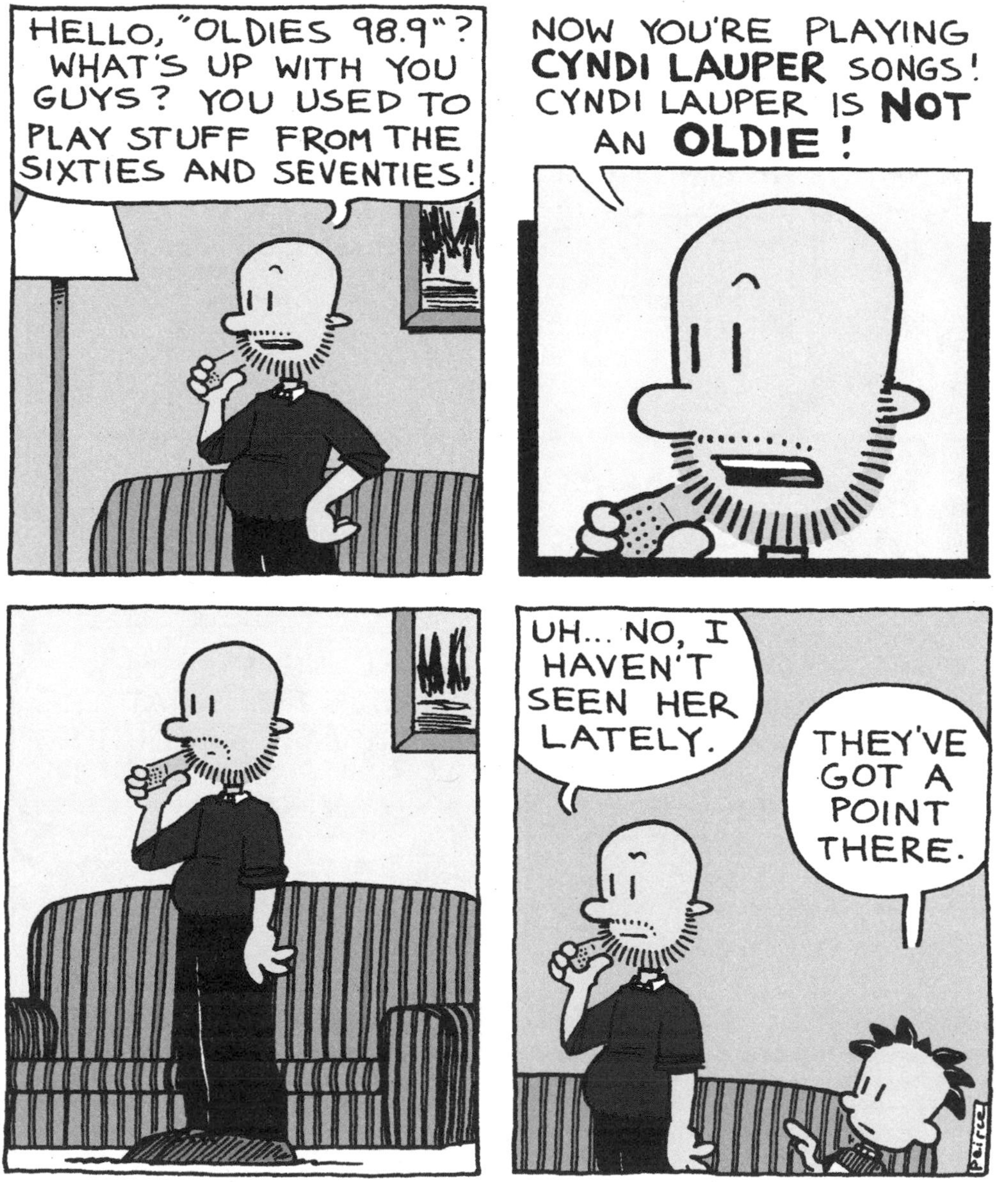
HELLO, "OLDIES 98.9"? WHAT'S UP WITH YOU GUYS? YOU USED TO PLAY STUFF FROM THE SIXTIES AND SEVENTIES!
NOW YOU'RE PLAYING CYNDI LAUPER SONGS! CYNDI LAUPER IS NOT AN OLDIE!
UH... NO, I HAVEN'T SEEN HER LATELY.
THEY'VE GOT A POINT THERE.
Peirce

HI, "OLDIES 98.9"? CAN YOU PLAY "LITTLE BITTY PRETTY ONE" BY THURSTON HARRIS? WHAT?... WHY NOT?

YES, I **KNOW** YOU'VE CHANGED YOUR FORMAT, BUT... WHAT?... WELL, YOU'RE STILL CALLING YOURSELF AN OLDIES STATION! WHY CAN'T I REQUEST AN OLDIE?

WHAT DO YOU MEAN, "THAT'S **TOO** OLD"? LISTEN, YOU CAN'T... WHAT?... WHAT DOES IT MATTER HOW OLD **I** AM? LET ME TELL YOU SOMETHING, SONNY, I'M NOT... HELLO? **HELLO?**

I NEVER KNEW EXACTLY WHAT THE PHRASE "MIDLIFE CRISIS" MEANT UNTIL JUST NOW.

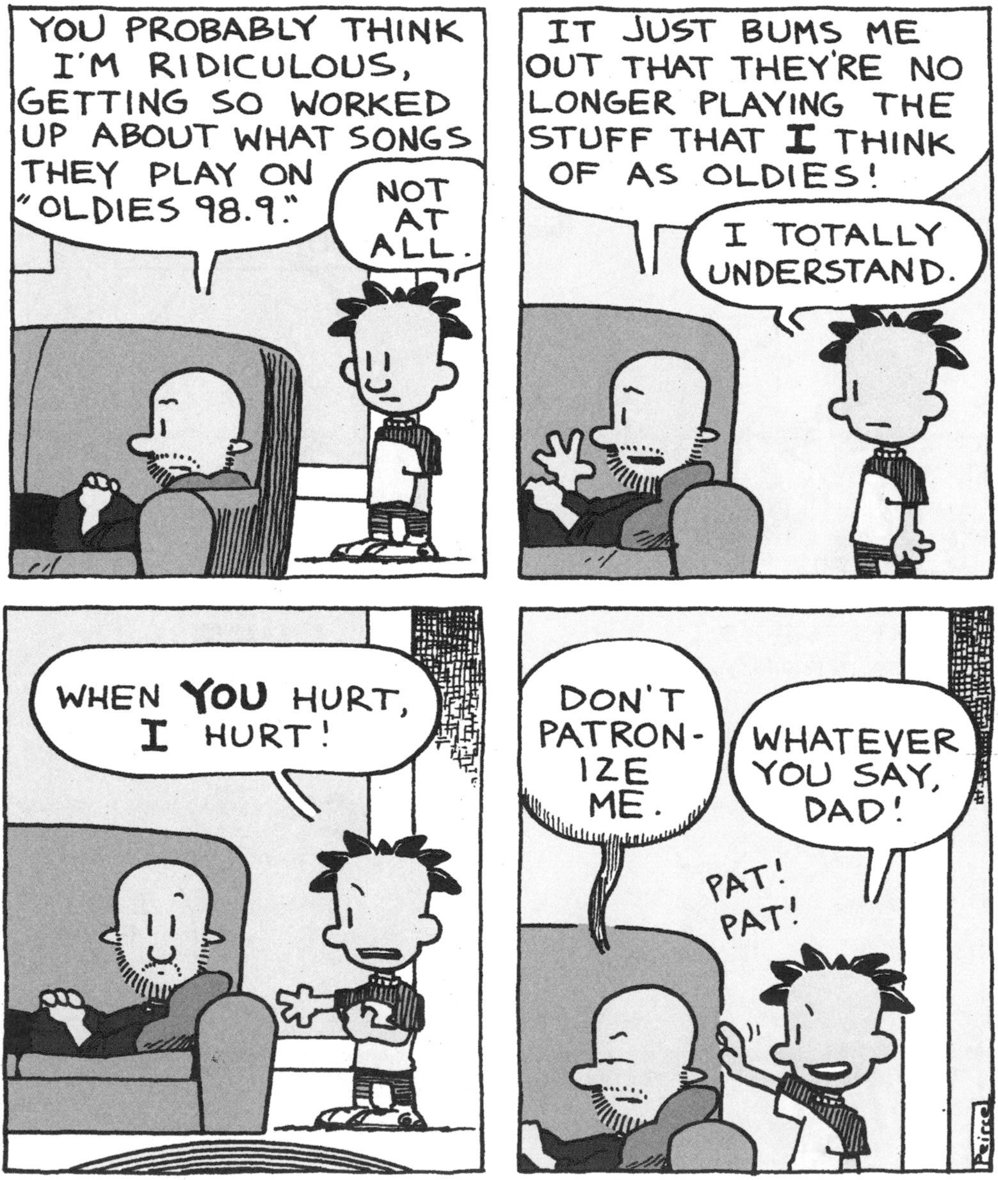
YOU PROBABLY THINK I'M RIDICULOUS, GETTING SO WORKED UP ABOUT WHAT SONGS THEY PLAY ON "OLDIES 98.9."
NOT AT ALL.
IT JUST BUMS ME OUT THAT THEY'RE NO LONGER PLAYING THE STUFF THAT I THINK OF AS OLDIES!
I TOTALLY UNDERSTAND.
WHEN YOU HURT, I HURT!
DON'T PATRON-IZE ME.
WHATEVER YOU SAY, DAD!
PAT! PAT!
Peirce

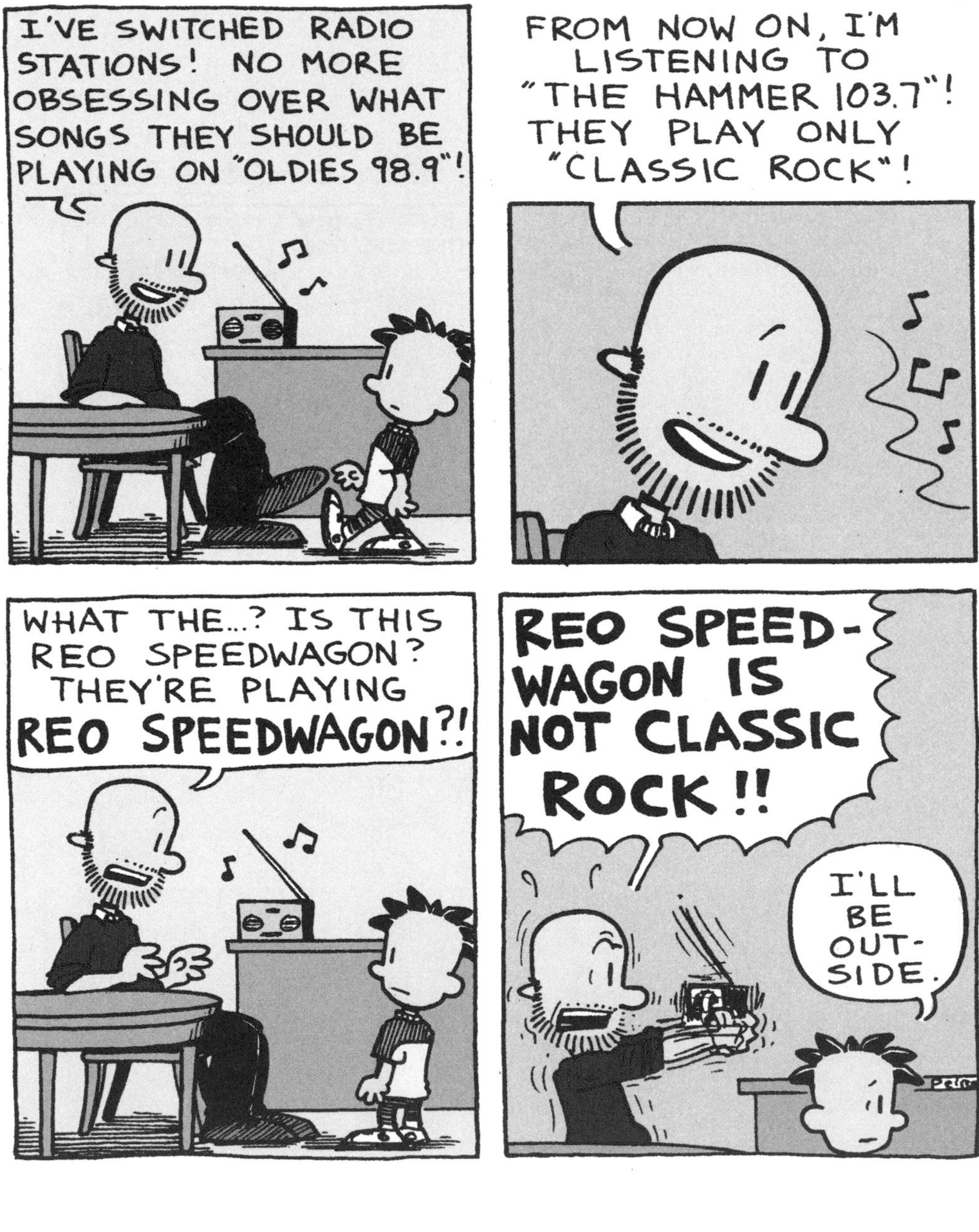
I'VE SWITCHED RADIO STATIONS! NO MORE OBSESSING OVER WHAT SONGS THEY SHOULD BE PLAYING ON "OLDIES 98.9"!
FROM NOW ON, I'M LISTENING TO "THE HAMMER 103.7"! THEY PLAY ONLY "CLASSIC ROCK"!
WHAT THE...? IS THIS REO SPEEDWAGON? THEY'RE PLAYING REO SPEEDWAGON?!
REO SPEED-WAGON IS NOT CLASSIC ROCK!!
I'LL BE OUT-SIDE.

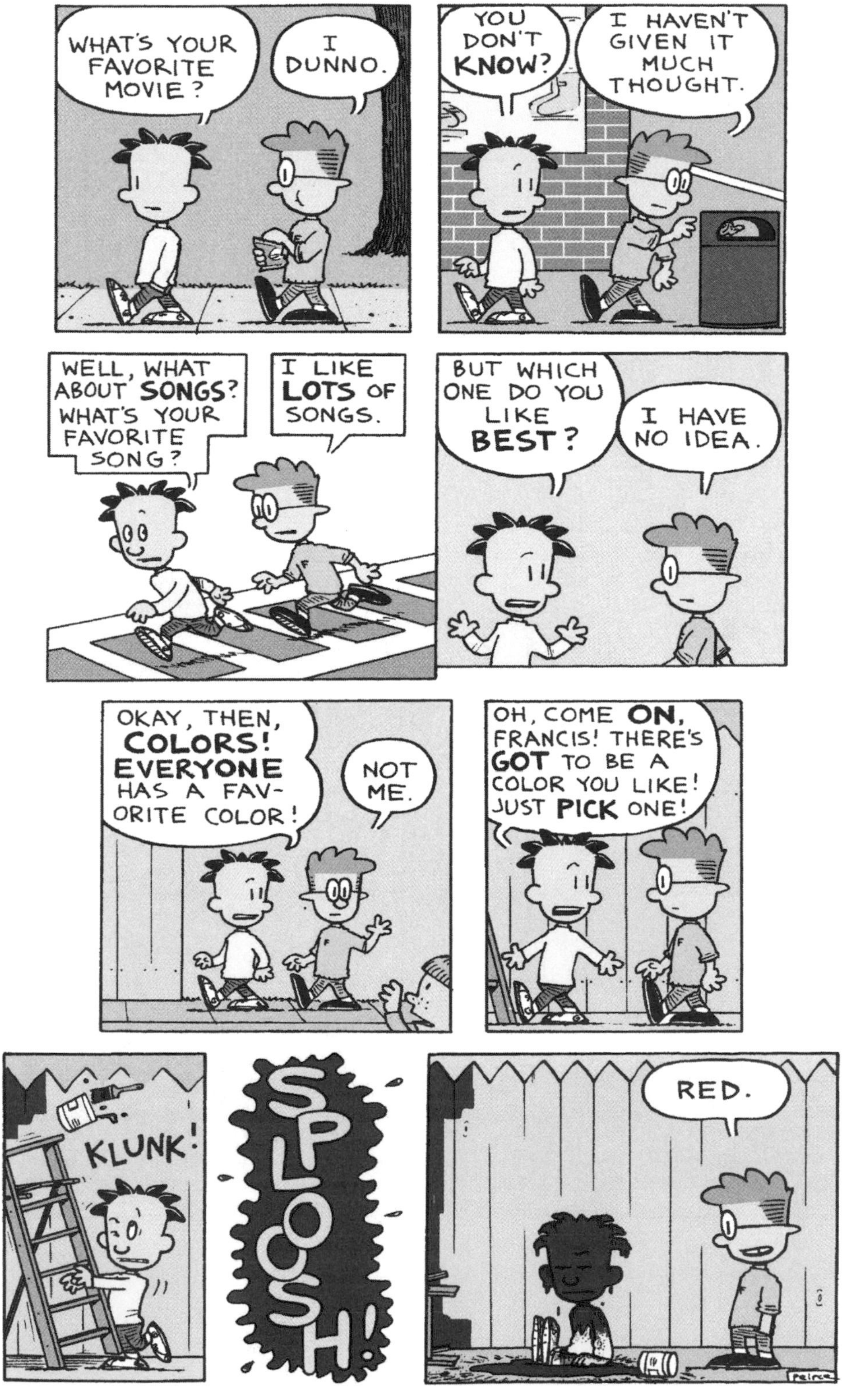
WHAT'S YOUR FAVORITE MOVIE?
I DUNNO.
YOU DON'T KNOW?
I HAVEN'T GIVEN IT MUCH THOUGHT.
WELL, WHAT ABOUT SONGS? WHAT'S YOUR FAVORITE SONG?
I LIKE LOTS OF SONGS.
BUT WHICH ONE DO YOU LIKE BEST?
I HAVE NO IDEA.
OKAY, THEN, COLORS! EVERYONE HAS A FAV-ORITE COLOR!
NOT ME.
OH, COME ON, FRANCIS! THERE'S GOT TO BE A COLOR YOU LIKE! JUST PICK ONE!
KLUNK!
SPLOOSH!
RED.
PEIRCE

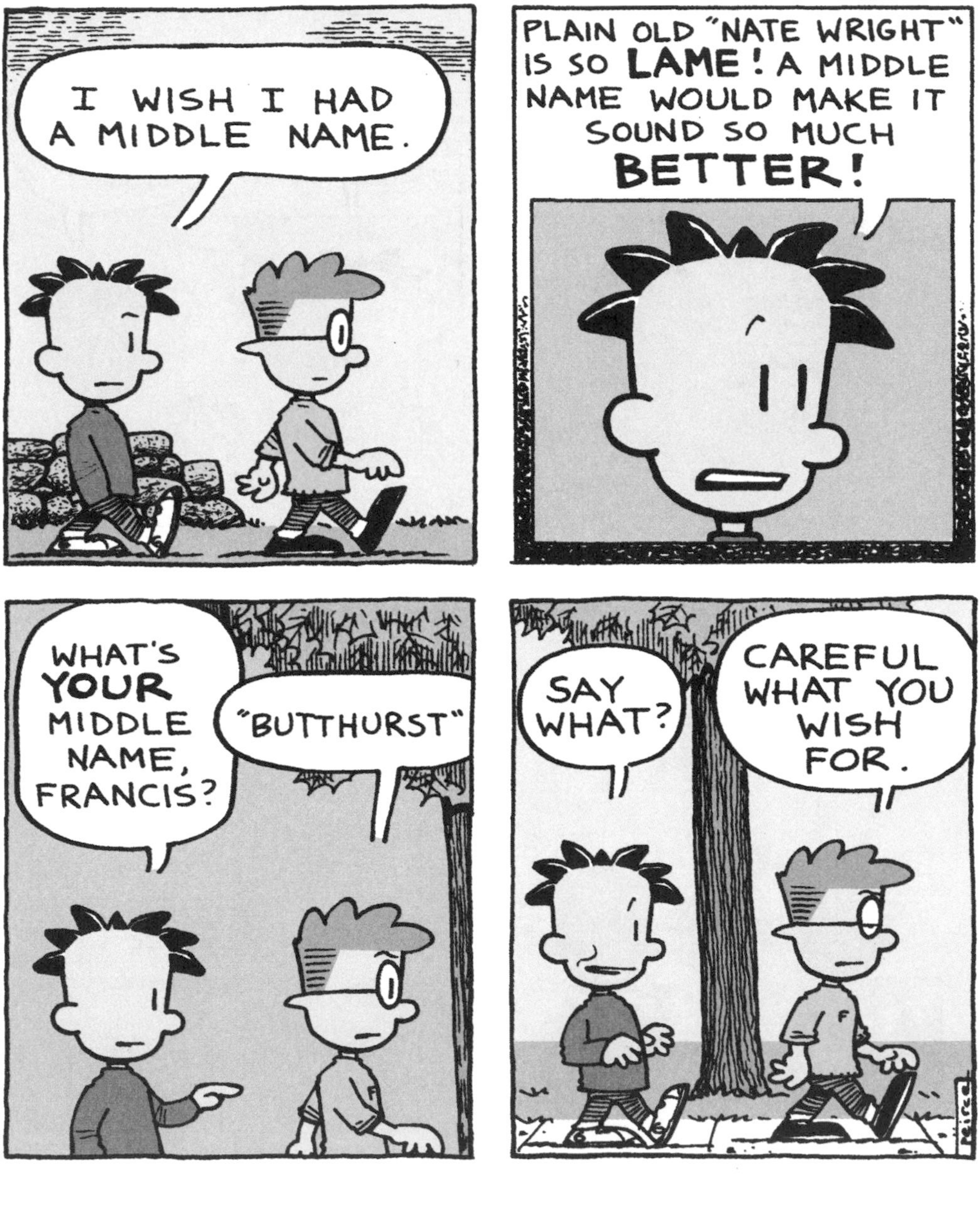
I WISH I HAD A MIDDLE NAME.
PLAIN OLD "NATE WRIGHT" IS SO **LAME**! A MIDDLE NAME WOULD MAKE IT SOUND SO MUCH **BETTER**!
WHAT'S **YOUR** MIDDLE NAME, FRANCIS?
"BUTTHURST"
SAY WHAT?
CAREFUL WHAT YOU WISH FOR.

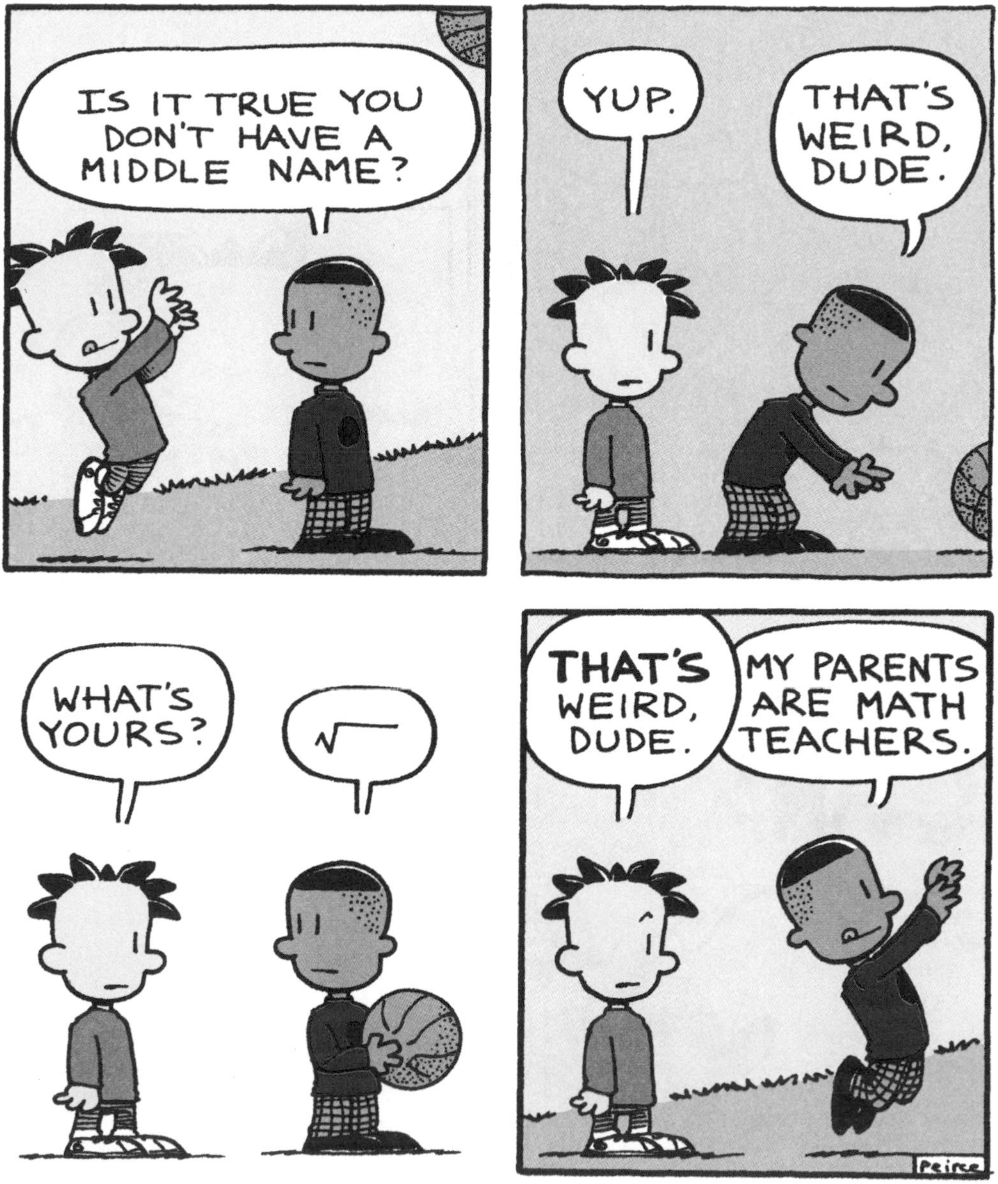
IS IT TRUE YOU DON'T HAVE A MIDDLE NAME?
YUP.
THAT'S WEIRD, DUDE.
WHAT'S YOURS?
√‾‾
THAT'S WEIRD, DUDE.
MY PARENTS ARE MATH TEACHERS.
Peirce

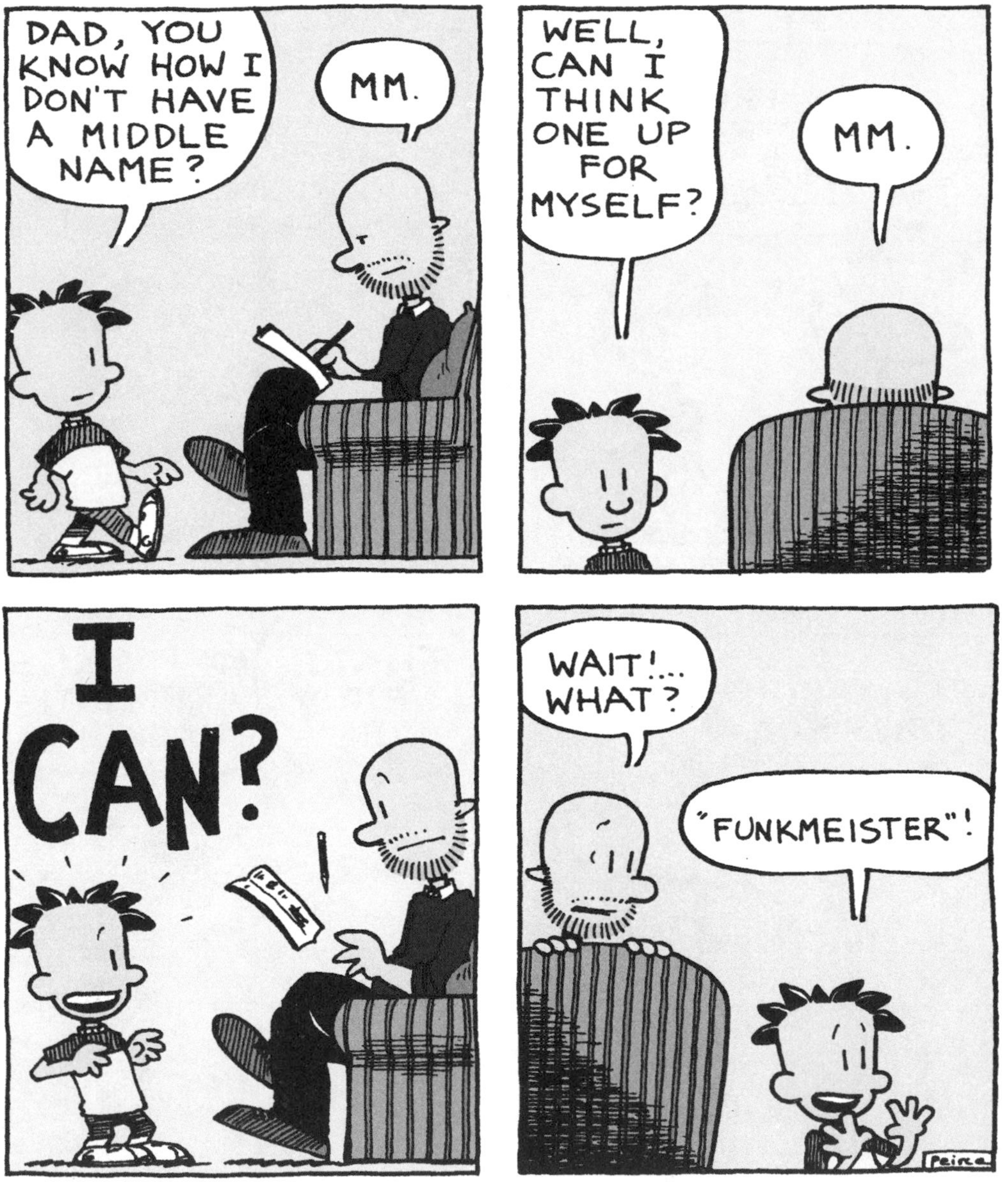
DAD, YOU KNOW HOW I DON'T HAVE A MIDDLE NAME?
MM.
WELL, CAN I THINK ONE UP FOR MYSELF?
MM.
I CAN?
WAIT!... WHAT?
"FUNKMEISTER"!
Peirce

GOOD NEWS, GUYS! MY DAD'S LETTING ME THINK UP A MIDDLE NAME FOR MYSELF!

I'M STILL MULLING IT OVER, BUT A CLEAR FRONT-RUNNER HAS EMERGED!

LET'S HEAR IT.

"MAXIMUS"!

VERY MODEST.

IS THAT A NAME OR A MALE ENHANCEMENT SUPPLEMENT?

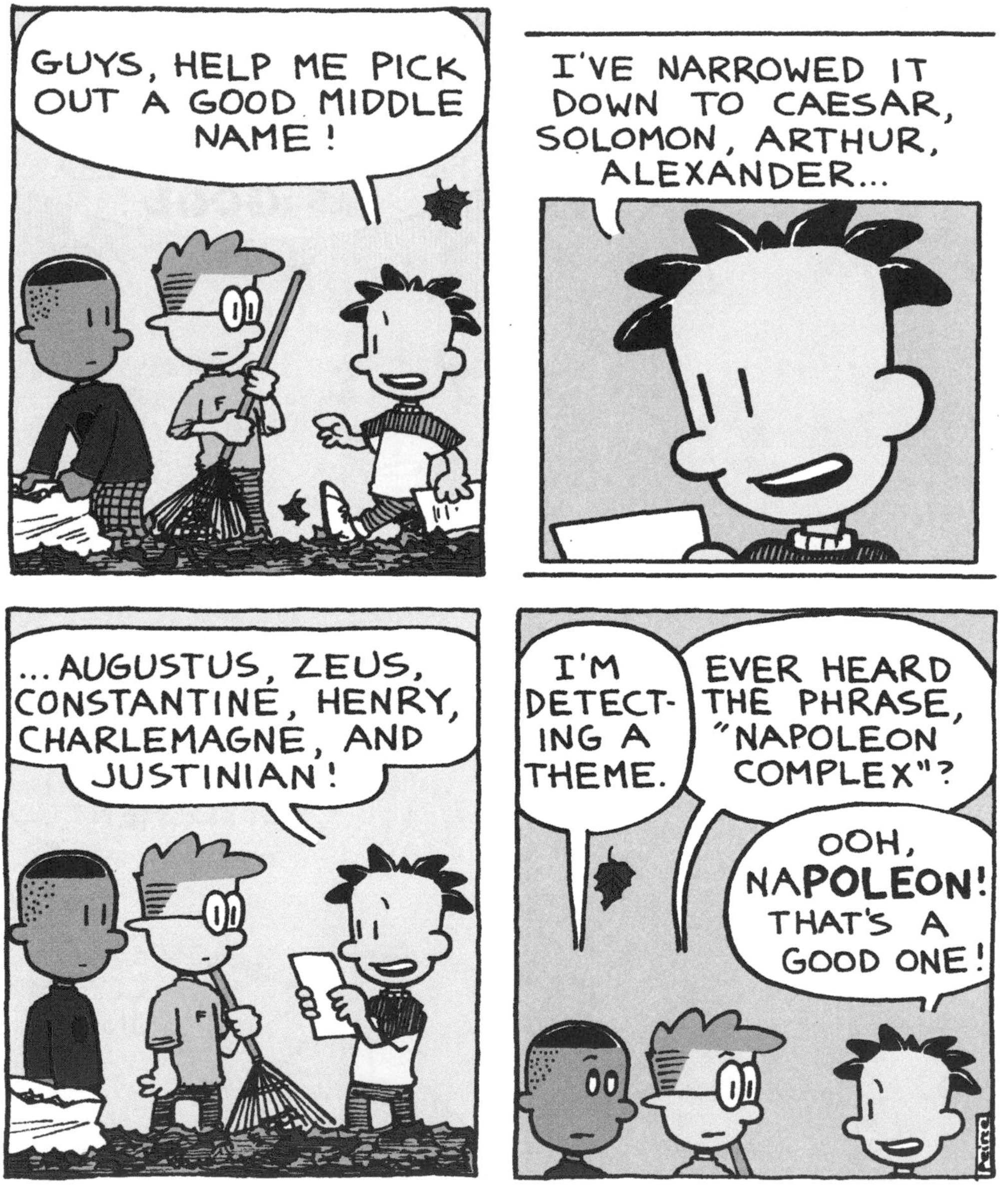
GUYS, HELP ME PICK OUT A GOOD MIDDLE NAME!
I'VE NARROWED IT DOWN TO CAESAR, SOLOMON, ARTHUR, ALEXANDER...
...AUGUSTUS, ZEUS, CONSTANTINE, HENRY, CHARLEMAGNE, AND JUSTINIAN!
I'M DETECTING A THEME.
EVER HEARD THE PHRASE, "NAPOLEON COMPLEX"?
OOH, NAPOLEON! THAT'S A GOOD ONE!

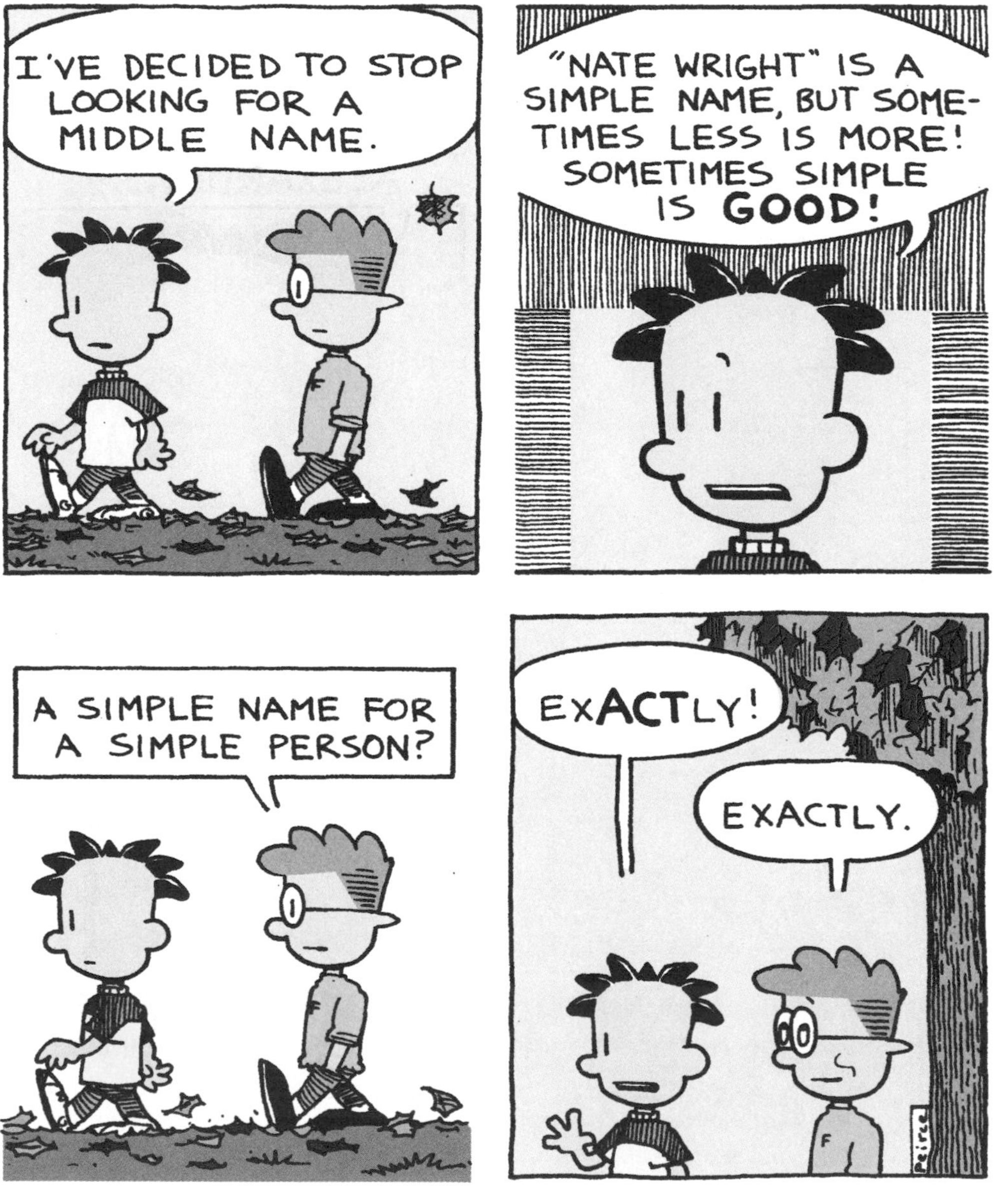
I'VE DECIDED TO STOP LOOKING FOR A MIDDLE NAME.
"NATE WRIGHT" IS A SIMPLE NAME, BUT SOMETIMES LESS IS MORE! SOMETIMES SIMPLE IS GOOD!
A SIMPLE NAME FOR A SIMPLE PERSON?
EXACTLY!
EXACTLY.
Peirce

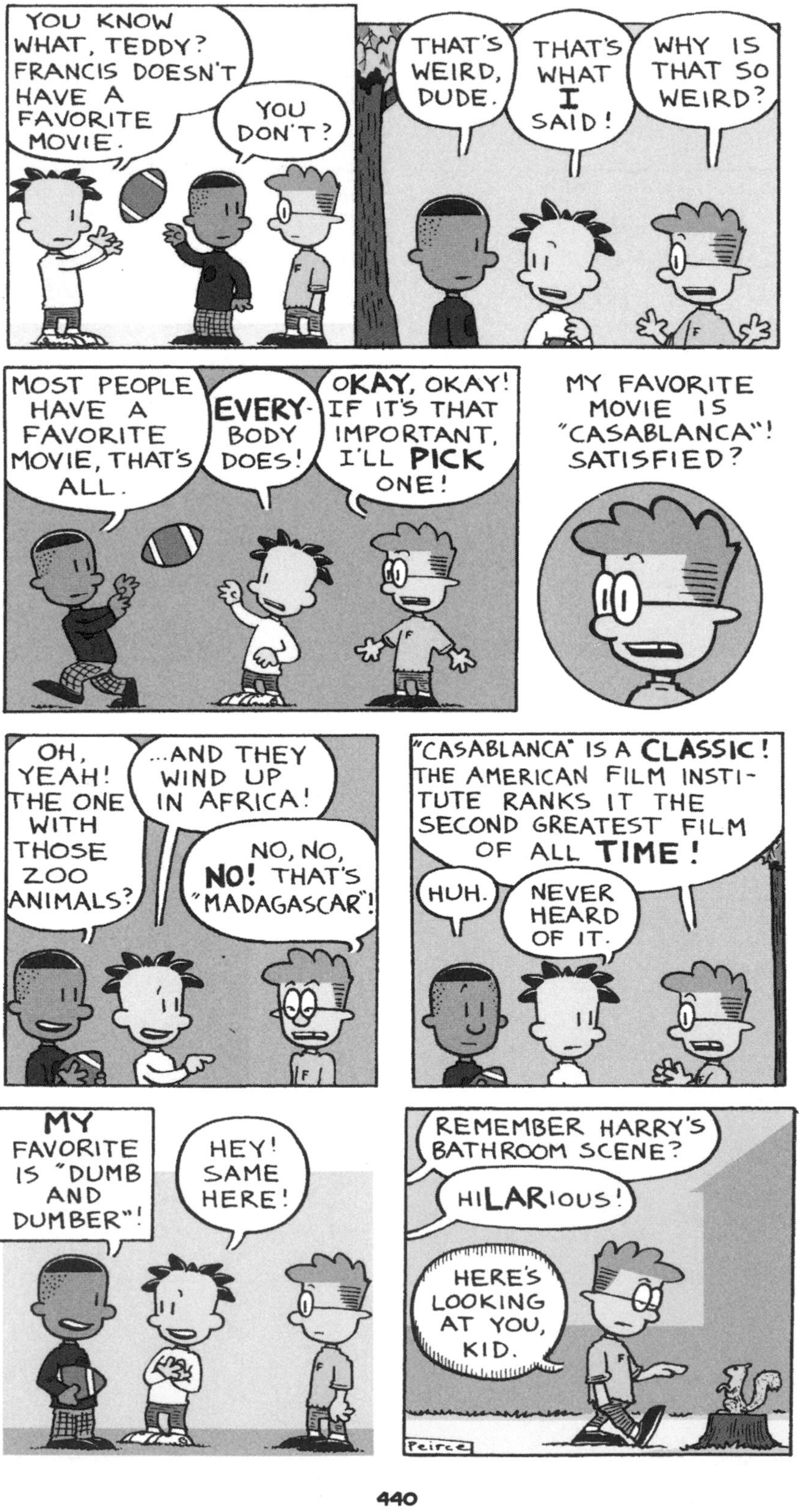
YOU KNOW WHAT, TEDDY? FRANCIS DOESN'T HAVE A FAVORITE MOVIE.
YOU DON'T?
THAT'S WEIRD, DUDE.
THAT'S WHAT I SAID!
WHY IS THAT SO WEIRD?
MOST PEOPLE HAVE A FAVORITE MOVIE, THAT'S ALL.
EVERY-BODY DOES!
OKAY, OKAY! IF IT'S THAT IMPORTANT, I'LL PICK ONE!
MY FAVORITE MOVIE IS "CASABLANCA"! SATISFIED?
OH, YEAH! THE ONE WITH THOSE ZOO ANIMALS?
...AND THEY WIND UP IN AFRICA!
NO, NO, NO! THAT'S "MADAGASCAR"!
"CASABLANCA" IS A CLASSIC! THE AMERICAN FILM INSTI-TUTE RANKS IT THE SECOND GREATEST FILM OF ALL TIME!
HUH.
NEVER HEARD OF IT.
MY FAVORITE IS "DUMB AND DUMBER"!
HEY! SAME HERE!
REMEMBER HARRY'S BATHROOM SCENE?
HILARIOUS!
HERE'S LOOKING AT YOU, KID.
Peirce

DAD, IT'S ALMOST HALLOWEEN.
THAT'S RIGHT.
YOU'RE NOT GOING TO RUIN IT, ARE YOU? YOU'RE NOT GOING TO HAND OUT RICE CAKES OR TRAIL MIX OR...
RELAX, NATE! THIS YEAR I'M HANDING OUT SOMETHING **SWEET**!
SOME-THING SWEET?
SWEET **AND** HEALTHY!
PLEASE TELL ME YOU'RE NOT HANDING OUT RAISINS.
EVEN BETTER! **PRUNES**!
Peirce

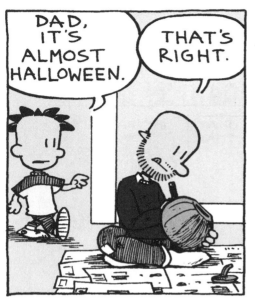

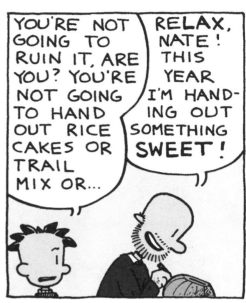

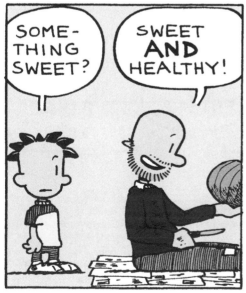

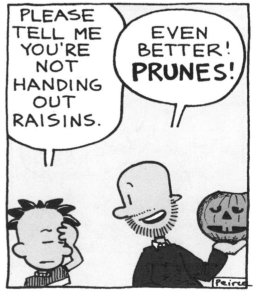

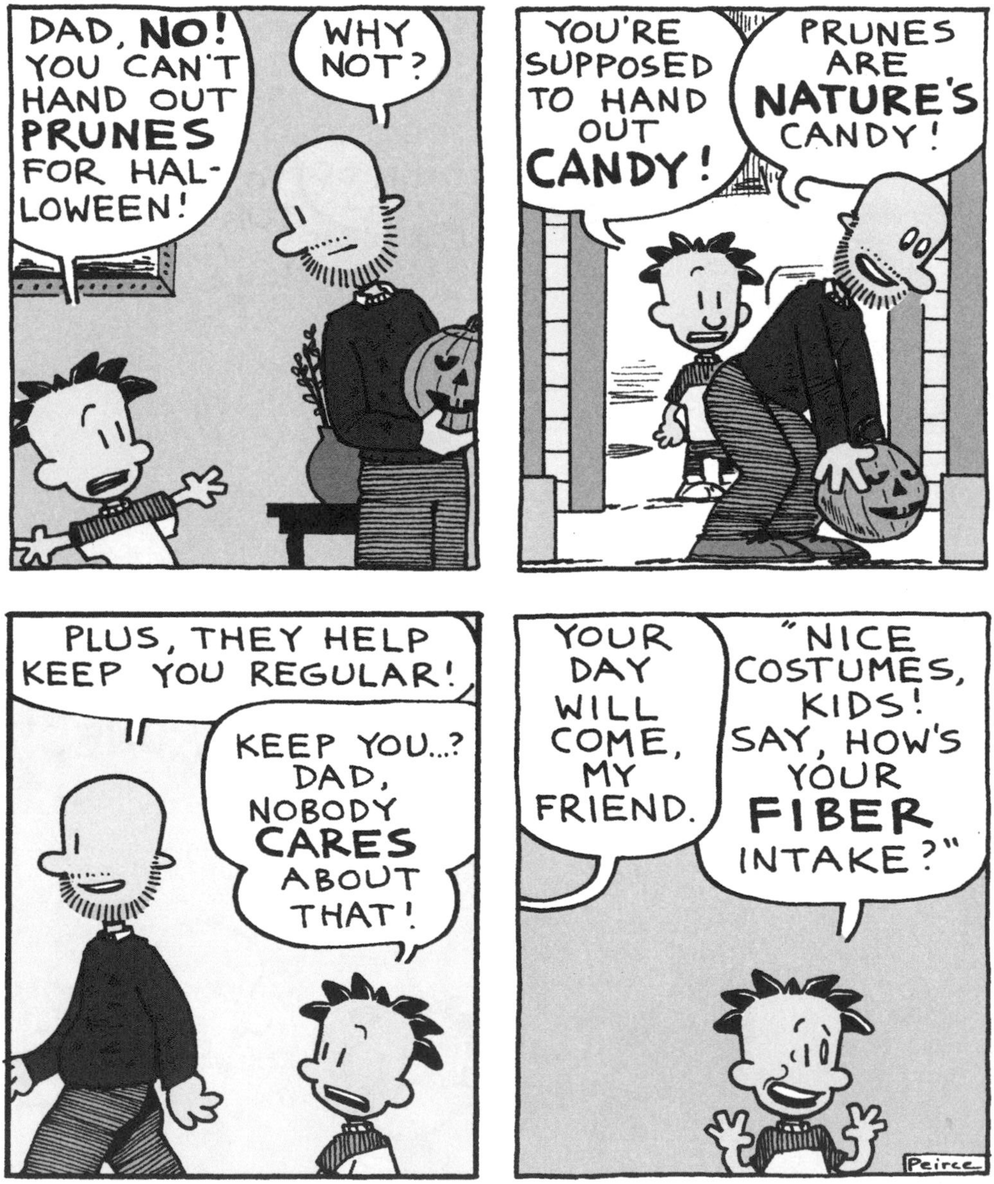
DAD, NO! YOU CAN'T HAND OUT PRUNES FOR HALLOWEEN!
WHY NOT?
YOU'RE SUPPOSED TO HAND OUT CANDY!
PRUNES ARE NATURE'S CANDY!
PLUS, THEY HELP KEEP YOU REGULAR!
KEEP YOU...? DAD, NOBODY CARES ABOUT THAT!
YOUR DAY WILL COME, MY FRIEND.
"NICE COSTUMES, KIDS! SAY, HOW'S YOUR FIBER INTAKE?"
Peirce

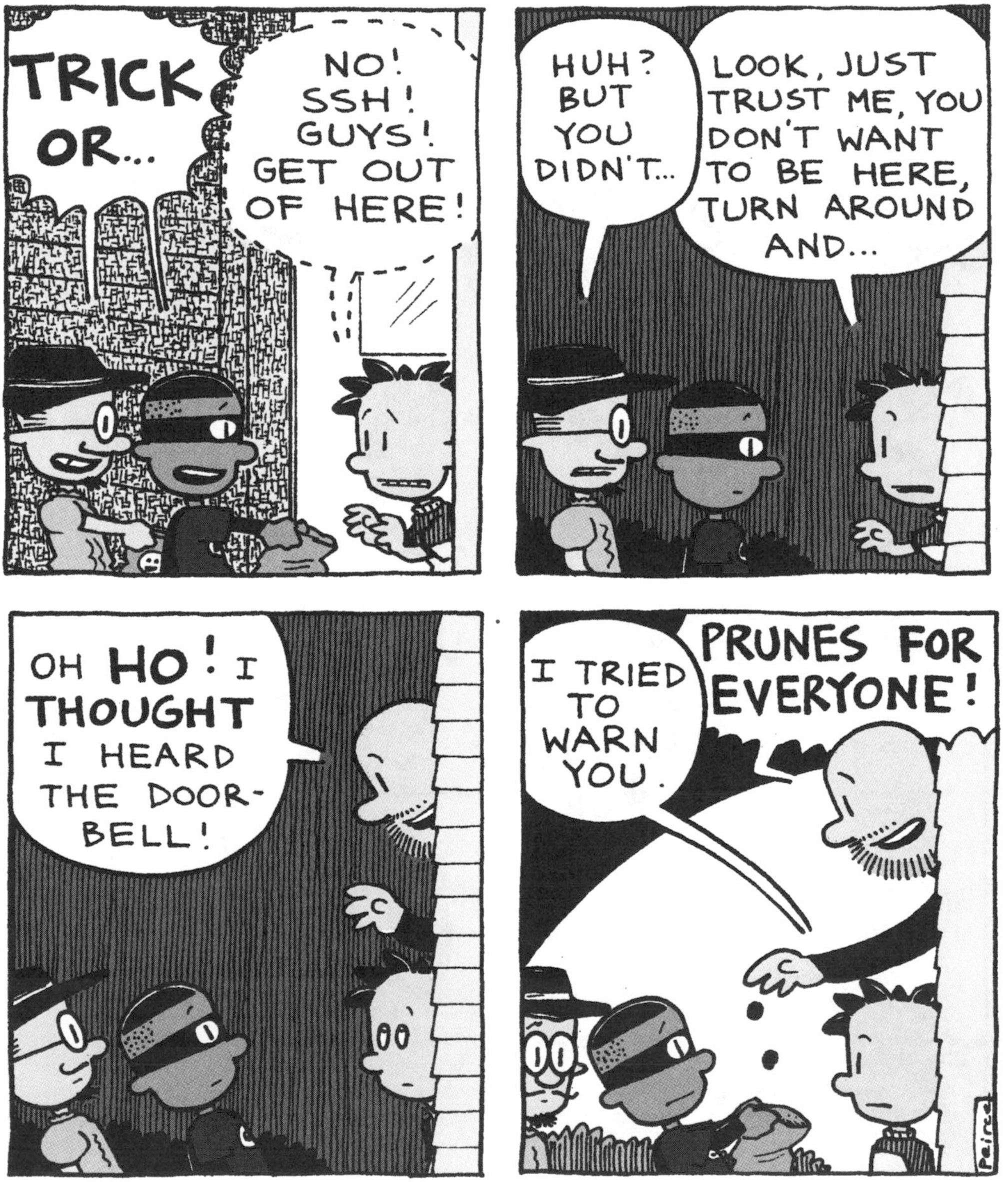
TRICK OR...
NO! SSH! GUYS! GET OUT OF HERE!
HUH? BUT YOU DIDN'T...
LOOK, JUST TRUST ME, YOU DON'T WANT TO BE HERE, TURN AROUND AND...
OH HO! I THOUGHT I HEARD THE DOOR-BELL!
I TRIED TO WARN YOU.
PRUNES FOR EVERYONE!
Peirce

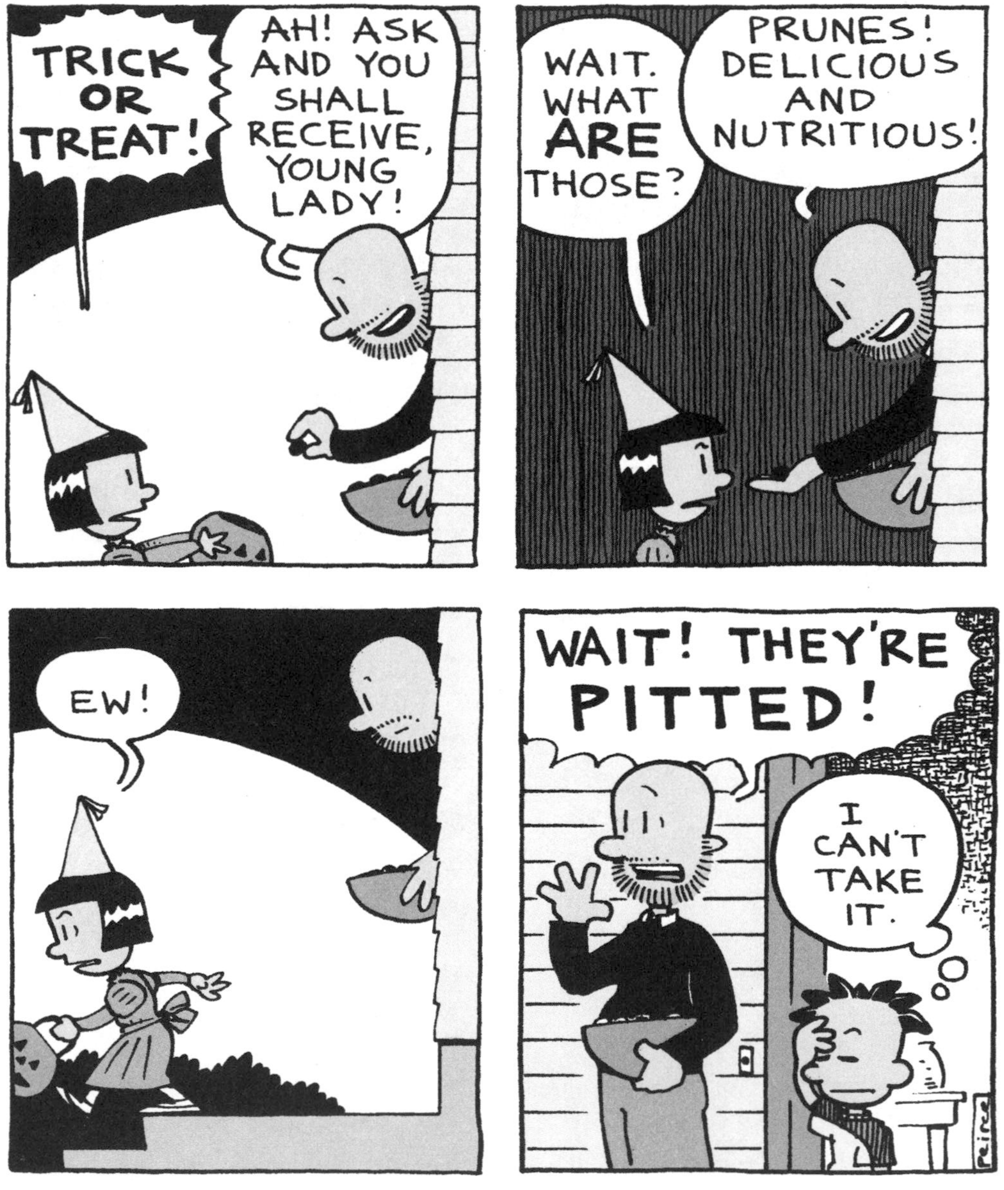
TRICK OR TREAT!
AH! ASK AND YOU SHALL RECEIVE, YOUNG LADY!
WAIT. WHAT **ARE** THOSE?
PRUNES! DELICIOUS AND NUTRITIOUS!
EW!
WAIT! THEY'RE PITTED!
I CAN'T TAKE IT.
PEIRCE

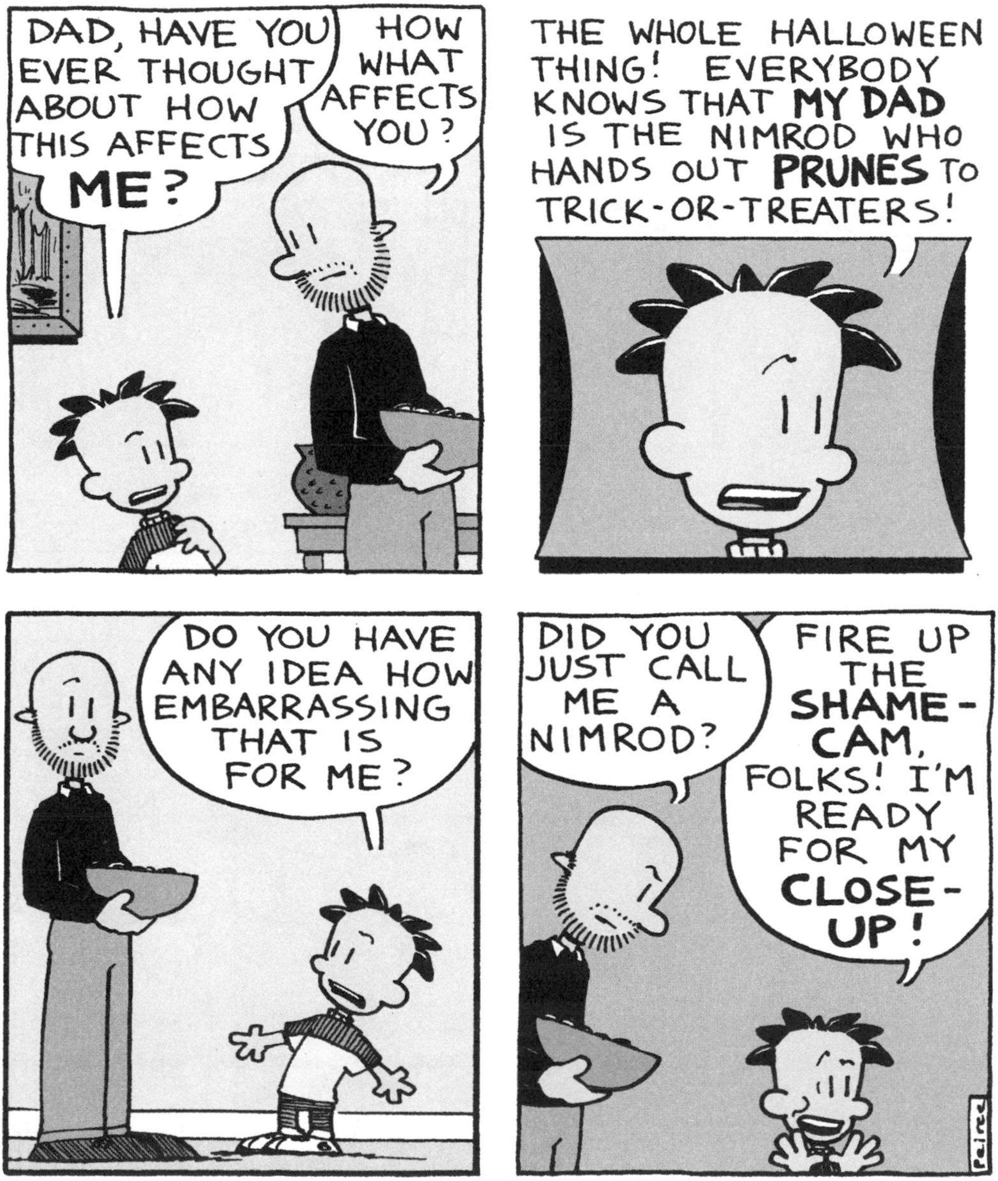
DAD, HAVE YOU EVER THOUGHT ABOUT HOW THIS AFFECTS **ME**?
HOW WHAT AFFECTS YOU?
THE WHOLE HALLOWEEN THING! EVERYBODY KNOWS THAT **MY DAD** IS THE NIMROD WHO HANDS OUT **PRUNES** TO TRICK-OR-TREATERS!
DO YOU HAVE ANY IDEA HOW EMBARRASSING THAT IS FOR ME?
DID YOU JUST CALL ME A NIMROD?
FIRE UP THE **SHAME-CAM**, FOLKS! I'M READY FOR MY **CLOSE-UP**!
Peirce

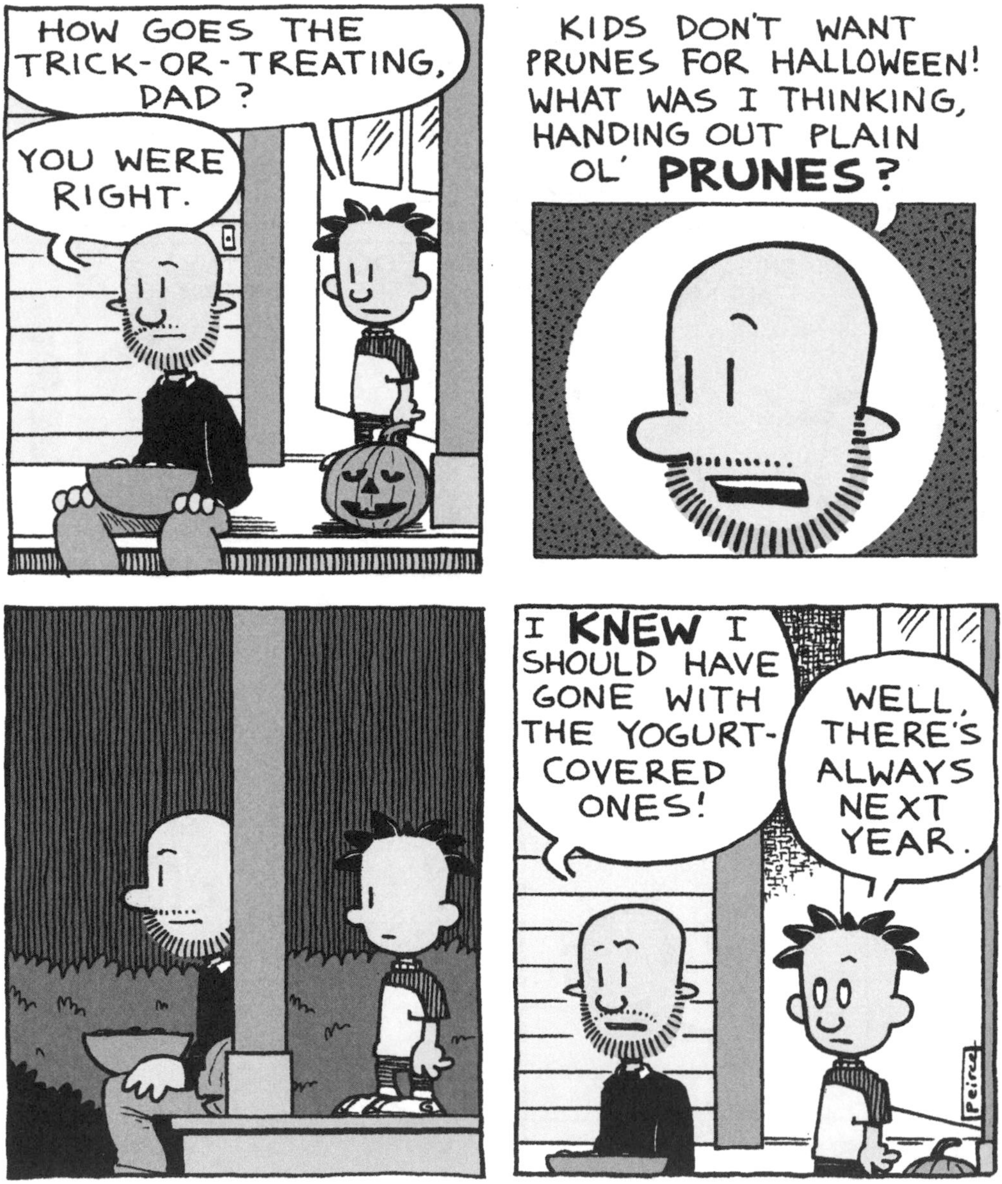
HOW GOES THE TRICK-OR-TREATING, DAD?
YOU WERE RIGHT.
KIDS DON'T WANT PRUNES FOR HALLOWEEN! WHAT WAS I THINKING, HANDING OUT PLAIN OL' PRUNES?
I KNEW I SHOULD HAVE GONE WITH THE YOGURT-COVERED ONES!
WELL, THERE'S ALWAYS NEXT YEAR.
Peirce

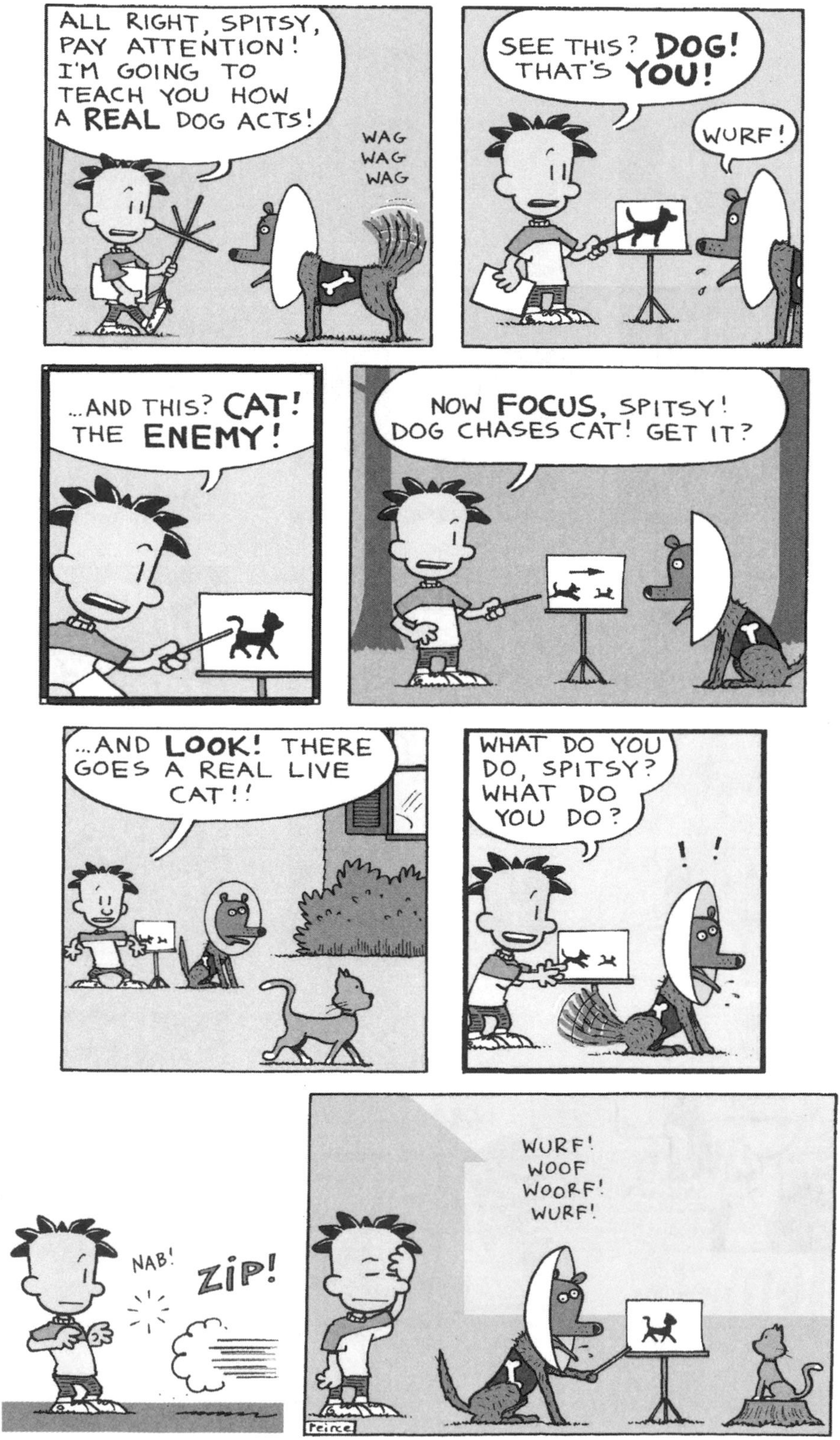
ALL RIGHT, SPITSY, PAY ATTENTION! I'M GOING TO TEACH YOU HOW A REAL DOG ACTS!
WAG WAG WAG
SEE THIS? DOG! THAT'S YOU!
WURF!
...AND THIS? CAT! THE ENEMY!
NOW FOCUS, SPITSY! DOG CHASES CAT! GET IT?
...AND LOOK! THERE GOES A REAL LIVE CAT!!
WHAT DO YOU DO, SPITSY? WHAT DO YOU DO?
! !
NAB!
ZIP!
WURF! WOOF WOORF! WURF!
PEIRCE

Look for these books!

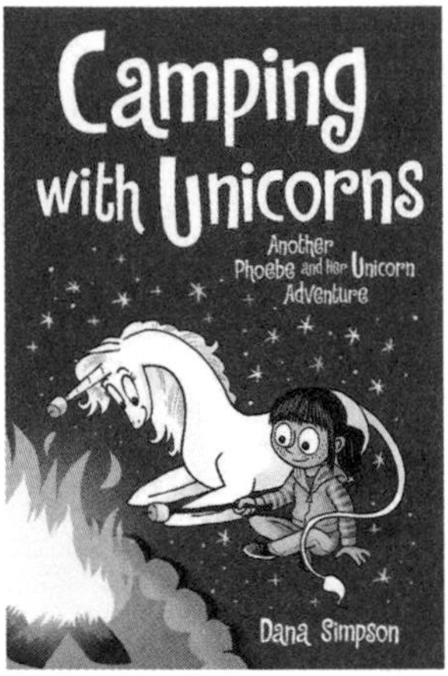
Camping with Unicorns
Another Phoebe and Her Unicorn Adventure
Dana Simpson

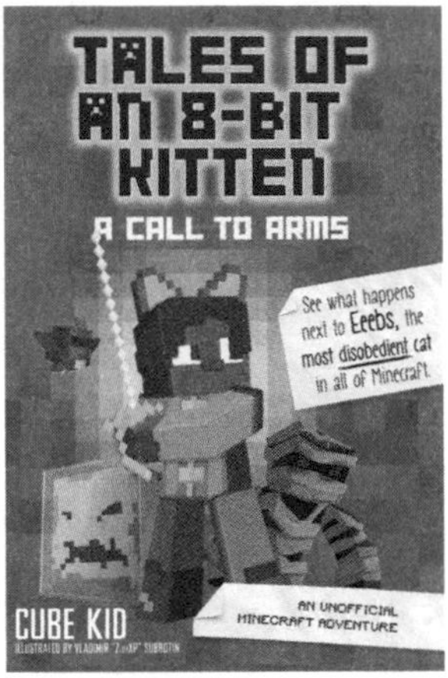
TALES OF AN 8-BIT KITTEN
A CALL TO ARMS
See what happens next to Eeebs, the most disobedient cat in all of Minecraft.
CUBE KID
AN UNOFFICIAL MINECRAFT ADVENTURE

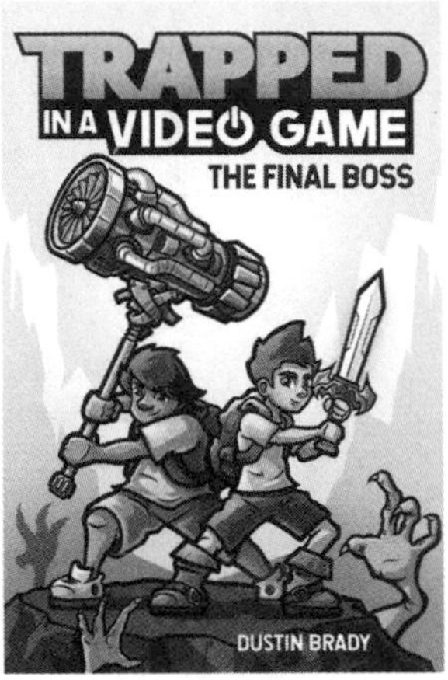
TRAPPED IN A VIDEO GAME
THE FINAL BOSS
DUSTIN BRADY

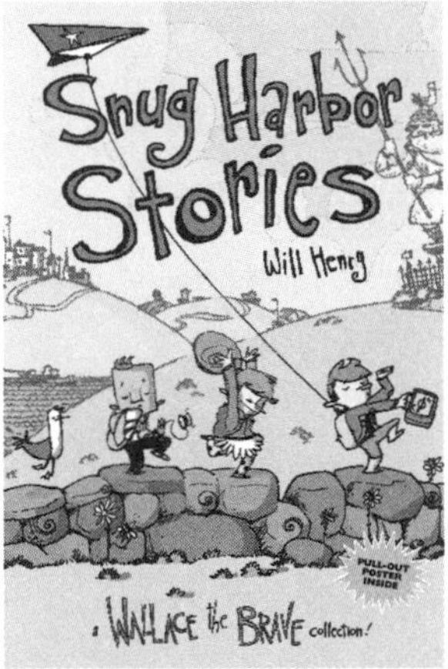
Snug Harbor Stories
Will Henry
PULL-OUT POSTER INSIDE
A WALLACE the BRAVE collection!

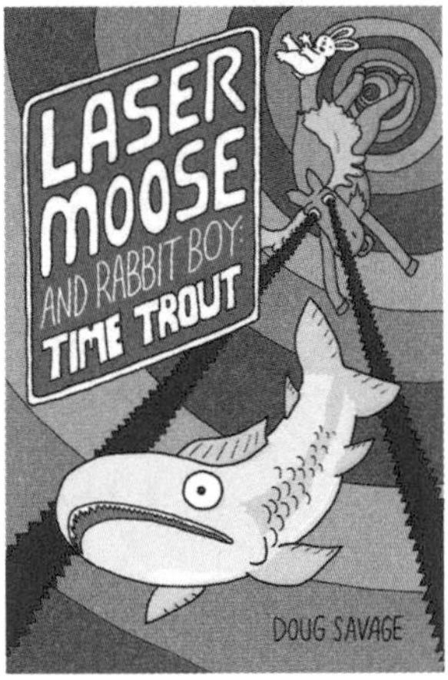
LASER MOOSE AND RABBIT BOY: TIME TROUT
DOUG SAVAGE

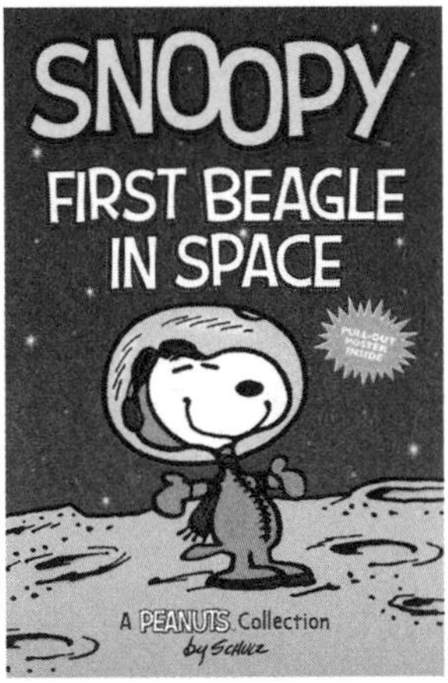
SNOOPY
FIRST BEAGLE IN SPACE
PULL-OUT POSTER INSIDE
A PEANUTS Collection
by Schulz

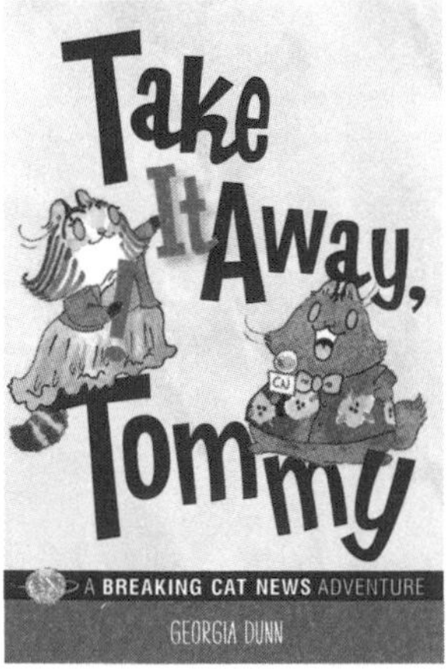
Take It Away, Tommy
A BREAKING CAT NEWS ADVENTURE
GEORGIA DUNN

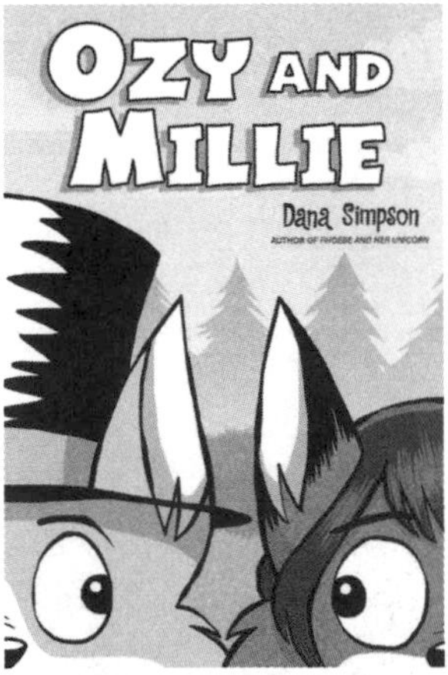
OZY AND MILLIE
Dana Simpson
AUTHOR OF PHOEBE AND HER UNICORN

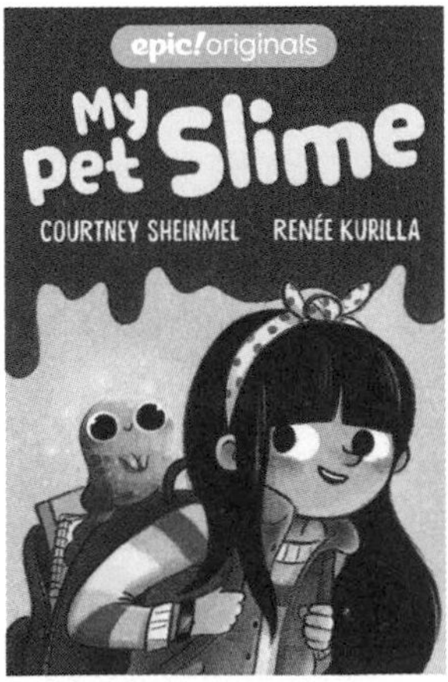
epic! originals
My pet Slime
COURTNEY SHEINMEL
RENÉE KURILLA